Vunderlich

Sydenham Society: on the
ature in Diseases

ginal.

| ISBN: 978-3-38210-101-5

print of Outlook Verlagsgesellschaft mbH.

ok Verlag GmbH, Zeilweg 44, 60439 Frankfurt, Deutschland
uthorized to represent): E. Roepke, Zeilweg 44, 60439 Frankfurt, Deutschland
emand GmbH, In de Tarpen 42, 22848 Norderstedt, Deutschland

Dr. C. A. W

The New Sydenha

Temperature

Vol

Dr. C. A. V

The Nev

Temper

Vol. 49

Reprint of the o

1st Edition 2023

Anatiposi Verlag is an

Verlag (Publisher): Out
Vertretungsberechtigt
Druck (Print): Books on

Ana

THE NEW SYDENHAM

SOCIETY.

INSTITUTED MDCCCLVIII.

VOLUME XLIX.

ON THE

TEMPERATURE IN DISEASES:

A MANUAL OF

MEDICAL THERMOMETRY.

BY

DR. C. A. WUNDERLICH,

PROFESSOR DER KLINIK AN DER UNIVERSITÄT LEIPZIG, K. SÄCHS GEHEIMEN
MEDICINALRATH, COMTHUR UND RITTER, ETC.

TRANSLATED FROM THE SECOND GERMAN EDITION

BY

W. BATHURST WOODMAN, M.D.,

ASSISTANT-PHYSICIAN TO THE LONDON HOSPITAL, AND PHYSICIAN TO THE NORTH-EASTERN
HOSPITAL FOR CHILDREN.

WITH FORTY WOODCUTS AND SEVEN LITHOGRAPHS.

THE NEW SYDENHAM SOCIETY,
LONDON.

MDCCCLXXI.

PRINTED BY
J. E. ADLARD, BARTHOLOMEW CLOSE, E.C.

I MAY, perhaps, be allowed a few words of introduction to the following pages. For the last sixteen years my attention has been uninterruptedly directed to the course pursued by the temperature in diseases of various kinds. The thermometer has been regularly employed at least twice daily, and in febrile patients from four to eight times a day, and even oftener, in special circumstances, for all the patients in my wards. I have also experienced the applicability of this method of investigation in very numerous cases in private practice. In this way I have gradually got together a material which comprises many thousand complete cases of thermometric observations of disease, and millions of separate readings of the temperature. The more my observations were multiplied the more firmly rooted did my conviction become of the unparalleled value of this method of investigation, as giving an accurate and reliable insight into the condition of the sick.

Not a few of the results obtained have already been published, partly by myself and partly by my assistants and the students who attended my clinique.

From many quarters, and repeatedly too, I have been urged to collect them together in a complete and connected form. I have at last resolved to do so, though recognising fully the extreme difficulty of the task; to abstract and formulate well-founded general principles from the mass of separate cases, whose enormous number

makes it simply impossible to devote special consideration to each case, and to present a *coup d'œil* of these intricate and complicated affairs.

For although theoretical questions as to human temperature and kindred subjects must not be overlooked, and well deserve to be explored, my immediate purpose has been to write a *practical* book, and to lay before my medical brethren as impressively as I could the eminent usefulness of thermometric observations. A knowledge of the course of the temperature in disease is highly important to the medical practitioner, and, indeed, indispensable :—

Because all the phenomena of the sick are deserving of study;—

Because the temperature can be determined with a nicety which is common to few other phenomena ;—

Because the temperature can neither be feigned nor falsified ;—

Because we may conclude the presence of some disturbance in the economy from the mere fact of altered temperatures ;—

Because certain degrees indicate that there is fever ;—

Because the height of the temperature often decides both the degree and the danger of the attack ;—

Because thermometric observation may serve to aid in the discovery of the laws regulating the course of certain diseases, and may enable us to learn them ;—

Because when once the normal course of certain diseases has been determined, thermometry is able to simplify, confirm, and certify the diagnosis ;—

Because thermometric investigations indicate most rapidly and most safely any deviations from the regular course of the disease ;—

Because the behaviour of the temperature during the progress of the disease discovers to us both relapses and ameliorations before we should otherwise recognise them ;—

Because in this way thermometry is able to regulate the results of our therapeutical efforts ;—

Because it puts us on our guard against the injurious influences which affect our patients in the course of their illness ;—

Because it is able to indicate the transition from one stage of the disease into another, and particularly the commencement of convalescence and its complete establishment ;—

Because it reveals the existence of complications, and shows how far recovery is from being yet complete ;—

Because it generally reveals the fact of a fatal termination being imminent ;—

Because it often announces the impossibility of a continuance of life, and thus gives an absolutely fatal prognosis with great distinctness ;—

And lastly, because it furnishes a certain proof of the reality of death, when this is otherwise uncertain.

If I succeed in diffusing yet more widely the conviction of the truth of these propositions, and if I am able to offer to my medical brethren a useful and usable clue to enable them to discover the true value of thermometric data, the object of my work is already obtained.

Dr. WUNDERLICH.

Leipsic; *March*, 1868.

AUTHOR'S PREFACE

TO THE

SECOND EDITION.

A Second Edition having become necessary, I have revised the text to the best of my ability, and have once more carefully compared the propositions it contains with the original observations, and have added also a considerable quantity of new material, partly original, partly selected. I hope that my book is thus not only bigger but better, and that this new Edition will meet with as friendly a welcome as the former one.

W.

Leipzic; *Feb.*, 1870.

THE

TRANSLATOR'S PREFACE.

I REGRET the delay which has occurred in the publication of this volume.

It has been partly due to the alterations necessary to make the translation correspond with the Second German Edition, and partly to the nature of the work itself, which abounds with numerals and foreign proper names. The translation has been done by me in the midst of other engagements, and with somewhat feeble health. Some few Germanisms and a few errors of the press have, it is to be feared, escaped notice. As to the rest, I have not aimed at fine writing, but simply at conveying the Author's meaning, as I understood him, to the English reader.

Professor Wunderlich, in a letter acknowledging the receipt of the first eight sheets, stated that he had no additional matter which he could incorporate with this Edition, the whole of his time being devoted to the supervision of three military hospitals for the wounded in the present Franco-German war.

The Centigrade scale has been retained for two reasons—

1st. Because in this way the original diagrams have been presented without any alteration, except some slight improvements in their execution, for which I have to thank the artist, Mr. Tuffen West ; and

2nd. Because the convenience of this scale will probably shortly lead to its general adoption by all scientific men, and then the value of this work for reference will still be unimpaired.

I have quoted English authors but sparingly, because I considered that the readers of the New Sydenham Society did not need more than a general reference to such. Had my task been to continue the History of Thermometry, the names of Drs. Clifford Allbutt, Aitken, Sydney Ringer, Grimshaw, E. Long Fox, and many others, would have occupied a larger space in these pages.

To Mr. Hutchinson, whose own researches on the effects of nerve-section are amongst the most interesting and important recent contributions to our knowledge, I am indebted for many kind and valuable suggestions.

Two new woodcuts (Nos. 39 and 40) have been specially designed for this Edition.

W. B. W.

10, FINSBURY PAVEMENT, E.C.;
February, 1871.

TABLE OF CONTENTS.

PAGES

CHAPTER I.
Fundamental Principles . . . . 1— 19

CHAPTER II.
History and Bibliography . . . 19— 48

CHAPTER III.
Value of Thermometer in Medical Practice . . 48— 58

CHAPTER IV.
The Art of Medical Thermometry . . 58— 80

CHAPTER V.
On the Temperature in Health . . . 80—120

CHAPTER VI.
Causes of altered Temperature in Disease 120—160

CHAPTER VII.
Local alterations of Temperature in Disease . 160—170

CHAPTER VIII.
Typical Forms with altered Temperatures . 170—202

CHAPTER IX.
Diagnostic Value of Single Observations . 202—226

CHAPTER X.
Daily Fluctuations of Temperature in Disease . 226—241

CHAPTER XI.
The Course of the Temperature in Febrile Diseases . 241—288

PAGE

CHAPTER XII.

On the Temperature in Special Diseases . 288, &c.

I.—Abdominal Typhus (Enteric Fever) . . 292
II.—Exanthematic Typhus . . . 327
III.—Relapsing Fever . . . 333
IV.—Variola (Smallpox), &c. . . 337
Varicella . . . 341
V.—Measles . . . 342
VI.—Scarlatina . . . 346
VII.—Rubeolæ . . . 351
VIII.—Erysipelas . . . 351
IX.—On a peculiar Remittent Fever . . 354
X.—Febricula and Traumatic Fever . . 355
XI.—Pyæmia . . . 361
XII.—Catarrhal Affections of Mucous Membranes . 365
XIII.—Croupous and Diphtheritic Inflammations . 367
XIV.—Pneumonia . . . 368
XV.—Amygdalitis (Quinsy) . . . 385
XVI.—Parotitis (Mumps) . . . 387
XVII.—Meningitis . . . 388
XVIII.—Pleurisy, Endo- and Peri-carditis, and Peritonitis . 391
XIX.—Acute Rheumatism . . . 394
XX.—Osteo-myelitis . . . 403
XXI.—Nephritis and Bright's Disease . . 404
XXII.—Hepatitis and Yellow Fever . . 404
XXIII.—Lues (Constitutional Syphilis) . . 405
XXIV.—Glanders and Farcy . . . 408
XXV.—Acute Miliary Tuberculosis . . 409
XXVI.—Acute Phthisis . . . 410
XXVII.—Trichinosis . . . 415
XXVIII.—Malarious Diseases (Ague, &c.) . . 416
XXIX.—Cholera . . . 419
XXX.—Injuries of the Spinal Cord . . 423
XXXI.—Neuroses . . . 424
XXXII.—Chronic Disorders of Blood, Tissues, and Secretions 427

CHAPTER XIII.

On the Effects of Altered Temperatures on the System 436

Appendices on Influence of Rest and Work, and Atmospheric Pressure—Table of Thermometric Equivalents—Temperature of Animals—Effects of Pinching—Respiration—and Supplemental Bibliography . 445

MEDICAL THERMOMETRY.

CHAPTER I.

FUNDAMENTAL PRINCIPLES.

§ 1.—There are two well-ascertained facts, which not only justify us in endeavouring to determine the temperature of the body in diseases, and render the use of the thermometer both a duty and a valuable aid to diagnosis, but form the basis of all our investigations. The first fact is *the constancy of temperature in healthy persons,* or, in other words, that healthy human beings of every age and condition, in all places and in all circumstances, and exposed to all kinds of influences, provided these do not impair health, have an almost identical temperature.

The second fact is *the variation of temperature in disease,* for in sick persons we are constantly meeting with deviations from the normal temperature of the healthy.

§ 2.—The *average normal temperature* of the healthy human body in its interior, or in carefully covered situations on its surface, varies, according to the plan of measurement, from 98·6° to 99·5° Fahr. (37° to 37·5° C.). It is about 98·6° in the well-closed axilla, and a few tenths of a degree higher (·5—1½ or 2° Fahr., ·7° Fahr. average) in the rectum and vagina.[1]

§ 3.—The temperature of healthy persons is almost constantly the same, although not absolutely so. Indeed, there are spontaneous variations in the course of every twenty-four hours, but these seldom exceed half a degree of the Centigrade scale (= ·9° Fahr.)

[1] The arrow to indicate the normal temperature is placed at 98.4° Fahr. on most English thermometers; from numerous observations, and comparison of various statements, I am inclined to believe that the author is correct in placing it higher.—[TRANS.]

1

for each individual. Unusual conditions, and external influences, may indeed cause variations of temperature, but these are never very great, as long as they produce no disturbance of health. Any elevation of the axillary temperature above 99·5° (37·5° C., or any depression below 97·2° (36·5° C.) is always very suspicious, and whether it appear to be spontaneous or induced by external circumstances, can only be considered normal when all the facts of the case are known, or in very exceptional cases.

The maintenance of a normal temperature under varying conditions, or, in other words, a constant temperature of the body in any individual, is a proof of a sound constitution.

§ 4.—A normal temperature does not necessarily indicate health, *but all those whose temperature either exceeds or falls short of the normal range, are unhealthy.*

§ 5.—There are certain limits, which are rarely exceeded, in the range of temperatures observed in disease. The highest temperature yet met with in a living man, noted by a trustworthy observer, amounted to 112·55° Fahr. (= 44·75° C.), whilst the range of lower temperatures is less accurately determined. But if we put aside cases which are quite exceptional, the range of temperature in the most severe diseases is between 95° Fahr. (35° C.) and 108·5° F. (42·5° C.), and it is very seldom that it exceeds 109·4° Fahr. (43° C.), or sinks below 91·4° F. (33° C.).

§ 6.—Deviations from the normal course of temperature are certainly to be regarded as significant, and as never occurring without due cause, whether we regard their origin, their amount, the course which they pursue, or their cessation. Many of these deviations may be referred to fixed laws or rules, even now (which I may call pathological thermonomy), but we sometimes fail to discover these, because in disease even much more than in health, animal heat or the temperature of the body is the result of many different, and, in fact, mutually antagonistic, factors. Besides the essential phenomena of disease, many accidental and collateral influences may alter the sick man's temperature.

§ 7.—Influences which in no ways disturb the temperature of a healthy man, have often a very remarkable effect in causing variations of temperature in diseased conditions of body, although the diseased condition itself may affect this but slightly. *Mobility of temperature as the result of external influences is, therefore, a sign of some diseased condition of body.* The discovery of abnormal temperatures in men who have previously exhibited a normal degree of heat is, therefore, a means of discovering or confirming the existence of latent disease.

§ 8.—Alterations of temperature may be confined to *special regions of the body,* which are *the seat of diseased actions* (local inflammations), whilst the general temperature remains more or less normal. These circumscribed variations, in topical diseases, are of very little practical moment. They consist for the most part of elevations or depressions of temperature of very moderate extent, seldom exceeding a degree Centigrade (1·8°, or less than 2° Fahrenheit), over a larger or smaller area. These local changes are almost invariably accompanied with other obvious phenomena, which, in a practical point of view, are far more useful for diagnostic purposes than the locally abnormal temperature.

§ 9.—The general temperature of the body (blood-heat), registered by the thermometer in interior parts, or in perfectly sheltered spots on the surface, not locally affected, is the *expression* of the result of a number of processes, which on the one hand tend to the production of heat (chemical processes, so-called tissue-changes), and on the other hand promote the giving up of heat (cooling by various means and apparatus, changes of heat into motion). However varied the combinations of these processes, and however their several values may change almost momentarily, so that they appear dependent on almost countless accidental circumstances; yet experience shows, not only that the final result (the animal heat, or specific heat of the body) remains almost always the same, in health; but also that in *disease* the variations of temperature, if not absolutely trustworthy, are yet the safest standard for estimating the condition of the whole body. Variations of temperature coincide with other functional and structural disturbances of the diseased organism, but none of them can be determined and measured with such accuracy as the temperature. None of them are so independent (comparatively speaking) of trifling and subordinate surrounding influences as the temperature. Very often these variations of temperature are conspicuous long before either functional or structural changes can be recognised.

§ 10.—The average temperature or specific heat of the whole body may be normal in disease, or increased or diminished, whilst the distribution of heat is unequal as regards various regions of the body. *A normal temperature in sickness is only to be considered as a relative sign*, as a symptom which may exclude certain forms of disease, and may justify, but never by itself lead to a positive diagnosis. *A fall of temperature below the normal range* is persistent in very few diseases only, but occurs as a temporary phenomenon in many favorable and unfavorable circumstances. Precisely parallel is the case of an unequal distribution of animal heat. In a majority of cases, however, this must be considered an unfavorable symptom. Abnormal *elevations* of temperature furnish the most important material for purposes of diagnosis and prognosis.

§ 11.—Abnormal variations of temperature, except such as are only momentary, are generally associated with certain common typical states of (ill) health (modalities, or typical forms.)

A rapid increase of the temperature of the body from a chill, or in the normal warmth of the hands, feet, nose, or forehead, is commonly associated with strong feelings of chilliness and convulsive movements ("*cold shivers;*" *rigors;* "*fever-frost*").

A more or less permanent and noticeable rise of temperature amounting to 101·3° Fahr. (38·5°) or more, is generally accompanied with subjective feelings of heat, and lassitude; and usually with thirst and headache, as well as with increased frequency, and rapidity of the pulse; and after lasting a little longer, with diminution of body-weight ("*Feverishness;*" *pyrexia; fever; fever-heat*).

Any considerable diminution of warmth in the extremities or in the face, or in separate exposed parts; with a high or simultaneously falling temperature of the trunk, is generally associated with a small pulse, sunken features, feelings of weakness, and nausea (Unlust), with much sweating, especially local, principally on the cold parts of the skin (*Collapse*).

§ 12.—The *amount* of temperature changes, the *relation* of these changes to one another, and their *alterations in the course of the dis-*

case [Quantity, type, and relation], although often modified by accidental influences, are commonly *determined by the nature of the disease:* and, indeed, the more typical and well-developed the diseased processes are, the more certainly is this the case. Many separate kinds of disease correspond to *well-marked types* of *altered temperature.* These answer to well-known varieties of disease.

In opposition to these there are certain *atypical* or irregular forms of disease, in which the temperature also is irregular. The contrast between typical and atypical forms is, however, not always sharply defined, so that many affections may be considered as standing on a sort of neutral ground, between typical and ill-defined forms.

True typical states of disease, that is, those which almost invariably show more or less clearly a characteristic type, and in which there is seldom if ever a complete deviation from the typical form, are illustrated by enteric fever (abdominal typhus), true exanthematic typhus, and apparently by relapsing fever, smallpox, measles, and scarlatina, primary (croupous or lobar) pneumonia, and recent malarious fevers.

The group of *approximatively typical* forms of disease, in which, indeed, characteristic types may be certainly recognised in the abstract, but which, although in certain stages they exhibit great regularity, yet occasionally deviate very widely from the typical, and almost constantly display a great breadth and laxity of behaviour is less easily defined. Yet we may include under it febricula, pyæmia, and septicæmia, varicella and rubeola notha, facial erysipelas, acute catarrhal inflammation, tonsillitis (cynanche tonsillaris), acute rheumatism (rheumatic fever), basilar meningitis, and meningitis of the superior convolutions; cerebro-spinal meningitis, parotitis (mumps), pleurisy, acute tuberculosis, fatal neuroses in their last stages, and the trichina disease.

Another group is formed by those diseases which in certain circumstances conform to a regular type, but which generally run their course without fever: when, however, fever supervenes a regular type is generally displayed. To this group cholera, acute phosphorus-poisoning, acute general fatty degeneration, and syphilis especially belong.[1] Even diseases which we are forced to include under the designation of atypical or irregular do occasionally, in exceptional cases, show a close approximation to typical forms in their

[1] Under these headings some observations will be made in the notes, which will, I believe, tend to show that this group is probably superfluous.—[TRANS.]

progress. Of these we may mention diphtheria, dysentery, pericarditis, peritonitis, acute and chronic suppurations (abscesses), and phthisis.

§ 13.—The course of the temperature in many special diseases almost invariably follows a single typical form (*monotypical* or *uniform* diseases).

Other maladies, according to their intensity, or from other special causes, follow various types of temperature (*multiform*, or *pleotypic* diseases). The study of thermometry can define these variations of disease far more accurately than has yet been done, and thus enable us to discover and differentiate varying types of the same disease. Smallpox, enteric fever, scarlatina, pneumonia, and malarious fever, are diseases which occasionally assume the multiform type (*pleotypism*), although as a rule they decidedly follow a single pure type. Those diseases which usually exhibit only an approximatively typical course of temperature, show still greater tendencies to assume a multiplicity of ill-defined types.

§ 14.—Any disease, however fixed may be its typical form, may exhibit deviations from this in special cases [irregularities.] They are determined by more or less lasting individual peculiarities and circumstances (idiosyncrasies), by external conditions, or therapeutical influences, whether favorable or unfavorable, and by the supervention of complications. These irregularities are circumscribed within certain limits, and their form and extent are more or less determinate. By means of the thermometer it will be possible to learn more of these irregularities than is yet known, to assign them to their proper causes, and give them their due weight in prognosis. And it will help us better to fix the time when a patient's disease, which has appeared to run an irregular course, reassumes a typical form.

§ 15.—*A single observation of an abnormal temperature*, however great, or however small the deviation from the normal may be, is *not by itself conclusive as to the kind of disease* from which the patient suffers. All we learn from it is—

1. That the patient is really bodily ill.

2. When there is considerable elevation of temperature, we know that there is fever.

3. When there are extremes of temperature, we know that there is great danger.

We may indeed assign the following general significance to single observations of temperature (in a conventional sense).

A. *Temperatures much below normal* (*collapse* temperatures), below 96·8° F. (36° C.).

(*a*). Deep, fatal algide collapse, below 92·3° F. (33·5° C.).

(*b*). Algide collapse, 92·3° F. to 95° F. (33·5 C. — 35°), in which it is possible for life to be saved, but which indicates the greatest danger.

(*c*). Moderate collapse, 95° — 96·8 F. (35 — 36° C.), in itself without danger.

B. *Normal, or almost normal temperatures.*

(*a*). Sub-normal temperatures, 96·8° to 97·7° F. (36 — 36·5° C.).

(*b*). Really *normal* temperatures = 97·88° to 99·12° F. (36·6 — 37·4° C.).

(*c*). Sub-febrile temperatures = 99·5° — 100·4° F. (37·5 — 38° C.).

C. *Febrile temperatures.*

(*a*). Slight febrile action = 100·4° to 101·12° F. (38 — 38·4° C.).

(*b*). Moderate degree of fever, 101·3° to 102·2° F. (38·5 — 39° C.). in the *morning*, and rising to 103·1° (39·5° C.) in the *evening*.

(*c*). Considerable fever, about 103·1° F. (39·5° C.) in the *morning*, and about 104·° in the *evening* (40·5 C.).

(*d*). High fever is indicated by temperatures above 103·1° (39·5° C.) in the *morning*, and above 104·9° (40·5) in the *evening*.

D. *Temperatures which in every known disease, except relapsing fever, in all probability indicate a fatal termination* = 107·6 F. (42° C.) or more. (Hyperpyretic temperatures.)

§ 16.—By taking into consideration other circumstances and symptoms of the sick, a single observation of temperature may sometimes lead to a diagnosis, or serve to *exclude* the existence of a supposed malady.

And a single observation of temperature (due regard being had to all the circumstances of the case) may sometimes help us to pronounce on the *severity*, or if the temperature of the disease be not dangerously high, on the comparative *safety* of the attack.

§ 17.—As there are *variations* of temperature in the course of twenty-four hours in *health*, so also they occur in *disease*. The *daily fluctuations in disease* are commonly *much greater* than *in health*. These are subject to rule—and partly depend (in febrile disease) upon the kind, stage, and degree of severity of the disease, and upon these improvement (or crisis) depends. If the daily temperature deviates from the normal type, it is generally due to the individual circumstances of the patient, to an abnormal type of disease, to complications and sudden relapses, to constipation or diarrhœa, to sudden emptying of an over-distended bladder, to a spontaneous or therapeutic loss of blood, to profuse perspirations, to moving the patient, or his over-fatiguing himself, to mental excitement or to sleep, to errors in diet and thermal influences, or the operation of medicines and other therapeutic agencies.

§ 18.—The daily fluctuations may be either simply ascending or descending, but almost always describe a *curve* with one or more *elevations* of temperature (*daily exacerbations*) and intercurrent *falls of temperature* (daily *remissions*). The number of degrees (or parts of them—the extent of the *excursus*) between the daily *maximum* and the daily *minimum* is the daily *difference* or *range* of temperature : and when the difference is trifling, we call the course of temperature continual ; when the daily fluctuations are considerable, we call it remitting. The *mean* between the *maximum* and *minimum* temperature is the *average* daily temperature, and the height of this shows the intensity of the fever. Typical forms of disease have, for the most part, during their intensity, a determinate average daily temperature, and seldom sink below a certain minimum or rise above a certain maximum, unless shortly before death.

§ 19.—*Continual observations* of temperature, repeated several times a day, through the whole course of a disease, or for a considerable period of its duration, afford the best materials for diagnosing and prognosticating the nature and results of any disease, when this is associated with considerable elevations of temperature We learn from them what is *conformable to law* or *normal* in the course of febrile diseases, thus gaining a solid basis for diagnosis in individual cases. They may often, in themselves considered, afford a perfectly *correct diagnosis of the kind of disease;* or, to say the least, they furnish the most important and trustworthy materials for a diagnosis, and are sometimes the only possible means of deciding in doubtful cases.

They point out to us the *stages* or periods in the course of a disease, and show the transition of one stage into another.

They afford the best means of judging as to the severity of a disease, and of recognising ameliorations and exacerbations. We learn from them the *irregularities* displayed by the disease in its course—dependent partly on accidental causes, partly upon complications, and partly upon the influence of therapeutic agents. They therefore furnish us *criteria* for the progress of the disease, and are checks or controllers of our therapeutics. By means of these daily observations we know when the diseased actions have come to an end; and very often, from the way in which this happens, we can decide (by looking at the chart of the temperature) upon the kind of disease, and whether it has been complicated or not, and judge of the *restoration to health* whether perfect, or as yet incomplete. Either in combination with other symptoms, or sometimes by themselves alone, the temperatures point out the approach of a *fatal termination;* and they either give assurance of undisturbed convalescence, or give the first signals of threatened relapses.

§ 20.—In the course of febrile diseases, we may distinguish the following stages or periods in the range of temperature:

A. Periods preceding the termination of the disease.

1. The period of development (initial period or pyrogenetic stage), which may be longer or shorter, but must be considered at an end with the development of a localised process, or when the lowest average daily temperature *characteristic* of the disease is reached.

2. The period of full development of the disease (the acme, the fastigium), during which the fever maintains the characteristic daily elevations of temperature.

3. The period of perturbation (amphibolic or doubtful stage) usually follows this in severe diseases, in which the temperatures generally show a more or less irregular course.

B. Periods in cases which recover.

1. The *crisis* (perturbatio critica, or stage of decrement) or period of decided, but as yet insufficient, decrease.

2. The period of return to normal temperature (stage of defervescence or cooling).

3. The epicritical period and the period of convalescence, in which the temperature is normal, or below normal, or sometimes even a little above the normal.

c. Periods of the fatal termination.

1. The pro-agonistic period (period preceding the death struggle), during which the more or less peculiar character of the temperature or other circumstances point out the commencement of a fatal termination.

2. The agony or death struggle.

3. The *act of dying* and the post-mortem changes of temperature.

Very often these several stages are very brief, and escape observation more or less entirely.

§ 21.—The initial period in many forms of disease has a constant and characteristic type, but very commonly escapes observation, on account of its brief duration. The type is varied by the fact of the fever either preceding or following a localised morbid process.

In those cases where a patient is previously ill and already feverish, the type of the stage preceding a new attack is very vague and undetermined.

The *intensity* of the symptoms (temperature, &c.) in the initial period will only lead to a correct decision on the intensity and degree of danger of the disease it ushers in, in cases of quite exceptional severity.

§ 22.—The next period, or *fastigium*, affords us *characteristic data* for a correct *diagnosis* in three ways — (a) from the height of the temperature, (b) by the alterations it undergoes, (c) and by the duration of this stage. It is especially by the positive *elevation of temperature*, by its long continuance at abnormal heights, and by deviations from the normal type (irregular progress), that we learn the *intensity* and *degree of danger* of a disease. On the other hand, when the elevation of temperature is moderate, when the duration of the *maxima* (high temperatures) is short, and the remissions occur early, we judge that the disease is of a *mild* type. *Irregularities* in the course of the temperature, even when they indicate an abatement of fever, must generally be regarded as unfavorable, and can only be considered as signs of a mild attack in certain special cases. A *rise of temperature towards the end of this stage* generally betokens some *complication* of the original malady.

§ 23.—The amphibolic or doubtful stage (of perturbations) is seldom absent in cases which, without terminating fatally, take a severe form, and the more regular the course in the fastigium the more plainly is this stage to be recognised. It is a period of improvement, marked by variations, sometimes easily traced to their source, at other times apparently capricious. During this stage we often get complications ushered in by noticeable elevations of temperature. *This period of perturbations* is always *a sign of a severe form of disease,* and should always indicate a *guarded prognosis* as long as it lasts, whether this be only a few days or some weeks. The occurrence of an exceptionally high or low temperature on a single occasion is *less significant,* but its recurrence, or the fact that the temperature remains abnormally high or at a moderate elevation, renders a relapse or convalescence probable.

§ 24.—At the conclusion of either the fastigium or the amphibolic period there is very commonly a *final rise of temperature,* which more or less exceeds those met with at an earlier stage, sometimes taking place in an afternoon, or is even shown by a *slighter* morning remission, but in many cases lasts two or three days. This rise of temperature is always associated with other marked symptoms, and gives in every way a deceiving impression that there is a relapse, or even that danger is imminent—*perturbatio critica.* It is, indeed, quite impossible to predicate its favorable character, which can only be judged of by the further course of the temperature and the progress of the case.

§ 25.—The stage of decrement, the period of preparatory moderation, is wanting in many cases of recovery, for in these the fastigium or doubtful period terminates the febrile process suddenly or after a critical disturbance.

The first time the temperature fails to reach its previous elevation, rather than any sudden change, is a characteristic of this stage. This may occur either at the evening exacerbation, or in the morning temperatures, or with both. It is not unusual in this stage to observe a single sudden descent of temperature even *below* 97·7° (36·5° C.), which is very often associated with all the symptoms of collapse. It may occur only once, and the temperature may return to its former, perhaps moderate elevation, or it may repeat itself daily, while the intervening exacerbations are still but slightly moderated.

§ 26.—The *period of defervescence* or cooling may conclude the fastigium or the amphibolic stage, or follow a critical disturbance, or be ushered in by a period of preparatory moderation. The temperature in this stage *returns to the normal*, and there are *two well-marked* and *different types*, although one may possibly sometimes pass into the other. Defervescence taking place rapidly, perhaps in a single night, or, at all events, in about thirty-six hours :— rapid defervescence or *crisis* ; or the fever may abate gradually, the process occupying several days even—protracted defervescence or *lysis*.

The defervescence may consist of either a continuous fall in temperature, which, however, when it lasts more than twelve hours, is less marked in the afternoon ; or of a fall in a remittent fashion, that is, interrupted by daily evening exacerbations. It is very common to meet with a state of *collapse* in the course of the defervescence, in which the extremely low temperature is accompanied with other deceptive and seemingly very dangerous symptoms. These cases, however, although protracted, constantly end in recovery.

§ 27.—The more rapid and complete the stage of defervescence has been, the more clearly defined is the *epicritical period* (commencing convalescence). Sometimes the temperature returns completely to the normal, and exhibits the same daily fluctuations as in health. But there is generally increased mobility, and a certain fickleness in the behaviour of the temperature. Once now and then the temperature remains below the average normal level. In some cases, and regularly in many diseases (especially in polyarticular rheumatism), it keeps above the usual height. Besides this, we sometimes meet with isolated, transient, but very significant rises of temperature (of 2, 3, or more degrees Centigrade, = 4, 6, or more degrees Fahr. nearly), of which the causes are sometimes nearly unknown, or seem but trifling. Real relapses, and secondary diseases, which also very frequently develop themselves at this special period, are also speedily recognised by the renewed rise of temperature. The duration and termination of the epicritical stage is not to be determined by the course of the temperature, because the actual true convalescence occurs without material alteration of temperature.

§ 28.—In the convalescent stage, or period of recovery, when this has been fairly entered upon, and the disease has left no sequelæ or complications, the temperature is much the same as in health. Every rise of temperature above normal, and every abnormal fall, shows that the convalescence is imperfect or deceptive. Very sudden elevations of temperature indicate a fresh complication, or a new disease; and slighter, continuous elevations are the expression of the fact that the disease has left a residuum [sequelæ] behind it.

§ 29.—In cases which terminate fatally there is generally some sign of the approaching end (pro-agonistic stage), which may either succeed the fastigium, or the amphibolic period (period of perturbation), or may unexpectedly develop itself during convalescence. The temperature is then very variable, sometimes rising, sometimes falling, sometimes continuing as before, sometimes wholly irregular. Other symptoms, such as the state of the pulse, will serve to denote this period.

§ 30.—During the *agony or death struggle*, the temperature either *alters but little*, or *remains* at its former elevation; or it *sinks* considerably, either to normal or even below it (especially in death by starvation); or it *rises* very rapidly to more or less enormous heights, to heights which in the previous course of the disease it has never reached, and, perhaps, not even approached.

§ 31.—Just about the *moment of death* the temperature sometimes *falls*; but commonly, even in cases where it has been rapidly rising for some time before, it continues to rise till death, and in some persons for some minutes, or even an hour or more *after death*. In the first class of cases the temperature falls rapidly after death; in the latter the process of cooling is tedious, so that even twelve hours after death the warmth of the corpse may be considerably greater than that of a healthy man.[1]

§ 32.—In reviewing the *course* or *progress* of febrile diseases,

[1] This section has reference (as will be seen by the context) to cases of *disease*. It has, therefore, but slight bearing on cases of *homicide*, or suicidal deaths, of which more will be said further on.—[TRANS.]

we find that the duration and succession of the febrile phenomena constitute five principal groups.

1. Cases of fever running a short course (febricula, ephemera, and terminal fever.

2. Fevers which are essentially *continuous* in their course (continued fevers), which exhibit but slight daily differences of temperature during their fastigium or acme, and defervesce rapidly (by crisis).

3. Acute fevers, which have an essentially remittent course or character, which when their intensity is not too great, exhibit even at the height of the disease, or at least in the commencement of defervescence, considerable daily differences of temperature (mostly evening exacerbations and morning remissions), and only fail to do so when complicated, or if there is a tendency to death. Their defervescence is also of a remitting type (gradual, or lysis).

4. The intermitting and relapsing types of fever.

5. Chronic or protracted forms of fever, which extend over several weeks, or even months, sometimes in an uninterrupted, but generally in a remittent or intermittent type, or sometimes with considerable intervals (free from fever).

§ 33.—Febricula and ephemeral fevers are those which last but a brief time, are moderate in degree, and terminate rapidly.

The temperature in these cases may rise, with or without rigors, to as much as 104 or 104·9° (140° or 40·5° C), or even more, but seldom exceeds this; and sinks in rapid defervescence, in all cases, with a short unbroken line of descent. The fever lasts from half a day to two or (seldom) three days. This type occurs in traumatic fever, in the brief childbed fever [ephemera or weed of Ramsbotham, Trans.], during convalescence in slight cases of catarrh, and in moderate inflammatory changes in tissues, and in many other occasional, and more or less recognisable circumstances. The *paroxysms* of intermittent fever assume this type.

In other cases the temperature rises but little at first, and either returns to normal after a day or two, or rises gradually after from two to five days to its culminating point, which seldom exceeds 104° (40° C.), and terminates rapidly in *defervescence*. This type is seen under similar circumstances to the former, but never occurs in intermittent fever.

§ 34.—Fevers which terminate a disease (terminal fever),

though widely different in their significance, much resemble those described above.

In the period shortly before death, of apyretic diseases, or in the death struggle itself, there is a rapid elevation of temperature at the point of culmination, or after a slight fall during the last moments, death ensues. This type is found at the conclusion of fatal neuroses, and in many cases of poisoning, and the temperature may thus reach a great elevation, even above that in life.

§ 35.—Fevers with *continued elevation* of temperature usually begin suddenly, with rigors and shivering. During the fastigium (or height of the fever) the average temperature varies (according to the severity of the case) between 102·2° and 104° Fahr. (39 and 40° C.), and seldom much exceeds or falls short of this. The difference between the daily maximum and minimum is only exceptionally above 1° Centigrade (1·8° Fahr.), more commonly it is only half a degree Cent. (·9 Fahr.). The length of this stage is usually less than a week. Defervescence is commonly rapid, or at least tolerably so. The most perfect representative of this group is primary uncomplicated croupous (lobar) pneumonia (although this disease sometimes assumes other types). A similar course obtains in the eruptive fever of smallpox, in scarlatina (in which, however, defervescence is less rapid), in parenchymatous tonsillitis (cynanche tonsillaris), in meningitis of the convolutions (of the convexity), and in typhus fever (exanthematic typhus), but in this case the fever lasts longer; in the beginning of facial erysipelas; and lastly, but very frequently, in very intense febrile diseases of all kinds (acute diseases), in which the temperature, previously remittent, assumes a continuous type simultaneously with the increase of heat.

§ 36.—In fevers with a *remittent* course of temperament, the initial period or stage of incubation may be either short or protracted. The average daily temperature is very varied, because both slight and severe forms assume this type, and may be either 101·3° (38·5° C.) or less, or may rise to 104·9° (40·5° C.) or more. In the latter case, so to speak, *exacerbations* may occur, but no true remissions, because the *minimum* temperature always continues truly febrile. The duration of the remittent type of fever temperature is less limited than that of the continued, and may occupy several weeks. Defervescence is generally by lysis, and of a remittent type.

Typhoid or enteric fever (abdominal typhus) is the best representative of this group. A remittent type is also displayed by febrile catarrhal affections, influenza, catarrhal pneumonia, febrile rheumatic affections, by measles, by the commencement of basilar meningitis, in acute tuberculosis, and often, at least, by acute (pulmonary) phthisis, and in acute trichinosis, &c.

§ 37.—*Intermittent* and *relapsing* types of disease have this peculiarity, that in the *intervals* of the brief, or, at all events, not protracted accessions of fever (paroxysms), there are periods of completely normal temperature. In the intermittent fevers, the actual paroxysms of fever are always short, and seldom extend through a whole day, and the temperature rises higher than in any other disease of similar intensity, where there is similar absence of danger; that is, temperatures of 105·8° F. (41° C.), or 106·7° Fahr. (41·5°) are common, and sometimes there are one or two tenths (Cent.) more (= 4° to 5° Fahr. nearly). The intermissions (apyrexiæ) are also short, yet vary from a few hours to three days. Paroxysms and intermissions alternate with each other, with more or less regularity, and this periodicity is the distinguishing feature of these diseases.

In the *relapsing* forms the paroxysm is of less limited duration, and the temperature in this stage varies; the intermission is longer, and the *relapse* or repetition of the paroxysm commonly happens *once* only, sometimes *twice*, and more rarely a *greater number of times*.

Malarial fever (ague) is the best example of the intermittent type, whilst relapsing fever (fièvre à rechute) is the best representative of the recurrent form. But many diseases seem with more or less regularity to approximate to one or other of these types, especially pyæmia, erysipelas, true smallpox, many cases of lobar pneumonia, and not unfrequently acute tuberculosis, basilar meningitis, and acute phthisis.

§ 38.—*Chronic* diseases, and those marked by *hectic*, are distinguished by their long duration, and cases are not wanting in which the fever has apparently persisted whole years.

Their course is sometimes very irregular, yet they generally approach some definite type, which although, perhaps, exchanged for another in the course of the disease, is still marked for a considerable space of time with considerable regularity. Their type is usually remittent, with one or two *exacerbations* in the course of every day. These exacerbations are sometimes slight, but sometimes severe or even extremely so, so that the temperatures daily or twice daily reach a similar elevation, and in the remission fall again to normal or even below it. Sometimes there is what I may call a tertian rhythm, or, in other words, there may be intervals of a day between the exacerbations, or the rhythm may be still more extended. When death approaches, or when complications occur, the remitting type often changes into a continuous one. This is best recognised in those chronic inflammations of the lungs and bronchi which are classed together clinically as phthisis, chronic ulcerations of the bowels, prolonged suppurations, in chronic inflammations of serous membranes, and in prolonged admixture of embolic or infecting materials with the blood.

§ 39.—An elevated temperature, be the cause what it may, has undoubtedly in itself an influence on the *functions of the body*, on the *nutrition* of the *tissues*, and upon secretions.

When the temperature is only slightly raised, it is not possible to distinguish the amount of this in particular cases. When the elevation of temperature, however, is considerable, the most certain result will be a diminution of the weight of the body. Besides this, the pulse and respiration will be accelerated, the brain will exhibit functional disturbances, the secretions of the skin, and the elimination of *urea* will be increased. There will be tendencies to local congestions, and their results; perhaps, also, to rapid fatty degenerations, and even destruction of tissue (mortification). Yet these results are not proportionate to either the amount, duration, or rapidity of the elevation of temperature, and their absence is not an unusual circumstance. The most remarkable elevated temperatures are incompatible with the continuance of life. The reason of this is at present unknown.

§ 40.—Very sudden alterations of temperature may influence the functions of the body. Very rapid rises of temperature, especially when the warmth of the trunk considerably exceeds that of the extremities, are commonly associated with *rigors:* with rapid falls of temperature, where this has previously been high, we find severe disturbances of health, dyspnœa, delirium, or appearances of collapse.

2

§ 41.—Diseases which, instead of displaying elevations of temperature, are characterised, on the contrary, by an abnormally low temperature, never conform to regular rules as regards the course of the temperature, which is never constant.

Many cases of inanition, of scleroma, cancer, chronic intoxication, and of serious mental disease, belong to this category.

Exceedingly low temperatures are, however, very commonly met with in the following cases:

In the remissions of a remittent fever;

In consequence of loss of blood, or powerful evacuations;

In the course of defervescence, when this is excessive;

And sometimes in the death-struggle.

Abnormally low temperatures may seriously disturb the various functions of the body; and when the fall is very considerable, it may render the continuance of life impossible.

CHAPTER II.

HISTORY AND BIBLIOGRAPHY.

§ 1.—In the earliest ages of medicine the significance of temperature as a symptom of disease was fully recognised. By *Hippocrates*, in common with most of the ancient writers, and those of the middle ages, and even of comparatively modern times, the heat of the body was deemed to be the chief and most diagnostic sign of acute diseases. Most of them considered heat as a pathognomonic symptom of fever, and the Greek and Latin names signifying fever point to the elevation of temperature as of the greatest importance.

It is somewhat remarkable that after the lapse of two thousand years, during which an increased temperature was recognised as a characteristic and important symptom of fever, without any controversy, the true significance of the phenomenon should first fail to be recognised, and as it were, fall into the background, in an age in which accurate thermometry first became possible by means of instruments, and that in a school which introduced the study of physical signs into pathology, and by which the use of the thermometer in the observation of disease was first recommended and introduced. We can, however, explain this. The Iatro-mechanical theories of medicine directed the chief attention of observers to the phenomena presented by the altered conditions of the circulation in fevers, and, moreover, these were precisely the symptoms which most exactly agreed with the current theories of disease. And further, as modern medicine developed itself, it so happened that as observation became more precise and difficult, attention was diverted from those common symptoms, which were difficult to determine precisely, to those topical changes which had been neglected by earlier observers. The increasing number of aids to diagnosis, which were continually being discovered and perfected, and thus revealed *local* alterations of structure, seemed to give such a certainty of diagnosis, that in contemplating this positive gain one forgot the loss sustained by neglecting to observe the amount of *general* disturbance of the bodily functions. And in this way, just as accurate thermometry was rendered possible by the discovery of instruments for determining the degree of heat, the study of temperature was more and more neglected, only a few isolated observations being taken here and there, till it had fallen quite into oblivion, and has only lately been revived.

§ 2.—*Sanctorius* (died about 1638), the fore-runner of the Iatro-mechanical school, was the first to apply a thermometric instrument of his own discovery and manufacture, to the determination of temperature. It is interesting to notice that Sanctorius was fully aware of the importance of determining the *body-weight* as well as the *temperature*, and considered these the two principal criterions for the changes affecting the whole body. [He invented a weighing-chair, and strongly advised the use of the balance in other ways, in the study of disease. He was Professor of Medicine at Padua, and afterwards practised at Venice. His treatise 'Ars de Statica Medicina' was published in 1614.—TRANS.] Another century, however, passed before the measurement of temperature was again revived—with improved and practically perfect instruments.

The great *Boerhaave* was the first to profit by this. Although he sought for the essential nature of fevers in disturbances of circulation, and amongst other things, remarks in his 581st Aphorism, "Velocior cordis contractio, cum auctâ resistentiâ ad capillaria, febris omnis acutæ ideam absolvit;"[1] yet he remarks in the 673rd Aphorism, "Calor febrilis thermoscopio externus sensu ægri et rubore urinæ internus cognoscitur."[2]

Van Swieten, one of Boerhaave's pupils, speaks yet more plainly; for although he too, in his second book of 'Commentaries on Boerhaave's Aphorisms' (Leyden, 1745), p. 26, says, "Signum patho-

[1] "An increase in the rapidity of the heart's contractions, and an increased resistance of the capillaries, complete our idea of every acute fever."
[2] "External febrile heat is recognised by the thermometer; internal by the sensations of the patient, and by the redness of the urine."

gnomonicum omnis febris est pulsus aucta velocitas," [1] yet he adds to the other aphorism of Boerhaave's the note, "The estimate of temperature by the hand is uncertain." [2] "Omnium ergo certissima mensura habetur per thermoscopia, qualia hodie pulcherrima habentur, et portalia quidem, fahrenheitiana dicta a primo inventore : accuratissima imprimis illa sunt, quæ argentum vivum loco alterius cujuscunque liquidi continent. Tali thermometro, prius mensuratur calor hominis sani, et plerumque in indice affixo ille gradus notatus est ; deinde hoc cognito, si idem thermometrum a febricitante ægro manu teneatur, vel bulbus ejus ori immittatur, vel nudo pectori aut sub axillis applicetur per aliquot minuta horæ, apparebit pro varia altitudine ascendentis argenti vivi, quantum calor febrilis excedat naturalem et sanum calorem." And in the commentary on section 476, "Datur in corpore hominis sani caloris gradus, thermometris mensurandus, a quo nec liquidis nec solidis aliquid noxæ accidit. Raro etiam in fortissimis hominibus calor ille nonagesimum sextum gradum thermometri Fahrenheitiani excedit. Ubi vero ultra centesimum gradum in morbis ascendit, incipit sanguis ejusque serum ad coagulationem disponi; si autem centesimum et vigesimum gradum æquat calor, serum sanguinis coagulatur."

In contrast with these limited researches another celebrated pupil of Boerhaave's, and a colleague of Van Swieten's, *de Haen*, the first clinical teacher at Vienna (and indeed in all Germany), greatly extended the practical application of thermometry in disease. Although he too defined fever, as a disease which was commonly to be recognised by a more or less quickened pulse, yet he availed

[1] "Increased rapidity of pulse is the special diagnostic symptom of every fever."

[2] "By far the most accurate measurements of heat are by thermometers, which are now to be had both elegant and portable, and are called after Fahrenheit, the first inventor of them. Those which contain quicksilver instead of other fluids are the most accurate. When such a thermometer, first used on a healthy man, and marked accordingly on the scale, is either held in the hand of a fever patient, or the bulb placed in his mouth, or laid on his bare chest, or in his axillæ, for some minutes, the ascent of the mercury to different elevations will show how far the fever heat exceeds the natural and healthy." "Let it be granted that the degree of heat, to be measured by the thermometer, in healthy men, is one at which no injury accrues to either liquids or solids ; for it is rare indeed, in even the strongest man, to find the temperature exceed 96° F. But when it rises above 100° in diseases, the blood and its serum are disposed to coagulate. If, however, the temperature equals 120° the serum of the blood is coagulated."

himself of the use of the thermometer in the observation of febrile
disease very extensively.

His method of thermometry was very peculiar, because he was
accustomed to leave the instrument seven and a half minutes *in situ*,
and then add 1° or 2° F. to the temperature registered, because he
had found that the mercury would rise as much if left longer. In
spite of this imperfect method of procedure, the thermometer
afforded him very valuable data, which for the most part have been
confirmed or even re-discovered in modern times. His researches are
dispersed through the fifteen volumes of his ' Ratio Medendi.'
Those chiefly deserving notice are: tom. ii, cap. 10, " De supputando
calore corporis humani;" tom. iii, cap. 3, " De sanguine humano,
ejusdemque calore;" tom. iv, cap. 6, " De sanguine et calore humano;
tom. vii, cap. 5, " Varia," § 3; tom. x, cap. 1, " De febribus inter-
mittentibus; cap. 2, " De morbis acutis;" tom. xii, cap. 2, " Historia
pulsus," &c.

De Haen made a number of observations of temperature on healthy
people of various ages, and very numerous investigations in sick
people, so that he could fairly judge of its significance. " Non
antem semel deciesve, sed pluries ipsissima experimenta iterata sunt
et semper idem docuerunt." [1] He remarked constantly the remarkable
fact of the high temperature of the aged. In various parts of his
work we discover how valuable an aid to prognosis and diagnosis de
Haen found thermometry to be. He was aware of the morning
remission and evening exacerbation of temperature in fevers; the rise
of temperature during febrile rigors (fieber frost) (tempore frigoris
homini intolerabilis cum pulsu contractiore minore, thermometum
signat octo gradus ultra calorem naturalem,[2] tom. ii, p. 142.)

He was familiar with the elevations of temperature, after intermittent fevers have been apparently cured, which are often unaccom-
panied with any other noticeable symptoms (tom. iii, p. 326); he
was aware of the discrepancies between pulse and temperature in
many patients, the common contrast between subjective feelings of
warmth (or the reverse), and objective elevations of temperature; he
used the changes of temperature as a controller or director for his

---

[1] " Not once only, nor even ten times, but very many times were the experiments repeated, and always with the same result."

[2] " During the cold stage, so intolerable to the patient, along with a
diminished force of the pulse, the thermometer registers eight degrees above
the natural heat."

therapeutics, and regarded the return to a normal temperature as a proof of convalescence.

The causes of animal heat were discussed by him at considerable length, and with some ardour, in opposition to any mechanical theory of its origin.

In spite of the influence of this celebrated Vienna Professor, his contemporaries appear to have neglected medical thermometry.

§ 3.—In England, however, about the year 1740, *Ch. Martin* published the first accurate observations on temperature in healthy men and animals ('De animalium calore').

The followers of *Haller* also turned their attention to this subject. (*Haller-Marcard*, 'Dissert. de generatione caloris et usu in corpore humano,' Göttingen, 1741. *Röderer*, 'Dissert. de animalium calore observ.,' Göttingen, 1758.) A dissertation by *Pickel* is also quoted, 'Experimenta med. physica de electricitate et calore animali,' Würzburg, 1778, in which experiments on the influence of bathing in rivers on the temperature are recorded.

One of the most remarkable and important facts of physiology, as regards temperature, was, however, established in 1774, *Blagden* ('Philosophical Transactions,' 1775, p. 111) demonstrated the maintenance of temperature of healthy men in rooms heated to the boiling point of water (212°), and *Dobson* remarked the same at a still higher temperature. These communications led *John Hunter*, the great surgeon and physiologist, to publish his experiments, begun in 1766 (Philosophical Transactions, 1775—78). He showed that animals were able to resist external cold, because they produced in themselves heat enough to counterbalance the loss.

John Hunter also, who was the first to remark local elevation of temperature in inflammation (first after an operation for hydrocele, Hunter's Works, edition 1837, vol. iii, p. 338), combatted the view that the temperature was produced by the circulation of the blood. He says, "It is very evident that warmth depends on a different principle, which is intimately connected with life itself, and is a power which maintains and regulates the machine, independent alike of the circulation, the will, and of sensation. However, he was not fortunate enough to discover the seat of this power, and he was inclined to locate it in the stomach.

Shortly after this, the celebrated work 'Sur la chaleur, mém. de l'académie' (1780) was published in France, by the celebrated

Lavoisier, the discoverer of oxygen, and the reformer of chemistry. [1]
In conjunction with Laplace, he investigated the causes of animal
heat, and ascribed it to the chemical combinations of oxygen with
hydrogen and carbon in respiration. He says, " The animal
machine has three regulators : respiration, which consumes hydrogen
and carbon, and produces heat ; transpiration, which according
to the necessity of the case, lowers the temperature and cools the
body ; and digestion, which restores to the blood what it has lost.
Although he considers the combustion of hydrogen and carbon to be
sources of animal heat, he does not entirely exclude other chemical
processes. He places the seat of warmth production (combustion)
in the lungs. An Englishman also, *Crawford* (' De calore animali,'
1779, ' Experiments and observations on animal heat,' 1786, and
second edition, 1788) seeks the source of heat in the chemical processes in the lungs, whilst he admits that there may be an overplus
of heat, because the capacity of the atmospheric air for heat may
exceed that of carbonic acid for the same. He also turned his
attention to some pathological changes of temperature, and also to
the temperature of special inflamed parts, seeking to explain what he
found by the help of his theory.

§ 4.—Towards the conclusion of the last century (1797) there
appeared a work which was singularly free from mere theories, and
in the highest sense of the term, practical. For the first time since
the observations of de Haen, temperature observations were made
available for medicinal purposes, especially for the therapeutic indications they afforded, and as a means for controlling therapeutic
experiments. This was James Currie's ' *Medical Reports on
the effect of water, cold and warm, as a remedy in fever and other
diseases.*'

Observations of temperature are almost invariably added to the
clinical reports of the cases, and thermometry pervades the whole of
Currie's practice. He tests the action of warm and cold baths, of
digitalis, opium, alcohol, and restricted diet, by the alterations of
temperature they produce. He regards perspiration as a regulating
apparatus for temperature (p. 620). The value which Currie set
upon temperature as diagnostic and prognostic in the case of fevers,
will appear from the following passage (which the German translator

[1] Oxygen was so *named* by Lavoisier, but was *discovered* in 1774 by Scheele
in Sweden, and Dr. Priestly in England, independently.—TRANS.

Hegewitsch says he should have suppressed, were it not that it appeared to him a "glaring instance" in proof of the miserable state of medicine in England !):—

"Though I am far from thinking that fever, properly so called, consists merely of a series of phenomena originating in a morbid accumulation of heat in the system, yet this symptom evidently occurs more or less early in that disease," (p. 624), and further, "that some advantages are to be obtained from a strict attention to the state of the heat in fever, and to the proper function of the perspiration, this volume affords, if I do not deceive myself, important proofs. A careful attention to the changes of the animal heat, and to the state of those functions on which it depends, and by which it is regulated, though more requisite in febrile diseases, perhaps, than in others, is however of importance throughout the whole circle of diseases " (p. 621). Although *Currie's* work ran through several editions in England, and was very favorably reviewed, yet it influenced his contemporaries and countrymen but little. Its influence in Germany was still slighter. *Michaelis's* translation of the first part fell almost still-born from the press, and *Hegewitsch*, who undertook to translate the second part, complained that the first part was almost unknown amongst German medical men. A similar fate befell himself, as regards his share in the translation, and it was not till half a century later that *Hufeland* again rescued Currie's work for a brief space from the oblivion into which it had fallen.

§ 5.—Whilst practical men in various countries, with the exception of those above named, concerned themselves but little with the temperature of the sick, physiologists for the most part were quite satisfied with the chemical theory of warmth-production, as explained by *Lavoisier*. It is true there were one or two exceptions, as *Vacca Berlinghieri* ("esame della teoria di Crawford"), *Buntzen*, and others.

But the experiments of *Coleman* ('Dissertation on suspended respiration,' 1791), and *Saissy* ('Recherches sur la physique des animaux hybernans,' 1808) adduced some interesting facts which appeared to contradict this chemical theory.

Sir Benjamin Brodie, in 1811, entered the lists as an opponent of the theory of the production of warmth by respiratory processes (see his paper on "Some physiological researches respecting the influence of the brain on the action of the heart, and on generation of animal heat," 'Philosophical Transactions,' 1811, p. 36, and also "Further experiments and observations on the influence of the brain in the generation of animal heat," 'Phil. Trans.' 1812, p. 378). His experiments had shown him that, in decapitated animals, when the cervical vessels were ligatured, and artificial respiration was maintained for some hours, in spite of the conversion of venous into arterial blood, maintained for so long a time, the temperature of the body sank more rapidly than in those cases in which (after decapitation) artificial respiration was not tried.   He deduced the conclusion that no heat was evolved in the conversion of venous blood into arterial by respiration, and that the source of heat must be sought for in the nervous system.   This explanation led not only to a lively discussion but to further investigations as to temperature.   *Dalton* at once opposed *Brodie*, and *John Davy*, in particular (' Philosophical Transactions,' 1814, p. 590), published experiments on the capacity of arterial and venous blood for heat, and comparative researches on the temperature of both kinds of blood, as well as that of different parts of the body.   A communication of *Hale's* (in Meckel's ' Archives,' iii, 429), and one by *Legallois* (Ibid., 436) may also be mentioned.

On the other hand, *Nasse*, the translator of Brodie's tractate (Reil & Autenrieth's ' Archives,' 1815, Bd. xii, 404—446) pronounced strongly in favour of *Brodie*.

Earle also believed that Brodie's theory was supported by pathological observations.

Chossat (see ' Mém. sur l'influence du système nerveux sur la chaleur animale.' Thèse de Paris, 1820) considered the opinion that the source of animal heat was to be sought in the sympathetic nerve, established by a great number of experiments.   In the course of this discussion the French Academy offered a prize for a treatise on the source of animal heat.   The essay of *Dulong* (read December, 1822), and that of *Despretz* (read January, 1823) were published.   Both of them decided for Lavoisier's theory.   They estimated the oxygen absorbed by animals, and the carbonic acid which they exhaled, ascribed the overplus of oxygen absorbed to formation of water; estimated the total production of heat by the combination of oxygen and carbonic acid, and that of the ascertained excess of oxygen combined with a calculated quantity of hydrogen, in proportion to form water, and compared these results with the total heat-production in animals, as determined by calorimetry (now for the first time made use of for determining physiological questions) ; as, however, an excess of heat was found to be produced (as compared with the estimated amount), the conclusion was arrived at that there must be other sources of heat than the combustion-processes of the animal body.

§ 6.—During these theoretrical discussions but few observations were made of temperature in human beings. *Gentil*, however, published some on the variations of temperature according to age, sex, temperament, and the time of day ('Diss. sur la chaleur animale,' quoted by *Deyeux* in 'Annales de Chimie,' xcvi, p. 45). *Thomson* also reported on the production of heat in an inflamed part (communicated in Meckel's 'Archives,' v. 405).

Shortly after, two practical works appeared in Germany, which followed Currie's plan. *Hufeland*, in 1821, offered a prize for the demonstration of Currie's experiments on the influence of the water treatment of febrile diseases. One of the requisitions of the giver of the prize was, that the essays should contain "a series of original experiments, in order to moderate febrile heat by the external use of water, by Currie's method. The use of the thermometer before and after the application of water, and counting the pulse, appears to be an essential part of the experiments."

These prize essays were published in Hufeland's 'Journal' for 1822. The third of these (by *Pitschaft*) appears to be valueless. On the other hand, the one by *Anton Fröhlich* (of Vienna), and that by *Reuss* (of Aschaffenburg) both contain many valuable contributions to pathological thermometry. Some thermometric observations are contained in *Lucas'* Dissertation at Bonn, 'Experimenta circa famem,' 1824.

Bailly wrote a "Mémoire sur l'altération de la chaleur animale dans les fièvres algides" ('Revue Méd.' 1825, v, 384).

Sir Everard Home (in 'Philosophical Transactions,' 1825, p. 257), in a paper "On the influence of nerves and ganglions in producing animal heat," adduced some incredibly high temperatures (as much as 118° Fahr. = 47·7° C.), which *Grainville* asserted to have observed in the uterus during labour.

Edwards, in 1824 ('De l'influence des agents physiques sur la vie') gave a résumé of all that was then known about temperature.

§ 7.—During these thirty years only a few methodical or comprehensive observations on the relations of temperature to health and disease were published.

The celebrated researches of *Becquerel* and *Breschet* (published in

1835 in the 'Annales des sciences naturelles,' second series,
"Zoologie," tom. iii, iv, and ix) belong to this category, although they
regarded pathological conditions but slightly. They tested the variations of temperature in different parts of the bodies of animals, by
means of extraordinarily sensitive thermo-electric apparatus. These
experiments found the temperature of inflamed parts to be higher
than that of the rest of the body.

Another work, which concerned itself still less with pathology,
was the zoo-physiological treatise of Berger, which treated of the
determination of temperature in various species of animals ("Faits
relatifs à la construction d'une échelle de degrés de la chaleur
animale," in the 'Mémoires de la societé de physique et histoire
naturelle de Genéve,' tom. vi, part 2, p. 257; and 1836, tom. vii,
p. 1).

Edwards furnished a comprehensive article in ' *Todd's* Cyclopædia,'
vol. ii, p. 648, 1836—39.

The specially medical publications of this period were far less
valuable.

Collard de Martigny, in 1836, wrote, ' De l'influence de la circulation génerale et pulmonaire de la chaleur du sang, et de celle de ses
fluides sur la chaleur animale,' in the ' Journal Conplénation,' tom.
xliii, p. 286.

The article on warmth in the thirty-volume ' Dictionary ' of 1834
had for its authors, for the physiological part *P. H. Bérard* (tom.
vii, p. 175), and for the pathological part (p. 212) *Chomel*, then the
first practitioner of his day in France. *Chomel* laid great stress
upon temperature, but believed the hand to be the only proper
instrument to determine it, and that the thermometer only gave imperfect ideas of its elevation, and was unable to give any indications
of its special modifications.

Bouillaud, however, declares that he made more than three
hundred thermometric observations (' Clinique Méd.' i, 294, and iii,
428).

Donné (' Archiv. Géneral:' 2 série, ix, 129) investigated the
temperature in various diseases, and compared it with the pulse and
respirations.

Piorry (1838, ' Traité de la diagnostie,' iii, p. 28) recognises the
necessity of a measurement of the skin temperature " dans plusieurs
cas," and cites the following from *Biot*, " Lorsq'un voit tant de
résultats obtenus par le seul secours d'un peu de mercure enfermé

dans un tube de verre, et qu'on songe qu'un morceau de fer suspendu sur un pivot a fait découvrir le nouveau monde, on conçoit que rien de ce qui peut agrandir et perfectionner les sens de l'homme, ne doit être pris en legère consideration." [1]

Piorry had a thermometer added to his stethoscope, and speaks very judiciously on the value of thermometry, only he gives so many cautions and difficult directions as to the use of the instrument as almost to deter people from using it. Notwithstanding this, his own observations are entirely untrustworthy, and indeed fabulous. He found the temperature in the axilla in healthy persons to be $32°$ Réaumur, and even more (= $104°$ Fahr.), and in a number of sick people, temperatures of 34—$36°$ R. (=$108·5°$—$113°$ Fahr.) and even $38°$ R. (=$117·5°$ Fahr.) in a case of typhus. In a case of prurigo, *free from fever*, he found a temperature of $34°$ R. (=$108·5°$ Fahr.) in the axilla, and $35°$ R. (=$110·75°$ Fahr.) at the epigastrium! He took temperatures in ninety-one individuals, but only once in any single case, and his observations were in various parts of the body. It is, therefore, obviously impossible to deduce any conclusions from observations so little comparable with each other.

Sir Benjamin Brodie made known his experiments on elevation of temperature after division of the spinal cord, and his case of traumatic hæmorrhage in the upper part of the cord, with enormous elevation of temperature, in the year 1837 (" Pathological and surgical observations relating to injuries of the spinal cord," in the ' Med.-Chir. Transactions,' vol. xx, p. 118).

In the same year (1837) a somewhat valuable dissertation by *Wistinghausen* was published at Dorpat (' De calore animali quædam') treating of the sources of animal heat, and the causes of its constancy.

Fricke, of Hamburgh ('Zeitschrift für d. gesammte Med.,' 1838), made experiments on the axillary and vaginal temperatures before and during menstruation, and found a slight elevation of temperature during the flow of the catamenia.

Friedrich Nasse published in 1839 (in ' Untersuchungen zur Physiologie and Pathologie,' von F. and Hermann Nasse, Bd. 2, Heft i, p. 115), some new experiments on the dependence of animal

[1] " When one sees such results obtained by the sole aid of a little mercury in a glass tube, and reflects that the discovery of the New World was owing to a little bit of iron suspended on a pivot, surely nothing which can supplement or perfect the operations of our senses should be held in slight estimation."

heat upon the nervous system, and *Hermann Nasse* (Ibid., p. 190), " On the dependence of animal heat on the brain and spinal cord."

Gavarret (' Journal l'expérience,' 1839), confirmed what *de Haen* had already found, although it was even then not generally known that the temperature of the trunk during the rigor of fever (Fieber-frost), was much elevated, and not less than in the hot stage (Fieber-hitze). We are indebted to *Dr. John Davy* for the most important additions to the facts of thermometry, at least in healthy persons at this period. He republished his earlier statements in ' Physiological and Anatomical Researches' (1839).

But during the whole of these forty years, the work done in animal temperature was but scanty, and *H. Nasse* (loc. cit. supra), has very justly remarked of this period : " For some years past the science of thermometry has been more neglected than formerly, and indeed remains almost in *statu quo.*"

§ 8. About the year 1840, there commenced in good earnest a series of not-again-interrupted painstaking investigations on the temperature of the body both in health and disease. The facts relating to temperature in both these conditions were now first collected in greater numbers, and in a much more methodical manner. As regards the practical application of thermometry to clinical observation, which holds itself free from all theories, we find several observers had already recognised the importance of thermometric observations in order to decide on the severity of a disease or its amelioration or exacerbation (diagnosis and prognosis), whilst others had considered an elevated temperature worthy of notice, either by itself or in relation to other single symptoms (the pulse, &c.) ; but no one, since the time of *Currie*, had made the attempt (or even believed in its possibility), to evolve practical laws from the *course of the temperature*, and, as it were, to *map them out* for others (und sie auschaumg zu bingen). *Andral* (whom we consider as in every way the leader of the march of progress in his day), first recognised the aspect of medical thermometry, and in the year 1841 he formulated a considerable number of fixed rules for the elevation of temperature in disease, in his ' Lectures on general pathology.'

Still more valuable was the dissertation by *Gierse* which appeared in 1842. The medical faculty at Halle had offered a prize for an essay on the question " Quænam sit ratio caloris organici partium inflammatione laborantium, investigetur experimentis accuratius faciendis." [The cause and reason of organic heat in inflamed parts to be investigated by careful experiments.]

Gierse extended his subject, and carefully measured the temperature, not only in artificially or spontaneously induced inflammations of the skin and mucous membranes, but also in various febrile affections (intermittent fevers, scarlatina, measles, &c.), not once but several times, and also the temperature during menstruation and pregnancy, making observations on his own temperature at various times of the day, and adding thermometric observations on plants.

Gierse's observations have long been regarded and quoted as the best comparative ones, and are not devoid of value at the present time.

Not less important, although somewhat neglected, were the observations of *Hallmann* scattered through his treatise on the proper treatment of typhus ('Uber eine zweckmässige Behandlung des Typhus'), 1844. He was deeply impressed with the importance of thermometry in medicine, and the necessity of its introduction into clinical researches, and has not only incorporated the result of his observations on the variation of temperature with his recommendations of the water treatment of fevers, but has also added a number of observations on the variations of temperature in the healthy, under various conditions and circumstances (p. 54).

In *France*, *Chossat's* " Experimental researches on inanition," which were for the most part communicated in 1838, were republished during the year 1843. ('Mémoires de l'académie royale des sciences,' tom. viii, p. 438.) In the second part (p. 532 *et seq.*), he investigated the influence of starch on animal heat, and incidentally discussed carefully the daily fluctuations of temperature in the normal condition. *Chossat* regards the difference between the day and night temperatures, as a proof that " les combinaisons d'ou résultent les dégagements de la chaleur animale, se font essentiallement sous l'influence nerveuse" (p. 554).[1] He investigates the decrease of temperature in complete starvation, as well as in the case of imperfect nutrition, and gives the lowest point to which the temperature falls in fatal cases of starvation.

The investigations of *Henri Roger*, although they have a limited basis, and are not guarded by those precautions necessary to perfectly trustworthy results, are yet highly important. (" *De la température*

---

[1] " The combinations which give rise to animal heat are essentially under the influence of the nervous system."

chez les enfants à l'état physiologique et pathologique," published in
1844 in the 'Archiv Génér.,' série 4, tom. iv—ix, [and republished
separately. There is a copy in the Obstetrical Society's library, of
which I have availed myself.—TRANS.]). After some preliminary
observations on the methods of thermometry, *Roger* adduces observations on the normal temperature of children (at birth, during the
first seven days, and at a later period), as well as in ephemera, intermittent, and typhoid fevers, smallpox, scarlatina, measles, erysipelas,
rheumatism, pericarditis, cardiac hypertrophy, stomatitis, enteritis,
dysentery, meningitis, encephalitis, laryngitis, bronchitis, pleurisy,
and pneumonia; and still further, in tuberculosis, hooping-cough,
chorea, dropsies, rickets, and paralysis; not to mention thrush and
the œdema (scléréme) of newly born infants.

Finally, at pp. 261—297 of tom. ix, he sums up the results
obtained in a very practical manner, in their application to diagnosis
and prognosis. Such a wealth of thermometric fact had never
before been accumulated, and *Roger* himself was well aware of the
practical importance of his experiments. If, however, we are forced
to confess that his great work does not express the full value of
pathological thermometry, the explanation must be sought in the
fact that the observations were not reported sufficiently often in the
several cases (very often the temperature was only taken once in the
disease), and especially in the fact that *Roger* strove rather to estimate and compare the positive rise or fall of temperature in various
diseases, than to indicate the course of the temperature in any given
disease, which is far more important. None the less, on this
account, are *Roger's* summaries and deductions of great interest
even in the present day, and they contain many fine observations.

Demarquay published a contribution to experimental pathology,
in which he investigated the influence of pain, of loss of blood, of
the ligature of blood-vessels, of traumatic inflammations, of obstruction of the bowels, and of various toxic agents on the temperature of animals. (Récherches expérimentales sur la température
Dissert., 1847), and conjointly with *Dumérril*, " Experiments on the
effect of ether and chloroform in lowering temperature" (1848,
'Arch. Génér.,' 4 série, tom. xvi, p. 189.) About this time, *George
Zimmermann*, an army surgeon at Hamm, began to make very
numerous observations on temperature. His first publications are
to be found in the 'Med. Zeiting d. Vereins f. Heilkunde in
Preussen,' 1846, Nos. 30 and 40, and almost immediately after,

very numerous ones in the same journal for 1847, Nos. 19, 21, and 35, 36; in the 'Archiv für physiologische Heilkunde,' 1847, p. 735, and in the 'Prager medicin. Vierteljahrschrift,' 1847, Bd. 4, p. 1. In the 'Archiv für Chemie und Mikroskopie,' 1847, and in his paper, 'Über die Analyse des Blutes,' 1847, further observations will be found.

In the year 1850, this surgeon published a new series of papers; first, in the 'Archiv für physiologische Heilkunde,' 1850, p. 283; next, in the first part of his own 'Archivs für Pathologie und Therapie,' 1850, in the 'Deutsche Klinik,' 1851, No. 36, and 1852, No. 9, in the 'Prager medicin. Vierteljahrschrift,' Bd. 4, p. 97; in 'Med. Zeitung des Vereins f. Heilkunde in Preussen,' 1852, but especially in a brochure which he published, entitled, 'Klinische Untersuchungen zur Fieber-Entzündungs-und Krisen-Lehre,' 1854 ('Clinical Researches in Fevers, Inflammations, and Crises').

Zimmermann undoubtedly rendered a great service to medical thermometry by his untiring observations, made at a time when its importance was generally neglected by medical men. His harsh and fearless denunciations of his colleagues, for neglect of so important a means of observation, were not entirely unfounded. Besides, he has furnished a great number of very valuable facts. The very copiousness of his works has, however, deterred people from following in his steps. Independently of the mass of facts which they contain, his works are, however, of value, because he first especially pointed out the dependence of elevated temperature upon local processes of inflammation, and the rise of temperature developed in them.

It is almost certain that the dissertation of *J. Peter Schmitz,* which appeared at Bonn, in 1849, 'De calore in morbo,' and contained about 300 observations of temperature in various diseases, owed its publication to the influence of *Nasse,* who was almost the only German clinical teacher who took a lively interest in the subject of temperature.

We ought, perhaps, to supplement this catalogue with the further observations of *Dr. John Davy,* on the temperature of healthy persons, as offering a simple basis for other observations, free from all theoretical propositions. He had published a number of papers from the years 1844 to 1850, of varying value, and in 1863 he published them in a collected form in his 'Physiological Researches.' They treat of the temperature in advanced age, of the influence of various

temperatures of the external air on animal heat ; of the diurnal fluctuations, the influence of seasons, of active and passive movements,
of concentrated attention, of increased alimentation, and of the
effects of sea-sickness on the temperature, and all these points are
discussed as regards tropical as well as northern climates, and incidentally many other less important subjects are considered. Although
not, perhaps, the most exact observations possible, they are collec-
tions of materials of great value.

Other pathologists devoted their attention to special features of
animal temperature. *Foureault*, *Flourens*, and especially *Magendie*,
made experimental researches on the physiology of temperature.

Bergmann, although a chemist, furnished a contribution of a
physical character to the literature of the subject in his " Beitrag
zur Kritik der Lehre von Calor Animalis" in Müller's ' Archiv,' 1845,
(p. 300), and again in 1847 (' Göttingen Studien,' p. 595), he published a treatise, " Über die Verhältnisse der Wärmeökonomie der
Thiere zu ihrer Grösse" (" On the size of animals as affecting their
comparative temperature.)"

In 1846, *Helmholtz* published a very valuable and comprehensive
article on warmth, in the Berlin ' Encyklopädische Wörterbuch der
medicinischen Wissenschaften,' Bd. 25, p. 323, and in 1848, the
same investigator furnished a demonstration of the production of
warmth by muscular movements. In 1847, there appeared a translation from the Dutch of *Donders* on " The tissue changes as a
source of heat in both plants and animals."

Friedrich Nasse's treatise on ' Verbrennen und Athmen,' 1846
(' Respiration and Combustion'), belongs to the physiological series.

§ 9. But the greatest advance was made at this time, in respect
to the theory of warmth, and of animal heat in particular. New
principles are developed which appeared at first to influence opinion
but slightly, but soon acquired an indisputable supremacy over all
views which had been previously entertained.

This appears to me the place to mention the views of *Liebig* upon
the sources of animal heat, views founded less upon direct experiment
than upon a bold and original conception of genius. He considers the
source of animal heat to be the combination of the constituents of the
food, with the oxygen carried by the blood-streams (v. ' Die organische Chemie in ihrer Anwendung auf Physiologie und Pathologie,'
1842). Although some of *Liebig's* conclusions are untenable, and
the distinction drawn by him between tissue-forming (histo-genetic)

material, and warmth-producing (respiratory, thermo-genetic) food, extremely difficult to maintain in its strict signification (although still accepted by many), and although his inroads upon the province of pathology have not all been successful, yet the deliberate reference of the ultimate source of animal heat to chemical processes, and especially to a slow combustion (eremacausis), maintains its ground. The basis laid by *Lavoisier* was extended and fortified, as well as adorned, by *Liebig*.

The recognition of the essential unity of the so-called imponderables (of chemical forces and of motion) ; the reference of all chemical processes to a single force or power, which sometimes appeared as light from the sun, its unquenchable source; was sometimes continued as chemical difference, sometimes changed into heat, sometimes into a mechanical effect (motion), and sometimes transposed into electricity, preserving all the while in inorganic as in organic nature, a constant magnitude—this doctrine of the unity and correlation of forces was a *perfectly new idea*, which we owe to *Dr. J. R. Mayer*, a surgeon practising at Heilbronn, who first published this idea, which marks an epoch in physics, in a short pamphlet, 'Bemerkungen über die Kräfte der unbelebten Natur,' in ' Wöhler und Liebig's Annalen,' May, 1842, and afterwards in a little book, ' Die organische Bewegung in ihrem Zusammenhang mit dem Stoffwechsel,' 1845. His teachings in regard to motion as the mechanical equivalent of heat, although disregarded at first, were gradually recognised in all their correctness and grandeur of conception, and are now the basis of the views entertained on the nature of heat, and especially on the forces of nature, as regards their mutual equivalency and preservation. And although they had but little influence in changing the current theories of heat-production till ten years afterwards *Helmholtz* had expressed substantially the same ideas, yet almost every one in the present day agrees that *Mayer* was the true discoverer of the mechanical theory of the forces of nature. " Ex nihilo nil fit, nil fit ad nihilum " (says *Mayer*, ' Die Organische Bewegung,' p. 5). " The effect equals the cause : the operation of force is again force in its turn. In real truth there is but one single force, which runs through an eternally changing round, in dead as in living nature. There, as here, there is no progress, unless the force changes its form (p. 6). Heat is a force, it becomes changed into motion (p. 10). Chemical difference is a force (p. 28), the changing of chemical difference into heat results from combustion

(p. 35). In all chemical and physical changes the given power always maintains a constant magnitude (p. 32). The sole cause of animal heat is a chemical process, a kind of oxidation (p. 46). The chemical force, which is contained in the food ingested, and in the oxygen inhaled, is the source of two manifestations of power, viz., motion and warmth; and the sum of the physical power of any animal is equivalent to that of the simultaneously produced chemical processes (p. 45). Since that time these views have been generally and fully accepted in physics, as well as in physiology, and they must doubtless be accepted in pathology, although their application to the ceaseless complications of disease processes is extremely difficult. In the pamphlet quoted, Mayer has very lucidly discussed the application of his theory to some pathological and many physiological processes.

He has also attempted a further application to pathology in his treatise on fevers ('Archiv der Heilkunde,' 1862, p. 385).

Soon after *Mayer, Joule,* of Manchester, experimentally demonstrated the absolute and unchangeable relation between heat and mechanical power, and showed that a given quantity of power produced a determinate quantity of heat, as on the other side, that the quantity of heat which would raise a given quantity of water one degree in temperature, would perform exactly a certain amount of mechanical work. The use, and indeed the name of the word kilogrammeter, originates from this principle in order to designate the mechanical power which is equivalent to, and necessary for raising 1000 grammes to 1 meter in height, or 1 gramme to 1000 mètres, for he found that the heat which would raise 1 kilogram of water 1 degree (Centigrade) will raise 424 kilogrammes 1 metre; and if converted, the same mechanical power which produced the latter effect will raise the temperature of a kilogramme of water $1°$, or in other words, that the mechanical equivalent of the heat (that required to raise a kilogramme of water, $1°$ in temperature being taken as a unit) is 424 kilogrammes.[1]

---

[1] Or, in another form :—That the quantity of heat capable of increasing the temperature of one pound of water (weighed in vacuo, between 55° and 66°) by 1° Fahr., requires for its evolution the expenditure of a mechanical force represented by a fall of 772 pounds, through the space of 1 foot. Or, the heat capable of increasing the temperature of 1 gramme of water by 1° C. is equivalent to a force represented by the fall of 423·55 grammes through the space of 1 mètre. This is consequently the effect of "a unit of heat." See Fowne's 'Chemistry,' 10th Ed., p. 64.—[TRANS.]

Hirn, in Colmar, showed by direct experiments, that whilst at work the production of heat never corresponded to the oxygen consumed, much of it being changed into work. Whilst during perfect rest 30 grammes of oxygen were consumed in an hour, and 155 units of heat produced, it was found that work equivalent to 27450 kilogrammetres done in another hour led to 132 grammes of oxygen being consumed, whilst only 251 units of heat were produced. One was increased four and a half times, the latter only one and two-third times. But in place of the missing heat so much work was done.

It would occupy too much space to discuss this subject in further detail. Enough has been said to indicate the direction which Mayer's initiation has given to the theories of warmth-production.

§ 10. In the beginning of 1850, medical thermometry entered on a new phase of development. Two medical men in Germany published some highly important, and, as regards medical thermometry, novel observations in the years 1850-51. Their names were *Bärensprung* and *Traube*.

It is somewhat doubtful which of them can claim priority.

Traube, indeed, published his first measurements of temperature in his treatise on the effects of digitalis, and especially on the influence of that drug on the temperature of the body in febrile diseases, ('Annalen der Charité,' 1850, p. 622), but it appears from other local publications of the same year, that in March and even up to June, he had never taken the temperature in pneumonia. His first case, in which measurements of temperature were given, was a case of typhoid fever, of the date 18th June, 1850.

Bärensprung's work "Untersuchungen über die Temperatur verhältnisse des Fötus, und des erwachsenen Menschen in gesunden und kranken Zustande," appeared in 1851 in Müller's 'Archiv,' at a later date than *Traube's* publication. But a careful consideration of his cases leads to the conclusion that his investigations were commenced at an earlier date than Traube's. Any decision as to priority, however, is unimportant. Both investigators doubtless commenced their observations independently, and the important services rendered by each remain the same, whoever may have been the first in the field.

Bärensprung's treatise is an eminently classical work. He has determined all the principal points of thermometric experience, and displayed their manifold relations, so that the accuracy of his results has been confirmed by later observations. What was previously known only in an imperfect, unsatisfactory, and fragmentary form, as regards single instances, has been raised by him to the dignity of a comprehensive, well constructed, and, in many respects, complete doctrine. The reason of his failure in influencing the medical profession in a degree corresponding to its merits, must be sought for in the fact that it is somewhat too minute and circumstantial, and surrounded with too many precautions, qualities, however, which are imperatively required in a scientific observer. His use of two decimal places in his measurements of temperature, the importance he attributed to deviations of one tenth of a degree (centigrade = $\frac{1}{5}°$ Fahr. nearly) or even less, and the recommendation of employing half an hour for every thermometrical observation, were slight recommendations of thermometry in general practice, rendered the use of the instrument too burdensome, and, indeed, almost impossible in ordinary medical use, and only exceptionally possible in hospital practice.

On the other hand, *Traube's* thermometrical investigations, which are evidently those of an earnest questioner of nature, had for their object the decision of questions which, though partly theoretic, were also very practical (the effects of digitalis, crises, and critical days, &c.), and have clearly shown that the thermometer is a most valuable means, and often the only one, of deciding difficult and debated questions in the art of medicine.

§ 11. Ever since October, 1851, *I, myself,* induced by *Traube's* spoken recommendations, have introduced the use of the thermometer in my clinique.

Used at first only in a few selected cases, an increasing appreciation of its value has led to its more extended and rational employment. For the last fifteen years there have been no patients in my hospital wards whose temperature has not been taken; and, although at first this was only done twice a day, for the last ten years from four to six daily observations have been made in cases of fever, and in special cases even more frequently. The number of cases of illness in which thermometric observations have been taken in my clinique, amounts to nearly 25,000, and the number of single observations to some millions.

The object which I had in view at first, was to determine the actual facts as regards the temperature of the sick, uninfluenced by special theories, and irrespective of special questions and objects in order, by accumulating a mass of observations, to eliminate the influence of accidental circumstances. When the number of observations fairly reached more than 100,000, they appeared to me to furnish a basis for the determination of to me the most important and most decisive question in pathology: the question, namely, *Do certain diseases in their progress obey fixed laws or rules, and can this be determined and displayed by the course of the temperature?*

The affirmative answer to this question was first afforded by our commonest form of severely acute disease, abdominal typhus (enteric or typhoid fever), and also by a slight epidemic of exanthematic typhus, imported into Leipsic, which was almost entirely under my own observation, and of short duration only. But afterwards, the regular course of other forms of disease was evident to me, after most careful consideration, and most painstaking observations: and the conviction of the immense and almost incalculable value of the thermometer in a practical point of view, hitherto unrecognised, took fast possession of me, a conviction which I am bound to endeavour to wake and confirm in the minds of others.

I considered, however, that it was not well to publish observations of such importance in a crude form, or before they had been carefully tested. On this account, with the exception of the communication of my former assistant (*Dr. Thierfelder*) on Abdominal Typhus, and my own on the subject of True Typhus, and the references to the importance of the thermometer in special forms of disease, in my 'Handbuch der Pathologie und Therapie' (2nd edit.), I waited six or seven years from the commencement of thermometric observations in my clinique before communicating the most important results and considerations to the common stock. Since then, however, I have constantly sought to adduce fresh examples of the practicability and usefulness of this method of investigation in the varied domains of pathology, and the innumerable questions of medical diagnosis.

The collection of this immense mass of observations now at my disposal, which has rendered it possible for me to determine common principles, and to discern what is normal and regular in disease, would have been impossible had I not been aided by a host of faithful and accomplished assistants, who worked day and night with the greatest devotion, taking and superintending thermometric observations. Many of these have themselves elucidated several important questions, partly by their own independent observations, and partly by the comparison of the results of sixteen years' materials collected together in the archives of my clinical wards.

I must especially express my thanks for their aid to my former assistants, *Drs. Thierfelder* (now Clinical Professor at Rostock), *Uhle** (first Clinical Professor at Dorpat, and afterwards at Jena), *Friedemann** (in general practice), *Rotter, Nakonz, Geissler** (Tutor and Clinical Assistant), *Wolff, Blass, Thomas* (at present Director of Policlinik), *Siegel* (now District Surgeon in Leipzig), *Schenkel*, and *Treibmann, Drs. Friedländer* and *Heinze*, as also to my present assistants, *Drs. Heubner, Stecher*, and *Hankel*, as well as to a great many earlier students, who have published valuable contributions to medical thermometry, especially to *Drs. Seume, Michael*, and *Hübler*.

I cannot omit saying that our labours have not been in vain. The thermometric observations which, on their first publication, many thought fit to ridicule, and which a French critic declared to be an empty wind-bag (lit. *eine unfruchtbare düftalei*), which could only amuse physicians in those little German hospitals where the number of the staff almost equalled that of the patients, these measurements are now customary in every clinical service in Germany, in the majority of hospitals, and with a great number of busy practitioners, and are regarded as an essential part of the observation of every case of fever. Let the scope and importance of this branch of science be regarded as it is now, and as it was ten years ago, and it will be seen to have reached a development which few theories have attained in so short a time.

The circumstances affecting the temperatur of the body, and its relations to other phenomena, have attracted the greatest attention from those who have investigated this subject.

The variations of temperature in *healthy people*, and the influences which cause them, have been to a great extent determined by the beautiful experiments of *R. Lichtenfels* and *R. Fröhlich* (see Bibliography, p. 45) ; and further contributions to our knowledge have been made by *Damrosch, Knauthe, Dr. W. Ogle*, and *Jürgensen* (for titles see p. 45).[1]

---

* Those marked thus are since dead.

[1] See also a paper by Drs. Sydney Ringer and A. P. Stewart "On the Temperature of the Human Body in Health," in the 'Proceedings of the Royal Society,' vol. xvii. No. 109, p. 287; and another by Mr. A. H. Garrod "On

The modifications of temperature induced by *pregnancy, delivery,* and the *post-partum period,* as well as those met with in the *newly born,* have all been very carefully investigated, as will be seen in further chapters. And the behaviour of the *temperature in cases of injuries,* has been investigated with equal care, especially by *Billroth* and *O. Weber.* Thermometry has been introduced into *surgical practice,* not for a day or a year, but "for all time" (lit. für alle Zeiten).

As regards *internal diseases,* very many observations of temperature have been published. And although perhaps no very great discovery has been added to the facts established by *Bärensprung, Traube,* and those of my own clinique, yet the confirmation, by numerous observers in different places, of the principles already laid down, are of great value, and have served still further to elucidate some special points. Details will be found under the several diseases treated of.

Drs. *Jenni, Wolf,* and *Uhl* and *Wagner* have all published comprehensive abstracts (see on pp. 46 and 47 for titles).

The application of the thermometer to patients has undoubtedly had an influence in inducing a rational use of cold baths in abdominal typhus (enteric fever), and some other diseases. Towards promoting the cooling treatment of febrile diseases, after *Brand* (of Stettin) had once broken the ice (lit. die Bahn gebrochen hat), *Bartels, Jürgensen, Liebermeister, Ziemssen, Obernier, Wahl, Barth, Mosler,* and *Immermann,* have all contributed, especially the two former.

Into other European countries also [besides Germany] medical thermometry has been introduced. The ice has been broken, so to speak, in Holland, Russia, France, Italy, and England, as well as in North America; and although I find my communications and those of my pupils and assistants simply reproduced (sometimes with acknowledgment, sometimes not!) in not a few publications in all these countries, yet in all there are independent and original workers. In *Russia,* especially, there are celebrated medical men, of German extraction, who have published important material, which must receive more detailed notice further on. In *Holland,* the observations of *Fokker* (see on p. 46) deserve special mention.

In *France,* besides numerous theses by *Maurice, Spielmann, Fouqué, Aronssohn, Hardy, Duclos,* &c., other distinguished practitioners, well acquainted with German literature, have recognised

some of the Minor Fluctuations in the Temperature of the Human Body when at rest, and their Cause," 'Proceedings of the Royal Society,' vol. xvii, No. 112, p. 419.—[TRANS.]

the great value of thermometry at the sick bed, especially *Charcot* (in numerous works), and *Jaccoud* (in his 'Leçons de Clinique Médicale,' 1867, and his 'Traité de Pathol. interne,' 1869, pp. 72-92). *Lade*, of Geneva, has published a good book (see p. 47). *Ladame*, of Neuchâtel, has also published a work, called 'Le thermomètre au lit du malade, recherches physiologiques et pathologiques sur la temp. de l'homme," in 'Bull. de la Société des sc. naturelles de Neuchâtel, 1866.' In *America*, according to *Lewick* ('Pennsylvania Hospital Reports, 1868,' i, p. 382), *Bennett-Dowler*, of New Orleans, had already in 1851 made a number of "Experimental researches into animal heat in the living and dead body," and published them in the July number of the 'New York Medical Gazette,' as well as later ones (in 1856) in the 'New Orleans Med. and Surgical Journal.'

Seguin, in particular, has made our experience well known in America ('Medical Record,' i. 516) ; and since then thermometry has been still more extended and recognised there.

In *England*, *John Simon* at first, and *Sidney Ringer* in particular (especially in his work 'On the Temperature of the Body as a means of Diagnosis in Phthisis and Tuberculosis,' 1865), and *Aitkin* (who quotes my observations and curves in almost all febrile diseases, in his 'Science and Practice of Medicine'), have all declared most strongly the practical value of thermometry, and introduced its significant results to their countrymen. Medical thermometry has in recent times found great acceptance with a host of intelligent medical men, towards which, no doubt, the Germans practising there, particularly *Weber* and *Baümler*, have contributed not a little. Compare the articles of *Compton* ('Dublin Journal,' August, 1866), *Grimshaw* (Ibid., May, 1867), *Warter* (since dead, in 'St. Bartholomew's Hospital Reports,' 1866), *McCormack* ('Medical Times and Gazette,' 1866), *Gibson* ('British Medical Journal,' 1866), and *Smith* ('Edinb. Medical Journal,' 1866), and many others. [See also the Supplemental Bibliography.—TRANS.]

§ 12.—The number of newer works on thermometry is so great that it is impossible for me to enumerate them all. But it may not be superfluous, at the end of this short historical résumé, whilst overlooking those occupying themselves with special circumstances and forms of disease, which will be mentioned in their place hereafter, to introduce the following works to the reader's notice, as appearing in the last fifteen years, as being generally important and necessary to complete one's knowledge of human temperature in both health and disease. The following comprehensive works, abstracts, and pamphlets on Heat itself, and particularly on Animal Heat, may be noticed :

H. Nasse, on "Animal Heat," in Rud. Wagner's 'Handwörterbuch der Physiologie,' 1853, Bd. iv, p. 1.

Gavarret, 'De la Chaleur produites par les êtres vivants,' 1855.

A. Fick, 'Medicinische Physik,' 1856, p. 162.

G. A. Hirn, 'Recherches sur l'équivalent mécanique de la Chaleur,' Colmar, 1858 ; 2nd edition, 1865.

G. Zeuner, 'Grundzüge der mechanischen Wärmetheorie, mit besonderer Rücksicht auf das Verhalten des Wasserdampfes,' 1860, (2nd revised edition, 1866).

C. Ludwig, 'Lehrbuch der Physiologie des Menschen,' 2nd edition, 1861, Bd. 2, p. 719-758.

R. Clausius, 'Abh. über die mechan. Wärmetheorie,' 1864.

John Tyndall, "Heat considered as a mode of Motion," (French translation, by the Abbé Moigno, 1864).

Berthelot, "Sur la chaleur animale" (1865), in Robin's 'Journal de l'anatomie et de la physiol. normale et pathologique,' ii, 652, and 'Gazette Méd. de Paris,' C. xx, 474.

Onimus, "De la théorie dynamique de la Chaleur" (1866) in 'Comptes rendus de la Soc. des Sciences Biologiques.'

R. Mayer, 'Mechanik der Wärme' (Collection of his earlier publications, 1867). Compare also the abstracts of the subject in the more recent text books of medicine and physiology.

The theory of the Relations of Animal Heat (to other forces) has been especially the subject of numerous and increasing discoveries. The influence of the nervous system on the production of warmth, the question of warmth-regulators, and the further elucidation of *Mayer's* theories of the conservation of forces, have all been the subject of numerous works. The most important of these are—

Claude Bernard, "De l'influence du système nerveux grand sympathique sur la chaleur animale" (1852), in 'Comptes Rendus,' xxxiv, 472. "Experimental researches on the vascular and calorific nerves of the great sympathetic (1862), in Ibid., lv, 228, and in the 'Journal de Physiologie,' v, 383 ; "On the influence of the great sympathetic in calorification" (1853), in the 'Mémoires de la société de Biologie,' p. 84 ; "Recherches sur le grand sympa thique, et spécialement sur l'influence que la section de ce nerf exerce sur la chaleur animale," 1854 ; " Leçons sur la physiologie et la pathologie du système nerveux," 1858, ii ; " Leçons sur les propriétés physiologiques et les altérations patholog. des liquides de l'organisme," 1859, i, 50-162 ; " Recherches sur le grand sympathique" (1863) ; in the ' Ann. des Sciences naturelles Zoologie,' xix, p. 101.

Brown-Séquard, " Experimental Researches applied to Physiology and Pathology," 1853 ; especially in the abstract " On the increase of animal heat after injuries of the nervous system," p. 73 : besides an immense number of papers in the ' Medical Examiner' of Philadelphia ; in the ' Journal de Physiologie,' &c.

M. Schiff, " De l'influence du grand sympathique sur la production de la chaleur animale, et sur la contractilité musculaire," in the ' Gazette hebdom.,' 1854, p. 421, and his " Untersuchungen zur Physiologie des Nervensystems mit Berücksichtigung der Pathologie," 1855 (especially the 2nd abstract) ; " Über den Einflusz der Nervenlähmung, auf die Erhöhung der thierischen Wärme," p. 124-228 ; " Neue Versuche über den Einfluss der Nerven auf die Gefässe und die thierische Warme" (1856) in the ' Mittheilungen der Natur forschen den Gesellschaft,' of Bern, p. 69, "Uber die Fieberhitze (1859)," in ' Allg. Wiener med. Zeitung,' Nos. 41 and 42.

Knoch, ' De nervi sympathici vi ad corporis temperiem,' Diss Dorpat, 1855.

Van der Beke Callenfels, " Ueber den Einfluss den vasomotorischen Nerven auf den Kreislauf und die Temperatur" (1855), in the ' Zeitschrift für rationelle Medicin,' N. F. vii, 157.

Kussmaul and *Tenner*, " Ueber den Einfluss der Blutströmung in den grossen Gefässen des Ohrs beim Kaninchen, und ihr Verhältniss zu den Wärmeveränderungen, welche durch die Lähmung und Reizung des Sympathicus bedingt werden" (1856), in ' Moleschott's Untersuchungen,' i, 90.

Liebermeister : " Die Regulirung der Wärmebildung bei Thieren von constanter Temperatur " (in ' Deutsche Klinik,' 1859), and " Physiologische Untersuchungen über die quantitativen Veränderungen der Wärmeproduction," (in Reichert's ' Archives,' 1860—62.

J. Beclard : " De la contraction musculaire dans ses rapports avec la température animale," 1861 (' Archives génerales,' E. xvii, 24).

Heidenhain: 'Mechanische Leistung, Wärmeentwickling und Stoff-umsatz bei der Muskelthätigkeit,' 1864.

Kernig: ' Experimentale Beiträge zur Kentniss der Wärmeregulirung beim Menschen ' (1864).

J. Vogel: " Uber die Temperatur-Verhältnisse des Menschlichen Körpers mit besonderer Rücksickt auf ihre Ursache und auf die Versuche, den Werth der Letzeren numerisch zu bestimmen," in the ' Archiv. des Vereins für wissensch. Heilk.,' 1864, p. 441.

Walther of Kiew : " Studien im Gebiete der Thermophysiologie," in ' Reichert's Archiv,' 1865, p. 25.

Ackermann: " Die Warmeregulation im höheren thierischen Organismus " (1866), in the ' Deutsch. Archiv fur Klinische Medicin,' ii, 359.

Tscheschichin, " Zur Lehre von der thierischen Wärme," in ' Reichert's Archiv,' 1866, p. 151.

Falkland : " On the source of muscular power," Royal Institution of Great Britain, weekly evening meeting, 8th June, 1866.

Dupuy: " De la chaleur et du mouvement musculaire " (1867), in the ' Gazette Méd. de Paris,' Nos. 32, 34, 37, 38, 42, and 44.

The subject of temperature in healthy persons, with its fluctuations, and the circumstances which affect it, were investigated by—

Rud. Lichtenfels, and *Rud. Fröhlich,* " Beobachtungen über die Gesetze des Ganges der Palsfrequenz und Körperwärme in den normalen Zuständen, sowie unter dem Einfluss bestimmter Ursachen;" in the ' Denkschrift der Wiener Academie, 1852, Mathemnatur-wissenschaft classe,' Bd. iii, Abt. 2, p. 113.

Damrosch, " Ueber die täglichen Schwankungen der menschl. Eigenwärme in gesunden Zustand," in the ' Deutsche Klinik,' 1853, p. 317.

Hoppe, " Ueber den Einfluss des Wärmeverlustes auf die Eigen. temperaturen warmblüt. Thiere," in ' Virchow's Archiv,' 1857, xi, p. 453.

Knauthe, " Halbstündliche und Viertelstündliche temperatur curven von Gesunden," in the ' Zeitschrift für Medicin,' 1865. Heft 8.

W. Ogle, " On the diurnal variations in the temperature of the human body ;" ' St. George's Hospital Reports,' 1866, i, 221.

Jürgensen (1867), in ' Deutsches Archiv. für klin Med.,' iii, 165.

As regards the thermometry of disease, with comprehensive observations and discoveries of abnormal temperatures (exclusive of treatises on special forms of disease, or on some special question), the following books may be consulted with advantage:

Jochmann, 'Beobachtungen über die Körperwärme in chronischen fieberhaften krankheiten,' 1853.

Virchow, article "Fever," 1854, in 'Handbuch der spec. Pathologie und Therapie, i, p. 26.

Lasègue, "De la température du corps dans les maladies," (1856), a retrospective article in the 'Archives Gén. de Médecine.'

Maurice, "Des modifications morbides de la température animale dans les affections fébriles" ('Dissertation,' 1855); and *Spielmann*, "Des modifications de la température animale dans les maladies fébriles aigues et chroniques" ('Dissert.,' 1856). (Both drawing chiefly from German sources).

Wunderlich, "Die Thermometrie bei Kranken," in the 'Archiv. fur physiolog. Heilkunde,' 1857, and "Ueber den Normal Verlauf. einiger typischen Krankheitsformen" (Ibid., 1858).

Fouque's Dissert. "Du Thermomètre en Médecine," 1858.

Aronssohn's Dissert. "De la Fièvre," 1859.

Hardy's Dissert. "De la temp. animale dans quelques états pathologiques," 1859.

Wunderlich, "Ueber die Nothwendigkeit einer exacteren Beachtung der Gesammtconstitution," in the 'Archiv. d. Heilk.,' 1860, and his "Vorlegung einiger Elementarthatsachen aus der praktischen Thermometrie und Anleitung zur Anwendung der Wärmemessung in der Privatpraxis" (Ibid.).

Jenni, "Beobachtungen über d. Körperwärme in Krankh.," 1860.

Smoler, "Ueber das Verhältniss von Pulsfrequenz, Respiration, und Temperatursteigerung in einigen acuten Krankheiten," 1860, in 'Prager Virtaljahrschaft,' lxvii, p. 111.

John Simon, article "Inflammation," in Holmes' 'System of Surgery,' 1860, vol. i, p. 40—53.

Billroth, in the 'Archiv. für klinsche Chirurgie,' 1862, and 64.

Förster, "Ueber Thermometermessung ber Kindern," in 'Journal für Kinderkrankheiten,' 1862.

Traube, "Zur Fieberlehre," in 'Allgemeiner medic. Centralzeitung,' 1863, 1864.

Fokker, "Over de Temperatuur van den Mensch.,' in 'gezonden en zieken. toestand,' 1863.

Behse, "Beiträge zur Lehre vom Fieber," 1864.

Duclos, "Quelques recherches sur l'état de la temp. dans les maladies" ('Dissert.,' 1864).

Wolf, "Rückblick auf die bisherigen Temperaturbeobachtungen," n the 'Archiv. des Vereins für wissenschaft Heilk.,' 1864.

O. *Weber,* "Ueber die Wärmeentwicklung in Entzündeten Theilen, und experimentelle Studien über Pyämie, Septicämie, und Fieber," in 'Deutscher Klinik.,' 1864, and 1865, and article on Fever in 'Pitha and Billroth's Chirurgie,' i, 1865.

Liebermeister, "Klinische Untersuchungen über das Fieber," (1865), in the 'Prager Vierteljahrschr,' lxxxv, 1, and lxxxvii, 1.

Wachsmuth, "Zur Lehre vom Fieber," 1865, in 'Archiv. der Heilkunde,' vi, p. 192.

Uhle and *Wagner's* "Handbuch der allgem. Pathologie," 3rd edit., p. 537—560 (1865).

Wunderlich, "Vorträge über Kranken-thermometrie," 1865 to 1867, in 'Archiv. der Heilkunde,' vi—viii.

Ladé, "De la temp. du corps dans les maladies," Geneva, 1866.

Frese, "Experimentalle Beiträge zur Aetiologie d. Fiebers," 1866.

Tscheschichin, "Zur Fieberlehre," 1867, in "Deutsche Archiv. für klinische Medicin,' ii, 588.

NOTE.—It has been thought best for the purposes of reference, not to translate the *titles* of books in the Bibliography. The respective questions discussed by each author will appear from the body of the book, and a supplemental list of still more recent works will be found at the end.—[TRANS.]

CHAPTER III.

THE VALUE OF THE THERMOMETER IN MEDICAL PRACTICE.

§ 1.—The tendency of modern medicine to set the highest value, for diagnostic and prognostic purposes, upon *objective* symptoms, and amongst these upon what are called *physical signs*, is undoubtedly a step in the right direction.

Now, the temperature of a sick patient is both an "objective" and "physical" symptom, and the use of the thermometer must be classed with the "physical diagnostic" methods of percussion, auscultation, &c.; and whatever may be claimed for these as regards their significance and practical value may be claimed for thermometry with equal justice.

Thermometry, however, has this advantage over all these applications of acoustics, an advantage of almost priceless value, inasmuch as it gives results which can be *measured*, signs that can be *expressed in numbers*, and offers materials for diagnosis which are incontestable and indubitable, which are independent of the opinion or the amount of practice or the sagacity of the observer—in one word, materials which are physically accurate. Amongst all the phenomena of disease there is scarcely another which admits of such accuracy or is so reliable as the temperature.

The results afforded by thermometry have yet another advantage over those of the other physical methods of diagnosis. Whilst the latter aids to our judgment indicate, for the most part, somewhat permanent changes, or at all events slowly changing phenomena, the measurement of the temperature gives us a peep, as it were, into a *scene of continual changes*—changes, indeed, which, in the normal states, are but as slight oscillations of a pendulum, which in disease, by its sudden and powerful swing, points to similar perturbation in the domestic economy. The temperature is both a *more accurate* and a *more delicate* measure of the changes undergone by the animal organism than other symptoms, which may slowly become evident, perhaps at a much later period of the disease.

There remains a third advantage in favour of thermometry, which amply vindicates its claim to a high position amongst physical methods of investigation.

Whilst nearly all the other methods of this kind have for their object the discovery of topical changes only, their indications are summed up, as it were, by thermometry, which presents to our judgment a *phenomenon dependent upon the whole of the vital processes of the entire body*; and whilst it places accurately measured observations at our disposal, opens up to us for our investigation regions of pathology (literally, "a domain of sick life") which were inaccessible to other methods of exploration. Indeed, thermometry renders these general changes available for *prognosis*, and the importance of this is great in proportion to the amount and significance of the general morbid processes.

The *use of the thermometer in disease* is, therefore, an *objective, physical method of investigation*, which gives *exact* and accurate *results*, in *signs which can be measured* and *expressed numerically*; which is *delicate enough to follow every step* of the changing processes of the organism, and places at the disposal of the practitioner a *phenomenon dependent upon the sum total* of the organic changes in the body.

§ 2.—The determination of the patient's temperature in disease may be regarded as a valuable contribution to pathology from three different points of view.

(*a*) It appears desirable and *necessary per se*, because any deviation from the normal or healthy condition is an essential element of the study of disease (des Krankseins, the state or condition of the sick), and of all deviations surely that which may be determined with objective physical accuracy.

(*b*) So far as the temperature obtained is a phenomenon common to the whole body, equally diffused, and apparently a result of the entire processes of life, its variations are *symptoms of general disturbance of function*, and its determination is the more important as it is the only speedy, accurate, and delicate method of following some of the sudden alterations of the general morbid condition.

(*c*) As the temperature affords us indications which can be measured of the general disturbances of function, however sudden, or

4

whenever they may occur; it also enables us, by a comparison of its course in a multitude of similar cases, to decide the question, "*Is there not, in many forms of disease, a fixed law which regulates the course of the general disturbance?* and as a corollary to this to discuss what deviations from the given law may occur, and by what they are occasioned.

In deciding upon the practical value of thermometry in disease, we must not lose sight of this threefold aspect of the question.

The human body has a temperature of its own, almost independent of the medium in which it is placed. A simple and accurate procedure shows us that this temperature does not remain at the same degree in certain conditions of health and disease. By further trials we learn that in health the temperature remains nearly the same under all circumstances, whilst in disease, with certain limits, we find considerable variations.

These facts are of the highest interest in themselves alone. We are almost impelled to serious reflection when we see that the temperature of the human body cannot be much increased or diminished without more or less injury to health, and that the temperature varies only within the limits of a few tenths of a degree (Centigrade), however the quantity or quality of the ingesta, of muscular or mental activity may vary, in all sorts of atmospheres, by any process of waste and expenditure, whatever the age, temperature, stature, body-weight, or other outward influences, so long only as health is not impaired.

On the other hand, is it less wonderful to see in the manifold varieties of disease, alterations of temperature occurring more or less suddenly, and to observe that the very presence of a diseased process gives rise to a speedy alteration of temperature, or at the least confers on the body an aptitude to exhibit fluctuations of temperature, under the influence of varied, but in themselves unimportant, circumstances?

If any facts at all relating to the organism deserve our attention, surely this contrast between the temperature of the sick and the healthy deserves it; and even if at present it appeared entirely devoid of practical results, we could scarcely be indifferent to so remarkable a circumstance. But the fact is the practical importance of this phenomenon is almost incalculable. This is strikingly evident (sie erhellt sofort) when we consider the bearings and relation of this phenomenon to the various processes carried on at one and the same time in various parts of the body.

If we admit the proposition, that the general condition of the system, or, in other words, the sum of the tissue changes in disease, is of considerable importance for diagnosis, it must surely be of the highest importance to avail ourselves of a simple physical phenomenon, the slightest changes of which admit of easy measurements which can be expressed in number, and thus give an index or a gauge of these otherwise recondite processes. The value of this symptom for the estimation of tissue changes would indeed appear entirely illusory, if we considered that the height of the temperature did not depend on the production of warmth in the body or indicate the result of chemical processes, and it would be still more difficult to come to an accurate conclusion if the radiation or giving off of heat were to be disregarded. The degree of heat (die Höhe der Eigenwärme) in an animal is a complex phenomenon, produced by the most varied, often incalculable, and partly antagonistic factors. On this account the immediate theoretic application of temperature-relations in disease is almost completely nugatory, and all endeavours in this direction are, à priori, hopeless and illusive. On this account it is possible that the opinion may be entertained that, although alterations of temperature do indeed generally betoken a disturbance of the customary order and regularity of the economy, all further deductions from them, and especially from any given degree of temperature, are worthless. But *experience teaches a different lesson.*

For this reason the greatest gain accruing to thermometric observation was undoubtedly the discovery that the *alterations of temperature in disease are subject to fixed laws ;* or, in other words, the *value of pathological thermometry* is chiefly *determined by the evidence afforded by an extended experience, founded on very numerous observations, that the alterations of temperature, however slight and insignificant, are determined by strict laws.* In fact, the circumstance that the body is warmer or colder than in health, whether the change be great or small, must not be considered in the same way as the indication that one weighs so much or more, feels strong or weak, sleeps well or badly, coughs frequently or but seldom, has much pain or the reverse, &c., &c., but the *deviation from the normal temperature is to be considered,* in more than one aspect, *as closely related to the various processes going on in the body generally* (im organismus).

As soon as thermometry attains to the discovery of these laws, it conquers a fresh territory for pathology, and reveals a " new world,"[1] vainly sought by other routes, and declared, indeed, by many who have attempted to reach it by other methods as the sanguine dream or fabled region of adventurous spirits—the domain of *law in disease*.

One difficulty meets us at once, when we endeavour to draw rigorous conclusions or to estimate the value of the data in given cases, and that is, that the alteration of temperature in disease is sometimes due to the morbid process, and sometimes to accidental, and perhaps only momentary, influences affecting the sick man's constitution. This difficulty is sometimes very great, but it may be conquered by increasing the number of observations, and by a proper use of our judgment and careful consideration of the surrounding circumstances.

When once these difficulties are overcome, thermometry will, doubtless, lead to entirely new views of many diseases, and no small part of our pathology will have to be " radically reconstructed."

§ 3. — The true position of thermometry in medicine clearly appears from these considerations. *It is a part of our method of diagnosis or observation of disease* which is *indispensable* in all the cases where the temperature varies, very useful in many doubtful cases, and an auxiliary in almost every case. The medical attendant who undertakes to decide a case of fever or febrile disease, without knowing the facts of thermometry, and without taking the temperature, is like a blind man trying to find his way in a fresh locality. With much practice, if very intelligent, he may often find it out correctly, but he will be more often deceived, and, at the best, will only discover, with much difficulty and very imperfectly, that which is patent to those gifted with sight.

But thermometry can and must do more than this; it ought to discover the laws which regulate the cause of disease; and when it has fully attained this—when thermometry becomes thermonomy, then, and not till then, will the strictly practical applications be attained in their full development.

§ 4.—After thus attempting to portray the true significance of

---

[1] " Unerreichbares Ziel." Wunderlich has changed the metaphor here. I have ventured to restore the original simile.—[TRANS.]

thermometry as it truly exists, although only partially known as yet, it is perhaps not quite superfluous to mention some of the *really practical applications* of this method of observation.

(*a*) A normal temperature is no proof of health, *per se*, but *the maintenance of a normal temperature under varied conditions and influences*, or, in other words, a *constant normal temperature*, may be *regarded as an evidence of a sound constitution*. A healthy man may have scanty or luxurious fare, he may fast or feast, drink water or stimulating liquors, he may remain quiet, or exert himself vigorously, both bodily and mentally, and do other things of the like kind, and yet have almost the same temperature, as long as his health is unimpaired. Even taking medicines and losses of blood, if he remains well, do not influence his temperature much, for in such circumstances the variation is only a few tenths of a degree (Centigrade). The less a man's temperature is disturbed by various modes of living and numerous other influences, the more confidently may we pronounce him to be healthy.

(*b*) In actual every-day life there are numerous occasions on which it is necessary, or at least desirable, to *ascertain whether a particular person is really ill, or at least indisposed*. Taking the temperature, when it shows a deviation from the normal, is one of the most rapid means of ascertaining the existence of some disturbance in the economy. It is an objective symptom, applicable to every one, very convincing, and often of almost incalculable value. Suppose a patient's complaints are vague, and his account of his symptoms confused, if we find an abnormal temperature, we may be quite sure that he is neither imposing on us, nor over-anxious about himself, and that his complaints are deserving of further investigation. We may find patients unwilling to confess that they are really ill, or whilst still suffering from the dregs of a disease they consider themselves quite cured, but if the thermometer still shows an elevated temperature, we may confidently affirm that they really are ill, or that they are only partially convalescent, as the case may be.

Not only does the surgeon himself obtain indications for his future guidance, but he may also by this means be able to convince the patient of the necessity of caution and of further treatment.

(*c*) In general, however, we wish to know more than the mere fact of the existence of disease, we want to know the *importance or degree of severity of the affection*. Very often the thermometer enables us to do this with an accuracy quite unattainable by other methods. If the temperature remains normal, or only slightly elevated, we may, after making allowance for any entirely local affection, which may generally be easily recognised, regard the general condition without alarm. But if, on the contrary, we find the temperature markedly abnormal, the case is to be considered far more serious. In this way the thermometer becomes an invaluable aid in accurately prognosing the severity or slight nature of a complaint. For example, in the frequently occurring cases of obscure symptoms in young children, the physician is either impelled to superfluous or over-vigorous treatment, or loses valuable time, or at least defers active treatment to a late period of the disease. The thermometer will clearly show in these cases whether the symptoms are of little consequence, or, on the other hand, indicate the development of a serious illness; and, indeed, in the hands of an intelligent nurse or relative, may serve as a useful criterion to judge whether it is necessary to summon the doctor instantly, or whether his visit may be postponed to a later period. Very often the thermometer alone indicates serious and yet latent disturbances. If a patient feels only "a little poorly," but shows a very high temperature, the attack is never to be slighted, as it generally masks the commencement of a very serious illness.

(*d*) When the malady has developed itself, and sometimes even in the first day or two of illness, a certain *diagnosis of the kind of disease* may be made from the *course of the temperature*. And still more frequently, when a concurrence of symptoms appear to indicate a special disease, the thermometer decides our diagnosis; or in other words, gives certainty to otherwise doubtful cases. There is no other aid to diagnosis which gives so many trustworthy indications, none which can so frequently correct premature conclusions; and further (a matter of great interest), when we have the complete map or course of the temperature before us, we can often, by this means alone, determine from what disease the patient has been suffering.

(*e*) But the mere making of a diagnosis or giving a name to the disease is far from being the most important or only matter on which the practitioner has to decide.

The varied modifications diseases exhibit, the passage of one stage into another, the times of exacerbation and remission, the development of complications, the severity of the attack, and the amount of danger, are at least of equal importance.

Thermometry in these cases serves as a clue or indicator to the practitioner at an earlier period, and more trustworthily than any other method of investigation.

(*f*) As long as the temperature *conforms to a normal type*, in the course of any disease which admits of recovery, the practitioner may almost always be confident that everything is going on favorably, and may often dispense with any further investigations ; and, on the other hand, whenever an unusual *alteration of the course of the temperature* occurs, this is an important symptom, and very often the first signal of danger, and ought to induce a careful search for the causes of the irregularity. Complications which would be otherwise unnoticed may often be discovered in this manner.

(*g*) *During convalescence* the course of the temperature is equally available, as the most certain method of discriminating between real and apparent improvement, and of recognising what seems to a careless observer to be a relapse—as a stage in the process of recovery. When there is improvement in all the other symptoms, but the temperature still continues high, complete recovery is far from being attained. On the other hand, a favorable "turn" (or crisis) is often accompanied with such alarming symptoms, that only the accuracy with which the temperature indicates the commencement of recovery makes us confident that this is really the case, in spite of the impression made by the severity of the rest of the patient's symptoms.

(*h*) Observations of temperature are exceedingly valuable as *controllers of our therapeutics*, or, in other words, as enabling us to judge of the real efficacy of medication in many diseases. Acute diseases, which contain in themselves the conditions of compensation (die Bedingungen zur Ausgleichung, or vis medicatrix naturæ), and therefore generally tend to spontaneous recovery, render it very difficult for us to demonstrate the advantages of medication.

No other method of observation except temperature affords so certain a means of proving the favorable influence of therapeutic agencies, or, on the other hand, of showing their failure to influence the disease.

Even in cases which terminate at a later period in death, observation of the temperature is often able to prove that the remedies applied have at least initiated a curative action. All active medication in febrile diseases must be tested, and judged almost entirely by the results of thermometric observations.

These examples must suffice for the present; it would be easy to multiply them greatly; but the practical advantages of thermometry, in almost every aspect of the question, will be further elucidated when we come to the consideration of special diseases.

§ 5.—There are many persons who freely admit the advantages of thermometry in hospital practice, and for clinical teaching, but who think it little suitable for private practice, or consider that it cannot be made use of in the latter.

The number of these sceptics is much diminished of late years, for there are a great many places where the general introduction of the thermometer into private practice has been already accomplished by energetic and accomplished practitioners. That the cost of instruments is by no means excessive, and that the use of them offers no insuperable difficulties, is now generally admitted. How far the time required for the observation may be abbreviated, so as to render the use of the thermometer possible for the busiest practitioners, will be considered under the heading of "The Methods of Observation," and no one maintains that the busy practitioner must take the temperature of every case he sees, or at every visit.

In a certain sense, however, *the thermometer may be said to be a saver of time,* for the observations of this one phenomenon will often lead to conclusions which could scarcely be arrived at otherwise, or only by lengthy interrogations and investigations. Indeed, we may safely affirm that just in the same way as one who is well versed in percussion and auscultation can dispense with their use on account of the lessons they have taught him, so the surgeon who has attained to great experience in thermometry can safely draw conclusions, in many cases of illness, without using the thermometer at all, from other diagnostic signs—conclusions which it would have been impossible to arrive at without his previous experience of temperatures.

The difficulties on the part of patients anticipated by many are entirely without foundation. Similar objections were made at first, as regards percussion and auscultation; but now-a-days our patients are scarcely satisfied unless these methods of exploration have been employed, so thoroughly is the general public imbued with a sense of their necessity.

Just in the same way the laity (if I may so call them) are deeply interested in observations of temperature, which can be taken without fatiguing the sick, and without any violations of propriety.

They derive satisfaction, not only from the little inconvenience this method of observation causes, but also from the favorable results which they experience from a diminution of febrile temperatures. Everywhere the thermometer has speedily become popular whenever it has been introduced, and there has never been any objection to its use on the part of the public.

To render thermometry generally useful we must next consider the methods to be employed, in order to secure trustworthy results from the observation of the temperature in disease; and we must not neglect the lessons derived from experience as to the temperature of the healthy.

CHAPTER IV.

THE ART OF MEDICAL THERMOMETRY.

§ 1.—Various instruments and methods may be employed to determine the temperature of the human body. In order to secure trustworthy results, or at least to form a judgment as to the degree of accuracy secured, it is necessary to consider the *sources of fallacy in observation*, and to know the *general rules which enable us to avoid them*.

Absolute accuracy of observation is unattainable, and if it were possible to secure it, it is *unnecessary* for the purposes of *medical thermometry*; and indeed the apparatus, and the precautions requisite to secure absolute accuracy, would be unsuitable for the practical applications demanded by the medical art. Whilst it is quite certain that unless we can secure trustworthy observations, no useful results can be obtained, and it will be impossible to deduce any rules for practice from them, it would, on the other hand, be absurd to require, or even to apply, an invariable method, of what I may term *painful* accuracy, in all sorts of cases.

Whilst requiring that the observations should be exact, and trustworthy, *we must always bear in mind what is required by the circumstances of the special case*, for *there is no single method which is equally good and appropriate in every case*. It is therefore requisite to have clear ideas as to the degree of exactness required for particular purposes.

Repeated observations of only moderate correctness, may be more valuable for some purposes, than single or scanty observations of irreproachable accuracy. And for many practical uses, a rapidly-secured indication is more desirable, however imperfect, than one which, while anxiously guarded from errors, is prodigal of time. Methods of investigation which make too excessive demands, have the effect of preventing the application of this method of research, and in endeavouring to give "sharpness" to the results, make the number of the observed facts too small to afford a safe basis for

xperience, and render any deduction of general principles im-
)ossible.

If we are only anxious to ascertain quickly *whether a patient has
'ever or not, and whether the fever be mild or severe*, in order to
atisfy our minds as to the nature of the case, or to learn the neces-
ity for more careful supervision, a somewhat superficial examination
uffices.

For *practical purposes* generally,—that is, to determine the nature
nd progress of any disease; or in other words, to form the usual
liagnosis and prognosis,—a somewhat greater degree of care is required; but even in this case, the frequency of the thermometric
observations, and the degree of accuracy required, must vary with
he special circumstances of the case. So long as the course of the
liseases varies little from that of which we have previous experience,
o long as nothing unusual or unfavorable occurs, so long as the
liagnosis is clear, and the disease runs its usual course, approxima-
ively accurate observations, repeated at considerable intervals of
ime, may suffice. Errors which do not exceed half a degree Cen-
igrade ($\cdot 9°$ Fahr.), are scarcely worth mention in this point of view;
nd if the proper time of day be chosen, twice a day, or sometimes
ven once, is often enough to take the temperature. But even in
eneral practice, in cases where the thermometer is used to clear up
difficult *diagnosis*, or a *doubtful prognosis*, or to prove and *regulate
he working of therapeutic agencies*, greater accuracy of observation,
nd more frequent repetitions of the process, are required. But even
n this case, generally speaking, errors of one or two tenths of a
legree Cent. ($\cdot 2$—$\cdot 4°$ Fahr. nearly) do not much matter. Only if the
emperature reaches unusual elevations (about $41°$ C.$= 105\cdot 8°$ F.),
tenth of a degree Centigrade ($\cdot 2°$ Fahr. nearly) becomes worthy of
notice, and especially so as regards prognosis. But the necessity
of accuracy, and of frequent repetitions of the observations, becomes
greater if we propose to formulate our observations into rules, and
o lay down the laws of disease, or to criticise those previously
leduced.

As regards questions of this kind, all those whose measurements
of temperature have been made but seldom, and are not sufficiently
accurate, must simply be ignored (haben einfach zu schweigen);
yet frequent repetition of the measurements in the course of the day
s to be insisted upon, more than the absolute accuracy of the observations. Errors of observation which only amount to one or two

tenths of a degree Centigrade ($=\cdot2-\cdot4°$ Fahr. nearly), or sometimes a trifle more, may be unimportant, as soon as one accumulates
a mass of observations, either of similar kinds of disease, or made
under tolerably similar circumstances; and these observations may
be valuable, if we set out with the principle, that not the absolute
height of the temperature, but its *course* (the curve of temperature
in the chart), is the object we have in view. But observations of
temperature made at rare intervals give a distorted and unfair impression of the progress of the temperature in cases of disease.

Finally, there are *questions of purely scientific interest*, for the
solution of which the highest possible accuracy is required, and consequently every kind of error in observation is to be carefully
avoided. In such cases, the slightest deviations are of great significance.

But as I have said before, absolute freedom from error is unattainable, and for practical purposes is not to be expected. We must not
require impossibilities; and in thermometry, as in all other affairs of
life, we must be content with possibilities.

§ 2.—The *means or instruments for determining the temperature of*
the body differ much in their value and suitability; but every one of
them may, under varying circumstances, find its place and application in medicine. The *use of the hand as a standard of temperature*
is by no means a reliable method. Any one unaccustomed to thermometric observations, may very easily be most grossly deceived by
this method; and even after many years' experience, corrected by
continual verification by the thermometer, one is often enough deceived, and can scarcely estimate a quarter of a degree Centigrade
($=\frac{9}{20}°$ Fahr.) correctly. If the observer's hand is cold, no confidence can be placed in its sensibility to heat, and the most experienced may make mistakes amounting to half a degree, or even a
whole degree Centigrade ($=\cdot9$ to $\cdot1\cdot8°$ Fahr.).

However, the use of the hand to estimate the temperature of the
skin, may afford a superficial knowledge of its warmth, and may
serve to indicate the necessity or otherwise of taking a thermometric
observation. But for this purpose it is never enough to feel the
hands or face only of the patient, but parts of the body protected by
clothing must be handled, because only these will give a correct
indication as to elevation or otherwise of the temperature.

§ 3.—The only *observations of temperature* which can furnish trust-worthy results, are those made by *instruments* for the purpose.

(*a*) The best instrument for ordinary medical purposes, is a good *mercurial thermometer*, which need not be too delicate, but such as, only rightly applied, can satisfy all practical requirements, though it fails to measure very sudden changes of temperature. This is to be preferred to a spirit thermometer, because the latter is not re-liable when the temperature is much elevated.

The following are desiderata in a thermometer which is to be used in medical practice :—

The reservoirs of metal (*i. e.* the bulbs) must be neither too large, nor too small. If the bulb is too large, it is wanting in sensitive-ness ; if too small, it is difficult to retain it in close apposition to the body. A diameter of about $\frac{1}{2}$—$\frac{1}{4}$ of a centimetre ($\frac{1}{10}$—$\frac{1}{4}$ of an inch nearly), seems the most convenient size. A globular form should be preferred for measurements in the axilla, or at least if the bulb be cylindrical, the long axis should not greatly exceed the shorter, but should approach to the form of a spherical bullet. For measurements in the rectum and the vagina, a conical reservoir is to be preferred, for a contrary reason, and the lower end should be tapering. A hemispherical form, with the flat surface downwards, is recommended for investigations on the surface of the skin, and is very convenient for any purpose, but the results are not trustworthy, and indeed scarcely of any use. The glass of the bulb should not be too thin, or it will be easily broken, or squeezed flat ; but if too thick, the instrument loses in delicacy.

The tube or stem of the instrument must have an even bore throughout, and be of such a diameter that the distance between any two-tenths of a degree C. can be easily divided by the eye into half and quarter parts (so that $\frac{1}{10}^{\circ}$ to $\frac{1}{20}^{\circ}$ Fahr. can be easily read). The length of the tube must be such that the degrees on the stem are at least 12 centimetres ($4\frac{3}{4}$ inches nearly) from the bulb, in order that the height of the mercury may be easily read *in situ*. For the sake of portability, however, it is well not to have too long a stem ; and it will be found sufficient to have a tube a little longer than the probable height to which the mercury will rise when applied to a living human being. The zero may very well be placed in the reser-voir (or bulb), and it is quite unnecessary to have the tube long enough to mark the boiling point of water (212° F. $= 100^{\circ}$ C.) ; and it will be quite sufficient, even for bathing purposes, if the stem comprises from $32.5°—45°$ C. ($= 90.5°—113°$ F.): or perhaps even $44°$ ($= 111.2°$ Fahr.) may be enough,[1] if the $35°$ Cent. [$= 95°$ F.] is 12 centimetres (about $4\frac{3}{4}$ inches) from the bulb.

Only the degrees given above ($90°—113°$) need be marked on the scale. Whether one uses Réaumur's or Celsius' (the centigrade) division is quite indifferent. On the Continent, Fahrenheit's scale, which was formerly employed, is quite gone out of use.[2] It is quite sufficient for ordinary medical purposes if the scale is divided into fifths of a degree centigrade [$= .36°$ Fahr. nearly, or about two fifths].

The marks for both the degrees and their divisions should be clearly defined and legible, and those for the degrees should be longer than those for their component parts.[3]

[1] "Etwa noch der 24 Grad," in my copy, which seems a misprint for 44.— [TRANS.]

[2] Réaumur's scale is only used in Russia, Sweden, and some parts of Germany. Fahrenheit's scale has been, and still is very generally used in all parts of the British Empire, and in the United States. It is, however, not generally understood on the Continent, and it is greatly to be wished that English medical men would learn to use the Centigrade Scale, which is almost universally employed by chemists and other physicists. (Messrs. Casella, Negretti and Zambra, Harvey and Reynolds, and others, supply thermometers with both notations, to facilitate the acquirement of this scale. See note in appendix.—[TRANS.]

[3] The thermometers made for medical use by English makers are generally divided into fifths of a degree Fahrenheit = ($\frac{1}{10}°$ Centigrade nearly), and can easily be read to half of that = $\frac{1}{10}°$ Fahrenheit; their range is from 85° or 90° Fahrenheit (29.4° or 32.2° Centigrade) to 110° or 115° Fahrenheit (43.3°—46.1° Centigrade). They vary in length, from about 5 to 10 inches or more. Nearly all the surgical instrument makers supply them; but Messrs. Casella (at the suggestion of Dr. Aitkin), I believe, were the first to make a registering maximum thermometer for medical use, by enclosing a little air between the mercury in the bulb and that serving as the index. To use these thermometers, the index must first be set, i.e. the mercury in the bulb should first be warmed (either between the thumb and forefinger, by warm water, or otherwise, so that the mercury rises about an inch above the bulb—then, holding the instrument in the hand, with the bulb a little lower than the other end, raise the hand to the shoulder, and bring it down again to the side with a smart swing—repeating this once or twice if required, till the index is about 95° (or sometimes lower); or, holding the upright thermometer lightly in the right hand, tap the bulb gently on the palm of the left a few times, which will shake down the index. Care must be taken not to shake the index down into the bulb, and it is better to carry the thermometer upside down in the pocket. I have tried the thermometers of Messrs. Casella (Hatton Garden), Negrett

An indispensable condition for accurate investigation by means of any instrument is, that the instrument itself should be accurate. The *accuracy of a thermometer*, however, depends more upon the *perfect equality of the divisions upon the stem* than upon the numbers affixed to them; it is desirable, indeed, that the *degrees* should be marked correctly, but it is easy to correct any error in this respect, for it is only necessary to compare the thermometer for each degree by placing it in a water-bath with a correctly marked (or *standard*) thermometer, and to notice the difference, if any, which exists between them, and make the necessary correction when the former is used. If the difference between the thermometer employed and the standard instrument is the same for every degree, we are at once aware how much is to be added or subtracted for each degree, and then the results, after this correction, will be as accurate as if the standard instrument itself were employed. In this way instruments of moderate price may be made useful, which renders thermometry accessible to men of moderate means. This is especially important, because for practical purposes it is far more desirable to have a considerable number of thermometers than to possess a few of absolute accuracy. Only care should be taken by the observer to be perfectly acquainted with the necessary corrections to be made for each instrument. But if, on the contrary, the scale is so badly divided (*i. e.* the degrees marked so unequally) that the error varies for each degree, the use of such an instrument becomes very awkward, and it is better not to make use of it at all, since it is difficult to avoid errors if a separate calculation has to be made for every degree.

Even the best instruments, with the most correct markings, should be *tested again* by a standard instrument about a year after they are made, and occasional testings should be had recourse to as long as the instrument is made use of for medical purposes, for even the glass of which it is made is subject to slight (molecular) changes in its condition by the lapse of time, until an equilibrium is established, if indeed that is ever attained. In this way the calibre of the bulb or reservoir is altered; and it may happen that a thermometer, which was perfectly correct in its markings at first, differs

and Zambra (Holborn), Harvey and Reynolds (of the Briggate, Leeds, the first to make a six-inch portable thermometer of this kind, at Dr. Clifford Allbutt's suggestion, although the Casellas were the inventors), and find them very good.—[TRANS.]

from a standard one by one or two tenths of a degree (Centigrade
= one or two fifths Fahrenheit nearly) after a year or so. It is
possible, also, that the handling it undergoes for medical purposes
and pressure upon a thin bulb, may cause a slight diminution of the
size of the reservoir in the course of time. On this account the
more frequently clinical thermometers are employed the more often
they will be found to require occasional comparison with a standard
Sometimes it is well, when meeting with an exceptional and hardly
credible temperature in the course of observation, to test the instrument, in order to make certain that it has received no damage. It
is scarcely necessary to observe that we must always be on our guard
against obvious injuries or accidents to the instrument, such as division of the mercurial column or loss of the mercury [or the index
being lost in the bulb in registering thermometers.—TRANS.]

It is always well to *use the same thermometer, if possible, for any
given patient,* and to note the number of the instrument in the
clinical notes, or on our memoranda. In this manner it becomes
easy, should any errors be discovered at a later date in the instrument, to see what observations are untrustworthy. It is always
requisite to *have a considerable number* of good instruments, and to
mark each with a number. In private practice, a thermometer
should be left with every patient who requires continuous observations of temperature. In hospitals, it greatly facilitates thermometric observations if there are a sufficient number of thermometers to
allow of one being applied to every patient in the ward at the same
time.

As a standard, it is quite enough to have one accurate (normal)
thermometer, which may be occasionally compared with another
standard instrument (say one belonging to a meteorological obser-
vatory or a philosophical institute, &c.). For many purposes it is
convenient, or may even be necessary, to possess one or more instruments on which hundredths of a degree (Centigrade = $\frac{1}{50}$ Fahrenheit nearly) can be easily read. But for private practice this is quite
superfluous, and, indeed, for really practical questions has hitherto
appeared unimportant.

(*b*) Very considerable accuracy of observation may be attained
(more, indeed, than is required in private practice) by the use of the
metastatic thermometer of Walferdin. The mercurial reservoir of
this is very small, and the very narrow tube is divided at pleasure
into equal divisions. To the upper end of the tube, namely, that

opposite to the reservoir, another bulb is affixed, and where it joins the capillary tube there is a narrowing of the latter. The calibre of the instrument is such that a variation of $3°$ or $4°$ (Centigrade $= 5\cdot4°$ to $7\cdot2°$ Fahr.) expands the mercury so as to fill the whole of the tube. The quantity of mercury in the instrument must be such that at the lowest temperature one intends to experiment with, the reservoir, the whole tube, and a part of the upper bulb shall be filled, and that with $1°$ or $2°$ over the highest temperature expected the whole of the upper bulb shall be filled (i. e. the whole instrument). For instance, if it is only desired to measure temperatures under $42°$ C. ($107\cdot6°$ F.), the instrument is to be warmed a little above $42°$. The quicksilver fills the whole tube and a great part of the upper bulb; then one sets it in a bath of $42°$, leaving it there till the mercury is expanded correspondingly to this degree. Then it is taken out of the bath, and given a smart *tap*, which causes the quicksilver to part or be divided at the narrow part of the tube, whilst that in the rest of the tube retracts considerably, in which it is not followed by the mercury in the upper bulb, and the metal is not again united till it is again exposed to a temperature of $42°$. The instrument is now ready for all observations under $42°$ ($107\cdot6°$), and the only requisite now is to compare the degrees with those of a standard thermometer in a water-bath. The only advantage of this thermometer is the length of the single degrees (allowing of very fine divisions), with its comparative cheapness. Walferdin made metastatic thermometers in which one degree centigrade ($1\cdot8°$ Fahr.) corresponded to a length of ten centimetres ($=$ nearly four inches). As we are able with the unassisted eye to conveniently distinguish distances of half a millimetre ($= \frac{1}{50}$th inch nearly), we are thus enabled to read off $\frac{1}{100}$th of a degree Centigrade with the naked eye, or $\frac{1}{1000}°$ even by the help of a lens ($= \frac{1}{100}$th and $\frac{1}{50}$th Fahr. nearly). Such minimal differences of temperature are of no practical moment in thermometry in cases of disease, and it is doubtful, even for purely scientific or theoretical purposes, how far they are of use.

(c) The *thermo-electric apparatus* offers considerable advantages for many investigations. The principle on which this is founded is, that in any metallic circuit, composed of two different metals soldered together, there is an electric stream or current produced whenever the two points of junction, or places of soldering have different temperatures; and although the difference may be very slight, the current may be rendered visible, and even measured by the magnetic needle. *Becquerel* was the first to use such an apparatus for physiological experiments, especially for ascertaining the differences of temperature between different parts of the body, and *Dutrochet* perfected it. They used only a single pair (iron and copper), whilst *Helmholtz* (Müller's 'Archiv,' 1848, p. 147) employed three elements joined together (of iron and virgin silver). Not only is the delicacy of the thermo-electric apparatus very considerable (Dutrochet's apparatus registered $\frac{1}{20}$th of a degree Centigrade $= \frac{1}{50}°$ Fahr. nearly), but if the solderings are sharpened to a point, it allows the difference of temperature between any two points of the surface of the body to be estimated with an accuracy of which the mercurial thermometer is incapable, because, in applying the latter, it is necessary to cover the skin and protect it from loss of heat by radiation, which alters the condition of things, and furnishes erroneous results.

Lombard ('Archives de la Physiologie normale et Pathologique,' 1868, I, 498) describes (but not very clearly) an apparatus with which he accurately indicated differences of temperature amounting to ·00025° Centigrade ($= \frac{1}{2000}°$ Fahr. nearly).

Gavarret has recommended that thin plates (of copper and bismuth) soldered together should be used instead of the needles for estimating the temperature of superficial parts. The thermo-electric apparatus is especially useful in indicating sudden changes of temperature, and serves for the measurement of heat of individual parts of the skin; and besides, as the needles can be introduced into internal organs, the temperature of these can be determined, and thus the thermo-electric apparatus is applicable where the mercurial thermometer cannot be introduced.

[See also some observations by Dr. Edward Montgomery with a platinum and steel apparatus, in the article on Inflammation, by Mr. John Simon, in Holmes's 'System of Surgery,' vol. i, p. 18.]

(*d*) In order to make *continuous observations of temperature*, and to secure the accurate and automatic registration of these by the instrument employed, *M. Marey* has invented a *thermograph* ("Le thermographe, appareil enregistreur des températeures," 1865, in Robin's 'Journal de l'Anat. et de la Physiologie normal et pathologique,' ii, 182). It is an *air*-thermometer, the copper chamber of which is connected by means of a very small-bored copper tube ($\frac{1}{3}$rd millimetre in diameter $= \frac{1}{100}$th inch nearly), with a glass tube, bent in a half circle, which is open at one end, and fastened to a metallic wheel moving easily on its axis, the glass tube having a globule of mercury just filling its calibre. As soon as the air becomes warm, it is expanded and moves the mercury, and as this always seeks the lowest level, it moves the wheel and tube, and this gives motion to an indicator or needle, which inscribes or registers the changes of temperature on ruled paper, moved by clockwork at a regular rate of motion. The use of this instrument in cases of disease has not as yet been tested, and it is doubtful whether we can expect it to be practically useful, since it is to be feared that when placed on any part of the body, without any one to superintend the process, some hitch might occur in the working of the instrument, which might destroy the whole value of the observations. For similar reasons the electric registering thermometers, invented, for example, by *Zecchi* and General *Morin*, are hardly likely to be introduced into practice.[1]

§ 4.—The *determination of units of heat* or *caloric-units*, that is, of the quantity of heat required to warm a given measure of distilled water (say one grain or one kilogramme, or so many ounces or pounds, as one chooses) one degree (Centigrade or Fahrenheit) is quite a different thing to measurements of the degree of temperature. These investigations, interesting as they are from a theoretical point of view, and much as they would add to our knowledge of warmth-production in disease, are yet, on account of the many details involved, and because, in spite of the precautions taken, absolute accuracy has not yet been attained—not available for practical purposes.

If one shows the increased warmth of the water of a bath, in which a living body is immersed, during a given period of time; one obtains the warmth given off by the body in the given time (or more properly only a portion of this) : in this manner endeavours have been made to estimate the warmth-production of the body during this time, by comparing the height of the temperature at the beginning and end of the experiment. Such calorimetric investigations have been industriously made by *Liebermeister, Kernig, v. Wahl, Leyden,* and *Rembold.*

---

[1] A portable and easily applicable apparatus which could be worn for stated periods of time, and consist of a registering *maximum* and a registering *minimum* thermometer seems to be the greatest practical desideratum in Medical Thermometry. The latter appears the chief difficulty. It would then be easy for the general practitioner to take the daily *excursus,* or extremes of temperature in any given case.—[TRANS.]

§ 5.—The *most suitable place for the application of the instrument* is by no means invariably the same under all circumstances, and, according to the purpose the observer has in view, he may select one or another spot at pleasure.

When the object is to take the *temperature of a particular part* of the body, the measurement must naturally be taken at the place in question. If this is on the surface of the body, the indications of the mercurial thermometer are always somewhat uncertain, because if the instrument is exposed (uncovered) during the observation the external air will continually tend to cool it; but if, on the other hand, the instrument and the part are covered, the warmth-relations (so to speak) of the latter, or the circumstances of the case, are materially modified. For this purpose, therefore, the thermo-electric apparatus is to be preferred.[1] But if, as generally happens, we want to determine the general temperature of the body (or blood-heat), the mercurial thermometer is the most practical instrument; but it must be so disposed that it is surrounded on all sides (as far as regards the bulb) by some portion of the body. We may avail ourselves of several places for measurement of temperature, of which each spot has its advantages and disadvantages, and may be chosen according to circumstances. The introduction of the thermometer into the *well-closed axilla* appears to be the most convenient method in the great majority of cases. Its use in this situation is attended by scarcely any difficulties, does not fatigue the patient, and no objection can be made to it on the score of decency. On the other hand, in very thin people or restless patients, the results are uncertain, and besides this, the axillary temperature is a trifle lower than that of most of the other accessible spots, and on this account its indications are less delicately sensitive than those of mucous membranes. If these imperfections, which may sometimes be very evident under certain circumstances may sometimes lead us to prefer other places for the thermometer, yet, in the majority of cases, the axilla will be found the most suitable place. The application of the instrument in the *inside of the mouth* apparently affords uncertain indications, because the cool air inspired may easily lower the tem-

---

[1] It appears to me that the author's objections do not apply to observations made on parts of the surface *usually* covered (*e. g.* the abdomen or thorax), nor to *comparative* observations on parts equally exposed, as, for example, two ears, two hands, &c. &c., when the object is to determine the *difference* rather than the absolute *height* of the temperature.—[TRANS.]

perature, and in cholera especially, it gives lower readings than many other places of observation. However, the mouth must be employed, if other regions are inaccessible (as, for example, in baths, or in patients who are "packed" or closely swathed for any purpose, &c.).[1]

Taking the temperature in *the rectum*, so warmly advocated by many observers, is repulsive, can seldom be repeated often enough to satisfy the exigencies of the case, may provoke the action of the bowels, and perhaps produce prejudicial chills by the necessary exposure. Besides this, if the bulb, as may happen, should be pushed into a mass of fæces, a false impression would be given of the temperature. And *Billroth* avers that powerful contractions of the *rectum* may be induced by the mere introduction of the instrument, which may thus affect the result. On the other hand, it is generally allowed that the mercury registers the maximum temperature more quickly in the rectum than elsewhere, and that this method may be advantageously employed in new-born infants, little children, very emaciated patients, and in collapse, when the peripheral temperature often differs greatly from that of internal organs; and in some other special circumstances.[2]

Still less suitable is the introduction of the thermometer into the *vagina*, except for special reasons (as in Obstetrics). Although certainly more trustworthy than observations in the rectum, there are very few individuals in whom it could be repeated sufficiently often. It seems most applicable to *cholera* cases, and when the temperature of the internal genital organs is to be estimated. *Levier* took temperatures in the *groin*, for a special purpose, which, however, is scarcely more suited for general use than *Mante-*

---

[1] In Germany it is still customary amongst the lower orders, at least, to roll young infants up in "swaddling bands"—a custom which still prevails in some country districts in England, and perhaps Ireland. Whilst agreeing with the author as to the general objections to the mouth, I believe that for auto-thermometry (as by Dr. Ogle, Dr. Garrod, and others) it gives good results for comparative observations.—[TRANS.]

[2] My own experience (which I am glad to see confirmed by Dr. Finlayson) is strongly in favour of this method, when a single observation has to be made in a young child, for *diagnostic* purposes. I find that if the child be in short clothes, it is only necessary to lay it comfortably on one side (the left usually) on the mother's lap, and the bulb of the thermometer, slightly oiled, can generally be introduced without giving any pain, often without *waking* the child even.—[TRANS.]

gazza's proposal to take the temperature of the freshly passed *urine* as a standard.

Holding the thermometer in the closed *fist*, is an entirely unreliable method of ascertaining the general temperature, but may be valuable as a means of comparing the temperature of the trunk with that of the extremities, or of comparing that of the two sides of the body.

[The clefts of the fingers and toes (in cases of paralysis of *one* nerve-trunk), and the elbows, and popliteal spaces, may, under special circumstances, and for special objects, be chosen as the places of observation. For similar reasons, the thermometer may be introduced into sinuses, wounds, the bladder, &c., &c., in special cases. Wunderlich's object, however, is to recommend those methods which will (approximatively) give the average general temperature of the body. —TRANS.]

§ 6. The *mode of using* the instrument may contribute much to the *accuracy*; or, on the contrary, the *worthlessness* of the observations. The following precautions must be observed, when the temperature is taken in the axilla.

When there is much perspiration, the axilla must first be carefully wiped dry. It is then advisable, as *Liebermeister* has recommended, to keep the axilla *closed* (by bringing the arm to the side) some time *before* the thermometer is put there. He has pointed out that the time taken by the mercury to reach the maximum, was reduced by this means to from four to six minutes ('Prager Vierteljahrsch.' lxxxv. p. 13). But sometimes this preliminary closure of the axilla may cause loss of time. The thermometer should first be warmed a little in the hand (to 85° or 90° F. in most cases, and if a registering one, the *index must be set*—see note, p. 62), then introduced deep into the axilla (under the anterior or pectoral fold), and the axilla closed, by close pressure of the arm against the thorax, which always gives the arm an inclination towards the breast (*i. e.* to the median line).

If the thermometer does not keep its position nicely,—if the patient is restless, unruly, sleepy, or forgets himself, or if he be very much emaciated, the arm and thermometer must be kept in apposition by the person who takes the temperature. In any case, it is well to make sure occasionally that the instrument is in good position.[1]

[1] The *pons asinorum* of young observers is generally found in the *necessity*

We can often judge whether the mercury is likely to rise to any considerable height, by the rapidity or slowness of its ascent during the first minute or two; and even the first few seconds often enable us to give a good guess as to the presence of fever, or its intensity. The mercurial column seldom becomes stationary, in measurements taken in the axilla (unless that has been kept closed for some time before) in less than ten minutes, or oftener a quarter of an hour, sometimes it takes twenty minutes, or even longer. It is noticeable, as regards this, that the mercury rises more quickly at first than afterwards, and for the last one-tenth of a degree, the time occupied in rising from one tenth to another tenth may even occupy some minutes.[1] In order to make accurate observations, it is therefore desirable to allow the thermometer to remain some minutes after the mercury remains stationary. This period, however, must not be unduly protracted, for it appears that in many sensitive sick people, the forced and uncomfortable position of the arm, and perhaps the persistent contraction of muscles, cause slight elevations of temperature after the mercury has (apparently) attained a stationary point, quite independent of fluctuations due to the disease. Besides this, in some minute investigations, it must not be forgotten that in some cases, chiefly on account of the not inconsiderable daily variation, the mercury never comes to rest at all. In such cases, therefore, these changing values must be noted for a given number of minutes. For

that the thermometer should be quite free of the clothes (which are bad conductors), and in contact with *the skin all round.* I have known mistakes of 3—4° Fahr. easily made in this way, where the arm-hole of the dress was tight.—[TRANS.]

[1] See a very interesting paper in the 'British Medical Journal,' August 21st, 1869, "On some Points concerning the Method of observing the Temperature of the Body," by Dr. Charles Bäumler, who finds from various experiments that the time required in the axilla for the mercury to *"settle"* or become steady, varies from eleven to twenty-four minutes. In the rectum from three to six minutes only were required. He quotes Dr. Liebermeister as follows:— "When a thermometer is placed in the axilla, its temperature gets there as quickly as in the rectum or any other place of application, into equilibrium with the surrounding temperature, and after a few minutes that point is reached which corresponds to the temperature of the unclosed axilla. Meanwhile, however, the axilla has, by enclosing in it the thermometer, been transformed into a closed cavity; its temperature therefore begins at once to rise, and continues rising until the temperature is reached, which would correspond to that of a point of the body lying in the same depth under the surface. The mercury too must therefore continue to rise until the temperature of the axilla has become that of a closed cavity."

most purposes, the observation may be terminated when the mercury has remained stationary for five minutes. In general practice, it is sufficient to wait for two or three minutes after it has appeared to stop rising.[1] It is scarcely necessary to observe (that *except in the case of registering thermometers*) it is *necessary to read the instrument in situ*; and yet I have known men of some eminence commit this mistake, and then criticize thermometry!

It is possible to shorten somewhat the time required for investigation, although at expense of accuracy, by previously warming the bulb, before introducing it, a few degrees higher than the expected temperature. However, there is not much to be gained by this, for *Liebermeister* has shown that unless the axilla has been previously closed for some time, the mercury first sinks below the temperature of the body, on account of the cooling of the axilla, and then begins to rise again. When there is much elevation of temperature, however, this disadvantage is less considerable; and the method (of previously warming the thermometer) may be recommended as sufficiently accurate in these cases, whilst in lower temperatures it is less advisable, unless the axilla has been closed beforehand.

If the thermometer is used *in the month*, the bulb should be placed under the tongue, the mouth closed, and breathing should be carried on through the nose. In observations of temperature made in the *vagina* and the *rectum*, it is enough to introduce the well-oiled bulb about two inches;[2] and it stands to reason that care must be taken to guard against such a mishap as the instrument breaking because it was not strong enough, or for want of some other precaution.

§ 7. A few *cautions must be added* as regards the taking of observations.

If the patient a short time previously, or just before the observation, has been affected by any unusual circumstances,—if he has had

---

[1] This direction is very different from the directions placed on some thermometers, directing them to be *retained* for three minutes only (altogether). I cannot but think that this direction is well-calculated to bring the instrument into contempt, if not disuse.—[TRANS.]

[2] Thomas (in the 'Jahrbuch f. Kinderheilk,' N. F. II, 239) gives the useful advice, to warm the thermometer two or three degrees (Centigrade = 4—6° F. nearly) above the temperature expected, and to introduce it quickly, in which way useful results are obtained in from a quarter to half a minute. This does not apply to registering thermometers. These, however, may be warmed to 98 or 100° F. before introducing, by which time is saved.

copious stools, or hæmorrhage, or has vomited, or just had a meal, or taken a considerable quantity of any heating or cooling drink, or if he is perspiring at the time, all these circumstances must be carefully considered and estimated, because they may all affect the temperature.

It is generally unimportant to note the temperature of the surrounding air at the time, because most observations are taken in temperatures which vary but little (i. e., in a sick chamber, which commonly has a temperature of 15°—20° Centigrade = 59°—68° Fahr.) It is only when the temperature of the surrounding air is very hot, as sometimes happens in summer, that it may be as well to note this also.

For a similar reason, any consideration of the barometric pressure is unimportant in the majority of cases where the thermometer is used in disease.

On the other hand, it is desirable to *note carefully* both the *day of the month*, and the *time of day* at which the observation is taken, as without this the whole of the observations may be useless.

§ 8. The circumstances of the case, and the objects sought to be attained, must decide the question of the *time*, and the *frequency* of repetition of the observations. Under most circumstances, it is desirable to repeat the observations, at a similar time of the day; and for most medical objects, it is enough to make observations twice a day, which is best done between seven and nine a. m., as probably the time of the lowest daily temperature; and in the evening, between four and six o'clock, as being probably the time of *highest* daily temperature. But if experience has shown that the daily remissions and exacerbations of a given case occur at other periods, the measurements should be taken at such times.

In cases of great importance, or when any special question has to be decided, the measurements should be repeated every two or four hours, especially in very acute diseases; and sometimes in the very commencement of a disease, in order to find out the periods of exacerbation and remission; in cases of doubtful diagnosis; and in cases where variations from the normal course or type of the temperature occur.

And besides this, the temperature should be taken whenever anything special is noticed in the patient, or occurs to affect him.

In order to learn accurately the real course of temperature in any illness, it is not enough to take observations only twice a day; they should be taken at least four, perhaps six or more times daily. For these observations, the following times are most suitable:—From seven to eight, and nine to ten in the morning; from twelve to one at noon; from three to four and from six to seven in the afternoon; and from ten to eleven at night. To these may be added an observation in the early morning hours, if the fever be very severe, or its course exhibits great fluctuations of temperature. When very sudden changes of temperature occur in a disease,—as, for example, in a rapid crisis, or in a case of intermittent fever,—hourly or half-hourly, or even continuous observations may be required to exhibit the actual progress of the case.

Such severe demands upon time seldom concern the private practitioner, but must be met, if it is desired to speak authoritatively on the laws of disease, or the course of a malady.

§ 9. The question—*By whom shall the observations of temperature be taken?*—is not an unimportant one.

Although it might appear that only the results obtained by a practised medical man, or a trustworthy medical assistant, could be relied upon, we must remember that this devolves an immense amount of labour upon the medical man.

The chief objection which has been made to the practical usefulness and applicability of thermometry to medical uses, rests on the supposition that the doctor must always take the observations himself,—a measure which is considered to involve too much expenditure of time.

So long as only one or two daily observations are taken, even in severe cases, this objection is of little value, since almost any medical man can afford to spare a couple of quarter-hours, for very acute cases, which do not occur so very often in private practice. If he cannot spare this amount of time, he had better not undertake the cases. The logic of this objection is scarcely better than that of an accoucheur, who would not wait to the termination of a difficult labour he had undertaken, for want of time!

But, on the other hand, it is quite certain that no busy practitioner can make six or seven daily observations in the same patient, except as a very exceptional thing indeed, and it is not very often that he would be able to *personally* take observations twice daily in the same cases. But indeed it is not necessary that he should do so.

It is only necessary that he should know by whom, and how the observations were taken, and that his knowledge of pathological thermonomy should be sufficient to enable him to control (or rightly estimate) the results obtained.

Any trustworthy, honest, and intelligent man, with good sharp sight, or provided with spectacles if necessary, can be very quickly taught to take temperatures with sufficient accuracy. The *rôle* of the surgeon is not merely taking observations, but the superintendence, control, and right interpretation of them. The mere reading of thermometer degrees helps diagnosis no more than dispensing does therapeusis.

Even in observatories and meteorological stations, the thermometric and many other observations are often made by those who have no direct interest in their interpretation. A trustworthy, attentive man, with good will, and conscientiousness, without any special medical knowledge, will indeed often make less errors than many a medical man. He will have no preconceived opinions to prejudice him, as many practitioners have, and thus he will take cognizance of things as they really occur.

In this way trustworthy and well-trained attendants on the sick, in private practice, or intelligent relatives, make very good and useful colleagues for the work of medical thermometry. I have generally found that the relatives quickly appreciate the value of these observations, and go to work with painful anxiety; and are often inclined, if they err at all, to do so by disturbing the patient too frequently to take his temperature. But whoever may be entrusted with the thermometer, must be carefully taught how to use it, and assiduously overlooked. Any carelessness on their part is a sign that they are not fit for their post; and the medical man ought to be so familiar with whatever regards medical thermometry, that any deviation from customary routine may be regarded as an indication for care, and as requiring that he should personally repeat the taking of the temperature. It is easily to be understood, that the indications thus obtained, although sufficient for private practice, cannot be considered satisfactory data for enunciating general principles or laws of disease. If the facts thus ascertained appear to be in contradiction to those obtained by better (*i. e.*, more accurate) observations, we must at least wait until we are convinced that such a deviation often occurs as the result of laws learnt by other means, or is in accordance with the other circumstances of the case.

§ 10.—The *shortest and simplest method* of obtaining useful results also varies with the circumstances of the case and the objects
sought.

In *private practice* the *axilla* will almost always be chosen as the
place for the thermometer. The medical attendant should place the
thermometer there as soon as he comes to the bedside. The axilla,
if necessary, is to be first wiped dry, and the thermometer previously
warmed slightly by the hand. Great care must be taken to avoid
the linen [or other underclothing] getting between the skin and the
bulb of the thermometer; or directions may have been given that it
should be so applied a quarter of an hour before his visit. The
moment of introducing the thermometer should be noted by a watch
or clock. While the thermometer is thus lying in the axilla, the
doctor can ask the necessary questions, feel the pulse, see the tongue,
and inspect the dejecta or excreta. If he has himself placed the
thermometer in the axilla, he may, after about two minutes, look to
see if the mercury is quickly rising, or if the thermometer is in good
position.[1] It is advisable, for many reasons, to look every two
minutes or so, and if from three to five minutes have elapsed since
the mercury became stationary, the instrument may be removed and
the observations concluded.

In private practice it is seldom necessary to know the absolute
height of the temperature, and therefore the observations may be
made more quickly than if we had to determine this. A fifth of a
degree Centigrade ($= \frac{1}{3}°$ Fahrenheit nearly) minus the proper temperature affects our diagnosis or prognosis very little. Just as in
regard to the pulse, it is generally of little moment whether a patient
has a pulse of 80 or 84, of 100 or 104, of 140 or 150 a minute, so
for the questions which arise in private practice, except in cases of
extremely high temperature, one or two tenths of a degree Centigrade
($=$ two to three tenths Fahr. nearly) usually matter but little. The
physician should know when it is of importance, and when not, and
so, very often the time for taking a temperature may be still more
abbreviated. In private practice the thermometer may be previously
warmed, which can be quickly done by a match, and the mercury
allowed to fall to the temperature of the body. In this way, two or
three minutes may suffice to give, not very exact, but quite satisfactory results. When it seems desirable, in private practice, to repeat

[1] One finger will feel if the bulb is all right, without opening the axilla, and
a glance at the stem is generally all that is necessary.—[TRANS.]

he observations more frequently than the surgeon himself can conveniently do (as, for example, in all severe cases of fever, in intermittents, and in chronic forms of fever), the duty should be entrusted
to an intelligent relative, first informing him or her of the importance of the results thus obtained for guiding our treatment of the
sick and judging of his condition.   When he has been shown and
told how the manipulations are effected, he must be allowed to take
some temperatures under supervision, and then he may be allowed
to make the observations independently, the surgeon *testing* (so to
speak) his accuracy, by occasionally *repeating* the observation, especially if anything unusual has happened, or any startling result has
been procured.   The attendant must put down his *reading* of the
degrees, the *time* at which the temperature was taken, and how long
the thermometer was kept in the axilla.   Such observations become
a great help to private practice, and if nothing further were learnt
from them than the times at which remissions and exacerbations
occur, they would serve as a very useful finger-post to indicate the
necessity of further visits and thermometric observations.   But much
more important lessons can be learnt from them without much
danger of self-deception, for by means of these we may often get the
first indication of tendencies (or complications) in the disease, the
early knowledge of which is of the last importance, and not to be
attained at an equally early period by any other means of observation.

I need hardly say that the thermometer left with the patient must
be an instrument which is in good order, and has been previously
tested.

In the *wards of large hospitals* a methodical process, with the
view of saving time, is even more necessary than in private practice.
For the regular daily observations, the same time must be chosen.
Before the doctor enters the ward, a thermometer should be applied
to every patient in it, and he should go round quickly, and ascertain that the instruments are in good position, correcting them
when necessary.   Whilst making other observations (pulse, &c.),
he may from time to time correct the position of the thermometer
or of the patient's arm, &c. If a patient is inclined to be restless, or
let the thermometer slip out of his axilla (which very seldom
happens in patients possessing consciousness, who generally show
deep interest in the temperature being properly taken), a nurse or
other attendant may attend to the instrument.   After about twenty

minutes, a clinical assistant, or an intelligent nurse or wardsman, goes round quickly, and notes the temperature of every case.

Meanwhile the instruments are left in the patients' axillæ for about five minutes more, when the doctor reads the temperature for himself. If the degrees he observes differ from those obtained just before, the thermometer in the given case is left still longer, till the mercury has become stationary. In this manner, the temperature of every patient in a ward containing twenty beds, can be accurately determined in less than an hour, and much of this time can also be usefully employed in simultaneously making other observations [pulse, tongue, respirations, questions, &c.]. In a well-organised corps of attendants on the sick, there will always be some found who make perfectly trustworthy *readers* of temperature, and their services may be made use of at least for cases of ordinary kind, and for times when no medical or surgical visit is to be expected. We must always remember that a physician who has much thermometric experience, will not be very easily, or at least for long together, deceived by false results, or imperfect takings of temperature, and that only the novice in thermometry has to fear being much misled by others.

Naturally enough, there will still be some cases which require more time to be devoted to them, either because the ascertained temperatures appear on some grounds suspicious, or because the special circumstances of the case render a more than common amount of accuracy and care desirable. We must devote more time and care to these, in thermometry, just as in other ways, some patients both claim and secure more detailed investigation of their cases than others do.

He who has learnt the value of thermometry will not reckon either his time or his trouble in these cases thrown away.

§ 11. Whatever the nature of the thermometric observations, if they are to be of any use at all, it is essential that the *results obtained should be continuously recorded*. This can be best done, and the course of the disease rendered most evident, by indicating it *on a chart*, or ruled map, as a *continuous curved line*. On this chart, both Réaumur's and Celsius' (the Centigrade) degrees may be marked. [Those used in this country generally have the Centigrade and Fahrenheit scales instead.] It is convenient to note the frequency of the pulse, and the number of the respirations, in a

similar manner, but in different colours. This may be conveniently
done by coloured pencils. Other memoranda, of other symptoms
and appearances which are highly important, may be exhibited on
the same chart. (See Model, Plate I.)   In this way the entire
course of the disease, with all its fluctuations, complications,
tendencies, and changes can be seen at a single glance. No memory,
however retentive, however life-like and true to nature, affords so
"speaking" a likeness of the course of the disease as such a chart.
The comparison of many such charts together exhibits the uniformity of the general course of diseases, lets the laws of disease promul-
gate themselves, so to speak, and exhibits all the variations and
irregularities of the malady, and the working of therapeutic agents
in so striking a manner, that no unprejudiced mind is able to resist
such a method of demonstration.

CHAPTER V.

ON THE TEMPERATURE IN HEALTH.

1. It is almost self-evident that our knowledge of the *tempera-ture of healthy human beings* must be *the basis of all our conclusions* as to the *temperatures met with in disease*. Although observations of temperature in healthy persons have now become very numerous, yet the facts are still insufficient in number, and as yet far from sufficiently reliable, to completely satisfy our wishes on all the points which it is desirable to elucidate.

These observations are for the most part concerned with differences of only a few tenths of a degree $[\frac{1}{10}^{\circ}$ Centigrade $=\frac{18}{100}^{\circ}$ Fahr. $=\frac{1}{5}^{\circ}$ nearly].

Very often indeed, we may fairly question, whether the persons who are the subject of experiment are *perfectly healthy* or not; and particularly in those cases, when the supposed healthy temperature is tested under the influence of unusual conditions and circumstances, it may be doubted whether these influences and conditions have affected the health of the subject of experiment—whether the in-fluences to which he is exposed have proved overpowering in them-selves, or that the individual subject to them has not been sufficiently healthy to withstand the effects of a novel diet, or prolonged baths, and such like. And it is no less true that whole series of personal observations have become of doubtful value, owing to the subsequent illness of the experimenter (as for example those of *Gierse*); and in many cases the unusual deviations from the recognised standard allow us confidently to assert that the experimentees were not in perfectly sound health. In this way, facts and observations made with the greatest care and precision, as regards the method of obser-vation, are subject to considerable drawbacks when regarded as materials for judgment on the temperature of health. Many of these observations, however, have been somewhat *negligently made*, and the precautions which are rightly considered essential for pathological thermometry have been neglected in the experiments made on the temperature of the healthy. It is, however, essentially wrong to found our principles of physiological thermometry upon *materials so scanty*. If a great number of observations, under all sorts of circumstances were accumulated, many errors would thus be compensated or eliminated. Instead of this, it has been attempted to solve the problem by a few isolated observations, or by observations made on a few persons, a solution which cannot be accepted unless further confirmed by general laws.

It is easy, too, to comprehend that it is difficult to pursue these investigations on normal temperature through a sufficiently extended period of time—most of the furnished data referring only to brief periods. It is equally necessary to accumulate a long series of facts in medical thermometry, only it is easier to find materials. Physiological thermometry generally tries to decide important questions in short periods of time, and on a small number of facts, which could not be accepted as a basis for conclusions as to the temperature in disease. We must not overlook the fact that it is difficult to get a sufficiently large number of thoroughly healthy people for our experiments, and even if we could secure them, it is more difficult to guard them from undue extraneous influences than it is in the case of sick persons confined to their beds in a hospital ward.

In the absence of a sufficient number of healthy persons to serve as subjects of experiment, recourse might be had to observations on animals; but those which are generally chosen for this purpose (dogs, rabbits, &c.) do not exhibit an equal constancy of temperature with healthy men, or in other words their normal temperature is not confined to such narrow limits; and therefore the results of observations on them cannot be accepted as conclusive in the case of human beings, without further investigations. The *results of physiological thermometry*, as regards trustworthiness, and the number of experiments on which they are founded, must be considered to lag greatly behind the principles which the observations of the last twenty years have established as regards the temperature of the sick.

§ 2.—But even when every precaution has been taken in making the observations, it is *impossible to draw a hard and fast line to indicate by the temperature the exact limits of health and disease.*

6

So long as no other signs of disease are present, the decision as to what degree of temperature is normal appears to be quite an arbitrary one. All that justifies the establishment of such a limit is the fact that the occurrence of temperatures which exceed certain limits, is generally quickly followed by symptoms of disease, even when none such are observed at the time of using the thermometer. But we cannot always determine absolutely that such and such evidences of disturbed health are really symptoms of a disease. However, this difficulty in disease is only met with occasionally. It only occurs when man, or some other of the mammalia is brought under the effect of unusual circumstances, or powerful influences are brought to bear on them. In such cases, a physiological effect may simulate a pathological one, and it is, in fact, often difficult to say whether the compensatory-heat of healthy bodies is much affected by outward influences, or whether the insufficient compensation is to be considered a sign of a really diseased, although artificially induced condition. We may perhaps be justified in considering the effect to be normal or healthy, when the normal temperature is very speedily restored, immediately after the disturbing element is eliminated, provided no other signs of functional or textural mischief present themselves. But such cases of experiment must often be considered to be on the border-land between health and artificially-induced disease. A similar remark applies to certain cases not yet regarded as diseased conditions; for example: extreme fatigue, menstruation, pregnancy, and parturition, and the more doubtful we are as to the absolute healthiness of the individual, the more difficult does it become to decide on the category to which these belong.

§ 3.—The untrustworthiness of the observations of healthy temperature, owing to the difficulty of excluding previously existing slight, or (although latent) serious disturbances of health in the subjects of experiment, and the impossibility of sharply severing pathological effects from physiological ones, prevent our positively determining the *range of temperature in healthy human beings*; yet we may accept, as not far from absolute truth (supported as it is by the very numerous observations we have the opportunity of making in convalescence), the statement that the *range of normal temperature in the axilla* is from $97\cdot25°$ Fahr. ($36\cdot25°$ C.) to $99\cdot5°$ Fahr. ($37\cdot5°$ C.) *and that the mean normal temperature*$=98\cdot6°$ F. ($37°$ C.). At least anything above or below this must be looked upon as suspicious, and only considered normal under special circumstances and conditions.

Since the temperature of the human body can only be considered as the result of continual production and losses of heat, of varying amounts, it appears a very remarkable fact that the sum total (Facit) should always remain so nearly the same (under the operation of so many, and doubtless every moment changing processes and influences), that the internal temperature varies by little more than a degree Centigrade(= 1·8° Fahrenheit).

What *Lavoisier* has said of the body-weight—" Quelle quantité l'aliments que l'on prenne, le même individu revient tous les jours après la revolution des 24 heures au même poids à peu près qu'il avoit la vielle, pourvu qu'il soit d'une forte santé, que sa digestion se fasse bien, qu'il ne s'engraisse pas, qu'il ne soit pas dans un état de croissance, et qu'il évite les excès,"[1] may be said with still greater propriety of the temperature of the body. So long as the bodily health is good, it maintains the same temperature in spite of slight fluctuations, or quickly returns to the same degree of heat; and even when special influences have determined a greater deviation, the normal temperature is soon reached again, if health is not injured; and even when an illness has been thus induced, as soon as ever recovery takes place, the temperature is again found to be normal. Human beings are not singular in this respect. Many other animals, and especially those nearest related to us in structure, exhibit the same phenomenon.

A specific temperature is indeed a peculiarity of every living being. Every animal, although subject to the laws which regulate the diffusion of heat, has the peculiarity that as long as it retains life it does not necessarily acquire the same temperature as the bodies with which it is brought into contiguity, or in other words, the temperature of the fluids or gases in which it is placed; under normal conditions it has a higher temperature than that of the medium which surrounds it, and if it happens, as it may exceptionally, that the temperature of this medium exceeds 104° or 107·6° Fahr. (40° = 42° C.) it does not acquire this temperature.

---

[1] "Whatever the quantity of food taken, the person taking it will be found to have regained almost exactly his original weight after the lapse of twenty-four hours, provided that he has done growing, that his health is good, and his digestion vigorous, that he is not getting corpulent, and that he avoids other excesses."

Mammalia and birds exhibit the still more remarkable peculiarity of a more or less *constant temperature* ; that is their temperature is independent, or almost independent of the warmth of the medium in which they are placed, whilst other animals are very materially influenced by this.

The expressions "warm-blooded" and "cold-blooded" animals are intended to denote this, but it is more correct to indicate the distinction between them by the terms, animals with "*constant*" temperature, and those with "*variable*" temperature.[1]   This constancy of temperature is however by no means absolute, and indeed many animals whose temperature is generally constant, exhibit considerable alterations of their specific heat, under certain circumstances—for example, amongst mammalia the hibernating animals closely approximate to the temperature of the surrounding medium during their winter-sleep, or hibernation.   Man belongs to the class of creatures in which the constancy of temperature is almost invariable—yet this must not be understood absolutely—in every man there are slight variations, under many different conditions, and in some persons, under special circumstances there are wider deviations from the normal, and this may be more particularly manifest in disease, which sometimes exhibits a great breadth of such deviations.

[1] From a comparison of statements by various authors, I believe that the temperatures given below are a fair average of the results of various experiments :—

Animal.		Mean temperature.	
Birds	=	$\{$	105·8° — 111·25° F.
			(41° — 43° C.)
Mammalia	=	$\{$	96° — 105° F.
			(35·5° — 40·6° C.)
Fish, Reptiles, and Amphibia $\}$	=	$\{$	50° — 52° F.
			(10° — 13·6° C.)

Or two or three degrees only higher than the surrounding medium (air or water).

Molluses and other Invertebrata $\}$ A few fractions of a degree higher than the surrounding media.

Insects, when excited, gain from 2°—10° Fahr. (= 3·6°—18° C.) in heat. A hive of bees has been known to have a temperature of 48·5° Fahr., whilst the surrounding air was 34·5°, and when annoyed the temperature of the hive rose to 102°. (Newport.)

The following temperatures are taken chiefly from Dalton's 'Physiology,' p. 255 :

§ 4.—This phenomenon of specific heat, and its constancy, is the *result, on the one hand, of the continual production of warmth*, which occurs in almost every part of the body, *and on the other hand of the ceaseless loss of heat*, processes which are always going on simultaneously, whilst life remains.

The fact that heat is generated in the human body, especially during life, is easily understood. There is no doubt that there is no other source of independent heat in the body except those processes which are called chemical. A fresh *creation* of heat no more happens in the body than a fresh creation of material—it is an exchange of forces which occurs in the organism. The forces which are changed into heat in the body, are the chemical affinities of its own substance, and of the materials introduced into it from without. In every process in which stronger affinities than before come into play, and are, so to speak, saturated, or satisfied (gesättigt), *force* is liberated (in the form of *heat* or *motion*). Since the tissues of the body, and the materials introduced into it, enter into fresh chemical combinations, which possess much less chemical power of combination (Spannkraft) or none at all; since the oxidisable ingesta (food of all kinds), and the inspired oxygen, are combined into carbonic acid, or eliminated as oxidised excreta, their previously existing chemical affinities are changed into (or pass over as, übergehen) heat

	Animal.						Mean temperature. Fahrenheit.	
	Swallow	.	.	.	.	.	$111.25°$	
	Heron	.	.	.	.	.	$111.2°$	
Birds	Raven	.	.	.	.	.	$108.5°$	
	Pigeon	.	.	.	.	.	$107.6°$	
	Fowl	.	.	.	.	.	$106.7°$	
	Gull	.	.	.	.	.	$100.0°$	
	Squirrel	.	.	.	.	.	$105.0°$	
	Goat	.	.	.	.	.	$102.5°$	
	Cat .	.	.	.	.	.	$101.3°$ — $102°$	
	Hare	.	.	.	.	.	$100.4°$	
Mammalia	Rabbit	.	.	.	.	.	$103.0°$	
	Dog .	.	.	.	.	.	$99.4°$ — $101°$	
	Guinea-pig	.	.	.	.	.	$102.0°$	
	Ox .	.	.	.	.	.	$99.5°$	
	Ape .	.	.	.	.	.	$95.9°$ — $98°$	
Reptile	Toad	.	.	.	.	.	$51.6°$	
Fish	Carp	.	.	.	.	.	$51.25°$	
	Perch	.	.	.	.	.	$52.10°$	

[TRANS.]

and motion.[1] *The innumerable chemical processes* going on in the system, and especially the *combinations* of the *alimentary materials converted into blood and*, although in a less degree, *of the tissues*, with the *oxygen inspired*, the oxidation of this material, the so to speak, continuous slow combustion of the blood, and of all the materials introduced into the body, or of those in it capable of oxidation—these are the sources for a ceaseless, and indeed copious development of heat.

The blood, on account of its capacity for taking up oxygen, is in every case the agent of heat-production. It is also, on account of its circulation through the entire body, the means of assimilating the unequal temperatures of different regions, and thus equalising the general temperature of the body. Whether the blood itself is not the principal seat of this interchange of chemical affinities which produces warmth, and whether the generation of heat in the parenchymatous tissues is due to this, and in what degree, is for the present of much less consequence. *Mayer* says, that " Not a hundredth part of the combustion-processes goes on anywhere else but in the blood-vessels themselves," and physiology has already begun to justify the statement. Yet it is generally admitted, that with the exception of the horny tissues (hair, nails, epithelium, &c.), all parts of the body contribute to the production of heat, by the changes their substance undergoes. The glands, the intestines, and the muscles, are the especial seats, or furnaces, (Heerde,) so to speak, of this process, although it is not possible to assign the exact share due to each.

It is equally impossible to express accurately in figures the *sum-total* of all the warmth produced in a given time in a healthy man under ordinary circumstances (that is, [amount of calorie, or] the number of warmth-units which are furnished by the human organism in any given time), because the loss of warmth in the same space of time can neither be prevented, nor exactly estimated ; and further, because the attempt to estimate the warmth produced, by calcu-lating from the products of metamorphosis, or from the combustion-heat of the materials of nutrition (that is, the amount of heat pro-

[1] It may perhaps be objected that this (although a description of a physical process) is couched in somewhat metaphysical language, and that a rather vague meaning is attached to the term *affinities*. This is, however, inseparable from the imperfection both of our knowledge and of language itself. Compare Groves 'On the Correlation of Forces,' and Professor Tyndall on ' Heat con-sidered as a mode of Motion.' —[TRANS.]

duced by their combustion), is beset with almost insuperable difficulties; and last of all, because the oxygen consumed is no measure of the warmth produced, since the materials to be oxidised have not all the same combustion-point; and because the whole of the *force* set free by oxidation, does not give rise to *heat*, but some of it appears as *motion* [Arbeitsleistung], and is to be calculated as so much *work*. The estimates we sometimes meet with, of the amount of heat produced by human beings in a given time, appear for the most part to rest on arbitrary data. For example, *Helmholtz* (in the 'Berlin. Encycl. Wörterb.,' xxxv, p. 555) calculates that a man weighing 82 kilogrammes (or about 13 stone) produces daily 2,732,472 "Calorien," or heat-units (*i. e.*, "*Gramm*-calorien" or heat-units in the sense of the quantity of warmth required to make 1 gramme [= 15·44 grains nearly] of distilled water 1° Centigrade [= 1·8° Fahr.] warmer than before) ; or, in other words, that every gramme of his body-weight produces *daily* sufficient heat to raise the temperature of 33¼ grammes of distilled water by 1° Centigrade (= 1·8° Fahr.), or in one *hour* enough to warm one gramme of distilled water about 1·4° Centigrade (= 2·52° Fahr.)[1].

§ 5.—As there is a continual *production* of heat in the body, there is also a continuous *giving off* or *loss* of heat. This loss of heat occurs—

By radiation (from the surface),

By conduction, or transmission to other bodies,

By evaporation of secretions in a gaseous form ;

And lastly, by the furnishing of mechanical work (or change of heat into motion).

[1] Wunderlich's figures are 38½ grammes and 1·6° respectively, instead of 33¼ grammes and 1·4° as above ; but a simple calculation appears to show that this is a clerical error. For the English reader the statement may be more familiarly put by saying that every pound of body weight produces heat enough in every 24 hours to make 6 gallons of water 1° Fahr. hotter than before ; in one hour enough heat to warm a quart of water to the same extent. Béclard estimates that a man produces daily heat enough to raise 55 lbs. (5½ gallons) of water from 32° to 212° Fahr., which indeed differs but slightly from the former statement. Other calculations by Despretz, Dalong, Barral, Nasse, and others, are referred to in Dr. Otto Funke's 'Lehrbuch der Physiologie,' Band I, pp. 492—508. See also Dr. Carpenter's 'Principles of Human Physiology' (edited by Dr. H. Power), pp. 437-8, where, apparently on the authority of Scharling, the daily number of heat-units is estimated at 2,464,154, or heat enough, if converted into mechanical force, to raise 1,166,000 kilogrammes (= 1147½ tons) 1 metre (= 39·37 inches) high.—[TRANS.]

The chief seat of the losses of heat, and consequently of the cooling process, is the surface of the body. It is here that the losses by radiation, and by transmission of heat to the surrounding media, and finally the loss of heat by the evaporation of water (perspiration) take place. The quantity of heat lost from various parts in this way depends partly upon the nature of the surroundings (Umgebung), their relative coldness, or conducting-power, &c.; and next on the form of the organs—(the nose, ears, fingers, quickly grow cool). But it depends also on the thickness and quality of the epidermis, and especially on the fulness, or otherwise, of the blood-vessels, and especially on the moisture of the skin, and the amount of perspiration. There is also a loss in the air-passages by the air which is inspired abstracting heat, and also by evaporation of water from the lungs. As, however, the air-passages are also the chief seats of heat-production, loss and gain are constantly going on together in them. In a less degree, there is also a loss of heat in the *stomach* (at such times as cold substances are introduced into it, correspondingly to their quantity and temperature), and in the *rectum* (by masses of fæces). Finally, in the action of *muscles*, a part of the heat is changed into *movement* (mechanical effect) ; but here again the account is balanced to some extent, by the production of heat in muscular contraction. It is estimated that from 60 to 70 per cent. of the heat lost must be assigned to radiation and conduction from the surface (from the skin), from 20 to 30 per cent. to evaporation of water, from 4 to 8 per cent. to loss through the air respired, 1 to 2 per cent. to loss in the excretion of urine and fæces, and about 2 per cent. to the introduction of cold articles of food.[1] The sum total of loss in a given time, cannot be determined any more certainly than the sum total of production ; this only we know, that in health one is equivalent to the other.

[1] *Barral*, on somewhat arbitrary data, makes the calculation that in a man of 29 years of age, in an atmosphere of 20° C. (68° Fahr.), the amount of heat production and loss amounts to the following figures :—

Heat-units produced = 2,706,076.

Loss of heat, in units and in per centages of the production :—

By evaporation, 699,801.   25·85 per cent.

By warming the air inspired, 100,811.   3·72 per cent.

By warming the food and drink taken, 52,492.   1·94 per cent.

By the solid and liquid excrements, 33,020.   1·22 per cent.

By radiation, conduction, and mechanical work, 1,819,952.   67·22 per cent.

See Funke's ' Physiologie,' *loc. cit.*—[TRANS.]

§ 6.—Although there is now pretty general agreement, and but little doubt as to the condition of warmth production, and the processes by which heat is given off, or lost; yet the real causes which maintain an even temperature in the body, or in other words, the *regulators of warmth*, are not at all well known.

As regards this, it is indeed quite conceivable that the production of heat is regulated by the concurrent increase or diminution of the losses of heat; and that man is instinctively led, when he loses much warmth, to try and limit this (by better covering himself) and to recover the lost heat by a richer production (through taking in food); or that, on the other hand, when the heat produced is excessive, he may seek to reduce it by such means as cold drinks, washing, bathing, &c. It is also conceivable that a number of contrivances may exist in the body, which unknown to the individual himself, come to the help of his instinct; as for example, in increased production of heat, the circulation is quickened, the blood-vessels of the skin become fuller, and the consequent loss of warmth from the skin greater, which is augmented by perspiration; the respiration is also quickened, and the consequent loss of heat from the difference of temperature of the inspired air becomes greater: whilst on the other hand, when the production of heat is less, the cutaneous vessels contract, become less rich in blood, and in this way the loss of heat from the skin is diminished. An uncompensated [einseitige = onesided] alteration of warmth-production, or an uncompensated change in the amount of heat lost, quickly induces, and indeed necessitates an alteration in the height of the temperature. But in a state of health, when the respective apparatus for heat-production, and heat-destruction [if one may use such a term], are in good order; or in a word, when the organism is under normal conditions, the compensatory changes are so suddenly made, that an equilibrium is quickly reestablished. Any considerable (uncompensated) increase of temperature is generally followed by a somewhat excessive loss of heat, and any unusually considerable loss is generally more than compensated by an over-production, so that after either a rise or fall of temperature, the temperature fluctuates somewhat, in opposite directions, till an equilibrium is attained. But all this does not make it any more evident, why the temperature in health so constantly maintains a particular degree, why this degree in human beings should be just about 37° C. (= 98·6° Fahr.); why other creatures, also provided with apparatus for the production, and means

for getting rid of heat, should either less perfectly, or not at all,
maintain an equally constant temperature with man; or what these
contrivances, so intimately blended one with another, really are,
by whose instantaneous and correct co-ordination, or working
together, the constancy of temperature (i. e. the regulation of it)
really depends.

Even *Ludwig* ('Physiologie,' II, 754), who sets out with the
"Means for the preservation of the normal degree of temperature,"
allows, that although the organic conditions, which determine the
balance between gain and loss of heat can be at least partially discovered, the mechanism of this connection is yet quite unknown.
There still remains this remarkable enigma, that these various and
changing factors in the healthy body, constantly produce so uniform
a result, as regards the degree of heat; and that thus, however
varied the amount of heat production, or whatever the amount of its
loss, there is constantly in the healthy body a regulator, which instantly steps in, and never allows it to rise much above, or sink
much below a determinate limit. The problem is not simplified by
our observing that this regulator only displays its full power in the
healthy, and that any disturbance of health makes itself known to
some extent by disturbing this regulating power also.

Yet, on the whole, the process is scarcely more mysterious than
that by which the blood maintains a constant similarity of composition in health, notwithstanding the varied ingesta and secretions ;
or that in which the totality of organic life, all the conversion of
tissue-materials to the composition (building up) of definite organic
forms, all compensation in living nature, whether in great things or
in little, all preservation of the individual, the equality (number-
relations) of the sexes, and the preservation of species (in spite of
slaughter, losses, and accidents), all alike depend. So long as the
organism is healthy, every *plus* on the one side is met by this
regulating power, with a *minus* on the other : and in health
the warmth production exactly compensates the amount of heat
lost through outward influences or in other ways, and in just a
similar way if the production of heat is either excessive or diminished, very numerous contrivances soon rectify the account. Just
as it is necessary for the due and orderly continuance of life that the
balance should be maintained between the *food taken in* [ingesta] and
the excreta, so it is with regard to this force. The undisturbed
continuance of life demands an equality as regards the production

of heat, and its loss or application in other ways, and on this equilibrium of heat health depends.

For this orderly arrangement (Ordnung) there is no need of *special regulating apparatus*, or organs for the purpose, or of any mystical working of these on the chemical processes of the economy, any more than the regularity of the rest of the system depends entirely on the domination of any special part of the body. The maintenance of the accustomed order depends much more upon the integrity of the function of all the parts where tissue changes are carried on, or, at least, on their practical (approximate) integrity, for the organism is fashioned with such artistic perfection, that a slight injury of one part sometimes disturbs the order of the whole body. But as regards the maintenance of the general functions of the body in their accustomed order, all parts of it are not of equal importance; so as regards an equilibrium of temperature, the integrity of some parts is much more important than that of others. Yet it must be allowed, indeed, that if there be (whether accidentally or designedly [artificially] induced,) too considerable hindrances to compensation; if the operation of single important organs deviates too widely from the necessary standard, there may then be very serious disturbances in the balance of production and loss of heat, and thus very considerable deviation from the normal temperature may occur. It will then depend upon the extent and duration of these deviations, whether we should consider them as within the limits (Breite) of health or not. Up to a certain point, indeed, we may choose to call it so, as has been said before, but it is no less true that with any considerable or continuous alterations of temperature, other signs of disturbed health are not long in making their appearance.

It is almost self-evident that such disturbances of the accustomed order may arise from various points and different processes of the economy. But that anomalies in the working of the nervous system (Anomalien der Thätigkeit der Nerven), are generally concerned in them, is easily understood, when we consider the extraordinary, complicated, and sensitive influence of this apparatus over all parts of the body. This, however, does not justify us in attributing to the nervous system or to any part of it, the function of regulating exclusively the heat of the body. The nervous system is, indeed, concerned in this function of regulation, first, because it is a part of the body; but it is especially concerned in it, and in a high degree, just because its relations with all the remaining parts of the body are so numerous, manifold, and important (einfluss-reiche) ; and it is further particularly concerned in the disturbances of equilibrium, because its own anomalies even when they are but slight, generally extend further than those of most other parts of the body ; and because the change in the calibre of the smaller vessels, and, consequently, the blood-supply (Blutfülle) of all the organs, depends upon one part of the nervous system itself.

§ 7. *Constant as the temperature remains in healthy men*, when re-garded as a whole (im Groben und Ganzen), yet, *it admits of some slight fluctuations (lit.* of a certain breadth of movement).

Many facts have been discovered which show the causes producing the minor deviations from the normal temperature, which are con-stantly occurring within certain limits.

The temperature of different *parts or places* of the same body, taken at any given time, is not quite uniform.

The temperature of any part of the body depends—

(1) On the amount of heat it receives.

(2) On the amount of heat generated in the part itself (an Ort und Stelle).

(3) On the local losses of heat.

As these conditions are not identical at any one time, in all the various parts of the body, since the copious or more sparing access of warm blood, the stronger or weaker local production of heat, and the topical radiation of heat, and cooling of the part may be more or less considerable, so the temperature of various parts will vary at one and the same time.

The *blood* itself, in different parts of the circulatory system ex-hibits variations of temperature. The cutaneous veins generally have the blood less warm than that of the arteries of the extremi-ties ; whilst, on the other hand, the venous blood of the kidneys and liver is warmer than the blood which is brought to these organs. The blood in the mucous membrane of the intestines is sometimes warmer, sometimes cooler, than that of the vena porta, and that of the veins of the salivary glands and muscles, in relation to their arterial blood, exhibits similar changes.

The blood of the jugular vein is warmer than that of the carotid artery.

The blood of the inferior cava is warmer than that of the superior, and than the mixed blood of the right side of the heart; but the latter is warmer than the blood of the veins in the extremities. The contents of the right ventricle are warmer than those of the left.

It is clear that in organs in which much warmth is generated, the venous blood leaving them is warmer than the arterial blood they receive; whilst in parts which give off a good deal of heat, the converse holds good. The arterial blood becomes colder in the extremities, whilst, on the other hand, the blood which passes through the organs of the abdomen, returns from them warmer than before, and make the blood of the inferior cava warmer than that of the superior, and even warmer than arterial blood itself.

Although these facts have no *immediate practical value*, yet they point, so to speak, to the furnaces (auf die Heerde,) where vital heat is produced, as well as to the refrigeration of the economy (die Stellen der Abkühlung); and now and then they may be used for purposes of comparative physiology. The following are the most important of the numerous investigations and experiments on the temperature of the blood in different blood-vessels: Those of *Becquerel* (' *Gavarret*, de la Chaleur,' p. 107); *G. Liebig* ('Uber die Temperaturunterschiede des venösen und arteriellen Blutes, Giessen thesis,' 1853); *Cl. Bernard* ('Comptes Rendus,' xl, p. 331 and 561, and his "Leçons sur les propriétés physiologiques et les altérations pathologiques des liquides de l'organisme," 1859, i, p. 54); *Savory* ('Lancet,' April, 1857), and *Wurlitzer* (' Thesis at Greifswald,' 1858). *Colin*, however, has obtained somewhat different results by means of very delicate Walferdin's maximum (metastatic) thermometers, as regards the blood of the heart. In 93 comparative measurements of the temperature of the blood in the two sides of the heart in horses, ruminants, and dogs, he found the temperature identical on both sides in 21, the blood of the right heart warmer in 45, and that of the left warmer in 27. He explains the latter by the production of heat in the lungs. He admits, however, that the temperature of the heart depends not only on that of the blood it receives, but also upon the varying conditions as to warmth of the stomach and intestines ('Annal. des Sciences, Zoologie,' vi, 83—103.

As regards the temperature of *internal organs* in healthy human beings, we can easily understand that direct experiment is wanting.

It is supposed, with some reason, that they have about the same temperature as accessible, but well sheltered spots.

Jacobson and *Bernhardt* ('Centralblatt,' 1868, p. 643), found the left heart in fifteen cases about ·12° to ·42° Centigrade (= $\frac{1}{4}$° to $\frac{7}{8}$° Fahr. nearly) warmer than the right, and the same temperature only in two cases. They found normal pleural cavities about ·1° to ·2° Centigrade (= $\frac{1}{5}$° to $\frac{4}{10}$° Fahr.), cooler than the abdominal cavity, and about ·2° to ·5° Cent. (= $\frac{1}{3}$° to $\frac{9}{10}$° Fahr. nearly), cooler than the left heart.

The *differences of temperature in those parts which are most capable of serving us in practical investigations* are apparently very slight when carefully measured. Amongst these, the temperatures of the vagina and the unloaded rectum are the highest, being from one to four tenths of a degree Centigrade (= $\frac{1}{5}$th to $\frac{7}{10}$ths of a degree Fahr. nearly), higher than that of the axilla.

The temperature of the interior or cavity of the mouth, if there is no disturbing element, occupies an intermediate position (between the axillary and vaginal or rectal). We may safely allow that when the mean temperature of the *axilla* in a healthy person is 37° (98·6° Fahr.), that of the *mouth* will be 37·1° to 37·2° (98·78° to 98·96° Fahr.), and that of the *vagina*, or unloaded *rectum* 37·3° to 37·5° (99·14° to 99·5° Fahr.). Yet the results of various observers are somewhat contradictory. Compare on these points *L. Fick* ("Temperaturtopographie des Organismus" in Müller's 'Archiv,' 1853, p. 408). *Winckel* (in the 'Monatsschrift für Geburtskunde und Frauenkrankheiten,' 1862, xx, 473). *Ziemssen* ('Pleuritis und Pneumonie im Kindesalter,' 1862, p. 10). *Schröder* (Virchow's 'Archiv,' xxxv, 253.)[1]

The differences between the temperatures of imperfectly protected situations on the surface of the body are far more considerable. As cooling takes place to a greater and more fluctuating extent, the differences observed in customary measurements are almost valueless for practical purposes. We learn, however, from thermo-electric determinations of temperature of various parts of the skin, that

[1] In some *diseases* (notably in cholera, pneumonia, pelvic and abdominal diseases, &c.) much greater differences will sometimes, as might be expected, be found. This is also the case occasionally in parturition. From 2° to 3° Fahr. (= 3·6° to 5·4° C.) difference between the axillary and vaginal or rectal temperatures occurs in some of these cases. Some of the discrepancies which have been recorded are, however, doubtless due to the methods of observation being imperfect.—[TRANS.]

here are constant variations of temperature, in one and the same place, within certain not very considerable limits, corresponding with the amount of blood-supply, and that this ebb and flow is almost continuous, and determined by various circumstances. For example, *Lombard* has found such variations in the temperature of the skin of the occiput produced by the influence of moderate mental exertion (Experiments on the relation of heat to mental work[s]— analysis by Brown-Séquard in 'Archiv de Physiol. Normale et Path.,' 1868, i, 670).

§ 8. The *variations* in the temperature of *healthy persons under varying conditions* are very slight, and are comprised in the limits of a few tenths or fractions of tenths of a degree. [This is true, whether we take the Centigrade or Fahrenheit scale.] With very few exceptions the temperature in the axilla, in health, under the most varied circumstances and influences, moves between 36·2° and 38° (Centigrade = 97·16° to 100·4° Fahr.), and if it exceed this a little, does so only for a moment. *Dr. W. Ogle* (On the diurnal variations in the temperature of the human body, 'St. George's Hospital Reports,' 1866, ii, 221,) gives a somewhat lower *minimum*, and a somewhat higher *maximum* temperature; however, he found the minimum at 36·1° (96·98° Fahr.), on a winter morning, and the maximum at 38·1° (100·58°) in a Turkish bath. In some individuals (healthy in other respects) of greater delicacy, especially women and children, the mobility of temperature is somewhat greater, and under corresponding conditions the variations may somewhat exceed the above limits.

It must, however, always be remembered, when we find more considerable deviations, that the apparently healthy cannot always be safely considered as really so. Very numerous observations have been made in the effect of varied circumstances and influence on the temperature of the healthy. Any extended *résumé* of these would be unsuitable for my purpose, on account of the very varying value and importance of these observations. In the following pages, notice will only be taken of the most important observations and experiments.[1]

[1] Mr. A. H. Garrod (in 'Proceedings of the Royal Society,' vol. xvii. No. 112), publishes a series of observations which are intended "to show that the minor fluctuations in the temperature of the human body, not including those arising from movements of muscles, mainly result from alterations in the

§ 9. The influence of *age upon temperature.*—Before birth the infant's temperature is a trifle higher than that of the mother's uterus or vagina (Bärensprung). The difference, although very

---

amount of blood exposed at its surface to the influence of external absorbing and conducting media." He says: "It has long been known that cold contracts and heat dilates the small arteries of the skin, respectively raising and lowering the arterial tension, and thus modifying the current of blood in the cutaneous capillaries. But modifications in the supply of blood to the skin must alter the amount of heat diffused by the body to surrounding substances; and so we should expect that by *increasing* the arterial *tension*, thus lessening the cutaneous circulation, the blood would become *hotter*, from there being less facility for the diffusion of its heat, and that by *lowering* the tension, thus increasing the cutaneous circulation, the blood would become *colder* throughout the body, from increased facility for conduction and radiation." The paper is accompanied with sphymographic tracings to show that "by *stripping* the warm body of clothing, *in a cold air*, when the tension was low (bounding, weak pulse), the *temperature* and *tension rose* at the same time the surface of the body became colder. Simply heating the feet in warm water of 110°—114° Fahr. (43°3—45°6° C.), lowers the temperature and tension together, and is accompanied with feelings of chilliness." The subject of the experiments was a young man, aged 22, and thin. The temperatures taken in the mouth (usually for five minutes), the temperature of the external air never over 66° Fahr. (= 18°9° C.); and the skin was uniformly dry.

The following are examples:

No. I, sitting in room of 66°, temperature in mouth from 10.30—11 p.m. = 98°7° Fahr. (37°1° C.). He then stripped, and remained nude till 11.40. Fifteen minutes after stripping, his temperature was 99° Fahr. (37°2° C.). He then (at 11.40) covered the skin with a warm blanket, and at 11.55 the temperature was again 98°7° Fahr. (37°2° C.).

No. III, same subject standing in room, the temperature of air in which was 52° Fahr. (11°1° C.), from 11 to 11.30 p.m., the temperature of mouth was 98°75° Fahr. (37°19° C.). He then stripped, and by 11.50 p.m. his temperature = 99°5° Fahr. (37°5° C.). He went to bed at 12.2, and by 12.30 his temperature was only 98° Fahr. (36°7° C.).

It fell to 97°75° Fahr. (36°5° C.) by 12.50 a.m.

No. V, sitting in a room (temperature of air 58° Fahr. (14°9° C.), all the time, warmly clad till 11 p.m. Temperature in mouth = 97°75° Fahr. (36°5° C.). Nude at 11.2. From 11.15 to 11.45 p.m. the temperature varied from 99° to 99°4° Fahr. (= 37°23° to 37°45° C.). After putting on warm flannel, and sitting in front of fire, it fell again by 11.55, p.m., to 97°75° Fahr. (36°5° C.).

This author explains the facts obtained by Dr. Ogle, Sydney Ringer, and others, as to the temperature falling at night, and being lowest at from 12—1 a.m., and then beginning to rise by the loss of heat, though going to bed, given to cold bed-clothes, which gradually become warm, &c. [But this fall will take place without going to bed at all, or stripping at all, and in a warm room

slight, is significant in a theoretic point of view : it indicates not only that the unborn infant has its own proper sources of heat, but also, that widely as the fœtus differs from the adult, as regards the means of cooling, or getting rid of heat, the sum total, or final result, is not much different from what is found in the maternal organism. During birth (according to Bärensprung, children exhibit an average temperature (in the rectum) of 37·75° C. (= 100° F. nearly). Of thirty-seven newly born infants twenty-six had a temperature exceeding 37·5° Cent. (= 99·5° F.), and only one under 36·75° Cent. (= 98·15° F.) *Schäfer* ('Greifswald Thesis,' 1863) found the rectal temperature of new-born children, before the division of the funis in twenty-three cases, higher than the vaginal temperature of the mother in sixteen cases, and lower in only two cases ; and the average temperature of these cases was 37·8° C. (100·04° F.) with an average temperature of 37·5° C. (99·5° F.) in the maternal vagina. (See also *Wurster*, Berlin. Klinische Wochenschr, 1869, No. 37.)

Soon after birth, especially after the first ablutions, infants lose on an average from ·7 to ·8 of a degree Centigrade (= 1·26° to 1·44° Fahr.) ; and exhibit an average temperature of 37° C. (= 98·6° Fahr.) Of twenty-two new-born children, there were only three whose temperature was above 37·5° C. (99·5° F.), and eight of them were under 36·75° C. (98·15° F.), according to Bärensprung. In the next ten days the rectum temperature again rises somewhat, and pretty constantly remains between 37·25 C.

or a cold one indifferently almost; also in summer or winter, as I have often found by experiment,—which is confirmed by a number of observers.

Drs. Sydney Ringer and the late Andrew Patrick Stuart ('Proceedings of the Royal Society,' vol. xvii, No. 109, p. 287), have drawn the following conclusions as to the temperature in health. "The average maximum temperature of the day in persons under 25 years of age is 99·1° Fahr. (= 37·3° C.); of those over 40, 98·8° Fahr. (37·1° C.). The highest daily point = 9 a.m. until 6 p.m. About this time it slowly and continuously falls, till between 11 p.m. and 1 a.m. it again rises, and reaches nearly its highest point by 9 a.m. The diurnal variation in persons under 25 equals about 2·2° Fahr. (1·2° C.) In persons between 40 and 50 it is very small, the average being not greater than 0·87° Fahr. (= ⁴⁄₉° C. nearly), or on some days no variation whatever occurs.

In young persons the diurnal fall occurs at night, in older persons at any hour. They do not believe in the influence of food as causing diurnal variations. Nor do hot or cold baths, although *at the time* the former may reduce the temperature to 88° Fahr. (31·1° C.), and the latter increase it to 103° or 104° Fahr. (39·5° to 40° C.).—[Trans.]

(99·05° F.) and 37·6° C. (99·68° F.), or a trifle higher than that of
grown-up people. From the sixth to the eighth day after birth, it
is very common to meet with temperatures even a little higher than
this. (See also *Förster* in the 'Journal für Kinder-Kr.,' 1862).
Besides this, the *variations of temperature* met with in different
observations, made at various times on *newly born children, are
much greater* than those met with in observations made on *adults.*
Even the act of crying will cause a rise of temperature. New-born
infants very commonly show an evening rise of ½ a degree Centigrade
(= ·9° Fahr.), and a still greater elevation at noon. In apparently
healthy new-born infants, although but rarely, we sometimes meet
with elevations of temperature amounting to as much as 2° C.
(3·6° Fahr.), which are not found in healthy adults. This may
be explained either by supposing that they exhibit less *constancy of
temperature* than adults, or that they are subject to disturbances
of health which are more easily overlooked (*i.e.* less easily diagnosed).

Throughout childhood the same mobility of temperature may be
recognised.

Dr. Finlayson ('On the Normal Temperature of Children,' 1869)
remarks that the daily fluctuations of temperature in children are
greater than in adults.[1] As the *age increases,* there is but little

---

[1] Dr. Finlayson places this daily range at from 2°—3° F. (= 1·1°—1·6° C.).
He lays especial stress *on a fall of temperature in the evening, as always occurring
in healthy children,* amounting to 1°, 2°, or 3° F. (= ·9°, 1·8°, and 2·7° C.); and
states that this usually commences about 5 p.m., but is most strikingly seen
between 7 and 9 p.m.—it often begins at 5 p.m. and continues till after midnight. The *minimum* temperature in children is usually reached at or before
2 a.m.; between 2 and 4 a.m., whilst still sleeping soundly, it begins to rise, and
fluctuates between 9 a.m. and 5 p.m., but only slightly. The observations of
M. *Henri Roger* on newly born infants and young children, agree in the main
with those of *Bärensprung* given in the text. Thus, at the moment of birth, he
found the temperature from ½° to 1° C. (= ·9° to 1·8° F.) *above* that of the
mother (*axilla*). The mean of 33 new-born children (1—7 days after birth)
was 37·08° C. (= 98·75 F.); in 13 children from 4 months to 6 years, a mean of
37·21° C. (= 98·97° F.), and in 12 cases varying from 6 to 14 years, a mean of
37·31° C. (= 99·15° F.)."—*Archiv. Général,* vol. v, Series 4, p. 293.

"*Dr. Finlayson* found a mean of 99·41° F. (37·4° C. nearly) in 21 children under
6 years, the temperature being taken in the *rectum* between 7.30 and 9 a.m.,
before breakfast. Dr. Cassel's average = 97·75° to 97·47° F. at an earlier
hour."—*Glasgow Med. Journ.,* Feb., 1867.

See also an interesting paper by Dr. William Squire, on "Infantile Tempera-

appreciable difference between the temperature of healthy individuals—the most that we can say being, that the average temperature falls one or two tenths of a degree Centigrade ('2—'4° F. nearly), from early infancy to puberty, and from puberty to fifty or sixty years of age, in about the same proportion; but about the sixtieth year it begins to rise again, and notably about the eightieth year the mean temperature approaches that of infancy. This *relatively high temperature of the aged*, is a very remarkable circumstance, when we take into consideration the varieties (not inconsiderable in themselves) of respiration, of tissue changes, of the quantity of carbonic acid exhaled, and the traditional notions (Vorstellungen) as to the degree of vitality (Lebensactivität) belonging to this period of life. This may perhaps depend on diminished loss of heat from the skin, on account of this being less supplied with blood (mehr anämischen Beschaffenheit). See *Dr. John Davy* on the 'Temperature of very Aged Persons' ('Philosophical Transactions,' 1844, p. 59).

§ 10. *The Influence of Sex.*—No noticeable difference of temperature can be ascribed to sex. It may be that grown up women are a trifle warmer than men of an equal age; but the number of observations is insufficient to enable us to lay down a safe general rule on this point. However *Davy* arrived at an opposite conclusion, from a very small number of facts ('Medical Times,' v. 24, Sept., 1864).

[Dr. Ogle's *continuous* observations of a single case, in the daytime only (*i.e.* from 9 a.m. to 12 midnight), made in the summer months, confirm Wunderlich as to a *slightly* higher temperature in the female, never exceeding ¼° F. (= '45° C.) ('St. George's Hospital Reports,' vol. i.)—[TRANS.]

§ 11. *Influence of Race, Station in Life, and Occupation.*—*Livingstone* ('Travels in South Africa,' p. 509) has observed that the temperature of Africans was 2° F. (= 1·8° C.) less than his own. On the other hand *Thomsen* ('Ueber Krankheiten und Krankheitsverhältnisse auf Island und den Faröerinseln,' p. 24) makes the temperature of the Icelanders somewhat higher (on an average 37·2° C. (= 98·96° F.) under the tongue).

There are scarcely any facts, up to the present time, which justify us in ascribing any differences in temperature to the situation

ture in Health and Disease," in the 'Transactions of the Obstetrical Society,' vol. x, p. 274.

in life, as, for example, to the difference between the poor and the well-to-do, notwithstanding their different diet.

In the same way different *occupations*, so long as health is not impaired, appear to be entirely without influence on temperature.

Consequently we must conclude that the almost certain difference in the amount of heat *produced* in differing circumstances of life, is compensated in health, by a corresponding difference in the amount of heat *given off*.

§ 12. *Individual Peculiarities, or Idiosyncrasies.*—Apart from age, sex, race, and all accidental modes of life, and incidental influences, it appears that the mean (average) temperature of healthy persons *is not absolutely identical in every individual.* In this point of view observations in sufficient numbers of absolutely healthy people are wanting. But if I may be allowed to draw any conclusions from the circumstances of those who have been ill, but have perfectly recovered, all living under similar circumstances, as for example, all in the same ward of a hospital, and taking the same diet, &c. I must conclude that the mean temperature of different individuals is not absolutely identical, and indeed may vary from 36·5° C. (97·7° F.) to 37·25° C. (99·05° F.) I have not been able to associate this somewhat considerable difference of average temperature in various individuals with any other special peculiarity of constitution, or habit of body. But it is of some practical importance to remember, that we may not make the mistake of ascribing what may be only an idiosyncrasy, to a continuous, or latent pathological condition. In experiments on animals, still greater differences of temperatures have been noticed, between individual animals of the same kind, than occur in the human subject.

§ 13. *The Daily Fluctuations of Temperature in the Healthy.*— The *temperature varies* a little even in healthy persons, *according to the time of day.* Many observers have directed their attention to the fluctuations of temperature, occurring in the healthy, during the course of a day. According to *Lichtenfels* and *Fröhlich* (loc. cit.) these amount, on an average, to scarcely half a degree Centigrade (= ·9° Fahr.) They state that the *lowest* temperatures occur in the night between 10 p.m. and 1 a.m., and in the morning hours, between 6 and 8 a.m. ; the highest temperature occurs between 4 and 5 o'clock in the afternoon.

According to *Damrosch* ('Deutsche Klinik,' 1853, p. 317) the temperature rises in the morning from 7 to 10 o'clock, about $\frac{1}{4}$° C. (·9° F.); falls till 1 p.m. about $\frac{1}{10}$° to $\frac{2}{10}$° C. (·2°—·4° F. nearly). From thence till 5 p.m. it rises from $\frac{2}{10}$° to $\frac{3}{10}$° C. (= ·4° to ·6° F. nearly), and then falls again till 7 p.m. by about $\frac{3}{10}$° to $\frac{5}{10}$° C. (= ·6°—·9° F.) Occasionally the afternoon fall is absent. The morning elevation of temperature (7 to 10 a.m.) and the evening fall (from 5 to 7 p.m.) are the most constant. The temperature at 7 in the evening is sometimes the same, sometimes lower than that of the same hour in the morning.

According to *Ogle* ('St. George's Hospital Reports,' 1866, i, 221) the temperature is lowest about 6 a.m., and then a rise begins, which continues till late in the afternoon. This rise and fall is independent of sleep.

Jürgensen (in the 'D. Archiv für Klin. Med.,' 1867, iii, 165) says that the daily *maximum* occurred between 4 and 9 p.m.; the daily minimum between 2 and 8 a.m.[1]

[1] As Dr. Ogle's observations were continued for many months, and appear to have been exceedingly carefully made, the chief results obtained have been tabulated, as follows:

Time of day.	Male.	Female.	Time of day.	Male.	Female.
9—11 a.m.; before breakfast.	97·73	98·7	12.30 a.m.— 1 a.m.; bed at 1 a.m.	97·9	
11 a.m.— 2 p.m.	98·2	98·56			
3 p.m.—5 p.m.; lunch at 3 p.m.	98·36	98·75	3 a.m.—5 a.m.	97·5	
6.30 p.m.—7.30 p.m.; dinner at 7 p.m.	98·63	98·6	5.30 a.m.—6.30 a.m.	97·2	
9 p.m.— 10 p.m.	98·0	98·45			
12 p.m.—12.30 p.m.	97·96	98·0	8 a.m.—9 a.m.	97·66	

No observations taken during the night

The temperatures were taken *under the tongue*. The *day* observations in summer. The *night* in winter. The numbers given in the table are the *means* of the *monthly* results.

Dr. Ogle finds the average variation to be 1½° Fahr. (= $\frac{5}{6}$° Centigrade.) He found the minimum = 97° F. (36·1° C.) at 5.30 a.m. on a winter's morning, and the *maximum* 100·6° F. (= 38·25° C.) in a Turkish bath, a variation of 3½° F. (= 1·94° C.) He found the morning rise *not* to be due to the temperature of

§ 14.—*Influence of menstruation, of pregnancy, and of the puer-peral state* (Wochenbett) *upon temperature.* Normal *menstruation* in healthy women, according to the observations of all trustworthy observers (which agree with what I myself have found to be true), is as a rule, without any influence at all upon the general temperature o the body. On the other hand, we sometimes find elevations o temperature during the flow of the catamenia, which cannot be con sidered as anything but decidedly febrile, and which are sometime accompanied with other functional disturbances, and sometimes not without any special pathological process being either indicated o: induced (sich anschlösse).[1]

Pregnancy has next to no influence (so gut wie keinen) on the bodily temperature. Only during the last two months the vagina temperature appears to be slightly elevated: the *morning* mean being 38·15° C. (100·5° F.), the minimum 37·9° C. (100·2° F.), and the maximum 38·35° C. (100·9° F.); whilst the *evening* mean i: 38·22° C. (100·8° F.), the minimum 38·1° C (100·5° F.), the maxi-mum 38·65° C. (101·5° F.).

Schröder ('Virchow's Archiv,' xxv, 253) estimates that the tem-perature of the gravid uterus is about ·3° C. (½° Fahr. nearly higher than that of the axilla, and on an average about ·15° C. (¼ Fahr. nearly) warmer than the vagina, which is doubtless independen of the warmth of the fœtus.

Immediately before the beginning of the *labour pains*, no eleva-

the room, but coincident with increased CO_2 exhaled, and urea excreted (see Dr. E. Smith's Paper, in 'Proceedings of Royal Society,' 30th May, 1861). I was *not* due to light.

General conclusions.—*Minimum* at 6 a.m. *Maximum* late in afternoon. A *rise* produced by both food and exercise. *Tea* retards the fall. *Alcohol* causes a fall, but probably the reaction reaches a higher temperature than if no alcohol were taken.—[TRANS.]

[1] In young women, otherwise healthy, who suffer from dysmenorrhœa, or sometimes in the *first* menstruation, I have often found swelling, redness and pain in the fauces and *tonsils*, with temperatures of 103°, 104°, and 105° F. (= 39·5, 40°, and 40·6°), with extreme depression, restlessness, perhaps semi-delirium, and occasionally vomiting, without being able to trace any scarlatinal or other febrile poison. These cases differ from scarlatina in their *sudden* onset, their equally sudden *recovery* (being well as soon as the catamenial flow ceases, or is *fully* established), and their having no desquamation of the cuticle, or other sequelæ. The sympathy between the *tonsils* and the *generative organs* has been known from great antiquity, but I do not know that this pseudo-amygdalitis has ever been described before.—[TRANS.]

tion of temperature is noticed. During the pains there occurs a rise of some tenths (Centigrade) ·2 to ·25 ($\frac{1}{3}$ to $\frac{9}{20}$ Fahr. nearly), in such a way that *in* the pains, and immediately after, the temperature *rises* somewhat; and in the pauses *between* the pains it *falls* again. However, the daily healthy fluctuation is not much affected by labour. The temperature during *labour* exhibits a mean rise of ·18° C. ($\frac{4}{7}$° F.) in the morning hours, and ·25 C. ($\frac{9}{20}$° F.) in the evening hours, as compared with the preceding period, and in the second stage of labour about ·07° ($\frac{1}{16}$ F.) above the temperature of the first stage. According to *Hecker*, the elevation of the temperature is proportionate to the intensity of the pains, and the quickness with which they succeed one another. However, his materials afford too scanty data to settle this point.

Schröder found that during labour the excess of the uterine temperature over the axillary and vaginal was somewhat greater than in pregnancy : ·83° C. (= 1·49° F.) more than in the axilla, and ·175° C. (·32° F.) more than in the vagina. In a later work he considers the temperature of women in labour to be very changeable, and expresses a strong opinion that this chiefly depends upon the amount of heat lost in various ways being more or less. Immediately *after delivery* a fall of temperature has been observed by *Bärensprung*, even as low as 36·2 C. (= 97·16° F.), and on an average about 37·1° C. (98·78° F.) and, indeed, especially when the birth happened between midnight and mid-day; while *Winckel* has only verified this fall in those cases where the birth fell within the time of the daily remission.

Schröder found the lowest temperature in those who had given birth to children at eleven in the morning.

In the first twelve hours after delivery *Winckel* found a moderate rise, in the second period of twelve hours a corresponding fall.

The average minimum of the normal lying-in period is estimated by *Grünewaldt* at 37° (98·6° F.). Amongst 57 lying-in women he found temperatures of 36·6° C. (97·8° F.) three times, of 36·8° C. (98·24° F.) nine times, and of 37° C. (98·6° F.), or more, forty-five times. The maximum temperatures often exceeded 38° C. (100·4° F.) especially in cases of constipation, and when there was distension of the mammary glands, but the above-named observer considers that all temperatures above 30·2 R. (= 100° Fahr. or 37·8 Cent.) in lying-in women are very suspicious. Schröder points out that lying-in women, even when they have subsequent puerperal mischief, may exhibit a perfectly normal temperature in the first period (*i.e.*, a few hours after the birth).

He further remarks that the course taken by the temperature after delivery is composed of two factors; on the one hand, of the regular daily fluctuation (a rise towards 5 p.m., a fall from then till 1 a.m.), on the other hand of the rise induced by the process of labour in the first twelve hours, and the fall in the second period of twelve hours. On this account the course or curve of the temperature will vary with the hour at which birth occurs, so that if the birth happens in the forenoon, the temperature will reach its highest point from 5 to 8 p.m.; the lowest about midnight, when the birth has fallen within the early morning hours, because, in the first instance, the daily rise and the first puerperal elevation, in the latter case the daily fall and the first puerperal diminution coincide. *Winckel* further propounds that at the end of the first four hours, after the beginning of the fall of temperature, the temperature begins to rise slowly again, and the evening temperature is on this account commonly higher than the morning, but the daily *excursus* (or amount of variation) less, so that as a rule the rise of temperature keeps pace with the secretion of milk, and on this account is most evident on the third, fourth, or fifth day, and that as soon as the draught or flow of milk is established : or, if the mother does not suckle, with the drying up of the milk a gradual decrease of temperature is noticeable; further, that nursing women, and those who do not suckle, primiparæ and multiparæ do not differ from one another as regards their temperature, and that normal after-pains are without any influence at all! Lastly, that the mean temperature of puerperal women is a trifle higher than the average normal temperature of other healthy women.

In so far, however, as the puerperal state is admitted to exhibit a great mobility of temperature, it must be considered as belonging to pathology. However, according to *Winckel*, the differences between the axillary and vaginal temperatures in lying-in-women are wholly without parallel, even in cases of disease of the uterus or vagina. *Schröder* found that in puerperal women the difference between the temperature of the uterus, as compared with the axillary and vaginal temperatures, amounted to only ·28° C. (·5° F.) above the axillary, and ·11° C. (·19° C.) more than the vaginal.

See also besides Bärensprung the following authors on the temperature in pregnancy, labour, and the puerperal state—*Hecker*,

'Annalen des Charité-Krankenhauses,' 1854, p. 333; *Winckel*, "Temperatur Studien bei der Geburt und im Wochenbett" (in the 'Monatsschrift für Geburtskunde,' 1862, Bd. 20, p. 409, and 1863, Bd. 22, p. 321); Grünewaldt, "Über die Eigenwärme Gesunder und Kranker Wöchnerinnen," in the 'Petersburg Med. Zeitung,' 1863, Bd. 5. p. 1; "Oscar *Wolf*, "Beiträge zur Kenntnisz der Eigenwärme im Wochenbett," Marburg Thesis, 1866; *Baum-felder*, "Beitrag zu den Beobachtungen der Körperwärme, der Puls und Respirations. frequenz im Wochenbette," Leipzig Thesis, 1867; *Schröder* (loc. cit., and especially in 'Schwangerschaft, Geburt, und Wochenbett,' 1867, p. 117; *Squire*, in the 'Lancet,' 1867, No. 10, and in the 'Obstetrical Transactions,' vol. ix, p. 129.[1]

§ 15.—*The Influence of Rest, of Muscular Activity, and of Work* (Arbeit) *upon the Temperature.*

The contrast between movement and rest, as regards their respective influence upon temperature, is by no means a simple fact, nor can it be elucidated by a bare recital of facts.

It has been shown by *Helmholtz* that the contraction of a muscle is accompanied by a rise of temperature, and in later times especially, *Solger, Heidenhain, Meirstein*, and *Thiry* have investigated it, and found, amongst other results, that in the first moment of stimulation the muscle itself actually becomes a little colder (negative warmth-variation, afterwards contradicted by *Heidenhain*), and then begins to grow warmer, but that the degree of warmth generated is never entirely proportionate to the mechanical work done; and,

---

[1] Dr. Squire's temperatures were taken in the vagina. After the sixth month of pregnancy he finds the temperature to be a little over 99° F. (= 37·3° C.).

He considers the vaginal temperature and the axillary to differ by only $\frac{1}{3}$° or $\frac{1}{5}$° except during labour. He found the temperature to gradually rise till the birth of the child, and soon after to slowly decline during the 24 hours after, to normal, or even below it. The most constant disturbance ushers in, and accompanies the formation of milk—it attains a certain prominence 48 hours after delivery. As soon as milk flows freely there is a considerable fall.

He objects to the *axilla* as not furnishing trustworthy details after labour.

It is probable that he omitted to *close* the axilla *previously*, as recommended by Wunderlich. The whole paper, however, is well worthy of study.— [TRANS.]

further, that the muscle when stimulated develops more heat, if its
contraction be hindered (or resisted) than when this is not done,
and that with equal weights, the heat developed by continuous contractions decreases as the muscle gets "tired out," and this more
quickly than the mechanical results would lead us to suppose, and
that by increasing the weight the heat increases up to a certain
point, and then decreases again.

According to the theory of *J. R. Mayer*, we must admit that
during rest the chemical affinities (spannkräfte) or combining
forces, which are set free through the combination of oxidisable
substances with oxygen, are perfectly changed into heat, whilst
during work of any kind, some part of these summed-up forces
are translated into mechanical results by means of them. Therefore, during rest, the heat produced should be greater, to which
must be added that the loss of heat by respiration, and transpiration, is also less during rest. Indeed, *Mayer* quotes from *Douville*,
the fact that the latter found a temperature of 40·2° C. (104·36° F.)
in a negro, who lay lazily basking in the sun, whilst the temperature
of the same man, when hard at work in the sun, was only 39·75° C.
(102·88° F.). Whilst, however, during active bodily work, a part of
the force set free by chemical processes, is so far lost, as regards
the production of heat, by being changed into mechanical results,
and producing motion ; so, on the other hand, there is a simultaneous
diminution of the amount of tissue-changes, the amount of oxygen
is increased by the quickening of respiration, and by the more rapid
circulation of the blood, the number of blood-discs brought within
the range of the oxygen in a given time is increased, as well as
the chemical action, on which the warmth-production depends, more
complete and more rapid, and indeed the increased production is
not entirely compensated by the conversion of a part of the total
force into mechanical results ; but the force generated or liberated
by the action of the muscles, through the coincident increased
chemical action is doubtless in general greater than that consumed
by conversion into work done (Arbeit). In addition to the
mechanical results there is therefore an overplus of warmth. *Hirn*,
whilst at rest, produced 155 calorien (or heat-units) per hour, and
251 whilst working in the treadmill. But a long series of contrivances carries off the overplus of heat in a healthy man. This
is effected by more rapid breathing, quicker circulation of the blood
through the skin, and therefore quicker cooling there, and by sweat-

ing, &c. And so it comes to pass that the opposing conditions of the loss of force (kraft-summe) by mechanical work, and by quicker cooling, and, on the other hand, the overplus through augmented chemical action, is compensated in health, so that *the final difference of temperature during rest and during labour is extremely trifling.*

John Davy made numerous direct experiments on the effects of bodily movements upon the temperature. He found, after active exertion, under widely differing circumstances, that the temperature under the tongue was between 98·7° F. and 99·4° F. (37° and 37·5° C.); whilst in travelling in a conveyance (in wagen) the temperature remained between 97° and 97·7° F. (=36° and 36·5° C.). In tropical climates, after active exercise, the temperature sometimes rose still higher, whilst in travelling in a waggon the minimum reached was almost the same, and, on the other hand, reached a maximum on one occasion of 99·7° F. (37·6° C.).

Breschet and *Becquerel* (*loc. cit.*) found by means of the thermo-electric apparatus, that the elevation of temperature in the working muscle, after 5 minutes' work, was about 1° C. (1·8° F.) In *Speck's* experiments (1863 'Archiv des Vereins für Wissenschaftl. Heilkunde') it appeared that during strenuous continued muscular action the temperature of the body rose somewhat. From the considerable increase of the elimination of carbonic acid, one might expect to see the body produce considerably more heat.

The sudden fall of temperature with cessation from exertion proves, also, how instantaneously the equalisation of the general temperature occurs ("dasz die Momente zur Ausgleichung der Körpertemperatur rasch und intensiv wirkten.") A moment ago, the body was, so to speak, taken by surprise, but how soon the cooling processes have brought back its normal temperature, or even reduced it below the normal. In a few other experiments, in which there was no perspiration during the exercise, there was but little elevation of temperature, and the maximum degree of heat occurred in those trials in which there was most sweating.

According to *Kernig* ("Experim. Beiträge," p. 41), the temperature in the axilla, when quietly lying down, was less by a few tenths of a degree (Centigrade) than it had been before, or was after in the erect or sitting posture.

Obernier has lately ('Der Hitzschlag.,' p. 80, published in 1867) made experiments on the influence of bodily exercise upon temperature. Marching for 30 to 35 minutes raised the temperature about half a degree C. (= ·9° F.) or less, whilst the pulse, one case excepted, when there was no effect produced, was much more strikingly affected—rising from 20 to 44 beats. A "quick march" of 1½ hour raised the temperature 1° to 1·2° C. (1·8° to 2·16° F.), (the pulse 30 to 48 beats). An observation made at the same time in a pedestrian, in which after a very fast walk of 1 hour, a temperature of 39·6° C. (= 103·28° F.), was observed ought not properly to be placed with the effects of muscular exertion on the temperature of the healthy, since this performer exhibited other evident signs of imperfect health. According to Mayer's theory, when muscular contraction brings about a mechanical result, it rather diminishes the production of heat by tissue changes (erhält eine Abzugs-quelle). *Beclard* has confirmed this ingenious proposition by actual observations. He found ("de la contraction musculaire dans ses rapports avec la température normale," in 'Arch. Gén.' 1861, xvii, p. 21—40, 157—180, and 257—279) that the amount of heat generated by muscular contraction is greater when the muscle contracts *statically;* that is, independently of mechanical work, than if the contraction produced a mechanical result (travail mécanique utile) ; and further, that the amount of heat which escapes (verschwindet) from a muscle in a mechanical effort, is in direct proportion to the mechanical effect (or work done) ; and he arrives at this further conclusion, that the products of muscular contraction, *i. e.,* the heat, and the mechanical results, are conjointly the expression or equivalent of the chemical action which goes on in the muscle.

Liebermeister denies that voluntary changes in the depth and frequency of the respirations have any influence on the temperature ('Reichert's Archiv.,' 1862, p. 661).[1]

§ 16.—The influence of *mental exertion* on the temperature is even less than that of bodily exercise. According to *Dr. John Davey,* the temperature during mental exertion in northern climates reached a height of only 98° to 98·7° F. (= 36·6° and 37° C.) ; while on the other hand, under similar circumstances in tropical climates, the temperature reached a much greater elevation, as much as 98·1° to 104° F. (= 36·7° to 38° C).

According to *Lombard* ("Experiments on the Relation of Heat to Mental Work" [s], Anal. in 'Archiv. de la Physiologie,' I, 670),

---

[1] That the temperature is *momentarily* affected in this way, is, however, readily shown by a delicate thermometer.—[TRANS.]

during a state of mental repose (Ruhe), the fluctuations of temperature were frequent, although inconsiderable ($\cdot$01° C = $\cdot$18 or $\frac{1}{7}$° F. nearly). Everything which excites the attention causes a slight rise. Very active mental exertion causes the temperature to rise from a quarter to half a degree Centigrade (= $\frac{9}{20}$° — $\frac{9}{10}$° Fahr.)

Sleep, in itself, so far as is known, has no influence on the temperature of healthy people; in other words, production and loss of heat preserve their mutual relations even in sleep.

§ 17. *Thermal influences*, and the effects of *air*, *water*, and *moisture*. The influence of external *cold* and *heat* on the temperature of the healthy body, simple as it may appear, really offers for the most part a complicated problem for our investigation, and we must separate the accompanying influences from one another, before we can rightly estimate the results of experiments. For, generally, it is not simply heat and cold which affect the organism, but they are connected with a medium, the simultaneous working of which must not be overlooked. With regard to hot and cold baths, the influence of the water in cold or warm atmospheres, their dryness, or the degree of their moisture, their movement, and their (barometric) pressure; in cold and warm drinks, the water and the other constituents of the solution must be taken into account, and it is not always easy to accurately determine how much is due to the thermal influences, and how much to collateral circumstances.

But, setting all these aside, there is much to be considered as regards the effects of cold and warm applications only. Their results are, indeed, far from simple; they are manifold and complicated. The phenomena of thermal influences are not only complex, but appear in succession.

The first *physical effect*, the direct and immediate operation of cold, is to abstract heat and to cool, whilst the effect of higher degrees of heat is to hinder cooling, or indeed to impart heat. Accordingly the temperature of the body may be lowered by cold, and raised by heat.

But in close conjunction with the immediate physical effect, is a simultaneously operating physiological one, which produces consequences more or less opposite to the former.

The impression made by cold brings about a constriction of the minute vessels of the skin, through which they become partially

emptied of their blood; in this way the cooling of the blood, which
now circulates less through the superficial parts of the body, is
hindered, and in this way the direct cooling operation of the outward cold on the general temperature of the body is considerably
diminished.   The operation of external warmth, on the other hand,
is followed by dilatation of the blood-vessels (of the skin) by which,
as long as the external heat is less than that of the blood, the
cooling of the blood, and thus of the whole body is promoted. Moreover, by the influence of warmth, the secretions of the skin, and the
evaporation of water is promoted—another powerful method of
cooling.

And indeed any remaining overplus of cooling by the operation
of [external] cold is soon compensated, so long as the organism
retains its normal condition or anything approaching to it, by an
increased production of heat, whilst in reduced or diminished cooling
the production of heat is lessened.

Every diminution or elevation of temperature which momentarily
occurs through thermal applications, is therefore only transient, and
and is speedily neutralized by the altered warmth-production.   It
does not follow that there is an immediate restoration of the *status
quo ante*, more often the increased production of heat, which follows
an artificial cooling, is greater than necessary [for mere compensa-
tion], and therefore the depression of temperature is followed by
increased heat.   And when artificial means have been made use of
to limit the loss of warmth, the production of heat generally becomes
less in amount than is necessary to restore an equilibrium of temperature, and so it may easily happen that a fall succeeds the
elevated temperature induced by the influence of higher degrees of
external heat.   Thus, for example, a high temperature (of the body)
commonly follows a cold bath, and after a warm bath on the other
hand increased coolness is noticed, and in tropical countries, and
very hot seasons, no means of cooling is so lasting as a bath, or a
douche (Uebergiessung) of very warm water. This secondary effect
(lit. back-stroke-working) is indeed partly compensated by the fact
that the cutaneous blood-vessels are dilated by the reaction after
the cold, and thus favour the giving off of the overplus of heat
which exists; but comparatively insignificant circumstances may
assist either the one effect or its opposite, and thus suffice to induce
disturbed action. The effect may be more or less *permanent*, although
very healthy individuals, gifted with the power of resistance, may

not show it, because their temperature still remains normal, whilst under opposite circumstances the effect would be evident in further deviation from normal temperature. Still further differences arise from the fact that the influence of thermal operations differs much according to the place of application (parts to which hot or cold water, ice, or poultices, &c., are applied), but extends from that to subjacent and *neighbouring parts*, and then to the *whole organism*, and the parts remotest from the place of application; and as commonly these operations on the different parts are not exactly similar, the combinations will be very numerous [*i.e.* the factors combining to produce the sum total will be many, and thus the operation of thermal application is complex].

Lastly, we must notice that individual *constitution* (Dispositionen des Individuums) of the subjects of thermal experiments must not be left out of consideration, or indeed in estimating the effects of other external influences. It is true that there is more diversity of constitution apparent amongst sick people, but still the influence of constitution (Diathesis) makes itself evident even in health, and as this occurs in regard to the direct or primary operation of thermal influences (baths, &c.), it does so still more as regards their secondary operation.

If *moist air*, or a *solution* is the vehicle (der Träger) of the thermal influences, the circumstances are still more complicated. Solutions of low temperature, or moist air, in contact with the surface of the body, abstract warmth from it far more than dry, cold air does, and their cooling effects are far more evident than those of the latter—and the secondary (opposite) effects may be still more considerable. Further, very much depends on the *duration* of the [thermal] influence on application on its remaining the same, or changing, and on the cooling medium being in a state of repose, or motion. In this way the results as affecting the temperature of the body may be much modified in various ways.

All these things go to prove that the effects of thermal influences are by no means so simple as they might at first sight appear. This consideration affords a key to the numerous contradictions met with in the results of different observers, and also serves to indicate that one should hesitate, before formulating as laws, the results of even careful observations on man, or on animals, chosen for experiment.

A few of the more important observations on the effects of

heat and cold are adduced here more as examples of what has been done than as exhausting the subject.

As regards the outward application of cold water, for instance, *Fleury* found the temperature in a cold bath sink to 34°, or even 29° Centigrade (= 93·2° or 84·2 Fahr.) *Speck* (in the Archiv für gemeinschaftliche Arbeiten, 1860, p. 422) found at the beginning of the application of a cold shower bath a slight rise of temperature, but after 10 minutes' continuance of the bath (at 22° C. = 71·6° F.) there was a decrease in the temperature of the mouth of about 1·23° C. (= 2·2° F.) *Liebermeister* has made the most painstaking investigations and observations on the influence of baths. He found that as regards the influence of cold water on the surface of the body of a healthy man, the other conditions of whose life were normal, that during a moderate length of exposure to this influence, the temperature in the well-closed axilla never sank at all. This resulted from the increased warmth-production. In a bath of 20°—23° C (= 68°—73° F.) the production of heat was three or four times more than usual; in a bath of 30° C. (86° F.) double the ordinary mean product. In a bath at blood-heat the warmth-production is very slightly more than usual. *Kernig* has made very extended experiments on the production of warmth in baths of 25·7° to 36° C. (78·26° to 96·8° F.) and comes to the conclusion, that the more heat is lost (the colder the bath) the greater is the amount of heat generated [in the body], and *vice versa* (Experimentalle Beiträge zur Kenntniss der Wärmeregulirung beim Menschen, 1864, p. 169). *Schuster*, of Aix-la-chapelle (in the 'Deutsche Klinik,' 1846, No. 22) found in some trials with baths at 37·6 to 41° (= 99·7 to 105·8° F.) made on himself and an assistant, that during the baths the rectum temperature rose considerably. He published further observations in Virchow's 'Archiv,' 1868, xliii, 60.

On the other hand the cooling influence of baths on completely exposed parts of the body (nose, forehead, hands, and feet) is much more considerable, and may amount to 6° or 7° C. (= 10·8 to 12·6° Fahr.), and, indeed, *Tholozan* and *Brown-Séquard* ('Journal de Physiologie,' J., p. 497) found that one hand immersed in water of a low temperature lost in a few (3—17 minutes) from 10—18° of heat (C. = 18°—34° Fahr.), and that it required far longer time to regain the lost heat (for 3 minutes' immersion 38 minutes, for 10 minutes' immersion in ice-cold water more than an hour); and on the other hand that the influence of this lowering of [local] temperature is quite unnoticeable as regards the general temperature, and, indeed, sometimes seemed to raise that; but that the hand which remained free in the air generally became cooler, in proportion as the impression of the cold on the hand immersed became painful. Bärensprung has shown that running water abstracts more heat from the body than water at rest, and that wet clothes, fluttered by the wind, produce the greatest amount of cooling. Hoppe (Virchow's 'Archiv,' xi, 462) observed that moisture diminishes warmth production, by hindering evaporation, and that on the other hand, a loss of heat excites fresh production. He found further, that in a dog who was set in a strong current of air of 60°—70° C. (140°—158° F.) the temperature in the rectum rose after 35 minutes about 1° C. (1·8° F.), after 41 minutes about 2·1° C. (3¾° F.). After retiring into common air, the temperature had fallen in a quarter of an hour to its original height, after a few minutes it was even below normal. The same fall below the normal was shown after a warm bath; and, indeed, the temperature fell more quickly, and to a lower level, in proportion to the height it had previously obtained. Finally, he remarked that persistent considerable losses of heat keep the blood temperature at its maximum, but continued losses of heat of less amount allow it, on the contrary, to fall below normal.

Lehmann, Böcker, and *Kirejeff* have studied the effects of local (Sitz) baths. The latter (see Virchow's 'Archiv,' xxii, 496) found a slight elevation of the general temperature in a warm Sitz-bath; after the bath was over the temperature returned directly to its usual height. In a cold Sitz bath the general temperature fell about 2° (3·6° Fahr.), but when the bath was over, it began to rise, overtopped the normal, and reached, after two or three hours, its highest point, which was 1° C. (1·8° F.) higher than the normal, and ½° C. (=·9° Fahr.) higher than the maximum temperature previously reached by the subjects of experiment on days when they did not bathe.

Hagspiel has shown that ice-bags applied to the body lower the temperature of the abdominal contents, and of the rectum ('Leipzig Dissertation,' 1857). The temperature of the rectum, after an hour's application of ice, fell from 37·25 C. (99·05 Fahr.) to 36·5° C. (97·7° Fahr.), the temperature of the abdominal cavity from 37° C. (98·6° Fahr.) to 35·25 C. (95·45° Fahr.).

According to *Binz* ('Beobachtungen zur innern Klinik,' 1865,

p. 159), ice-bags applied to the belly caused a rapid fall of the mercury in a thermometer introduced beneath the abdominal wall, but no alteration of the temperature in the rectum.

The effect of *drinking cold water* on the temperature has been investigated by Lichtenfels and Fröhlich, who observed a slight diminution of temperature, with a " Seidel" (=12·4 oz. nearly) at 18° C. [=64·4° Fahr.] after six minutes, about $\frac{1}{10}$° C. [=$\frac{1}{5}$° Fahr. nearly]; with the same quantity at 16·3° C. [=61·3° Fahr.], about $\frac{4}{10}$° C. [=$\frac{7}{10}$° Fahr. nearly] in the same time. Some others also have made similar experiments, and particularly *Winternitz* ('Oesterr Zeitschrift für prakt. Heilkunde,' 1865, p. 130). In one experiment, after the enjoyment of 6 "Seidel" (=3¼ pts. nearly) of water at 40·48° Fahr. (4·6° C.) at intervals of ten to fifteen minutes, in the course of seventy minutes the temperature was lowered about 2·5° Fahr. (1·4° C.); but pathological symptoms followed (tendency to vomit, eructations, &c.). In another trial (p. 168) after four "Seidel" (=2¼ pts. nearly) of 6·7° C. (44° Fahr.) had been drunk in divided portions, at intervals of fifteen and twenty minutes, within one and a quarter hours, the temperature sank about 1·44° Fahr. (·8 C.), eructations being again produced.

In the summer the temperature of the human body is a trifle (about $\frac{1}{10}$ to $\frac{2}{10}$° C.=$\frac{1}{5}$ to $\frac{1}{3}$° Fahr. nearly) higher than in winter. In very hot summers this elevation may be still more considerable.

John Davy found in the transit from a hot climate to a temperate one, with a mean difference of 11·11° C. (=20° Fahr.) a decrease of temperature of ·88° C. (=1·58° Fahr.). *Brown-Séquard* ('Journal de Physiologie,' ii, 551) found, in a journey from France to the Isle of France, that eight healthy people, between seventeen and fifty-five years, whose temperature was taken under the tongue, whilst travelling in an atmospheric temperature of 8° C. (46·4° Fahr.), a mean body temperature of 36·625° C. (97·9° Fahr.). Eight days later, with the temperature of the air at 25° C. (77° Fahr.), the body temperature was 37·428° (99·4° Fahr.), and still further nine days later, under the equator, with an atmospheric temperature of 29·5° C. (=85·1° Fahr.) a mean temperature of 37·9° C. (=100·22° Fahr.) was shown, and six weeks later, in 37·4° S. latitude, with the external air at 16° C. (=60·8° Fahr.), the mean temperature had sunk to 37·23° C. (=99·04° Fahr.). *Eydoux* and *Souleyet* observed rather smaller differences ('Comptes rendus de l'Acad. des Sciences,' 1838, vi, 456).

John Davy ("On the Effect of Air of Different Temperatures on Animal Heat," in 'Philosoph. Transact.,' 1845, p. 61) has made some observations on temperature during long continuance (aufenthalt) in over-heated rooms, and believes that a considerable elevation is caused by this circumstance. His data are, however, scarcely sufficiently numerous or accurate to enable us to formulate a general law.

The same observer made observations on temperature in Constantinople at a time when the temperature of the air ranged between 31° and 94° Fahr. (—0·9 C. and 34·5° C.), and observed differences of temperature under the tongue, varying from 97° to 99° Fahr. (=36—37·2 C.). In his treatise ("On the Temperature of Man within the Tropics," 'Philosophical Transactions,' 1850), he arrives at this, amongst other conclusions, that the average temperature in tropical climates is one degree Fahrenheit (=·9 C.) higher than in temperate regions, and that the daily fluctuations are not identical. For further remarks on the effect of external temperature, see also the next chapter on the causes of altered temperature in disease.[1]

§ 18. Variations in *Atmospheric Pressure* appear to have no important effect upon human temperature; which does not vary with the changes of the barometer. Yet *Vivenot* (Jahrbuch der Gesellschaft der Aerzte zu Wien, xi, 113—146) found by experiments in a chamber where the air was compressed, that the temperature rises about ·4° C. (= $\frac{3}{4}$° Fahr. nearly) during the rising of the atmospheric pressure, whilst during the maximum of pressure in the chamber it falls again, and may finally fall to a lower degree than at the commencement of the experiment.

§ 19. The kind and amount of *Nutritious Material* introduced into the body, although indeed this is the chief means of warmth production, have very slight effect upon the temperature, so long as the body remains healthy. Beyond a doubt the very different kinds, bulk, and amount of ingesta [taken by different persons] must

___

[1] Dr. Ogle (in St. George's 'Hospital Reports,' vol. i), points out that the value of Dr. John Davy's numerous and laboriously collected observations, scattered through the 'Philosophical Transactions' from 1845—50, is seriously impaired by numerous and serious arithmetical errors—partly typographical, and partly perhaps errors of calculation. For instance, the means and averages given do not correspond with the data assigned as their sources. As,

very greatly affect and, indeed, determine the amount of heat *produced*, but manifestly this is compensated by a corresponding difference in the amount of heat got rid of, and the balance of production and loss is either not at all or but slightly disturbed.   In healthy people taking a *meal* has only a moderate effect on the temperature. According to Bärensprung, after dinner, between 2 and 6 p.m., the temperature rises, on an average about $\frac{6}{10}°$ C. ($=$ 1° Fahr. nearly). But even when no dinner is taken, there is a rise about this time. *Supper* (or an evening meal taken at 8 p.m.) is more likely to hinder the customary fall of temperature at this time in the evening.

Ogle remarked that the normal *rise* (in the daily fluctuation) was most evident after a good breakfast, less after lunch, and that the evening dinner (or principal meal of the day) only caused a delay in the fall which otherwise took place at this time of day.

The daily fluctuations are only slightly affected when the customary

---

however, those published in 1863 (founded on the others) are often quoted, I subjoin them.

Observations on himself in England August 1844, *to April,* 1845.

Time of day.	Temperature under tongue.	Pulse.	Respiration.	Temperature of Room.	Remarks.
7—8 a.m.	98·74°	57·6	15·6	50·9°	
3—4 p.m.	98·52°	55·2	15·4	54·7°	} Dinner at 5 p.m.
12 at night.	97·92°	54·7	15·2	62·°	

Observations in Barbadoes, July, 1845, *to November,* 1848.

Time of day.	Temperature under tongue.	Pulse.	Respiration.	Temperature of Room.	Remarks.
6—7 a.m.	98·07°	54·4	14·4	76·7°	Breakfast, 9 a.m.
12—2 p.m.	98·09	56·	15·4	83·6°	Dinner with wine at 5 p.m.
9—11 p.m.	99·° [·98·775]	60·3	15·	79·°	Tea, 7 p.m.

Evening temperature lower than morning in England by 0·82° F.
,,   ,,   higher   ,,   in Barbadoes by 0·93° (? 0·705°).

meals are postponed. If a meal produces a different effect it may be taken for granted that the individual in question is either not quite healthy or under entirely normal conditions; or that the meal itself has a detrimental effect upon health.

Jürgensen found, that a hearty meal taken after prolonged fasting is likely to cause a considerable elevation of temperature (rather more than $\frac{1}{2}$° C. $= 1$° Fahr. nearly) 'Deutsches Archiv für klin. Med.,' iii, 177. *Deprivation of food* has no considerable effect on the temperature, until the general health begins to suffer. According to Lichtenfels and Fröhlich, from the 10th to the 15th day of fasting the temperature fell pretty continuously with strong subjective feelings of chilliness, about $\frac{5}{10}$°—$\frac{8}{10}$° C. ($= \cdot 9$° to $1 \cdot 44$° F.), and then rose again spontaneously, with cessation of the chilly feelings till about the 20th day of fasting, about $\frac{5}{10}$° C. ($= \frac{9}{10}$° F.). The further effects of inanition through deprivation of food, first elucidated by *Chossat* fall appropriately into the pathological department.

§ 20. Effects of *ardent spirits* and other *luxuries* (Genussmittel) on the temperature.—In experimental trials with various kinds of these we must not forget the simultaneous action of the higher or lower temperature of the medium or vehicle.

According to Lichtenfels and Fröhlich, the use (genuss) of beer, containing from 3 to 4 per cent. of alcohol in quantities of a half " maas " to a " maas " [a " maas " is the German equivalent for our English " pot," and its size varies with the part of Germany where it is found—it averages a little over a quart—but may sometimes be found to contain about half a gallon English. The measure in the text probably means about 50 oz. ($2\frac{1}{2}$ pints)] lowered the temperature about $\frac{1}{2}$ a degree Centigrade ($= \cdot 9$° Fahr.) in not more than a quarter of an hour's time, and it remained thus low for $1\frac{1}{2}$ hour. In the same way wine and brandy have a lowering effect upon the temperature. Very numerous observers, the latest of whom is *Cuny Bouvier* (Pflüger's 'Archiv,' 1869, p. 370), have confirmed this fact and confuted the contrary opinion.[1]

[1] To the best of my belief, Demarquay and Duméril were the first to clearly point out the lowering effects of alcohol on the temperature, although Orfila, Ogston, Percy, and others, had noticed in general terms the coldness produced by poisonous doses. The translator had also (' Med. Mirror,' Feb. 1866) formulated the results of numerous experiments in the words, " The secondary

Bouvier has found that small doses of alcohol invariably lower the temperature of the body (whilst increasing the frequency of the pulse), but the effect does not last long; larger doses lower the temperature almost immediately several degrees (the pulse at the same time becoming fuller and more frequent). See also his latest work, 'Über die Wirkung des Alkohols auf die Temperatur,' 1869, and also *Godfrin*, 'De l'alcool, son action physiologique, ses applications thérapeutiques,' 1869. The cause of this effect of alcohol is not certainly known. It appears partly to depend on a retardation of the tissue changes, partly on an increased loss of warmth from the superficies of the body; but here the physiological and pathological (toxic) effects can scarcely be separated. Refer, therefore, to the next chapter.

Warm alcoholic drinks, on the other hand, may raise the temperature; punch about $50°$ C. ($= 122°$ F.) raises the temperature about ·1 to ·3 of a degree C. ($= \frac{1}{5}$ to $\frac{1}{2}°$ F.) for $\frac{1}{2}$ to 1 hour.

Carbonic acid (sherbet powders, &c.) causes a lowering of temperature equal to about $\frac{1}{10}$ or one or two more tenths of a degree ($\frac{1}{5}°$ to $\frac{1}{4}°$ F.) which is compensated in about half an hour. Strong *coffee* causes an elevation of temperature, which in about an hour reaches its maximum (2—4 tenths of a degree C. $= \frac{1}{3}° - \frac{1}{4}°$ Fahr.) *Tea* (drunk at blood-heat) acts in the same way, but less powerfully, and for a shorter time [compare Sydney Ringer, Anstie, &c.].

§ 21. The effects of *losses of blood* on the temperature of the healthy are not very considerable. But after a moderate venesection, the temperature rises a few tenths, and gradually returns to the normal after a day or two, and may even at a later period, sink below the normal (Bärensprung). After very copious bleedings (in animals) the temperature sometimes sank a great deal (*Marshall Hall*). According to *Frese* (Virchow's 'Archiv,' xl, p. 303) immediately after a moderate bloodletting, a fall of temperature of about $1°$ C. ($1·8°$ F.) ensued; but a few hours after the temperature

effect of alcohol appears to be invariably a great fall in temperature." Tscheschichin (Reichert's 'Archiv,' 1866, pp. 151—179) published a confirmation as regards animals poisoned with alcohol. In this country Drs. Anstie, B. Ward Richardson, Walter Rickards, Sydney Ringer, and others have further confirmed the statements in the text. Dr. Ogle also (*loc. cit.*) says, that alcohol at first lowers the temperature, and then raises it (perhaps higher than before).

began to rise and generally exceeded the temperature before the bleeding.

Unfortunately it is not easy to determine these facts by experiments on healthy men; indeed, it is now impossible [except in Italy?—Trans.]

§ 22. As stated in the introduction, all fluctuations in the height of the temperature in health, are very trifling (fast durchans minimal). Whether they arise spontaneously, or are induced by internal influences, these deviations from the mean (average) temperature are only transient. As soon as ever the temperature takes an upward or downward direction, a tendency to return to the opposite direction soon manifests itself. Whenever the production of warmth is increased in a healthy body, not only is the loss of warmth greater but there remains for some time after, a tendency to diminished generation of heat. When the production is very small the losses also are limited; when these are slight production is lessened; when these losses are excessive they are compensated by an increased warmth production.

Herein is the mystery of the organism, that so long as it is healthy, everything goes on in it with wonderful regularity (Ordnung) and all accidental disturbances are immediately and spontaneously compensated.

CHAPTER VI.

THE CAUSES OF ALTERED TEMPERATURE IN DISEASE.

§ 1. Thermometric observations show us *how narrow are the limits between health and disease, and how imperceptibly one passes into the other* (wie sie untrennbar in einander übergehen).

From temperatures which fall within the limits of health, to those which are decidedly morbid, the transition from the very first step is entirely undistinguishable; neither in theory nor in any given case can we discriminate a point where health ends and sickness begins. A sort of neutral territory, of no great width, intervenes impartially between the normal track, and that over the morbid nature of which no doubt can be entertained.

Just so it is with the causes which determine alterations of temperature. There are some influences which are nearly certain to produce morbid changes of temperature in those exposed to them.

But in a great number of other cases the effect produced depends very much on the constitution (disposition) of the subject exposed to the influence, and very often upon quite accidental circumstances. These influences, which in one healthy man either produce no effect upon temperature, or such effects only as fall within the range of health, may, in another healthy person, with less powers of resistance, or in a sickly person, whose temperature was not previously affected, cause more or less considerable, and more or less decidedly morbid alterations of temperature.

Various circumstances which influence temperature must be considered not only as converting normal temperatures into abnormal and diseased ones, but also as modifying temperatures which were previously abnormal. The self-same influences and circumstances which affect the normal balance of temperature, and thus prove causes of pathological temperature-changes, are able when the balance has once been disturbed, to induce further deviations from the standard. The causes of these cannot be severed one from the other, they may indeed be identical. But their effects on him whom they make ill, in the first instance, and on him who is previously ill, and constantly has an abnormal temperature, are by no means always alike; and the effect produced upon the sick is throughout to be distinguished, not only as regards the kind of influence brought to bear on him, but also from the effect produced by it on the healthy. As regards every kind of influence, the effect depends much, and indeed chiefly, upon the previous condition of the patient, and upon the "epidemic constitution" of the prevailing type of disease, upon the regularity or irregularity and intensity of the sickness, upon the degree of its development—in one word, upon the sum-total or aggregate of all the circumstances of the patient. And if, indeed, the effect of an influence affecting temperature and causing disease in a previously healthy person, in no ways depends upon the nature and degree of this influence alone, but very much upon the individuality, surroundings, and other conditions of the subject, and may be determined in part by accidental circumstances; so, also, in estimating the results of any influences affecting temperature in patients already abnormally warm, must the whole closely interwoven "complexity" of morbid conditions be taken into consideration.

On this account one and the same influence may possibly induce very different and even opposite effects.

§ 2. The common basis of the operations [or community of working] of those influences which affect temperature, does not depend on their increasing or diminishing either the production or the loss of heat, but rather on the fact that the *regulating power is less perfect* (die Regulation unvollkommener ist) than in health.

Even in health there may be a greater or less production of heat, but the giving off of heat regulates itself (so to speak) according to the plus or minus of production. The loss of heat may also be more or less than usual, even in health, but the warmth generated is proportionate to the amount lost. Therefore in health the sum total (Facit), or the height of the temperature, remains at a determinate point, just in the same way as the body-weight, the average daily quantity of urine secreted, the number of respirations, the composition of the blood, and the whole organism in its various parts, and as regards its most important groups of functions, remains substantially the same.

When we perceive in a patient whose general temperature conforms to the standard, a deviation from the normal temperature, produced by influences which do not affect the temperature of the healthy, we may conclude that the power of regulating his temperature possessed by him is sufficient for all ordinary purposes, but becomes inefficient under somewhat strange influences. Such great mobility of temperature in patients whose ordinary temperature is normal, may closely approximate to the fluctuations met with in health; but the " excursus " or curve of the temperature (vide § 18, chap. i) will be striking and exceed ordinary bounds, just in proportion as the resistance or controlling power is less or the influences overpowering. Influences which produce a morbid alteration of temperature in a healthy man either produce in him so considerable an uncompensated alteration of heat-production, and its loss, as makes compensation become impossible, or they excite an illness, which has for one of its elements an imperfect regulation of the balance between heat-production and the loss of heat. For every deviation of temperature is a proof that the compensation between production and destruction of heat is imperfect. There is still compensation, but the power of maintaining the normal constancy of temperature is lost. Sometimes heat-production and heat-destruction (or loss) are so evenly balanced that a certain equality is maintained between them—an equality, however, which stands on a different level (niveau) from that of the healthy, and an equality which it is always far more easy to disturb than it is in the case of good health.

§ 3. It is quite conceivable that the defective balance (Equilibrirung) of many functions which compensate each other in health may arise from very different sources (Ausgangspunkte), and from widely differing reasons.

The loss of heat may be so considerable that the most extreme over-production, or at least the greatest rise in production possible to the individual, may not compensate it.

The giving off (or radiation) of heat may be so much hindered in the bulk (in dem maase) that with a limited production of heat, or in a special case with even a diminished amount of it, an accumulation (Stauung) of temperature is certain.

The production of heat may be so much increased that all the contrivances to carry it off, or at least all the available contrivances in the organism in question, may not suffice to compensate the overplus. Or the generation of heat may be so much diminished that although the giving off of heat is limited in every possible way, no satisfactory compensation is attained.

Increased production of heat and diminished loss of it, or increased giving off of warmth and diminished warmth-production, may also be combined together, in different degrees, and their disturbing influences may accumulate. They may, even in different parts of one and the same organism, show themselves in different ways.

The antagonistic compensating processes, instead of going on swiftly and promptly in their relative order (Beziehung), may be hindered, interrupted, and dilatory.

And besides all this it is very evident that in sickness we have not to do with merely a *plus* or a *minus* of the heat-production (or loss) in health, but that there are *fresh sources* (Quellen) of heat-production developed unknown to the healthy body. And, on the other hand, *ways of getting rid of heat* offer themselves, which are wanting in the healthy body.

Amongst such new sources of heat-production, we may reckon the more or less rapid destruction of tissues, which we can only conceive of as chemical processes, the formation of abnormal chemical products of the metamorphosis of tissues (*End*-producte—such as oxalates, cystin, &c. &c.); and finally, it is not at all impossible, that independently of the oxygen in the body, some kind of fermentative process may be excited, which may become a fresh source of heat, as happens indeed external to the organism (so also perhaps in zymotic diseases). To the new methods of abstracting heat we must refer copious losses of the fluids of the body, and the deposit of larger, but less vitalized (belebter) masses, such as exudation and extravasation products in the body, in which warmth is not produced, but only expended, &c.

But even when the equilibrium is disturbed in disease, there is an adjusting power in the body which guards against a mischievous anarchy (Maassloswerden), and is able after a longer or shorter interval to bring about a restoration of the equilibrium—sometimes by a return of the excessive heat-production (or loss) to the normal, or even below the normal, and sometimes by the gradual strengthening of the active compensatory processes, till they become sufficiently strong for the purpose, and sometimes by the opening of new sources for the production of heat, or for its distribution. The [animal] organism is indeed full of the most varied and ingenious (sinnreichsten) contrivances and combinations for this purpose. For example, increased heat quickens the movements of the heart, which propels the warm blood more quickly through the vessels to the surface of the body, through which in a given time, a greater quantity of blood comes into contact with the surrounding coolness, and so becomes more rapidly cooled. Heat also increases the need of breathing [besoin de réspirer], the movements of the respiratory organs are quickened, and the cooling air is introduced in greater quantity. Anæmic people, with diminished blood corpuscles, produce less warmth, but their superficial vessels are contracted, and thus the cooling of their blood is less rapid. Other examples might easily be adduced.

Even in disease there is a certain amount of regulation, *but with more extended limits of fluctuation*, and in this way, when the original causes of the disturbance of equilibrium, or in other words, the sources of the disease, are exhausted, and no new ones have arisen in the course of the malady, the return to a state of equilibrium is provided for, and actually introduced.

When these natural aids (Selbsthülfen) are wanting, and artificial means prove powerless, and therefore the disturbance of the equilibrium between the production and the giving off of heat, proves overwhelming in power, then no restoration occurs, and the excessive disproportion, and extreme deviation towards one extreme or the other, as regards temperature, must terminate in death.

These propositions, which in the abstract are almost indubitable, can however very seldom be demonstrated in individual cases.

As it has already been shown that it is not practicable to determine accurately the sum total of the warmth produced, or eliminated (weggeschafften) in a healthy man in a given space of time, so it is still less possible to indicate even approximatively the sources, or amount of the heat production, or the quantity of heat lost, or to determine the several shares of the different parts in which the generation or dissipation of heat occurs, in any special form of disease, or any given case of sickness, or in any determinate part of the course of the disease. The combinations are so numerous, and so subject to almost momentary [instantaneous] change, and are generally, at any given time, built up, as it were, of such contrary-working forces

(Momenten), they partly concern such inaccessible regions of the body, and both the greater and the lesser modifications in the products [Leistungen] of the various organs are so manifold, and complicated, that even the loosest and most superficial calculations become either impossibilities or fiction.

We are therefore only in a position to determine the result or sum-total, the alteration in the height of the general temperature; the factors composing this result elude direct observation, and at the best can only be estimated approximately by conjectural methods.

Since then we are unable, and doubtless never shall be in a position to trace back the alterations of temperature to their true conditions, as a matter of accurate calculation; it is all the more necessary to endeavour, as far as possible, to determine accurately in an empirical manner the connection between the course of the temperature in disease, and determinate influences, conditions, circumstances, and processes.

§ 4. The primitive causes (Ursachen) which may lead to morbid changes of temperature, or modify those already existing, may be—

(a.) External influences.

(b.) The circumstances (surroundings) and constitution of the individual.

(c.) The processes going on in the organism itself.[1]

In any given case, these primitive causes may be very variously combined, and it would seem impossible, on account of their intricacy (Unentwirrbarkeit) to disintangle, from the combination of such varied influences and circumstances, the exact share of any one force, or to reduce these operations to elemental forms, or make them evident as matters of simple necessity (in ihrer einfachen Nothwendigkeit auschaulich zu machen).   And since the final decision as to the operation of primitive causes of temperature-disturbance, falls to the share of clinical observation, the latter is still further justified by the fact, that ever since the earliest period of observation of thermal phenomena in the organism, *experiments*, or the artifical production of simple morbid phenomena, have been made subservient to discovery.

The results of *experiments* on the influence of various circum-

---

[1] " Äussere Einflüsse,
      Die Verhältnisse und Anlagen des Individuums,
      Die Vorgänge in dem Organismus selbst."

stances on the temperature of animals or healthy men, in themselves of the highest and most undoubted interest, must however be estimated with the greatest caution and circumspection (*Vorsicht*, und *Besonnenheit*) when applied for the purpose of drawing conclusions as to the behaviour of the human organism under external injuries, or in diseases. Many of the results of experiments correspond exactly, or at least exhibit a close analogy with influences which make a healthy man ill when he is exposed to them, or are able to modify his temperature when already morbid.

But we must not forget to use caution when applying to man the results obtained in experiments on healthy animals—for human beings exhibit slighter normal fluctuations of temperature than most other mammals. Amongst these, for example, rabbits may give very deceptive results, because they show very extreme variations in temperature—and such are induced even by merely trying them securely [for experiment].

The same caution must be employed as regards experiments made on healthy men. It is indeed highly useful and important to study the operations of therapeutical agents on the healthy, but we must be cautious how we transfer results so obtained to the organism in sickness—for there the results may possibly be quite different, and are especially likely to vary with the pathological conditions. In many diseases conditions exist which cannot be induced experimentally. But experimental results serve capitally to direct attention to special operations—to afford us analyses as it were, of complex phenomena, and to prove selected theories from pathological facts—but if we except traumatic and toxic influences, for which they are apparently able to furnish us safely with pure analogies, the remainder must always be controlled by clinical observations.[1]

[1] Even in toxicology, the comparative immunity of certain animals to the poisonous effects of alkaloids must not be forgotten. See a paper by Dr. W. Ogle "On the Comparative Harmlessness of Atropine to Rabbits," *àpropos* of the case of Regina v. Sprague ('Med. Times and Gazette,' i, 1867, p. 466), where he shows that a middle-aged rabbit can live for six days at least on Belladonna leaves only, without inconvenience (See also 'Pharmaceutical Journal,' 2nd series, vii, 127, and the newspapers for 1866).

Pigeons also, and perhaps most birds, possess a *capacity* of resisting the effect of morphia, first pointed out by Dr. Weir Mitchell (U. S.) and confirmed by Dr. B. W. Richardson. It is also well known that some dogs will take

The amount of clinical material, setting forth general facts regarding the operation of certain influences, which induce morbid alterations of temperature, and regarding accidental circumstances incidental in the course of the disease, but not an essential part of it, yet influencing the track of the temperature, is indeed extraordinarily great; yet it is for the most part fragmentary, and therefore often unreliable. It requires great attention, and much thermometric experience, to evolve the simple facts from the conflict of combined circumstances. Amongst other things we must remember to separate the effects of accidental circumstances upon the temperature of the sick from the effects of such influences as immediately induce a true amelioration or deterioration in the sickness itself, or in its principal symptoms. It is clearly not the same thing, whether after some incidental operation the whole malady is bettered or made worse, or whether, without any special effect on the disease, only the course of the temperature is affected. In the same way we must seek to determine whether, after a result obtained on the temperature of a previously healthy person, this is the pure result of the experiment, or whether it depends upon the development of a determinate form of disease, of which an abnormal temperature is an essential element.

§ 5. The influences which operate as *depressors of temperature* do so either (*a*) by abstracting heat from the body, and especially increasing the amount of heat lost, (*b*) or by hindering or limiting the access of the (normally, sub-normally, or unusually) warm blood to the parts under observation, (*c*) or chiefly by diminishing the production of heat in the body.

It is not always easy to exactly determine of what kind the temperature-depressing influence may be, and no doubt one and the same cause often operates in different ways.

The very same cause may at one and the same time, or successively, operate in opposite ways—that is, it may even raise the temperature. In this way it may happen that the effect is so compensated that the height of the temperature remains apparently unaffected. On the other hand, the compensation must remain imperfect whenever through the influence of the original cause the temperature is depressed.

large doses of Prussic acid. It has recently been shown that some monkeys resist comparatively large doses of strychnia.—[TRANS.]

Experimental and clinical experiences of *elevated temperatures* are far more numerous, both as regards the general temperature and that of special regions.

Any elevation of general temperature above the normal must have as its basis either an over-production or a diminished loss of warmth, or both combined; but in elevated temperatures the respective shares of these conditions are not to be determined any more easily than in diminished temperatures.

Since, moreover, the very same causes which originally raise the temperature operate immediately on those which tend to depress it, and the effects of over-production, or diminished giving off of heat may be compensated in this manner, the [absolute] height of the temperature may be the result of very complicated, and widely differing factors.

In local elevations of temperature, especially when this is determined by observations made on the surface of the body [*i. e.*, with the ordinary thermometers], it is by no means always certain whether the temperature observed is a real elevation of temperature or only a relative addition to the [local] warmth; produced by the part, as compared with the general surface, having received a greater quantity of the warmth-bringing [although in itself of normal heat] blood—or whether the giving-off of heat is diminished in the spot where the temperature is measured.

§ 6. Extreme degrees of *external cold* are the most certain means of abstracting warmth from the body, and may, when their operation is very intense, and long-continued, depress the temperature so greatly that death becomes inevitable. *A. Walther*, of Kiev, has investigated the results of artificial cooling (Virchow's 'Archiv,' 1865, p. 25). The lowest point to which he could depress the temperature in rabbits, before they died was 9° C. (= 48·2° Fahr.) Animals which were cooled down to 18° or 20° C. (= 64·4° or 68° Fahr.), and then brought into a medium not warmer than their own temperature, were found to have lost the power of regaining their normal temperature. But on the other hand they were restored to their normal heat by artificial respiration. Some of the animals which had been thus cooled, and again artificially warmed, displayed for some days a febrile elevation of temperature (42° C. (= 107·6° Fahr.) or more).

As regards the direct effect of cold in producing disease in healthy men, accurate observations are wanting.   Apparently death from cold (congelation) takes place in a similar way to the death of *Walther's* rabbits, although perhaps by much less extreme degrees of cold.   Diseases which result from the influence of cold are always complicated with other circumstances; and the temperature in these must not be regarded as the immediate consequence of the operation of cold.   On the other hand the results of experience of the *effects of cold* on men whose temperature is *febrile* are far more reliable, and are of the highest moment, since cold is available as one of the chief antipyretic and antiphlogistic remedies, and has been applied as such, in modern times, in febrile, especially typhous and exanthematic diseases, and that most extensively.

The effect of cold drinks and cold injections on a morbidly elevated temperature is transient, and indeed rapidly so.   Constantly repeated applications of very cold water (washings), ice-bags, or cold compresses, and cold sitz-baths are far more effective.   Yet their influence extends but little beyond the place where they are applied, and the general temperature is but little or not at all affected.

Unlike these, the effect of the application of water, more or less cold, in the form of packing (Einwicklungen) in wet sheets, of full (complete) baths, and of douches, is far more considerable, intense, and permanent.   The advantages of an energetic and more or less methodical treatment of high degrees of fever with these measures have been abundantly proved since the zealous recommendations of *Brand*, and although without doubt there is another and an adverse side (Kehrseite) to this question, which at present is not fully discovered, yet this much is certain, that the effects are exceptionally potent, and that there is no therapeutic method which is capable of inducing such favorable modifications in the course of a severe fever, with equal power and trustworthiness (see Abdominal Typhus or Enteric Fever).   It may be freely conceded that the conditions, and indeed the very causes (Gründe) of the effect of cold in lowering febrile temperatures, and in shaping the course of the disease, are by no means accurately determined; and as regards the immediate and remote effects of this method, much remains to be done (sind noch Keineswegs die Akten geschlossen—the curtain has not yet fallen). Certainly much depends upon the kind of application, the temperature of the water used, and the duration of the operation; and on the other side upon the morbid conditions themselves, on the intensity and form of the disease, its stage, &c., &c. And the operation is by no means uniformly simple. At the moment of application, or when applied in an inefficient manner, the cold often causes the temperature to rise, and only after continual application, the temperature begins to fall. If repeated too seldom, reaction (lit. back-stroke-working) takes place the more certainly, in proportion to the intensity and newness of the disease, and the definitive (or desired) effect is only to be attained by a very energetic and continued application of the method. The true cause of the effects of the cold treatment has not yet been explained. It is no doubt an error to believe that the benefits derived in cases of fever depend simply upon the mere abstraction of a detrimental [over] plus of heat.

Schröder ('Deutsches klinisches Archiv,' vi, 385) has found that cold baths in typhus diminish the elimination of carbonic acid and urea, and retard all the tissue changes.

Wahl ('Petersburg. med. Zeitung,' 1867, xii) attributes the chief influence of cold baths to their influence on the nerves and the nervous centres; says that they fail whilst the temperature is still rising, and recommends that the cold should be chiefly applied in the remissions, or in extremely high temperatures, because the carrying away of the extremely accumulated heat acts beneficially.

The reaction which takes place after the external application of cold is so powerful, that we may very safely use short but energetic applications in order to raise an abnormally low temperature, or in other words, the temperature of collapse.

§ 7. Temperatures above *blood-heat*, or even approximating closely to this, have, when long continued, a decidedly morbid influence, and cause the temperature of the body to rise.

Claude Bernard ('Gazette Médicale,' xiv, p. 562, 1859) has found that animals exposed to a high external temperature, succumbed to the effects of the heat, whilst their own temperature rose, as soon as the latter exceeded their normal temperature, by 4—5° C. (= 7.2°—9° Fahr.). *Obernier* ('Der Hitzschlag,' 1867) has determined the rise of temperature in animals which were exposed for a lengthened period to the effects of an elevated external temperature. The temperature of animals generally fell at first (about $\frac{4}{10}$° C. = $\frac{3}{4}$° Fahr. nearly) when the surrounding temperature was raised continually for some time. When the surrounding temperature reached from 30°—35° C. (= 86°—95° Fahr.) the animal heat began to rise also, and commonly to a few degrees *above* that of the surrounding atmosphere. When the animal heat reached from 44° to 45° C. (= 111·2°—113° Fahr.) the animals generally died, although the air in which the animal was placed did not exceed about 40°—41° C. (= 104° to 105·8° Fahr.) The temperatures rose, post mortem, a few tenths of a degree in most cases. Animals whose temperature was raised to 41·6° or even 43·8° C. (= 106·88° or 110·84° Fahr.) might still be recovered.

A. Walther exposed rabbits, securely confined, to a direct solar heat of 30°—34° C. (= 86°—93·2° Fahr.). The temperature rose to about 46° C. (= 114·8° Fahr.). After death the temperature continued to rise till it reached 50° C. (= 122° Fahr.). The autopsy showed anæmia of the internal organs, but the lungs were hyperæmic, and the muscles rigid, as if cooked. *Walther* considers that the elevation of temperature in these experiments is only the result of diminished giving off of heat, and he attributes the post-mortem rise of temperature and the rigidity of the muscles to a development of heat (Bulletins of the Petersburg Academy, in the 'Berliner Centralblatt,' 1867, p. 391). A morbid elevation of temperature may often be observed in human beings as a consequence of unusually high atmospheric temperatures. In the hot summer of 1865 many of my fever patients exhibited unusually high temperatures, the cause of which, I have no doubt, was to be traced partly to the impossibility of keeping the sick-ward sufficiently cool, and partly to the insufficiency of the necessary giving off of heat by the patients themselves. From the 5th of July to the 1st August of that year, during which time the average temperature of the air at 2 p.m. was 26·6° C. (= 79·9 Fahr.), and was only six times less than 25° C. (= 77° Fahr.), whilst it exceeded 30° C. (= 86° Fahr.) on six occasions, the maximum being 34° C. (= 93·2), 25 patients in my clinique died. In 23 of them the temperature was taken at the moment of death; and of these six had normal or collapse-temperatures (3 cases of phthisis, 1 of heart-disease, 1 of marasmus, and 1 of small-pox); 3 sub-febrile and moderately febrile temperatures (2 cases of phthisis and 1 of cancer); and 14, which is more than half of the cases, exhibited temperatures of 40° (= 104° Fahr.) or more. The particulars of these cases are as follows:—

A case of pseudo-rheumatic osteomyelitis had a temperature of 40° C. (= 104 Fahr.) at moment of death.

2 cases of peritonitis a temperature of 40·5° C. (= 104·9° Fahr.).

2 cases of typhoid fever = 41·375° C. (= 106·47 Fahr.).

1 case of delirium tremens = 41·75° C. (= 107·15 Fahr.).

1 case of pneumonia and 1 case of a girl, aged 23, who died after a few days' severe fever, without any localised symptoms, and at whose autopsy no anatomical lesions of any kind were discovered, had temperatures of 42° C. (= 107·6° Fahr.).

1 case of typhoid fever, and 1 case of delirium tremens = 42·25° C. (= 108·05° Fahr.).

1 case of cholera (choleraic diarrhœa) (= 42·875° C. (= 109·175 Fahr.).

1 case of insolation (coup de soleil) = 43·25° C. = 109·85 Fahr.).

1 case of puerperal septicæmia and 1 of cerebral softening = 43·75° (= 110·75° Fahr.). Never, either before or since, have I seen so many high temperatures at the moment of death compressed within so short a space of time. Many observers have noticed sudden and remarkable elevations of temperature, in cases in which the complex symptoms of insolation (sunstroke) have been met with. *Schneider* ('Inaugural Dissert. on Sunstroke,' 1867) observed a temperature of over 40° C. (above 104° Fahr.) in a fatal case 2½ hours after admission to the hospital. *Helbig* ('Leipzig Dissertation on three cases of Sunstroke,' 1868) observed the same. *Ferber* ('Archiv der Heilkunde,' ix, 487) observed 40° C. (= 104° Fahr.) in a case which recovered. *Bäumler* ('Medical Times and Gazette,' Aug. 1, 1868) observed a temperature of 42·9° C. (= 109·22° Fahr.) in a fatal case one hour after admission. According to *Levick* ('Heat Fever in Pennsylvania Hospital Report,' 1868, i, 369) a case in a man of fifty-five, who recovered, showed a temperature of 42·8° C. (= 109·04 Fahr.); a similar case in one aged forty, the same. He also communicates a number of similar observations, amongst which one by *Dowler* is said to have reached as much as 45° C. (= 113° Fahr.).[1]

On the other hand, it is a matter of every day experience, that in

[1] See also a letter of Dr. Bäumler's in the 'Lancet,' August 6th, 1870, calling attention to the great benefit derived from rubbing with ice in case of sunstroke, as recommended and practised by Dr. Levick in the cases mentioned above: the same means proved successful in my hands in some cases admitted to the London Hospital, when I was resident medical officer there, with temperatures of 103°, 104°, and 105° (the latter temperature seems not uncommon), a few hours after the first attack. For another paper by Dr. Levick, see the 'American Journal of Medical Sciences,' vol. xxxvii, p. 40.—[TRANS.]

those whose temperature is sunk below the normal, bringing them
into a warm medium or surrounding them with warmth-giving
materials [hot-water bottles, &c.] is able to raise the temperature
of their bodies.

§ 8. The application of *external irritants* (Reizmittel) appears to
have the effect of lowering the general temperature rather than of
raising it. *Mantegazza* (Reference in Schmidt's 'Jahrbuch,' 1867,
i, p. 153) observed that pain had a tendency to lower the temperature both in man and other animals. Most observers agree that
there is no elevation of temperature in places rendered hyperæmic by
mustard, and *Naumann* (Prager's 'Viertelj.,' 1867, xciii, 133) even
states that he has found a lowering of the general temperature
consequent upon the application of mustard. *Heidenhain* communicated to the Innspruck Natural History Congress, that according to his experiments irritation of sensory nerves constantly and
suddenly lowered the temperature except after division of the
medulla oblongata from the spinal cord, or when fever was
present.

§ 9. When a *considerable hyperæmia* of any part is *artificially
induced* the temperature of the part may become elevated, and an
artificial *impediment to the access of blood* to a part may diminish
the temperature.

Kussmaul and *Tenner* (loc. cit.) have shown that ligature of the
arterial trunks which diverge from the vessels leading to a given
part, the part receiving a greater blood supply in consequence of
the operation (as, for example, the head, after ligature of both
subclavians), induces not merely congestion in the part, but an
elevation of temperature. Brown-Séquard ('Comptes Rendus,' 1854,
xxxviii, p. 117) found that when animals were hung up by the
hind legs, with the head hanging down, the temperature in the
head became raised.

On the other side narrowing, or compression of the vessels, has
on similar grounds the result of lessening the temperature in the
part concerned.

Therapeutics has long known how to turn to advantage the
results of artificially increased or diminished fulness of blood on the
temperature. [*e. g.* Local and general bloodlettings—influence of
position and compression, &c., on inflammation—ligature of arteries

for ditto (as suggested and carried into effect by Mr. Maunder)—
the effect of topical astringents—local warmth, &c., and cold, may
be adduced as examples. It must be remarked here, however, that
although the *immediate* effect of ligature of either arteries or veins
leading to or from a part is as *full* of temperature, there is a *rise*
again (often considerable) as soon as the collateral circulation is reestablished.—TRANS.]

§ 10. *Large losses of blood*, both in healthy people and in sick
persons, generally cause a rapid lowering of temperature, which is
however compensated pretty generally, after a few hours or days,
unless ending fatally, or, as may sometimes happen in the course of
a disease, terminating in a crisis. *Marshall Hall* observed the
temperature fall from $37.5°$ C. ($99.5°$ Fahr.) to $29.45°$ C. ($85°$ Fahr.)
in a house dog weighing 17 lbs., from whom he took 32 oz. of blood,
and the animal died. From another dog, weighing 19 lbs., he took
30 oz., and the temperature sank to $31.65°$ C. ($= 88.97°$ Fahr.).
Frese's experiments with moderate bleedings (see page 118) may
be contrasted with these.

After a copious hæmorrhage from the lungs, stomach, intestines,
or uterus, there ensues an almost immediate and very considerable
sinking of the temperature, even amounting to collapse-temperatures, when there has previously been a high febrile range. It
depends upon the circumstances of the case whether, how soon, and
to what degree the temperature again rises. Even a moderate
spontaneous loss of blood [such as epistaxis, &c.] causes a disproportionate fall of temperature in most fever cases.[1]

General bloodlettings in suitable cases of disease, and in a less
degree local abstraction of blood, have similar effects, and it not
seldom happens that the temperature, which just before was considerably elevated, or in other words, febrile, becomes normal, or
very nearly so just after. But the reaction is generally far from
insignificant. In most cases the temperature soon rises again to its
previous height, or even exceeds it. The temperature will remain

---

[1] For example, a girl under my care, aged 12, on the tenth day of typhoid
fever, had a morning temperature of $104°$; pulse, 130; R. 24. In the evening,
after a moderate bleeding from the nose, the temperature was only 100 ;
pulse, 100 ; R. 24 ; whereas the evening temperature of this disease is generally from $2°—3°$ higher than the morning, and was so in this case when there
was no epistaxis.

reduced just in proportion to the actual improvement which has taken place in the patient's condition (lit. in dem Krankheit s process, in the process of the disease) at or after the bleeding. It appears not to be very material whether the blood flows from capillary vessels, or from those of a larger calibre; but it is far more important, on the other hand, that the course of the disease should be sufficiently *forward* to allow of a lasting impression being made upon it by the abstraction of blood.[1]

If menstruation occurs in the course of a disease, we find it more commonly preceded by a rise of temperature than is the case in healthy people. The loss of blood itself is sometimes followed by a diminution of the previously elevated temperature induced by the disease. And besides this, the occurrence of the catamenia has often a disproportionate disturbing influence, especially on women of a nervous temperament, and may cause a previously high temperature to rise as well as causing greater mobility of temperature, and in some very susceptible individuals it may be associated with a species of febricula [see note to page 102].[2]

§ 11. *Chossat's* valuable researches and experiments on the effects of *deprivation of food* in lowering the temperature, were the first published on this subject (1843, 'Recherches expérimentales sur l'inanition. Mém. présentés à l'acad. des sciences. Sc. mathém. et physiques,' viii, p. 438), and on the effects upon temperature, further see page 532. Besides this *Schmidt, Lichtenfels,* and *Fröhlich*

---

[1] Dr. Christian Baümler ('Clinical Society's Transactions,' vol. ii, read Feb. 12, 1869) has called attention to the rise of temperature which takes place within a few (one or two) days after hæmoptysis, and to the necessity for watching such cases and keeping them quiet, even when occurring in previously healthy people. The paper is illustrated with several cases, and a chart of the temperature. There can be no doubt that this is a very important practical observation.—[TRANS.]

[2] It may not be out of place here to draw the reader's attention to the eminently practical therapeutic results and indications to which Wunderlich refers here and elsewhere, as the fruit of thermometry applied to medicine. I would especially single out the author's remarks on alcohol, bleeding, baths, calomel, digitalis, diet, ice, and purgatives [see this, and the preceding and following chapters, and many other places passim, for which I must beg the reader to consult the index]. It appears to me that the effect on the candid reader's mind, however radical or revolutionary his pathology and therapeutics may be, will be to make him endorse the Horatian maxim, "Vixere fortes ante Agamemnona multi."

have experimented on the influence of hunger upon the temperature, and it has thus been established that by continuous deprivation of food, moderately extensive diminutions of temperature may be produced, without necessarily producing thereby any intercurrent relative elevations of temperature. In disease the effects of diminished diet are never simple, and therefore observation of this kind upon sick people are of little value.[1]

§ 12. The *introduction of nutritious material*, contrary to the rule of health, is often remarkable in its operation upon the sick. Not only those patients who have a more or less elevated temperature, but even those whose temperature is entirely normal, or has again become so, may exhibit very striking elevations of temperature consequent on taking nourishment; and for these we do not need any special error of diet, or an increase of nourishment before the appetite is restored, but they may occur on the introduction of very moderate quantities: sometimes with the first enjoyment of animal food, during convalescence, at a time when the appetite is extremely sharp (in hohem grade lebhaft), it is not uncommon to meet with a rise of temperature of two or more degrees (Centigrade $= 3.6°$ F.), and it may remain at this height for two or three days or more.

§ 13. *Constipation*, if it lasts a few days, and sometimes even the absence of an alvine evacuation for only twenty-four hours, especially after previous diarrhœa or catharsis, may give rise to elevations of temperature in disease. *Retention of urine* and *suppression of the catamenia* have a similar effect. So when a pathological hæmorrhage occurs, the temperature usually rises a few hours previously.

Very relaxed motions generally lower the temperature, and when artificially induced, more than when they are spontaneous. Even a single copious evacuation may do this, if there has been long-standing constipation, and the temperature has been previously high. After the relaxation however, the reaction is generally considerable,

---

[1] For a very interesting account of various experiments of Bidder and Schmidt's, and others, on the effects of starvation, see Otto Funke's 'Lehrbuch der Physiologie,' i, 607. See, also, Dr. Carpenter's 'Principles of Human Physiology,' pp. 54—56, 434—5, sixth edition, and Taylor's 'Medical Jurisprudence,' p. 742. Also the medical journals of the current year on the case of Sarah Jacobs, "the Welsh Fasting Girl."—[TRANS.]

and the subsequent rise may exceed the height of the previous temperature. The kind of purgative, however, appears to have but slight influence on either the amount or the permanence of the depression of temperature.

Vomiting depresses the temperature far more than the action of the bowels. Indeed the act is often accompanied or followed by collapse-temperature. In this case also there is, for the most part, a certain amount of reaction, inducing a rise of temperature.

§ 14. *The lowering of temperature* consequent on the *toxic effects of alcohol* agrees with what has been said before of its effects in health, although as long as health is unimpaired the effects are far slighter (see page 117).

With poisonous doses of alcohol the depression of temperature may be very considerable,[1] as Duméril and Demarquay first pointed out, and many others have confirmed. It appears that the ingestion of alcohol diminishes or retards the tissue changes. Yet we must notice that after the employment of brandy the fall of temperature is usually followed by a very strong reaction. But in febrile conditions the effect of alcohol is to lower temperature, as several English observers have announced, from clinical observations, and *C. Bouvier* has lately proved by experiments (Pflüger's 'Archiv,' 1869, p. 381). Habitual "soakers" have as a rule, under parallel circumstances, a lower temperature than other persons, and collapse-temperatures are met with in them, both in different kinds of fever and in non-febrile diseases also, very commonly, and the collapse is often very marked. This is not incompatible with the fact that very high temperatures are often met with at the termination of fatal cases of delirium potatorum (D. tremens). A variety of other more or less poisonous substances depress the temperature. *Demarquay* has demonstrated this as regards *Ether* and *Chloroform*. Brown-Séquard (1849, 'Comptes rendus des séances de la Société de Biologie,' Nr. 7, p. 102) reckons opium, hydrocyanic acid, hyoscyamus, digitalis, belladonna, tobacco, euphorbium, camphor, acetic acid, oxalic acid, sulphuric, nitric, and hydrochloric acids, amongst the agents which lower the temperature.[2]

---

[1] In cases of acute alcohol poisoning admitted to the London Hospital, I have several times noted a temperature of only 90° F. (32·2° C.) in cases which recovered.—[TRANS.]

[2] Chloral-hydrate must also be reckoned amongst temperature-depressors.

Many medicines, when administered to patients suffering from fever, have the effect of lowering the previously elevated temperature. This is most certainly correct as regards digitalis (employed in quantities amounting to from 3 to 6 grammes (grs. 46 to 93) in

See Dr. Otto Liebreich's monogram, 'Das Chloral Hydrat,' &c., Berlin, 1869. Also papers and notices by Mr. Spencer Wells, Dr. B. W. Richardson, and others, too numerous to mention, in the 'Edinburgh Medical Journal,' 'Lancet,' 'Medical Times and Gazette,' 'The Practitioner,' 'Pharmaceutical Journal,' and other medical publications at the close of 1869 and commencement of 1870.

I may also specially mention a paper on its use in tetanus, by Mr. Waren Tay, in the 'British Medical Journal' for April 2, 1870, p. 329); other papers in same journal, pp. 301, 433, and 413. It is not at all uncommon for the temperature to fall 3 or 4° Fahr. (= 1·61° to 2·2° C.), or even more after a full dose (40—80 grains) of chloral hydrate.

Dr. R. P. Oglesby, of Leeds, has made a series of experiments on various animals (cats, dogs, rabbits, and guinea pigs), which tend to prove that the action of morphia and atropine, administered hypodermically, is almost identical, regard being had to the difference of activity (see the 'Practitioner' for January, 1870). He finds that the first effect is to lower the temperature, but it rapidly rises again; and he believes that in these drugs, so used, we have a reliable remedy for the collapse of cholera, summer diarrhœa, &c. The following examples may serve to explain and illustrate his statements.

No. 1.—A young cat. Temp. in rectum 101° before operation; ⅛ gr. bimeconate of morphia at 9.30 p.m.

10 p.m.	Temperature	99·1°	1 a.m.	Temperature	100·3°
11 p.m.	,,	99·0°	2 a.m.	,,	102·1°
12 night	,,	99·4°	4 a.m.	,,	102·3°

No. 2.—A terrier. Temp. in rectum 102·3°; ½ gr. morphia at 4.30 p.m.

5.0 p.m.	Temperature	101·4°	7.0 p.m.	Temperature	102·1°
5.30 p.m.	,,	101·1°	8.0 p.m.	,,	102·4°
6.0 p.m.	,,	101·1°	9.0 p.m.	,,	103·1°*
6.30 p.m.	,,	101·4°			

* In spite of vomiting, this temp. continued several hours.

No. 3.—A guinea pig. Temp. in rectum 101·2°; ⅛ gr. bimeconate of morphia at 4.0 p.m.

4.30 p.m.	Temperature	101·2°	6.0 p.m.	Temperature	103·0°
5.0 p.m.	,,	102·2°	8.0 p.m.	,,	104·1°
5.30 p.m.	,,	102·4°			

No. 4.—A cat. Temp. in rectum 103°; $\frac{1}{50}$ gr. atropine at 6 p.m.

6.15 p.m.	Temperature	102·4°	8.30 p.m.	Temperature	103·1°
6.30 p.m.	,,	102·3°	11.30 p.m.	,,	104·0°
7.0 p.m.	,,	102·3°	1.30 p.m.	,,	104·0°
7.30 p.m.	,,	102·2°			

Similar results were obtained in rabbits.—[TRANS.]

divided doses, spread over some days), veratria, quinine, antimony, and calomel. Acids, saltpetre [potassium nitrate], and other salines show this action less decisively. But children and delicate women exhibit greater sensitiveness than other patients in this respect, and exhibit more clearly the temperature-depressing effects of these remedies.

[Hence the old-fashioned treatment of fever by salines, and the more modern use of mineral acids both find a justification. Dr. Robert Barnes, who has paid great attention to therapeutics, expresses himself very strongly on the beneficial effects of salines ('Lectures on Obstetric Operations,' p. 493, and elsewhere). *Liebermeister* of Bâle has published in the 'Deutsches Archiv f. Klinisch Medicin,' vol. iii, parts 5 and 6, on the effects of *Quinine*, to which he ascribes a decided and almost invariable temperature-reducing effect. Dr. F. Stabell in the 'Report of the Medical Department of the Royal Hospital, Christiana,' for the year 1867 ('Norsk Magazin for Lægevidensk Aben,' xxiii Bd., 1 Heft) gives details of two cases supporting the same view. In one woman, aged thirty-one, a case of fever, with rose spots and petechiæ, without diarrhœa, the temperature fell 8°, 5°, and 9° nearly after three doses of ɘj each of quinine. Dr. Bäumler, however ('Klinische Beobachtungen über Abdominal-typhus in England'), found but slight effects from quinine, except perhaps in the last period of enteric fever; indeed ɘj doses of quinine had no effect at all in one case in which that dose was several times administered.

Dr. Bäumler's paper also contains remarks on the effect of port wine, calomel, and other medicamenta, and is full of interesting observations on the course of the temperature in enteric fever, &c.—TRANS.]

§ 15. On the other hand, a great many *substances* have a direct effect in *raising the temperature*, which are partly to be observed after "toxic incorporation" in healthy people, and partly in diseases when the temperature is either abnormally high or depressed. *Coffee, musk, and camphor*, belong to this group. The effects of *curare* (Woorara) have been most accurately investigated. After *Claude Bernard* had made the discovery that it acted on the vaso-motor nerves first, and that then the temperature rose, *Voisin* and *Liouville* ('Gazette des Hôpitaux,' 1866, Nr. 109 and 111, and 'Journal de l'Anatomie et de Physiologie,' 1867, p. 114), by means of sub-

cutaneous injections of this drug, induced a complete artificial fever
in human beings, with rigors, heats and sweatings, the temperature
rising to 40·4° C. (104·8° F.), accompanied with all the signs
of febrile circulation and secretion, and disturbance of the nervous
system. *Tscheschichin*, on the contrary, found that in animals, some
minutes after the injection of curare, there was a slight decrease of
temperature, which continued till cramps set in, when the temperature began to rise unmistakably. *Fleischer*, however (Pflüger's
'Archiv,' 1869, p. 441), confirmed the effect of curare in raising
the temperature.

§ 16. *Billroth* and *Hufschmidt, O. Weber*, and *Frese*, have all
pointed out the *temperature-raising* (pyrogonic) effects of *certain
animal substances, when introduced into the circulation.*

Billroth and *Hufschmidt* ('Archiv für klin. Chir.,' vi, 392)
found that in all the cases in which putrid solutions (jauchige
Flüssigkeit), or recent pus, were injected into the subcutaneous
cellular tissue, or into the blood, there was a rise of temperature in
the rectum, which was considerable even within two hours after the
injection, and reached its maximum in from two to twenty-eight
hours; that the minimum exceeded the normal temperature by
1·6° C. (2·88° F.), and the maximum by 2·2° C. (3·96° F.) ; and
that if the injection were only done *once*, a rapid defervescence
generally set in, shortly after the acme had been reached ; whilst, on
the other hand, after repeated injections, death constantly occurred,
generally with very high temperatures.

Soon afterwards, *O. Weber* (in 1864, 'Deutsche Klinik,' p. 495,
and 1865, p. 13, 21, 33, 53) determined by similar experiments the
pyrogonic (and phlogogonic, or in other words, heat-producing and
inflammatory) effects of *pus* injected subcutaneously, or into serous
cavities, or into the blood; of fluids from inflamed tissues, and
further, of the injection of pyæmic and septicæmic blood, and even
of the blood of an animal merely suffering from simple inflammatory
fever. However, in the last case, the elevation of temperature was but
slight, and amounted to only 0·65° to 1·15° C. (1·17° F. to 2·07° F.).

Frese (1866, 'Experiment. Beiträge zur Ætiologie des Fiebers.
Diss.') made still more numerous experiments. He showed that
the blood of animals suffering from fever, whatever kind of fever it
might be, when introduced into the circulation of a healthy animal of
the same species, induced a rise of temperature.

This followed the injection pretty speedily; in one case, after two hours and a half, the temperature was already 1° higher (= 1·8 F.). Yet according to Frese, the rise of temperature was by no means enormous. In the three cases uncomplicated by accidental introduction of part of the injurious blood into the connective tissue (which then set up local inflammation) the temperature only exceeded the maximum temperature of healthy animals by 0·7 to 1·3° C. (= 1·26° to 2·34° Fahr.). The rise of temperature lasted only a short time (1½, 4½, and 6 days), and thus only attained the very minimum period held to constitute a state of fever in the human subject.

Frese further discovered or confirmed—

(1) That products of decomposition and of inflammatory tissue-destruction, when introduced into the circulation, induce a rise of temperature—whether they are obtained from the body experimented upon or from that of another animal.

(2) That this depends not upon the pus-corpuscles, but upon the serum of the fluid.

(3) That even boiling and subsequent filtration does not destroy this property.

(4) That very recent fresh serum of pus possesses this property in a high degree.

(5) That no fever is induced by the injection of healthy blood, but that the blood of an animal suffering from fever has pyrogenic effects (induces rise of temperature).

(6) Since beating up ("whipping," German "Quirlen") of the fever blood and subsequent filtration does not deprive it of this property, the effect cannot be due to the fibrin.

More recently *E. Bergmann* (1868, 'Petersburger med. Zeitschrift') has made a great number of experiments on the effects of decomposing and inflammatory products, and has found that after the injection of a moderately small quantity (according to circumstances) of the deleterious material, there is always induced a very exact and identical typical alteration of the course of temperature (an immediate rise after the injection, a maximum attained in from 2—5 hours, and a return to the normal in 3—6 hours). Local disturbances thus originating may hinder the process of restoration, and cause modifications of the course of the temperature. All the experiments are parallel, whether decomposing materials, or products of inflammation, or only the results of the customary tissue changes, are injected. Indeed it appears to this observer (p. 84) that after the injections of large quantities of water, or smaller quantities of irritating substances, there may be a very similar (analogous) alteration of temperature, to that which occurs after the injection of solution of decomposing or inflammatory products.

Those unknown influences which excite *specific morbid processes* in the person attacked must have something in common (schliessen sich an) with those results of experiments on the pyrogonic action of animal substances introduced into the system. However, except in the case of pyæmia and septicæmia, the resemblance is not very close [lit. die Aehnlichkeit ist doch nur eine beschränkte].

Our knowledge is still very far from being in a position to clearly comprehend the peculiar course of the temperature produced by the operation of these unknown but doubtless specific influences, or to be able to trace clearly the connection between the original specific causes and the altered temperature.[1]

[1] The conclusions arrived at by M. *Andral* on the relation of the constituents of the blood, &c., to temperature, are stated as follows in the 'Medical Times and Gazette' of January 1st, 1870. 1st. As to *fibrine*. When the blood contains more than $\frac{1}{1000}$ths of this, the temperature rises, and in a corresponding ratio. Thus, of all diseases, pneumonia is marked with the greatest increase of fibrine, and is the highest in temperature of all the phlegmasiæ. In 85 cases in only 13 was the temperature below 39° C. (102·2° F.); in 44 it was between 39° and 40° C. (102·2° F. and 104° F.); in 26 between 40° C. (104° F.) and 41° C. (105·8° F.); and in 2 rose to 41·2° C. (= 106·16° F.). In acute pleurisy, in which there is always less fibrine, the temperature only once reached 41° C. (105·8° F.), and usually oscillated between 38·5° C. (= 101·3° F.) and 39·5° C. (103·1° F.). M. *Andral*, however, admits exceptions, as in erysipelas, when there have been only $\frac{7}{1000}$ths of fibrines, the temperature has been 41·8° C. (107·24° F.). Still there are high amounts of fibrine never seen without a corresponding rise of temperature—thus the fibrine never exceeds 10 parts in a thousand without the temperature exceeding 40° C. (104° F.). But he does not consider these as cause and effect, for in pyrexia, where there is no excess of fibrin, the temperature is as high or higher than in phlegmasiæ. Thus 42·4° C. (108·32° F.) has been reached in typhoid; 42° C. (107·6° F.) in the onset of smallpox, the hot stage of ague, and in glanders, &c. Indeed, the highest degrees are reached in diseases when there is the least fibrine in the blood.

2. The number of red globules does not much affect it. In a woman exhausted by hæmorrhage, with only 21 parts of globules in the blood, the temperature was maintained at 37° C. (98·6° F.), and a chlorotic patient with only $\frac{1}{1000}$ globules kept a temperature of 37·9° C. (100·22° F.). Of 20 cases with 38—117 per 1000 globules, the temperature varied from 37° to 38·4° C. (98·6° to 101·12° F.).

3. When the albumen escapes in the *urine*, theory would lead us to expect

§ 17. Breschet and Becquerel (Session of the Academie des Sciences, 18th Oct., 1841) were the first to point out the remarkable depression of temperature in animals, the *surface of whose body is covered with an impermeable coating*. They made the communication,

diminished temperature. More facts are wanted, however, to establish this. Of 7 cases, the temperature was diminished in 5, and 2 had intercurrent inflammation.

4. On the relations of the amount of *urea* in the urine to the temperature, M. *Andral* considers that the increased temperature generally means an increased amount of urea in the urine. Notably in fevers. He considers 10—15 per 1000 normal. In 53 patients whose temperature was normal, the urea did not exceed $\frac{12}{1000}$th in more than 8 cases. In 45 others with non-febrile diseases it ranged from 4 to 12—1000ths. But in 23 analyses in intermittent fevers, the urea ranged from 13—32 per 1000. In pneumonia 20—29 per 1000, &c. Urea is increased also in cirrhosis of the liver."

With regard to the artificial production of tuberculosis in animals, by inoculations, and the injection of various irritants, the scope and purpose of this work do not allow me to do more than refer the reader to the following sources of information.

For an account of M. *Villemin's* experiments communicated to the French Academy in 1865—6 see the 'Edinburgh Medical Journal,' Feb. 1867, pp. 756—765.

For further experiments, English and Foreign, see also—

Dr. *Wilson Fox*,—'The Artificial Production of Tubercle in the Lower Animals.' (Macmillan, 1868.)

Dr. J. *Burdon Sanderson*,—'Appendices to Reports of the Medical Officer of the Privy Council,' 1868—9, and his article, "Recent Researches on Tuberculosis," ('Edinburgh Medical Journal,' Nov. 1869, p. 385.) See also—

'British and Foreign Medico-Chirurgical Review,' April, 1870, p. 389, ("Tuberculosis and Pulmonary Consumption.")

Niemeyer's 'Clinical Medicine,' American edition. (Henry Lewis, Gower Street).

Niemeyer's 'Clinical Lectures,' (translated by Dr. Bäumler, New Sydenham Society).

The number of German and French writers, and other contributors, is too great to allow of more than mentioning the names of Virchow, Cohnheim, Buhl, Ziemssen, Bastels, Chaveau, Cornil, Ranvier, and Petersen, and quoting the following titles :

"Die Tuberculose, die Lungenschwindsucht, und Scrofulose, &c.," von Dr. L. *Waldenburg*, Berlin, 1869.

"Manuel d'Histologie Pathologique," MM. *Cornil* and *Ranvier*, p. 204.

Dr. Julius *Petersen's* "Thesis for M.D.," Copenhagen, 1869, entitled, "Lungesvindsotens og Tuberculosens omtvistede Contägiositet og Inoculabilitet."

This appears to me a fitting opportunity of doing justice to the labours of two of our own countrymen, who have been somewhat unfairly neglected (per-

that rabbits whose shaved skin was covered with a coating of glue, or tallow and rosin, lost from 14—18° C. [25·2°—32·4° Fahr.] of their proper temperature, in the course of 1 or 1½ hour, and soon after died. These observers themselves remarked that what they thus propounded was apparently contradictory to the received notions about the functions of the skin. However, the observations themselves have been lately fully confirmed by *Gerlach* (in Müller's 'Archiv,' 1851, p. 467), *Valentin* (in 'Archiv für Physiologische Heilk.,' 1858, p. 433). *Edenhuizen* (in 'Zeitschrift für rationelle Med.,' 1863, p. 25).

Valentin has also shown that in animals thus treated, the respiratory movements are diminished to a third or even a quarter of what they were. The taking in of oxygen and the giving out of carbonic acid became diminished in a greater degree (to $\frac{1}{6}$th); but that on the other hand, if the air which the animals breathe is raised in temperature the refrigeration is checked, the breathing becomes stronger, the animals become more lively, and the fatal termination is retarded although not prevented. *Edenhuizen* found that the animals [rabbits] perished after only a part of the skin was thus treated, as soon as more than ⅓th or ½th of their superficies was thus covered. The more the surface was thus coated, the quicker and more remarkable was the sinking of the temperature, and the more rapidly death set in. When a considerable portion of the surface was left free, the temperature, pulse-frequency, and frequency of respirations were all diminished at first; but the first two soon recover again, and may even exceed the normal, while the frequency of respiration still remains lessened. If a yet larger surface (⅗ths to ⅔rds) was left uncovered, the frequency of respiration was diminished at first, but soon became increased, but did not exceed the normal so long as the temperature and pulse did. If only ⅕th to ¼th of the surface was covered in this way, the quickened breathing was the chief symptom, whilst the temperature and the frequency of the pulse were less affected. *Laschkewitzch* explains

haps by accident) by the writers of some of the articles referred to—I mean Dr. Andrew Clark, and Dr. Edwards Crisp. A paper by the latter will be found in the 'Transactions of the St. Andrew's Med. Grad. Association,' vol. i, p. 110. With regard to Dr. Andrew Clark, I can state from personal knowledge, that his experiments on the artificial induction of tubercle were carried on long before the publications of those who have ignored his labours.— [TRANS.]

these symptoms by the increased loss of warmth in consequence of paralytic dilatation of the cutaneous vessels.

§ 18. Very numerous experiments and investigations have been made with the view of elucidating the *influence of the nervous system upon temperature.* Numerous very remarkable facts have been added to our knowledge, partly by experiments and partly by means of clinical observations. It is however not possible as yet to deliver a comprehensive and satisfactory judgment on the mode in which the nerves affect the temperature. Long ago there were numerous observations, showing that after experimental division of the spinal cord, or after severe injuries of it, there followed a peripheral elevation of temperature, particularly by *Chossat* (1820, 'Mém. sur Influence du System. Nerveux sur la Chaleur Animale'), by *Sir B. Brodie* (1837, ' Medico-Chirurg. Transac.,' XX, 146[1]), by *Macartny* (1838, 'Treatise on Inflammation,' p. 13), by Fr. *Nasse* (1839, ' Untersuchungen zur Physiologie and Pathologie,' II, 115), and especially by H. *Nasse* (ibid. II, 190).

In opposition to these, *Flourens* and *Magendie* observed, that the temperature fell after injuries to nerves, and this fall was local when nerve trunks only, general when nerve centres were damaged. *Claude Bernard* gave in his adhesion to the latter proposition, which he erroneously considered a constant phenomenon, when he published his astonishing discovery of the effects of dividing the cervical sympathetic (1852, 'Comptes Rendus de l'Acad. des Sciences,' XXXIV, p. 472). He discovered that after the division of the connecting branches between the superior and inferior cervical ganglia, there commenced an immediate increase of heat in the whole corresponding side of the head, which could be especially well seen in the ear of a rabbit. He also found that merely laying bare, or disturbing, or pressing on the ganglia of the sympathetic nerve was followed by great congestion, and increased development of heat. More lately ('Comptes Rendus,' lv, 232) he made further communications, according to which section of the lumbo-sacral plexus, or of the sciatic nerve, was followed by an elevation of temperature in the posterior limb thus treated, and also that section of the brachial plexus about the first rib, was followed by a rise of temperature in the

---

[1] Sir B. Brodie's first paper was in the 'Philosophical Transactions' for 1811. It is referred to by the author, p. 25.—TRANS.

corresponding anterior extremity. *Bernard* built upon these results the theory of a special influence of the sympathetic on the blood-vessels, and upon calorification, and distinguishes the sympathetic system from the motor and sensory nerves, as being vaso-motor, and calorific nerves.

In his "Leçons sur la Physiologie et la Pathologie du Système Nerveux, ii, 490" (1858). Bernard formulated his ideas as follows :—

1. La section des nerfs du sentiment outre l'abolition du senti-ment, produit la *diminution* de la température des parties.

2. Celle des nerfs du movement outre l'abolition du mouvement donne lieu également à un *refroidissement* des parties paralysées.

3. La destruction du nerf sympathique qui ne produit ni l'immo-bilité des muscles, ni la perte de sensibilité amène une *augmentation de température* constante et trés considérable.[1]

The most important questions arising out of these results of experiment are :—

(1.) Whether the increased heat is proportionate to the excess of blood in the part which occurs when the sympathetic is divided?

(2.) Although the temperature (as compared with the other ear, and with its height before the section of the nerve) may be consider-ably increased, does it remain within the range of temperature which is proper to the internal organs of animals? If these ques-tions are answered in the affirmative, this phenomenon has only a subordinate, mediate, and almost insignificant relation to the pro-duction of heat. In that case, the section of the nerve merely acts by producing a hyperæmia, and the consequence of this hyperæmia is, that the normal blood heat is more perfectly attained and exhibited by the parts thus more richly supplied with blood.

(3.) Finally, this question arises—Are they really the proper fibres of the sympathetic, or those which although mixed with it, are derived from the spinal cord, upon which the phenomena depends? Is the sympathetic the special vaso-motor nerve (as

[1] " 1. Division of nerves of *sensation*, besides producing anæsthesia, dimi-nishes the temperature of the parts supplied.

" 2. Division of motor nerves, besides causing paralysis, gives rise also to *coldness in the paralysed parts*.

" 3. Destruction of the sympathetic nerve, which neither produces muscular paralysis nor loss of sensation, is accompanied with a constant and very con-siderable *elevation* of temperature."

Bernard supposes) or are the movements of the vessels dependent on the cerebro-spinal centres?

On all these points, the majority of experimenters have decided against Bernard.   Brown-Séquard first entered the lists against Bernard's conclusions.   Before the publications of the latter in the 'Comptes Rendus,' the former had communicated the experiment that galvanization of the divided portion of the cervical sympathetic caused contraction of the vessels in the corresponding part of the head, and in consequence of that, anæmia, and diminution of temperature and of sensation (in 1852 in the 'Medical Examiner of Philadelphia,' p. 486, of the vol. for that year).   Shortly after (in 1853, in 'Experimental Researches,' p. 9) he expressed the opinion, that the results of section of the cervical sympathetic ought to be attributed only to a paralytic dilatation of the cephalic blood-vessels, and the increased warmth referred to the increased congestion, through the larger amount of blood flowing to the part.   He pointed out that hanging up the animals by their hind legs had almost the same effect as division of the sympathetic.   He concludes the abstract ('On the Increase of Animal Heat after Injuries of the Nervous System') as follows (p. 77) :—

(1.) An injury to the nervous system may cause either an increased or diminished temperature in the parts which are paralysed, by it.

(2.) It appears that the respective shares of the sympathetic and cerebro-spinal nervous systems in producing these, cannot well be determined.

(3.) The degree of temperature of paralysed parts depends on the quantity of blood which they contain, and this quantity varies with the condition of the arteries and capillaries of the part.

(4.) It is a matter of fact, hitherto unexplained, that the arteries and capillaries of paralysed parts may be either dilated, normal, or contracted.

Budge (1853. 'Comptes Rendus,' xxxvi, 377, and 'Med. Ztg. von dem Verein für Heilkunde in Preussen,' xxii, 149) has pointed out, that this elevation of temperature is not only produced by division of the sympathetic, but that injuries of that part of the spinal marrow which lies between the seventh cervical and the third dorsal vertebra, which thus includes the eighth cervical, and the first and second dorsal nerves, has the same effect on the temperature of the head.

Waller also ('Comptes Rendus,' xxxvi, p. 378) attributes the rise of temperature simply to the paralysis of the circular fibres of the smaller arteries, and the hyperæmia thus induced, caused by the section of nerve.

De Ruyter ('Dissert. de actione Atropæ belladonnæ,' 1853) remarked also, that he had noticed no alteration of temperature which could not be explained by the increased access of blood; and *Donders* ('Aanteekingen van het Utr. Gen.,' 1853) remarks that in these experiments the temperature of the ears very seldom exceeds that of the rectum, that it is high just in proportion to the amount of blood sent to the ears—that it diminishes when they are congested—and that after ligature of the carotid the temperature of the ear on the side of the section is no higher than that of the other side, and that if the ears are forcibly rubbed the temperature in both is alike.

Schiff discussed the question from the most advanced point of view, and made a number of fresh experiments (1855, 'Untersuchungen zur Physiologie des Nerven Systems,' i, 124). He has observed that the difference of temperature of the two sides of the head (of the ears) may be very considerable, and may amount to even 12° or 16° C. (= 21·6° to 28·8° Fahr.); that the difference of temperature was proportionate to the difference in the quantity of blood in the parts, and that when (as exceptionally occurs) the section of the cervical sympathetic has no effect on the vessels of the ear, there is also no elevation of temperature. He seeks to prove that the increased fulness of the vessels depends upon paralysis of the blood-vessels, and that the larger quantity of blood circulating through the part, causes the local elevation of temperature. He also propounds that the sympathetic is not the sole and exclusive vascular nerve of the head, but that the cervical auricular, the facial, and the trigeminus nerve have their share; and also that the part of the vaso-motor nerves of the head, which is actually contained in the sympathetic, consists entirely of the spinal nerve fibres contained in it; that the vaso-motor nerves pass through the spinal cord, and that a part of the medulla oblongata must be regarded as a centre for the vaso-motor nerves, because those of the head and trunk both meet there. He maintains that in complete spinal paralysis of a part, the temperature of this must be elevated, whilst in incomplete (*i. e.*, paralysis of motion only) the temperature must be diminished (p. 226); a conclusion which has since been at least partially confirmed by pathological facts.

A further very important conclusion of *Schiff's* in its relation to the pathology of fever, is this, which he claims to have established by experiments : that the vaso-motor nerves of the face, and of the distal portions of the extremities on the one hand ; and those of the trunk, the arm (above the elbow), and the upper part of the thigh, on the other hand form two distinct groups, which keep perfectly separate in their course through the spinal cord, so that the latter group of vascular nerves, decussates laterally, as does the corresponding group of the other half of the body, which those of the first group fail to do ; and further, that when one cuts across the left half of the spinal cord near the medulla oblongata, the vascular nerves of the skin of the face, of the hands and feet, and the lower part of the forearm, and of the leg (below the knee) of the left side, and on the other side (the right) those of the trunk, the arm (above the elbow), and the upper part of the thigh are paralysed.

Some further experiments of *Schiff's* which he published afterwards in the 'Allgem Wiemer Med. Zeitg.,' 1859, p. 318, are of very great interest. He excited fever by injection of pus into the pleura, or into the vascular system, in animals in whom he had previously divided the left cervical sympathetic, or resected the nerves of one extremity. As soon as the fever set in, the parts unaffected by the section of the nerves began to rise in temperature, whilst in the parts suffering from vaso-motor-paralysis, which were previously warmer, the temperature either did not rise at all, or only very slowly ; and when the febrile temperature was fully established, the organs which before were warmest (the nerves of which were divided) were colder than the corresponding parts of the other (uninjured) side. He concluded from this, that the [paralytic] hyperæmia (Blutüberfüllung) induced by the nerve-section, and that induced by fever (and congestion) do not depend on the same process ; that the latter is of a much more active nature, and that therefore (as for that matter, *Claude Bernard* himself admits, as regards the submaxillary glands, see 'Comptes Rendus,' 1858) there must exist in the nerves of the blood-vessels, such elements as, when stimulated, cause [an active] dilatation (durch ihre *Erregung* eine Erweiterung bedingen) ; but that, after section of the nerves, this is no longer possible.

Kussmaul and *Tenner's* researches (in Moleschott's 'Untersuchungen zur Naturlehre des Menschen und der Thiere,' 1856, i, 90—132) had considerable influence in again referring the pheno-

mena of warmth to the amount of blood contained in the vessels.
They obtained the important result, of constantly reducing the
increased warmth of the ear of the side on which the sympathetic
was divided, below that of the other ear, and even lower than its own
temperature before the section, as soon as (in addition to ligaturing
or compressing the carotid on the same side) they also ligatured the
two subclavians at their origin, and thus prevented the establishment
of the collateral circulation. On the other hand they procured an
elevation of temperature if they only ligatured the subclavians, and
thus increased the lateral pressure of the blood in the carotid. The
effect of compression of the carotid on one side, after previous ligature of the subclavians, had parallel results, whether the sympathetic
were previously divided or not, and the section of the sympathetic
produced no greater increase of heat than the increased pressure of
blood. However, both *Lussana* and *Ambrosoli* ('Gazz. Lombarda,'
1867, Nos. 25—33), after suspending animals by their hind legs, did
not find so great an increase of temperature in the ears as they did
after division of the sympathetic; and they think that in the latter,
a local pathological process of blood-dissolution (decomposition)
induced by the section of the sympathetic, causes the elevation of
temperature, and not mere hyperæmia, or increased functional
activity.

Brown-Séquard ('Experimental Researches, applied to Physiology
and Pathology,' p. 73) discovered also that complete division of
one lateral half of the spinal cord in the dorsal region was followed
by a rise of temperature in the hinder extremity of the corresponding
side, and a fall of temperature in the opposite limb.

Schiff (' Untersuchungen,' p. 196) confirmed this, but attributes
the (low) temperature of the opposite extremity to an accidental
injury of one half of the spinal cord in performing the section of the
other half.

Tscheschichin, after complete section of the spinal cord in a
variety of situations, has always observed a suppression of the active
operations of the vessels, and a sinking of the general temperature,
in addition to the loss of voluntary movements (Reichert's 'Archiv,'
1866, p. 152); and he considers the primary cause of this *diminished
warmth*, to consist in the paralytic dilatation of the vessels, their
overfullness of blood (and especially in the veins), in the hindrance
to the free circulation of the blood, and consequently in the increased
radiation [or loss] of heat. He found that the rapid sinking of the

internal temperature after division of the spinal cord might be diminished or even prevented, by enveloping the body in bad conductors of heat [wool, cotton, &c.], and thus hindering the loss of heat from the surface of the body.   When Tscheschichin, however, divided the medulla oblongata in a rabbit, near to its junction with the pons, he found that immediately after the operation, the general temperature began to rise, and the pulse and respirations were greatly quickened. After half an hour, the temperature was from 39·4° to 40·1° C. (102·92° to 104·18° F.); after an hour it rose to 41·2° C. (106·16° F.), whilst the respirations ranged from 78 to 90, and the pulse became uncountable.   Immediately after the operation, the reflex phenomena began to be unusually evident, and reached so extreme a point, that the least touch excited convulsive movements of the whole body of the animal.   After an hour and a half, the temperature reached 42·2° C. (107·96° F.); after two hours 42·6° (108·68° F.; more rapid breathing and convulsions set in, under which in half an hour more the animal died.

Tscheschichin connects these facts with the theory of centres of control (Moderationscentren) which have their seat in the brain, in order to regulate the activity of the spinal cord.   By the ceaseless activity of these, the intense activity of the spinal cord is diminished; when they are destroyed or isolated, the activity of the spinal cord is morbidly increased, and for some time exhibits itself in excess of functional activity (increased reflex action, quickened respiration, acceleration of the cardiac systole (Herzschlag), and increased animal heat).

Naunyn and *Quincke* (Reichert's 'Archiv,' 1869, p. 174), asserted that after crushing of the upper part of the (spinal) cord, remarkable elevations of temperature were only met with when the animal was prevented from losing heat, otherwise there was always a rapid sinking of temperature, lasting till death.   They propound the view that injuries to the cord have a two-fold operation—an increase of warmth production, and an increase in the amount of heat given off.   By these contrary forces they explain the contradictory results obtained by different observers.   They further observed, that when the cervical portion of the medulla was divided, the rise of temperature was more rapid than when the section was in the dorsal portion.   Naunyn and Quincke have lately published other interesting experiments, and have shown, that after division of the spinal cord, the temperature can be kept at a low degree by means of quinine [by limiting the warmth-production]. Fischer ('Einfluss der Rückenmarksverletzungen auf die Körperwärme.' Orig. Mittheil in Centralblatt, 1869, p. 259), believes that he has met with cases which justify him in concluding that there is a centre in the cervical portion of the cord for limiting the temperature [ein Temperatur-hemmungscentrum], by irritating which we get a decrease of temperature; by paralysing it there is increased heat obtained; and that this centre is to be looked for in the anterior fibres of the cervical portion of the spinal cord.

Remotely, and one might almost say negatively related to all these experiments are those of *Breuer* and *Chrobak* (1867, 'Wiener medic. Jahrbücher,' xiv, p. 3) who have investigated the question whether the nerves of a part supply the stimulus which causes the febrile elevation of temperature in an inflamed part; by means of experiments on animals, in whom they have as far as possible divided all the nerves of one part of the body. After the injuries caused by the operation have healed, they have set up local inflammations in the nerveless part; and they think themselves justified in concluding that the fever of the traumatic inflammation is *independent* of the nervous connections of the inflamed part with the nerve centres.

Clinical observations furnish us with only a few cases exactly analogous to the results of experiments on the relations of the nervous system to the temperature of the body. However, we may consider the following as analogous spontaneous conditions:—

(1.) The local alterations of temperature in neuralgias, during the paroxysms of pain.

(2.) Observations on temperature in paralysed parts.[1]

(3.) Observations on variations of temperature in those forms of disease which are considered as vaso-motor neuroses.

(4.) The effect of mental exertion, or excitement in elevating the temperature in cases of disease, the effect of different kinds of delirium, and the moderation of febrile temperature, which is sometimes observed after a quiet sleep.

---

[1] Mr. Earle published a paper entitled " Cases and Observations Illustrating the Influence of the Nervous System in Regulating Animal Heat," in vol. vii, of the ' Medico-Chirurgical Transactions' (1816), in which the following cases appear sufficiently interesting to justify quotation:—

CASE I.—A sailor had paralysis of the left arm after an injury. The temperature of the right (uninjured) hand was 92° (F.), of the left (or paraly-

(5.) The great elevation of temperature in acute (rapid) inflammation of the brain.

(6.) The more enormous elevation of temperature in injuries destructive of the spinal cord.

(7.) The very disproportionate rise of temperature at the end of tetanus and other fatal neuroses.

These facts are indeed very favourable (völlig genügend) to the theory that a large share in the regulation of heat belongs, at least in

tic) hand only 70° (F.) ; after electricity for ten minutes it rose to 74° (F.). On another occasion the temperatures were,

		Before electricity.	After electricity.
Paralysed limb	Hand	71°	77°
	Arm (at elbow)	80°	83½°
	Axilla	92°	93°
Healthy limb	Hand	92°	92°
	Arm (at elbow)	95°	95¼°
	Axilla	96°	96°

CASE II.—Excision of portion of ulnar nerve (about one inch) for neuralgia. Five years after the cleft between little and ring fingers of that hand $= 57°$; other parts of hand 62°. Between little and ring fingers of other hand 60° ; other parts of hand 62°, as before.

He also states that a friend of his examined twenty-five cases of paralysis in the Bath Hospital, and always found the paralysed limbs colder than normal. See, also, a paper by *Dr. Yelloly* in vol. iii of same 'Transactions.'

More recently *Mr. Jonathan Hutchinson* has published a series of accurate observations on temperature (inter alia) after injuries to nerves in the 'London Hospital Reports,' vol. iii, p. 305—324. The following results seem especially worthy of selection.

CASE III.—Injury to median nerve supplying the forefinger. Difference of 10° F. (5·5° C.) between that and adjacent thumb.

CASE IV.—Section of ulna and median nerves of right hand—latter partial only. Temperatures—Fourteen weeks after the accident the following remarkable difference was noted : " Cleft between little and ring-fingers, left 83; right (paralysed) 64°" $= 19°$ F. $= 10·4$ C. Twenty-one months after there was still 10° difference in this situation, and 5° between the right and left hands in the cleft between fore and middle fingers—the paralysed parts being that much colder.

He records other cases with a difference of 2°, 4°, 5°, 9°, 10°, 11°, &c. See also a case of injury to cervical spine, in a boy aged 6, under *Dr. Fraser's* care (in the 'London Hospital Reports,' vol. ii, p. 365). I myself saw a case of division of the *median* nerve, in which nine months after there was a difference of 13° between the healthy and paralysed hand (between the middle fingers—the paralysed $= 75°$, the other 88°). Dr. Powell kindly verified this for me.—[TRANS.]

complex cases, to the nervous system.   The influence of certain
nerve-tracks on the activity of the heart on the one side, and on the
circulation on the other, is indeed indubitable.   On this account it
may be safely assumed, that alterations in the amount of blood in
the peripheral vessels, influence in more ways than one the warmth
of the places concerned, and of the general temperature also.

A great part of the pathological phenomena of warmth, may
be only the expression of the action (verhalten) of the vaso-
motor nerves.   And, perhaps, even in actual diseases of the
nervous system, the fluctuations of temperature, particularly if
slight, must be attributed to an alteration in the circulation.   But
we learn from another series of observations, those namely with
enormous elevation of temperature, that some hitherto unknown
power has sway over animal heat, since the most remarkable
alterations of temperature occur with profound disturbances of the
nervous system, without corresponding anomalies of circulation, and
it is perhaps not too much to affirm that the integrity of certain
parts of the central nervous apparatus is more necessary for the
regulation of animal heat, than that of any other parts of the body.

§ 19. *Muscular exertions* generally cause a very considerable
rise of temperature, in cases where there is any previously existing
morbid condition, however slight.   On this account *we are quite
justified in feeling anxiety about the health of any one whose temperature exceeds the normal after only moderate exercise, however
cheerful and apparently well he may seem in other respects.*

During convalescence, however, the temperature generally rises
one or more degrees (Centigrade = 1·8° Fahr. or more) on the first
occasion of rising from bed, and sitting up, even when this has not
been permitted at all too soon.   If the sitting up has been disproportionate to the strength of the patient [*i. e.*, too long at any one
time], the temperature generally rises again, so that in this way we
have a useful criterion as to how far we may allow the patient to
relinquish his couch.   In confirmation of my own publications on
the enormous elevation of temperature in the fatal termination of
cases of tetanus, *Leyden* in 1863 ('Beiträge zur Pathologie des
Tetanus,' in Virchow's ' Archiv,' xxvi, 538), and *Billroth* and *Fick*
in the same year ('Versuche über die Temperaturen bei Tetanus,' in
the 'Schweizerische Vierteljahrschrift,' viii, 427) instituted experiments on animals, which they artificially tetanised, and found that

the temperature in these cases was increased as much as $5°$ or $6°$ C. $(= 9°—10\cdot8°$ Fahr.).

The removal of a sick person, and the sum-total of the influences then brought to bear upon him [$i. e.$, the mental and physical conditions induced by the transfer of the patient], have almost always a disturbing effect upon the temperature, and it is about equally common to find a rise of temperature, or a reduction of a previously high one. It may therefore be laid down as a rule, that an observation of temperature taken immediately after the removal of a patient to a fresh place [admission into a hospital ward, or after a journey of any kind] is by no means decisive.[1]

An athlete, who whilst running a (foot) race, became faint and insensible, and was brought into my wards, showed a very remarkable rise of temperature in consequence of his strenuous muscular exertions. His temperature was $40\cdot5$ C. ($104\cdot9°$ F.), and his pulse 128 per minute. The urine contained $\frac{1}{10}$th of its volume of albumen. Two hours afterwards the temperature had fallen to $39\cdot1°$ C. ($102\cdot38°$ F.) On the second morning the temperature was normal, and remained so, whilst the albumen in the urine rapidly diminished, and after a few days entirely disappeared.[2]

On the share which post-mortem rigidity of muscles takes in the temperature of the dead body, see further on.

§ 20. It seems almost superfluous to remark, that this enumeration of the influences which affect the temperature is by no means exhaustive. For not only is the material furnished us by

[1] The author does not of course mean that *no* importance is to be attached to a high temperature, or a low one, after removal of a patient—the preceding paragraph (in italics) forbids this—but simply that for purposes of prognosis, or even diagnosis, we must reject such temperatures, or at all events give them a subordinate value—since the mere *transport* of the patient is sufficient, in his weak condition, to disturb his temperature—either from the muscular exertion, or the mental excitement—or the exposure to cold or heat, &c.—[TRANS.]

[2] Dr. Robert Barnes, in his clinical lectures at the London Hospital, laid special stress upon the development of a febrile state, by excessive uterine (muscular) action—especially in delicate women—and adduced this as one of the best arguments for skilled interference in protracted labour. I remember a lad of nineteen who walked seventy miles in two days, who had a temperature of $105°$, with a pulse of 130 next day, with enormous quantities of lithates in the urine. In three days his temperature was normal. Another youth, a little older, walked from Dover to London in about the same time, and was similarly affected.—[TRANS.]

experiment and clinical observation to be regarded in all its detail, and in every possible point of view [*lit.* in its infinite nuances], but there are also, no doubt, numerous real causes (Ursachen) of alteration of temperature, as yet quite unknown, or only partially anticipated.

This is especially true of the original causes of altered temperature in the diseases which are said to arise spontaneously, and also in many which originate in contagion (Infectionskrankheiten). It is very evident that the more or less extensive tissue-changes which occur in severe diseases, and especially those complete destructions of the parenchyma of organs, which have lately become accessible, as it were, to improved methods of research, must have a very important share in the production of high temperatures. It is, however, very difficult to accurately investigate them, on account of the complexity of the phenomena. It is also very apparent that changes in the *blood* itself, processes akin to fermentation, often occur, which are equally capable of increasing the amount of heat produced; as, on the other hand, some things in the blood may contribute to limit the chemical processes on which the warmth-production depends, and either to hinder or promote the giving off or loss of heat.

But from this general idea of the possibility or probability of the influence on the temperature of morbid processes in the tissues or blood no particular good results at present. We cannot indicate the special chemical processes which influence the production of heat; we cannot say why the temperature is such and such in one form of disease, or why it differs from that of another disease. We ask in vain why in many severe disturbances in the economy, accompanied with very extensive (reichlicher) tissue changes, the temperature, as a rule, remains normal. Sometimes the absence of any influence on the temperature appears to depend upon the slow and tedious development of the changes, and in such cases the commencement of a change in the temperature either heralds the approach of a complication, or indicates the more rapid development of a previously existing morbid process.

On the other hand, in some affections of remarkable chronicity, alterations of temperature may be noted for months, and even years, and these not inconsiderable ('Forms of Chronic Fever').

Moreover, we must not forget, that for the most part we are accustomed to observe only the results of two factors, namely, that of warmth-production, and that of the giving-off, or loss of warmth, and not the factors themselves, so that many a case of over-production of heat may escape observation, because the giving-off of heat is simultaneously increased.   So that a previously existing over-production of heat may suddenly become noticeable on account of some subordinate influence on the parts which give off heat, whereas before it had been latent, on account of a satisfactory compensation.

§ 21. Besides the external influence mentioned, and in addition to processes occurring in the organism itself, there are also *individual circumstances and surroundings*, which have their share in causing deviations of temperature, and especially in affecting the facility with which they occur, and the extent of the variations themselves. Whether the disease which affects the patient necessarily modifies the temperature in itself or not, we may remark in almost every sick person, a greater sensitiveness to accidental influences.   Even when the temperature has been unaffected by the disease, the most varied influences will seem to disturb the equilibrium, and may sometimes cause very considerable rises or falls of temperature.   These may either be partial, or extend over the whole body.   Diseases in which the temperature is always affected, exhibit a similar sensitiveness and mobility of temperature.   Yet there is a great difference in the degree of sensitiveness to accidental influences.   The more decidedly typical, regular, and uncomplicated the course of a disease is, the less is it affected by accidental influences.   On the other hand, in a typical form of disease, in slight cases of illness, and in such as constantly admit of deviations from other causes, accidental influences operate most markedly.   The severity and stage of the disease affects the stability of the temperature; or in other words, its dependency upon accidental influences.   At the real commencement of an acute typical disease, outward influences affect it but little; the less decisive the symptoms which usher it in, the greater effect external influences will have.   Mild cases of disease are chiefly thus affected from their commencement, to about their acmé.   In the further progress of the disease, there is also a distinction as regards the mobility of temperature, in response to external influences.   The more variations the disease itself exhibits, the longer convalescence is protracted, the greater effect of these on the temperature, whilst in rapid recovery very powerful external influences are often quite powerless to disturb the temperature. In convalescence, the outward influences often become once more of considerable importance, but especially when convalescence is only partially established, and when the embers of the disease are, as it were, still smouldering.

The direction in which an accidental influence tends, is not unimportant [*i. e.*, whether it tends to raise or lower the temperature]. If this is in the same direction as the natural course of the disease at the time, the effect is all the more certain : if the operation of the cause is in an opposite direction, the effect is less certain. Even the "daily fluctuation" has an influence in this point of view. Circumstances which *raise* the temperature operate most certainly at noon, and in the afternoon, whilst those which *depress* the temperature, act most surely at night or in the early morning.

§ 22. Apart from all previously existing or special morbid conditions, the degree of sensitiveness to accidental influences on temperature is very varied in different persons.

In *children* the temperature exhibits great mobility in disease. Not only do slight ailments induce a great amount of disturbance, and not only are the daily fluctuations greater than in older patients, but influences of all kinds also have a more powerful effect.

In the *female sex*, even in adult life, there is a resemblance to children in this respect. Indeed great mobility of temperature is most perfectly developed in women. Apparently causeless elevations of temperature occur in them with the rapidity of the recoil of a spring, and outward accidents exert a wholly unusual influence. This is especially seen in those individuals who exhibit the nervous temperament (hysterical persons, and the like).

In the *male sex*, also, we find certain individuals, whose temperature is far more impressionable by external influences than that of others, and in general these also are of the nervous temperament.

Men of *advanced age* differ in this respect from younger adults. It is more common to meet with a sluggish course of temperature in them, than with increased susceptibility. In very old people, it is common in various diseases, to find the temperature half a degree or more (C. = $\frac{2}{10}°$ Fahr.) lower than is common in similar circumstances in younger people.

Individual susceptibility is also sometimes strongly shown under certain influences, and but slightly under others. This may depend upon many personal peculiarities (idiosyncrasies) ; and it appears very clear that, on the one hand, repetition of certain influences may augment the sensibility of the temperature, whilst on the other hand the repetition of certain influences may weaken, or blunt this susceptibility.

CHAPTER VII.

ON LOCAL ALTERATIONS OF TEMPERATURE; AND ALTERATIONS OF THE GENERAL TEMPERATURE IN DIFFERENT DISEASES.

§ 1. THE variations from the normal temperature occurring in sick people, are partly local, confined to special regions of the body, and partly general, that is, extending more or less over the whole body.

This antithesis must not be interpreted too strictly. It is very seldom, perhaps never the case, that with any considerable local alteration of temperature, that of the whole body remains perfectly normal in all respects, not only as regards its absolute height, but as regards its stability and freedom from fluctuations (Festigkeit und Unveränderlichkeit), notwithstanding adverse influences.

On the other hand, when the general temperature is much affected, it is very seldom that the increased heat is distributed quite impartially over all the different regions of the body. Indeed, in the commencing period of the disturbance of temperature, and afterwards when it is still more affected, the contrast, as regards warmth, between various parts of the same body, is often well-marked.

But the contrast between local and general alterations of temperature is sufficiently indicated by the fact, that sometimes the one and sometimes the other is the most important.

§ 2. Since even in health, different parts of the same body differ from one another in their temperature, in disease the contrasts are still more marked.

The temperature may be locally elevated, in contrast with other parts of the body, or with even the general temperature; or it may be lower in one part than that of the rest of the body. Although it has been rendered indubitable by separate observations, that some local elevations of temperature in parts specially affected, actually exceed the temperature of the blood, although only very slightly, yet in other cases it is certain, and in very many others at least possible, that the local rise of temperature is only apparent, and that the parts with high temperature only exhibit the degree of blood-heat more perfectly than other accessible regions of the body. We must not overlook the fact, that we do not accurately know the temperature of the blood, and that that is possibly even higher than our observations taken in the most sheltered spots appear to show; and if Brown-Séquard's previously quoted opinion on the true temperature of human viscera be confirmed, this will very seldom be found exceeded by any local elevation. The local increase of heat in so far as it is a more complete exponent of the true blood-heat, may depend either on a freer access of blood to the part, or of a less perfect degree of cooling, or on both combined.

§ 3. *Local elevations of temperature* have been met with in the following conditions—

(*a*). In inflammations.

According to theory, and the subjective feelings of the patient, and even when estimated by the objective method of laying the observer's hand on the inflamed part, there is a very considerable elevation of temperature in a part which is inflamed, and this opinion has gained general credence. Direct measurements [by the thermometer] have however shown that this does not always occur, and that the local elevations of temperature which are sometimes met with, are even then very moderate in amount.

We owe the first observation of increased local temperature from inflammation to *John Hunter,* as has been remarked previously. After an operation for hydrocele, he found the temperature of the tunica vaginalis to be 92° F. (= 33·33° C.). "The cavity was filled with lint, dipped in salve." The next day the temperature was found to be 98¾° F. (= 37·1° C.); which was indeed a very considerable elevation of temperature, yet not exceeding that of the blood.

John Hunter made many similar observations, yet in experiments which he made on animals, after artificially induced inflammation, he did not discover any alterations of the local temperature.

Numerous examples of locally elevated temperatures were published by *Breschet* and *Becquerel* (in 1835, loc. cit.) They were furnished by a thermo-electric apparatus. In a scrofulous girl, the temperature of whose mouth was 37·5° C. (99·5° F.), they remarked in an inflamed glandular swelling in the neck a temperature of 40° C. (104° F.) In other cases there was also a difference between the heat of inflamed parts, and the general temperature. Yet it was always much less than that above. Many doubts however have been raised against the accuracy of these experiments.[1]

Gierse's experiments show an increase of heat in inflamed parts amounting to half or even a whole degree Centigrade (= ·9 to 1·8° F.).

Bärensprung found no rise of temperature in an artificially induced erythema, but in a case of crural phlebitis he found the temperature in the patient's diseased thigh, at the lower part, 1° R. (= 2·25° Fah.) hotter than in the healthy limb.

John Simon has published some very important observations in Holmes' 'System of Surgery,' 1860, article, "Inflammation," vol. i, p. 43 [2nd edition, 1870, vol. i, p. 18, &c.] They were made by the help of a thermo-electric apparatus [of platinum and iron, connected with a galvanometer, devised by Dr. Edward Montgomery]. Mr. Simon found—

(1). "That the *arterial blood* supplied to an inflamed limb is less warm than the focus of inflammation itself;

(2). "That the *venous blood* returning from an inflamed limb, though less warm than the focus of inflammation, is warmer than the arterial blood supplied to the limbs; and

(3). "That the venous blood returning from an *inflamed* limb, is warmer than the corresponding current on the opposite side of the body."[2]

Billroth and *Hufschmidt* only obtained negative results. The figures are added up incorrectly in the original. But it appears from the observations themselves, that in 37 comparative measurements of temperature in a wound and in the rectum, the heat of the wound was less than that of the rectum 28 times; the two temperature were alike 8 times, and the temperature was only once higher

[1] Especially by *Helmholtz*, and *Ludwig*. See note to *Mr. Simon's* article, quoted above.

[2] Mr. Simon's article on "Inflammation" gives a very interesting *résumé* of what is known of the relations of temperature and inflammation. The same volume of the 'System of Surgery' also gives charts of the temperature in tetanus, traumatic fever, &c., &c.

in the wound (by $0.3°$ C. $= 0.54°$ F.) than in the rectum, after the wound had been irritated by turpentine.

In 9 comparative observations on the temperature of an inflamed vagina and that of the rectum, the temperature of the vagina was 5 times lower than the rectal; both temperatures were alike 3 times, and once the temperature of the vagina was $\frac{2}{10}°$ C. ($= 0.36°$ F.) higher than that of the rectum.

Billroth remarks, that although hyperæmic parts may on that account appear warmer, because there is greater fullness of the blood-vessels, than in healthy parts, yet there is not necessarily any greater production of warmth in the inflamed parts.

In four observations on a man suffering from a very extensive diffused abscess in the subcutaneous connective tissue (diffused cellulitis) the temperature of the wound was lower than that of the rectum or axilla.

O. Weber in 1864 published a number of observations in the 'Deutsche Klinik' (Nos. 43 and 44), which, however, furnish equally dubious results. In 12 thermometric observations on men suffering from wounds (from operations) the temperature of the wounds was six times higher, three times lower, and three times the same as that of the mouth and the axilla. However in the first class of cases the temperature was only $\frac{6}{10}°$ C. ($= 1.08°$ F.) in favour of the wound. It was also noticeable that the temperature of the wound was most markedly elevated where the superficies of the wound lay somewhat protected, and towards the interior; whereas when the wound was in an exposed part, it was much less— owing perhaps to cooling and evaporation. He also remarked that with continued and profused suppuration, the temperature of the wound decreased.

In a series of 31 experiments on dogs and rabbits, the thermometric observations showed the warmth of the wounds (or inflamed parts) to be higher than that of the rectum 9 times, equal to it 6 times, and less warm 15 times. The maximum difference in favour of the wound was $1°$ C. ($1.8°$ F.) in rabbits, and $0.35°$ C. ($= 0.63°$ F.) in dogs. Besides this, *O. Weber* has repeated and confirmed *Simon's* experiments, and agrees with Simon's conclusions.

We may at least conclude from these experiments that the greatest heat in inflamed parts only exhibits a moderate rise of temperature—and it still remains open to discussion, how much is due to hyperæmia, and how much to true local production of heat, respectively. In a great number of cases there was no increased heat in the wound, and it was much more common to meet with a lower temperature than that of the rectum.

Jacobson and *Bernhardt* (1868, 'Centralbl. Orig. Mitth.,' p. 643) have also pointed out that the temperature in inflamed serous cavities (pleura and peritoneum) may be *lower* than the heat of the same parts when healthy, or than the temperature of the heart.

So also *Landien* (1869, 'Centralblatt Orig. Mitth., p. 291) found that the temperature of the skin, however deeply inflamed, and that of the muscles, even in their deepest layers, was never so high as the temperature of the interior of the body, and he found [in opposition to Simon] the temperature of the arterial blood higher than that of the focus of inflammation to which it was streaming.

(*b*). That an elevated temperature may be caused by simple hyperæmia, or at least a temperature relatively high under the circumstances, in relation to other parts of the surface of the body, appears from the above quoted experiments on division of the sympathetic, with ligature of the subclavian, and of suspending animals by their hind legs. In the human subject, however, we have no trustworthy observation of a rise of temperature through simple hyperæmia : and it is particularly to be noted, that the local application of mustard does not cause a rise of temperature.

(*c*). In the *exanthemata*, the inflamed parts of the body appear to show a higher temperature than those parts free from the ex- anthem, as the experience of *Gierse* and Bärensprung indicates.

(*d*). In *neuralgiæ*, and local *cramps*, the temperature of the skin of the painful or cramp-affected part, appears to be somewhat raised ; which generally coincides with great reddening of the skin, and must apparently be attributed to increased afflux of blood, but perhaps also to local diminution of cooling, although in cramps there may very well be increased warmth-production.

(*e*). As regards *paralysed parts*, *Schmitz* has observed a slight diminution of temperature ; *Bärensprung* also, in four cases, found the temperature of the paralysed parts less in three cases, and a trifle higher in one case, than in the healthy parts. *Nothnagel* (Berliner 'Klinische Wochenschrift,' 1867, p. 537) found in the hollow of the hand of a paralytic arm a temperature of 2° C. (= 3·6° F.) *lower* than in the healthy side. [See also note to page 152 for experi- ments of Earle, Hutchinson, and others.]

On the other hand, *Folet* (in the 'Gaz. Hebdom.,' Nos. 12 and 14 for 1867) made continuous observations on hemiplegic patients, and came to the following conclusions—

(1). In the immense majority of cases, the commencement of hemiplegia is accompanied with an increased temperature on the affected side ; both sides are very seldom alike, and a diminished temperature on the diseased side is hardly ever noticed.

(2). The rise of temperature varies between $\frac{3}{10}°$ and $\frac{9}{10}°$ C. ($\cdot54°$ and $1\cdot62°$ F.) but seldom exceeds $1°$ C. ($= 1\cdot8°$ F.).

(3). The presence or absence of contractions has no influence on the thermometric results.

(4). The thermometric difference may be greatly augmented by various primary causes.

(5). The original cause of the hemiplegia has no effect upon the result (?).

(6). Recovery from the paralysis tends to equalize the temperature again : if the paralysis continues, the height of the temperature varies greatly, and in one case may return to the normal in a few months; in others, may continue unequal for even years together.

(7). Undoubtedly paralytic atrophy necessitates depression of temperature.

(8). In an old hemiplegia, when the affected side exhibits a high temperature, and the other side becomes paralysed at a later date, either the two sides become equalized in temperature, or the side last paralysed now becomes considerably hotter.

(9). The general temperature of hemiplegic patients is not usually above the normal, but exhibits an average height of $37°$ C. ($98\cdot6°$ F.), except in the last hours of life, when it generally rises.

Lepine ('Gazette Méd.,' 1868, p. 501) states that he has found—

(*a*). That in a recent case of hemiplegia, the paralysed limb is at first warmer than the healthy one; and on exposure to a certain amount of cold, loses more heat than the sound one ; with a still greater degree of cooling, however, it loses less heat than the other.

(*b*). On the other hand, in a very old case of hemiplegia, the paralysed limb appears colder than the other, but remains relatively warmer than the healthy one when exposed to cold, and with artificial heat becomes less warm than the sound limb, thus exhibiting less extensive fluctuations either upwards or downwards under external thermal influences.[1]

FIG. 1.

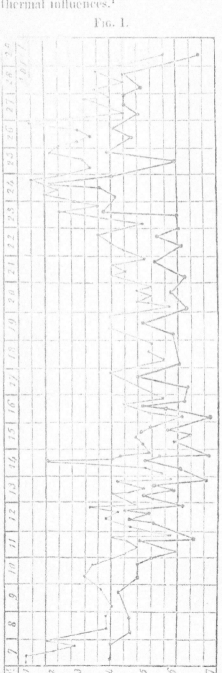

§ 4. An *increased temperature* extending *all over one half of the body* without any evidence of any local diseased process going on on either side of the body, has been many times, and very persistently observed by me, in a person suffering from apparently hysterical spinal disease.

This girl, who was 18 years old, was often attacked with partial (*i. e.*, right-sided) hyperæmias, and urticoid eruptions, local sweatings, and very changeable and varied symptoms in different internal organs. Besides this, at other times than the local hyperæmias of the skin, she exhibited all over the surface of the body, from $\frac{1}{5}$ to $\frac{1}{2}$ C. ($= \cdot 36°$ to $\cdot 9°$ F.) higher temperature than in the vagina; in the

[1] If these observations should be confirmed by further experience (as I believe they will, for the most part), it is clear that our means of diagnosis in cases of feigned or doubtful paralysis, have received a valuable addition. I believe, myself, that the temperature mainly depends on the amount of cerebral or spinal irritation, or in other words, on the more or less active changes going on in the central portions of the nervous system, at or around the seat of the lesion.—[Trans.]

right axilla (as well as in the right groin) there was a persistently higher temperature than in the left; the difference being sometimes only a few tenths of a degree (Centigrade), sometimes as much as $1 \cdot 1^\circ$ C. ($= 2 \cdot 7^\circ$ F.).

There were occasional, apparently purposeless (unmotivirte) elevations of temperature as much as to $39 \cdot 5^\circ$ C. ($103 \cdot 1^\circ$ F.); through which the temperature of the two sides was sometimes approximated, and sometimes still more discrepant.

This very remarkable behaviour of the temperature, which lasted almost a year (and of which the accompanying curve (fig. 1), represents a short period) could scarcely mean anything else but a disturbance of the vaso-motor nervous system, which whilst it affected both sides, affected the right much more than it did the left.

§ 5. More or less extensive *partial depressions* of temperature, occur pretty commonly, especially in mortified (gangrenous) parts, also in œdematous and indurated conditions, and in disused parts of the body [ausser Activität gesetzten Körperstellen—probably the author means in limbs disabled by accident, or paralysis, or purposely kept inactive, as in the limbs tied up by fakirs, or impostors], and especially whenever the access of blood to a part is diminished, or its cooling becomes excessive. In direct contrast to the internal temperature which is often excessively high, the surface of the body often shows more or less extreme depression of temperature, particularly after cold applications, in febrile rigors, and in all collapsed conditions. It would however be very erroneous to regard the partial depression of temperature in these cases as an isolated phenomena, it ought indeed rather to be regarded as part of a very complicated process.

§ 6. It need scarcely be remarked that *alterations of the general temperature* are the most important phenomena in pathological thermometry whether we regard them theoretically, or practically.

The temperatures taken in either the axilla, vagina, or rectum (provided these are not affected by any local processes of disease) approximate as closely as is possible in a living man, to the temperature of the blood, and also to the general temperature of the individual.

This general temperature (Temperatur des Gesammtkörpers) in its manifold, and often extremely rapid changes, is not the only standard we possess, but it is at least a very delicate gauge (Mass-stab) for the general condition of the system (Allgemeinver-halten) in disease.

Then the question immediately occurs—what importance ought we to attach to the general condition of the system? and further, what are the processes which are connected with the temperature?

The general condition in diseases (setting aside new growths [neoplasms]), and the loss or severe injuries of parts essential or very important to life, and the obliteration or closing of channels (Canälen) which cannot safely be dispensed with [urethra, alimen-tary canal, thoracic duct, &c., &c.], and some other conditions of overwhelming local importance (Einflusse), is of all other things the most important in furnishing us with rules for safely prognosticating and judging of the fate of a patient, or the course and duration of his disease, and his prospect of recovery or dissolution.   And it is just the same in practical therapeutics, which has its strongholds (Angriffspunkte) not in the local disturbances which so frequently give a name to the disease [e. g. pneumonia], but in the general condition of the system, which our therapeutic helps must assist and direct.   Here also exceptions must be made, as regards determinate (causalen) urgent symptomatic, and specially important topical indica-tions.   (I may refer here to my treatise ' Ueber die Nothwendigkeit einer exacteren Beachtung der Gesammtconstitution bei Beurthei-lung und Behandlung der Kranken," in the ' Archiv der Heilkunde,' 1860, Bd. i, 97. [On the importance of particular attention to the General Constitution of the Patient, in the diagnosis and treat-ment of Disease.]   When all this has been more or less fully conceded, we are still met by the difficulty of discovering how far the fluctuations of the general temperature depend upon certain organic processes.   On what fixed laws does the temperature depend?   How can we explain the fact that some disturbances which undoubtedly affect the whole organism do not alter the temperature? whilst on the other hand others invariably do so? What forces (Motive) determine the varieties of temperature? Where are the regulators which, even in sickness, keep these within certain limits?   In my opinion no definite answer can be given as yet to these questions,[1] and we must be satisfied for the

---

[1] Nach meiner Meinung sind alle diese Fragen nicht spruchreif.

present to deduce empirical rules from the copious stores of experience. But only the most painstaking and comprehensive study of the special details of the subject can place us in a position to extract from them the common principles which are illustrated by the normal course of disease.

CHAPTER VIII.

ON THE TYPICAL FORMS OF CONSTITUTIONAL AFFECTIONS ASSOCIATED WITH ALTERATION OF TEMPERATURES.

§ 1. In many diseased conditions, the anomalies of temperature consist solely in its *increased mobility*. Very slight influences suffice to determine very considerable deviations from the normal heat of the body; the daily fluctuations show a wider "excursus" [or range of temperature]; and when slight accidental disturbances of general health occur, they are associated with unusual, though brief elevations of temperature, or with similar depressions; and the increase or decrease of heat often takes place in an apparently spontaneous, and purposeless manner, either as an isolated pheno-menon, or recurring in an entirely anomalous fashion. Such changes often vanish as casually, and as inexplicably as they appeared. The diseased conditions in which the temperature exhibits this behaviour, are very numerous—and do not consist merely in well-marked, definite diseases to which we can give names, but also in very many conditions in which no accurate diagnosis is possible, and in which it is only possible to recognize a disturbance in the general health. Cases of slight illness (Kränklichkeit), general irritability, persistent feelings of lassitude, slight disturb-ances of all the [bodily] functions, impaired digestion, imperfect respiration, convalescence, &c. The actual and well-defined diseases in which these occur, are usually chronic in their nature, confined within certain limits, or so slightly developed, that extreme anomalies of temperature do not occur, or they are brief intervals of not quite undisturbed repose intervening between the phenomena of severe disease (nicht ganz reinen Pausen—"not quite pure pauses"); or the "residua" (so to speak) of various morbid affections; or they may be diseases of short duration and of moderate severity; or lastly, they may be fresh complications, which do not conform to rule, and only produce lasting or considerable alterations of temperature, when they become intensified.

§ 2. It is not unusual to meet with cases, in which the *temperature of a patient remains a little above the normal*, either persistently, or in the form of a nightly rise.

In addition to this, we may have the increased mobility previously mentioned, and also isolated and apparently causeless elevations of temperature. This "course" of temperature also occurs in ill-pronounced disturbances of health, in convalescents (especially after articular rheumatism); in the decline of various affections, as for example, after the exacerbations which occur in phthisis, as well as in many sub-acute, and pre-eminently atypical forms of disease.

It is far less common to meet with cases in which the temperature takes the *descending* type, and remains constantly *below the normal*, or is so at least in the morning hours. And in these cases also, either with or without recognized cause, the temperature may sometimes exhibit intercurrent elevations. This form of temperature also is met with in chronic, and declining diseases, principally in such as are marked with the character of inanition, in marasmus, cases of cancer, in diabetes, and extreme degrees of anæmia, only exceptionally in phthisis; in cases of mental disease according to *Williams* ('Medical Times,' 1867, No. 896) both in the stage of depression, and in chronic, uncomplicated, though incurable forms; and, according to *Wolff*, especially in melancholia attonita [Lypemania].

§ 3. In real, though not very apparent relation to these less conspicuous alterations of temperature (*i. e.*, approximating to these through their "middle term," which one may place either above or below the normal line) we may consider those constitutional affections which are connected with alterations of temperature, *which assume definite and characteristic types*. These are generally much more strongly marked, and are generally separated by a sharp line of demarcation from the ordinary course of health.

Such definite general types, in which constitutional anomalies specially affect the temperature, are illustrated by—

(*a*). Rigors (Fieberfrost).

(*b*). Fever-heats [flushings, hot stages of fever], pyrexia.

(*c*). Collapse.

It would be a great error to suppose that alterations of temperature are the sole characteristics of these pathological processes. Each of them forms a complex assemblage of manifold and more or less essential phenomena. Every one of them is a condition of the entire body, in which every organ and every particle (Punkt) of the body has its share, and the share of each is infinitely "many-sided" (und dieser Antheil bietet unendlich viele Seiten dar). The physiology of rigors, of febrile heat (pyrexia), and of collapse, is as comprehensive, and as little comprehensible, as the physiology of healthy men; indeed far less so, because confirmation from experiments is almost entirely wanting. In this complexity, our purpose is chiefly to regard the part played by temperature. As to other phenomena, they will only be considered so far as is necessary to the comprehension of the subject.

§ 4. During a rigor (Fieberfrost) when well marked, we usually find the general temperature of the body very greatly increased (amounting usually to about 40° C. (104°), or even more); on the other hand, the parts of the extremities which are farthest from the trunk (the hands, forearm, feet, and the legs below the knees), and also parts of the face (nose, chin, ears, and frequently the forehead), very commonly show more or less considerable decrease of warmth. Along with this contrast of the high temperature of the trunk, and the heat of the body generally, with the coldness of the parts named above, there is experienced a subjective feeling of chilliness (shivers), which is often very extreme.

Several other phenomena are associated with this, the most constant being pallor of the skin, with bluish (cyanotic) coloration of the nails and some other parts, automatic and convulsive movements (yawning, chattering of the teeth, tremblings, &c.), thirst, headache, and extreme malaise, and colorless, watery urine.

As a rule, rigors occur in the beginning of a febrile disease, or of an accession of fever, but by no means exactly at the commencement of the rise of temperature in the trunk, the increased temperature generally preceding the rigors a little (see fig. 2.) As soon as the heat has exceeded the previous temperature (whether that has been normal, sub-normal, or sub-febrile), either a little, or it may be by nearly 2° C. (3·6° F.), during which the warmth of the extremities, and of certain parts of the face, has not kept pace with that of the trunk, and has indeed even fallen; the phenomena of chilliness set in, and increase in intensity with the rise of temperature of the trunk, till the increased heat has extended to the nose and the fingers and toes.

Then the phenomena of the "cold stage" disappears. Shortly after they cease; they can, however, be rapidly re-induced, simply by exposure of the hands, arms, or feet, which causes rapid cooling.

When the temperature, after reaching its maximum (which may occur in the rigor itself, or in the succeeding hot stage), begins to fall again, there is, as a rule, not a trace of the feelings of chilliness, or of the phenomena peculiar to rigors; and it seems to make no difference in this respect, whether the sinking is rapid or protracted, whether the temperature becomes nor-

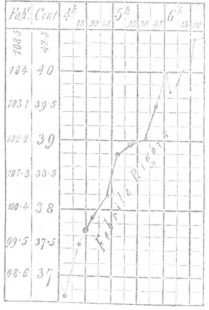

Fig. 2.

mal or remains above it, or whether it sinks below normal, and the case goes on into collapse.

This is the usual progress (Verhalten) of a rigor ["cold stage"], especially in those cases in which it attains its fullest and most decided development, and runs a well-defined course of half an hour to two hours.

But in forming a right opinion on the subject of rigors, we must not overlook those forms which are less marked in their commencement (initial stages) and their indications; those rarer modifications, and less perfect forms, which often occur. In overlooking these, we lose, as it were, the key to the whole process.

We must bear in mind those rigor-like phenomena, which occasionally occur in very nervous people, without any alteration of temperature at all (nervöser Frost). We may grant that the latter pursue no definite course, and therefore our experience of these gives us little insight into the actual significance of the phenomenon; but at least they show us, that all the other phenomena of rigors may occur without any objective alteration of temperature.

With these we must associate those cases, in which a severe rigor occurs after any sudden impression made on some sensitive spot (which most commonly occurs during the passing of a catheter). In this case, there are either no objective alterations of temperature, or they are at all events inconsiderable, and these cases must also be ranked with nervous rigors.

Very similar symptoms often show themselves immediately after the introduction of toxic agents into the blood, without actual objective alteration of temperature.[1]   So also in slightly indicated and rudimentary developments of a true rigor (chilliness, shiverings, "cold water running down the back," &c.), the objective coldness of the extremities is very often wanting, or but very trifling, whilst the rise of temperature in the trunk makes rapid progress.   Pallor of the skin is often absent: and indeed there is sometimes nothing at all objective to be noticed about the patient, whilst he himself has a decided feeling like a rigor: and these, in delicate and susceptible personages, may easily pass into severe rigors under the influence of slightly unfavorable circumstances.[2]

But rigors also occur occasionally with falling temperatures— collapse, rigors; these are, however, for the most part, imperfectly developed, or have some other origin than the fall of temperature, probably identical with that of nervous rigors.

But there are some cases of rigors which occur in the very midst of an elevated temperature, occasionally without any fresh exciting cause, and usually without the extremities being chilled, as for example in pyæmic patients.   It must specially be noticed, that whilst the

---

[1] The convulsions of epilepsy, and [the so-called] uræmic poisoning, ought clearly to be reckoned in this category.   I have traced the history of very many epileptics in whom there was no *history* of convulsions before puberty, and have found that the first "fit" followed the ingestion of an inordinate quantity of alcoholic stimulants in a very large proportion of the cases.—[TRANS.]

[2] It is exceedingly common to meet with imperfect rigors in middle-aged patients living in malarious districts, and in some places not commonly reckoned as such [notably in the East of London]: as many of these patients are women, in whom the catamenia are beginning to be irregular, or ceasing, and the rigors are very imperfectly marked, being chiefly subjective, and described as "heats and flushes" (the chilliness being often absent or very transient), these symptoms are very commonly attributed to "the change of life" even by their medical attendants; and the patient is led to believe that they are either incurable, or at least of uterine or ovarian origin, whereas I believe this pathology to be erroneous, and I know that the symptoms can generally be cured by either quinine, arsenic, or a change of residence.—[TRANS.]

temperature remains high, and in those periods of the disease in which it is making progress, rigors occur more easily than in those periods which either precede or constitute convalescence. The more recent a disease is, the more easily does mere stripping of the body, or a draught of air, prove distressing; and in delicate and sensitive individuals, at such times, rigors are easily and suddenly thus induced, in spite of the high temperature.

Very complete rigors may also occur when the temperature rises rapidly, although the rise may take place from an abnormally low temperature, and may never rise above the normal level. I have seen cases of chronic starvation, in which, so to speak, habitual collapse-temperatures of about $35°$ C. ($= 95°$ F.) were met with, but there was a rise of about $2°$ to $3°$ C. ($= 3·6°$ to $5·4°$ F.) occurring every evening, which raised the temperature just to normal. This evening-rise was very commonly accompanied with strong sensations of cold, shiverings, and "chattering" of the teeth, in spite of the fact that the rise of temperature was only relative. Nor on the other hand, must we overlook the fact, that the temperature of the trunk may rise with equal rapidity, and to as great a height as in a complete rigor (Schüttelfrost), without being accompanied with any subjective feelings of chilliness, and without any other particular phenomenon except that of increased heat. Such simple elevations of temperature very commonly occur once or twice after an intermittent fever has been apparently cut short by quinine; and they may also be noticed in transient accessions of fever, during convalescence, and in many other conditions. The temperature may even rise as high as $41°$ C. ($105·8°$ F.) with equal suddenness, and in a similar manner to a complete rigor; and in intermittents, as well as in the former, may again as rapidly fall. In like manner objective coldness may often be noted in the forearms and hands, the lower part of the legs and feet, along with more or less increased heat in the trunk, without the least feeling of chilliness [on the part of the patient]. It is not therefore the coldness of the extremities and remote parts which causes the feeling of chilliness and the other phenomena of rigors. The extremities may be very cold without a rigor, and they need not be cold (in spite of the one-sided statements often made) even although rigors are present, and indeed this is often the case. Nor is it the increased heat of the trunk which causes a rigor. This may be present to a very great extent, quite as much as in a febrile rigor without this phenomenon. And on the other hand a rigor may occur in cases where the temperature is normal only, or but slightly above it.

Nor do rigors depend merely on the contrast between the high temperature of the trunk and the low temperature of the extremities. This may occur equally in collapse without the feeling of chilliness. And it is absent in nervous rigors.

When the difference between the coldness of the hands and feet and the temperature of the trunk sets in suddenly and continues to increase, this appears to play a far more important part in the constitution of a rigor. It is not when the hands and feet are cold, whilst the trunk is excessively warm, but when the temperature of the trunk rises rapidly, whilst that of the hands and feet remains stationary, or even falls, that a rigor occurs; and especially when with a rapid rise of the internal temperature the warmth of the surface of the body, and particularly of the extremities, is rapidly abstracted in great quantity; then a rigor follows almost instantaneously.

People who go to bed at the very commencement of a severe febrile attack are often attacked with very severe rigors, because the cold bed rapidly abstracts the heat from the surface of their bodies, and thus the contrast between the heat of the interior of their bodies, and the coldness of their extremities and surface (Peripherie) is very quickly intensified.

Yet even the sudden increase of the difference between external and internal temperature will not explain everything; and there are cases of rigors, with both normal and abnormal temperatures, in which there is no fluctuation or alteration of temperature during the rigors (nervous rigors).

All this undoubtedly indicates that a febrile rigor is a complex phenomenon, the several elements in which, viz. the altered temperature, the subjective sensations, and the remaining functional phenomena, do not pursue a parallel course, and are thus not necessarily dependent one upon another. The more perfect, or so to speak normal, the process is, which constitutes a rigor; so much the more perfectly are all the elements not only present, but developed; any one of these may, however, be wanting, whilst the rest may be very strongly developed.

Those cases of rigors where there is a rapid rise of the temperature of the trunk to decidedly febrile or extreme degrees of heat, are usually followed by a longer or shorter hot stage. In the remaining forms of febrile rigors this may be either present or absent.

§ 5. The pyrexia ("hot stage" or fever heat, Fieberhitze) may follow a well-marked rigor, or slight feelings of chilliness; but it may also develop itself out of a normal temperature without the slightest indications of either of these.   Sometimes the pyrexia affords no other result to our means of observation than the mere increase of temperature, which not unfrequently amounts to a rise of $2°$ to $3°$ C. $(3·6° = 5·4°$ F.) or more (as for example in the ephemeral (transient) febrile attacks of convalescence, and in the *paroxysms* of temperature, after the apparent cure of an intermittent fever, &c.).   There may be no subjective feeling of discomfort whatever, no thirst, nor languor (at least if the patient lies in bed), no quickening of the pulse, nor any change in that, nothing unusual in the peripheral circulation, or in the respiration, no altered secretions, and no change in the functions of the nervous system, only the altered temperature. These are facts which all who have used the thermometer much at the bedside must have verified; and facts which are of extreme value in a theoretic point of view.

In other cases, however, besides considerable elevations of temperature, there may be indications of particular complications, which may be easily overlooked on account of their being slight in degree; yet still the phenomenon of abnormal heat bears no special relation to the other symptoms.

In both classes of cases it appears that although the temperature may reach no great height under conditions of perfect repose, and the absence of external influences, yet it generally rises greatly as soon as functional forces [disturbances], or powerful external influences come into play; and then we generally find other and complex phenomena superadded.

In contrast to the cases where there is only an elevation of temperature, we find in the great majority of diseases a complex group of other disturbances of the general health, of functional anomalies, and of varieties of impaired nutrition.   Of these the most striking are alterations of the pulse, of the urinary secretion (which becomes scanty, and, therefore, concentrated), and of respiration; and added to these, subjective feelings of heat, thirst, and loss of appetite, loss of power, malaise, disturbed sleep, and interruption to the continuity of mental operations; the muscular system is affected, and digestion is also impaired—there is a decrease in the number of blood-corpuscles, and in the body-weight. These are the phenomena, which without special disease of the organs concerned, generally accompany the morbid elevation of temperature, and are grouped together by the general name of *fever*.

But in opposition to the loudly expressed opinions of many, I would most emphatically assert that there is generally no exact parallelism between the height of the temperature on the one hand, and the kind and degree of the remaining phenomena on the other, neither regarded as a whole, nor yet as concerns any single phenomenon : that neither the feeling of depression, nor the thirst, nor the quality or frequency of the pulse, nor the pallor or injection of the skin, nor the amount or quality of its secretions, nor the frequency of respiration, nor the quantity or quality of the urine or of any of its ingredients, nor the functions of the nervous system, nor, finally, the diminution in the weight of the body, usually stands in any definite general proportion to the rise of temperature. It is only in a few special forms of disease, that we can establish a relation between the height of the temperature, and this or that morbid symptom, so long as the course of the disease is normal ; but the experience and rules obtained from any special form of disease, cannot be applied indiscriminately to other forms of disease.

This want of congruity between the temperature and the other symptoms of febrile diseases might lead to the conclusion, that the temperature is either no guide at all, or a very deceptive one, to the general condition of the system ; but experience shows, that whatever the kind of sickness may be, a careful observation of the temperature, and of its course, offers a far more reliable stand-point (Anhaltspunkte), or basis for judging the progress of a disease, than any other phenomenon, or even than all the other complex phenomena of fever united. All mere theoretical considerations must be put to silence by this simple empirical fact, although we may be quite unable to explain it.

In the pyrexia of fevers we commonly meet with a general elevation of temperature, but this does not preclude some parts of the body from both appearing and really being warmer than other parts. Not only is the trunk often warmer than the extremities, because they cool more rapidly, but we also notice (what seems contradictory) a similar increase of heat commonly occurring in the head, the ears, the cheeks, and the hands, especially in the palms of the hands. Not only can the increased heat of these parts be noticed earlier than in other places, in contrast to the still slight elevation of the heat of the trunk, and especially so in the cases in which the pyrexia has not been preceded by rigors; but when the febrile movement is only moderate, it is often limited, or almost entirely so to these parts, which generally appear colder during a rigor. During the pyrexia, the height of the temperature may be very varied. This depends, as will be subsequently shown, not only on the intensity of the disease, but also very materially on the kind or type of the disease; and so much so, that in certain kinds of disease, however mild and favorable their course, the temperature reaches an elevation which in other diseases never occurs, or only when the case is exceptionally severe. The conditions which regulate the height of the temperature (die Bedingungen für das Niveau der Temperaturhöhe) seem therefore to be partly determined by the specific nature of the progress of the actual disease. Free perspiration generally diminishes fever-heat very considerably; indeed, in parts which sweat much, the temperature of the skin may fall below normal. But this is a purely local effect, and it entirely depends on circumstances, whether the increased blood heat itself is diminished, or remains the same, or only returns to the normal height with the cessation of the perspiration.

There are some cases of enormously increased temperature, which deviate in many ways from the usual course of pyrexiæ. They are, partially at least, cases of disease in which there is often [for some time] either no pyrexia or but very little, and the tremendous increase of heat generally occurs with the near approach of a fatal termination—the subjective phenomena which generally accompany the pyrexia, are wanting; the functional disturbances of the heart indicate the beginning of paresis, the products of tissue-changes are deficient in the urine. It is doubtful whether we ought to regard these cases as extreme degrees of pyrexia, on account of their frequent and sudden development out of cases where there is no previous fever—or whether we ought to exclude them altogether from the category of fevers.

§ 6. *Collapse* sometimes occurs by itself (isolirt), sometimes in the middle of pyrexiæ of various degrees, very often in the sequelæ of fevers, very seldom during rigors, although these have many phenomena in common with collapse

Collapse is not a disease any more than a rigor, or pyrexiæ. It is a more or less isolated process, occurring in the course of a disease; yet, when it attains a certain degree of severity, it may temporarily acquire an all-absorbing interest, may demand every available remedy for its treatment, and rightly cause us to wholly forget for the moment the disease under which the patient is labouring.

Without doubt, collapse is a symptom which never occurs without very sufficient reasons, but these are such as for the present, receive no elucidation from direct anatomical investigation.

Like rigors and pyrexiæ, it is a general disturbance, affecting the whole of the system. But in spite of its character as a constitutional anomaly, the alterations of temperature occur in collapse, as they do in rigors and pyrexiæ, at first locally only, make themselves visible only in particular places, and extend to the whole body only when the phenomena of collapse are fully developed.

Collapse is more transient and less eventful than pyrexia or even rigors, and when it is relatively protracted, it still forms only an episode, or the last act [of a drama] of relatively short duration. It presents a contrast to pyrexia in many of its phenomena, but it is not essentially the opposite of this, for it may occur in the middle, as it were, of pyrexia, and the fever, although modified by it, pursues further course in company with it.

In the slighter degrees of collapse, the patient conplains of nothing particular, there is no special alteration in his appearance; in company with the preceding period, the fever may persist, or may have ceased; the pulse and respiration present no particular deviation from the previous course, nor does the general condition; but the nose and cheeks are cold, often only locally, and perhaps on one side only, and the coldness may be noticed in the forehead, ears, and hands and feet. Although the circulation in these parts need not be visibly interfered with, although they may not always have been exposed to any greater degree of external cold, than the rest of the body, their temperature is often considerably diminished, without the patient being himself conscious of it. From this first and slightest degree of collapse, there is an almost imperceptible transition (accompanied with an access of more and more numerous and severe symptoms) and extreme degrees of collapse, in which the patient lies pale, sunken, motionless, and almost without signs of life—like a corpse, and perhaps soon to be one in reality; icy-cold, so to speak, both in the head and limbs, and sometimes in the trunk also—with an almost imperceptible pulse, feeble action of the heart, and scarce visible breathing, whilst the skin, which has lost its plumpness, is bedewed notwithstanding, and bathed with a copious perspiration which stands on it in big drops, and almosts pools of sweat—(in grossen Tropfen und Lachen). Unpleasant subjective sensations are sometimes met with in the slighter degrees of collapse, sometimes at the very commencement of the severer forms. Not pain indeed, nor rigors, but generally still more disagreeable feelings—the feeling of the most extreme weakness and faintness (Unmacht), with anxiety, and a sense of oppression (suffocation), with a "beaten feeling" in the limbs, and often thirst also, giddiness, with disordered vision and hearing, and confusion of thought. Collapse often occurs as the immediate sequel to particular events, such as vomiting, profuse diarrhœa, after losses of blood, and with perforations of serous membranes. The collapse in these cases is significant in itself, only just in the degree in which the circumstances which cause it involved anger; when this is not the case, it usually passes off quickly, without any after-consequences. In the same manner the significance of the collapse which accompanies extreme debility (Unmacht) depends upon the original causes which produced it, and upon the particular bodily disorders which accompany it. The collapse of [Asiatic] cholera is generally unusually severe and protracted; it may indeed occur in sporadic cases, both in children and adults, but much more frequently in epidemic and infectious cholera.

In chronic diseases, also, collapse is often observed, either transient or prolonged, and it is not unfrequently repeated.

The kind of collapse which occurs in acute febrile diseases, is of a much more peculiar character. In such cases its beginning is almost imperceptible to the patient; but occasionally he feels a slight shivering, or a general feeling of malaise; and it is generally only when the collapse is deep that very distressing sensations are complained of. In the very beginning of collapse, we may recognise it only by the nose, the chin, the forehead, and the extremities becoming cold; but as soon as the collapse becomes deeper, the face becomes very pale, sometimes yellowish or livid (blue) and the integuments lose their elasticity. The face appears flaccid and sunken, the eyes look hollow, and the features deformed; the posture and movements of the patient indicate extreme feebleness, his voice is weak and has no timbre (no ring in it), and his skin is either dry or more or less bedewed with sweats, particularly noticeable on the forehead, which is covered with numerous big drops of moisture.

Whilst, however, the face and the extremities appear more or less cold, the temperature of the trunk may be either increased, or normal, or diminished. This distinction is very important, yet a prognosis can scarcely be founded on this alone, for collapse with diminished temperature, and that with increased temperature may be equally dangerous, although in different ways. The temperature in both may be equalised, and this again happens in various ways. Cases of collapse with a falling temperature in the trunk are those most commonly met with in febrile diseases, and these require to be watched with the most painstaking care. The previously more or less high temperature sinks near to or quite to normal, and very often indeed more or less considerably below it (most often between $35°$ and $37°$ C. $(95°$ and $98·6°$ F.)). The fall is usually sudden, within a few hours, and often in still briefer time.

The diminution of temperature, in the course of half a day, may amount to as much as $6°$ or $8°$ C., or even more $(= 10·8°$ to $14·4°$ F.). Cases of collapse with sub-normal temperature may last a few hours only, or be prolonged through several days; and the temperature may either become normal or rise to a more or less considerable degree of pyrexiæ, or the patient may die in the collapse.

Such cases of collapse in which the temperature of the trunk falls, occur :—

(a) During the stage of defervescence, most commonly in pneumonia, but also in acute exanthems and other diseases; in these cases the condition of the patient may give rise to more or less anxiety, but is generally quite devoid of serious danger;

(b) During the remission of fevers, most common in enteric fever (abdominal typhus);

(c) In the transition stage from intermittent fever to an apyretic condition, especially in pernicious forms of malarial fevers, and in pyæmia;

(d) During rigors, especially in pernicious forms of malarial fevers, and also in other very severe diseases, or in very delicate and susceptible individuals;

(e) As accidental (spontaneous) or artificially induced Episodes (Epistrophen), especially after bloodlettings, vomiting, very copious evacuations, and also after overloading the stomach, and with extreme nausea, with extreme degrees of pain, very rapid or copious exudations, and perspirations—perforations of the pleura, or peritoneum—and the formation of coagula in the heart;

(*f*) In many kinds of intoxication (poisoning of various kinds), and in the cold stage of cholera;

(*g*) In the pro-agonistic period, and in the [death] agony itself.

Cases of collapse with elevated temperature in the trunk are scarcely to be met with except in severe cases of fever, and it appears as if a very elevated temperature directly predisposed to such collapses (Geneigtheit und Veranlassung geben könne).

Refer to the following abstracts on the subject of collapse, and especially to a treatise by the Authors, entitled, 'Der Collaps in fierberhaften Krankheiten' (1861, 'Archiv der Heilkunde,' II, 289).[1]

§ 7. If the course of the temperature in relation to these three general forms of constitutional disturbance be compared, and the whole summed up, the following is the result. The temperature may be *above* the normal in all sorts of cases: it is always high in pyrexia, highest of all in febrile rigors, and generally above normal in collapse.

No distinction can be drawn between them from the mere height of the temperature. Normal and sub-normal temperatures often occur in collapse, but only exceptionally in cases of incomplete rigors.

The extremities (peripheral parts) are always cold in collapse, and generally so in rigors.

A rapid rise of the temperature of the trunk, with coldness of the extremities, is generally associated with rigor.

A rapid and very considerable fall of the temperature of the trunk generally goes along with collapse.

---

[1] The internal temperature (as measured in the rectum and vagina, in the collapse of cholera), is often very high, relatively to that of the axilla. See some very interesting observations by assistant-surgeon F. M. Mackenzie, in vol. iii 'Lond. Hosp. Reports' (for 1856), p. 457. For instance, in a female, æt. 35, with an axillary temperature of 90·2° F., that of the vagina and rectum was 102·4° F. In a female, æt. 32, the temperature in the axilla was 93° F., and that of the vagina 102·8° F., &c. &c. See also other papers in the same volume, and Dr. Sutton's Report in the 'Ninth Report of the Medical Officer of the Privy Council.'—[TRANS.]

The recurrence of warmth in particular parts of the body whilst the temperature of the trunk remains high, is peculiar to collapse.

§ 8. We are met by insuperable difficulties when we try to explain theoretically the true meaning of all these varieties of temperature. Previous attempts at explanation have concerned themselves entirely with the theory of "Fever," and have in so doing ignored the interesting and practically important condition of collapse.

Even as regards attempts to explain fevers, many of them have been very partial. Many persons, setting out with the opinion that fever is identical with elevation of temperature, have only regarded the latter in framing their theories. This view is repelled by logic as well as by facts. Some have taken rigors, and others again pyrexia, as the basis of their several explanations, and thus only one-sided views have been promulgated. The theories of others have been founded upon the course of very perfectly developed cases of fever only, and their conclusions therefore are not suitable to slighter and less typical forms. Indeed, so infinite have been the "practical judgments," founded on a mere observation of the circumstances of temperature in febrile diseases, that one might almost doubt whether the theory of fever has made any real progress through thermometric observations. Indeed, we can hardly help doubting, when we see how widely divergent, and even directly contradictory to one another many of the theories are; and how many of them are not only one-sided, but stand in direct opposition to the facts of every day experience; and how strong an inclination there is to reintroduce that old, and frequently recurring fallacy (Irrweg) of medicine,—the attempt to explain the complex phenomena of the organism by one simple and short ("cut and dried") formula.

An unprejudiced consideration of the phenomena of fever leads us rather to ascribe the chief share in them to the agency of the nervous system, than to lay particular stress [Hauptaccent] on the increased heat. (See my treatise, 'Das Fieber,' 1842. 'Archiv für Physiolog. Heilkunde,' ii, p. 6.)

After the great significance of temperature in febrile conditions had been incontrovertibly demonstrated by thermometric observations, *Virchow's* theory of fever, and his explanation of the mutual relations of the phenomena (propounded in 1854, in his 'Handbuch der Speciellen Pathologie und Therapie,' i, p. 33, ff.), agreed very well with the general views, because he distinguished the rise of temperature as the most constant phenomenon of fever, and again ascribed it to increased combustion of the blood-constituents; and also prominently insisted that the rise of temperature in fevers was not merely increased heat, but an increase of heat from a special cause, and that this cause could be found nowhere else but in the nervous system.

This explanation appeared to give general satisfaction; and *Zimmermann's* theory, which ascribes pyrexia to local centres (foci) of inflammation, was almost entirely disregarded. Fever was held to be a process produced by increased tissue-decomposition, leading to increased heat, and the influence of the nervous system on this process, although it could not be determined with precision, remained undisputed.

Claude Bernard, in an article on fever (communicated in the 'Allgemein Wiener med. Zeitung' for 1859, Nos. 23 and 24), has sought to utilize his experiments on the effect of section of the sympathetic nerve upon animal heat, and to apply them in explanation of fever. He considers that whatever may be its origin, a fever must be regarded as a purely nervous phenomenon, and indeed as a transient and incomplete paralysis of the sympathetic system (which, according to him, is the sole vaso-motor nervous apparatus).

Certain transient impressions produce feelings of chilliness, *i.e.* a disturbance of common sensation; a reflex activity of the sympathetic causes a rigor, and to this succeeds a relaxing (Erschlaffung) of the nerves, which entails increased activity of circulation, temperature, perspiration, &c. He is inclined, therefore, to look upon a rigor as a general irritation, and upon pyrexia as a general weakening of vascular nerves of the whole surface of the body.

The rigor is accordingly looked upon as the primary condition, and, in fact, the only active process, the heat being only the result of the activity, a sort of sequel to it, and in some sort a new creation of the other.

Schiff opposed these views in an article contained in Nos. 41 and 42 of the 'Algem. Wiener med. Zeitung,' 1859. He very justly propounds, that rigors and heat (pyrexia) are two separate (independent) phenomena, and that the former does not explain the latter, and that any theory which represents the one as the necessary consequence of the other is incorrect and incomplete. He comes to the conclusion, that the vaso-motor nerves (which according to him are by no means to be regarded as fibres of the sympathetic nerve only), by which the vessels are contracted, also contain within themselves an active element, by which the vessels can be dilated, and that pyrexia is an active condition, an increased activity of those dilating nerves; whilst in a rigor a portion of the contracting fibres are in activity (*i.e.* those which do not decussate in the spinal cord, the vaso-motor fibres belonging to the face, hands, and feet. He propounds, further, that both contracting and dilating fibres go to the medulla oblongata, where accordingly all vaso-motor nerves find a point of reunion; that powerful and direct impressions chiefly excite the activity of the contracting nerve-fibres, rather than that of the dilating, and thus excite a rigor, but that the dilating nerves are more easily excited in a reflex manner by slighter impressions than the contracting ones require, and are more persistently active than these, which require powerful irritants. But whilst *Schiff* thus believes in an active condition in both rigors and pyrexia, he expressly declares that he does not deny that there may be pathological forms of increased temperature, which may be due simply to paralysis of the vaso-motor nerves.

Whilst either by silence, or by express declination, there was a general consent to the doctrine that the increased heat in fever was to be regarded as the immediate (Wesentlichen) consequence of an increased production of heat, *Traube* (who had shared the same opinion in 1855, 'Deutsche Klinik,' No. 46, for the year 1865) asserted, in opposition to all previous theories, that he considered the essence of fever to consist not in *increased production* of heat, but in *diminished giving* off of the same ('Algemein medic. Centralzeitung' for 1863, xxxij. Nos. 52, 54, 102). He says:—
"The elevated temperature, and the other phenomena of fever are induced as follows: Under the influence which the primary cause exciting fever exerts upon the vaso-motor nervous system, which I regard as a stimulating (erregende) influence, the muscular fibres of the vessels, which are well known to be most developed in the small arteries and arterioles, are thrown into stronger contraction. This diminished calibre of the small arteries and arterioles must have a twofold result: it reduces the quantity of blood which the capillaries receive in a given period of time (Zeiteinheit) from

the systemic circulation; and simultaneously with this, it diminishes the pressure on the interior of these minute vessels. From the first movement there results (along with a decreased access of oxygen to the tissues) a diminished cooling of the blood by conduction and radiation to the surface (periphery) of the body: from the second movement we get diminished transudation of liquor sanguinis, by which I mean the fluid which is forced through the walls of the capillaries by the pressure within them, and which furnishes to every tissue not only the oxygen, but other vital necessaries, especially the materials appropriate for furnishing to the secreting apparatus materials for both secretions and excretions. The diminished supply of water to the superficial layers of the skin, and mucous membrane of the lungs (Lungenschleimhaut), is necessarily followed by a diminished transpiration on both these surfaces, which is another cause for the diminished cooling of the body." In continuation, he endeavours to explain the varied circumstances and phenomena of fever in harmony with this theory. In this way *Traube* has taken a rigor with its tetanic contraction of the smaller vessels as the starting point of his theory of fever. He explains the rise of temperature preceding a rigor, and the commencement of fever without rigors, by supposing that the agents which excite fever act with varying intensity on the vaso-motor nervous system; so that in the first case the dose (quantum) of the primary fever-excitant is but small at first, and therefore is only able to excite a slight degree of contraction in the vessels; and, on the other hand, when it is more potent, stronger contraction is induced; and in cases of fevers, which begin without rigors, he supposes that the fever-poison itself is less active.

The results arrived at by *Behse* partly coincide with this view. (See his 'Beiträge zur Lehre vom Fieber,' 1864.) He sums up his views in the following words :—" By fever we must understand an increase of tissue-changes, induced by alterations in the nervous system, and connected with a general disturbance, in which the temperature-regulating machinery of the body, which is dependent upon the nervous system, is so affected, that the loss of heat is diminished in proportion to the amount of warmth produced."

Auerbach combatted *Traube's* theory, and criticised it sharply, with considerable completeness and pertinency (Erwägungen über die Ursachen der Eigenwärme, in the 'Deutsche Klinik,' Nos. 22 and 23 for 1864). He points out that the full force (Möglichkeiten) of the original causes of an increased temperature in fevers cannot be explained simply by the alternative of increased production or diminished loss ; that the contraction of the smaller arteries in fever has never been demonstrated, and particularly that the pallor of the skin may arise from contraction of its own muscles ; and that this arterial contraction is especially inapplicable to explain the hot stage of fever, and that the increased heat in this stage has been scarcely explained in any way by *Traube*, and that the length of time usually occupied by this stage makes it impossible for us to derive its increased heat from the preceding short stage of rigors ; and that even in the latter the economy of warmth from the contraction of the small arteries is affected by a variety of circumstances, and can never be sufficient to produce the increased height of temperature. *Auerbach* finally comes to the conclusion that during fever, especially in chronic febrile diseases, the relative amount (*Bruchtheile*) of heat generated in the body of an animal, exceeds the normal, perhaps very greatly, on account of the combustion of hydrogen, and that the absolute amount of heat generated by the combustion of hydrogen in fever greatly exceeds the normal.

The proposition that fever depends upon a diminished cooling of the body was also combatted by *Liebermeister* (Prager Vierteljahrschrift, 1865) and *Immermann* (1865 Deutsche Klinik, Nos. 1 and 4), who attempted to show by calculations that during the stage of rigors (cold-stage) the temperature rises more than could be accounted for by a mere diminished loss, and that therefore there must of necessity be an increased production of heat.

Wachsmuth, on the contrary, explained (in the ' Archiv der Heilkunde' for 1865, vi, p. 211) that neither increased production nor diminished loss of heat constitute fever, or at least neither occurring by itself, but that fever depends upon a disturbance of the regulators of warmth—that this is the *essentia febrium*. Fever, according to him, is the result of at least two influences, one of which increases heat-production, and the other paralyses the nervous system.

In opposition to all these theories which seek to explain fever by regarding it from one point of view only, *Billroth* endeavours to explain the varied forces which may cause an elevated temperature, and thus constitute fever (see the ' Archiv für klinische Chirurgie' for 1864; vi, p. 429). According to him, the following conditions may be met with:

I. The heat-supplies may be increased, the conditions which determine the giving off of heat remaining identical, and for the foci (lit. furnaces) of increased heat-production, may be :—

(*A*). Local only ; or,

(*B*). All the processes of oxidation may be increased, either by (*a*) an increased amount of oxygen in the inspired air, or the nutritious material ingested, or (*b*) by an increased amount of oxidisable tissues (material) in the body, or (*c*) by an increase in the capacity for oxidation of all the materials in the body which generally take up the oxygen, or lastly (*d*) by an increased rapidity of change (Bewegungsgeschwindigkeit) in the oxidisable materials.

(*C*). Amongst subordinate forces seeming to maintain a constant temperature in the body, are the friction of the blood and the walls of the vessels, friction in the joints, of the muscles on one another, &c., &c. Of far more importance is the development of warmth produced by muscular contractions.

II. The circumstances which conduce to the giving off of warmth may be less favorable, and thus heat may become accumulated in the body, and so the blood-heat may be increased.

Billroth further investigated the conditions which are able to excite fever. According to him, three kinds of excitants of fever are conceivable :—

(*a*). Decompositions may arise in the blood without any particular action of the nervous system, which may allow of increased combustion, or bodies may be introduced into the blood which may excite and maintain such decompositions ;

(*b*). The poisoned (lit. intoxicated) blood may irritate the nerve centres, and thus excite fever ; (*aa*) the poisoned blood may irritate the trophic nerves (nerves of nutrition) and the latter may operate directly to produce increased oxidation of tissues ; (*bb*) the poisoned blood may stimulate all the vaso-motor centres, and thus (*a*) in every part of the system the tissue-changes, and processes of oxidation may be augmented ; (B) contraction of the small arteries and arterioles may ensue, tissue-changes may be diminished, and thus the general temperature may rise in consequence of the conditions being unfavorable to the giving off of heat ;

(*c*). Or the blood may have nothing to do with the origination of fever, it may be caused by a direct specific irritant (Reiz) acting on peripheral nerves, by which the vaso-motor nerves may be excited in a reflex manner.

This somewhat diagrammatic analysis has at least the merit of calling attention to the great multiplicity of circumstances which may possibly be concerned in the production of fever.

O. *Weber*, in 1865 ('Pitha und Billroth's Handbuch der allg. und spec. Chirurgie,' i., 599), explained fever as a general increase of the tissue changes, associated with elevation of temperature, which is produced by a poisoning of the blood by the products of tissue decomposition, which operate after the manner of ferments, and induce a rapid decrease of the weight of the body. How one-sided and partial this explanation is, is self-evident (liegt auf der Hand). However well it may suit some cases of fever it suits others just as little.

On the other hand, *Tscheschichin* has propounded some ideas which deserve the most careful consideration : (" Zur Fieberlehre " in the ' Deutsch. Archiv für Klin. Medicin' for 1867, ii, 588). He considers fever to be a morbidly increased activity of the spinal centres in consequence of an affection (weakening or paralysis) of the moderating portions of the brain, by which a number of chemical processes are increased to an extent which is never attained under normal conditions of the functions of the brain. Without being entirely reliable as regards fever in general, this hypothesis sheds considerable light upon certain of its processes, and is well worthy of consideration in some cases of extreme febrile temperatures at the close of severe diseases of the nervous system (such as tetanus) or of pernicious infections.

More recently two works deserve special mention in reference to the relations of the production and loss of heat to fever :—

Senator (Virchow's 'Archiv,' xlv, 351), adopts Traube's theory, whilst *Leyden* ('Deutsch. Archiv,' v, 273), arrives at the following conclusions by calorimetric investigations. The loss of heat in fever is greater than usual, and this is true whether the temperature remains the same, or rises, or falls. An increased generation of heat must, therefore, undoubtedly occur. In very high fever the loss of warmth is from one and a half to almost double the normal amount. It is most extensive in the stage of crisis with a rapidly falling temperature ; it then amounts to two or two and a half, or even three times the normal quantity (lost). The defervescence always occurs with well marked perspiration and exhalation of water, whilst in increasing fever no evaporation of water can be demonstrated even under an impenetrable covering.

§ 9. These varied attempts to explain the primary cause and processes of fever, widely differing as they are, do certainly throw light on many points connected therewith. Most of them fail because they take such partial (one-sided) views of the process, and almost all are spoilt by dwelling upon some one special phenomenon of fever which they seize upon, and whilst seeking to explain this, the authors fancy they explain the whole process of fever, and they all omit one important circumstance, the impossibility of explaining all the phenomena! In the foreground is the question, "On what does the abnormal temperature depend?" But this is by no means identical with the question—what constitutes fever?

Fever is a complex assemblage of very varied phenomena, of which one of the most important is the increased temperature, if, indeed, this be not the most important; whilst it is not possible to derive all the other phenomena from the elevation of temperature.

The true value and significance of the several symptoms must be first separately determined before we are in a position to comprehend them in their complex entirety.

As regards the *course* of the temperature more particularly, it is very varied, and on this account also may well have very varied determining causes (Ursachen). Even when the course of the temperature is identical [in two cases of fever] it by no means follows that both originate in the same way. It is, on the contrary, highly probable, that the opposing circumstances of production and loss [of heat] in different cases, or at different periods in the same case, and even with an identical height of temperature may vary greatly. It is more pertinent to inquire, What are the primary causes of a given degree of temperature in a given individual, at any given time? or, to say the least, what are the true reasons of the course taken by the temperature in a given form of disease at any one period? and when progressing in any particular manner (bei einer bestimmten Artung), than it is to ask, why is the temperature altered in fever? These questions can certainly only be answered as regards particular cases and special forms of disease, by careful consideration of the possible conditions by which alterations of temperature may be produced during life, a method which up to the present time has only been hit upon (eingeschlagen) by *Billroth*, and by further reflecting on the particular share which the varied primary causes affecting temperature have in different pathological conditions.

Amongst those alterations of temperature which must be considered as signs of constitutional disease, we may consider the following :

(1) A general rise of temperature (all over the body).

(2) An increased temperature in the greater part of the body, with diminished temperature in certain parts of it.

(3) A general diminution of temperature all over the body.

§ 10. As far as our present knowledge extends, *an increase of temperature all over the body* (which is the commonest phenomena of a fairly commenced febrile disease which is still running its course) is determined by :

(*a*) An accumulation of heat caused by deficient abstraction of warmth. Diminished giving off of heat may itself be determined by a variety of causes. Yet we can scarcely admit that during a long continued duration of febrile heat any such circumstances could be continuously realised as a considerable accumulation of normally produced warmth, and we cannot but admit that if any such storing of heat supervened on the customary methods by which it is dissipated, either the production would soon decrease or new methods of getting rid of it would present themselves ; and it is a matter of every day experience that those suffering from fever make all their bedding, and whatever surrounds them, quite hot, however often these are changed. On the other hand, it is quite conceivable that a transient case of fever might arise from accumulated heat, and that during a rigor the deficient cooling of the blood through the anæmia of the skin may have a great share in causing the increased heat of the internal organs. It is further very apparent that in many cases the accumulation of heat, through deficient carrying off of warmth, may assist in producing the high temperature.

(*b*) It is further conceivable, when a local centre or focus of increased warmth-production is set up in any part of the body, that from this the overplus of heat is communicated by means of the circulation to the entire body ; and thus the latter has its own temperature increased. Such centres (foci) let the mode of increased production of heat be what it may (centres of inflammation or hyperæmias) are always very limited in comparison to the bulk of the whole body, and it can at the most only be admitted that the local overplus of production may effect a very moderate increase in the general temperature, which moreover, unless special disturbing influences come into play, is easily and speedily compensated through the means of giving off heat in the same manner as very considerable physiological over-plusses of heat are got rid of through these channels.   Besides this, in contradiction to any view ascribing the origination of every fever to local processes, we have the fact that it is just in the very cases where the highest febrile temperatures are met with, that is in the severest forms of fever, that the pyrexia generally precedes the occurrence of localised disturbances, whereas when it follows the latter the temperatures observed throughout the disease are, on an average, very moderate in height.   We must not say that local over-production of heat contributes nothing to the general elevation of temperature; but the contribution is by no means large, and where it is at all considerable there must be complications at work which hinder the compensation [which would otherwise occur] of the local overplus of warmth.

(c) A general elevation of temperature may arise from increased activity of the normal processes for the production of heat. Here, too, it is very evident that the means of giving off heat will prevent this disproportion from lasting long, or becoming very great, unless further complications in the organism arise to hinder the activity of the heat-abstractors.   And it must be remarked that there is not a single fact which would warrant us in concluding that in any case of fever the simple circumstance of increase or acceleration of the normal chemical processes is present; and, on the other hand, the results of direct determination of the normal products of decomposition in fever patients (of the carbonic acid exhaled, and of the urea excreted) are by no means uniform, and indeed only very partially correspond with the amount of increase in the temperature; and, again, the weight actually lost by the body in fever corresponds just as little with the amount of destruction of the constituents of the body which might have been preconceived as resulting from the increased production of heat.

(d) A general elevation of temperature may also occur through an extensive over-production of heat, resulting from chemical processes which are more or less unknown (fremd) in the healthy body (Leben), by means of which so much heat may be generated that the channels of heat-abstraction are quite unable (ausser Stande sind) to compensate it, whilst in these also, through the extension of the disturbance, irregularities and anomalies may be developed.   Very much, indeed, may be said for this, and something of this sort occurs in very many cases of fever; but we are still very far from being

13

able to determine with precision what actually happens, or to calculate its exact share in the production of warmth. It appears, however, that the following special processes may occur: an increased combustion of hydrogen in fevers which, from the very high combustion heat of hydrogen (which is more than fourfold that of carbon) may tend very greatly to raise the temperature (*Auerbach*); a widely diffused sudden organic decomposition (Zerfall), by which it is possible free caloric may be produced, a circumstance, however, which is so suddenly deadly that it can only be realized at the conclusion of a fatal illness, with the dying rise of temperature, or in terminal fever; an over-production of heat by violent, persistent, muscular contractions not furnishing any mechanical results (tetanic spasms), which, however, only occurs in a few special cases, and, as shown by experience, also only towards the fatal termination of the disease, and so doubtless concurrently with other conditions, is uncompensated, and thus induces a rapid elevation of temperature (der Eigenwärme).

The development of new combinations of the constituents of the body, associated with increased generation of heat, but not necessarily dependent on increased oxidation (*Gährungen*, zymoses, fermentative processes), which cannot indeed be exactly demonstrated; but whose occurrence is very probable, although we cannot always tell what diseases to rank in this class: for example, should the development of fever by the transfusion of fever-blood, by the introduction of products of inflammation and of tissue destruction [pus, and putrid materials] be attributed to zymotic (fermentive) processes; and how far are we justified in accepting the theory of fermentation (zymosis) in cases which terminate in recovery?

(*e*) Alterations in the degree of activity of the vaso-motor nerves must, if they are sufficiently extensive and persistent, almost necessarily have an influence upon temperature, and that in more ways than one, and quite as much by altering the conditions of production, as by affecting the giving off, or loss of heat. In reality, many phenomena indicate that the blood-vessels are in an abnormal condition, not merely in the stage of rigors (cold stage) but also during pyrexia, and it is scarcely possible to attribute this entirely to the changes in the contraction of the heart, or to the temperature itself in other ways. It would rather seem that in many cases the condition of the vessels was rather the prime cause of the increased temperature than its consequence. But we are met by insuperable difficulties in ascribing warmth to the activity of the vaso-motor nerves as long as we suppose that an isolated direct stimulation of the vascular nerves absolutely determines (feststeht) the contraction of the smaller arteries. For active contraction (Zusammenziehung) of the smaller arteries can only be considered certain in a very brief space of time during the course of a fever, and if their dilatation, which results in hyperæmia and increased calorification, is made to depend simply upon paresis or upon debility and exhaustion, this explanation may easily be accepted in the case of certain fevers of great intensity; but for many other cases, indeed for the majority, it is unsatisfactory.

A great part of the difficulty would be removed, should *Schiff's* conclusions be confirmed, that besides the *contractile* elements in the vascular nerves, there are also such as induce a *dilatation* of the vessels when they are stimulated. It is easily explicable, on this hypothesis, that on the first onset and determined attack (Zurwirkungkommen) of the primary cause inducing the disease, such an excitation of the central vaso-motor organs may ensue, as may give predominance to those elements which produce contraction of the vessels; and that at a later period, or when the primary causes of fever are in less force, more gradual in their approach, and milder in their operation, the influence may be such as may chiefly make itself manifest in the dilating elements of the vaso-motor nerves, just as under powerful stimuli applied to the motor (locomotorischen) nerves, the action of the extensor muscles usually preponderates, whilst with a less powerful, or longer continued stimulation, the contractions are principally shown in the flexor muscles, and their previous antagonists appear inactive. Further opinions of *Schiff* as to the two distinct properties or functions (Gebieten) of vaso-motor nerves, are no less striking. According to him, the state of vascular contractions is not generally met with at any given time all over the body, but is probably limited to the face and extremities (Extremitätenenden,—hands and feet); and this view agrees extremely well with many pathological conditions; as for example, with the distribution of warmth and cold on the surface of the body, even without rigors, and with the spread of many exanthems [the evolution of the eruption], &c. &c.

(*f*) Elevation of temperature may occur in consequence of a morbidly increased action of the spinal centres, in consequence of loss of power in the moderating portions of the brain,—a process, however, which we can scarcely be confident in accepting as true,

unless we meet with other symptoms of a suspension of the normal
influence of the brain during the course of the illness.   This
explanation deserves some consideration in very severe diseases, in
lesions of the upper part of the spinal cord, and in many terminal
fevers.   On the other hand, it is not applicable to moderately severe
cases of fever, in which there is often no indication at all of any
brain disturbance.

(*g*) The rise of temperature is doubtless brought about by
several of these conditions combined, or in varied succession;
indeed, it is probable that such combinations occur in the majority
of cases; and thus the precise determination of the relative shares
of the primary causes becomes quite impossible (eine reine un-
möglichkeit); and, indeed, the mere indication of the several
causes in operation may become for the most part hypothetical.

When we consider the probability, and for many cases indeed
the certainty of the co-operation of more causes than one [for
the production of febrile heat], we can understand that in two
different cases, or at two separate periods of the same case, one
and the same high degree of temperature may have a very varied
significance.   The same height of temperature may indicate very
different amounts of over-production of heat, according as the
amount of heat given off is diminished, normal, or increased; and
it is very apparent that the consequences, *i. e.* the disturbances of
functions, and the waste of tissue (consumtion), may be very
different in one case where the high temperature remains, in spite
of large losses of heat by the usual channels, from another case
which maintains a similar height, but in which the production of
heat is only moderate, and the result is attained by simultaneous
retention or accumulation (stauung, lit. stowing) of heat.   In this
way we may explain the fact, that in some cases of long-continued
high temperature the final products of tissue changes [urea, &c.]
are greatly increased, and the body loses a great deal of weight,
whilst other cases, with equally long-continued, and equally high
temperature, waste but little, and furnish but few such products.

The hand of the observer laid upon the patient does not always
receive the same sensation (adequate to the degree of heat) from
the same temperature in fevers when there is great increase of heat.
Sometimes, without being really higher than at other times, there
is a peculiar and lasting impression of a "burning" quality in the
heat (calor mordax).   It is conceivable that this phenomena of

calor mordax belongs to those cases in which the high temperature chiefly depends upon increased production of heat, and in which the hand of the observer is therefore less able to place itself in equilibrium with the heat of the patient's skin, because the continual over-production compensates for the heat lost by conduction; and the fact that the phenomena of calor mordax is chiefly met with in zymotic diseases agrees very well with this view [1].

§ 11. An *elevated temperature which extends over the greater part of the body, whilst the temperature of certain parts is lowered* may arise from

(*a*). An unequal distribution of the heat produced in the body; or,

(*b*). From an unequal cooling, through variations in the amount of heat lost in various parts, especially on the surface of the body, in contrast to the continual increase of warmth-production in internal parts.

(*c*). But especially from unequal fulness of the (blood) vessels. The very common distinction which is, however, by no means uniformly present between the temperature of the trunk, the (upper) arms and the thighs, on the one hand, and of the forearms and legs (below the knees), on the other hand [see page 149], is well explained by *Schiff's* view of the different centres, and different course pursued by the corresponding vaso-motor nerves; and it is easy to understand that in the first beginning of an illness, and again in a sudden relapse during its course (as in the collapse of defervescence), both groups of vaso-motor nerves may not be affected in the same way, or in the same degree, and that thus there may be an actual contrast between the blood-vessels influenced by them, and so of the warmth of the parts to which they are distributed. *Schiff's* theory, indeed, does not explain a rigor, for this may occur without this contrast, but it does explain one of the phenomena of rigors, which is, indeed, very common, viz. the contrast between the coldness of the forearms, and (lower part of the) legs, with the high temperature of the trunk.

[1] By many English observers this pungent heat of skin, at least in its most characteristic form, is believed to be almost pathognomonic of *pneumonia*. I have myself been accustomed to attribute it to increased *acidity* of the cutaneous secretions. It is best recognised by a slightly *moist* hand, and the almost painful feeling induced, sometimes requires the hand to be washed to get rid of it.

It is further very evident that the great variety of causes of unequal distribution of warmth vary greatly in their importance as
regards the functions and special relations of the organism generally. A patient in a rigor, and a patient in collapse, feel very
differently notwithstanding the fact that the contrast between the
temperature of the trunk and that of the extremities may be identical. It may be conjectured that it depends more upon the differences in the original causes than upon the degree of their operation, as to what further symptoms may accompany the phenomena
of difference of heat, and one may even venture to affirm that when
no difference of temperature is manifest, because the exciting cause
has operated too feebly, yet other corresponding special effects are
associated with the cause in question.[1]

§ 12. *A lowering of temperature* all over the body, can only be
induced (bedingt) by

(*a*). Diminished warmth-production, or,

(*b*). Increased loss of heat, or,

(*c*). Both these conditions together.

Such a depression of temperature below the normal warmth, may
occur after a previously normal temperature of the body, or after
this has been previously above normal. In the latter case, in some
points of view, a fall of temperature which does not even reach
the normal level (Niveau), may have the same significance, and be
followed by similar results, as a descent below the normal temperature would have under other circumstances.

In most cases, if not in all, it is quite impossible to assign the
respective shares of diminished production or increased loss, with
anything like accuracy. But we may sometimes arrive at tolerably
correct conclusions, as to the chief cause of the decreased heat,
from the circumstances of the case, from the suddenness with which
the temperature falls, and from the mode in which certain remedies
act when applied.

§ 13. The remaining phenomena of rigors, of collapse, and of

[1] It is scarcely necessary to remind the reader that fæcal accumulations, and
pelvic or abdominal tumours, &c., may cause coldness of the *lower extremities*.
It is also no less true that in such cases the corresponding parts of the
upper extremities are also affected. The former from diminished blood-supply—
the latter by sympathy (?)—[TRANS.]

pyrexia, present us with a very complex assemblage of functional disturbances, and in part also of chemical and textural changes. Although, indeed, many of these may be attributed to the altered temperature itself, a great number of them still remain which indicate that in the three conditions named above, the different organs of the body are placed at once in abnormal conditions, by the immediate operation of the original exciting causes (Ursachen), and the disturbing effect of the complications thus induced is so penetrating (innig) and complete, that a variety of interdepending and, perhaps, opposite circumstances arise, which, however the temperature may affect them (or whatever its relations to other special complications may be), undoubtedly affect the temperature. For example, if increased temperature effect certain definite changes in the movements of the heart and respiratory organs, it is just as certain that an altered rhythm and force of the heart, and changes in the respiration affect the temperature. An inexplicable interdependency of influences and operations, and, therefore, incalculable results and consequences might fairly be expected to ensue, were it not that even disease itself is a part of the "domain of law" which we can discover by oft repeated and laborious observations, but apparently never succeed in codifying [lit. ergründen].

§ 14. Thus, a rigor presents itself as a complex Initial—very rarely as a process complete in itself—in certain types of disease, and recurring paroxysms. In the one case its occurrence is the rule; in the other case it requires for its production a certain intensity of the disease (as regards its exciting causes) or a certain *predisposition* on the part of the individual attacked. If this predisposition be highly developed, forms of disease which usually exhibit no cold stage may set in with one, and a rigor may even occur in the midst of their course, although usually it only marks the commencement of fresh disease or new attacks of old ones.

There is no doubt that a rigor is most sure to be developed when the temperature of the trunk rises so rapidly that it soon creates a considerable contrast with the slowly rising or perhaps falling warmth of the extremities.

But this condition is not inseparable from a rigor, and even when it exists, there may be no rigor. In men who are not very impressionable, or in such as have their capacity for impressions diminished by medicines (*quinine*) or by disease, no rigor may ensue, in spite of sudden rising of the trunk temperature. In very sensitive people, on the other hand, it does not require any very marked contrast to induce a rigor, and the same condition (stimmung) of internal parts which is brought about by the contrast of temperature, may doubtless be induced in other methods and by other primary causes. For even in health, a sensation like a rigor (feelings of chilliness, &c.) is induced by slight but sudden changes in the objective warmth of the media in which we find ourselves (a draught of cold air, or in summer, passing out of an atmospheric warmth of 30° C. (86° F.) into a room at 22° C. (72° F. nearly); but there is a very remarkable difference between one person and another even as regards the predisposition to shiver under such circumstances.

§ 15. If we regard a rigor as an expression signifying the rapid development of new conditions, and especially of such as are accompanied with a rise of temperature, we must look on *pyrexia* as a state in which these conditions have arranged themselves more or less in a kind of relative equilibrium—not indeed an equilibrium on the same plane (niveau) as in health, but such a balance of power as is brought about by the pathological processes which are occurring —an equilibrium in which the temperature either remains persistently high, or exhibits daily fluctuations with more or less considerable excesses over the normal daily maxima of health. It is not difficult to understand that in those cases in which this relative equilibrium is very gradually brought about, or in which the increase of temperature always keeps within certain limits (maass) and remains tolerably constant, the transition from health into the febrile condition may occur without any rigor or " cold stage," and the " hot stage " (pyrexia) may begin at once—or at least only slight indications of a rigor (chilliness and the like) may precede it. The maintenance of a certain equilibrium of temperature in the course of a disease, does not prevent the occurrence of " changes of level" in the temperature. If they do not occur too suddenly, they generally have no other consequence than an increase or decrease of the other symptoms. When a fresh and rapid rise of temperature sets in, and the temperature in other parts of the body does not keep pace with it, a fresh rigor may occur.

§ 16. *Collapse* may occur relatively as a primary phenomenon, (after the operation of certain causes and influences), or as an episode of brief duration in the course of pyrexia, and also in the fatal close of a disease; or, lastly, in its transition into health. The relatively primary collapse, to which also belongs the collapse of rigors (that is, the kind of collapse which sometimes occurs in very intense cases of rigors), doubtlessly depends essentially upon an effect produced on the nervous system, and with this we find rapid losses of warmth (generally with very profuse perspiration), uncompensated by increased production of heat.

The kind of collapse which occurs as an episode during pyrexiæ is sometimes only the result of special influences, or occurrences, or of predisposition on the part of the individual, or it may be induced by circumstances in the course of the disease, which induce greater losses of heat than can be immediately compensated all over the body, particularly at its periphery, owing to imperfect circulation; notwithstanding, an overplus of heat may be actually produced. It is, therefore, chiefly met with where there is much sweating, along with a feeble contraction of the heart.

Pro-lethal collapse may rest on similar grounds, and it is even possible that the production of warmth in disease may actually fall below the normal.

Collapse during the transition from disease to health only occurs when a rapid fall of the previously high temperature sets in—whether this fall be definitive or followed by a fresh rise of temperature. An overplus of heat has nothing to do here; but, doubtless, at the same time the means of giving off heat are greatly increased. (Perspirations, &c.). The favorable nature of the process in these cases is guaranteed by the fact, that in the closing periods of the sickness, compensation for the losses of heat by normal production very soon becomes established, because the increased temperature itself is no longer continuously fed by morbid processes.

CHAPTER IX.

THE DIAGNOSTIC VALUE OF SINGLE (DETACHED) THERMOMETRIC OBSERVATIONS.

§ 1. A *single observation* of temperature is always an *imperfect and unsatisfactory* standard—and taken by itself must almost always lead to incorrect conclusions. It may chance to coincide with a point of time, in which the state of temperature is of the highest importance (entscheidende); but, on the other hand, it may just as well happen at a moment when the temperature is no standard at all. Notwithstanding this, however, detached observations claim our first attention for the following reasons :—

(*a*) A single observation may enable us to decide whether a person is fairly (wahrscheinlich) healthy, or decidedly unwell; whether the complaints of the patient are probably feigned, or undoubtedly justified by circumstances, although the disorders may be mistaken, or even appear improbable.

(*b*) It may enable us to form a decided opinion upon the severity and urgency of a general disorder (Störung), which occurs suddenly, although dependent on a previously existing and undoubtedly local disease.

(*c*) Supposing it to be the first thermometric observation in a given case of illness, it is still of considerable value; for when certain precautions are taken, it assists us in diagnosing the kind of disease which is present, and in excluding some forms of disease, with even greater certainty.

(*d*) And sometimes, especially when the other symptoms and circumstances of the case are taken into consideration, a single temperature may itself enable us to make both a diagnosis and a prognosis.

(*e*) The divergence (heraustreten) of a single temperature from the general course of the temperature in a given disease, is of very great importance, and may furnish us with many valuable aids [in treatment; *lit.*, werthvolle Anhaltspunkte] when guided by the rules of experience.

(*f*) Finally, it is necessary to form a right estimate of separate observations, because the whole course of the temperature in a given disease [as known to us] is composed of a consecutive series of single [thermometric] observations; and because, of necessity, the separate observations thus become the very foundation (das letzte Fundament) of all empirical rules.

The conclusions derived from a single temperature will be reliable in proportion to their extent, and to the precautions observed against deception.

Although in ordinary cases, when continuous observations of temperature are taken, very extreme accuracy is not so important in a practical point of view; it may easily be understood that, when a single temperature is to be made a diagnostic or prognostic *basis*, the correctness of our conclusions must chiefly depend upon the accuracy of the observation. In such cases every precaution against deception in taking the temperature, both as regards the instrument and the method, must be used, if we are to attach particular importance to the single thermometric reading. Yet it is consolatory to know, that even here we need not concern ourselves much with hundredths of a degree; and indeed, in the majority of cases, an error of observation amounting to one or sometimes even two tenths of a degree (Centigrade $= \frac{1}{5}°$ to $\frac{1}{3}°$ Fahrenheit, nearly) is of no great consequence, and will not materially affect the practical value of our conclusions.

§ 2. It has already been remarked (in § 5, Chapter I) that, with very few exceptions, the temperatures observed in human beings during life are limited to a range of about 8° (Centigrade $=$ less than 15° Fahrenheit).

The extreme *minimum* of the general temperature, or that of the blood, can scarcely be determined with even approximate accuracy. It is precisely in the lower degrees of temperature that errors of observation are most likely to occur, and the observations made in accessible situations, even when such parts are fairly sheltered, do not allow us to conclude that the temperature of the blood, or that of internal organs, is precisely similar. In the great majority of cases, the temperature of the well-closed axilla exceeds 35° (C. $= 95°$ F.), and indeed it is very seldom that we observe a depression of temperature there as low as $33°$ C. ($91.4°$ F.) or $32°$ C. ($89.6°$ F.); and although in certain cases of cholera, temperatures of $26°$C. ($78.8°$ F.), or even lower, have been observed on the surface of the body, we may be almost sure (from other observations in the same disease) that the rectal and vaginal temperatures were considerably higher.[1]

Very recently *Löwenhardt* has published four cases of insanity, in which lower temperatures occurred than any hitherto observed (see the 'Allg. Zeitschrift für Psychiatrie' [for 1868] XXV, 685). Before death, and indeed for several days, they showed temperatures of $25°$, $29.5°$, $23.75°$, and $28°$ Centigrade! ($= 77°$, $85.1°$, $74.7°$, and $82.4°$ Fahr.) They were very old people, who got out of bed in the coldest time of the year, and ran about naked, and from their dirty habits were constantly being bathed, and who took hardly any food—in one case the pulse was only 45, in another only 23 strokes per minute. *Magnan* ('Gazette des Hôpitaux' for 1869, No. 82) states that he found that the vaginal temperature of a drunken woman who laid out exposed to sleet all night, was only $26°$ C. ($78.8°$ F.). After two days it became normal.

The *maximum* of temperature has hitherto never been accurately observed to be higher than $44.75°$ ($112.55°$ F. in a case of tetanus measured by myself). Even approximative degrees (leaving fabulous accounts out of sight) are very seldom observed. But *Currie* found a temperature of $44.45°$ ($112°$ F.) in a case of scarlet fever.[2] *Simon* ('Charité Annalen,' XIII, B. 8, 1865) observed $44.5°$ C. ($112.1°$ F.) in a case of variola hæmorrhagica, although indeed the temperature was taken after death. *Lehmann* (Schmidt's 'Jahrbücher,' C. XXXIX, 236) noted $44.4°$ C. ($111.9°$ F.) in a tetanus case just before death; *Quincke* ('Berlin. Klin. Wochenschrift,' 1869, No. 29) $44.3°$ C. ($111.74°$ F.) in a case of acute rheumatism; *Brodie*,

---

[1] Reference has previously been made (p. 183) to the observations of assistant-surgeon F. M. Mackenzie and others on the vaginal and rectal temperatures in cholera. Confirmatory evidence will be found in the third vol. of the 'London Hospital Reports,' and in the 'Ninth Report of the Medical Officer of the Privy Council,' from the Observations of Drs. Sutton and James Jackson, Mr. J. McCarthy, Drs. Bathurst Dove, N. Heckford, and myself.—[Trans.]

[2] In the 'Medical Mirror' for February, 1865, I have put on record some *fatal* cases of scarlet fever, in which the temperature amounted to $115°$ F. ($= 46.1°$ C.). The observations were made with one of Negretti and Zambra's thermometers, divided into fifths, which had been recently compared with a standard.—[Trans.]

in his case of destruction of the lower cervical portion of the spinal marrow, 43·9° C. (111·02° F.). I myself have seen several cases where the temperature reached 44° C. = 111·2° F., or approached it very closely. Just after death the temperature may sometimes be still higher : 57 minutes after death, the temperature in the case of tetanus I mentioned above, amounted to 45·375° C. (113·675° F.).

Even temperatures between 42·5° and 43·5° C. (108·5° and 110·3° F.) are exceptional (gehören zu der Seltenheiten), and only occur under special circumstances. In the great majority of cases, the temperatures met with in disease, even when they prove fatal, do not exceed 41·5° C. (106·7° F.).

Narrow, however, as the limits are within which the temperature ranges, very decisive conclusions can be derived from them.

§ 3. All possible precautions having been taken to ensure accuracy, the fact of the temperature being APYRETIC (or, in other words, the axillary temperature being *less than* 38° C. (= 30·4° R., or 100·4° F.)), is of the greatest importance [in a diagnostic point of view] ; it proves the absence of fever at the moment of observation at all events; yet it must be borne in mind, that the nearer the temperature approaches the confines of fever-degrees, the more probable is it that it may soon overstep the boundaries. Whenever, therefore, a given temperature nearly approaches fever-heat, it is important to repeat our observations at short intervals. Yet there is no sharply defined line of demarcation dividing the febrile condition from the non-febrile. It may depend entirely upon other circumstances in the case, whether we admit that there is fever or otherwise. If the comparatively high temperature be observed in the morning, before taking food, and after having been in bed some time, fever is far more probable than with a similar degree observed in the evening, or after the mid-day meal, or after the enjoyment of alcoholic beverages, or after exertion, &c. So that the complexion (ausdruck) of the complementary phenomena must be studied before making the diagnosis of fever.

All temperatures which exceed 38° C. (100·4° F.) must be looked upon with *suspicion*, as probably febrile. We may consider one of 38·4° C. (101·1° F.) as indicating a mild febrile movement; anything over this indicates decided *fever*. To determine whether very moderate, considerable, or extreme degrees of fever are present, regard must be had principally to the time of day at which the temperature is taken. The very same temperatures may be important or otherwise, according as they occur in the morning, and at the usual times of remission (ebb-tides) or otherwise.

Sometimes very high temperatures occur, which exceed, sometimes even considerably, those common in high fever, which cannot, however, in spite of this, be regarded as the true expression of an unusually severe degree of fever, for they often occur under circumstances where there is no corresponding development of fever. Either other symptoms are wanting, of those which we are accustomed to group together under the general name of fever, or they are at all events not developed in a corresponding degree to the height of the temperature. On this account, such temperatures may fairly be called *hyper-pyretic*.

Whenever the temperature exceeds $41°$ C. ($105.8°$ F.) we may suspect that we no longer have to do with a simple case of fever; as the temperature rises, this suspicion will be strengthened, and indeed becomes a matter of moderate certainty with temperatures above $41.5°$ C. ($106.7°$ F.)

The circumstances under which such high temperatures occur, differ widely from one another:

(*a*) They occur in some specific forms of disease, which doubtless depend upon infection; but which, in spite of the high temperature, are some of them quite free from danger, and others by no means so dangerous, as might be inferred from the enormous elevation of temperature. Malarious intermittent fever (ague) and relapsing fever, are examples.[1]

In these, the temperature often rapidly rises, and generally more than once in the same cases, to $41°$ C. ($105.8°$ F.), or even more, without being at all dangerous. In cases of relapsing fever which recover, rises of temperature to $42°$ C. ($107.6°$ F.) may occur, and even a few tenths more. In this disease the temperature may remain rather longer above $41°$ C. ($105.8°$ F.) than in ague, but not often for more than about a day.

(*b*) In other diseases of a favorable type, terminating in recovery,

---

[1] With every respect for the opinion of so illustrious an observer as Professor Wunderlich, I cannot but feel that he speaks rather lightly of the danger of intermittent fevers. Although a *first attack* in young healthy adults is perhaps never fatal, it is far otherwise with the very young, the aged, the enfeebled, or those who have suffered from repeated attacks of ague, or the swamp-fevers of Europe, Asia, and Africa, to say nothing of the American Continent.—[TRANS.]

t is much more exceptional to meet with temperatures of 41 C. (105·8° F.), or more; and when they do occur, it is only for a briefer time. No satisfactory explanation of this occurrence can be given; they sometimes immediately precede the *crisis* (perturbatio critica).

(*c*) There are some diseases, of which the chief common charac-teristic is best designated by the term *malignancy*; some of these are specific infections, whilst in others we are unable to prove the pre-sence of any infection: in such diseases it is very common to meet with very high temperatures, and it remains open to doubt whether these should be regarded as the cause of this malignancy, or merely as its expression (Grund oder Ausdruck). Such cases most commonly occur in typhus, acute exanthems [scarlatina, measles, &c.] pyæmia, parenchymatous hepatitis, malignant pneumonia, puerperal fever, meningitis of the convexity, and fatal rheumatic affections. The rise of temperature in these cases sometimes happens somewhat abruptly (ziemlich schroff, *lit.*, rather rudely), and it seldom remains at this height for any number of days. The degree of temperature very commonly decides the prognosis in these cases. If the temperature rises to 41·5° C. (106·7° F.), the prospect of recovery is always small; and if it rises to 41·75 C. (107·15° F.), death is almost certain.

(*d*) In many cases of disease, even such as are not febrile in themselves, during the last hours of life the temperature rises enormously, generally by a sudden spring, to over 41° C. (105·8° F.) up to 42·5° C. (108·5° F.), or more, or even above 44° C. (111·2° F.)

They are generally diseases in which the central nervous system is seen to be implicated, and generally severely so, before the rise of temperature. Tetanus, in particular, pursues such a course, and so do epilepsy and hysteria when terminating fatally; and so, also, inflammatory affections of the brain and medulla spinalis, as well as injuries of the upper part of the medulla; and once, now and then, diseases in which there had been no previous evidence of the nervous system being implicated.

As regards COLLAPSE-TEMPERATURES we must not forget, that collapse itself is not identical with collapse-temperatures—for these may occur without the special phenomena of collapse, and symp-toms of collapse may occur, with an elevated temperature of the trunk.

§ 4. Any special diagnostic or prognostic value based upon the *absolute height* of a given temperature merely, apart from what has previously been stated, is in every way doubtful (misslich). Only extreme degrees of high or low temperature can be regarded as in themselves certain indications of danger, or even of the certain approach of death, with this limitation, that in certain forms of disease, extremely high degrees of temperature, which in other cases would signalise a death-agony, may in them permit a favorable prognosis. In both typhus and typhoid fevers, higher temperatures are borne [safely] than in pneumonia, and higher in scarlet fever than in measles ; yet, whilst in all these types of disease a degree of temperature above 42° C. (107·6° F.) allows us scarcely any hope—in relapsing fever, such an occurrence is almost free from danger in itself. The highest temperature noted in a case of recovery, in recent times, is given by *Mader* (Session of the [Vienna] Imperial Surgical Society, June 5, 1868). In a soldier returned from Mexico, previously suffering from an irregular intermittent, after repeated hæmorrhages, and the most extreme debility and deafness, the temperature rose to 43·3° C. (109·94° F.) (?). Transfusion of blood saved him, and the next day the temperature was almost normal (' Wiener Wochenblatt.,' xxiv, 233.) Cases of sun-stroke with temperatures of 42·8° C. (109·04 F.), ending in recovery, have been published by *Lerick* (see page 132.) In cases observed by myself, I can only remember two (of relapsing fever) with a temperature of 42·2° C. (107·96° F.) which ended in recovery ; all the rest, which exceeded a temperature of 42·125° C. (107·825° F., occurring in the rigor of abdominal typhus) ending fatally.

It is less easy to define the limits of temperature in a downward direction. The lowest temperature I find recorded amongst those cases of mine which recovered, is 33·5° C. (= 26·8° R., or 92·3° Fahr.), the pulse at the same time being only 62 per minute (in the collapse of defervescence in a case of enteric fever).

§ 5. In all less extreme degrees of temperature particular attention must be paid to the other circumstances of the case.

The *idiosyncrasy* (Individualität) of the patient is to be chiefly regarded.

In CHILDREN the significance of temperature in disease is in the main identical with that of adults, but children much more frequently exhibit sudden and extensive changes of temperature than those of

THEIR VALUE AND SIGNIFICANCE.

more advanced age. They show more sudden "plunges" (Sprünge), and in febrile diseases an earlier rise, and a somewhat higher temperature all through, than grown-up people.

Their temperature is affected more rapidly and more considerably by accidental influences. So that if we note a high febrile temperature in a child, it has not generally the same serious import as it generally is in the adult, but may, apart from malarious intermittent fever, belong to a brief, paroxysmally occurring affection, and may occur without much danger in diseases in which, in the grown-up person, it would almost warrant a fatal prognosis. Yet any considerable elevation of temperature in a child must always call for the most careful and anxious supervision ; although we see often enough, that considerable rises of temperature, occurring after a few hours' illness, give place either to normal or moderate degrees of heat, after some twelve or twenty-four hours.

Cases of ephemeral fever, without any very serious foundation (bedeutungsvolle Begründung), are particularly characteristic of the period of childhood. Therefore in children's diseases, even when we find a very high temperature, we must be very careful in drawing conclusions from the first [or a single] observation. At this age also more or less high temperatures may occur at stages [Punkten] in the course of a disease in which we generally find very moderate or normal temperatures in the adult. And even in *convalescence*, especially after muscular exertions, very considerable elevations of temperature are sometimes met with in children.[1]

On the other hand, very old people and aged men very often show temperatures in disease, which are from a half to a whole degree C. (= ·9 to 1·8° F.) under the average height, or even under the minimum height exhibited by the same disease in younger people— and this kind of advanced age (betagte Alter) occurs in febrile disease somewhat sooner than we generally reckon ; at a time, indeed, which a healthy man considers as his prime of life, though earlier in some than in others. Between forty and fifty the majority of men begin to exhibit the senile character in the degree of temperature in febrile diseases, and in not a few this modification of age begins to show

---

[1] If any confirmation were wanted, I might mention that I have several times found a temperature on the second day of a child's illness, of 106° F. (41.1° C.), whilst on the third or fourth day the temperature was not only normal, but the child was also to all appearance well, and *continued so.*— [TRANS.]

itself about their fortieth year. This senile character is so peculiar,
that the nature of the disease being previously determined, one can
diagnose the age with tolerable certainty, merely by a glance at the
course of the temperature. On the other hand, if we disregard this
[physiological] age of the patient, the moderate elevation of temperature may easily lead us into error, as to the kind and degree of
danger of the disease, especially in a first observation, or before the
diagnosis is otherwise determined. On the other hand, aged men
are much addicted (incliniren) to collapse-temperatures, and in them,
these often sink to a very low level. For some details on the conditions of temperature in fevers, in very old people, consult *Charcot*
(de l'état fébrile chez les vieillards, in Nos. 69 and 74 of the
'Gazette des Hôpitaux,' 1866) and *Bergeron* ('Récherches sur l
Pneumonie des Vieillards,' 1866.)

Many *women*, and sometimes also men, of delicate, somewh e
feminine build and constitution, occasionally exhibit a similar cou
of temperature to that shown by children. They are generally de
cate, sensitive, nervous natures, and those of hysterical temperam .th
in whom we meet with sudden elevations of temperature, o or
reaching high degrees on slight provocation, and sometimes a ar
rently without any " motive" [any apparent cause], degrees of t a-
perature which they sometimes exhibit for unusually prolong n
periods. In such persons, when no other decisive symptoms a
present, we must suspend our judgment for awhile. But a
unusual height of temperature must always afford a good reason 1
careful and continued supervision of the case.

§ 6. In estimating the diagnostic value of a thermometric rea
ing, the *time of day* at which it is taken must never be left out of
consideration. (Refer on this subject to the sections on Daily
Fluctuations of Temperature.)

The period of *digestion*, which generally causes a more considerable rise of temperature in sick people than in the healthy,
and other accidental influences, must always be considered, even
in a solitary observation. We must particularly remember that
thermometric readings, just after the removal of a patient, are
always untrustworthy, since the mere act of removal (transport) is
just as likely to raise the temperature as to depress it.

§ 7. It is especially important [although we may not be able to draw absolutely decisive conclusions from a single thermometric reading] to devote special attention to the *other symptoms* of the patient, and particularly to consider whether they agree or contrast with the temperature we discover.

In order rightly to estimate the relations of temperature to the other symptoms discovered in the patient, we must endeavour to realise how varied and many-sided these relations may be.

(*a*) The altered temperature may be produced by a disease of some organ, which in itself gives rise to more or less striking symptoms. The behaviour of the temperature in such a case is the result of the topical malady.

(*b*) The altered temperatures, and a larger or smaller number of other symptoms may be the common result of one definite primary cause, *e.g.* of an infection (contagion), of an intoxication (poisoning), other external morbific operation.

(*c*) Alterations of temperature, especially such as greatly exceed normal, or are of long duration, in themselves produce very erous functional disturbances in most portions of the body, even alterations in the tissues, if very long continued; so that 1 in high degrees of fever and in collapse the foundation may laid for a copious semeiology, which may base itself on the ered temperature, and exhibit itself in changes in the circulating, spirating, secreting, and nutritive systems, as well as in the actions of the nervous system. But it must not be forgotten that ere is in no way an exact parallelism between the morbidly vated or depressed temperatures on the one hand, and the ecial symptoms on the other; but empirically we learn that the most important indications (Kundgebungen), particularly as regards the nervous system, coincide not with the actual height, or the equivalent condition of the temperature, but with *rapid changes* of the same.

(*d*) [Almost] innumerable circumstances and conditions may cause a discrepancy between some one or more of the patient's other symptoms, and the course of the temperature.

In particular cases it is first necessary to carefully consider how far the temperature observed agrees with the remaining symptoms. If the temperature *harmonizes* with the patient's whole condition, and with all the rest of the several symptoms, and with the diagnosis derived from them, as to the kind, degree, and character of the disease, it is, as regards this diagnosis, simply an additional, but indeed very valuable and decisive confirmation.

§ 8. If, on the other hand, we notice a [marked] *contrast* between the temperature, and the rest of the symptoms, we ought, in those cases in which the contrast is considerable, to lay the chief stress upon the temperature. On the other hand, if the temperature be less than we should expect from the other symptoms, our first duty is to verify the thermometric reading, and having done so, to consider, as far as we can, what accidental, therapeutic, and other influences and events have occurred, which may either depress the temperature, or exalt the other symptoms. And in considering the apparent contrast between the slight deviation of temperature, and the severity of the other symptoms, we must inquire whether the type or stage of the disease may not be the concealed cause which is signalised by this course of tempeaturre.

If no such explanation is possible, the contrast between the temperature and the other symptoms generally furnishes us with proof, either that no very pronounced type of disease is present, that an advanced stage of it has been reached, or that some peculiar development is masked; or perhaps the lowness of the temperature may even indicate that the patient is just bordering upon collapse.

§ 9. Although the temperature may contrast strongly with the general feelings of the patient (Allgemeinbefinden), even should these be more or less uncomfortable (schlechte), still if the heat of the body is only normal, or slightly abnormal, there may indeed be some irregularity or disturbance in the economy; but it is at most not very acute; and sometimes, if the disease has only lasted a short time, the association of loud and varied complaints with normal temperature gives us good reason to suspect simulation or exaggeration.

If, on the other hand, the subjective condition [*i.e.* the patient's own feelings] and the temperature exhibit a considerable contrast (Abweichung), we are at once justified in concluding that the disease is probably severe and extensive. In typhöus and other infectious diseases the contrast between subjective feelings of comfort (Wohlbefindens), and a high temperature is not unfrequently met with.

At the very moment of a favorable crisis of severe febrile diseases a very miserable (unbehagliche) feeling sometimes occurs with normal, or even sub-normal temperatures, especially when defervescence degenerates into collapse. We should not allow ourselves to be easily deceived in these cases by the uncomfortable (schlechte) feelings of the patient, but may safely conclude that convalescence has commenced.

§ 10. There is very often a contrast between the temperature and the *frequency of the pulse*.

We may lay down as a rule for febrile conditions in grown-up people that slight febrile temperatures coincide with a pulse of 80 to 90, moderate degrees of fever with one of 90 to 108, considerable fever with a pulse of 108 to 120, and that in more extreme degrees of fever the frequency of the pulse exceeds 120 per minute. Yet these numbers have only an approximate value.[1]

In children and very delicate and nervous individuals this relation is materially altered, and the frequency of the pulse is generally much greater.

[1] Dr. Aitkin ('Science and Practice of Medicine') says, "As a general rule the co-relation of pulse and temperature may be stated as follows: namely, "*An increase of temperature of* ONE DEGREE *F. above* 98° *F. corresponds with an increase of* TEN *beats of the pulse per minute, as in the following table:*

Temp. Fahr.	[Centigrade.]				Correspond to a Pulse of
98°	= [36·6°]	.	.	.	. 60
99°	= [37·2°]	.	.	.	. 70
100°	= [37·8°]	.	.	.	. 80
101°	= [38·4°]	.	.	.	. 90
102°	= [38·8°]	.	.	.	. 100
103°	= [39·9°]	.	.	.	. 110
104°	= [40·0°]	.	.	.	. 120
105°	= [40·6°]	.	.	.	. 130
106°	= [41·1°]	.	.	.	. 140

[I have added the Centigrade equivalents for convenience sake.]

Liebermeister gives the following numbers ['Schmidt's Jährbuch.,' Bd. 142, pp. 42, 91]:—

Pulse.	Temperature.	Pulse.	Temperature.
78·6	37° C. = 98·6° F.	105·3	40° C. = 104° F.
88·1	38° C. = 100·4° F.	109·6	41° C. = 105·8° F.
97·2	39° C. = 102·2° F.	121·7	42° C. = 107·6° F."

Both statements substantially agree with the author's in the text.—[TRANS.]

Sometimes very great contrasts occur between pulse and temperature,—the former generally *follows* the temperature when there is any improvement; and increased frequency of the pulse generally precedes the rise of temperature in exacerbations.

A somewhat infrequent pulse, as compared with the temperature, may be regarded as a favorable sign, as it indicates a tranquil nervous system; a disproportionately low pulse-frequency with a high temperature, allows us, on the contrary, to predicate the presence of some special conditions, which must be discovered by some other method, *e. g.* pressure on the brain, biliary constituents in the blood, medicines which affect the pulse (depressants), and such like. A temperature which is disproportionate to the great frequency of the pulse, points to local complications in the heart, or to mischiefs arising from the organs of respiration, the thorax, or the pelvis, or to the heart being influenced by the nervous system; we must, however, not forget that any movement, however slight, will accelerate the pulse considerably in many of our patients.

On all these grounds the frequency of the pulse, taken by itself, is a bad guage of the amount of fever present.

In general that which affords us the best standard, is the circumstance (Moment) which appears the most unfavorable. With rapid pulse and moderate temperature the former, with slower pulse and high temperature the latter—and this rule (Verhalten) will be found most applicable when the contrast between the two is greatest. A sub-normal temperature co-existing with a not excessive frequency of pulse does not, however, indicate an unfavorable prognosis.

§ 11. The *number of respirations* per minute corresponds with the temperature far less than the frequency of the pulse. In collapse-temperatures there is generally increased frequency of respiration, but it cannot be laid down as a universal rule.

It is equally impossible to apply any rule in this respect to hyperpyretic temperatures, whilst on the one hand respiration may be much accelerated, on the other it is not uncommon to meet with cases in which it is less rapid than normal. When the temperature is nearly normal, and in moderate degrees of fever, respiration is scarcely influenced at all; only in children, even with moderate fever, there is sometimes increased frequency of breathing. [In others] when we meet with quickened respiration, we must look for local causes. In ordinary degrees of fever there is generally a moderate increase in the number of respirations, amounting to some 20 or more respirations (Zügen) per minute, and in children even to 40 or 50 in the same time. In considerable, and extreme degrees of fever, the number of respirations generally rises to 30 or more, and in children even above 60 per minute, without the organs of respiration being specially implicated.[1] The frequency of respiration in fever-patients is also considerably increased by every movement of the body.

§ 12. Between the temperature, and *cerebral symptoms*, there is sometimes a certain parallelism (correspondence), and at others there is a considerable contrast to be noted. With regard to these brain-symptoms, no doubt individual peculiarities play the most important part. In slight or moderate degrees of fever, in grown-up people, the brain is usually but little implicated; but in children and very old persons much more striking cerebral symptoms are met with. Even with more considerable degrees of fever in adults, the functions of the brain are not generally so much disturbed as to produce confusion of ideas, or involuntary utterances during the daytime. Delirium and special disturbance of brain-function chiefly occur with very high degrees of fever. If, therefore, there is a moderate temperature, with considerable symptoms on the part of the brain, we must attribute the symptoms to a local and independent affection of this organ, in the case of most patients, but not if the patient be either a child or a very old person.

This conclusion is justified in proportion as the temperature approaches to normal, and the less "peculiarities" mark the individual.

When the temperature is falling rapidly, as occurs in collapse, and in many cases of defervescence, there sometimes occur, during the change, alarming cerebral symptoms, particularly fierce delirium and maniacal outbreaks, which under these circumstances have far less

---

[1] It is scarcely necessary to remind the reader, that much of this is due to diminished muscular power, and more perhaps to the fact of the mechanical disadvantages under which much of the work of respiration is performed, and the *increased* work thrown upon the lungs, owing to other organs being *hors de combat*. These remarks apply of course to fevers without special pulmonary complications.—[TRANS.]

importance than those not familiar with the circumstance would ascribe to them. However, it is no less true, that similar symptoms occur during the collapse preceding death (Agonic-collaps.) And here the distinction between the two sets of cases must be made upon other grounds [than mere temperature or delirium].

§ 13. *Significance of the result of a single thermometric observation in a person considered to be healthy.*—The fluctuations, which generally occur in such, are very trifling. Yet there are cases, in which one finds very considerably excessive temperatures. During menstruation and lying in (Wochenbett), during suckling, during dentition, unusually rapid growth, in conditions of extreme fatigue, of psychical depression, and such like, the temperature is often increased. In such circumstances, therefore, the maintenance of a normal temperature is a capital guarantee of the resisting powers [Widerstandsvermögen, staying powers, or capacity of endurance] of the organism, and therefore that no pathological process is going on. On the other hand, when the normal limits are exceeded, the significance depends on the amount of excess, and upon the idiosyncrasies of the patient. In every case, every deviation from the normal should be a motive for further careful observation.

A sub-normal temperature in apparently healthy people is, as a rule, without much importance; although it will always raise the suspicion that either some unfavorable influence is working upon the individual in question,[1] or that the apparent health masks some concealed disorder.

The commonest deviation from normal temperatures which occurs in apparently healthy people, without any very exceptional circumstances, is a sub-febrile temperature. It indicates that the subject of it is not quite in good order, and that at all events there is a morbid susceptibility (Empfindlichkeit).

In children, particularly, the younger they are, such temperatures can generally be caused through slight external influences, by movements, &c. In adults, particularly, if they seem pretty robust, such febrile temperatures render it very probable that some latent mischief exists. When such are found, they should urge us to further examination, particularly of the lungs, heart, bowels, renal secretion, &c., and to continued vigilance, and particularly to repeat

---

[1] The temperature is often sub-normal in chronic alcoholism, saturnine intoxication, and the intermissions of malarious fevers.—[TRANS.]

the application of the thermometer. Febrile temperatures occur pretty frequently in men reputed healthy, but certainly as a rule only moderately febrile degrees. They are a sure sign of some existing mischief,—either of some anomaly from the operation of an external cause, or the beginning of some acute disease, which has not yet revealed itself in any other way, or finally, that some chronic mischief, although present, is concealed (latent).

It need scarcely be remarked that such a state of things calls for the most vigilant supervision.

§ 14. *Significance of a single observation of temperature in cases of apparently slight indisposition.*

Cases of indisposition, which afford as yet no diagnosis in other ways, exhibit the value of the thermometer as a rapid method of acquiring information (zu einer raschen Orientirung) in a very striking manner. When the temperature is found to be normal, the slight character of the illness is confirmed; yet it is well in all cases of indisposition with normal temperature to use the thermometer again a few hours after, and particularly at such times as are commonly marked by exacerbations (in disease).

Even a sub-normal or sub-febrile temperature allows us to conclude that the malady is not very serious, provided the observation is not taken at the very commencement of the disorder. But as soon as the temperature reaches the fever limit, increased vigilance is necessary. Yet such a febrile elevation need not necessarily entail a severe illness; for children, women, delicate persons, those suffering from chronic diseases and phthisical patients, commonly show a transitory febrile temperature during slight attacks of indisposition.

But a very high temperature should at least always prepare our minds for the development of a serious illness. Under these circumstances, therefore, the patient should be confined to bed, and requires at least prudence and vigilant nursing.

§ 15. A diagnosis is seldom possible at the very *commencement of an acute* febrile disease.

If we find the temperature normal, or the fever only moderately high, we may with tolerable certainty exclude acute true pneumonia (croupöse lobäre Pneumonie), small-pox, and scarlatina.

If the temperature is normal, or only slightly febrile, the illness is certainly not typhoid fever (so ist die Erkrankung kein Typhus). [Our petechial typhus is rare in Germany.—Trans.]

If, on the other hand, with the development of the other early symptoms, the temperature at once shows considerable fever, the "area of probabilities" is much more extended, and includes the exanthemata, acute tonsillitis, pneumonia, pleurisy, intermittent fever, ephemera (febricula), pyæmia, meningitis of the convexity of the brain, petechial typhus, &c.; but we may at least conclude with great certainty that there is no enteric (typhoid) fever present. Influenza (eine Grippe) is also improbable, and so is diarrhœa, except some special injurious influence has attacked the bowels. In the same way acute articular rheumatism is very improbable when the temperature is very high at the onset of a disease.

§ 16. In many cases, the diagnosis of an acute disease is still very doubtful during the *first half of the first week*. Thermometry is sometimes able to assist in the diagnosis, by means of a single observation, but not always. Subnormal and collapse temperatures only occur in diarrhœa, cholera, hæmorrhages, perforations occurring internally [as of intestine], sometimes with gastritis from toxic agents, and even in peritonitis.

If in spite of symptoms suggesting the idea of fever, one finds on any of the early days, particularly in the evening, a normal temperature, we are justified in suspecting an intermittent fever to be present; at all events, such a course of disease excludes both typhus and typhoid (enteric) fevers, and acute exanthems before the eruptions (except measles, rubeola notha [rötheln], and varicella.) The development of severe inflammations is also improbable under such circumstances; and above all, a normal temperature in the evening in the early period of the disease, points to a speedy termination of the process. If the morning-temperature is also found normal, unless some special circumstance operates to keep the temperature low, we may conclude against any disease at all with tolerable certainty.

Catarrhal affections, measles, pleurisy, acute tuberculosis, granular (tuberculous) meningitis, and acute rheumatism, may however be present with a normal morning temperature. Sub-febrile temperatures, and those of a slight febrile movement have about the same significance, except that on either the first or second morning they do not exclude the possibility of abdominal typhus (enteric fever). When acute exanthems are very rudimentary [in the early stage], especially in measles, such moderately febrile temperatures may occur before the eruption. In catarrhal and rheumatic affections they are the rule for the first few days; on the other hand, we do not find them in intermittent fever, unless we accidentally take the observation at the beginning or end of a paroxysm.

A considerable or high febrile temperature, when it is observed as early as the first or second day, renders enteric fever improbable, or proves that it began longer ago than the other symptoms seem to indicate. This conclusion is still more probable if the high temperature be found in the morning. For the rest, a single observation of temperature indicating a high degree of fever, scarcely allows us to form a conclusion as to the kind of [morbid] process going on, for the first few days; but if we are able to exclude the possibility of an intermittent fever, we may with great probability expect a very severe illness.

If, however, the diagnosis of the disease can be made from other data (Momenten) during the first few days, the degree of the temperature obtained may enable us to form tolerably accurate conclusions as to severity of the case, since extreme temperatures indicate a severe form, whilst a temperature less than the *mean* (*vulgò*, average) temperature of the disease at any given hour of the day, indicates the probability of a mild course of the disease.

§ 17. Even in the *second half of the first week* of illness of a febrile character, the diagnosis may still be very uncertain. We may have to do with the protracted [initial or] prodromal fever of an exanthem, with abdominal or exanthematic typhus [typ*hus* or typ*hoid* fever], relapsing fever, a tardily developing pneumonia, severe influenza, capillary bronchitis, acute miliary tuberculosis, intermittent fever, tubercular meningitis, epidemic cerebro-spinal meningitis, hepatitis, internal suppuration, osteo-myelitis, acute lues [syphilis.]

A solitary reading of temperature can give us but scanty aid in forming a diagnosis in such cases. If we find, however, the *evening* temperature normal, sub-febrile, or moderately febrile only, and no temperature-depressing influence has been at work, we may correctly assume that neither the prodromal fever of an exanthem nor typhus is present.

If we find a considerable, or very high degree of fever heat, we can with great probability exclude tubercular meningitis.

If a hyper-pyretic temperature is present, either an intermittent fever, or some malignant form of infectious disease is masked, and there is imperative necessity for further anxious supervision and renewed application of the thermometer. Temperature is in all these cases a valuable auxiliary) in diagnosis, but to remain satisfied with a single observation of the thermometer, must always lead to imperfect results, and we ought to be particularly careful not to found rash conclusions on such.

§ 18. When an *exanthem* [eruption] appears, in cases when the diagnosis has previously been doubtful, its kind and the symptoms while occupying it must naturally be the groundwork of our diagnosis; but we may sometimes still be uncertain for a little while, whether we should consider the commencing eruption to be that of small-pox, measles, scarlet fever, exanthematic [true] typhus or a syphilide. In these cases the thermometer may help us to a diagnosis, at least, so far as this, if the symptoms have been very severe, and after the eruption the temperature becomes low, we may conclude for small-pox, and, indeed, if it become perfectly normal, we may be almost sure that we have modified small-pox (varioloid). With a syphilitic exanthem the temperature falls also, but the distinction is that the preceding fever-symptoms are moderate also in that case. In measles, scarlatina, and exanthematic [true] typhus, the fever continues, on the contrary, at the commencement of the eruption.

§ 19. During the *further course* of an acute febrile disease, when the diagnosis appears certain, or is so, the *temperature* continues to afford most important and desirable information on which to found our conclusions, only this thermometric observation must be continual and consecutive.

Yet sometimes a single thermometric observation may be of great importance : it may serve to confirm a diagnosis; it may remove or mitigate a doubt; it may decide on the severity of the disease, and may indicate its modifications, as well as the dangers and complications which attend it.

In order to avail ourselves of the full value of a single thermometric observation, we ought to be well acquainted with the usual course of temperature of the disease which is present. A high degree of temperature, in proportion to the remaining symptoms, must especially be regarded as a sign of a severe attack, even when it is only noticed once. Comparatively low degrees of temperature are not, however, corresponding signs of safety, or of a mild form of the disease, because even in the worst cases a temporary improvement may occur, the cause of which is sometimes evident, sometimes unknown.

An isolated observation of temperature taken in the course of a disease, only allows us to form just conclusions, after the most careful consideration of all the other circumstances and symptoms of the case.

We can scarcely admit the presence of typhus [enteric?] fever, when at any time between the third and tenth days of the disease the temperature is not at least moderately febrile, and considerably so in the *evening* (at least 39·6° C. (103·28° F.) unless some strong fever-moderating influence has been at work just before (such as copious hæmorrhage, diarrhœa after previous constipation, &c.), or when the patient is aged. A low temperature, contrasting strongly with the previous course of the temperature, may at once raise the suspicion of internal hæmorrhage, before any blood has appeared externally. Even later, and up to the middle of the third week, *enteric fever* is very doubtful if the *evening* temperature (apart from the influence named above), is less than 39° C. (102·2° F.). High febrile *morning* temperatures (which approach 40° C. (104° F.), or even *evening* temperatures of 41° C. (105·8° F.), are, in this disease, signs of great severity and threaten danger. And the danger is very great, if the temperature of the trunk is very high along with symptoms of collapse. But a normal temperature in the morning, at a later period, is in no way a sign that the fever is over [for it still rises in the evenings].

In *measles* it is a sign of a threatened or existing complication, when temperature remains febrile, after the eruption begins to fade and even a sub-febrile temperature is suspicious.

In *scarlatina* the same rule applies, although at a little later date.[1]

---

[1] I have found the *noon* temperature of typical non-maliguant scarlatina in a great many cases to be nearly as follows:—

Day of eruption.	Temperature. Fahrenh.	Centig.	Day of eruption.	Temperature. Fareuh.	Centig.
1st	105° =	40·5	4th	102° =	38·9
2nd	104° =	40°	5th	101° =	38·4
3rd	103° =	39·5	6th	100° =	37·8

About *two days more* being required to regain the normal.—[TRANS.]

In *small-pox*, when the temperature still continues febrile after the eruption has fairly come out, a variola vera (*i. e.* the disease with the stage of suppurative fever), or a complication may be predicted with great certainty.

In primary croupous and lobar [true] pneumonia, the occurrence on a single occasion of a normal or sub-febrile temperature is no proof that the [inflammatory] process is over. All high-febrile temperatures in pneumonia are deserving of consideration, and must cause the cases in which they occur to be regarded as very severe. If they are found in the later period (after the sixth day) this is still more true. Only it must be borne in mind that a striking rise of temperature sometimes precedes the favorable crisis. In the advanced stage of *pneumonia*, in spite of alarming symptoms, if the temperature shows itself normal or sub-febrile, there is, usually speaking, no danger, and one may predict [favorable] termination of the process with great confidence.

In *facial erysipelas* a febrile temperature indicates that the process is still going on, and that further extensions or complications will occur.

In *influenza* and *bronchitis* considerable or high-febrile temperatures are always very suspicious, and the more so if they occur in the morning or later on in the course of the disease. They indicate with great probability an extension to the finer bronchi, or the supervention of pneumonia; but they also sometimes occur in cases in which the bronchitis simply masks the deposit of acute [gray or miliary] tubercle.

In *hooping cough* any febrile temperature indicates a complication, the first period of its development being excepted.

In *acute (articular) rheumatism* a single observation of temperature aids diagnosis hardly at all, not even to discover the existence of complications. Very high temperatures, however, in this disease, generally show the case to be a dangerous one.

When symptoms of *meningitis* are present, a considerably febrile or high-febrile temperature points specially to disease of the convexity or summit of the brain. Weak febrile, or apyretic temperature, on the contrary, indicates the granular form of meningitis of the base of the skull.

In *cerebro-spinal meningitis* the temperature may reach [almost] any height.

In *pleurisy, pericarditis, endocarditis,* and *peritonitis,* a high febrile temperature always indicates great danger at whatever time it may occur, whilst a tolerably moderate degree of fever, or even an apyretic temperature by no means ensures a favorable prognosis. In presence of a *gastro-intestinal catarrh*, if the patient has been previously in good condition and not exposed to any special prejudicial influences, a single observation if it shows us a high temperature must always excite a suspicion of enteric fever (abdominal typhus), or of some latent inflammation. Yet a second thermometric observation of a high temperature is required to make us certain that a severe disease is present.

Unless the temperature at the conclusion of the cold stage (rigor) or the commencement of the hot stage reaches nearly 41° C. (105·8° F.), or more, it is very doubtful whether we have to do with an *intermittent fever*. But if it exceed a height of 41·8° C. (107·24° F.), the diagnosis of an intermittent is again very improbable. And the diagnosis is further doubtful unless the temperature be normal in the apyrexiæ (intermissions). Although the attacks (paroxysms) may have ceased, and no other morbid symptoms are present, as long as the temperature still shows itself febrile the intermittent is not cured.

§ 20. During *defervescence*, isolated observations of temperature afford no satisfactory results, although a low temperature occurring in the evening is in some sort a proof of the cessation (*lit.* winding up) of the fever. When the fever is just about to take its departure, and shortly after, the temperature often exceeds the normal bounds, especially in severe illnesses, and in weak, sensitive individuals, often falls for hours together, or even for a whole day, to a depth which may easily cause anxiety. These collapse [conditions] are sometimes associated with other symptoms, more or less severe, and sometimes can only be recognised by the temperature. The closer to the crisis such a collapse occurs, the less danger does it indicate, and the more safely can it be pronounced to be the collapse of defervescence.

§ 21. After the *termination* of the disease, and in true *convalescence* (Reconvalescenz) the temperature is generally normal, but convalescents are rather subject to transitory collapse-temperatures. They are not without special significance, and the more so, the farther off they are from the crisis; and in that case, we must endeavour to determine whether an internal hæmorrhage, or perforation of the bowel has caused the collapse. Simple subnormal temperatures often occur during convalescence, without any special unfavorable significance, yet they indicate that the convalescence is not yet consolidated, and leave room for suspecting that nourishment is not proportionate to the necessities of the case.

Moreover, the temperature of *convalescents* is very mobile, and easily affected by insignificant influences, so that we may not unfrequently be surprised by more or less considerable elevation of temperature at this period. Such rises of temperature indicate that convalescence is not quite complete (lit. rein.), or that it has been interrupted.

If we find a febrile temperature in convalescence, it may depend upon subordinate influences.

(*a*) From some relative errors in diet, especially a premature use of flesh-meat, or spirituous liquors, or from overloading the stomach.

(*b*) From some exertion too much for the strength of the patient; from too early leaving, or too long staying out of bed; and many convalescents show an immediate rise of temperature on first getting up.

(*c*) From constipation.

(*d*) From other more or less trifling influences to which the convalescent has been exposed.

(*e*) But it may be caused by serious, it may be persistent, although not yet diagnosable disordered conditions (such as imperfect resolution (Abheilung) of the diseased process, partial extensions of the disease, latent chronic affections, or a fresh disease); but a single observation is not decisive on these points, and can only serve as a beacon or sign-post, to point out the necessity of further observations, and of the most watchful solicitude.

§ 22. When any *considerable change* (Wendung) occurs in the course of an acute febrile disease, a single observation of temperature may sometimes decide whether a fatal termination is imminent or not. Such an event is very probable, if the temperature is hyperpyretic, or if, on the contrary, it is moderately febrile, or falls to normal, or even below it, whilst the remaining symptoms exhibit great severity.

§ 23. In *diseases* which are *not* in themselves *of a febrile character*, the discovery of an elevated temperature is always specially noteworthy.

In *affections of the nervous system* (epilepsy, chorea, hysteria, tetanus, neuralgias and apoplexies) it may depend on the supervention of a new febrile disorder, or be the beginning of a fatal termination.[1]

In *jaundice* a high febrile temperature is always a very suspicious circumstance. In diseases accompanied by vomiting, diarrhœa, and particularly collapse, a febrile temperature of the trunk indicates the commencement of *reaction*. And in all these non-febrile diseases the occurrence of a febrile temperature may indicate an exacerbation or complication.

On the other hand, in all these affections, collapse temperatures, if they are very extreme, are of very great importance.

§ 24.—In *chronic* cases, with persistent fever, it is naturally to be expected that nothing important as regards diagnosis will flow from a single observation of temperature. Continuous observations must, therefore, be made as soon as the results of a single observation are observed to be divergent from the usual course of the disease.

If collapse temperatures occur in chronic diseases they are more significant than in acute cases, unless such subnormal temperatures correspond to the kind of disease present.

---

[1] In some cases of chorea, and perhaps of epilepsy, the high temperature is probably to be regarded as the result of muscular action, or in other words of the metamorphosis of the muscular tissue, and not in itself unfavorable.—[TRANS.]

CHAPTER X.

THE DAILY FLUCTUATIONS OF TEMPERATURE IN DISEASE.

§ 1. In disease the height of the temperature varies more or less even in the course of one day. It never remains stationary at any one point for twenty-four hours continuously, and observations which represent the temperature as remaining a whole day at the same elevation are undoubtedly false.

The daily fluctuations of temperature, which have already been remarked as occurring even in health, are still more evident in disease. In sick persons the temperature commonly varies from 1 to $1\frac{1}{4}°$ Centigrade ($= 1·8°$ to $2·7°$ Fahrenheit), and it may very well change as much as $5°$ or even $6°$ ($= 9°$ to $10·8°$ Fahrenheit), or more. When the temperature is rather high, or very high, and the daily variations are very slight, the course of the disease will be more or less continuous, and, *cæteris paribus*, a severe attack of illness is indicated.

The daily fluctuations in different diseases, and in different patients suffering from the same disease, assume very different forms (*lit.* form a varied picture), yet they all have certain points of agreement, and are regulated by certain laws. The daily fluctuations when projected diagrammatically take the form of waves, with crests and furrows (*lit.* hill and dale], or not infrequently of combinations of waves. The daily fluctuation is a curve, with one, two, or even more secondary curves. In order to become acquainted with it, it is clear that numerous observations must be taken in the course of the day. According to the purpose one has in view, and partly according to the nature of the case, it may sometimes suffice to take from two to four temperatures in a day—sufficient at least to form an opinion on the special case in accordance with general principles previously learnt. Indeed, beginners are sometimes puzzled by the complex combinations of curves (Wellensystem) derived from very frequent observations, and don't know how to find the longitude of the case, so to speak [sich zu orientiren], whilst they easily do so from double or fourfold daily observations, which must, however, of course be taken near the periods of daily exacerbation and remission.   But such sparse observations must make us overlook and fail to recognise many very important and critical events [Momenta], and very numerous observations, six or eight at least in the course of a day, and in some conditions even a continuous observation of temperature, is indispensable if we want to learn the laws or, in other words, the common facts of the daily fluctuations in disease.

§ 2. The *average value* of all the temperatures of a given day, or (which is less accurate but more practical) an equal division of the sum of the daily maximum and daily minimum is the *mean daily temperature*. This must be considered in the first place if any conclusions are to be drawn from the daily fluctuations.[1]

The daily *difference* is the extent of the *excursus* between the *maximum* and *minimum* temperature of the day.

All the elevations of temperature which occur in the course of the day, and exceed its mean temperature, may be designated its *exacerbations*, whilst all falls of temperature below the daily mean, may be called its *remissions*.

The moment (during an exacerbation) in which the rising temperature changes to a falling one (which is thus, as it were, the crest of the wave), is the acmé of exacerbation (Exacerbationsgipfel).

The temperature may happen to fall the moment it has reached its highest point, = pointed or acute exacerbation ; on the other hand, it may chance to linger at the height attained before sinking = less-acute (*lit.* broad-topped) exacerbation. Sometimes the exacerbation shows a sinuous outline, caused by two or more

---

[1] Vol. xi of the New Sydenham Society (published in 1861) contains some interesting papers on "The Importance and Value of Arithmetic Means and their Applications to Medicine," by Professor Radicke, of Bonn; translated by Dr. F. T. Bond from Wunderlich's ' Archiv. für Physiologische Heilkunde,' new series, vol. ii, part 2, 1858, as well as other papers by Professor Carl Vierordt of Tübingen, and Dr. F. W. Benecke, of Marburg, translated from the same source, and bearing on the same subject, by the same accomplished translator. The reader is referred to them for explanations of the difference between a simple average, or arithmetic mean, and the true value.

slight falls interrupting the ascent = double or triple-peaked exacerbation. The highest point in such cases is *the maximum of the exacerbation*. When several exacerbations occur in the course of one day, there may be maxima of exacerbation which need not coincide with the maximum of the day. [These phrases refer to the curves projected by the temperature on the charts.] The moment during a remission at which the falling temperature reaches its lowest point, is the *depth* or *nadir* of the *remission*. When several remissions occur in the course of one day, these low-points may differ, and the lowest of them corresponds with the day's minimum. The time between the moment at which the rising temperature exceeds the daily mean, and the moment in which the once more falling temperature again touches the same point represents the extent of the exacerbation; and just in the same way the period between the moment in which the sinking temperature oversteps the daily mean, and that in which by its again rising from the lowest point of remission it reaches the same point again, shows the extent of the remission.

There is a great difference in different cases between the length of time in which the temperature remains near to the high or low points respectively; sometimes it remains a long time high (or low), sometimes only a very short time: = duration of proximity to the high (or low) point.

The moment the temperature begins to rise from the low-point of the remission, it has begun its true ascent. This ascent (the daily *ascendance*) is sometimes moderate, sometimes extreme, and interrupted, sometimes tedious, at other times very sudden.

The daily *descent* begins the moment the highest point of the exacerbation is reached. If the line of exacerbation presents two or more elevations, the beginning of the descent is to be reckoned from the last elevation, even when this is somewhat lower than the former one. The descent may be gradual or precipitous, and may be interrupted; it may take place slowly or suddenly.

Through the occurrence of two or more exacerbations in the course of a day, morning, noon, or evening descents may be met with.

§ 3. *The form assumed by the daily fluctuations depends—*

(A.) Upon the elements which constitute the morbid processes, and chiefly, (*a*.) on the kind of disease;

(*b*.) on its intensity;

(*c*.) on the stage it has reached;

(*d*.) on the regularity or irregularity, or other peculiarities of its course;

(*e*.) on the improvement or relapses of the patient;

(*f*.) on the occurrence of complications or special events;

(*g*.) on the progress towards health; or,

(*h*.) on the fatal crisis.

(B.) It may also depend—

(*a*.) on the idiosyncrasy of the patient;

(*b*.) on interstitial external influences;

(*c*.) on therapeutic agencies.

Thus the daily fluctuations exhibit very complex phenomena; but notwithstanding this, they furnish us with very numerous and valuable indications.

In cases where the diagnosis is tolerably clear, the daily fluctuations greatly extend our bases of observation, and our means of forming a judgment, but in obscure cases they are far less reliable. The mere observation of the fluctuations of one day of twenty-four hours, only permits us to draw satisfactory conclusions under special circumstances. It is generally necessary to watch them for some days, in order to either a safe diagnosis or prognosis; and a comparison of one day with another, of variations, or of their symmetrical repetition, gives the surest and the plainest indications. We can never positively determine the nature of the disease from seeing the temperature-curves of a single day, but it is sometimes possible to *exclude* the presence of an otherwise probable disease from such an examination. But a single day's fluctuation may often suffice to determine the degree of severity of a disease which has been diagnosed in other ways.

It may also afford a tolerably ample means of judging the *stage* of certain forms of disease.

In the same way an irregular course of the malady may be sometimes learnt from a single day's curves, whilst the regularity of the course indicates that the disease will probably be of some days' duration. An examination and comparison of the curves of several days is necessary in order to decide as to ameliorations or relapses.

In general, more than one day's fluctuations are needed to establish the presence of complications, whilst the commencement of convalescence may be sometimes recognised in the fluctuations of a single day.

In like manner, in special cases, a fatal termination may be prognosticated from the curves of a single day, especially when corroborated by other symptoms.

But the individual peculiarities of a patient can scarcely be determined from only one day's fluctuations.

And the operation of accidental external causes can only be recognised by a comparison of the day's fluctuations with those of preceding days.

The operation of therapeutic agencies also requires a comparison of one day with another for its determination. Notwithstanding these limitations, the daily fluctuations are an important element in the general constitution of diseases, and form, so to speak, a very solid substratum on which the remaining circumstances of the case are superimposed.

§ 4. The conclusions to be drawn from the *average temperature* of a single day.

An important distinction must be made, between fluctuations upon a high *level* and those of a medium or lower level. Whilst the base-line, or plane (Durchschnittsniveau) of the daily fluctuations in health is 37° C. ($98\cdot6^\circ$ F.), it is seldom so low in disease, but generally more or less elevated; and it is only in a few forms of disease, which are distinguished by their low temperatures [such as cholera], or in advanced stages of others, where there is a casual sinking of temperature below the normal, or in cases attended by collapse, that the mean daily temperature of the sick is found to be lower than that of health.

The daily mean temperature furnishes us at once with tolerably certain indications as to the degree of fever present.

In moderate degrees of fever, the mean daily temperature should not exceed 39° C. ($102\cdot2^\circ$ F.) ; and when the average temperature of a day is between 39° and 40° ($102\cdot2^\circ$—104° F.) the fever must be considered somewhat high; indeed, this is the case in remittent types with a mean of 39° to $39\cdot5^\circ$ C. ($102\cdot2^\circ$—$103\cdot1^\circ$ F.), and in continuous fevers with one of $39\cdot5^\circ$—40° C. ($103\cdot1^\circ$—104° F. If the average temperature of the day exceeds 40° C. (104° F.), a very high degree of fever is present.

Many diagnostic and prognostic conclusions depend upon this.

Highly febrile daily-means above $40°$ C. ($= 104°$ F.) are met with in pernicious (malarial) fevers; in typh*us* and typh*oid* fevers, in their fastigium; in relapsing fever, and in severe cases of pneumonia. All these, notwithstanding the height of the temperature, may possibly terminate in recovery. On the other hand, when a like average daily temperature is met with in other diseases, we may reasonably conclude that death is imminent.

A considerably febrile daily mean-temperature ($39°$—$40°$ C. $= 102·2°$ to $104°$) is generally met with in all well-developed forms of pyrexia, and in many inflammatory diseases during the fastigium; and in general the only safe conclusion to be drawn is, that a very severe febrile affection is present, yet there are certain forms of disease in which such a temperature deserves the most careful consideration, and is of the highest importance. In this category we must include all forms of catarrh, acute (polyarticular) rheumatism, cerebro-spinal meningitis, all the neuroses, the post-choleraic stage of cholera, trichinosis, diphtheria, dysentery, pleurisy, pericarditis, peritonitis, and all the diseases which are suspected to be tubercular or phthisical.

Daily-mean temperatures which are only moderately febrile, may be of very varied significance. They occur in continued and remittent febrile diseases, when these attain only a rudimentary development; also in the commencement (initial period) of such diseases, or on the contrary, when a favorable crisis has occurred; but chiefly in cases in which in the course of a single day, the temperature sinks from a considerable height till nearly normal, or even subnormal; as well as in many favorable and unfavorable irregularities which occur in the course of these diseases, after an uncompensated fall of temperature in consequence of some potent influence, as in febrile collapse, and so forth; as well as in most inflammations of mucous membranes, rheumatic affections, and inflammations of serous membranes; and not infrequently in the death-agony itself, especially when this is brought about by pressure on the brain, suffocation, anæmia, or inanition, or occurs during collapse.

When the daily-mean is much affected by some special occurrence, or some momentary alteration is induced by active remedial measures very great caution must be exercised, if we attempt to draw any conclusions from it.

§ 5. The *daily-difference*, or the extent of the excursus between the maximum and minimum of the day, may vary greatly, and the significance of the same number of degrees may be very different, in proportion as the daily mean at the same time is high or low.

In a daily mean of 37° C. (98·6° F.), daily excursus of 1° C. (1·8° F.) are of no importance—they seem at most to show only very slight disturbances of health, and may even occur in quite healthy people. On the other hand, if they amount to 1½° C. (2·7° F.) they are at least suspicious.[1] When the daily mean is 37·5° C. (99·5° F.), daily excursus of 1° C. (1·8° F.) indicate disordered condition with far more certainty; and such as amount to 1½° C. (2·7° F.) undoubtedly show some disease to be present, although not always a decidedly febrile one.

If the daily mean temperature is as much as 38·5° C. (101·3° F.), or more, the daily difference becomes of far higher importance. If the daily difference is less than ½° C. (·9° F.) a *continued fever* is to be diagnosed, when less than 1° C. (1·8° F.) a *sub-continual* fever.

The fever must be considered *remittent* when the difference is more considerable, especially when, at the same time, the day's minimum does not exceed 39·5 C. (99·5° F.).

But when the daily minimum remains at a considerable fever height, even when in the exacerbations this is only exceeded by about 1° C. (1·8° F.), or a little more, such a course has no longer the same significance as that of a truly remittent fever; it is rather a sign of a very high degree of fever, in which there is yet no trace of a disposition to a favorable termination; and it is far preferable in such cases to denote such a course by the phrase of an " Exacerbating daily fluctuation."

If the daily minimum reaches the normal, there is, in truth, an *Intermission* introduced into the febrile curve of the day, yet we are not generally accustomed to reckon such cases with intermittent forms of fever, but generally class them with remittent, more particularly when such daily minima first occur when the dis-

---

[1] As I wish to render Prof. Wunderlich's meaning perfectly clear to every reader, I will put this in another form:—If the average temperature of the day (*i.e.*, the *sum* of the highest and lowest, divided by the number of observations) be normal, *i.e.*, 98·6 F., then a range of nearly two degrees Fahrenheit (*i.e.*, anything between 97·7° and 99·5°, or in the same proportion) is quite compatible with health. But excursions of more than 2° Fahr. are probably morbid.—[TRANS.]

ease has reached its acme, and convalescence has commenced.   In like manner we are accustomed not to admit an intermittent type when the lowest degree falls under the normal, although there may be more or less considerable degrees of exacerbation, although the daily difference may thus amount to 6° C. (10·8° F.), or more.   Such an event indicates collapse, which may actually be an excessive remission, or a true intermission, which may, however, be intercurrent in the course of a fever of continuous type.

Real *intermissions* are only to be admitted when *all* the symptoms of fever abate and the return of febrile symptoms assumes a paroxysmal form; they are founded on the whole course of the disease, and not upon the fluctuations of a single day.   (See the next chapter.)

Whenever, in a fever of tolerable severity, the daily differences are but slight, they are generally a sign either that the disease is in an early stage, or that exacerbations or complications are present.

The occurrence of remissions during the height of an illness almost always indicates an improvement, or the transition towards convalescence.   A continuance of the remissions, and especially an increase in the amount of the daily difference, proves that convalescence is progressing, whilst an interruption to the remissions, combined with a continuance of a febrile daily mean, indicates either a relapse or a complication.

When the difference becomes greater, by the daily minima falling more and more (increasing difference, with a decreasing mean temperature), this is a sign, in acute diseases, that convalescence has made good progress.

But when the difference is augmented so that the elevations (*lit.* peaks) on the charts become more acuminated (increasing difference with rising daily means), this is, on the contrary, a sign of the patient's getting worse.

When the difference is augmented, through the temperature becoming sub-normal in the period of remission, it may be either a favorable, indifferent, or dangerous symptom.

When the remissions are unduly protracted, in relation to the customary course of the malady, this indicates a tendency to protracted defervescence and to sequelæ.   Especially is this the case when the patient in all other respects [except temperature] seems fairly convalescent, for then the continuance of a remitting temperature is a sign that disease has still a hold upon him, and that true recovery is yet incomplete.

A diminution of the daily difference is a favorable sign when the exacerbations become less severe at the same time (decreasing difference with decreasing daily-means); it is an unfavorable symptom when the remissions are less marked (decreasing difference with increasing mean temperature); whilst when both exacerbations and remissions are more limited in range (decreasing differences with stationary means), the significance is doubtful. The differences may remain the same, in spite of the progress or diminution of the disease; in the first case, because the exacerbations rise to a height corresponding to the fall of the remissions (stationary difference with increasing means); and in the second case, by the exacerbations decreasing in proportion to the increasing depth of the remissions (stationary difference with decreasing means).

The daily difference is usually slight, or in other words, a continuous or sub-continuous type is met with in the following diseases : in very severe typhoid fever (abdominal typhus), in true (exanthematic) typhus, in the prodromal stage of smallpox and its congeners, in scarlatina at its height, in the majority of cases of croupous and lobar (true) pneumonia, in the last stage of acute fatty degeneration, in facial erysipelas, in meningitis of the convexity of the brain, and in the last stage of fatally-ending neuroses.

On the other hand, the daily differences are generally considerable in typhoid fever of moderate or even medium severity, and even in severe cases for the first few days, and again when they are beginning to convalesce, sometimes in the recovery from true typhus, in the suppurating stage of smallpox and its allies, in measles, and all catarrhal affections, in acute polyarticular rheumatism (rheumatic fever), in basilar meningitis and acute tuberculosis, in pleurisy, pericarditis, in acute and chronic suppurations, in pyæmia, the various forms of phthisis, and in trichinosis.

Daily differences which alternate between normal and sub-normal and considerable or high febrile temperatures, occur in the advanced stage of recovering typhoid, sometimes in the suppurating stage of small-pox and its allies, occasionally towards the end of lobar pneumonia, in all malarial diseases, in pyæmia and septicæmia, and sometimes in acute tuberculosis and chronic forms of fever.

Such a change may also occur in the course of a single day's fluctuations, through some special occurrence or seizure (after hæmorrhages and such like.)

Daily differences between moderately high temperatures, and such as are normal or subnormal, are extremely common in many fevers of moderate severity, especially those progressing towards recovery, or with a protracted defervescence (lentescirenden).

§ 6. In the majority of cases we find on a *single day*, *i.e.*, in 24 hours, only one exacerbation, [whose curve] displays one, two, or three peaks, and one remission with one minimal descent. This, which is the simplest form, is by far the commonest in all sorts of diseases. Only in complicated cases of intermittent fever the fluctuation, which comprises the paroxysm with the apyrexia or intermission, has ordinarily a duration of 48 hours (tertian type).

We generally find the remission begin in the time between the late evening and the early morning; and last through the later hours of the morning (morning-remission). The exacerbation begins in the late morning-hours, or even the first hours of the afternoon; and lasts till late on in the evening, till midnight perhaps, or even later (evening exacerbation). The remission generally reaches its lowest point from 6 to 9 o'clock in the morning. and the daily maximum generally occurs in an afternoon, or early hour of the evening (3 to 6 p.m.) sometimes indeed at noon, and once now and again near midnight. Such is the general course of the temperature in almost all kinds of diseases in all stages; with the exception of malarial fevers, which far most frequently have their exacerbations at other, or at alternating times of the day, and also pyæmia, the paroxysms of which are confined to no hour of the day. Sometimes, also, we must include with these the hectic of phthisis and tuberculosis, which also not infrequently shows morning exacerbations. Occasionally, too, in particular cases of other kinds of disease, we meet with a different arrangement, *i. e.*, the rise of the temperature in the early morning hours, or at least after midnight, and remissions in the afternoon. If this only happens on a particular day, we may regard it as an irregularity, which often indicates the approach of a relapse, or a complication, although it may sometimes herald, or occur in the very moment of a favorable crisis. Yet we meet with cases in which, without affecting the results, the daily fluctuations are misplaced (as regards the time of their occurrence) throughout a considerable period, or even through the whole course of a remittent fever (in typhoid fever, or in influenza for instance), the exacerbations occurring in the morning, and the remissions in the evening—individual peculiarities which at least sometimes result from the habits and mode of life of the patient—when during health they have slept by day, and worked by night (as bakers do, for example).

In cases of *collapse*, also, we may meet with an extraordinarily low minimum in the evening.

§ 7. The *time at which the daily maximum and daily minimum occur*, may be available for diagnosis and prognosis, when we can compare several consecutive days' fluctuations. When the daily maximum occurs very early (about noon) it is generally a sign of the disease being nearly at its height, and also of its being a very severe one, whilst the occurrence of the maximum late in the day indicates that the disease is already moderated, or is of a trifling character, in the majority of cases. The occurrence of the daily minimum at an early hour, may be considered a sign of improvement, although it is not infrequently brought about by collapse in the evening, and before midnight, and cannot by itself be regarded as a decisive element for prognosis.

Far more important than the mere moment at which the maximum or minimum is reached, are the *periods* in the daily fluctuations, especially if they are preponderating in either direction, when the *daily rise of temperature begins* (ascent) on the one hand, and *when the temperature begins again to fall* (daily descent) on the other hand. The more punctually (when the rhythm of the fluctuations is not otherwise disturbed) the ascent begins in the course of the day, the more intense is the disease, and the more remote from convalescence. It is therefore always an unfavorable sign, when even in the early morning hours (before 9 a.m.) the temperature begins again to rise considerably ; and if, from comparison of several days' fluctuations, we find that the moment of rising becomes earlier day by day, an increase of the disease may be anticipated with great probability.

On the other hand a postponement of the ascent is decidedly favorable. It shortens the duration of the exacerbation, especially if in the evening hours there is a gradual moderation (remission), and we may with great probability conclude that there is improvement, although the daily maximum is yet in no degree diminished. On the other hand the later the exacerbation begins to decline (as for example first towards midnight or even later) the more severe and extreme will the disease generally be.

§ 8. The *suddenness* with which the daily rise or fall occurs, may sometimes afford materials for judgment, especially when the daily differences are considerable. The *first* rise of temperature is generally gradual, and some hours are occupied in rising a few tenths of a degree only, then a rapid rise occurs, and towards the conclusion of the process, the rise is again very gradual.

An unusually rapid rise occurs in the early stages of acute diseases, and principally in very severe ones, but especially in the cases in which intense fever-paroxysms interrupt the course of an apyrexia (or intermission) without, in the latter case, necessitating an unfavorable prognosis. On the other hand, when a rapid rise occurs half-way on in the course of a remitting disease, this is unfavorable, unless the remissions at the same time become more decided; this indicates either a great intensity of the disease, or some accidental influences causing the temperature to rise, relapses, or complications, and the like, and must in all cases call for the most careful and continued observation of the case. Just before a favorable crisis, we not infrequently meet with an unusually protracted rise of temperature, which is then generally the last of its kind, and immediately precedes defervescence. In such cases the ascent is sometimes broken by a short descent. A very rapid fall of temperature may occur in cases of convalescence, or may on the other hand be due to collapse. When the fall of temperature occurs very slowly, it is to be feared that the next day's remissions will be less marked, or entirely absent. Defervescence may be inferred with considerable probability, when we find the morning-fall interrupted in the afternoon by either a stationary temperature or a slight rise, but again resuming the descent in the evening.

In fevers of some severity the temperature generally lingers less in the vicinity of the lowest temperatures, than it does at the higher degrees; and it may therefore be regarded as a favorable symptom, when the extreme points (peaks) of temperature are very quickly attained, and very suddenly again deserted.

§ 9. The duration of the variations of temperature above the daily average, the *latitude of the exacerbations*, is in slight and even moderately severe cases, but inconsiderable, as is also the duration of the daily movement *below* the daily average (*the latitude of the remission.*) If the former be longer than the latter, the case is to be regarded as severe, without further evidence. This happens particularly in the early stages of severe diseases. The more a disease approaches to recovery, the more equality is evident, and it is therefore no slight matter, when in spite of a late period of the disease, the latitude of the exacerbations preponderates. In advanced convalescence the [curves of the] remissions become daily broader and broader, whilst [those of] the exacerbations become more pointed (steep curves). Exacerbations of great extent generally show [curves with] double or multiple summits; these elevations especially occur about midday, the early hours of afternoon, the late hours of the evening, and after midnight. If there are only two elevations (or summits) they generally happen at noon, and in the evening—sometimes in the evening, and after midnight. In the double-peaked exacerbation the evening elevation is generally the highest; in the triple-pointed the maximum-point is sometimes the first, sometimes the second, but very seldom the third of them.

These many-crested (mehr-spitzigen) daily fluctuations generally indicate a considerable exacerbation, and are therefore unfavorable; if, however, during the preceding days, the exacerbations have presented an unbroken line, their occurrence may be regarded as a sign that the fever is moderating.

§ 10. Those cases in which two or more exacerbations succeed one another in the course of twenty-four hours (*duplex and triple exacerbations*), are closely related to these multiple-peaked exacerbations just described. In many forms of disease, the afternoon exacerbation is followed by another about midnight. Very commonly the evening remission in such cases occurs with all due punctuality, and may be erroneously taken as a favorable symptom, although an observation at night would indicate a fresh exacerbation. In general a daily fluctuation, which is marked by several waves, is a sure sign that the course of the disease is complicated, or influenced by some special circumstance, or has some special tendency.

It occurs principally in very severe cases, and these are always more or less complex. It occurs in a relapse, yet it may be the prelude to convalescence; yet, indeed, the two cases present a different aspect. It is often induced by some special, and powerfully operating symptom of the disease itself, or is preparatory to such:

constipation, or very copious stools, vomiting, hæmorrhages, nervous disturbances, and sleeplessness. It may be a consequence of some injurious influence, of a more or less unsuitable diet, of catching cold, or of undue exertions in proportion to strength. It may also be induced by therapeutic operations.

The nature of a daily fluctuation marked by several waves, especially requires the most careful simultaneous investigation of all the other circumstances of the case, in order to a right estimation of its significance. Its meaning varies :

(*a*) According to the degree of the daily difference ;

(*b*) According to the type of the fever, whether that be continuous, exacerbating, or remittent.

(*c*) In proportion to the height of the daily mean, whether that indicates a very high, considerable, or moderate degree of fever, or shows a sub-febrile condition.

(*d*) In proportion as the general tendency is either to a rise of temperature or to a fall, or the disease has already entered on the period of defervescence.

In fevers exhibiting a continuously high degree of temperature, the daily fluctuations have no special (prognostic) significance, and therefore their waves, however numerous, assist us little in forming our judgment. It is only when one of the waves much overtops the other, or when, on the contrary, an unusually deep depression occurs, that one is able to draw an unfavorable conclusion from the former, and a favorable one from the latter.

In exacerbating fevers of great intensity, in which the lowest temperatures are still considerable, and the intercurrent elevations enormous, a repetition of such elevations in the course of one twenty-four hours is always more unfavorable than one solitary rise. In remittent fevers of great intensity, in which the remissions may descend to moderately febrile, or even sub-febrile, temperatures, whilst the exacerbations are very strongly marked, the occurrence of a duplex daily exacerbation, the preceding fluctuations having been simple, is an unfavorable symptom.

If the exacerbations, on the other hand, are duplicated from the very commencement, the type of disease is generally mixed, and of itself affords grounds to suspect complications.

In moderate degrees of fever, a daily fluctuation marked by numerous waves is always a suspicious symptom, and either causes us to suspect complications and disturbing causes, or at least indicates great susceptibility on the part of the individual affected. Their occurrence, when we might otherwise hope for a favorable termination, must always render this doubtful.

In the period preceding death (pro-agonistic stage) the fluctuations of temperature are often marked by a wavy outline, and we must be careful not to deceive ourselves by false hopes in such cases.[1]

[1] The whole of this chapter requires frequent reference to the charts of the temperature in various diseases, which are placed at the end, and to the diagrams, in order to understand the allusions to the varied types of the daily fluctuations.—[TRANS.]

CHAPTER XI.

THE COURSE OF THE TEMPERATURE IN FEBRILE DISEASES.

§ 1. FEBRILE diseases exhibit great variety as regards the course pursued by the temperature, but, in spite of all their differences, we can recognise certain rules as regulating their behaviour; and it is also true that the very differences they exhibit furnish us with most important data for distinguishing the several forms of disease and their varieties.

The temperature in febrile diseases may remain continuously above the normal, at least till they have passed their maximum development, or only descends below it from some special accidental circumstances, in which case it speedily regains its abnormal height = *continued* fever. Or the elevations of temperature are interrupted once, or several times, by apyretic temperatures = *intermittent* and *relapsing* fever. In such cases each interval of time, separated by the period free from fever (apyrexia), may be regarded as a fever in itself, and all that belongs to continuous fever may be attributed to this fever-abstract (so to speak); for although the disease is by no means terminated by this single paroxysm of fever, yet the paroxysm itself behaves exactly as a longer or shorter course of continued fever, and exhibits all the peculiar characters which are common to such cases.

The fever is an essential part of the disease, at least in a part of its course, in so far as it is never absent in the given forms of disease, except under very exceptional individual circumstances.

Sometimes the elevated temperature is more accidental, depending on the severity of the disease, on idiosyncrasies of the patient, and on numerous collateral circumstances.

These differences affect the course of the fever in a decided manner,

16

since in the former case this is decided by the type of disease, and in the latter principally by accidental circumstances.

The category of diseases in which fever is an essential part includes most well-marked types, besides many others which are only approximatively typical. Many of the latter, however, only show occasional elevations of temperature. This is equally true of diseases which are occasionally typical and of those which are atypical.

§ 2. The course pursued by the temperature in febrile diseases may be determined, first, by the *nature of the disease;* the more typical the form assumed by the disease, the more preponderating its influence on the course of the temperature. This influence is, indeed, not the only one, even in typical forms of disease, but it has greater force in proportion as the disease shapes itself in a pure, uncomplicated, and, so to speak, normal fashion; that is, in proportion as a previously disposed healthy individual is attacked by the original specific cause of disease without admixture of other injurious influences, and the less other disturbing influences come into play during the course of the disease. (Refer to Fundamental Principles, §§ 12 and 13.)

Secondly, the course of the temperature is determined by the *intensity* of the *disease.* Even in typical forms of disease this considerably modifies their course, and may sometimes prove the cause of a particular variety of type. It is still more decisive in approximatively typical diseases, but has only a partial influence in atypical forms.

Thirdly, the course of the temperature may be determined by *individual circumstances.* These are of limited influence only under certain conditions, *e.g.* in little children deviations of temperature are very frequent; in aged persons alterations of temperature are tardy, and the height of temperature under otherwise similar circumstances remains less considerable; whilst a freshly acquired febrile affection has very great influence on the course of the temperature of a previously existing fever; and, lastly, certain peculiar modifications of constitution, as, for example, the hysterical temperament, very commonly modify the course of the temperature.

Fourthly, the course of the temperature may depend on *accidental influences*, under which we must include many therapeutic undertakings! The degree in which these operate depends on the one side upon the potency of the influence itself, and on the other hand on the susceptibility of the individual, or of the form of disease from which he suffers. As regards the latter, truly typical forms of disease are capable of being thus influenced in only a very slight degree. Not only do accidental influences very commonly fail in influencing the course of the temperature at all in typical forms of disease, but even when they do affect it they do so in this way—either that the alteration induced by the accidental influence is only temporary, or that the modification of the course thus induced itself takes on this type of the disease.

Fifthly and lastly, the course of the temperature is especially modified by *complications* supervening on the disease, and these are sometimes able entirely to obliterate the original type of the temperature, and, indeed, to destroy all appearance of type of any kind; whilst they sometimes introduce a new and peculiar type of their own, and lead to mixed conditions; whilst sometimes their effect is only transient. An intimate knowledge of special details is required in order to estimate the working value of complications in themselves and in their relation to special diseases, and to decide in a complicated case of disease what is to be attributed to the original and essential disease and what to the particular complications which have occurred.

§ 3. The course of the temperature in febrile diseases may be divided into a number of *periods* or *stages*, which vary much in their significance, as well as in expression, and can be very clearly recognised in the form assumed by the course of the temperature. (See Fundamental Principles, § 20.)

In many diseases, and in many special cases, these stages are very strongly marked, whilst in others the lines of demarcation are very indistinct.

§ 4. The *pyrogenetic* stage, or initial-period, the first development of fever in a patient, assumes various forms, depending somewhat on the fever either preceding the development of the local affection, or running its course almost without any localised disease, or succeeding to a local morbid process. In the first case the fever begins more or less severely, and very commonly reaches a considerable height even before the appearance of any local disturbances. In these cases the initial-period generally terminates as soon as the lowest daily average temperature characteristic of the type of disease is reached, or as soon as the local affection is developed.

In the second case (if there are hardly any localised morbid processes) the beginning of the pyrogenetic stage is very indistinct, and in the same way the boundary line between it and the fastigium is more or less arbitrary, especially in less typical forms of disease.

We can easily understand that the material for observations in this stage is but scanty, from the nature of things, since few patients seek medical aid till their disease has made some progress. As regards the form of the initial stage, different cases of disease vary.

(a) There are forms of disease with a *short pyrogenetic stage*. The temperature rises suddenly, and in one line, or at least in a short interrupted line, and reaches the characteristic height in a few hours, or from one day to a day and a half. (See figs. 3 and 4.)

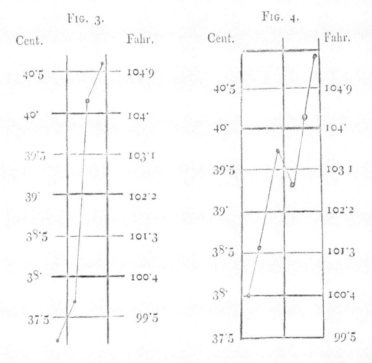

FIG. 3.   FIG. 4.

In these cases the temperature generally rises more rapidly in the trunk than in the extremities, particularly as regards the fore-arms, hands, legs (below the knees), feet, and even face. These parts still appear cold, whilst the temperature of the trunk has already risen considerably (see p. 149). In such cases there is therefore very commonly a strong feeling of chilliness, with shuddering move-ments (shivering and shaking), chattering of the teeth, and the like, to be met with, which ceases as soon as the temperature of the extremities has approximated to the elevated temperature of the trunk.

Attacks of illness which begin with a short pyrogenetic stage have for the most part but short paroxysms of fever, lasting from a few hours to a few days, with a sharp elevation of temperature (akmeartiger), or with a continuous course, not lasting more than a week, and terminated by death or by a fall of temperature. The latter happens in such cases with great rapidity (by crisis) if no disturbing influences come into play. On the other hand, these cases often exhibit a proclivity to repeated accessions of fever, or these may be a principal feature of the kind of disease present.

This kind of initial-stage is commoner in some forms of disease than in others, whilst there are forms of disease in which it never occurs at all.

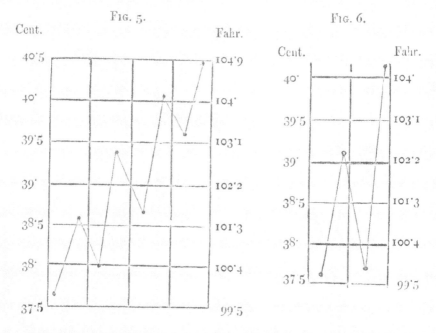

Fig. 5.

Fig. 6.

It is the rule in variolous affections (smallpox, &c.), in scarlatina, in primary croupous and lobar [true] pneumonia, in malarial attacks, in pyæmia, and in relapsing fever. It is excessively common in true exanthematic typhus, in febricula, in facial erysipelas, in tonsillar angina, and meningitis of the convexity of the brain.

It never occurs in abdominal typhus (anglicè typhoid fever), in basilar meningitis, in catarrhal affections, nor in acute polyarticular rheumatism.

(*b*) Forms of disease with *protracted pyrogenetic stage*. The rise of temperature generally happens thus : it begins to ascend in the evening, in the morning hours it moderates again, to rise again more considerably the following evening (fig. 5). It may thus happen that the normal temperature is again reached in the morning of the first day (fig. 6), or even that the initial-stage is interrupted by a still longer interval free from fever (apyrexia, fig. 7).

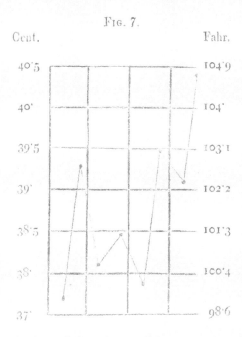

FIG. 7.

In this type the initial-stage lasts three or four days, but seldom more than a week. If the temperature is not high by that time, the illness will remain slight, and quickly pass away ; if the temperature, on the other hand, rises to a considerable height, we must not expect so sudden a termination to the illness.

This type occurs most constantly in typhoid fever, and so much so that the diagnosis can be safely based upon the initial-stage only [the other symptoms being conformable].

This kind of initial-stage is common enough in some other diseases, such as measles, acute bronchial catarrh, catarrhal pneumonia, basilar meningitis and cerebro-spinal meningitis, in acute tuberculosis, in polyarticular rheumatism (rheumatic fever), as well as in most of those cases in which fever begins to supervene on an already existing local affection, supposing the next type to be mentioned is not predominant.

(c) In many cases the development of fever is more *insidious*. Such attacks of illness do not generally conform to rules, or have at best only an approximatively typical course (fig. 8).

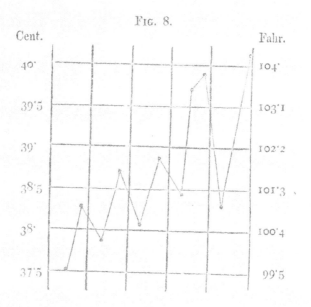

FIG. 8.

This is the common type in acute (polyarticular) rheumatism, in pleurisy, in pericarditis, in peritonitis, in lues,[1] in chronic cases of suppuration, and phthisical affections, as well as in numerous atypical affections, particularly when the fever only depends upon the gradually increasing severity of the local disturbances.

§ 5. The *fastigium* (or acmé) is that period in which the fever is most fully developed. In this stage, more especially, the temperature of the sick exhibits great variations, which may depend on a variety of influences—in fact, on all those which affect the course of the fever.

(A) The variations in the height of the temperature in the fasti-

---

[1] Syphilis has become a name so commonly known that the author prefers to use the name of Lues for its secondary and tertiary manifestations, as less calculated to produce domestic misery, in case our observations on a patient's case are overheard or our diagnosis read by unprofessional readers.—[TRANS.]

gium may be in relation to the *height* of the *maximum temperature*
(of the highest point reached by the temperature in the given case
of disease), which depends in part upon the kind of disease, and
partly on the degree of its severity; yet this circumstance, on which
people were at first inclined to lay the chief stress, is really of subordinate importance, since an isolated rise of temperature to unusual
heights may be induced by accidental collateral circumstances. Of
course, if the temperature be one incompatible with life, or even
indicating great danger—as, for example, a temperature of 42° C.
(107·6° F.), or above this—it must greatly affect our judgment of
the case.

In special forms of disease it may be worth while to determine the maxima of numerous separate cases, in order to learn the
limits between which the maxima may vary in individual cases, in
order to determine, for purposes of diagnosis, that any elevation of
temperature above those limits excludes the presence of a given form
of disease. The lower ranges of the maxima of a special form of
disease must always be less useful and less trustworthy, because one
can be by no means certain, in an individual case, whether one has
obtained the maximum temperature from the observation. Yet (for
example) by the careful observation of a brief accession of fever
one may be pretty sure that the case is not one of intermittent fever,
if the lower range of maximal temperature of intermittent fever has
never been reached. In like manner, by very painstaking observation
of a case we may exclude typhus [and typhoid] fever if a temperature of 39·5° C. (103·1° F.) has never been met with.

(B) The variations in the height of the *daily means* (average daily
temperatures) are far more important. Like the former, they also
depend on the kind and severity of the disease, and also on a multiplicity of other influences which modify the course of the disease.
The sum (total) of the daily means furnishes us with the general
average height of the whole fastigium, which is far more symptomatic than the mean of single days.

The general average height of the temperature in the fastigium
fashions itself somewhat as follows, according to the kind of disease:—

(*a*) In typhoid fever (abdominal typhus), according to the severity
of the case, it is between 39° and 40·2° C. (= 102·2° and
104·36° F.).

(*b*) In typhus fever (petechial, or true typhus), between 39·2° and 40·5° C. (102·56° and 104·9° F.).

(*c*) In the eruptive fever of smallpox and its allies, between 39° and 40° (102·2° and 104° F.).

(*d*) In measles about the same, yet very commonly somewhat lower, on account of the extent of the morning remissions.

(*e*) In normally developed scarlatina, about 40° C. (104° F.).

(*f*) In primary croupous (true) pneumonia, from about 39·2° to 40° C. (102·56° to 104° F.).

(*g*) In meningitis of the convexity (of the brain), to 40° C. (104° F.), or more.

(*h*) In articular rheumatism, without complications, generally from about 38·5° to 39·5° C. (101·3° to 103·1° F.).

(*i*) In acute influenza, from 38·5° to 39·2° C. (101·3° to 102·56° F.).

(*j*) In facial erysipelas, from 39·5° to 40° C. (103·1° to 104° F.).

(*k*) In parenchymatous tonsillitis, somewhere about 39·5° C. (103·1° F.).

Meanwhile the general average height of the fastigium temperature may very easily be modified by the circumstance that, especially when this stage is short, a single accidental remission may essentially depress the general average, whilst a single accidental exacerbation may considerably raise it. It is better, therefore, to entirely disregard such manifestly intercurrent variations of temperature, when seeking to determine the general average height.

Within certain limits the degree of average height is the chief factor in determining the intensity of the disease. The limits here set down relate only to such cases as are pretty perfectly developed. Unusually slight cases, and, on the other hand, very malignant ones, may much exceed or fall short of the limits assigned above to their average temperatures.

(c) The most valuable data, for both diagnosis and prognosis, are obtained from the *general course* of the temperature during the fastigium.

The course of the temperature during the fastigium is [when projected on a chart]—

(*a*) Either *acuminated* in form, and consists in the rapid reaching of a point at which it rapidly begins to fall, or which terminates fatally; or—

(*b*) It is a *continuous* persistence at a given height (which does not, however, preclude slight fluctuations, not exceeding $\frac{1}{2}°$ C. (·9° F.); or—

(*c*) The course is *interrupted* by considerable fluctuations in a single day, or by differences manifesting themselves in the course of different days.

(*a*) An acuminated course of temperature during the fastigium occurs in all one-day fevers, and in some whose duration is only a few days, as well as in all paroxysms of intermittent fever of short duration; in ephemeral fever, in malarial fever (ague), in pyæmia, sometimes in erratic erysipelas, seldom in pneumonia; also in herpetic eruptions and varicella, as well as in many of the daily attacks of fever in acute tuberculosis and chronic fever, and, lastly, in all terminal fevers. The fastigium may thus exhibit only a single pointed summit (fig. 9), or it may show a broad-topped maximum

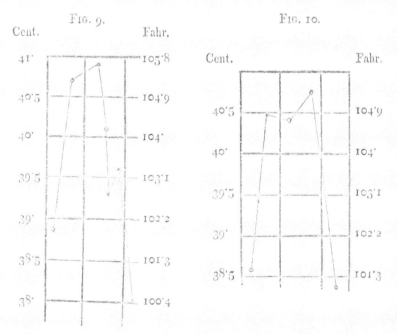

Fig. 9.　Fig. 10.

(fig. 10), or the heights may have several peaks (fig. 11). The duration of this kind of fastigium is generally only a few hours, but not infrequently it extends over more than one day.

The pyramidal fastigium either ends in death, as happens in terminal fever (fig. 12), or a downfall of temperature occurs soon after reaching its acmé, which under such circumstances is generally very rapid. In the latter case there are generally two or even more attacks of fever (paroxysms) to be expected. Such repetitions of the fever are sometimes more or less essential to the special form of

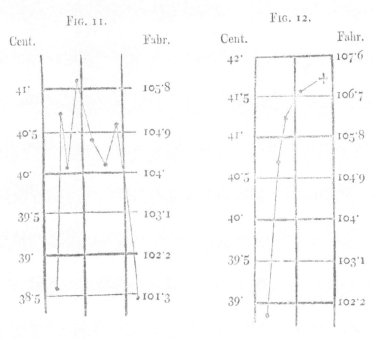

FIG. 11.   FIG. 12.

disease, e. g. malarial fevers, pyæmia, intermittent pneumonia; often customary in erratic erysipelas, acute tuberculosis, and chronic fevers; and, moreover, when a fever terminates so abruptly a relapse very frequently occurs.

(b) A *continuous course* of temperature during the fastigium seldom consists in an absolute and perfectly steady persistence of

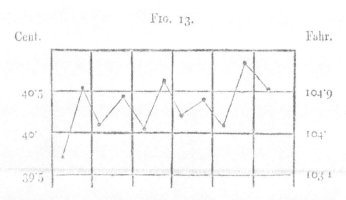

FIG. 13.

the temperature at one and the same height, but it is far more general to meet with slight fluctuations, and they may very well amount to $\frac{1}{2}°$ C. ($9°$ F.), or even a little more (fig. 13).

A *continued* course [of temperature] occurs in the fastigium—

(*a*) In every very severe acute disease.

(*b*) In most cases of severe complications supervening on a previous disease.

(*c*) And also in very mild cases of almost all kinds.

Besides this there are some diseases in which there seems to be a predilection (so to speak) for this type of fastigium, which is sometimes perfectly developed, sometimes only partially so, and always in proportion to their severity, for when they are milder the fastigium fashions itself after a non-continuous type. The forms of disease in which a continual course of temperature predominates are especially true exanthematic typhus, scarlatina, primary croupous (true) pneumonia, the prodromal stages of variola and its allies, and acute severe secondary pneumonia, facial erysipelas before it begins to extend, parenchymatous tonsillitis (angina), meningitis of the convexity of the brain; severe general febrile affections, in which, although not localised, slight microscopic pathological lesions are sometimes discovered; and chiefly diseases which have a short initial stage of rigors.

When diseases which usually exhibit a remittent or non-continuous course assume a continuous type, it must always be regarded as an unfavorable symptom.

The height of the average temperature is of great importance in forming a judgment of the intensity and danger of the disease in such as have a continuous type. The continuous course of temperature is either persistent at one level, or in favorable cases descending (fig.

FIG. 14.

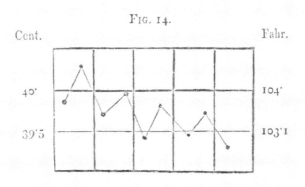

14), or sometimes at first, and in unfavorable cases, ascending (fig. 15).
It is often broken into two distinct parts, of which the first is generally the more severe, and the second milder.

FIG. 15.

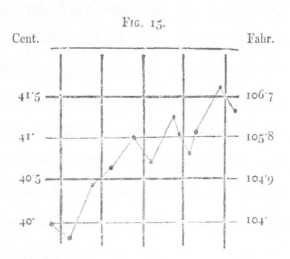

They are generally divided by a considerable fall of temperature
(*pseudo-crisis*).

The continued course of temperature usually lasts but a short
time, seldom more than a week.

It either terminates fatally or remissions set in, which are for the
most part a sign of improvement, provided that the exacerbations do
not much exceed the previous height of the temperature; but these
remissions may sometimes announce the commencement of a fatal
end, or the continuous course may merge into defervescence, which
is generally rapid, though sometimes protracted. This defervescence
may either immediately succeed the continued fastigium, without any
further change, or it may be divided from this by a period of critical
perturbations, or by a preparatory decrease of temperature (*lysis*).

This continuous course of temperature may sometimes be repeated,
and is then interrupted either by a more or less lasting and considerable moderation of temperature, or sometimes by a remitting
course.

(c) In the great majority of diseases the course of the temperature
is *non-continuous* during the fastigium.

This is the rule in many diseases, as in abdominal typhus (*typhoid
fever*), catarrhal affections, catarrhal and putrid pneumonia, measles,
polyarticular rheumatism, osteo-myelitis, meningitis without much

affection of the summit of the brain, pyæmia, suppuration-fevers, the secondary fever of variolous affections, trichinosis, lues (constitutional syphilis), and chronic fevers, and more or less commonly so in other diseases.

The fluctuations between most of the evening exacerbations and morning remissions may be more or less considerable, and, therefore, the absolute height of the *daily maxima* may be very varied. In cases of moderate severity the morning remissions fall more or less below the average height of the fastigium of the particular disease (remittent type, fig. 16), whilst in severe cases the morning remissions

FIG. 16.

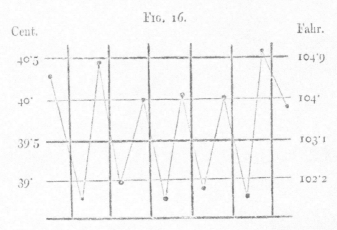

generally remain above the average level of the disease in question, or rather of its stage of fastigium, whilst at the same time the evening exacerbations are more or less considerably removed from, and rise above, this average level (type with exacerbations, fig. 17).

FIG. 17.

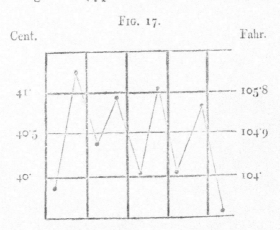

The extent or *excursus of the fluctuations* between the morning and evening temperatures may be very varied, ranging from $\frac{3}{4}°$ to 3 or 4 degrees Centigrade ($= 1\cdot35°$ to $5\cdot4°$ or $7\cdot2°$ Fah.). See fig. 18.

FIG. 18.

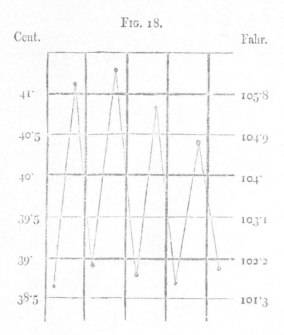

The alternations (*lit.* exchange) between exacerbations and remissions are sometimes more or less *regular*, and, indeed, in acute diseases may repeat with the utmost regularity the same daily height of exacerbations and depth of remissions for a whole week together, or even more; and in chronic fevers this regular alternation may go on even for months with perfect, or nearly perfect, identity. Yet this does not preclude the occurrence of two periods, even in the non-continuous fastigium, the first with slighter and the second with more extended excursions or fluctuations [or inversely as the continuous type]. But occasionally, and especially in complicated or otherwise abnormal cases, as well as in special forms of disease (particularly in pyæmia), the non-continuous course of temperature exhibits more or less striking *irregularities*. Sometimes it continues an even course for only a few days preparatory to abnormalities. Such irregularities may occur from accidental influences, individual circumstances, and many other conditions. These irregularities may consist in—

(*a*) The remissions and exacerbations occurring at irregular times

—sometimes earlier, sometimes later in the day, or lasting for a longer or shorter time on a given day.

(*b*) Or in a want of correspondence between the depth of the remissions and the height of the exacerbations.

(*c*) Or of intercurrent and powerful *retrograde movements* of temperature, sometimes taking the form of isolated falls of considerable extent, sometimes of more or less lasting, but not strongly marked decrease of temperature, such as often occurs through favorably operating influences, and is induced by many accidental events. In some diseases, however, this may often occur spontaneously, and must not then be regarded as a favorable symptom.

(*d*) In intercurrent *elevations* of temperature, which either occur once or consist in more or less lasting intercurrent rises of temperature, which are for the most part the result of unfavorable influences or the development of complications.

(*e*) And occasionally, though but seldom in this stage, the irregularities consist in intercurrent *collapse*.

Generally speaking, the irregularities proceed from a combination of two or more of these; and when once irregularities have broken in upon the regular course, and destroyed its typical character, the regular type is seldom resumed again, or only imperfectly. Sometimes the course of the temperature appears quite anomalous, fluctuating hither and thither with sudden elevations and equally sudden falls, and with occasional alternations of the continuous and non-continuous type (commonest in pyæmia).

The *varieties in the non-continuous course of temperature during the fastigium* result, for the most part, from the nature of the disease and the degree of its severity. But the absence or presence of complications, events occurring perhaps only once, accidental and also therapeutical influences, and finally the individuality (idiosyncrasy) of the patient himself, all contribute their share in determining the nature of the fastigium in the non-continuous type.

Of all the diseases which exhibit a non-continuous course in their fastigium, abdominal typhus (typhoid fever) is the most clearly typical. It has clearly defined minimal limits to its exacerbations ($39 \cdot 5$ C. $= 103 \cdot 1°$ F.); tolerably well-marked limits to the daily excursus (which does not much exceed $1\frac{1}{2}°$ C. $= 2 \cdot 7$ F.); an extremely regular course (at least in normal uncomplicated cases); and a very accurately defined limit to the duration of its fastigium (not under eight nor over seventeen days). This disease may, indeed, be affected by individual circumstances, but these do not easily affect the range of its temperature, and still less often its duration.

All the remaining forms of disease, with a non-continuous type of fastigium, exhibit greater varieties, and the influence of collateral circumstances is more strikingly shown.

The *absolute height* of the *maxima* of the *exacerbations* is generally very considerable in the non-continuous part of the course of recurrent fever, in the suppurating fever of variola, in measles, catarrhal pneumonia, pyæmia, osteo-myelitis, facial erysipelas, and acute tuberculosis. On the other hand, it depends more upon the severity of the attack, or upon the existence of severe complications, whether the height of the exacerbations is considerable in the following diseases:—Influenza, polyarticular rheumatism, pleurisy, cerebro-spinal meningitis, trichinosis, lues, and acute suppuration. The maxima of the exacerbations may remain inconsiderable in spite of very severe disease, in acute fatty degeneration, basilar meningitis, dyphtheria, dysentery, pericarditis, and peritonitis.

The *daily difference*, or the width of the excursus of the fluctuations, depends on the form and severity of the disease. Sometimes the extent of the excursus approximates closely to the type of intermitting fever (pseudo-intermittent), and sometimes the smallness of the difference imitates the continuous course. Cases of the latter kind must generally be considered severe, whilst the former (pseudo-intermittent), especially if the temperature is very high in the exacerbations, must be at least suspected of malignancy (*tückisch* = tricksy); they give rise to the suspicion of latent pyæmic or septic infections, or of successive embolisms, and are generally connected with secondary deposits [in the tissues], and particularly so in the suppurating fever of smallpox, in parotitis, acute rheumatism, endo-carditis, pleuritis, inflammatory affections of the liver and spleen, suppuration in any part, whatever the original cause; and always more so the higher the temperature goes in the exacerbations. Such latent self-infecting processes may occur also in other diseases, and, since many of them are, at least occasionally, impossible to diagnose, the development of remissions which almost amount to intermissions, followed by exacerbations of considerable height, becomes of very great importance, and must always make us dread danger, and more especially so when such a course lasts several days without the exacerbations moderating. This does not set aside the fact that in many of these cases recovery may occur without any subsequent

17

confirmation of the suspicion, yet in such cases it will generally be found impossible to discover any other ground for such a course of temperature. Exacerbations reaching a very high degree with almost, or entirely, apyretic remissions, occur in the fastigium, without any special danger, most frequently in the prodromal fever of measles, in severe influenza, in erratic erysipelas, and also in lues [constitutional syphilis]. On the other hand, if the temperature nearly reaches normal in the remissions, whilst in the exacerbations it exceeds the limits of moderate fever only slightly, or not at all, one may generally consider the case to be a mild one, unless, from the nature of the disease, great and perhaps unavoidable danger exists, apart from fever altogether. For this reason, moderate exacerbations, with almost perfect absence of fever in the mornings, do not justify a favorable prognosis in the following diseases :—Acute fatty degeneration, acute capillary bronchitis (bronchiolitis), basilar- and cerebro - spinal meningitis, acute tuberculosis, diphtheria, severe dysentery, peritonitis, and acute parenchymatous nephritis. Perfect *regularity* of alternation between exacerbations and remissions, as to both time and height, must not be expected in any other form of disease mentioned here, except abdominal typhus; or, in other words, no particular importance as a symptom is to be attributed to such irregularities in any other disease except abdominal typhus. The following diseases chiefly and generally exhibit more or less regularity of course : — Influenza, catarrhal pneumonia, on which account both may assume a great resemblance to typhoid fever (abdominal typhus) during their fastigium, polyarticular rheumatism (in which the temperatures are generally not so high in the exacerbations as in typhoid fever), pleurisy, cerebro-spinal meningitis, trichinosis, suppurations, lues, phthisis, and chronic fevers. Sub-acute tuberculosis sometimes follows a very regular course for some time, although just as often it shows most remarkable irregularities.

With so great a predisposition in the non-continuous fever-course towards irregularities, very trivial occurrences suffice to make their course irregular. This principally occurs from complications from special events in the course of the disease, and through influences and circumstances of either a favorable or an unfavorable nature.

Complications generally affect a non-continuous course, in such a way as to render the course of the temperature either temporarily or persistently continuous, or approximating to that type, although sometimes they change the remittent course into an exacerbating one.

Isolated events principally induce sudden springs or plunges, sometimes rises of temperature, sometimes—indeed, very often—falls of the same, and even collapse; the latter is particularly wont to be induced by hæmorrhages, vomiting, strong diarrhœa, immoderate perspirations, and perforations of serous cavities.

Influences of either a favorable or unfavorable kind may have either a temporary or a lasting effect. It is possible, in many cases, after long experience, to recognise a definite typical course as the result of certain therapeutical influences, at least in certain kinds of diseases, in this way; in typhus (enteric fever?), calomel, digitalis, and cold-water treatments each furnish us with, so to speak, typical and definite modifications in the course of the disease, and so does bloodletting in pneumonia.

The *direction taken by the temperature* when the course is non-continuous may in like manner differ; the fastigium may either continue to assume a *uniform* character, or sometimes it takes an *ascending*, sometimes a *descending* direction; (of the course modi), which in most cases sufficiently accurately corresponds with the severity and dangerousness of the disease.

The *ascending* direction may consist—

(*a*) In an increase in the height of the daily averages of temperature (fig. 19).

FIG. 19.

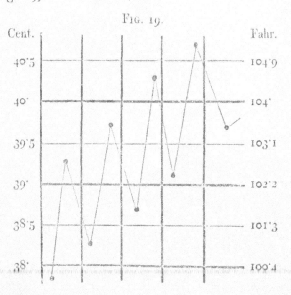

(*b*) Or in the remitting type approximating to a continuous or exacerbating one (fig. 20).

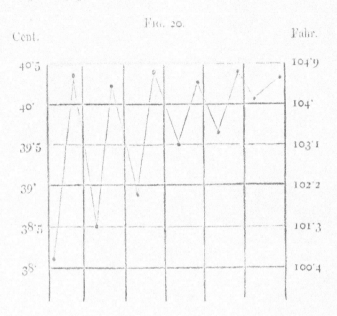

FIG. 20.

The *descending* type is to be recognised by exactly opposite symptoms. A change in the direction of the fastigium usually happens gradually and easily, but sometimes suddenly and rudely, and is generally led up to by very brief irregularities.

The fastigium may be broken into two abstracts, or phases, more or less sharply defined, through an abrupt change of direction, and these not infrequently correspond to a whole week, or half of one. When the fastigium lasts longer the various characteristic phases can be clearly recognised by the curves, and if an ascending direction is succeeded by a uniform course, and then a descending one makes itself evident, we are warranted in a favorable prognosis; but when, on the other hand, a uniform progress is lost in an ascending direction, the case is bad, although not yet on this account a lost one. The *duration* of the fastigium in the non-continuous type is, on an average, longer than in the continuous one, and very often depends on the kind of disease, and on the other hand very much on its severity. It is obvious that in most (that is, not suddenly fatal) cases a short duration of the fastigium indicates that the cases are not very severe. When the fastigium is much prolonged, it is always noteworthy.

The prodromal stage of measles, in favorable cases, has a particularly short fastigium.

In influenza, bronchitis, cynanche, tonsillaris, parotitis, catarrhal pneumonia, wandering erysipelas, the suppurating fever of smallpox, in peritonitis, and the reaction fever of cholera, the fastigium cannot last more than five or six days without the case becoming dangerous. The fastigium lasts one to two and a half weeks in abdominal typhus (enteric or typhoid fever).

Even in favorable cases the fastigium is, comparatively speaking, prolonged in polyarticular rheumatism, in pleurisy, in trichinosis, in suppuration, in cerebro-spinal meningitis, and in lues (constitutional syphilis).

In basilar meningitis the probability of a fatal termination is little affected by the length of the fastigium.

In septicæmia and pyæmia a protracted fastigium is rather a hopeful indication, and the same may be said of acute tuberculosis.

In phthisis and other chronic febrile affections the fever may persist in a remitting course for a great length of time, for months and even years, with great uniformity; although it may sometimes be spontaneously interrupted for some weeks, or in consequence of some influences brought to bear upon it, the former fluctuations often recur with great regularity, and with an identical height of the daily temperature.

(D) In most diseases the fastigium is simple; on the other hand, it may be doubled or repeated more than once in the following affections :—In typhoid fever with successive relapses, in relapsing fever, in smallpox, in irregular exanthems, in many cases of pneumonia (relapsing forms), in pyæmia and septicæmia (with apparent improvement intervening), in facial erysipelas (following an apparent relapse), in polyarticular rheumatism (in complicated cases), in basilar meningitis, cerebro-spinal meningitis, pleurisy, and phthisis.

When the fastigium repeats itself, the first differs from the second and successive stages. Continuous, remittent, and paroxysmal types may alternate with each other. The more continuously elevated these later stages are the more unfavorable, generally speaking.

(E) The *close of the fastigium* is sometimes clearly defined, sometimes it is indistinctly marked and merges into the other stages. Sometimes a brief rise of temperature occurs at the close of the fastigium. This was particularly noticed by the physicians of old times, and designated by them as the *perturbatio critica* (fig. 21).

FIG. 21.

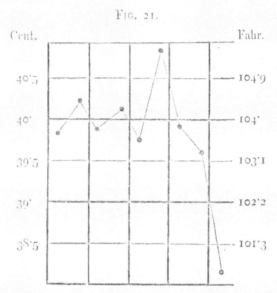

In other cases we meet with a considerable fall of temperature — preparatory decrease. In the prodromal stages of smallpox the fastigium ends as soon as the eruption becomes "shotty" (Erhebung zu Knötchen).

In measles it terminates when the eruption is at its height.

In scarlatina when the exanthem begins to pale.

In pneumonia when hepatization is completed, seldom before the third, or after the ninth day.

In true petechial typhus, towards the end of the second week, sometimes in the middle of the third week.

In abdominal typhus, or enteric fever, in mild cases in the middle or at the end of the second week, in severe ones in the middle or at the end of the third week, and sometimes not till the fourth week.

In influenza it generally ends after a few days.

In parenchymatous tonsillar angina after lasting from three to seven days.

In the remaining diseases the termination is more or less uncertain.

§ 6. The periods of development and completion of most diseases come to an end with the fastigium; that is, they either pass on at once to a fatal termination, or immediately begin the convalescent stage. Yet the fastigium is frequently followed by a stage of indecision.

This period of indecision (*amphibolic* stage) is most evident when the course of the temperature is most regular in the fastigium, whilst with an irregular course of temperature in the fastigium it becomes difficult to separate this from the amphibolic stage. Cases which, without quickly proving fatal, run a very severe course, almost always have an amphibolic stage. This is most strikingly severe and lasting in bad cases of enteric fever. It also occurs in severe and lingering cases of pneumonia, in exanthems with severe complications, in petechial typhus under similar conditions, in polyarticular rheumatism of great severity, and in epidemic cerebro-spinal meningitis.

The amphibolic period displays more or less want of regularity, and is marked by isolated changes of temperature, or such as last for a few days, and exacerbations and remissions of varying degree; the remissions, indeed, generally occur in the morning, but frequently at other times also, and the exacerbations are not limited to any hour of the day. Intercurrent collapse is often met with. The temperature rises suddenly, either from some recognised cause, or as it were casually, and slight improvements take place in a similar manner, and both sometimes last only a few hours, or frequently a few days, whilst now and again alterations take place on alternate days, generally in a very irregular fashion. Sometimes, when the amphibolic stage lasts some time, we notice on certain days of the disease, at the middle or end of a week (of the illness), certain special changes, which do not, however, last long enough to modify the general character of the course.

Notwithstanding all these irregularities, however, the temperature keeps within limits which permit some definition, and the separate temperatures seldom reach the maximal heights of the fastigium.

The amphibolic stage may last from a few days to a week or even more. It lingers longest in severe cases of abdominal typhus.

§ 7. When a disease is at its height, and in the amphibolic stage, the fever is more or less easily *influenced* by processes in the organism itself, or by causes which operate on it from without, sometimes injuriously and sometimes with benefit to the patient. It may be stated generally that those processes and influences which cause the previously high temperature to rise still higher are prejudicial, whilst, on the contrary (although not invariably), those which tend to moderate the temperature are beneficial. Therapeutics should therefore aim at utilising the latter, and also strive to greatly multiply them, but, above all, to determine as far as possible their true powers, and how far they may be safely employed. A *rise of temperature* may be induced in febrile patients by mental excitement, by movements of the body, by being kept too warm, by errors in diet, by persistent constipation, and by the occurrence of complications.

A *diminution of the high temperatures* can be brought about in the fastigium and in the amphibolic stage by the following causes:

By spontaneous hæmorrhages (v. p. 134).

By copious stools, by vomiting, and profuse perspirations.

Also by the respiration becoming impeded and imperfect, by paralysis of the heart, by pressure on the brain, and by starvation.

Sometimes, but by no means always, by tranquil sleep.

Still further by the proper application of cold to the body of the patient.

By medicinal bloodlettings; and finally, by the ingestion (incorporation) of a number of medicines, amongst which the following are already recognised as antipyretic:—Mercury (calomel), antimony (tartar-emetic), lead, digitalis, veratria, quinine, acids, and the so-called "cooling" salts, laxatives, and emetics.

The amount and safety of their operation is, however, by no means the same in all cases having a similar temperature, and the suceptibility of single cases is even yet more varied. One fever patient is very susceptible of their influences, and therefore quickly responds to the action of medicines and well-chosen therapeutic procedures. In other cases the fever has more resistance (so to speak), and all methods of procedure remain altogether, or at least for a time, without any effect.

The temperature is most easily affected when the fever is at its height and in the amphibolic stage, principally in children, in delicate individuals, in diseases of moderate severity, after spontaneously occurring falls of temperature, in temperatures with a non-continuous course, and in the natural daily remission. Robust adults, very severe diseases at their onset, and complicated maladies, the continuous type of fever, and the hours of daily exacerbation, on the contrary, exhibit more or less resisting power.

§ 8. The course taken by the temperature during *convalescence* may be more or less peculiar.

Diseases differ very considerably in the mode in which recovery from them generally takes place, and the difference is most charac-teristic when the course of disease is least complicated and, so to speak, most normal. In one disease the morbid process appears almost instantaneously exhausted and terminated, and what follows is merely compensatory, without being serious—the return to the old order of things follows quickly, and without hindrance. Such a course may be noted in petechial typhus, in varioloid, varicella, and measles, in primary croupous, lobar and uncomplicated pneu-monia, in febricula, in relapsing fever, in facial erysipelas, in parenchymatous tonsillar angina, in the fever of cholera-reaction without parenchymatous degeneration of the kidneys. In other forms of disease such alterations in the texture of the parts are induced by the morbid process itself, so many new products stand-ing in organic relation to another, and so much destruction of tissues is brought about, that there is need of long and laborious processes of reparation, easily permitting of renewed damage and dis-turbance, in order to restore again more or less of pristine order and regularity.

To such a category belongs enteric fever (abdominal typhus), and for the most part scarlatina, true smallpox, acute polyarticular rheumatism (rheumatic fever), all forms of meningitis, trichinosis, pleurisy, pericarditis, dysentery, &c.

That which occurs in these last-named diseases, from the essential nature of the morbid processes, may also be brought about by com-plications and unfavorable circumstances in the first class, although in a normal way recovery from them is sudden and without difficulty. Naturally enough, there are cases intermediate between these two types of rapid recovery and protracted and tedious reparation.

The course of the temperature corresponds to these varied re-lations, and therefore this allows us to draw conclusions as to the mode of recovery.

In cases of laborious convalescence very considerable rises of tem-perature may occur in the midst of the healing processes. This harmonises with the fact that in certain forms of disease the patient is most, and most often exposed to danger just at the very period of recovery.

On the other hand, in those diseases in which there are no great obstacles to recovery the fever also passes away with the disease.

The course of the temperature during the process of recovery may be divided into—(*a*) The period of decided, but still insufficient, decrease of temperature (stadium decrementi).

(*b*) The period of cessation of the fever, for which I have introduced the now generally accepted term " defervescence."

(*c*) And the period after defervescence, epicrital period, and recovery.

§ 9. The first stage in the restorative process, the period of decided, but still insufficient, decrease of temperature, cannot, indeed, be observed in all cases. When it is present it either closely succeeds the fastigium or immediately follows the amphibolic period, or after a precursive rise of temperature; then immediately succeeds for a day or two a slight fall, which is at once followed by unmistakable defervescence (see fig. 22). This preparatory

FIG. 22.

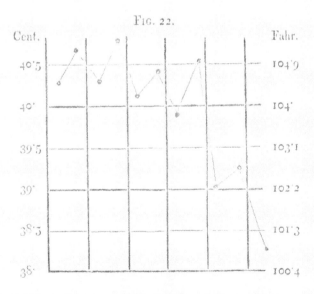

process of slight decrease of temperature may be gone through so imperceptibly, in acute cases, that it may be difficult to define the commencement of true defervescence. This preliminary decrease may amount to half or even a whole degree (Centigrade = 9 to 1·8° Fahr.) in very high fevers and pseudocrises; in the latter, indeed, it may even reach 3° C. (= 5·2° F.) or more. Sometimes it consists in a moderation, or perhaps entire absence, of the customary evening exacerbation, in such a manner that on the day of decrease the daily fluctuation is absent, and the morning elevation of temperature persists continuously;

Or it may consist of a greater morning remission, whilst in the evening the temperature reaches its previous height;

Or it may happen that the morning remission is more considerable, and the evening exacerbation is less marked, thus making the daily difference the same, whilst the average temperature of the day appears lower;

Or it may consist in a pseudo-crisis followed by a slight rise of temperature. It not infrequently happens that in this way for several days, or even a whole week, the daily averages may be actually lower than in the preceding time of the fastigium or of the amphibolic period, whilst at the same time a moderated febrile condition persists for several days, or subsides very slowly, before the proper defervescence.

Such a course is easily distinguished from the amphibolic stage, for in that which we are now describing no fresh aggravations occur, and the rises of temperature in the evening hours are nothing else but the expression of the daily fluctuations; they have no unfavorable significance, provided the morning remissions occur regularly. There are no forms of disease in which such a stadium decrementi may not be met with, and defervescence may succeed it either rapidly or lingeringly. Therapeutic efforts often manifestly hasten its commencement. On the other hand, the length of this stage varies with the kind of disease. In abdominal typhus the stadium decrementi may last from several days to a week or more, and the same may occur in the suppurating stage of variola. It is shorter in petechial typhus and in scarlatina, and shorter still in measles and lobar pneumonia. In forms of disease which are only approximatively typical the length of this stage may be very various, and affords less warrant for believing that it will be immediately followed by defervescence. And in these, without any fresh complications occurring, the temperature may begin to rise again, and the course once more assume the characters of the fastigium. In these cases a state of diminished fever has intervened between two periods of fastigium, and gives a deceptive appearance of recovery. Just such wholly deceptive and false moderations of temperature are met with in pyæmia and in the amphibolic stage of many diseases.

§ 10. The most clearly defined distinctions are met with in the period of defervescence, according to the kind of disease; and the deviations from the proper type of the special form of disease afford us very safe indications as to the anomalies and imperfections of the recovery.

(*a*) *Defervescence* may occur quite suddenly (rapid defervescence, *crisis*) in such a way that it is complete in four, twelve, twenty-four, or at the most thirty-six hours; the temperature falls during this time from 2°— 5° C. (= 3·6° to 9° F.), and, indeed, sometimes more than that, reaching to normal, or even below that (figs. 23 and 24).

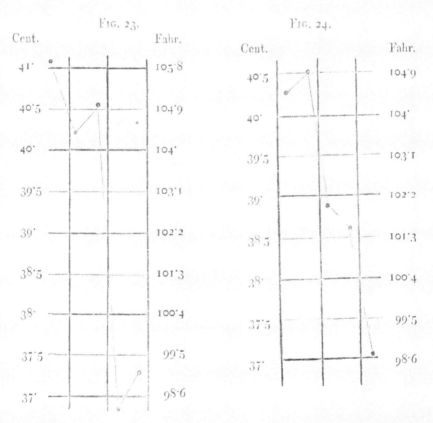

In this way the fever may terminate in the time between morning and evening, or in the course of a night, and already next morning perfectly normal temperatures may be reached; but the end of the fever is not to be assumed until we see that no fresh rise of temperature takes place on the next afternoon and evening. Such a rise is not uncommon, but it does not reach the height of the day before, and definitely passes on into the feverless condition on the next night.

This rapid defervescence may often extend over twenty-four hours. The temperature falls in the early morning more or less rapidly; in the course of the afternoon it falls still more, but more slowly, or the temperature remains the same, or even rises afresh, and the normal temperature is first attained on the morning after. It may also happen, even on the second evening, that the temperature rises again a little, but this rise is generally very trifling (see fig. 25).

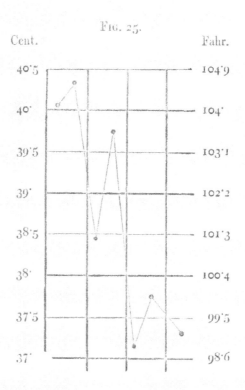

Fig. 25.

It happens, occasionally, that there is no disposition to defervescence to be remarked in the morning hours, or at most only a very moderate depression, and often, indeed, an unaccustomed height of temperature, and that defervescence begins in the afternoon or evening. In such cases the decrease is seldom considerable; very commonly the defervescence is to be recognised by the absence of the evening exacerbations, or instead of this a slight fall, amounting to $\frac{1}{10}$ to $\frac{3}{10}$° C. (about $\frac{1}{5}$ to $\frac{1}{2}$° F. or a little more), upon which the defervescence on the following evening may be based, or even then may require twenty-four hours in the way just described for its completion (see fig. 26).

Fig. 26.

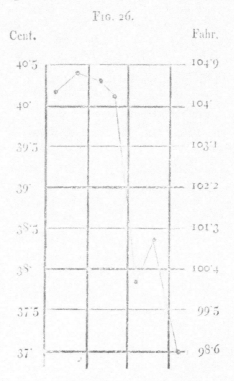

The temperature often falls below the normal, either almost to 36° C. (96·8° F.), or even below that, when defervescence is very rapid, and this is especially apt to be the case when therapeutic efforts have been made to reduce the temperature. But even such an immoderate depression gives no guarantee that the temperature may not rise again, and we cannot make sure of defervescence, unless the temperature on the next evening confines itself within normal limits. Symptoms of collapse are often met with in cases where there has been a very rapid fall from a previously extreme height of temperature, and the general disturbance in the economy is so great that the patient and those around him often consider the situation more critical than even at the height of the fever, and when it was really dangerous. By means of the thermometer we are able in such cases to recognise the transition towards health in these unpleasant and apparently unfavorable circumstances. Generally speaking, this uncomfortable condition, which may be accompanied by delirium, only lasts a few hours, yet it may continue for a day or two; and if the temperature continues to be normal, or subnormal, there is nothing at all to dread, unless the fall of temperature, instead of depending on the termination of the illness, is the result of the intervention of some severe and easily recognisable event, such as a copious hæmorrhage, perforation of the intestine, or perforation of the lung, &c. There is generally rapid defervescence (crisis) in those cases and forms of disease in which there is a very rapid rise of temperature in the initial stage, and which are thus for the most part free from complications of special cases. Relapsing fever exhibits the most striking and constant rapid defervescence, and the excursus is the widest (5° or 6° C. = 9° or 10·8° F., or more, in a few hours), and this is as true of the first attack as of the relapse. It is the rule in the uncomplicated cases of primary croupous pneumonia which do not last more than a week, in varioloid diseases and typical measles. It occurs also in ephemeral fever (febricula), in all fevers and febrile cases of acute kind (Akme-artig, i. e. in which the temperature assumes a pointed or a pyramidal outline). It is the rule in parenchymatous tonsillar angina, and also occurs in facial erysipelas, but is no guarantee in the latter that a new fever may not begin with further extension of the cutaneous inflammation. It also occurs very often in petechial typhus, less often in scarlatina and catarrhal fevers.

(b) In an opposite class of cases, defervescence takes place more slowly, in an *extended line*, or by *lysis*, and this may be—

(1) Either in a *continuous* but tedious fall of temperature, in which this generally falls rather less from morning to evening than it does from evening to morning, or may even remain stationary, or rise a little [during the day]. In this manner the decline occupies two to four days, and sometimes a whole week (fig. 27, on page 272).

This is particularly the case in scarlatina (see page 221), in petechial typhus, and sometimes in pneumonia, if the course of this disease is not quite normal or lasts over a week. This mode of defervescence only occurs exceptionally in abdominal typhus, and occasionally in catarrhal forms of fever.

Or lysis may exhibit a *remittent* type, in which morning remissions alternate with evening exacerbations, but on the whole either the daily maximum or the daily average is less from day to day.

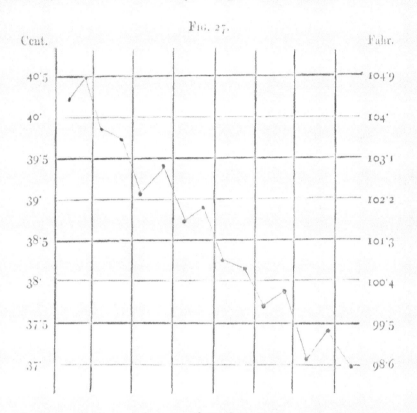

Fig. 27.

In this way it may happen that the evening exacerbations continue to reach their previous high degrees for some time, whilst the morning remissions become more marked from day to day, till at a later period the exacerbations also decrease in severity (fig. 28, on page 273).

Or the daily differences remaining the same, both the morning and evening temperatures may become lower (see fig. 29, on page 274); or the evening exacerbations may become less severe, and gradually approximate to the morning remissions (fig. 30, on page 275).

These various forms may succeed one another, and in this way the transition from one to the other may be sudden and abrupt (stoss- und schub-weiser).

Remitting defervescence may last from three or four days to a whole week or more, and interruptions to the regularity of its course are very commonly met with.

It is the characteristic type in enteric fever (abdominal typhus), is customary in the suppurating fever of variola, and very com-

FIG. 28.

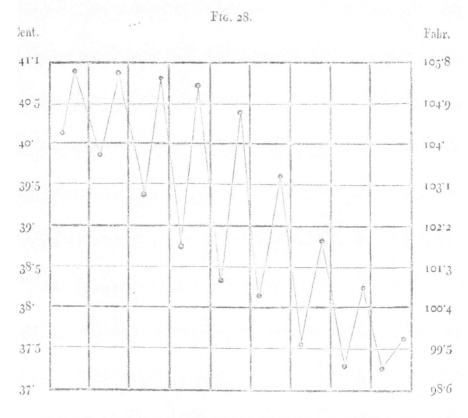

monly met with in severe forms of catarrhal disease. It also occurs frequently in acute polyarticular rheumatism, as well as in trichinosis, pericarditis and peritonitis.

Collapse not infrequently occurs in remitting defervescence, at least in severe diseases; and the way in which it happens is by the morning temperature falling considerably below normal, which is succeeded by the other symptoms of collapse. This state of affairs may last for several days.

§ 10. In the epicritical period, and especially in *convalescence*, when this has undoubtedly commenced, and remains undisturbed, the temperature is normal both in the morning and in the evening; and only the normal daily fluctuations which are met with in health occur. This behaviour of the temperature is the safest guarantee

18

that the healing process will be perfected. As long as ever such febrile temperatures are met with in the evening hours, convalescence is still imperfect; whilst if the temperature is above normal in the morning hours, it is a still greater argument against satisfactory convalescence having set in. Yet in special cases, and in many diseases, we find that the daily fluctuations, far on in the course of

FIG. 29.

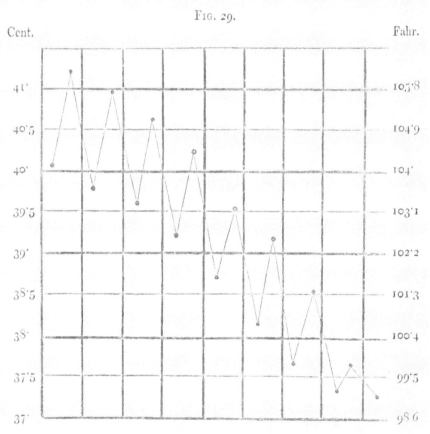

Cent.

Fahr.

convalescence, are on a somewhat elevated plane of daily averages, without the prospects of recovery being materially affected; for example, this is very common in articular rheumatism.

The temperature of convalescents is, however, almost always more mobile, and more easily influenced, than that of healthy people, and the daily fluctuations are somewhat greater than in health. Outward influences, little ailments, trifling errors in diet, little muscular exertions, such as the first rising from bed, cause sufficiently noticeable rises of temperature, and sometimes they occur without any assignable cause. For example, a rise of temperature is often met with when the convalescent is allowed animal food for the first time, especially if this be given a little too soon. (Fig. 31 on page 276.)

FIG. 30.

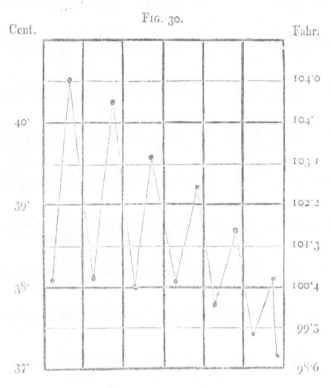

Such slight elevations of temperature, however, only last a very short time, and disappear after one or two days, or so, when everything else is as it should be.

Walking about will again induce temporary rises of temperature, amounting to $\frac{1}{2}$ a degree Centigrade ($= \frac{9}{10}$ Fah.), or a little more, which speedily compensate themselves when the patient lies down again. Whenever the temperature remains elevated, however slightly, and generally when the temperature rises still more, we may confidently assume that the healing process is yet incomplete, or that a fresh malady, a sequela, or a hypostrophe is being developed. And the incompleteness of the recovery generally shows itself either in continued evening exacerbations, or in the temperature remaining abnormal in the morning, or in occasional strongly marked relapses into fever, extending over several days, which often exhibit themselves only in the elevated temperatures. The beginning of an acute affection (whether a relapse, or some other complication) during convalescence, is generally shown by a suddenly occurring rise of temperature after the type of the new affection.

Fig. 31.

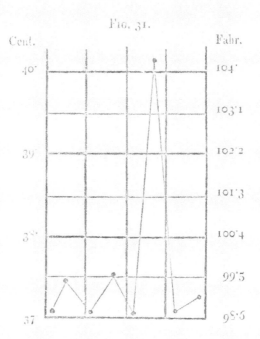

§ 11. If an illness, instead of recovering, or directly terminating fatally, is followed by *sequelæ*, the course of temperature just described as belonging to recovery may go on towards convalescence, and the sequela may set in after a longer or shorter duration of the convalescent stage, with or without a fresh occurrence of fever.

Yet in almost all these cases the healing process is imperfect, retarded, interrupted, and exhibits many deviations from the normal; for instance, in forms of disease which generally recover with rapid defervescence, the fever in these cases terminates by lysis; and in such as are accustomed to end in lysis, the process is protracted, fresh rises of temperature intervene, and there are pauses in the progress towards recovery; or even in apparent convalescence, the temperature does not become normal, or rapidly rises again without obvious cause.

The transition to a consecutive disease (sequela) may occur during the amphibolic stage, the stage of decrement, or at any point in the defervescence. The sort of thing that generally occurs is this: —after some slight and deceptive remissions of temperature have occurred (or even more considerable ones, though not equalling those which might fairly be expected, and it may be not easily traceable to any special influences), and have held out false hopes for a short time, the apparent lysis is proved to be only apparent, by a fresh elevation of temperature or the failure of further progress towards improvement. The further course is determined by the nature of the sequelæ, and the preceding disease has hardly any influence on the course of the fever which may accompany the consecutive disease.

§ 12. A *fatal termination* is often preceded by symptoms lasting for a longer or shorter interval, which are for the most part of an unfavorable and casual kind, but in other cases may easily be interpreted as apparent ameliorations. When such symptoms set in, we are seldom able to obviate the tendency to death by even the most powerful means at our command.

The *pro-agonistic* stage is very far from being simple; its *habit*, so to speak, differing more or less according to circumstances, from the earlier course of the disease, as it does also from the death agony itself. Its duration may be long or short. Thermometric observations aid our prognosis most, especially when the remaining symptoms are also taken into consideration. The course taken by the temperature, as well as the other phenomena in the pro-agonistic period, partly depends upon the actual disease and the extent of its development, and partly upon the numerous complications and terminal disturbances which generally accompany severe and fatal illnesses, although perhaps but slightly connected with the original affection.

If we take the course of the temperature as our clue, we shall find the pro-agonistic stage assume varied forms. The temperature rises continuously, although there may be morning remissions, until the occurrence of the agony, and it may be the very moment of death = the *ascending* form of the pro-agonistic stage; in such cases the commencement of this period may be more or less obscure, if the preceding course of the disease has had the same character, or even if an amphibolic stage has preceded.

Its commencement is however sharply defined if the disease has passed into the period of convalescence, or made more or less progress towards recovery, or when the temperature has been artificially affected by therapeutic agencies which lower the temperature. It is well marked also when the previous course of the temperature has been continuous. But it is most sharply defined when a pro-agonistic period begins with a very rapid rise, in a disease which was previously marked by no fever or by slight feverishness only.

In this ascending form we generally note the temperature continuously rising higher and higher, yet seldom quite uninterruptedly so, far more generally in a zig-zag fashion, so that in the morning hours there is a slight decline of temperature, which is however followed at the next evening exacerbation by a still higher rise; thus the daily average height of the temperature increases, and the daily maxima increased at the same time (fig. 32).

Fig. 32.

Cent.   Fahr.

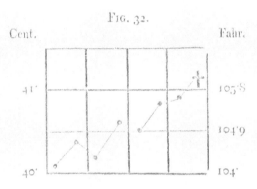

In this way it may sometimes happen that the temperature which had already shown a more or less constant tendency to rise, continues to do so with more or less regularity all through the pro-agonistic period. This is however comparatively rare ; or the rise may first begin when the pro-agonistic stage itself begins—these cases also are uncommon.

Or the decided rise of the pro-agonistic stage succeeds an irregular course, or follows the fluctuations of the amphibolic stage.

Or the pro-agonistic elevations of temperature occur, after a previously moderate or not truly febrile condition, or after more or less favorable events have occurred in the course of the disease, or even after convalescence has made considerable progress.

Or the pro-agonistic stage may set in after a fall of temperature which approximates closely to normal, or even descends below it, after a deceptive remission, or a state of collapse has existed for a short time.

In contradistinction to this steady rise of temperature it is common enough to find cases with rapid and extremely remarkable elevations in the pro-agonistic period, and they may occur either when the temperature is previously very high or when it is moderate, or when it is low and all fever is absent.

In the first case, which is common enough, the temperature before the beginning of the pro-agonistic stage has reached a height of 40° to 41° (C. = 104° to 105·8° Fahr.) or more, when a further rise of 1 to 2 degrees (C. = 1·8° to 3·6° Fahr.) sets in: in this case the pro-agonistic stage is short, and imperceptibly merges into the death agony (fig. 33).

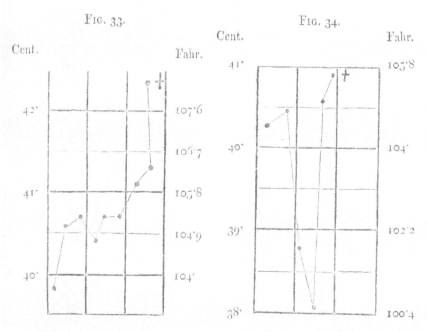

In the second case it may be an open question whether the fall of temperature which precedes the last elevation ought to be included in the pro-agonistic stage or not. The final rise is often very considerable when compared with the preceding fall, yet the absolute height is not always remarkable *per se ;* in these cases, too, the pro-agonistic period merges at once into the final agony (fig. 34).

Lastly, in the third category, to which terminal fever and hyperpyretic rises of temperature in fatal neuroses and diseases of the brain free from fever (non-inflammatory diseases) belong, we may consider the whole period in which the temperature is rising as the pro-agonistic stage. The rise is generally moderate in the beginning, but soon becomes rapid, and in the death-agony reaches enormous heights (fig. 35).

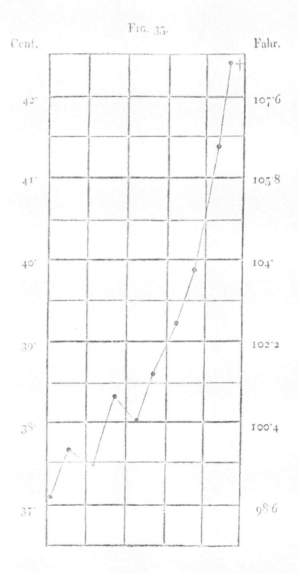

FIG. 35.

(*b.*) Far more common than the ascending form of the pro-agonistic stage is that with decrease of temperature (*descending type*), and it is much more important to regard this form, inasmuch as a superficial and partial consideration of the temperature only, might lead us to consider its decrease as a sign of amendment.

A careful attention to the state of the pulse is our best safeguard against this gross deception, for in such cases, along with the fall of temperature, the frequency of the pulse increases in the most striking manner.

Sometimes the pro-agonistic stage is very short in such cases, the fall of temperature occupying from twelve hours to about two days, and amounting as a rule to about 1° (C. = 1·8° F.) ; yet sometimes the decrease extends till even the normal temperature is reached, and then it often happens that immediately after such a pro-lethal moderation of temperature, there is a sudden and extremely striking rise of temperature in the death-agony itself, and the extremest ranges of fatal temperature are attained. With these must be associated the cases, where in consequence of some occurrence not essential to the disease (such as considerable hæmorrhage from the lungs or intestines, or perforation of the peritoneum) the temperature is much diminished, and the patient either dies at once, or may just before death exhibit a rapid rise of temperature (fig. 36).

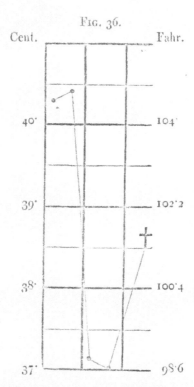

Fig. 36.

In other cases the remissions are periodical, and may be repeated

several times, whilst they are interrupted by fresh elevations of temperature. A certain irregularity is noticeable in these cases. It is
not the quiet, although zig-zag descent of defervescence by lysis, but
there are plunges up and down; sometimes the descent is absent, at
another time it is very marked. This form occurs in all sorts of
diseases, especially in cases where complications set in at an early
stage, or when nervous symptoms are unusually predominant, also
with bad nursing, or after the use of strong remedies.

Sometimes the combinations of rising and falling temperature
in the pro-agonistic stage are tolerably regular. The period begins
with a very decided fall, which may last one and a half or two and a
half days, but then the temperature rises again nearly to its previous
height, or may even exceed that. The approach of death may be
heralded in these cases by a still higher rise, or through an exceptional
fall of temperature.

But sometimes (and these are indeed the most difficult cases for
prognosis) the temperature for some days pursues a descending
course, whilst all the other severe symptoms continue. The patient
dies, whilst the temperature still continues to fall; or the temperature
suddenly sinks still deeper, or changes itself at once to a more or
less considerable fatal perturbation, in which the death-struggle can
no longer be overlooked (fig. 37). Such a course is common

Fig. 37.

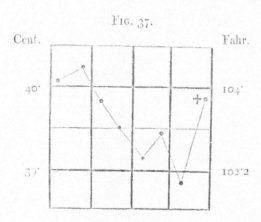

enough in almost all cases of long protracted disease—in basilar
meningitis, in exanthematic and abdominal typhus (typh*us* and
typh*oid* fevers), in acute exanthems with complications, and especially in scarlatina, but very seldom in pneumonia; and indeed there

arc cases which, in their very onset, arc distinguished by their ferocity, and may be considered in themselves as almost necessarily fatal, and cases in which death follows the very beginning of a temperature depressing treatment (such as venesection).

(c.) In rare cases the course of temperature in the pro-agonistic stage is not materially affected, and we must found an unfavorable prognosis on other data, especially on continuous rise of the pulse, which is not followed by a corresponding rise of temperature. Such are the cases particularly where, at the end of the disease, cyanosis occurs through insufficient respiration, although in these it is much more common to meet with the descending type of the pro-agonistic stage.

(d.) Lastly, the pro-agonistic stage is sometimes marked by very extraordinary fluctuations of temperature, repeating themselves more than once in the course of twenty-four hours, in which deep descents and enormous elevations of temperature suddenly alternate with one another, and the death agony sometimes begins during the fall, sometimes during the rise. Pyæmic affections, and those diseases which induce very energetic therapeutic measures on account of their great severity and almost certain hopelessness of cure, are those which more especially display such a course of temperature (fig. 38). For details on the course of the temperature during the pro-agonistic period, I may refer to my treatise, "Das pro-agonische Stadium in fieberhaften Krankheiten," in the "Archiv der Heilkunde" for 1868, Band ix, 1.

§ 13. In the *death agony* the course of the temperature is very varied.

In not a few cases the patient's temperature during the death struggle exhibits no particular peculiarity, and may even show the daily fluctuations very clearly. The patients usually die with a somewhat rising temperature, if the death-struggle occurs in the time of daily exacerbation; and on the other hand, if the death takes place during the time of the daily remission, the temperature at the moment of death will be rather moderate.

In most patients previously suffering from fever, we may note an elevation of temperature amounting to half a degree or a degree ($\frac{9}{10}$ths to $1 \cdot 8°$ F.) during the agony. If the fatal rise be only moderate, there is very commonly a recession of temperature amounting to a few tenths during the last few hours. As regards this, there are two very remarkable and by no means uncommon exceptions.

In not a few cases, whether the previous temperatures have been febrile, normal, or sub-normal, there occurs a fall of temperature in

FIG. 38.

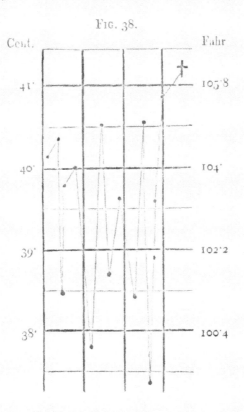

the death-agony, which, when the preceding temperatures have been above normal, may be rapid and very considerable: the patient dies in collapse. This happens in many cases of consumptive diseases, in death from inanition, as well as after profuse hæmorrhages, very copious evacuations of the bowels (cholera flux), and also when death rapidly follows perforation of the intestine, and sometimes also under other circumstances.

On the other hand, in other cases a rapid rise of temperature to extraordinary degrees occurs in the death-agony itself, both in patients who have before shown highly febrile degrees of warmth, and also in those whose illness has furnished us before with no remarkable elevations of temperature, or indeed with no febrile temperatures at all. Of these we have on the one hand, patients with malignant febrile affections, in which the diagnosis of an infectious character is very probable, especially abdominal typhus, exanthematic or true typhus, scarlatina, variola, pyæmia, septicæmia, and also .sunstroke; also measles, though less commonly, pneumonia, endo-carditis, general acute fatty degeneration, malignant peritonitis, facial erysipelas, malignant rheumatic fever (even if uncomplicated), osteo-myelitis, acute miliary tuberculosis; in all these cases very severe cerebral disturbances are often met with, but are by no means essential, in order to induce the excessive temperature in the death-agony; and it would rather seem that extensive (diffused) chemical processes, of a zymotic nature, were the causes.

On the other hand there are diseases in which the affection of the nervous centres appears to determine the essential, or one of the essential disturbances—partly coarse anatomical changes : e. g. meningitis of the convexity, softening of the brain; partly diseases without definite tissue changes : tetanus, epilepsy, hysteria, and other so-called central neuroses ; diseases in which the temperature generally begins to rise for the first time in the last days of life, and very rapidly reaches enormous heights. In these cases it may be questioned whether the fatal rise of temperature is a symptom and effect of the death-agony (and the processes which go along with it), or is this rise (and the processes which form its basis) the original cause of the agony, that is, of the fatal termination ?

Senator (Virchow's ' Archiv,' xlv, 412) thinks the latter is true, and says we may pretty safely conclude that the agony and death occur because from some cause or other the temperature rises to a height incompatible with life. However, the thing scarcely seems so simple. The high temperatures of the agony must be differently estimated, according as they take their point of departure from an immediately preceding highly febrile process, or on the other hand attain suddenly to enormous heights after preceding moderate temperatures. However, it must be conceded that a fresh state of affairs is inaugurated, a final process, which is indeed very frequently thus early and thus undoubtedly prejudicial from no other cause so much as from the enormous elevation of temperature.

§ 14. The *moment of death* is not indicated by any special alteration of temperature.

When the temperature is only moderate, or even low, in the

agony-period, it generally sinks most in the few last moments of life.

When the temperature is high during the agony, it often reaches a height at the very moment of death higher than any ever before attained; yet in some cases there is a minimal diminution of temperature just at the fatal moment, compared with what it was just before.

§ 15. *After death,* in the majority of cases, the temperature begins to fall, and the decrease is slow and tedious at first, then more or less quickened, and in general much more sudden when the patient has died with a low temperature than when the temperature was high at the time of death, and the rapidity of cooling increases as it goes on.

In a good many cases, however, a moderate rise of temperature, seldom amounting to more than a few tenths of a degree, may be observed after death, and this may continue from a few minutes to an hour, and then a short pause ensues, which is followed by a very tedious sinking of temperature, which afterwards becomes more and more rapid.

This *post-mortem* rise of temperature sometimes occurs in cholera, but especially in cases of disease which have terminated with hyperpyretic temperatures, and most especially in those in which the rise of temperature has continued to the very moment of death, yet it is met with in cases in which a slight and short-lasting pro-lethal decrease has moderated the hyperpyretic temperatures a trifle. Consult *Thomas* (1858, in the 'Archiv d. Heilkunde,' ix, 31).

This remarkable phenomenon of *post-mortem* rise of temperature is based on two causes.

When death occurs, the cooling that goes on by the introduction of air (in respiration) and by perspiration, comes to an end, whilst the warmth-producing processes of the economy are not so immediately terminated. And new sources of warmth are opened after death, by changes in the substance of the muscles, and by *post-mortem* decomposition, two sources which are foreign to the living body, and which are sufficient to maintain the corpse for a short time at an equilibrium of temperature, against the losses of heat it suffers, and sometimes even to raise the temperature a trifle. Compare on *post-mortem* temperatures: *Seume's* 'Leipzig Thesis, 1856' (" de Calore corporis humani in Morte observato "), *Wunderlich* (" Bemerkungen bei einem Fall von spontanem Tetanus, 1861," in ' Archiv der Heilkunde,' ii, 547), *Huppert* ("über die Ursache der post-mortalen Temperatursteigerung, 1867," ibid. viii, 321), *Thomas* ("Klinische Bemerkungen zur Thermometrologie, 1868," ibid. ix, 17), *Fick* and *Dybkowsky* ('Centralblatt,' 1868, 197), *Schiffer* ('Reichert's Archiv,' 1868, 442), *Ad. Valentin* (1869, 'deutsches Archiv,' vi, 200), which indicate that *post-mortem* production of heat is a process common to all corpses, and when it is more considerable than the simultaneous losses of heat it gives rise to the phenomenon of *post-mortem* elevations of temperature.

[Drs. Taylor and Wilks collected observations on the cooling of the dead body in 100 cases ('Guy's Hospital Reports,' October, 1863, p. 184). The temperatures were taken in the dead-house, by placing the bulb of a thermometer on the abdomen. The bodies had probably been washed before removal from the wards. The following summary is taken from Dr. Taylor's ' Principles and Practice of Medical Jurisprudence,' p. 6 :

	First period, 2—3 hours after death.		Second period, 4—6 hours after death.		Third period, 6—8 hours after death.		Fourth period, 12 hours after death.	
Number of observations .	76		49		29		35	
	F.	C.	F.	C.	F.	C.	F.	C.
Maximum temperature of the body . .	94°	34·4°	86°	30·0	80°	26·6°	79°	26·1°
Minimum temperature of the body . .	60°	15·5°	62°	16·6°	60°	15·5	56°	13·3
Average temperature . .	77°	25·0°	74°	23·3°	70°	21·1°	67°	19·4°

In cerebro-spinal meningitis, temperatures of 104°—111° F. have been observed just after death. *Simon* observed 104°—113° after death from variola. Assistant-Surgeon F. M. Mackenzie observed 106·2° in rectum after death from cholera ('Lond. Hosp. Reports,' vol. iii, p. 454).—Trans.]

CHAPTER XII.

ON THE TEMPERATURE IN SPECIAL DISEASES.

§ 1. A complete insight into the course of the temperature in disease can only be obtained by comparison of the curves of many thousand separate cases. It is only thus that the mind awakes to the conviction of their harmony one with another, and gains the faculty of finding itself at home in the manifold modifications and deviations which occur in the temperature of the sick.

When one studies the rules which may be deduced from the comparison of separate cases, one never feels quite satisfied, although they may be derived from one's own extended experience. These rules, however cautiously they may be drawn from a great number of separate observations, are never a complete, exhaustive or exact expression of the facts. All the faults of empirical abstractions are common to them : they fail to bear the stamp of inevitability, and fresh experiences of another kind may probably modify, and possibly overthrow them.

The fact that abstractions are to be deduced from a material which consists of definite quantitative values, is not in itself an advantage, but raises a very peculiar difficulty. We might imagine that the greatest exactness might be attained by calculating, in a statistical manner, the arithmetic means of corresponding numbers of single cases of the course of a given form of disease, and putting these forward as the expression of the average course of the temperature in the given form. Such a course, however, is quite inadmissible, and if practised must lead to quite erroneous and delusive results. The true characteristics are not to be sought in the absolute height of the temperature on a given day, but in the orderly succession of the temperatures in the whole course of the disease, or during a definite portion of it, in the rise of the temperature to a certain height at a casual moment, and in its fall to a certain depth at an equally occa-

sional or fortuitous time.   A mere statistical estimation of the curves
in the gross mass must obliterate all the peculiarities of the course
followed by the temperature, and a mere numerical treatment of the
numbers of different cases can only afford trustworthy data for the
answer of certain definite questions.

In order to extract the general facts from separate observations,
we must look less to the *numbers* than to the *form*, that is, to the
varied outline of the wave-systems which each separate curve furnishes us.   Only in this way are we able to construct a sort of model
curve, which may approximatively express the peculiarities of single
cases.   Yet even these, and the general rules of which they are the
image (so to speak), can never adequately express or attain to the
concrete actualities of the case.   Whenever I strive to formulate
such rules, I am perfectly convinced of the deficiencies and short-
comings incident to them, and it is only the copious stores of material
at my command, and constantly repeated proofs of the correctness of my principles which allow me to hope that they do not
caricature or contradict nature.   Although I do not arrogate to
myself the right to declare them to be the laws of pathological
action, I still believe they may serve as a very useful clue to those
who interest themselves in the thermometry of disease.

In order to present the reader with a solid foundation for the
exercise of his own judgment, a number of different cases are figured
in the tables (see lithographs at end) ; and although these are numerous, they are indeed only a very scanty selection from thousands of
observations, and can only furnish a partial view of the actual processes of disease.   The varieties met with in the thermometric
symptoms of disease are multiplied, like every other symptom, in
proportion as one follows them into detail.   It cannot be doubted
that a critical (*lit.* epicritical) exploration of individual cases is of the
highest utility.   But this is the province of clinical instruction.
Medical literature cannot concern itself with individual cases, when
these amount to many thousands, each of which has its own peculiarities.

The different types of disease, and their principal varieties, are the
only details which can be discussed in such a method of repre-
sentation.   I do not ignore the dangers of such a mode of regarding
diseases, a danger which especially consists in the fact that the so-
called special forms of disease are for the most part merely abstractions which find but slight justification in the actual facts, and

too often comprehend things which differ under the same name, and doubtless rudely separate things which are really closely related to one another.   But these abstractions are useful enough as current categories, which may be employed without any great danger of being misunderstood.

§ 2. Amongst the different forms of disease there are many in which each separate case of the same general form of disease exhibits more or less correspondence with others of the same kind, in the general course of the malady, in the parts of the body affected, in the complications which occur, and in their symptomatic manifestations. No unprejudiced person can deny this fact, and there is nothing contrary to reason or illogical in designating such forms of disease as *typical*, although the reason of such correspondence and harmony of symptoms may be quite inexplicable, and although the correspondence may vary greatly in degree.   These forms of disease may be to a great extent units based on some special cause, *i. e.*, depending upon some specific cause, which modifies and directs all the vital processes, so as to bring them within the control of one particular and definite force ; or at least we are justified in assuming with considerable probability the presence of such primary causes and conditions.

The course of the temperature in these forms of disease exhibits a similar correspondence as regards the special cases, a harmony of type which is sometimes more marked, and sometimes less so than is the case with other symptoms.   The notion of typical forms must therefore be extended so as to embrace the course of the temperature.   We are quite ignorant of the real cause of this agreement in the course and behaviour of the temperature ; we know neither more nor less of it than we do of the reason why the contagion of smallpox generally produces pustules, why that of measles produces a patchy eruption on the skin, or why in the latter case the respiratory track, whilst in the contagion of scarlet fever the pharynx is mostly attacked, or why idiopathic erysipelas generally fastens itself upon the face ; or lastly, why the primary cause of abdominal typhus should cause disease of the glands of the intestines.

The typical course of the temperature in many forms of disease is no mere speculation, but an acknowledgment of undeniable facts. It is only doubtful and, perhaps, optional, how many diseases may be included in such a classification.

When once we have admitted the fact of this typical behaviour of the temperature, we are confronted with the idea that there are such things as *normal diseases* (Krankeitsnormen). Those, namely, which most perfectly correspond to the abstract type of uncomplicated cases of the given form of disease.[1]

As far as I know, the distinction between normal and abnormal cases of typical form of disease was first introduced into modern pathology in the classical and incomparable treatise of *Rilliet* and *Barthez* on the diseases of children, with a full consciousness of the practical significance of this distinction.

These authors established it with great ingenuity in the varied forms of disease, as far as the symptoms they could then recognise allowed; and logically and correctly expounded the conception of normal courses of disease, that is of such as represent the uncomplicated results of a specific primary cause, in a previously healthy individual, and which appear as such to every reflecting mind; and *Rilliet* and *Barthez* rendered the practical value of this distinction between normal and abnormal cases very evident.

Above all other phenomena, the course of the temperature is able to distinguish what is normal and characteristic in the course of diseases, and thus to establish, confirm, and extend the distinction between normal and abnormal cases.

The fact that there are numerous cases which exhibit deviations from the typical course, and cannot be brought into harmony with it, and that even when one sharply defines the normal form of any form of disease, the abnormal cases may exceed the normal in number, will not appear to any reflecting mind as a valid objection against the reception of a type, or against the conception of normal diseases. It is so easy to weaken such objections by analogies derived from any other province of science not founded upon mathematics, that no space can be spared for its discussion.

But it is necessary to remember that in different forms of disease, the limits of the normal are sometimes boldly defined, sometimes faintly, and sometimes merge obscurely into others, and that, whilst fully recognising the principle, one cannot force all forms of the disease to conform to any given type.

[1] The reader who is familiar with the original will see that in this chapter, as elsewhere, I have occasionally altered the form, and sometimes the order of the author's language, with a view of conveying to the English reader what I believe to be the real meaning.—[TRANS.]

I. Abdominal Typhus.

(Typhoid or enteric fever, Dothinenteritis.)

§ 1. Abdominal typhus fever pursues its course with unmistakeable regularity. It is almost impossible to resist this conclusion when we compare a number of charts or curves of temperature of this form of disease, and next to relapsing fever and intermittents this disease affords the best proofs and the best justification of the theory of types.

In spite of this recognition of the typical character of abdominal typhus, it must be conceded that the course of particular cases may be very dissimilar, and yet, in spite of their differences, it is possible to recognise amidst them all the marvellous and noteworthy order and regularity of its course.

I will go further and say that in this pre-eminently typical disease not a single rule can be laid down which is not subject to exceptions, although these may, as regards some rules, be extremely rare. It must, however, be remarked that when a case proves to be an exception to some well-founded rule in some single point, it shows an agreement in all others, or at least in a great many others. The type is there, although it must clearly be understood that it is not to be considered as a model to be slavishly copied in all cases and at all times. On the contrary, deviations may occur in any segment, but they are neither so numerous nor so out of proportion in any given case as to prevent the typical peculiarities from being reflected in the greater portion of its progress, provided the observations are made with sufficient accuracy, and extend over a considerable period of the actual course of the disease.

But even where very painstaking observations are made, cases of abdominal typhus do occur, in which, so to speak, the disease remains latent, and where the nature of the fatal illness is first recognised in the dead body. Such cases are generally those in which the commencement of the disease is uncertain, generally secondary cases, and moreover irregular, or with severe complications.

There are also cases in which, although there is a suspicion of abdominal typhus being present, the diagnosis remains doubtful and cannot be decided until recovery, or even up to the time of death, especially cases of acute tuberculosis, many cases of basilar meningitis, and epidemic cerebro-spinal meningitis, of true petechial typhus, sometimes cases of pyæmia, whether puerperal or otherwise, cases of protracted catarrhal pneumonia, and severe influenza, trichinosis, and also cases of very decidedly localised disease, which have not declared themselves in life, and whose presence is not indicated by the sum total of the symptoms (for example, cases of myocarditis, endocarditis with ulceration of the valves, abscesses of the liver, acute affections of the kidney, &c.), all of which closely simulate abdominal typhus, as regards their course, especially resembling the more or less irregular forms, often so closely that the diagnosis is often impossible. Still more difficult is it to be sure whether abdominal typhus has supervened upon some other special severe form of disease. Even thermometry cannot resolve our doubts in some of these cases, but it can settle many a doubtful diagnosis which could not otherwise be decided. It can raise questions which, apart from thermometry, would scarce have been entertained. It may often confirm and certify our suspicion that the suspected abdominal typhus may be another form of disease, or that abdominal typhus is complicating another severe disease ; and it especially determines our power of replying to questions as to the diseases, and furnishes us with a standard for judging of the apparent propriety of the answers.

§ 2. In order to gain the full, *practical value* of thermometry in abdominal typhus, attention must be paid to the following points :

A single thermometric observation is never sufficient, *per se*, for the diagnosis of abdominal typhus.

A single observation, made at certain times, may, however, contravene the presence of this disease, or at least make it very improbable. We may with great probability assume,

That abdominal typhus is not present, when even on the first day, or on the second morning of the disease, the temperature rises to 40° C. (104° F.) ;

We may exclude abdominal typhus, when between the fourth and sixth day, the evening temperature in a child, or adult under middle age, never reaches 39.5° C. (103.1° F.), and indeed if it has failed to do so two or three times ;

Abdominal typhus may be excluded when as early as the second half of the first week considerable or progressive diminutions of the evening temperature are met with.

Very often the thermometric observations alone raise the suspicion, or help to justify it, that abdominal typhus is latent:

As in cases of slight subjective severity;

In cases where an unaccustomed localisation of the disease directs all our attention to the part affected, but the course of the temperature is able to show that the fever is not dependent upon the given local manifestation;

In the first week, or three or four days at least of the course of abdominal typhus;

In cases where this disease attacks one who was previously ill from some other cause, or who was just convalescent.

Only morning and evening temperatures, taken for several days, can decide the presence of abdominal typhus—in the beginning of the fever about three days', but in the fastigium from four to six days' observations, and in convalescence about the same time is required.

The temperature indicates the severity of the disease in most cases about the second week, generally at its middle, and only rarely as early as the first week. A single observation of temperature affords no certain sign as to the severity of the disease, but a whole day's, still more two or three days' temperatures often give very valuable indications.

Irregularities in the course of the disease are best and earliest known by thermometry.

The thermometer indicates complications at a period of the disease when they are recognisable by no other means of observation.

It is the first means of recognising a relapse after the patient has begun to recover;

The thermometer warns us of the tendency to death.

Thermometry is able to regulate the potency of therapeutic operations.

Thermometry shows the transition to convalescence with very great definiteness.

Thermometry points out complications during convalescence, and affords the only sure sign, by which we can certify ourselves of the patient's convalescence.

The disorders of the convalescing period, relapses, and new diseases are recognised earliest and most certainly by the thermometer.

We must not overlook the very important fact, that a large thermometric experience in abdominal typhus first gave us a

full insight into the course of this disease, and rendered possible a
certainty of diagnosis and prognosis in such cases (even sometimes
without using the thermometer at all), which without thermometry
would have been quite unattainable by any previous means of
observation.

§ 3. *Abdominal typhus is characterised by a fever which lasts for at
least three weeks,* unless we include very exceptional cases, and even
those which rapidly terminate fatally, seldom do so in less than a
week. The *maximum* temperature, with rare exceptions, is not less
than 39·6° C. (103·28° F.), and is more commonly between 40° and
41° C. (104°, and 105·8° F.), although it may rise to hyper-pyretic
degrees, but not easily above 43·5° C. (110·3° F.), and except
in fatal cases it is rare to meet with temperatures above 41·5° C.
(106·7°).

The *daily course* of the disease varies very much according to its
intensity and the period of the disease. It is either

Continuous, but with highly febrile daily elevations of temperature
when the disease is at its height, in severe cases; or

Sub-continuous, or continuous without any considerable intercurrent elevations of temperature at the height of the disease, or at
any part of its height in severe cases;

In all cases it is fairly remittent in type at the beginning of the
illness, and in moderately severe and in slight cases it is so even at
the height of the disease; sometimes it may almost be considered
remittent even when severe cases are at their height; and lastly, it is
so in all cases where they begin to convalesce;

The type of the disease is decidedly remittent (with sharp curves)
during the period of recovery, in the most severe as in the milder
cases;

The course sometimes repeats itself irregularly in many of the
severe cases, both at critical periods and after the occurrence of particular events, or the operation of special influences.

Accordingly the *daily average,* on which the daily fluctuations are
based, varies a good deal: in the continued form with exacerbations
it is 40·5° C. (104·9° F.) or more; in the sub-continuous, and continued forms, about 40° C. (104° F.), or a few tenths more or less; in
the milder remittent form seldom above 39·5° C. (103·1° F.), in slight
cases even as low as 39·2° C. (102·56° F.) at the commencement,
and in convalescence still lower; in the former with sharp curves
between 38° C. (100·4° F.) and 38·5° C. (101·3°).

When the fluctuations are irregular, the daily average is uncertain, and affords no indications. In the great majority of cases the *daily maxima* occur between noon and 11 p.m., most commonly between 4 and 7 p.m., or at least between 2 and 9 p.m.

The extent of the exacerbations is very considerable in severe cases and at the height of the disease, and the rise begins as early in the morning as between seven and nine. At the height of the disease, the exacerbation is generally a single-peaked curve, with a broad summit, yet it may sometimes be two, three, or four-peaked. From the third week on, the form with two or more peaks prevails, and the single peaks again in the period of advanced convalescence, and the peaks are more pointed, and thus the extent of the exacerbations is very considerably diminished.

In the form with curves of multiple peaks, the first peak or rise is between 9 a.m. and 4 p.m.; the second between 2 and 8 p.m., most commonly about 6 p.m., the rise at night is between 1 and 5 a.m. Sometimes the rise at night is doubled, one occurring about 11 p.m., the second between 1 and 5 a.m. In double-peaked exacerbations, we sometimes find the first the higher one, but sometimes *vice versâ* (in the period of increase the second is generally the higher one) ; when the exacerbation has more than a double summit, the first and third peaks are generally the highest. [These descriptions of the curves will easily be understood by a reference to the lithographs at the end.] The lowest point of the remission occurs between midnight and 10 a.m., most often between 6 and 8 a.m., and not seldom between 6 and 8 or 9 a.m. It is not very low, and assumes an acute curve (lasting only a few minutes) in severe cases as well as in recent ones, but increases in breadth with the progress of convalescence.

The rise of temperature is sometimes gradual, sometimes sudden, and sometimes one segment of it is tardy, the other rapid. The daily descent is slow, as a rule, and takes the form of an easel (Staffelformig), and is only rapid when the curves are sharp, or when there are irregularities. On the subject of the daily curves in abdominal typhus the following authors may be consulted :

Thomas ('Archiv der Heilkunde, v, 456, and viii, 49), *Jürgensen* (1866, 'Klinische Stúdien,' p. 56), *Ziemssen* and *Immermann* (1870, 'Kaltwasser behandlung des Typhus abdominalis,' p. 33), *Immermann* ('Zur Theorie : Deutsches Archiv für klin. Med.,' vi, 561). [*Bäumler* ('Deutsches Archiv für klin. Med.,' iii, Bd.

xxvii, p. 527, &c.)   For references to English authors see 'Supplementary Bibliography.']

§ 4. Abdominal typhus has *two principal types*, which agree with each other at their beginning, and again at their end, but differ from each other by the fact that one type has a brief and steady course, generally terminating at the end of three weeks; whilst the other, on the contrary, has a longer period of intense fever and fluctuations interposed between its commencement and its decline, by which its course is extended to four or four weeks and a half, and very commonly to five or six, or sometimes even to eight or ten weeks. These two principal distinctions correspond sufficiently closely to the anatomical changes met with, since the former, which lasts but a short time, occurs in those cases where only slight infiltrations of the plexus of glands in the intestines are met with (*plaques molles*), whilst, on the contrary, the longer fever corresponds with those cases in which copious and extensive deposits are developed in the bowel, and in which indeed there are often successive deposits.   In the one the restorative process is simple, and occurs easily by restorative retrograde metamorphosis; in the others, on the contrary, there is need of complicated processes of elimination, in order to dislodge the deposits; ulcers follow this dislodgment, and their healing may be more or less protracted.   As the period of febrile development is from its very nature most intense in these cases, so the process of restoration affords numerous opportunities for renewed extensions and intercurrent febrile attacks, for unfavorable events, for complications and dangers.

In characteristic cases, these two types exhibit a very pregnant difference (see Table II); but there are many cases which occupy a middle ground between these two forms, and sometimes resemble one, sometimes the other form most closely; and the anatomical changes may exhibit very different characters in different parts of the intestine, sometimes healing with facility, whilst in other spots, on the contrary, they take such a development that they can only undergo tedious and extensive processes of reparation.   An intermediate type of fever may also be shown in the course of cases when there are successive deposits in the bowel.

Sometimes there is a difference between the two forms even at the very commencement of the fever, but they are generally seen in the period when its development has reached its height, and in the stages of repair and restoration of the affected portions of the intestine. Whilst the latter process can be finished in a week in the mild and brief form, in the longer and severer form it may be very protracted, and many unfavorable and dangerous events may occur, so that at this period the life of the patient is indeed threatened on almost every side. The duration (*lit.* rapidity) of these two forms may vary in different places, and certainly varies at different times in the same place. The mortality [of an epidemic] depends chiefly upon the preponderance in numbers, of one or the other type, and all conclusions as to the results of therapeutic measures require to be modified in accordance with this rule.

§ 5. Besides these two principal distinctions, complications, and the circumstances of individual cases may cause many *irregularities* and *deviations* from the normal course of the fever. These, however, are less frequent, and of far less significance in the rapid form of abdominal typhus than in the protracted type.

It is noteworthy, that the most perfect typical course of the rapid form of abdominal typhus occurs in those who are again attacked at the close of a typhous fever after convalescence has commenced, or seemed about to do so. The *relapse* of abdominal typhus when its commencement dates from the period when the fever of the first attack has just left the patient, is marked by all the characteristic features of a normal attack of abdominal typhus.

A regular course of the fever is generally met with in persons whose previous health has been good, and whose age is from eighteen to twenty-eight, provided other circumstances are normal, and the fever is not of great severity, and provided also that they are not subject to other injurious influences.

On the other hand, in children (and the younger they are the more so), in people of more advanced age, whom the fever attacks first in their thirty-fifth or fortieth year, in those sick of some other disease (especially sufferers from phthisis and hysteria), in puerperal and scarlatinal cases, and those simultaneously suffering from any pronounced local disorder of any kind (especially endo- and pericarditis, pleurisy, and parenchymatous nephritis), the typical character of the course of the fever of abdominal typhus becomes more or less obliterated.

In particular epidemics, and at certain times, it is more common to meet with irregularities in the fever course than at other times, as has been remarked also of the remaining symptoms of abdominal typhus.

Extremely slight cases, as well as those of great severity, and cases which run a very rapid course, are for the most part irregular.

The character of the fever-course may also be more or less altered and affected by injurious influences, to which the patient may have been exposed either before or at the beginning of the attack ; by defects in nursing; through gross mistakes, and continued muscular exertions ; and by special events of great influence (very severe hæmorrhages, perforation of the bowels, and by complications of overwhelming severity).

Some therapeutic measures have also the power of modifying the type; and that in a way which is beneficial to the patients.

With the approach of death, the peculiarities of the course are often lost.

These deviations and irregularities are, however, not extravagant and unbounded; indeed, some indications of the reign of law may be recognised even here, and, above all, we can usually (unless a fatal termination be imminent), recognise a tendency to resume the normal course, or to run a course with certain modifications of the type agreeing with the definite circumstances of the case.

§ 6. Both in regular and in irregular cases, but most constantly in the former, we observe the course of the disease to be divided into more or less clearly defined *periods* or stages. *Two* well-marked *periods* may be distinguished as clearly separated from each other, and capable of being recognised by the thermometer with great certainty, in the course of typhoid fever ; the first corresponds to the deposition of the exudation and infiltration (in the intestinal glands), whilst the second corresponds to its elimination, and the restoration and repair of the diseased parts.

But both of the principal periods or stages are marked by points at which an alteration of the general fever course occurs, although no corresponding change in the anatomical characters can be recognised. These points can also be more clearly recognised by the the thermometer than by any other means of diagnosis.

It is, however, noteworthy, that in a very large number of cases, especially such as run a perfectly regular course, the duration of the separate periods or stages of the course pretty accurately corresponds in time with the division into weeks and half weeks, and that alterations in the complexion of the course, and transitions from

one stage into another, generally occur at the beginning or end of a
week of the disease, or else in the very middle. This hebdomadal
type is most decidedly shown in the brief and mild form of typhus
(abdominalis); in the severer and longer form it is less clearly
marked, or is preserved only in the third and fourth weeks. Complications also, and other irregularities may completely obliterate
this weekly type, or, at least, disturb it for a time.

§ 7. The period which appears to be the initial stage of abdominal typhus, does not always perfectly represent the first commencement of morbid symptoms. In not a few cases it is preceded for a
longer or shorter time (corresponding, doubtless, to the period of
incubation, according to the original causes in operation), by slight
and generally interrupted phenomena, which display themselves in
disorders of the bowels or of the head, or of the respiratory mucous
tract, or of the whole system, and even slight febrile movements, and
occasionally rigors may occur off and on as a kind of prologue to
the proper course of the disease. But all these symptoms are too
slight and too transitory to afford opportunity for careful medical
observation, and we have, therefore, to begin at a point from which
an unbroken series of pathological phenomena take their origin.
This *initial stage* of abdominal typhus, although for the reasons just
mentioned not always properly called so, runs its course with great
regularity.

Its course is always identical, whatever complexion the case may
afterwards assume.

The temperature always takes an ascending course, in a zig-zag
fashion, in such a way that during the three or four days occupied
by this stage it always rises about $1°-1\frac{1}{2}°$ C. ($1·8°-2·7°$ F.) from
every morning till evening, and falls again, from every evening till
the next morning, about $\frac{1}{2}°-\frac{3}{4}°$ C. ($·9°-1·3°$ F.) till, on the third
or fourth evening, a temperature of $40°$ C. ($104°$ F.) is reached, or
a little exceeded.

The formula for this ascent is nearly as follows:

First day, morning, $37°$ C. ($98·6°$ F.); evening, $38·5°$ C. ($101·3°$ F.).
Second day,   ,, $37·9°$ C. ($100·22°$ F.);   ,, $39·2°$ C. ($102·56°$ F.).
Third day,   ,, $38·7°$ C. ($101·66°$ F.);   ,, $39·8°$ C. ($103·64°$ F.).
Fourth day,   ,, $39·2°$ C. ($102·56°$ F.);   ,, $40·3°$ C. ($104·54°$ F.).

It is very seldom indeed that an attack of abdominal typhus, occurring in a healthy man, or even one free from fever, does not closely approximate to this type in its initial stage.

It is still more rare for any other form of disease except abdominal typhus to show a similar pyrogenetic stage. This course in the first half of the first week is thus in itself alone tolerably decisive for diagnostic purposes. In other words:

If the temperature in the evening hours of the second, third, or fourth day is only approximatively normal, we may exclude abdominal typhus;

If the temperature on the first three evenings, or only on two of them, is the same height, the disease is not abdominal typhus;

If the temperature on two of the first three mornings is alike, it is almost certain not to be abdominal typhus:

If the temperature on the first two days rises to $40°$ ($104°$ F.) or more, abdominal typhus may be excluded with great probability;

If the temperature displays a retrograde course only once on any successive mornings of the first half week, or on any successive evenings, we must exclude abdominal typhus.

The positive diagnosis is so much more certain in proportion as the course of the temperature in the first four days follows the formula given above.

Meanwhile we must not overlook the fact that here and there exceptions to this type of the initial period are met with.

The rise of temperature may very occasionally be completed by the end of two days, or, on the contrary, may take five days for its completion; in both events a severe course must be expected, and in the latter a favorable turn (crisis or lysis) must not be looked for before the middle of the third week. The temperature may sometimes return to the normal on the second morning, which is succeeded by a still greater rise on the second evening, than that of the first.

The rise of temperature on the first and second day is sometimes less, and then it is so much more on the third and fourth.

The height reached by the temperature on the third or fourth day is not always $40°$ C. ($= 104°$ F.), but may be a few tenths less; more often, however, it is a few tenths higher, and, indeed, may be a whole degree more ($= 41°$ C. or $105·8°$ F.).

When typhoid fever is a secondary disease attacking those already ill, and already suffering more or less from fever, the initial stage is very often obscure and unrecognisable.

The initial period decides nothing as to the mildness or severity of the subsequent course of the disease, for it is the same in mild cases as in severe. In the majority of cases, however, this stage does not come under medical observation; the disease has generally lasted some days before medical advice is sought for. But if the initial stage does not come under our notice, our diagnosis is deprived of a very powerful proof, and a longer period of the disease must be watched in order to make a positive diagnosis of abdominal typhus by means of the thermometer, with anything like the same accuracy.

However, we must remember also to guard ourselves against deception in respect to the day on which the illness began, since defects of memory often lead the patient into error as to the beginning of the disorder.

§ 8. *In the second half of the first week, and in the first half of the second week,* the course of the temperature, in the majority of cases, is pretty tolerably uniform; but it must be specially remarked that nothing decisive can be predicted from the course of the temperature, or the height to which it rises, as regards the intensity of its further course.

At this time, and, indeed, very often in the second half of the first week, the cases reach the maximal height of their temperature, which happens most commonly on the fourth or fifth, more rarely, in cases left to themselves, on the sixth, still more rarely on the seventh or eighth day, and generally amounts to between 40° and 41·5° C. (104° and 106·7° F.); most often between 40·2° C. (104·36° F.) and 40·8° C. (105·44° F.). This maximum is generally reached on one day only (usually between noon and evening), but sometimes on two days, rarely on three; in the latter case the third maximum is commonly reached on the seventh or some later day. During all the second half of the first week the maxima of the daily exacerbations remain in the neighbourhood of the general maximum temperature. All this time the morning temperatures, as a rule, are from ½°—1½° Centigrade (= ·9°—2·7° F.) lower than the evening ones, seldom less than this; greater differences may occur sometimes, but not often, except that sometimes, on a particular day, a transient deeper remission may show itself.

The first half of the second week, although agreeing in main with the course of the preceding half week, is very often marked, at least

in cases which show a favorable course, by its exacerbations being a
trifle less severe than those of the preceding period ; the remissions
also show a tendency to become somewhat more marked (deeper), so
that in such cases the fastigium divides itself into two segments—the
first distinguished by more severity in the exacerbations and less
considerable averages in its remissions, and the second by more
moderate exacerbations and somewhat more considerable remissions.

The end of the first half stage of the fastigium most commonly
falls on the seventh or eighth day, more rarely on the sixth, or
perhaps not before the ninth or tenth day.

During this course of the fastigium temporary diminutions of temperature often occur, generally on a single morning, once and again
in an evening.

Sometimes they are met with as early as the first week, most
generally not before the tenth day; are most common when the
course is mild, but by no means ensure such a course. Especially
must it be remarked that this period offers nothing decisive as to
the further progress of the disease, for from the middle of the first
week to the middle of the second week the course may be severe,
and yet be followed by speedy convalescence ; or be mild, and yet
lead to a severe and protracted course at a later date. Yet sometimes cases occur which vary from this type; sometimes the form
of the disease is mild, sometimes more severe; and then the further
development of the case may no doubt be predicated with tolerable
probability.

§ 9. Sometimes, indeed, *cases occur with an unusually mild course*
between the fourth and eleventh days.

The evening temperatures generally remain comparatively low
($39.6°$—$39.8°$ C. = $103.28°$ to $103.64°$ F.), or considerable intercurrent moderations of temperature may occur on particular
evenings.

Or the morning remissions may be more considerable ($1\frac{1}{2}°$ to $2°$ C.
= $2.7°$ to $3.6°$ F.).

Or the course appears to be cut short, and a retrocedent type
finds a very early expression, which may lead to complete defervescence even in the beginning of the second week.

In not a few cases it happens, after therapeutic measures at
the beginning of the disease, that this takes the desired turn very
early, even after a laxative. If the disease were previously well

pronounced, this termination is no reason for altering the diagnosis. But such early convalescences and mild forms of the disease may occur spontaneously, although much more rarely. Sometimes, in such mild cases, we notice a moderation of all the symptoms, whilst the course of the disease maintains the minimum duration of normal cases (three weeks), or only a little less.

In other cases a prejudicial increase of the fever again occurs, and we may then conclude that the typhous changes happened successively, on account of the first deposits (in the glands) being slight, and the later ones more intense. If, on the other hand, recovery takes place unusually early, the question may remain doubtful whether abdominal typhus has been present or not. *Post-mortem* confirmation cannot be obtained, and the remaining symptoms are not sufficiently decisive, and in such mild cases many of them are often absent.

In such circumstances ought we to pronounce the case one of abortive or exceptionally mild abdominal typhus, or should we admit some other disorder, such as febrile intestinal catarrh, and such like? This question is not only a difficult one in concrete cases, but is difficult to decide even in the abstract.

No one is quite certain that the course of abdominal typhus *must* have a fixed duration, or that it *cannot* occur without a certain number of the symptoms usually reckoned as pathognomonic. We can only say that in our times and our country it is, comparatively, very rare for a well-characterised case of abdominal typhus to exhibit any shortening of the febrile course to less than two and a half weeks, unless in consequence of powerful therapeutic measures; and still more, in the vast majority of cases, even a mild course of the disease does not terminate in decided defervescence before the twenty-first day.

Meanwhile it is quite possible that two essentially different diseases, very similar in many of their symptoms and in their anatomical relations, may be included under the common designation of abdominal typhus; the one may be a general disease, produced by infection, although localising itself in the glandular apparatus of the bowels; the other may be a local enteritis in which only for individual reasons the follicular apparatus of the bowels is attacked in a similar manner as in abdominal typhus, and thus a series of symptoms like those of the first form are evolved. What happens in scarlatina supports this, for not only do alterations in the follicles of the bowels occur in that disease similar to those of abdominal typhus, but during the period of convalescence a variety of symptoms and the course of the temperature closely resemble the latter disease, whilst without doubt no abdominal typhus is present.   Analogy with many other diseases leads to the same conclusion, for example, with cholera, in which the epidemic disease induced by contagion may be perfectly simulated by forms of disease arising from purely local conditions.   Now it is very conceivable that in the second forms, the further typhous development of the anatomical changes and of the general course may halt and stop at any given point, and that thus we may get affections beginning like typhoid fever, but ending much earlier.   Such cases must include merely intestinal catarrh, without any very precise limitations.

But even in the disease which originates in infection, we have no reason to deny that, provided the original causes were not very potent, or when the deposit is slight, rudimentary forms of the disease may be developed, as may be often observed in the case of other infectious diseases.   All this, however, only complicates the question for diagnosis; thermometry alone cannot settle it, yet it may give us considerable aid in the solution.   The ætiology, the circumstances of the special case, the remaining symptoms, must be taken into consideration.   Thermometry itself may afford the following aids to diagnosis in unusually mild cases :

If the temperatures, without any other particular reason, several times reach the evening ranges of abdominal typhus, this, especially if it occur with good nursing, is an argument for abdominal typhus.

Even if the temperatures are somewhat below the characteristic ranges, but still approximate to them very closely, and the general course resembles that of abdominal typhus, this is also an argument in its favour, and so much more so if the patient is more than thirty years old, or a child, or suffering from anæmia.   If such a type of disease lasts for a whole week, without special and satisfactory reasons, this is a powerful argument for the presence of abdominal typhus.

§ 10. However characteristic the fastigium stage may be, errors of diagnosis may occur very easily when the initial period has not been under observation, and still more easily when no information as to the commencement of the attack can be obtained, and we are thus left in ignorance as to the time the disease has already lasted.

These errors are likely to be most numerous when our observations are made on only a brief period of the fastigium. At this period it is common enough to confound abdominal typhus with the following diseases:

(*a*) With *pneumonia*, especially in cases where hepatization takes place slowly, and for two or three days at least it is impossible to differentiate such cases from abdominal typhus simply by the temperature. Even in cases of pneumonia, where the physical examination of the chest has determined the presence of changes in the lungs, it may still remain doubtful whether abdominal typhus may not co-exist with pneumonia. In such cases it is not possible to form a correct diagnosis, except by several days' observations.

(*b*) With *acute exanthems*, in which, however, it is very rare for a high fever temperature to persist longer than the fifth day, without either the exanthem or some local manifestation declaring itself.

(*c*) With *exanthematic typhus*, which sometimes is indistinguishable from abdominal typhus, as far as the temperature goes, during the fastigium; in general, however, the elevation of temperature is greater in true typh*us* than in typh*oid* fever, and the morning remissions especially are less considerable in the former.

(*d*) With *cerebro-spinal meningitis*, in which the observations of a few days only afford little aid to diagnosis.

(*e*) With *acute osteomyelitis*, which may run a very similar course to abdominal typhus, but differs from it by intense local phenomena developing themselves in the joints.

(*f*) With *acute tuberculosis*, which may sometimes exhibit a similar course to that of typhoid fever for several days together.

(*g*) With *trichinosis*, which, like the preceding, may exhibit a similar course of temperature.

(*h*) With *abscess of the liver* and *pyæmia*, which for some little time cannot be diagnosed from the fastigium of abdominal typhus.

(*i*) With *intestinal catarrh*; with moderately good nursing, however, this shortly exhibits a lower range of temperature than abdominal typhus.

(*j*) With *influenza*; like the preceding, however, with good nursing, it does not long maintain the high temperatures of typhoid fever, unless associated with catarrhal pneumonia.

Although thermometry does not always succeed in mastering the difficulties of diagnosis in these cases at this stage, yet it often enough does so, and by itself is able to procure us a means of decision, and to exclude abdominal typhus—(1) in young adults, when during the fastigium (especially if the other symptoms are severe) the evening temperature keeps under 39·6° C. (103·28° F.); (2) in all cases in which, during the severity of the symptoms, the temperature sinks to normal at any time of day (unless from powerful causes, such as copious hæmorrhages, perforations, &c.), which certainly happens in severe, or pernicious intermittent fever resembling abdominal typhus, does often at least happen in pyæmia, and sometimes occurs in pneumonia and acute tuberculosis.

Most certainly one is justified in positively diagnosing abdominal typhus in illnesses of moderate severity during the fastigium, when previously healthy persons of youthful or middle age, after being ill about five days or perhaps a week, exhibit evening temperatures of 39·7°—40·5° *C.* (103·46°—104·9° *F.), or a little higher, alternating with morning temperatures, which are* ¾°—1½° *C.* (1·35° —2·7° *F.) lower; unless some other disorder of any sort can be discovered to explain the height of the fever, or unless they have been the subjects of gross neglect immediately before coming under observation.*

In children, or persons who have been much neglected, and very old people, and where considerable local disorders are recognisable, even where the course of the temperature is conformable, the curves of the second week must be waited for, if the diagnosis cannot be established by other means than the thermometer.

§ 11. If the period of fastigium is marked by very extravagant temperatures, or, indeed, either by specially high temperatures (41° C. (= 105·8° F.) or more), or the morning remissions are wanting, this may depend, in the first place, upon the severity of the case, or on the want of proper care in nursing, or on manifold mistakes of various kinds, but less often at this period on the occurrence of complications.

In such cases, the same doubts and errors of diagnosis are possible as in cases of moderate severity, but the diagnosis is certainly more difficult in those extremely severe cases. But very extravagant temperatures are rather against than in favour of abdominal typhus. A positive diagnosis of abdominal typhus on the basis of thermometric observation can sometimes, under such circumstances, be obtained only by watching the case for a longer period.

§ 12. In the *middle of the second week*, between the ninth and twelfth days, slight and severe cases show a well defined difference.

In *slight* cases of abdominal typhus the fastigium then shows a tendency to terminate. Sometimes a brief perturbation, an unusually high evening temperature, or an absence of the morning remission, immediately precedes the crisis; more commonly, however, the decrease of fever immediately follows the fastigium. The favorable crisis (Wendung) generally happens from the tenth to the twelfth day of the disease, or even earlier now and again, especially after remedial measures have proved successful. On the tenth day, or most commonly on the twelfth, in favorable cases, the first considerable morning remission is wont to occur, and contrasts most satisfactorily with those which have preceded it. On the following day the remission may indeed again appear less considerable, but soon the remissions steadily increase in amount, whilst the exacerbations at the same time decrease in severity; the daily ascent begins later, and the corresponding fall begins earlier; the height of the exacerbations generally diminishes a little, a decidedly descending direction is taken by the temperature, and already at the end of the second week, or at the beginning of the third, the decrease of the evening exacerbations shows that convalescence is fairly established.[1]

The conversion of the short daily curves of the fastigium into the steep daily curves of the period of convalescence, when it occurs in the second week, may be regarded as a sign (which seldom deceives us) that the case will be a mild one. It is true it gives no absolute pledge as to the termination; for dangers threaten even in the mildest course of this disease, dangers which cannot be foreseen: perforations, hæmorrhages, cerebral irritations dependent on individual peculiarities, complications from the organs of respiration,

---

[1] It is interesting to notice how the thermometric results obtained by the author in many hundred cases of abdominal typhus and other fevers, confirm the observations of Hippocrates on *critical days*. The Father of Medicine considered the 3rd, 5th, 7th, 9th, 11th, 14th, 17th, and 20th as the critical days in fevers, and if allowance be made for the difference in the Oriental and modern methods of reckoning (by including both the day *from* which we date, and the day *on* which the change happens) we shall find his observation fully confirmed by our author's.—[TRANS.]

and so forth. But if the essential process assumes a favorable shape—and thermometry only guarantees this—the probability of such degenerations and accessory disorders becomes incomparably lessened, and to a great extent the patient may be guarded from such dangers by a careful vigilance.

Less favorable and less trustworthy than this transition of the temperature into steep curves, is a temporary considerable sinking of temperature, a considerable decrease of the evening exacerbations occurring unusually early, so that they approximate to the unaltered morning temperatures, or an apparently rapid transition into defervescence; in all these cases the course is usually irregular, and fresh elevations of temperature may be expected.

The commonest course taken by the temperature during improvement and convalescence, is that of increasing remissions in the morning hours, which are succeeded by exacerbations of less severity, so that in the course of from six to ten days the temperature approaches to normal in a sort of zigzag fashion. The difference between the morning and evening temperatures may thus remain the same for several days, or even a week, or it may become increased, through the morning remissions rapidly becoming greater. Then the daily differences become less, through the continuous diminution of the evening exacerbations, and at the end of the third week we generally find both the normal temperature and convalescence attained together.

If the course described above be taken, there can be hardly any doubt as to the diagnosis. Catarrhal pneumonia and very severe influenza may indeed recover in similar fashion, but they do so much more quickly, and the fever does not last to the end of the third week. On the other hand, when high temperatures are met with in recovering cerebro-spinal meningitis and trichinosis, convalescence indeed occurs in a remitting fashion, but it is more protracted, and is more commonly interrupted. Other affections which recover in this remitting type are distinguished by not reaching the same heights of temperature during the fastigium as abdominal typhus does. Deviations from the prescribed form of defervescence do indeed occasionally occur, and may make the diagnosis doubtful. With these we must reckon the accelerated return to freedom from fever, which happens once now and then in such a way that in the middle, or even in the beginning of the third week, normal temperatures are met with in the evening. This generally occurs after judicious therapeutic measures, and seldom, if ever, without them. In such cases, the diagnosis of the disease must not have been made from the general symptoms only, but from the temperature also, if it is to be maintained after such a recovery.

Other varieties of defervescence are less common when recovery takes place in the course of the third week. Sometimes the variation is only apparent. We are deceived by false statements of the patient as to the duration of his disease. If all the remaining conditions are perfectly *en règle*, we are often able to determine, from the course of the temperature, that the patient has deceived himself as to the beginning of his disease, and this thermometric indication is often subsequently confirmed when further demands are made upon the memory.

In such a course of temperature during convalescence we seldom meet with much trouble from complications, unless the patient was in a condition of imperfect health before being attacked; or special injurious influences induce them, or the "epidemic constitution" exhibits a temporary tendency to such complications. If a complication occurs, there results at some point of the course an arrest of the decrease in temperature, or a fresh elevation of temperature. Sometimes an unusually sudden and deep fall of temperature precedes this change, and is always suspicious.

On the other hand, it is not unusual in such cases, and especially in diseases which run a very mild course, to meet with relapses, and recrudescence of the morbid processes. There is here an essential distinction in the course and danger of the case, whether the renewal of the process begins in places which have hitherto remained intact, so long as the earlier deposits have not yet begun the healing process, or have made but little progress in it (recrudescence, typhous afterstroke, or relapse); or whether recovery has, on the other hand, made considerable progress, and freedom from fever has been obtained. In the former case, the commencement of recrudescence is either indicated by the temperature rising above the previously moderate height; or we observe all at once an alteration in type instead of the constantly descending course, the daily remissions begin to be more imperfect, the daily exacerbations begin earlier, become somewhat higher, and last longer, and in general a very severe and irregular course succeeds, which brings many dangers to the sick in its train. It is quite otherwise with the relapses, properly so-called, which begin after the patient is free from fever, and sometimes even in convalescence. They have (as has already been said), as a rule, a very normal, and generally favorable course, which usually terminates with the twenty-first day from the beginning of the relapse, more particularly when they occur after a mild primary attack.

§ 13. We may always, with great probability, expect a *severe course* of the disease as soon as morning temperatures above 39·5° C. (103·1° F.) are persistently met with, and evening temperatures of 40·5° C. (104·9 F.) are reached or exceeded, and the daily exacerbations occur with great punctuality, or prolong themselves beyond midnight, whilst the daily differences are slight, and so the course of the disease is sub-continuous, but the daily minimum exceeds the lowest limits of the range of typhus exacerbations (39·6° C. = 103·28° F.); and finally when moderation of the temperature does not occur about the middle of the second week, or at the latest about the twelfth day.

All irregularities in the second week are suspicious. All uneven elevations of temperature, as well as purposeless and excessive falls of temperature, and although a tolerably rapid recovery is possible in such cases, relapses, fresh elevations of temperature, complications, and hypostrophes are very common. The irregularity is especially unfavorable when no indication of an increase in the remissions is met with in the second week, although the evening temperatures *per se* may remain substantially inconsiderable, or even when the morning temperatures are higher than the evening.

It is an almost certain sign of a severe course when the morning temperatures reach 40° C. (104° F.), and those of the evening exceed 41° C. (105·8° F.), and especially when, towards the close of the second week, increasing rises of temperature are met.

The most unfavorable circumstance of all, however, is the occurrence of apparently purposeless fluctuations, along with such a course as has been described, even when such fluctuations consist in a sudden decrease of temperature not proper to abdominal typhus.

§ 14. It is in severe cases more particularly, that we meet with a *complicated course*.

The least dangerous form is that in which, without any particular or at least much moderation of temperature at the beginning of the second half of the second week, the evening exacerbations remain considerable (over 40° C. = 104° F.), and on particular evenings reach above 41° C. (105·8° F.) ; and on the other hand, morning remissions amounting to one degree, or a degree and a half Centigrade (= 1·8° or 2·7° F.), or even more, are met with ; and thus the course goes on into the third week, or even to its very end, with scarcely diminished severity. But if no complications occur, it is most customary, even in such cases, to find the exacerbations a trifle less in amount from the middle of the third week, and now and then a more considerable remission occurs, preparatory to a decided decrease of fever heat.

Sometimes, however, the temperature moderates in this way—the high temperatures of the second week do not recur, the temperature especially remaining about $\frac{1}{2}$° C. ($\frac{9}{10}$° F.) lower than in the second week, but still a high degree of fever remains, and the remissions continue to be inconsiderable. However, even in cases which may be considered pretty favorable, it is not infrequently the case that considerable remissions of temperature are postponed to the fourth week. Or the temperature may still remain as high as in the second week, or even rise still higher, and continue so till at least the middle of the third week, and often to the middle or even end of the fourth week. In such cases the evening temperatures continue to show themselves as high or almost so as in the earlier stages, the remissions are less, and the daily difference is commonly not above $\frac{1}{2}$° C. ($\frac{9}{10}$° F.), except when the exacerbations exhibit an exorbitant height of temperature. The morning temperatures, in particular, generally range between 39·5° and 40° C. (103·1° and 104° F.), or perhaps between 40° and 40·5° C. (104° and 104·9° F.), but are seldom above this, whilst in the periods of exacerbation the temperature sometimes exceeds 41° C. (105·8° F.), or may reach and even surpass 42° C. (107·6° F.). The *mean* daily temperature is generally over 40° C. (104° F.). The extent of the exacerbations is thus increased, and the daily rise of temperature begins in the morning, even as early as 9 or perhaps 8 a.m., and the high temperature continues till midnight or even later, commonly with two or more peaks [to the curve of elevation]. The morning remission is, correspondingly, of very brief duration, and lasts only an hour or two.

Or irregularities may occur in the course of the fever, which usually draw other irregularities in their train. Not infrequently these irregularities result from the severity of the case, from unfavorable conditions surrounding the patient, individual peculiarities, or the prevailing character of the epidemic. But in many cases the irregularities result from complications. If the complications are of a local inflammatory nature, such as intense bronchitis, pneumonia, parotitis, and such like, either the temperature rises notably, or at least the previous morning remissions, which have probably been considerable, become much less so.

When a patient suffering from abdominal typhus becomes attacked with *Asiatic cholera,* the course of the temperature is very peculiar. Cases of this, observed in my wards, have been published by *Friedländer* (in 1867, in 'Archiv der Heilkunde,' viii, 439). He has not only shown that cholera exerts a powerful influence in depressing the temperature, but also that in the patient suffering from typhoid fever, the first unmistakable fall of temperature occurs even thirty to thirty-six hours before the collapse of cholera, and as much as twelve to twenty-four hours before copious diarrhœa commences, and this fall of temperature therefore serves as the first symptom of cholera infection in such cases.

If severe *hæmorrhages* supervene in the course of abdominal typhus, particularly hæmorrhages from the bowels, a considerable fall of temperature may be met with, even to below normal; but the temperature usually rises again speedily to the previous heights, or even above them.[1]

The momentary elevations of temperature in the former cases, and its momentary falls in the latter cases, are by no means the sole effects of the complications: beyond this, they more or less completely destroy the normal characters of the course, and the numerous irregularities may themselves prove injurious even when the complications which caused them have been happily overcome.

In some special, and in many respects extraordinarily severe cases, considerable falls of temperature occur at the supreme moment of danger, without any particular collapse, and without assignable cause; these are by no means to be looked upon as favorable, but are on the other hand connected with an increase in other threatening symptoms, with weakness of the cardiac contractions and of the sounds of the heart, with enormous frequency of the pulse, severe delirium, and automatic muscular movements (floccitatio, carphology, subsultus tendinum, &c.), with coma, and the most extreme prostration, and bear the strongest resemblance to the fall of temperature in the pro-agonistic period, which will be described presently. They

[1] See page 134 and the foot-note.—[TRANS.]

do not accurately represent any favorable crisis of the disease; yet it sometimes happens that the fatal end, which seemed so imminent, is averted by energetic measures—upon which the temperature recurs to its previous heights, or even rises as the patient gets better. We may call these cases of pro-lethoid (pro-agoniform) fall of temperature. But even in cases which have become severe and irregular, the typical course recurs, as soon as affairs begin to mend. This does not so often happen at the height of the disease (or in the fastigium), but generally begins first during convalescence.

Unless death succeeds, all severe cases have this in common, that the fastigium period and the whole course of the disease is protracted. And therefore, in very many cases, there occurs, on a tolerably fixed day of the disease, a transitory moderation, and in others a particular elevation of temperature. The remissions seem to prefer the last days of the week, or the middle of a week (of the disease); the rises of temperature immediately *before* those days, or at the beginning of a fresh week. The commonest event of all is to observe, in such protracted cases, a striking rise of temperature about the twenty-fifth day, or sometimes a day earlier or later. This rise of temperature becomes more conspicuous, because about this time the course exhibits a visible remission, and the fever has even begun to decrease; and this decrease is very commonly interrupted on the twenty-fifth day by elevations of temperature which are wont to exceed the height attained on the preceding day by $\frac{1}{4}°$ C. ($\frac{9}{10}°$ F.) or more.

At this stage the diagnosis is seldom doubtful; only exceptionally acute tuberculosis, or cerebro-spinal meningitis, may be suspected, and particularly when the latter is epidemic, at which times especially many more or less striking cerebro-spinal symptoms are generally associated with typhoid fever, and thus increase the resemblance of the two diseases. On the other hand, the prognosis is an affair of practical interest at this period. Thermometry cannot always afford certain data on which to found them, but may give us very valuable hints (literally *winks*).

Generally speaking, every case is a dangerous one in which this (protracted) form of the disease is met with.

There is very great danger, as soon as the temperature reaches a height of $41·2°$ C. ($106·16°$ F.), and the best that can be hoped for is a very tedious recovery. With a temperature of $41·4°$ C. ($106·52°$ F.) the fatal cases are always nearly twice as numerous as the recoveries. With 41·5° (107·15° F.) and higher degrees, recovery is a rarity.

Fiedler ('Deutsch. Archiv. f. klin. Med.,' i, 534) declares 41·75° C. (107·15° F.) to be the maximum temperature admitting of recovery, which occurred in two such cases, all the rest with the same, or a higher, temperature ending fatally. However, in one of my cases of typhoid fever, recovery took place after a temperature of 42⅛° C. (= 33·7° R. = ·107·825° F.) had been reached (during a rigor in the course of the disease).

A repeated rise of temperature to very considerable heights (41° C. = 105·8° F.) increases the danger considerably. Yet these are much better borne by the patient if, in the morning hours, or intercurrently, there are considerable falls of temperature. Very high temperatures with intercurrent remissions of temperature are less dangerous than somewhat lower heights which continue both morning and evening with scarcely any break. If the temperature exceeds 41° C. (105·8° F.) in the morning hours, death is almost certain.

If the temperature in the third week is higher than in the second, or when an ascending direction is assumed in the third week, it must always be considered noteworthy.

All gross irregularities afford a bad prognosis; or, at least, one must be prepared for further complications.

§ 15. It is quite the exception for the course of a severe case to immediately terminate favorably by crisis; for more often there intervenes a period of changing fortunes—a period of uncertainty: the *amphibolic stage.*

This stage often intrudes into cases which seemed in the commencement to be of only slight severity, but which, in any case, must excite the suspicions of the well-informed practitioner; as particularly in cases of abdominal typhus of aged persons; in cases of previous ill-health; in cases of relapse, occurring before decided progress towards recovery has been made; in cases which displayed great irregularities at a very early stage, unless these necessitate an extreme mildness of the attack; in patients continuously exposed to injurious influences, or who are forced to make great muscular exertions in the earlier part of the illness; and such like. The amphibolic stage generally begins in the middle, rarely so early as the commencement, of the third week, sometimes in the beginning of the fourth week, and is preceded in many cases by a remission of unusual extent, or even by collapse, and makes itself known by more or less considerable irregularities, apparently casual improvements or purposeless relapses. In general the evening temperatures are still pretty high in this stage, although less so on the average than in the fastigium. And although on particular days the maximum of the fastigium may be reached or even exceeded, yet in the majority of cases the temperature in the evenings remains a trifle lower. Considerable remissions, which may extend to the evening, occur intercurrently, but exhibit no steadiness; and whilst the symptoms for several days may appear strikingly favorable, all at once relapses again occur. It is by no means common to find the intercurrent falls of temperature in this stage going on into collapse, without further and dangerous reasons for such a course; and, when such falls of temperature occur, they are almost always dangerous, or are at least followed by a fresh and striking rise of temperature.

Sometimes exacerbations of stationary height alternate for a longer or shorter time with deep remissions of temperature, which go down to normal or even below it; in the latter cases, symptoms of collapse are often met with. Although defervescence may establish itself by a gradual decrease of the exacerbations, after such an alternating course has lasted a whole week; yet what generally occurs is this— that after some time, the remissions become less, and even approximate to the exacerbations. In special cases, deep falls of temperature, or even collapse temperatures, occur even in the time of the exacerbation. It is not very rare to meet with a postponement of the times of exacerbation and remission—so that the former occurs in the morning hours, and the latter in the afternoon—which seems to have no bearing upon prognosis.

Very many complications commonly occur in this stage; most frequently their effect is not simply to raise the temperature, but also to abolish or at least mask the remissions.

Sudden and considerable falls of temperature are only observed with severe hæmorrhages and perforations in this stage.

Not infrequently recrudescence of the course takes place, with a renewal of the symptoms in the fastigium, apparently caused by a renewal of the anatomical lesions. It is in these cases, more particularly, that dangerous and fatal hæmorrhages and perforations are to be dreaded.

Rigors sometimes set in, with great rise of temperature; they generally indicate the occurrence of fresh complications (pyæmic and septicæmic processes).

This amphibolic stage sometimes lasts only three or four days (half a week), generally a week, or a week and a half; sometimes even longer.

§ 16. If the disease is tending towards death, the pro-agonistic stage generally commences with deceptive depressions of temperature, which, however, for the most part not only exhibit a contrast to the remaining symptoms, but also show a certain amount of irregularity.

In other cases, on the contrary, there is an unusual and persistent rise of temperature, particularly in the morning, which exceeds 41° C. (105·8° F.); or there ensues a sudden increase of temperature, amounting even to 42·5° C. (= 108·5° F.), or even more, only seldom reaching 43° C. (109·4° F.), or above that;

Or there occurs a sudden deep fall of temperature, accompanied with symptoms of extreme collapse.

The death-agony is not always preceded by a recognisable pro-agonistic stage. Sometimes, on the contrary, death happens very suddenly and unexpectedly in this stage. In the death-agony, and in the actual moment of death, the temperature may, according to circumstances, be very low, highly febrile, or even hyper-pyretic; which apparently depends chiefly upon the kind of condition which immediately determined the fatal result.

If the temperature rises in the death-agony, this generally happens with rapidity in proportion to the near approach of death, amounting sometimes to a degree and a half in a single hour (= 2·7° F.).

Death generally happens between 42° and 43° C. (107·6° and 109·4° F.).

Post-mortem elevations of temperature are met with, but they are generally inconsiderable, and only last a few minutes.

§ 17. When severe cases of the disease tend towards *recovery*, this generally occurs after a critical perturbation, which may be noticed for only a few hours, or may extend itself over a longer period, even lasting several days.

More commonly, however, a preparatory moderation of temperature precedes, in which case the commencement of true recovery is less clearly defined.

This preparatory moderation shows itself either in a single remission, somewhat deeper than others, or in a slighter exacerbation, or in a slightly descending direction taken by the temperature, which may spread over several days, by means of which, in severe cases, the type always remains sub-continuous, and the daily mean may continue about 40° (104° F.). Such a gradual descent may last for a half, or even a whole week, before any decided amendment occurs.

The amendment generally announces itself by a considerable fall of temperature, which commonly happens at the time of the daily remission, and is generally somewhat lower than the remission of the day which succeeds it.

The beginning of decided improvement in cases of moderate severity often occurs about the middle of the third week, but in very severe ones only seldom at the end of the third week, most often in the middle of the fourth week (immediately after the rise of temperature on the twenty-fifth day), and sometimes even later.

Defervescence occurs after the remittent type, just as in cases which recover at an earlier period, but the defervescence takes a longer time in most, but by no means in all cases.

The remissions are not infrequently so excessive as to induce collapse more than once.

Defervescence often induces a "stand-still," or even a slight relapse in the patient's condition.

Sometimes its even course is broken by single moderate or colossal fluctuations, sometimes through a solitary evening rise of temperature of considerable amount, sometimes by several such, between which, however, the temperature every morning returns to the normal, or sometimes the defervescence is interrupted by several days' subcontinuous elevation of temperature.

But actual relapses are often enough observed during the defervescence.

§ 18. Sometimes, instead of exhibiting a tendency to death, or instead of passing on into recovery, the amphibolic stage terminates in a protracted process (lentescirende[1] Process), which generally depends on continuous ulceration in the bowels, sometimes on

---

[1] "*Lentesco*, to cleave or stick like pitch, to grow gentle or supple."— AINSWORTH.

suppurative bronchitis, and other tardily recovering local affections, and once now and again by marasmus, it depends on advanced marasmus.

The course of the fever is chronic in such cases, with daily more or less high evening exacerbations and morning remissions, which reach even to normal. The duration of this stage is quite indefinite.

§ 19. Complete *recovery* in abdominal typhus is only to be admitted when the temperature shows complete freedom from fever in the evenings. The beginning of recovery is therefore to be established only by the thermometer, and we can only be assured of it when the lower temperatures have been met with for at least two successive evenings.

Very commonly, however, during reconvalescence, the temperature is actually somewhat *lower* than in the normal condition, being from $36°$ to $36.5°$ C. ($96.8°$ to $97.7°$ F.) in the morning, and under $37°$ C. ($98.6°$ F.) in the evening, which rather indicates the safe character of the recovery than any unfavorable course.

But very often the period of recovery is complicated.

The least significant disturbance consists in a brief, although often very considerable, elevation of temperature, occurring after the first indulgence in animal food, or other nutritious substances, or very often in abdominal typhus after the visit of a friend.

In many cases of abdominal typhus, and more commonly in severe cases than in milder ones, febrile movements or febrile relapses are met with without any known cause, and last from one to three days. They are not dangerous in themselves, but they retard recovery, and unless the patient be treated accordingly may have other injurious consequences as a sequel. The temperature is generally the only sign by which they can be certainly recognised, and it also indicates their termination most accurately. Sometimes it shows that at a certain period in the course of an epidemic the recovery of almost every case is interrupted by such relapses into fever, which may be repeated once or twice in one and the same individual.

Very frequently, in many periods, and less frequently at other times, true relapses or repetitions of the typhoid process occur during convalescence, and can generally be recognised only by the temperature for the first few days, since in general no other symptoms call attention to the relapse during the period.

They are rather to be dreaded if elevations of temperature above normal occur during convalescence, and may be developed eight days or even more after convalescence has occurred. With timely care and supervision they are not generally dangerous, and they furnish us, as already stated, with the most perfect example of a simple, favorable, and quickly recovering typhoid process.

Various hypostrophes[1] may occur during the recovery from typhoid fever, which are generally to be recognised earliest by a fresh rise of temperature; the kind of fresh complication can generally be determined after a few days.

On this account continued thermometric observations of convalescents from abdominal typhus, at least once every evening, are of the greatest practical value, and its usefulness becomes all the more evident when we reflect on the difficulty or impossibility of making a daily examination into all the symptoms, and that this easy method indicates with the greatest accuracy the moment at which it becomes desirable once more to make a more careful examination of the patient who was recovering.

§ 20. In *childhood*, particularly in very young subjects, the course of the temperature in abdominal typhus is generally somewhat irregular.

The commonest irregularity is a course of extreme mildness, yet in these cases the temperature for the first few days rises more suddenly than in the adult, and during the first week its average height is very considerable.

Cases of typhoid fever pass more quickly in the child into the remitting period, and the course of defervescence is usually more sudden. But complications are often met with, and where they show themselves the height of the subsequent temperatures may be very considerable.

These irregularities of temperature may render the diagnosis of abdominal typhus very difficult in children [and hence it is seldom made in England. Infantile *remittents* and a host of other spectres being conjured up in its stead.—TRANS.].

§ 21. When *people over forty years of age* are attacked by typhoid fever, their temperature is commonly lower than that of

---

[1] ‘Υποςτροφὴ, a return, a going back, the act of turning round or turning back—a relapse.

young adults. Even during the fastigium the height reached by the exacerbations is only from 39° to 39·5° C. (= 102·2° to 103·1° F.) ; 40° or more (104° F.) being quite exceptional, and in the morning hours it falls below 39° C. (102·2° F.)

More irregularities are met with in its course than in younger individuals.

The fastigium seldom lasts over the second week, but an amphibolic stage succeeds, or at least the period of recovery is protracted and inclined to complications. Collapse often occurs, and the temperature more often falls below normal during convalescence and in recovery than it does in younger people. The beginning of the fever, even in fatal cases, is often mild and deceptive, but later on the temperature may reach considerable heights. Death sometimes occurs with a high, still more often with a moderate or low, temperature. Such a course of temperature is very common in persons of forty years of age or more, and occurs in about half of those attacked at this age, and is generally absent only in those who are very well preserved in spite of their age; it is far less frequent in men of thirty-six to forty years (only in about one seventh of the cases), and still less frequent in men between thirty-one and thirty-five years (in about one tenth of the cases).

Compare *Uhle* (1859, in the ' Archiv für physiolog. Heilkunde,' xviii, 95).

§ 22. *Anæmic* people, especially when their anæmia is not too extreme, exhibit a modified course of abdominal typhus as a rule, and recovery happens comparatively early. This does not preclude anæmic people being greatly endangered by complications, or the temperature from shaping itself unfavorably in certain events—such especially as hæmorrhages (although not in themselves severe), affections of the lungs, severe brain-symptoms, parotid-gland affections, bed-sores, all of which have a more dangerous significance and a greater influence in anæmic people than in others.

§ 23. *Previously existing diseases*, of almost any considerable kind, which persist through the whole course of abdominal typhus, render its course irregular, with scarcely a single exception; and the irregularities may be so great that we may be doubtful of the diagnosis right through the disease, and even up to the time of death. In most cases of this kind the course is not only irregular, but at the same

time very severe. High temperatures are not very often met with in
the evening; remissions, and indeed very profound ones, are often
seen, but the succession of events in the course is disorderly and
obscure, and the fluctuations of the amphibolic stage are met with
almost at the beginning of the course. The principal diseases which
have this effect are pulmonary phthisis, extreme degrees of emphysema,
diseases of the heart, catarrh of the stomach, ulceration of the intestines, chronic nephritis when considerable, the hæmorrhagic diathesis, chronic alcoholism, chronic lead-poisoning, high degrees of
hysteria; and amongst the acute diseases in whose course abdominal
typhus supervenes are peritonitis, scarlatina, and cholera.

Pregnancy and the puerperal state have a similar tendency, but
not by any means in all cases.

§ 24. The energetic application of *cold* in the form of repeated
more or less cold baths, very cold douches, continued ice, cold
compresses over the trunk, or frequently repeated envelopment of
the body in cold wet sheets (so-called cold-water treatment) is in-
contestably the most powerful means of influencing the temperature
of abdominal typhus as yet known to us.

Besides the numerous other results which the above applications
produce on other symptoms of the disease, they have the following
effects, provided they are sufficiently often and energetically
applied.

(*a*) A more or less considerable, and more or less lasting depression of temperature after each application. A slight rise of temperature for the first few moments sometimes precedes the depression
of temperature; this is not, however, by any means invariable, for
sometimes it falls immediately after an energetic application; for
instance, after a complete immersion in a cold bath for a quarter of
an hour, after an hour's application of ice-bags, &c., the temperature
measured in the rectum is either very triflingly (a few tenths only)
or not at all elevated; generally speaking, however, one finds a
quarter or half an hour after the application of cold, that the temperature has fallen about 1 to 3 degrees Centigrade (= 1·8° to
5·4° F.), and sometimes considerably more; after this it begins for
the first time to rise again, and after from two to six hours, or even later,
it reaches intense febrile heights. Very often, under special favorable
circumstances, it never again reaches its previous elevation. These
varied effects depend partly on the kind and intensity of the applica-

tion, and partly, on the other hand, upon the surroundings of the case, and the form and stage of the malady.

The effect is in general greater and more durable in complete cold baths, and quickly repeated cold wet packs, especially in children; when the course of the fever is mild and remittent, in the absence of complications, in the later periods of the disease, and when the application is made at the time of the natural remission. The effect is less marked, or entirely wanting, when the applications are less energetic, also in grown-up people in the earlier stages, and when the disease is of a severe sort, when its course is sub-continuous, or complicated, and during the previously described daily ascent of temperature, or at the height of the daily exacerbations.

(4) The type of the course is more or less materially altered by an energetic and sufficiently frequent application of cold. First the natural daily remission becomes obscured, and the exacerbations are commonly enough *dislocated*.

It is quite an exceptional thing to have the course actually shortened, it is perhaps rather prolonged, but, on the other hand, very commonly rendered milder. The highly febrile exacerbations are at once interrupted, and a fresh rise of temperature is hindered; it is true indeed that as a rule, the latter recurs when the applications are left off prematurely. It also appears that when the course is sub-continuous, a repeated and consecutive application of cold causes a transition to the remittent type, though the form of this is perhaps anomalous at first, and the further progress is secured and accelerated by the occurrence of the remission.

As regards this, it is already evident that severe accidents and sequelæ of abdominal typhus may be guarded against, and moderated, and great dangers successfully combated, and thus many lives saved in abdominal typhus by the cold-water treatment. The other effects of this method of cure do not belong to my subject, but I may add that by the common consent of all observers, and in my own trials of the method, the mortality of the disease is very considerably diminished, and that in some desperate cases, favorable terminations which could scarcely have been anticipated have been obtained.

Consult on this subject *Hallmann* (*loc. cit.*), *Brand* ('die Hydrotherapie des Typhus,' 1861, and 'die Heilung des Typhus,' 1868), *Liebermeister* and *Hagenbach* ('Beobachtungen und Versuche über die Anwendung des Kalten Wassers bei fieberhaften Krankheiten,'

1868), *Jürgensen* ('Klinische Studien über die Behandlung des Abdominaltyphus mit kaltem Wasser,' 1866), *Ziemssen* and *Immermann* ('die Kaltwasser-behandlung des Typhus Abdominalis,' 1870).

§ 25. The early (*i. e.* in the first week) internal use of *calomel* in doses sufficiently large (30 Centigrammes, = 4½ grs. nearly), and although less certainly the use of other laxatives,[1] influence the course chiefly; producing especially an immediate more considerable remission than is accustomed to occur spontaneously at this period. After this fall, however, the temperature rises again, but not commonly to the former height; and in a tolerable number of cases, defervescence follows on the few days' modified course induced by these means, in the usual remittent fashion, and sometimes even more rapidly, and recovery takes place earlier than it does on an average in cases left to themselves, however mild. If calomel be given very early (*i. e.*, in the middle of the first week), a great remission takes place almost directly, but the rise of temperature which succeeds is sometimes (although not in the majority of cases) more considerable, and may exceed the temperature before the dose was given. It appears that by the early use of calomel the temperature is sometimes delayed in reaching the usual maximum heights, at least in such cases the maxima occur on the seventh or eighth day, or even later, and the efficacy of the method must generally be regarded as doubtful if temperatures of more than 40·5° C. (104·9° F.) are observed after its use. If calomel is not given till the second week, or later still, considerable remissions immediately succeed its use, but it is exceptional to find it affect the general course of the disease, and it does so less and less frequently the further advanced the disease was at the time it was exhibited.

Consult my treatise, 'Prüfung der Calomelwirkung beim enterischen Typhus' (1857, 'Archiv für physiol. Heilkunde,' xvi, 367.)

§ 26. *Digitalis*, in the quantity of two to four grammes (℥ss—℥j nearly), or even more (in divided doses, extending over from three to five days), given in the second and third week of a severe abdominal

---

[1] Dr. W. Tennant Gairdner, who has had considerable success in the treatment of typhoid, speaks highly of the use of sulphate of magnesia in small doses.—[TRANS.]

typhus, immediately produces a slight moderation of temperature in a great number of cases; or perhaps a considerable fall of temperature, which during the time of the exacerbation may amount to two degrees or more (C. = 3·6° F.)   This fall does not generally last more than about a day after the exhibition of the remedy.   Then the temperature rises again, and in cases favorably affected, does not again attain the previous height, but remains stationary, with very powerfully depressed pulse, at moderate heights, whilst defervescence takes place as usual; and the pulse first recovers itself from its artificial retardation, about four days after the use of the digitalis, whilst convalescence has meanwhile advanced.

Compare my article, ' Ueber den Nutzen der Digitalisanwendung beim enterischen Typhus' (1862), in the ' Archiv d. Heilkunde,' iii, 97); *Ferber* (1864, in ' Virchow's Archiv,' xxx, 290), and *Thomas* (1865, 'Archiv d. Heilkunde,' vi, 329).

§ 27. *Quinine*, in tolerably large doses (1·2—1·8 grammes = Ɔj ʒss nearly) divided into three doses given within a few hours, has a powerful effect in lowering the temperature in typhoid fever.   The first who made observations on this was *Wachsmuth*, who gave 0·6 grammes (= 9¼ grs. nearly) every three hours, on three occasions, and observed a rapid fall of temperature from 40·25° C. (104·45° F.) to 36·75° C. (98·15° F.)   After two days, the evening temperature rose again to 40·2° C. (104·36° F.), but in the remission it again reached the normal, and defervescence soon began and was rapidly completed.   In one of my cases in which one to two grammes of quinine (Ɔj nearly) were given, when the temperature between 5 and 12 p.m. had reached a height of 41° (105·8° F.), a rapid fall of temperature resulted in the night after toxic symptoms [cinchonism], and on the following morning there was a temperature of 37·1° C. (98·8°), and at noon it was actually only 36·25° C. (97·25° F.)   In the evening it rose again to 40·1° C. (104·18° F.)   A fresh exhibition of 1 gramme (15·44 grs.) in divided doses, spread over forty-eight hours, again depressed the temperature to 36·9° C. (98·42°), after which it rose again, but the disease from that time preserved a mild course.   The use of quinine in large doses does not however afford us any certainty of a favorable issue.   It is noteworthy, too, that *Quincke* has communicated to the Berlin ' Klinische Wochenschrift,' 1869, No. 29), a case in which a girl who was suffering from an attack of abdominal typhus, which did not appear of any great severity, was treated for several evenings with ℈j doses of quinine, and died suddenly in the third week of the disease with an excessively high temperature ($43°.4$ C. $= 110°.12°$ F.) More moderate doses of quinine (0.6 to 0.8 gramme $= 9$—12 grains nearly) may also cause the temperature to be reduced in abdominal typhus, but cannot be relied upon. [Compare p. 139, where the views of Dr. F. Stabell and Dr. C. Baümler are recorded. The former thinks the quinine ought to be given in large doses, with which the author seems to agree.—TRANS.]

See also *Wachsmuth* (1863, 'Archiv der Heilkunde,' iv, 74), *Thomas* (1864, ibid, v, 536), *Liebermeister* (1867, 'Deutsches Archiv,' iii, 26).

§ 28. There is no other form of disease in which such numerous investigations and facts are accumulated as there are in abdominal typhus. Amongst the first which deserve mention are the already quoted works of *Gierse, Hallmann, Roger, Zimmermann*, and especially *Bärensprung* and *Traube*, which either touch upon the course of the temperature, or are more or less exhaustive. Its thermometric relations are also treated of, *inter alia*, in most of the more recent accounts of abdominal typhus, as well as in most modern text-books, amongst which, besides my own treatise (*Wunderlich's* 'Handbuch der Pathologie und Therapie,' 2nd edit., 1856), I may especially mention *Griesinger's* account in his 'Infectionskrankheiten,' 2nd edit., 1864, as based upon very numerous independent thermometric observations. I may also mention the following:—
Thierfelder's article, from observations made in my wards (in 1855, 'Archiv für physiologische Heilkunde, xiv, 173), *Wunderlich* (1857, ibid, xvi, 367, and 1858, xvii, 19), *Uhle* (1859, ibid., xviii, 76), *Wunderlich* (1861, 'Archiv der Heilkunde,' ii, 433, and 1862, iii, 97), *Fiedler* (ibid., iii, 265), *Wachsmuth* (1863, ibid., iv, 55), *Thomas* (1864, ibid., v, 431 and 527; and 1847, ibid., viii, 49), *Ladé* ('De la Température du Corps dans les Maladies et en particulier dans la Fièvre Typhoide, 1866), Bäumler (1867, 'Deutsches Archiv für klin. Med.' iii, 365, which treats of typhoid fever in England), *Seidel* (1868, 'Jena'sche Zeitschrift.' iv, 480). Besides these, numerous notices of special points, or confirmations of previous statements, will be found scattered through various periodicals, &c.

See the Charts at the end, Tables I, II, and III, and the supplemental bibliography.

II.—EXANTHEMATIC TYPHUS.

(Spotted fever—petechial or true typhus.)

§ 1. As far as can be gathered from very accurate although not very numerous observations, the fever in exanthematic typhus has a very definite typical character, which can be recognised best in mild cases, and those of medium severity. The fever in this disease differs from that of all other diseases, and particularly from that of abdominal typhus (or *typhoid* fever), with which, however, it displays certain points of correspondence.

The fever of exanthematic typhus is of shorter duration than the shortest normal fever course of abdominal typhus; it lasts longer, however, than the fever in all the rest of the acute diseases which run a typical course.

In exanthematic typhus the initial stage, the fastigium (in which two distinct divisions can be distinguished), and the period of defervescence, are all characteristic. Observation of the temperature alone through any one of these stages sometimes allows us to diagnose typhus fever with great probability, whilst a continuance of such observations through any two of these periods almost always renders the diagnosis perfectly certain.

The course of the temperature furnishes a means of distinguishing mild cases, cases of moderate severity, and dangerous cases with tolerable certainty.

But in very severe cases the type sometimes becomes difficult to recognise, and this, or observation of only a brief period of the disease, may sometimes render the diagnosis, especially from other severe diseases, very difficult, and sometimes impossible.

Irregularities in the course, with or without complications, also occur in exanthematic typhus, but the sparseness of undoubtedly correct observations has hitherto made it impossible to characterise them more precisely.

§ 2. In the *beginning* of the illness, the temperature generally rises more suddenly than it does in typhoid fever, especially in cases which commence with a rigor.

The temperature generally reaches 40°—40·5°C. (104°—104·9° F.) as early as the first evening. On the following morning it recedes somewhat, and sometimes even approximates to the normal temperature, but most generally remains between 39·5° and 40° (103·1° and 104° F.). On the second evening it rises afresh, and often enough exceeds 40·5° C. (104·9° F.), and on the third evening it has risen to a still greater height, even to 41·5° C. (106·7° F.).

This increase continues at least till the fourth evening, on which the temperature is seldom under 40·5° (104·9°), generally about 41° C. (105·8° F.), and often more, and this indifferently in cases which die as in those which recover.

At this period of the disease, neither thermometry nor the remaining symptoms, however carefully weighed, are able to make a certain diagnosis; and in particular it is impossible to differentiate the disease from relapsing fever. On the other hand the diagnosis from typhoid fevers is very definite, because in the latter the temperature rises less suddenly. The positive diagnosis of true typhus can only be made with tolerable accuracy, by a consideration of the etiology (proofs of infection) during this stage.

§ 3. In moderate cases, and such as take a favorable course, the temperature has already reached its summit on the fourth day, and in the course of the second half of the first week, on the fourth, fifth, or sixth day, there occurs a turning-point, which, indeed, is announced by only a very trifling decrease of temperature. A somewhat greater remission succeeds, in favorable cases, on the seventh or eighth day. The temperature, it is true, rises again immediately in the second week, but only for a few days, and as a rule, in favorable cases, does not again reach the maximal heights of the first week.

This rise of temperature, in pretty nearly all the cases, begins about the eighth or ninth day, seldom later, and may be from ½° to 2° C. (1° to 3·6° F.). In favorable cases it lasts only a very short time, it may be only one day, or two to three days, and the temperature begins slowly to descend again. On the twelfth day, in fortunate cases, there commonly occurs a more decided, and, so to speak, *preparatory* remission, which sometimes lasts half a day, at others for two successive mornings.

A third, but generally very brief rise of temperature may succeed this, having the character of a perturbatio critica, and terminating immediately in definite defervescence.

Or defervescence may immediately follow the first inconsiderable diminution of temperature, which occurs in the middle of the second week, without any further rise of temperature intervening.

In these slight cases, the diagnosis generally remains doubtful during the fastigium, unless the etiology confirms it.   Thermometry only affords a fair probability in favour of exanthematic typhus, and against the presence of typhoid fever, based on the temperatures being uniformly higher in the second half of the first week, and not much less in the first days of the second week.   The probabilities are essentially strengthened, when with these high temperatures, the cerebral symptoms are considerable, and the remaining phenomena relatively unimportant.   The other symptoms indeed, taken by themselves, furnish a number of points in confirmation, but certainly afford no certainty of diagnosis.   However, if the case has been under observation from the very beginning till the first half of the second week, we may generally make the diagnosis with great confidence, merely from the thermometric course.

There is indeed one other disease, besides typhus fever, which begins in a similar way, and exhibits the same course during its fastigium, and, especially after high continuous fever, may even extend into the second week without any severe localisation ever taking place. The disease thus easily confounded with petechial typhus, is relapsing fever, although this happens but seldom; for in the great majority of cases of relapsing fever, the fever, properly so-called, does not extend into the second week.

§ 4. In severe or neglected cases of typhus, the continuous ascent in the height of the exacerbations continues all through the first week, and attains very considerable degrees (41·2°—41·6° C. = 106·16° —106·88° F. or more). The remission on the seventh day is absent, and the high fever persists through the whole of the second week, or at least for a great part of it, at very considerable heights, and in an exacerbating type; so that the morning temperatures are about 40° C. (104° F.) whilst in the evenings the heat may rise a degree or more higher (= 1·8° F. or more). In such severe cases, even the remission on the twelfth day is wanting, or is present only in a much less degree, and although in severe cases which recover, the temperature may become a trifle lower towards the end of the second week, yet very high degrees of temperature are met with both in the mornings and evenings till the beginning of the third week.

In severe cases the diagnosis during the fastigium is almost always more difficult than in the milder cases, especially the diagnosis from abdominal typhus: for severe cases of typhus and typhoid are in every respect more alike in the fastigium than milder cases of these diseases. The daily maxima of temperature are, however, as a rule, higher than even in severe abdominal typhus; the tendency to considerable remissions is far less, but these are mere *quantitative* differences, which are generally not sufficient to decide. If we add to this, that there may be a very great correspondence between the recurring symptoms of these two diseases in severe cases—that, for example, the rose spots may be very copious in typh*oid* and very scanty in typhus,[1] that the brain symptoms may be equally severe in typh*oid*, and that in typh*us* liquid stools and profuse diarrhœa are sometimes present; it is easy to understand the necessity of great care in making a diagnosis.

§ 5. The stage of *defervescence* is usually very characteristic in exanthematic typhus.

In the great majority of cases defervescence is preceded by a critical perturbation, which lasts only a very short time (one to two evenings), and consists in a rise of temperature amounting to from a few tenths to 2° C. (3·6° F.), or more, above that of the preceding evening, and often contrasting still more strongly with the already modified temperature of the morning of the same day.

Defervescence may either succeed this immediately in a precipitous manner, or in rarer cases the rise of the perturbation is immediately followed by a brief fall of moderate amount, and then a rapid descent.

In cases where there is no critical perturbation the temperature is usually moderated to a medium intensity as early as the second half of the fastigium.

Defervescence most commonly occurs between the thirteenth and seventeenth days, less frequently between the twelfth and thirteenth, and still more seldom at an earlier date.

Postponed terminations are rare and doubtful, unless the fever is

---

[1] To those who are familiar with typhus, this note may seem superfluous, but as the eruptions are so badly described in most text-books, it is perhaps not really out of place to remark, that the *first* appearance of the typhus rash is not only strikingly like the typhoid, but absolutely indistinguishable in some of the cases, both as to colour, form, and fading on pressure.— [TRANS.]

protracted on account of complications. Defervescence follows a
rapid course in the majority of cases. In many the temperature in
the course of a single night falls from a height of 40° C. (104° F.),
or even from higher degrees, down to normal ; or falls from 2°
to 3° C. (3·6° to 5·4° F.) or so, and from this time no longer rises
to febrile height [crisis]. But rather more commonly, especially in
severe cases, this happens: that the morning temperature after the
first evening decrease does not quite reach normal, but about 38°—
38·5° C. (100·4—101·6° F.) ; on the following evening it rises again
to 38·8° or 39·2° C., and reaches the normal point for the first time
on the following morning.

More rarely the defervescence continues during the night, although
the line of its march is extended, or it descends in the pattern of an
easel [see diagrams at end], and reaches the normal after a second
twenty-four hours ; or a somewhat slower though almost continuous
fall of temperature continues for some days, so that from three to
five days are occupied in reaching the normal temperature.

It is, however, quite exceptional for the defervescence to resemble
that of typhoid fever, because that exhibits remissions. And in these
cases also the normal temperature is in fact reached much more
quickly than in typhoid fever.

These varieties of defervescence distinguish exanthematic from
abdominal typhus in the most striking manner; and although other
diseases may defervesce in a similar fashion (cases of pneumonia,
variola, measles, scarlatina, &c.), yet the course and duration of the
fastigium is essentially different in these. Typhus on the other hand
is distinguished by the defervescence itself from relapsing fever,
because the decrease of temperature in the former is never so colossal
as in the latter. Defervescence, therefore, taken in connection with
the preceding course, may serve to distinguish exanthematic typhus
from every other form of disease with great accuracy ; and the cases
are quite exceptional in which complications during defervescence
weaken the potency of this method of proof.

§ 6. *Fatal cases* of exanthematic typhus generally announce themselves even from the very beginning by the enormous height of the
temperature (41·2° C. = 106·16° F., and even more). The transient remission at the end of the first week is wanting in these
cases.

Death may occur in the second week with continual high temperatures. If the case enters the third week, some remission may show itself on the fourteenth day, but this must not be regarded as a favorable symptom, and is very soon compensated.

Yet even in fatal cases the temperatures in the third week are not so high as at the earlier periods, at least till near the death agony. The daily maxima do not exceed 40·8° C. (105·44° F.), but are, for the most part, moderate. The danger to life during this third week is indicated not by the height of the fever, but by its continuance.

Just before death, and in the death agony, the temperature constantly rises in exanthematic typhus. In all my cases in which it was possible to make observations, there was a rise of temperature during the agony of at least 1·25° C. = 2½° F., in one case of even 3·6° (6·48°) ; and on an average about 1·8° C. (3·24° F.). During the agony the temperature was seldom so low as 40° (104° F.); more usually it was about 41—42° C. (105·8° C.—107·6° F.), and once 43° C. (109·4° F.).

§ 7. The course of the fever in exanthematic typhus was first demonstrated by myself in my article, ' Beobachtungen über den exanthematischen Typhus,' (1857, in the ' Archiv f. physiol. Heilkunde,' N. F. Bd. i, 177). My conclusions were confirmed in all essential points by *Griesinger's* Observations (1861, ' Archiv der Heilkunde,' ii, 557), by *Moers* (1866, in the ' Deutsche Archiv für klinische Medicin,' ii, 36), and by *Murchison* (in the ' Lancet' of Dec. 8th, 1866). Even the readings obtained by *Grimshaw* (' Dublin Journal,' 1867), unsatisfactory as they are, for he only took the temperature once a day and noted too many *whole* degrees, and adduced as they are by him as a contradiction to my conclusions as set forth by *Aitkin*, show clearly, at the first glance on the charts, that with all their imperfections they simply represent and confirm the views I have set forth.

[Dr. *Grimshaw* ('Medical Press and Circular,' 1866) speaks of *Collapse* temperatures of 95° and 96° F. preceding death in many cases of typhus. Dr. *Edwin Long Fox* thinks lysis the most common mode of defervescence. He thinks the author places the typhus temperatures too high (' Medical Times and Gazette,' February 5th, 1870), and Mr. *Squarey* ('Med. Chir. Transactions,' 1867), seems to be of the same opinion. He states that the evening temperature rarely exceeds 105° F. in the evenings. Whilst fully admitting that all cases are not alike, I can only account for the different results obtained by these observers and some other English ones, by supposing that the cause was the same as that mentioned in the note to page 105, or that the thermometer was retained for only three or four minutes. My own observations entirely confirm those in the text.—TRANS.]

See the curves of temperature in Table IV at the end.

III.—RELAPSING FEVER.

(*Typhus recurrens ; famine fever ; fièvre à rechute.*)

§ 1. Recurrent or relapsing fever shows itself in two forms—as a simple recurrent fever (*relapsing fever* of English writers) and as *bilious typhoid* (first introduced into pathology by Griesinger).[1]

The course of the fever in the simple relapsing form is in the highest degree typical, and is quite peculiar from the fact that two, sometimes three, seldom four, attacks of fever running a continuous course of several days, with very remarkable heights of temperature, are interrupted by intervals free from fever, which also last for several days; so that this disease pre-eminently deserves to stand as a model of the relapsing fever type.

In the other far rarer form of bilious typhoid the course of the fever has been far less accurately studied, but the type of the course may correspond pretty well with that of the other. Yet both in fatal cases and in those which recover, the second attack of fever is often wanting, and so the peculiar apyretic interval or interruption is wanting, and the peculiar character of the type is thus lost.

§ 2. The disease generally *begins* with the symptoms of a rigor with rapid rise of temperature, and thus on the second day the temperature commonly exceeds 40° C. (104° F.) or even 41° C. (105·8° F.)

The further course of the first stage of the fever is pretty practically continuous, although interrupted by solitary *peaks* of exacerbation, which may occur at any hour of the day, and may extend to between 41° and 42° C. (105·8° and 107·6° F.) Two elevations of temperature on one day are not uncommon. Actual remissions,

---

[1] Is not this the true "bilious fever" of our own older writers? [TRANS.]

i. e., a downfall of temperature as low as 39·8° C. (103·64° F.) do not occur during the principal part of the fever paroxysm, which as a rule lasts from five to seven days, or less frequently three to four, or eight to thirteen days. A decidedly descending direction is first perceived on the last, or last day but one, or if the paroxysm be protracted, on the third or fourth day before the critical period. This descending direction announces itself by a lasting, and considerable fall of temperature, or sometimes by the remissions becoming more marked, and being succeeded by slighter exacerbations. More particularly a very marked remission descending to nearly 38° C. (100·4° F.) sometimes occurs, just the day before the crisis, after which the temperature rises again more or less, but generally not to the height of the exacerbation of the preceding day, though sometimes it may even exceed this.

The height of the temperature immediately before the crisis is commonly between 39·8° and 40·5° C. (= 103·64° to 104·9° F.), and is thus actually less than the maximal heights, and it is only exceptionally that the heat rises immediately before defervescence to the level of the earlier maxima, in the manner of a critical perturbation. The downfall now occurs with extreme rapidity, with or without the co-operation of perspiration, so that within less than twelve hours the temperature falls in an unbroken line from 4° to 6° Centigrade (7·2° — 10·8° F.), and seldom less than 3° C. (= 5·4° F.), and hence it generally reaches sub-normal degrees. According to *Zorn*, the fever does not run so high in the *bilious form*, as it does in the simple, although it is obviously severe. The mercury seldom rises above 41° C. (105·8° F.), but generally fluctuates between 39° and 40·5° C. (102·2° and 104·9° F.), and it is common for peripheral parts to feel even cold, which is an immediate indication of a dangerous attack. In the bilious form, very many cases prove fatal even in the first attack. A similar rapid fall of temperature appears sometimes to determine a cessation of the fever in bilious typhoid; this sometimes happens after a fresh rigor, and with copious perspirations. Yet this is not the normal course. Some cases end at once in death, without any further progress, others have a protracted defervescence. *Herrmann* remarks, that either accidental complications or more profound localizations are to be dreaded in cases in which the perspirations are not critical, and lysis takes place, interrupted by fresh exacerbations.

§ 3. A period free from fever (apyrexia) follows the defervescence, and generally lasts from a half to one and a half weeks, rarely only one to three days, and sometimes as long as two to two and a half weeks. It is, however, exceptional for this period to exhibit a continuous course of normal temperatures, marked by healthy or convalescent daily fluctuations. As a rule, it is far more common to meet with interruptions to this even course of temperature, from more or less considerable elevations.

Very shortly after the temperature at the conclusion of defervescence has reached its lowest point, it rises again more or less rapidly, in many cases, not only from sub-normal to normal, but very commonly also to the level of a febrile movement, or even to moderate fever heat ($38 \cdot 5^\circ$ C. $= 101 \cdot 3^\circ$ F.) This fresh rise of temperature is usually ephemeral; after a few hours it falls again for half or a whole day till it reaches the normal. Sometimes a second, but less considerable elevation occurs on the next day, and these fluctuations may continue for as much as three to five days, whilst in other cases these rises of temperature are absent entirely, or do not transgress the limits of normal temperature, or the temperature may even remain below normal for several days.

Let the course of the temperature during the intermediate, or apyretic, stage be what it will, there almost always occurs about the middle of the stage a brief, sharply pointed (akme-artige) elevation of temperature, sometimes only amounting to about one degree C. ($= 1 \cdot 8^\circ$ F.), but sometimes to as much as 2° or 3° C. ($= 3 \cdot 6^\circ$ to $5 \cdot 4^\circ$ F.). The freedom from fever soon recurs, and very often it is only completely seen after the episodal elevation; at other times, however, the temperature is as truly normal before this as after.

This rise of temperature generally divides the apyrexia into two almost equal portions, of which the former has a special character of its own.

The apyrexia is indeed not wholly devoid of danger, and even in simple recurrent fever death may once now and again occur at this period, whilst in bilious typhoid such a termination is pretty frequently met with.

§ 4. The *second attack* or relapse is more often met with in the simple form than in the bilious, and in the former almost invariably in cases which recover, whilst, according to *Zorn*, it occurs only in about half of the bilious cases.

The beginning of the second attack is generally more or less rapid. It is sometimes preceded by a slight rise of temperature. Then the rise occurs in an abrupt line, and sometimes in a very few hours, or in other cases within twenty-four hours, the temperature has already reached its previous height. This, as a rule, amounts to from 40° to 41° C. (104° to 105·8° F.), but is almost always considerably under the maximum of the second fever period.

This second stage of the fever generally occupies three to four days. The temperature generally takes an ascending course, with more or less deep remissions; sometimes it is continuously ascending, more rarely it is actively intermittent with a tertian, or some other type, with two to four paroxysms; or rarely a solitary, short, and acutely pointed elevation of temperature.

The *peaks*, of which there is generally only one in the course of the day, though sometimes there are two, generally grow higher and higher: and the last usually represents the maximum of the second fever period, which is commonly rather higher than that of the first attack, and is seldom less than 41° C. (105·8° F.), generally between 41·4° C. (106·6° F.) and 42° C. (107·6° F.), and sometimes even still higher (in two of my cases it reached 42·2° C. = 107·6° F.).

Hardly any other kind of disease exhibits such high temperatures in cases which recover.

The intercurrent remissions are sometimes very inconsiderable, but in the majority of cases, one or more of the remissions (most usually the first or the last) is considerable, so that the temperature may fall about 2° or 3° C. (3·6° to 5·4° F.) within a few hours. But it immediately begins a fresh ascent, and very rapidly exceeds the level from which it had fallen. In the intermittent form only do the intercurrent lower temperatures last somewhat longer, whilst the paroxysms rise higher than in ordinary malarial intermittent fever or ague. The last elevation, which is generally also the highest point, is very often reached in the morning hours. Defervescence immediately succeeds, with or without perspiration, by a rapid and unbroken fall of temperature; that is, in the course of half a day it falls from 4° to 7° C. (7·2° to 12·6° F.), and very seldom less than 3½° C. (6¼° F.), generally even below the normal, which may occur without any symptoms of collapse. Isolated fluctuations are sometimes met with at the end of the fall.

The disease generally terminates with this second defervescence, which exhibits a greater fall of temperature than any other disease.

Once now and then some inconsiderable fluctuations of temperature succeed, which slightly surpass normal temperatures, but in general convalescence is definitively reached. Sometimes death may occur even after the cessation of the fever. Once now and then, after a fresh interval of apyrexia (generally lasting one to four days) a *third* or even a *fourth* attack (second or third relapse) may succeed.[1] But these renewed attacks are generally wanting; they occur but seldom in simple relapsing fever, and still more rarely in the bilious form. When they do occur they have the same character as the first two, but are generally less acute, and the temperatures are not so high, but are no less fatal on this account.

In cases which recover, the third attack lasts from two to four days, seldom more. Defervescence is rapid, but the fall of temperature is less considerable. Owing to the fever temperature being less extreme, the fall amounts only to from 1·6° to about 3° C. (2·88° to 5·4° F.).

§ 5. As regards the *fatal termination*, which may occur under various conditions, sometimes in the fiercest paroxysms of fever, at other times in the extremest collapse, or it may be under many other conditions, thermometric data are wanting. In the only fatal case observed by myself the second attack was succeeded by an amphibolic stage of fluctuation, which lasted a whole week, and the temperature finally rose again to 41·4° C. (106·52° F.).

As regards the fever in relapsing typhoid, I would specially refer to *Herrmann* ('Petersburg. Zeitschrift,' viii, 14), *Zorn* (ibid., ix, 16), *my own* account (in the 'Archiv für Heilkunde' for 1869, x, 314), *Wyss* and *Bock* ('Studien über Febris recurrens,' 1869), and numerous other authors.

[The English reader will find a good résumé in Dr. Russell Reynolds's and Dr. Aitkin's works on medicine previously quoted. —TRANS.]

See the charts in Table IV.

IV.—VARIOLOUS DISEASES.

§ 1. The fever in variolous diseases exhibits *two distinct types*, which closely correspond, however, at their commencement.

---

[1] Dr. Warburton Begbie (Reynolds's 'System of Medicine') and Dr. Aitkin ('Practice of Medicine') state that a fourth or fifth relapse is, although rare, sometimes met with.—[TRANS.]

These two types correspond to the two chief modifications of smallpox ; one a brief *continuous* form, belonging to the moderated and modified disease, or *varioloid*, occurring chiefly, although not exclusively, in vaccinated or inoculated persons; the other a *relapsing* type, which characterises the complete form, which runs its course with fever in the suppurating stage, or *variola vera*, which, for the most part, though not always nor only, attacks the unvaccinated. The course of the fever does not distinguish variolous disease from all others; in the initial stage more particularly, and in modified smallpox, the fever course may resemble that of some other diseases, and particularly that sometimes met with in pneumonia.

On the other hand, the course of the fever at the time of the eruption is so peculiar that this, taken in combination with the outbreak of the exanthem, even whilst this has not yet presented any distinctive characters, is able to afford a perfectly correct diagnosis.

Nor will the course of the temperature in the initial stage suffice to distinguish between variola vera and variolois. But as soon as the exanthem develops itself the course of the temperature is not only the most certain, but the only certain criterion by which true smallpox may be distinguished from the modified form. Not only is the occurrence of a more or less developed secondary fever (fever of suppuration) the most trustworthy means of diagnosis between the two forms, but the mode of defervescence of the eruptive fever gives an almost infallible indication as to the kind of further course we have to expect.

During the initial stage the temperature affords no aid in deciding on the severity of the disease, but the course after the eruption aids us very much. Complications, also, for the most part, may be recognised by the temperature, when occurring after the first commencement of the eruption.

§ 2. The initial period is common to both types. On the first or second day of the disease the temperature has already attained a considerable height (40° C. = 104° F., seldom below this, sometimes above it). This may, perhaps, occur in an unbroken line and with extreme rapidity (in which case there is generally a rigor and shivering), or perhaps it may occur more slowly, and reach this elevation in the second evening, after a retrocession on the morning of that day.

In patients previously ill (*e. g.* phthisical cases) this rise may be more protracted and less considerable.

On the second day the temperature may have already attained its maximum, or may still exhibit a moderate increase on the third or, indeed, on the fourth day, with which only very slight remissions occur in the morning hours.

The *maximum* temperature of the initial stage or prodromal fever is only exceptionally less than 40° C. (104° F.), generally somewhat above that, sometimes even 41° C. (105·8 F.), or, indeed, a few tenths more.

When the maximum has been reached a slight fall immediately ensues, which generally lasts only one day. At this time we may commonly notice the first traces of the eruption in the form of spots. This stage lasts from two to five days, and it is not possible at this time, from the course of the temperature, to discriminate smallpox from exanthematic typhus, relapsing fever, or from a pneumonia which as yet affords no local evidence of its presence; and even when the other symptoms are taken in conjunction, it is seldom that we can speak with complete certainty. Yet, on the one hand, every day that the fever lasts without the lung symptoms renders pneumonia less probable; and, on the other hand, if the fifth day of the disease pass over without any eruption making its appearance the presence of smallpox must be considered very doubtful.

§ 3. Soon after the first development of the variolous papules *the temperature falls more or less rapidly*. In rare cases of the disease this defervescence occurs as early as the second or third day of the disease, but generally from the fourth to the sixth day. The downfall either lasts only twenty-four hours or less, in which case it is continuous; or two, or, indeed, even three days, when it is generally not continuous or, in other words, it is interrupted by a moderate evening exacerbation.

In cases of uncomplicated *varioloid* the temperature quickly reaches normal by this defervescence, or falls even a trifle below it, and thenceforth remains normal, or pretty nearly so, unless the occurrence of some complication causes a fresh rise, which is but seldom the case.

When the eruption in modified smallpox (varioloid) is very copious there may sometimes occur a slight, scarcely febrile, and seldom decidedly febrile elevation of temperature at the time when the pustules are desiccating, but this does not last long in any case. This fall of temperature is the best characteristic of *varioloid*, especially when regard is had to the fact that the defervescence is not simultaneous with the full development of the eruption, but occurs soon after that begins, even at the time the spots begin to be papular, or to be distinctly felt as elevations. When this occurs, and the temperature begins to fall in this way with the beginning of the eruption, one may pronounce for smallpox with great certainty if the question be between smallpox or measles, or between the former and exanthematic typhus.

In the same way, one may be perfectly certain that not the so-called variola vera, or true smallpox, but a modified disease or variolois is present, if a normal temperature is very quickly reached during this defervescence.

§ 4. In variola vera the falling temperature after the prodromal stage either never gets down to normal, sometimes remaining sub-febrile, but generally at decidedly febrile degrees, and continuing in this fashion for several days, with or without considerable daily fluc-tuations; or the normal temperature is reached, if at all, tediously, and defervescence is by lysis.

With the beginning of the renewed congestion of the skin intro-duced by the suppuration of the eruption, the temperature again begins to rise.

The secondary fever (suppurating fever) is of indefinite duration, varied, indeed, according to the intensity of the disease; and at the same time its course and the height of the temperature differ according to the danger and severity of the disease. In smallpox of moderate severity the temperature in this stage scarcely reaches $39°$ C. ($102.2°$ F.) in general, and very rarely $40°$ C. ($104°$ F.) or more; there are morning remissions, and the duration is usually only a few days. In severe cases the temperature is considerably higher; the course is sometimes remittent with very marked exacerbations, and sometimes continuous with occasional isolated elevations of temperature.

Irregular fluctuations very often mark its course. If during the fever of suppuration the temperature several times exceeds $40°$ C. ($104°$ F.) it is a sign of great danger. In cases not fatal the duration of the secondary fever is seldom less than a week.

In favorable cases the fever defervesces by lysis, in a very gradual manner, and sometimes at the time of scabbing there is an occasional prejudicial but brief rise of temperature, or the fever may even continue till desiccation, and it may be even longer.

In *fatal* cases the temperature may rise rather quickly from moderate heights to very considerable degrees, and death may occur at 42° C. (107·6° F.), or even more, although during this stage the patient may sometimes die with only very moderate elevation of temperature. *Simon* ('Charité Annalen,' xiii, Bd. v) has published cases in which the temperature (which was, however, measured after death) was 43·75° and 44·5° C. respectively (110·75° and 112·1° F.).

§ 5. Serious complications may cause intercurrent attacks and irregularities in the temperature, which, however, presents nothing specially characteristic of smallpox.

Compare *my own* account of the disease (1858, in the 'Archiv für physiol. Heilkunde,' N. F. ii, 18) and a communication by *Leo* on an epidemic of smallpox in my wards (in 1864, in 'Archiv der Heilkunde,' v, 481); *Fröhlich* (1867, ibid., viii, 420); and *Körber* ('Petersb. Zeitschrift,' xiii, 303). For the curves of variolous fever see lithographs, Table IV.

VARICELLA.[1]

Thomas states (in the 'Archiv der Heilkunde,' viii, 376, and the 'Archiv für Dermatologie und Syphilis,' i, 309) that sometimes even in the incubation stage of *varicella* there are slight elevations of temperature, and that at the time of the eruption in many cases the rise of temperature is very trifling. In the majority of cases, however, sometimes at the beginning of the exanthematic period and sometimes after a copious eruption had been developed, he found a sudden and relatively considerable elevation of temperature, sometimes indeed only a few tenths over 38° C., or about 101° F.; in rather severe cases 38·5° C. (101·5° F.) to even 40° C. (104° F.), but

---

[1] I have removed this from No. VII, where the author places it with rubeola, and associated it with its congeners, because the experience of several epidemics of smallpox (in London, Herts, Warwickshire, and Hants) more and more forces upon my mind the essential identity of variola and varicella, a conclusion which is warmly contended for by Hebra (see Dr. Hilton Fagge's translation, New Sydenham Society).—[TRANS.]

seldom more. The high stage lasted from two to five days, and the
fever was remittent, and as regards the height of the temperature
corresponded pretty accurately with the copiousness of the eruption.
The maximum temperature occurred sometimes in the first, but more
often in the second half of the fastigium, and the morning remissions
after the maximum were sometimes somewhat more considerable than
they had been before. Defervescence was rapid, and commonly over
in half a day. [I have nothing to add to this very accurate
account, except that my own notes confirm it in every respect.—
TRANS.]

V.—MEASLES.

§ 1. The disease known as *measles* presents us with a fever
which precedes the exanthem, and accompanies it to its fullest
development. Its typical character is pretty strongly marked.

But inasmuch as measles is subject to manifold irregularities
of extraordinary number, and more especially so in certain epidemics,
when they seem to accumulate, it cannot be expected that the
course of the temperature should be absolutely regular and free from
deviations.

Still further, since measles is a disease which principally attacks
children or very young people, and since the temperature in childhood
is more susceptible of variations from accidental influences than at
any other age, it is perfectly easy to understand that one often
stumbles upon cases which exhibit more or less deviation from the
typical form which occurs when uncomplicated measles attacks previously healthy although predisposed individuals, who are not too
delicate and sensitive. The very beginning of measles has many
characteristics, and so have the maxima of temperature attained in it.
But the mode and the time of defervescence of the fever is particularly characteristic in measles, and very definitely distinguishes it
from other acute exanthematic diseases.

Even the forms which deviate from the normal show more or less
clearly some traits of this type of defervescence; and on the other
hand the imperfect correspondence of the descending temperature
with the type, or the irregularity of the defervescence in special cases,
affords us data for prognosis, and is an indication that the case is
abnormal.

§ 2. Even before the proper fever-stage in measles, in even the stage of *inculation*, and therefore at a time in which, although the infection has been taken, no ordinary means of observation suffice for its recognition, *Thomas* states that there is, in many cases, a short preliminary fever-course in the form of an ephemera, or of an ephemera protracta, in which the maxima of temperature are about 38·8° C. (102·84° F.) to 39·8° C. (103·64° F.), and that this is followed by a pause or interval of several days quite free from fever.[1]

§ 3. Decided and connected symptoms of the disease commence with a rapid and more or less considerable rise of temperature (initial-fever) which is complete in from twelve to twenty-four hours, and by which in the great majority of cases a temperature of 39·1° to 40° C. (102·38° F. to 104° F.) is attained in the evening; it is far less frequent to find only 38·1 to 39° C. (100·58° to 102·2°) according to *Thomas*. Yet it is exceptional for this first rise of temperature to reach the *maximum* temperature of the entire fever-period of measles. On the other hand, the degree of temperature attained in this preliminary elevation allows us to forecast the subsequently occurring elevations with very great probability, since these, on an average, are wont to exceed the height of the initial rise by about $\frac{7}{10}$ to 1° Centigrade = 1·5° to 1·8° Fahrenheit, and only exceed this a trifle even when most extreme.

The initial rise of temperature is pretty constantly followed by an immediate downfall on the next night, so that in the morning the temperature is normal, or only just a few tenths above it, and very seldom exceeds 38° (100·4°), except in very severe or anomalous cases.

This depression of temperature sometimes lasts for a few hours only, and sometimes a whole day (through an entire evening and the following morning).

The rise and fall of temperature in this initial stage are so rapid

[1] Dr. Wm. Squire (if I understood him correctly) expressed a similar opinion at a recent meeting of the Obstetrical Society, but extended it to a variety of other febrile diseases of childhood. Should this be generally confirmed (as I fully expect it will be), it is clear that in large schools or families, during an epidemic, a rise of temperature in a previously healthy child, accompanied, perhaps, by trifling symptoms of indisposition, may afford a seasonable warning and indications for precautionary measures, but the great mobility of childish temperatures must preclude our founding an absolute diagnosis or prognosis upon such a slender foundation.—[TRANS.]

that the case might be taken for an intermittent, did not the temperature remain rather too low to allow of this idea. On the other hand, it may easily be confounded with an ephemeral fever, and if the succeeding normal temperature lasts a little longer than usual the opinion may easily gain ground that the disease is already over! But in most cases the marked existence of other symptoms (particularly the ocular and pulmonary ones) allows us to recognise the disease which is developing itself.

§ 4. The true *eruptive fever* begins with a fresh rise of temperature, which henceforward till the exanthem is fully developed either exhibits no return towards normal or only very temporary remissions.

In most cases this eruptive fever is divided into two sections, a moderately febrile stage and the fastigium or acme.

The *moderately febrile stage* generally lasts from thirty-six to forty-eight hours, seldom less, and is made up of one or two exacerbations of moderate extent ($38°$ to $39°$ C. $= 100\cdot4°$ to $102\cdot2°$ F.), which do not generally reach the high level of the initial fever. When there are two exacerbations the second is the higher, and the morning remission which intervenes commonly descends less low than the retrocession after the initial fever, yet even at this stage the normal temperature may be reached on a single occasion.

The stage of *fastigium* is characterised by a considerable and persistent rise of temperature, which leaves behind for some time the preceding normal or moderately febrile temperatures (*Thomas*). The commencement occurs early in the day in some cases, in others in the evening. In the former case the evening temperature rises still more, which may or may not be followed by a trifling remission on the next morning, and the maximum occurs the next evening.

If the rise of the fastigium begins in the evening, there is similarly, the next morning, either a very slight remission or none at all. But in rare cases rather considerable remissions may be met with during the fastigium.

The *maximum* temperature of the fastigium, and also generally speaking that of the disease itself, is chiefly observed in normal cases at the very time when the exanthem reaches its maximum of development and extension. Yet there is a tolerable number of cases which are so far exceptions that the temperature reaches its maximum shortly after the first appearance of the eruption, and so between its beginning and its highest development; when the latter has been perfected, the temperature has already begun to sink somewhat. But the maximum of temperature almost always occurs closer to the maximum of the exanthem than to its beginning. And even if the maximum has been reached whilst the eruption is still progressing, the decrease of temperature up to the time of the fullest development of the eruption is almost always very slight. Moreover, it is not improbable that complications may contribute their share towards accelerating the acme of temperature. The maximum temperature usually occurs in the evening hours; and if it occur in the morning hours there is only a moderate fall the same evening; and it seems an optional thing whether we should yet call this the beginning of defervescence.

The whole fastigium lasts from one and a half to two and a half days, and thus the complete eruptive fever occupies from three to four and a half days. Its course may, however, be prolonged by complications.

§ 5. Decided *defervescence* begins, according to rule, in the night, and for the most part, and in normal cases, runs a rapid course. Either the temperature on the next morning has already fallen to normal, or even below it; or the fall during the night is less complete, and the descent continues, although less rapidly, all through the day, or the temperature rises again in the evening, and first reaches the normal on the following morning. In uncomplicated and normal cases the normal temperature is at least reached on the second morning, and from that time continues thus. One or two slight evening exacerbations rising to sub-febrile heights are the most that occur.

Very severe bronchitis, or complications, may protract the course of the defervescence. In the same way, cases of measles which begin irregularly may have an abnormal defervescence. Nor must it be forgotten that in young children trifling causes may suffice to elevate the temperature.

Sometimes a recrudescence of the fever is caused by a second attack (nachschub = after-stroke or recoil) of the exanthem. In this the elevation of temperature may almost or quite equal the height of the previous maximum, but if no other complication be present this rise of temperature is very transient.

§ 6. *Complications* may induce alterations in the course of temperature of measles, which in such cases shapes itself according to the kind of complication, and is no longer subject to the sway of the original disease. Only, if the complication precedes the development of the exanthem, there generally occurs along with and immediately after the eruption a further elevation of temperature, which is, doubtless, due to the exanthem. Since the fatal termination in cases of measles which go on to death undoubtedly always depends upon complications, the temperature in such circumstances is determined by the kind of complication present.

On the subject of the type of fever in measles, consult *my own* publication, " Ueber den Normal-verlauf einiger typischen Krankheitsformen" (1858), in ' Archiv für physiol. Heilkunde,' B. ii, 14) ; *Siegel* (" Beobachtnugen über Masern 1861 ausführliche Bearbeitung der in meiner Klinik vorgekommenen Fälle," in ' Archiv der Heilkunde,' ii, 521); *Ziemssen* and *Krabler* (1863, ' Greifswalder Beiträge,' i) ; *my own* remarks on them in 1863 (in ' Archiv d. Heilkunde,' iv, 331) ; *Pfeilsticker* (' Beiträge zur Pathol. der Masern,' 1863); *Monti* (' Jahrbuch für Kinderheilk.,' vii, 21 ; and especially *Thomas* (1867, in the ' Archiv der Heilkunde,' viii, 385).

For the curves of the fever in measles see lithographs, Table V.

VI.—SCARLATINA.

(*Scarlet fever.*)

§ 1. Scarlatina conforms far less closely and regularly to its type than the previously mentioned diseases do to theirs. Yet there is considerable correspondence in the course of the temperature even in cases which differ widely in other respects, and in this point of view the deviations appear to compose a minority of the cases.

§ 2. Cases of an abnormally mild course are tolerably common, and the symptoms of indisposition are sometimes so trifling that, especially at their commencement, they never become objects of medical care at all, although, indeed, in many such cases this want of care is punished by subsequent severe or even fatal sequelæ. I cannot from my own experience state whether any of these cases are so abnormally mild that either no alterations of temperature or next to none occur, because in cases which run a mild course all through I never had an opportunity of observing the commencement of the disease. *Thomas,* on the other hand, has lately stated, in a commu-

nication to the 'Archiv d. Heilkunde,' Heft ii (1870), that he has
seen cases which in the early stage, *i. e.* before or at the beginning
of the eruption, have not shown any febrile temperature. However,
I also know cases in which it was most strenuously asserted by their
guardians that the scarcely noticed and very slight eruption, which
was afterwards followed by desquamation, and indeed by severe
kidney-symptoms, occurred at first without any uncomfortable
or unusual feelings at all. But the course of the fever is very
often quite characteristic when the infection of scarlatina develops only
a rudimentary disease, or even only an angina without any eruption.[1]

§ 3. In all cases of scarlatina which are tolerably severe the
first symptom which shows itself, or, at all events, one of the first,
for other symptoms may accompany it or even sometimes precede
for an hour or two, is a rapid and continuous elevation of temperature, by which in the course of a few hours this reaches a considerable height (39·5° to 40° C. = 103·1° to 104° F)., generally accompanied by the phenomena of a more or less intense rigor or shivering.
Sometimes the commencement of the exanthem dates from immediately after this first rise, but the eruption commonly begins the next
morning (on the second day). If this delays to come out, the temperature continues to rise slowly, with very slight morning remissions, beyond the considerable height it obtained at first. It generally

---

[1] I think it possible that one explanation, applicable to some of the cases
alluded to above by *Thomas*, lies in the fact that just as there are some persons
who all through life have a relatively *slow pulse*, so there are others who all
through life have a relatively *low temperature*, or, in other words, *their* line of
normal temperature must be drawn one or two degrees Fahrenheit, or even
more (·9° to nearly 2° Centigrade), *lower* than the average normal temperature
of 37° C. or 98·6° F. I feel strongly convinced of this, and on looking over my
notes I find charts of several cases of scarlatina, measles, typhus, and typhoid,
in which the temperatures all through were at an unusually low level, although
other symptoms were fairly marked. *e.g.* Selina F—, a girl of 18 (said to have
been always very cold from infancy), had well-marked rash of scarlatina, sore
throat, and afterwards desquamation, albuminuria, &c. Her temperature was
never above 101° F. (38·3° C.), and when she recovered remained at or a little
below 97° F. (36·1° C.), although watched for several months.

J. A—, a man who died of typhus at 30, never had a temperature above
102·2° F. (39° C.) all through the fever, although there was no sign of collapse,
nor any hæmorrhage nor other symptoms to account for it. I also know one or
two people, apparently in good health, whose average temperature is 96·8° F.
(36° C.).

remains persistently high, or continues to rise strongly, till the exanthem has reached its maximum and covered the whole body, and sometimes even whilst the parts first attacked by the eruption have begun to grow pale. The duration of this rise may be very varied, and may continue from only half a day to four days.

The height finally reached by the temperature in this fashion is almost always above 40° C. (104° F.), very commonly over 40·5° C. (104·9° F.), but seldom in cases which terminate favorably exceeds 41° C. (105·8° F.).

In general the height of the temperature stands in tolerable parallelism with the intensity of the exanthem. Yet there are cases in which the eruption is but slight or almost wanting, with a very high temperature, but very few cases of copious eruption go with moderate fever.

The continuous course of the rising temperature, or when the eruptive stage is protracted, its dwelling upon almost stationary heights (disregarding the insignificant, and often enough totally absent, remissions), is only exceptionally interrupted by a solitary fall of temperature, which seems by preference to occur in cases where the eruption comes out in successive crops (Stössen). No definite moderation of temperature is generally met with before the eruption has attained at least the greater part of its development.

The rapid rise of temperature at the beginning of the disease on the one hand, and its remaining continuously high without any proper remissions on the other hand, allies scarlatina with many other diseases, and the diagnosis cannot therefore be made from this behaviour of the temperature taken by itself.

But scarlatina may indeed be very well distinguished by this course of the temperature from those affections with which, on account of the other symptoms, it is most easily confounded, and more particularly from measles (morbilli) and rubeolæ (Rubeola notha—Rötheln, or the so-called hybrid between measles and scarlatina), and, provided no exanthem can be noticed, from abdominal typhus, diphtheria, simple angina, and acute parenchymatous nephritis.

§ 4. When the eruption has passed its maximum, *defervescence* commences. The progress of this is not always the same. In cases with moderate elevation of temperature it may happen, although only exceptionally, that the temperature falls rapidly and reaches the normal height in half a day.

But in an overwhelming majority of cases defervescence is protracted, and requires from three to eight days for its completion. As a rule, it occurs in this fashion, that from day to day the temperature gets gradually lower, and slopes like an easel, or almost easel-like (Staffelweise), or goes down with trifling remissions, falling more especially at night, remaining about the same from morning to evening, or perhaps sinking a little till it reaches the normal. Sometimes elevations of a few tenths of a degree (Centigrade $= \frac{1}{4}$ to $\frac{1}{2}$ F. or a little more) in the evening break the fall, in which case the nightly descent is rather greater.

But it is only very seldom that a remitting defervescence produces a remote resemblance to that which is peculiar to abdominal typhus.

When defervescence is considerably delayed the downfall on the first, second, or even third day is often very slight, and a rapid fall is not noticed till afterwards.

Complications may still further retard defervescence, or even give rise to fresh elevations of temperature.

A sub-normal temperature is pretty commonly met with before the definite return of normal temperatures, and other symptoms of collapse may also be associated with this. The sub-normal temperature, however, seldom falls below 36° C. (96·8° F.), but often lasts for some days.

This form of defervescence, although not invariably met with, is tolerably characteristic of scarlatina, at least it does not so often occur in any other disease. A close resemblance to it is met with sometimes in exanthematic or true typhus, and in catarrhal pneumonia.

§ 5. An anomalous course of temperature is not infrequent in scarlatina.

The temperature, more particularly, sometimes remains rather low. This does not exclude danger, and by no means guarantees a favorable termination, which is very often missed on account of disorders which affect the temperature but slightly (diphtheria, croup, nephritis (q. v.), cerebral irritation, and parotitis). Here and there fresh elevations of temperature interrupt its descending course, depending on varied causes, and lasting for varying periods. Sometimes they can be traced to complications, but not always. In any case they retard recovery.

There is also a peculiar typhoid course of the disease, in which not merely transient but persistent cerebral disorders, diarrhœa, meteorism, and great enlargement of the spleen[1] are met with, and the duration of the disease may be extended a fortnight or more after the fading of the eruption. The fever thus remains more or less high, sub-continuous or remittent in form, yet in general it takes a descending course.

§ 6. During *convalescence* the temperature remains normal so long as it is undisturbed by complications or fresh diseases, or it may be by a second eruption. Therefore the persistence of a normal temperature is a pretty good guarantee for the absence of other disorders; the occurrence of fresh rises of temperature, on the other hand, may be regarded as a danger signal, and as a demand for a more careful examination and very painstaking supervision of the case. If any incipient disease provokes the fresh rise of temperature in convalescence, it will be found that the previous attack of scarlatina has no particular influence upon it.

§ 7. In *fatal cases* the course of the temperature may be very varied, and is chiefly affected by the time at which the tendency to death sets in, and by the disorders which induce the fatal result.

If death happens during the eruptive stage the temperature may reach very high degrees indeed, but it may also fall during the death agony.

If the fatal termination sets in after the exanthem has passed its maximum, and the temperature has begun to decline, the dying hour is generally heralded in by previous irregularities of the course. Whether fresh elevations of temperature precede death, and to what extent they do so, or whether, on the contrary, the temperature falls, depends chiefly on the nature of the processes which bring about the fatal result.

Cases also occur in which very suddenly, and without obvious motive, the temperature rises to enormous heights before death. (In one of my cases it rose to $43 \cdot 5^\circ$ C. ($110 \cdot 3^\circ$ F.).[2]

My own frequently quoted paper, "Ueber den Normalverlauf

---

[1] And lymphatic glands. I have seen several cases of leucocythæmia dating from scarlatina, also valvular disease of the heart.—[TRANS.]

[2] See note 2 to page 204. Also (as regards defervescence) the note to page 221.—[TRANS.]

einiger typischen Krankheitsformen," may be consulted on the temperature in scarlatina. Also *Hübler's* 'Beobachtungen über Scharlach' (Leipzig Thesis, 1861).

For the curves of scarlatina see lithographs, Table V.

VII.—RUBEOLÆ [and VARICELLA; see page 341].

§ 1. Rubeolæ (Rubeola notha, Rötheln, or the so-called hybrid between measles and scarlatina, sometimes called roseola also), which needs the experience derived from the observation of an extensive epidemic to carry conviction as to its peculiar characters, does not necessarily entail any fever at all, or only a slight transient attack before and during the eruption. The elevations of temperature are generally sub-febrile, or at the worst moderately febrile. And although in isolated cases more considerable elevations of temperature may be met with, they depend, no doubt, either upon complications or on the peculiar mobility of temperature which is characteristic of very young children.

Refer to *Thomas* ('Jahrbuch der Kinderheilkunde,' N. F. ii, 240).

[The English reader will also find a summary of what are supposed to be the distinguishing characters of this disease in Dr. Aitkin's 'Science and Practice of Medicine,' vol. i, 345 (chiefly from Dr. Robert Patterson, who was one of the first to clearly distinguish this disease).—TRANS.]

VIII.—ERYSIPELAS.

§ 1. Facial erysipelas is pre-eminently a polytypical disease, and in many cases it is quite atypical.

This probably depends upon the fact that undoubtedly the self-same anatomical changes are brought about by very varied conditions, and may thus vary greatly in their significance.

Purely local erysipelas, arising from the irritation of wounded parts; the kind that is brought about by local predispositions; the erysipelas which is connected with gastric and intestinal disturbances; protracted *erratic* or vagrant erysipelas; the kind analogous to an acute exanthem, especially the primary and spontaneous; and that arising from pyæmic infection; the erysipelas of glanders; the terminal erysipelas which is developed in cases of marasmus and severe disease, and precedes death only one or at most a few days; all these different forms, I say, are undoubtedly in great measure radically different diseases, which have hardly anything else in common except the localised dermatitis, and the name of the disease. It is easy to understand that the participation of the whole organism and the course of the temperature must needs differ widely in these cases.

But at present it is not possible to associate special forms of erysipelas, or special causes of it, with particular forms of fever curves, or at least to do so with anything like precision or accuracy.

Erysipelas in other parts of the body presents us with similar varieties—but quite atypical courses are rather the rule than exceptions in these.

§ 2. The disease begins, in an overwhelming majority of cases (excluding cases free from fever, with an atypical course) by an intense and rapidly occurring rise of temperature, generally with a strong feeling of chilliness.[1] So far as can be determined from the comparatively limited number of cases which afford an opportunity of examination at this time, the temperature rises in a few hours to a height of nearly 40° C. (104° F.) or even more. In most cases the inflammation of the skin of the face can be seen on the following morning, although, perhaps, it is not very evident yet, and liable to be confounded with the heightened colour of feverishness.

Much more rarely, a more gradual rise of temperature is met with, which takes from two to three days before any considerable degree of fever heat is attained.

§ 3. The greatest number of variations is met with during the *fastigium*. In just a few cases the curve of this consists of a single slender peak (Akmespitze), lasting a very short while.

Most frequently the high temperature persists in a continuous, or sub-continuous fashion, but still rising, and with but slight morning falls, so long as the inflammation simultaneously develops and extends itself. In this way the temperature in the evening hours is very generally above 40° C. (104° F.), and may reach as much as

[1] It is not very uncommon, even in adults, for convulsions of an epileptiform character to usher in erysipelas.—[Trans.]

41° to 41·5° C. (105·8° — 106·7° F.), or, although seldom, 42° C. (107·6° F.), whilst the morning remissions go a little below 40° C. (104° F.), though but seldom below 39° C. (102·2° F.). Yet sometimes cases are also met with which show a more remittent, or even intermittent, course in the fastigium, in which case the exacerbations generally run very high.

The *maximum* temperature does not generally occur at the end of this fever course, but one or two days before. And then a trifling moderation of the temperature succeeds (corresponding to a somewhat less rapid further development of the inflammation), which is, however, sometimes overlooked on account of a critical perturbation preceding defervescence. Sometimes a pseudo-crisis reaching to normal temperatures, or very nearly so, occurs towards the end of the course, which is succeeded by a transient and final rise of temperature to heights of 40° C. (104° F.) or even more.

§ 4. *Defervescence* succeeds this, and generally goes on with such speed that in the course of twelve hours, or a single night, the temperature falls to normal, or very nearly so. At other times, particularly when the previous temperatures have been very high, normal temperatures are not reached in the first twelve hours, but the temperature rises once more in the evening, and first reaches normal during the following night.

It is not very unusual for defervescence to be less rapid, and to occur rather in a sort of remittent form, but always far more rapidly, than in abdominal typhus. These cases are generally such as have been marked by considerable daily fluctuations during the fastigium, and in which dermal inflammation still progresses a little, even during defervescence. This remittent sinking may sometimes terminate in such cases with a final more rapid downfall, which completes the defervescence.

In the cases in which the eruption ends with defervescence this freedom from fever holds its ground, and convalescence sets in without any further disturbance.

§ 5. The cases in which the first well-marked fall of temperature goes on to definite defervescence, or in which more particularly the feverless condition maintains itself, are indeed pretty commonly met with. Yet it not infrequently happens that after a brief interval (of one to six days), whether the temperature has become perfectly normal or not, a *fresh and striking rise of temperature* occurs, which either accompanies or heralds in a new extension of the inflammation of the skin. This sort of relapse of the fever, which, however, does not generally last so long as the first fastigium, but usually only one or two days, may be repeated several times, and the more the erysipelas assumes the erratic form the more numerous are the repetitions. The fever does not cease till the erysipelas is checked, and for the most part there is no check to the eruption as long as fresh elevations of temperature are met with.

Yet one observes that the longer the affection lasts, and the more it wanders, the less elevated do the rises of temperature gradually become, and sometimes assume the form of only daily moderate evening exacerbations.

§ 6. In cases with a *fatal* termination death generally seems to occur with very high temperatures. At least it was so in the cases observed by myself. Consult *my own* publication, 'Ueber den Normal verlauf typischer Krankheiten,' p. 15; *Blass* ('Beobachtungen der Erysipelas,' Leipzig Thesis, 1863); *Eulenburg* ("Ueber Præmortale und Postmortale Steigerungen der Eigenwärme bei Erysipelas," an original paper in the 'Centralblatt' for 1866, p. 65); *Ponfick* ('Deutsche Klinik,' 1867, 20—26).

For the fever-curves in erysipelas see lithographs, Table V.

IX.—REMITTENT FEVER WITH PHLYCTENULAR ERUPTION (MILIARY FEVER?)

§ 1. Under this name I described in the 'Archiv der Heilkunde' for 1864, vol. v, 57, and 1867, viii, 174, a form of disease which appeared to me very peculiar, as well as previously undescribed, and I gave details at the same time of seven cases of my own, and one sent to me by *Ladé* of Geneva.

The disease is distinguished by an exanthem which is peculiar both in its form, its situation, and its course; and by a number of typhoid symptoms (especially affecting the nervous system and the spleen, but not so much the intestines), by considerable disorders of the respiratory organs, and finally by the course of the fever.

§ 2. There was no opportunity, in any of the cases, of observing the course of the fever during the first week. Its subsequent course was of great intensity, and unlike the type of any other exanthem. It neither declined with the appearance of the exanthem, like vario- loid, nor exhibited a fresh and injurious rise of temperature, like smallpox; nor did a rapid defervescence coincide with the maximum of the exanthem, as in measles, nor was there the protracted defer- vescence of scarlatina nor the irregularities of miliaria nor the rapid or rather rapid downfall of spotted fever (true typhus), which seems independent of the exanthem; nor a swift downfall, with ten- dencies to recrudescence, as in erysipelas.

It is a continuous remittent, with high degrees of temperature, generally marked by evening exacerbations exceeding 40° C. (104° F.), or even above 41° C. (105·8° F.), and with morning remissions of one or two degrees (1·8° to 3·6° F.), for the first two to eleven days of residence in hospital; then on one occasion as early as the eighth day, or else towards the end of the second or third week, the temperature began to decrease by large daily fluctuations, analogous to the period of improvement in abdominal typhus. From eight to fourteen days it ran on pretty much in this fashion—that from day to day the morning remissions became somewhat more marked, and the evening exacerbations generally became a trifle less from day to day, till the patient exhibited normal temperatures, first in the morning, and a little later on in the evening also. Slight and transient relapses interrupted convalescence in four of the cases. Thus, the course of these cases was considerably protracted, and in every one the exanthem lasted during the greater part of the fever. For details of these cases see the accounts quoted above.

For the curves see lithographs, Table V.

X.—FEBRICULA.

§ 1. Under the name of febricula we may include two different courses of temperature.

In the first place, febrile movements, which last for a longer or shorter time, but in which the temperature, even in the evening exacerbations, rises but very little above sub-febrile heights, or only occasionally reaches greater elevations.

And, secondly, we must include under this name brief fevers ending in recovery, which last only one, two, or at the most a few days altogether—*ephemera*. In this form a sudden rise of tempe-

rature accompanies the first feelings of indisposition, and the temperature in the course of a few hours rises as much as from 2° to 3° C.
or more (= 3·6° to 5·4° F.)   There may or may not be a rigor at
the same time.   Sometimes the highest temperature is not reached in
an unbroken line, or within a few hours, but in the course of one or
one and a half day, and is interrupted for a short while by a moderate
fall on the morning following the beginning of the sickness (ephemera protracta).   The fastigium lasts only a few hours, or at the
furthest one day, but the height of its temperature may be more or
less considerable, sometimes even 40° C. (104° F.) or more.   A rapid
decrease of temperature immediately succeeds, which in twelve, twenty-
four, or thirty-six hours, has already regained the normal.   During
this course of defervescence a slight interruption from a trifling elevation of temperature in the evening hours is not unusual.   Complete
restoration to a condition free from fever may also be somewhat
longer delayed, and from two to three days may be required in some
cases before normal temperatures are securely reached.

§ 2.   Both these courses occur under a great variety of circumstances.   The condition which follows *wounds* (of an operation, &c.)
generally involves a febricula, the course of which has been especially elucidated by *Billroth* ('Archiv für Klinische Chirurgie,' ii).

It is true, indeed, that a great number of lesions (sometimes by no
means inconsiderable in themselves) are not followed by any febrile
movement.

But in a great many cases, indeed in the majority of cases, a rise
of temperature is to be noted on the days succeeding any considerable
injury (*traumatic or wound fever*).

The fever which sets in most rapidly, that is, usually during
the first twenty-four hours after the injury, generally shows a
rapid rise of temperature, so that in the majority of cases the
maximum temperature is already reached on the first or second
day, or at all events between the third and sixth.   The rise of
temperature is generally continuous; it is only interrupted by
morning remissions when protracted.   The acme is usually reached
on some evening during the attack ; it is quite the exception for it to
occur in the morning hours, and the time of day at which the injury
occurred has no influence upon this.   The maximal height attained is
less than 40° C. (104° F.) in the great majority of cases, and very

often less than 39° C. (102·2° F.) ; it is quite exceptional for the temperature to rise to 40·5° C. (104·9° F.) or more.

When the maxima of the first two days are both alike, tolerably high, it is more favorable for the patient than when the temperature at the beginning of the attack remains only moderately febrile and later on rises all at once, in which latter case there may be reason to suspect some accidental inflammation or pyæmia.

There is no particular relation between the duration of the whole attack and the particular height reached by the temperature. The temperature keeps in the neighbourhood of the highest *peak* (*i.e.* near to the maximum) only a few hours on one day, in the great majority of cases. Sometimes very nearly the same peaks of elevation are reached in two evenings, which are separated by a morning remission.

If the temperature remains long at any considerable height, or a severe exacerbation is often repeated, we may suspect some complication, or internal inflammation, or that pyæmia is commencing.

Defervescence begins pretty commonly even on the first day of the fever, more often on the second, and pretty often on the third or fourth day, seldom so late as from the fifth to the seventh. It is sometimes rapid, sometimes protracted. In the latter case there are evening elevations of temperature. Both kinds appear to occur about equally often. During defervescence the temperature never sinks below normal.

The age and constitution, &c., of the patient appear to have no influence upon the height of the temperature, or upon the course of traumatic fever.

On the other hand, when the injury has been followed by considerable hæmorrhage, there almost immediately occurs either a slight or, in some cases, a considerable fall of temperature. This depression of temperature is only transient. The traumatic fever is not warded off by it, but succeeds in the course of a very few hours, and may be quite as severe as in cases where hardly any blood at all was lost.

Once more, if a chronic condition of fever existed before the injury or operation, the traumatic fever is usually acute, exceeds its accustomed heights, lasts longer, and is exceedingly prone to further complications. Patients, too, who, though free from fever, were suffering from chronic disease, such as consumptive patients without hectic, those with Bright's disease, or with amyloid degeneration, are affected by traumatic fever in the same way.

All immoderate elevations of temperature in the wounded, or after operations, for the most part announce the existence of further complications, greatly increase the hazards of the lesion, and commonly nullify the success of operations.

§ 3. Pretty often, although perhaps not in the majority of cases, the wounded are again attacked with fever after the fourth day— *secondary fever* (Nachfieber of *Billroth*).

The intensity and duration of the traumatic fever do not affect the genesis of the secondary fever, which may even develop itself when there was no (primary) traumatic fever. On the other hand, when the primary fever is protracted, it may be very difficult to distinguish it from this secondary fever. Sometimes no particular origin can be assigned for the secondary attack; in such cases it is usually slight and transient.

In the majority of cases, however, the secondary fever has a definite origin, and may even serve the useful purpose of drawing attention, and making us search after the causes which disorder the healing process. Retention of the secretions of the wound, progress of inflammatory changes in the subcutaneous or intermuscular cellular tissue, or retention of fæces or urine, or the development of some fresh morbid process, or inflammation of internal organs, are the principal determining causes of the fever which occurs later on. Secondary fever may set in on any day from the second half of the first week, or in any of the successive weeks, even up to the end of the sixth week.

The slighter cases occur almost imperceptibly, and particularly without rigors; their duration is brief, one or two days, or a week at the outside. The severer forms of secondary fever generally begin with a rigor.

The course taken by the temperature in secondary fever is very varied, because it is induced by such varying conditions, and because, in fact, these varied fevers have little else in common except the circumstances of their occurrence at a given time after the injury. They are the general constitutional expressions of very manifold slight or severe disorders to which the subject of a lesion is exposed for the first six weeks after the injury or operation. It is impossible, therefore, that they should follow any definite type, and their practical importance lies in the fact that they are amongst the first signs which indicate that some injurious influence or other, acting upon the increased disposition to morbid activity induced by the lesion, has led to disturbance of the healing process.[1]

§ 4. In cases of abnormal *uterine action* thermometry is in a condition to decide (as *Winckel* has pointed out) the important question between weak labour-pains and the so-called cramp-pains, or colicky pains.

During insufficient labour-pains the elevation of temperature proper to normal labour is wanting; the temperature, as a rule, is lower, and follows the fluctuations of health. In all cramping pains, from whatever cause they originate, the temperature rises in proportion to the duration of the anomalous pains. The elevation of temperature in any case is, however, inconsiderable, and seldom exceeds 1° C. (1·8° F.), but it persists quite unaffected by the normal daily fluctuations.

Immediately after the labour the temperature still remains high after cramping pains, but if no inflammation has supervened it falls within the next twelve hours.

§ 5. In *childbed* a temperature above 38° C. (100·4° F.) may not be a certain sign of a pathological process, but it is at least suspicious, whilst a normal temperature in the lying-in woman by no means ensures an undisturbed recovery.

Very many lying-in women show a slight rise of temperature in the first twenty-four hours after labour, a species of mild traumatic fever, without any indication of any local morbid process. The temperature in these slight febrile movements does not exceed 38·5° C. (101·3° F.) The rise generally lasts only one day.

Some of these patients exhibit a more intense fever, sometimes preceded by rigors. This more intense form usually begins on the second or third, sometimes on the fourth, fifth, or sixth days, and

---

[1] The English reader will find a good résumé (by Mr. Windsor) of Billroth on "Traumatic and Secondary Fever," in the New Sydenham Society's 'Year-Book for 1862,' p. 183. Reference may also be made to the articles on "Inflammation," by Mr. Simon and Mr. J. Croft, in Holmes's 'System of Surgery,' vol. i, pp. 2 and 287, and to numerous cases in the reports of various hospitals; also a paper on "Traumatic Fever" by Dr. Macdonald, 'Dublin Quarterly Journal,' Aug., 1869, p. 31.

therefore coincides with great distension of the breasts (so-called *milk-fever*).

This fever may reach its culminating point after only a few hours, or not before from two to five days, and this often reaches 40° C. (104° F.), then suddenly turns, if no unfavorable local complications exist, to defervescence, so that a normal temperature is reached very quickly indeed after the beginning of the fall of temperature.

From this time the temperature either remains normal, or a secondary fever sets in after from twelve to twenty-four hours or a longer interval of apyrexia; in this secondary fever the temperature may even rise to 42° C. (107·6° F.), and this again decreases after from one to two days' duration, and passes into the normal condition without further disturbance.

All deviations from such a course, either higher degrees or a longer duration of rising temperatures, are signs of more severe disease, which may be either a local inflammation or an essentially constitutional affection.

§ 6. A great variety of circumstances may induce attacks of ephemeral fever. They occur in weakly or sick people, and women and children, often without any recognisable cause.

They set in sometimes along with very rapid growth, dentition, exhaustion, and in menstruation.

Sometimes they indicate the beginning or the increase of some more or less latent and protracted [morbid] process.

They form the prelude to transient disorders of tissues; for example, a very intense ephemera often precedes the eruption of a herpes confined to the labial region.

A single attack not infrequently occurs during the incubation stage of infectious diseases.

They sometimes occur during the very time that a morbid poison is extending itself through the body by means of the lymphatics, although it may be followed by nothing more serious, or at the time of an embolic obstruction. When the contagion has been insufficient, or the individual exposed to it but little predisposed, an ephemera often represents the entire effect of the operation of a specific morbid poison.

Ephemerae may also occur, without any further results being necessarily entailed, after other potent causes of disease (such as severe chills, wettings through, or powerful emotions).[1]

[1] See note to page 155.

XI.—PYÆMIA.

§ 1. Pyæmic fever, that is the fever which accompanies acute multiple inflammations, very seldom originates as a primary or spontaneous disease, but generally succeeds other processes, such as severe lesions or the puerperal state; and, without doubt, has its genesis in infection, and either develops itself out of a condition entirely free from fever, or is preceded by a more or less considerable fever originating from the processes which precede it. In either case the commencement of pyæmia is (as a rule) sharply defined; in the latter case, however, one sometimes remarks a slight or sometimes more considerable fall of temperature, immediately before the beginning of the pyæmic symptoms; whilst in other cases there is a slight preparatory rise of temperature, and it is possible, and, indeed, not improbable, that these alterations of temperature constantly belong to the pyæmic attack, and are the first effect of the infection.

The first elevation of temperature with which unmistakable manifestations of the disease commence, which is generally accompanied also by a severe rigor, is generally very rapid, sometimes completing itself even in a few hours, or half a day, generally in the course of a day, seldom lasting more than one day and a half, or more, and amounting usually to $2\frac{1}{2}°$ to $3\frac{1}{2}°$ C. ($= 4\frac{1}{2}°$ to $6\frac{1}{3}°$ F.), or more, and only exceptionally less. During the rise the temperature almost always exceeds 40° C. (104° F.), generally, indeed, exceeds 41° C. (105·8° F.), and commonly enough approaches to 42° C. (107·6° F.).

To be more precise, this rise of temperature generally happens in this wise—that in the first twelve to fifteen hours, for example, from morning till near midnight, the temperature rises about 1° to $1\frac{1}{2}°$ C.) (1·8° to 2·7° F.), which (supposing any particular fever to have preceded it) resembles the daily fluctuation affected by this, and yet is somewhat different. This is followed, after midnight, by a more rapid rise, and in the morning the temperature is found to be considerably increased; in cases where there has been fever of any kind beforehand it is from $1\frac{1}{2}°$ to $2\frac{1}{2}°$ C. (2·7° to $4\frac{1}{2}°$ F.) higher than during the daily maximum of the days which preceded.

Sometimes a further, although moderate, rise persists on the days succeeding the night of fever. The rigor may occur at any point in the ascending temperature, and sometimes may occur even twice during the ascent.

In a minority of cases the rise of temperature during the first paroxysm is essentially more rapid, especially where there has been fever beforehand, so that in a very few hours the highest peak of the first paroxysm is reached.

§ 2. The first paroxysm of fever takes an acuminated form (akme-artig). After the temperature has reached the highest peak or maximum it begins immediately, just as rapidly, or perhaps more rapidly than it rose, to fall again; in a few hours, indeed, it sinks from two to four degrees Centigrade (= 3·6° to 7·2° Fahr.), so that, as a rule, the temperature is lower after the first paroxysm of fever in pyæmia than it was before it, even when a state of fever existed before the pyæmia set in. But after the first paroxysm the temperature seldom falls quite to normal, although, indeed, it comes very close to it, but generally falls only as low as 38—38·5° C. (100·4° to 101·3° F.) The low temperature which succeeds the first attack of fever, does not, as a rule, last long, scarcely half a day; in most cases, as soon as the temperature has reached its minimal depth, it begins to rise again immediately, and this fresh rise, whether a rigor is associated with it or not, is generally just about as rapid as the first; it does not, however, in general reach quite so great a height.

The first accession of pyæmic fever has many points of resemblance to the beginning of other acute diseases which are distinguished by a short pyrogenetic stage. But, on the one hand, the temperature in pyæmia reaches a greater height in a shorter time than it does in any other disease, and, on the other hand, the first pyæmic paroxysm may be distinguished from forms of continued fever at all events, by the temperature quickly turning back and falling rapidly as soon as it has reached the acme.

The diagnosis from a paroxysm of intermittent fever or ague is far more difficult. However, the rise of temperature in the first access of pyæmia is essentially more protracted than in a case of intermittent fever. And besides, after the paroxysm of pyæmia the downfall of temperature very seldom reaches the normal, but usually turns again before 37·5° C. (99·5° F.) has been passed, and often long before, to begin a fresh ascent.

§ 3. The following circumstances in the further progress of the course deserve notice :

(1) A "brusque" rise of temperature to more or less considerable heights, sometimes more, sometimes less, closely approximating to the summit of the first paroxysm, and sometimes even overreaching it by a few tenths of a degree. This is scarcely ever absent, and in the great majority of cases repeats itself more or less frequently, without any regular rhythm, sometimes twice or even three times in a day.

(2) A sudden turning back again of the temperature, after reaching the maximal point. Only very exceptionally it happens that the temperature lingers a half-day or more in the neighbourhood of the maximum; generally speaking, it goes rapidly downwards immediately after the summit is reached.

(3) Rapid downfall of temperature after the manner of a rapid defervescence, or even more rapid than this, not seldom reaching even to normal or below it, in the later attacks, although even then not infrequently pausing at 39° C. (102·2° F.) or even above this.

(4) Only seldom do we meet with pauses of apyretic, or approximating normal temperatures of half or a whole day in length.

(5) Intercurrently and, as it were, thrust in between the paroxysms of fever, more particularly towards the fatal termination of the disease, there are one or more days' fragments (Strecken) of a continuous or remittent course, with either an ascending or descending direction, or it may be of irregular progression.

The well-known rigors, or shivering fits, which are more or less frequently repeated, and generally coincide with the rapid rise of the temperature, yet are often independent of this, and are sometimes, though rarely, absent altogether. The course of pyæmic fever is very well characterised by this behaviour, and is thus distinguished from all other diseases. Amongst the manifold individual differences met with, diagnosis is much assisted (*lit.*, finding the longitude is furthered) by *Heubner's* setting forth the following principal forms assumed by the course of the disease :

(*a*) Cases in which the abrupt rises and downfalls of temperature very quickly succeed one another.

(*b*) Cases with widely separated febrile paroxysms, and apyretic or barely febrile intervals.

(*c*) Cases with continuous fever, and intercurrent sharp elevations of temperature.

The duration of pyæmic fever, as a rule, is about a week, seldom less than three or four days, seldom more than a week and a half.

Death is not generally preceded by any thermometric indications of a pro-agonistic stage, and sometimes it takes place with comparatively low, or even normal, temperatures, sometimes with those of medium height, and sometimes with high febrile temperatures. This is especially the case in rapidly fatal puerperal fever with hyper-pyretic temperatures.

§ 4. But the fact of *deviations* occurring in particular cases must not be overlooked.

In patients already suffering from severe disease death may occur even at the very beginning of the pyæmia, and thus the characteristic features of the course may be lost.

In rare cases pyæmia follows for a few days a continuous course, without rigors, or only marked by a rigor at the beginning. This course is sometimes met with in traumatic pyæmia, and still more commonly in puerperal fever, especially the form which kills quickly, and does not go on to the formation of abscesses.

Just about as rarely, at the beginning of pyæmia, we meet with a rise assuming a zigzag curve, or shaped like an easel, and extending over several days; or if there were a strong remittent fever present before pyæmia set in, there is a diminution of the remissions, which later on is followed by an almost instantaneous and extreme rise of temperature.

Many cases also, at least for a time, exhibit a certain amount of rhythm in the return of the paroxysms.

Sometimes the disease is protracted, and the paroxysms may even become less frequent and less severe for a time, but finally the case terminates fatally notwithstanding.

Lastly, cases occur with a very protracted course, in which for a long time occasional intense paroxysms of fever interrupt an apyretic or mildly febrile course, and sometimes have intervals of one or two weeks between, and so occupy a correspondingly long time. The febrile paroxysms may finally cease, and recovery take place, or death follows, whilst the paroxysms become more frequent, as at the conclusion of a short continued fever.

On the course of the fever of pyæmia consult *Heubner*, whose work is based on the material of my own wards and those of the

Surgical Clinic of Leipsic (1868, 'Archiv der Heilkunde,' ix, p. 289).

For pyæmic temperature curves see lithographs at end, Table VI.

XII.—CATARRHAL AFFECTIONS OF MUCOUS MEMBRANES.

§ 1. As regards the course of their temperature, catarrhal affections of mucous membranes generally follow no particular type.

In many cases there is either no alteration of temperature,[1] or it only shows somewhat greater daily fluctuations than are met with in health, so that in the evenings supra-normal, sub-febrile, or even moderately febrile temperatures, are met with.

Sometimes an ephemeral elevation of temperature, which leads to no further consequences, may be observed at the beginning of the disease, and occasionally during its course.

Here and there quite anomalous rises of temperature occur, which are generally connected with fresh malignancy or with accidental increase of the catarrhal affection.

They more particularly happen to very delicate people, or such as before being attacked by the catarrhal malady already suffered from some chronic disorder.

Little children also often exhibit high temperatures during catarrhal affections. When catarrh runs a chronic course there occurs in many cases a fever which assumes the form of hectic, especially when the chronic catarrh is marked for some time by exacerbations.

In many catarrhal affections the occurrence of an elevated temperature is a pretty safe sign of commencing complications; this is particularly the case in *hooping-cough*, in which, therefore, a continuous daily observation of temperature may be of great practical importance.

This behaviour of the temperature is common to catarrh of the pharynx, of the larynx, of the deeper organs of respiration (trachea and bronchi), of the intestinal canal, of the urinary apparatus, and of the female genitals. In all these cases fever is the sign of intense irritation of the mucous membranes, rises and falls with this,

---

[1] This is often the case as regards simple bronchitis and simple diarrhœa, as I have over and over again demonstrated to myself and others.—[TRANS.]

or depends on the surroundings, idiosyncrasies, injurious influences, and complications of the case.

The temperature may, however, display a more connected and almost typical course—(*a*) in intense and particularly in epidemic catarrhs of the respiratory mucous membrane, which are then generally associated with intestinal catarrh and more or less striking nervous symptoms (influenza); (*b*) in severe gastric catarrh and catarrhal affections of the mucous membranes of the bowels, and again more particularly during epidemics or in cases where these attacks have been grossly neglected.

§ 2. It is only in severe cases of *influenza* that any considerable alteration of temperature is met with.

The beginning of the rise of temperature is, therefore, seldom rapid. The temperature usually ascends in a similar course to that of the initial period of abdominal typhus (see page 300), not, however, with the same regularity, nor is the time so regularly kept, but sometimes more rapidly, at other times more slowly, it rises, but not generally to the identical heights of typhoid fever.

During the fastigium the course is very similar to that of the above disease, at least similar daily remissions and exacerbations are met with. The latter may be as high as in ileo-typhus, but are not generally quite so high.

Besides this, the fastigium is almost always of essentially shorter duration than in abdominal typhus, and after a few days, under good nursing, unless other disease supervene, the temperature shows a tendency to fall. In general, too, the defervescence follows the same remitting type (lysis) as in abdominal typhus, yet its decrease is generally more sudden than in that, and its termination takes place more punctually. On the other hand, it is not unusual, in influenza, for the temperature, after it has almost reached the normal, to linger for a certain time on a level somewhat above this, or at least to show somewhat greater evening exacerbations than are consonant with complete recovery.

The most important diagnostic question in connection with this behaviour is whether in a given case we have to do with a severe influenza or a case of typhoid fever (abdominal typhus), a question which is rendered still more difficult to decide by the fact that very often there is a general correspondence between severe influenza and ileo-typhus in numerous other respects (as regards the prostration, cerebral and nervous symptoms, and bowel symptoms), and that even when we find enlargement of the spleen it often remains doubtful whether this may not have existed before the present illness ; even the absence of the rose spots is not conclusive against the existence of typhoid. If the temperature remains decidedly below the ranges of abdominal typhus, the answer to this question is easy in young adults, and we must exclude typhoid fever.

But if the typhoid ranges are reached or exceeded, which occurs pretty often, particularly in severe epidemics of influenza, the differential diagnosis must often be deferred some days; but with moderately good nursing, if catarrhal pneumonia do not supervene, one may be certain that the high temperature will begin to abate, however severe the influenza, at an earlier date than in ileo-typhus. In favorable cases the defervescence also will be completed more quickly than in that. Even in unfavorable cases, where there is very intense bronchitis, bronchiolitis (capillary bronchitis) and peribronchitis, and even in fatal cases, the temperature generally returns to a level which is incompatible with typhoid fever, whilst at the same time other severe symptoms persist and contrast with the moderated temperature. As regards the course of the lung-infiltration which supervenes, see *Pneumonia*.

§ 3. The temperature in febrile gastro-intestinal catarrhs is pretty nearly similar, and elevated temperature chiefly occurs in greatly neglected cases, or with defective nursing, or in very delicate persons. We may notice in them the same type of rising temperature, the same remitting fastigium, and the same kind of zigzag defervescence, and the same practical question arises whether or not we have to deal with an ileo-typhus (or typhoid fever). The same criteria are decisive as in influenza, and, indeed, with moderately good nursing the temperature will be observed to begin to fall in febrile intestinal catarrh more quickly than even in influenza.

XIII.—CROUPOUS AND DIPHTHERITIC INFLAMMATIONS OF THE MUCOUS MEMBRANES.

In no other acute affections has the temperature so little significance as it has in croupous and diphtheritic affections—pharyngeal

diphtheria, laryngeal croup, intestinal croup, dysentery, and diphtheritic and croupous puerperal endometritis.

One may indeed regard very high temperatures in all these affections as adding very greatly to the danger.

But moderate or even normal temperatures do not give the slightest
guarantee for a favorable termination. The high temperatures may
even decline, whilst the disorder unhaltingly goes on to worse and
worse.

See *Richardson* on "The Temperature in Diphtheria" ('Medical
Record,' 1867, ii, 219).

XIV.—PNEUMONIA.

§ 1. The forms of disease which are comprehended under the name
of *pneumonia* exhibit a very varied thermometric course. In particular cases, even acute ones, the temperature is quite unaltered [?],
in others only a slight febrile movement is induced. In the majority,
however, a more or less sharply defined fever course can be observed ;
but even this, at least to superficial observers, shows the widest
variations—continuous, remittent, relapsing, and intermittent forms
being met with.

Yet it is possible to bring together groups of cases which perfectly coincide as regards the course of their temperature, and in
which, therefore, there is as much a typical character as in any other
disease.

It is clear that the varied types met with do not depend (as in
abdominal typhus and variola) on a distinction between simple and
complicated forms.

This manifold complexion of the course taken by the temperature,
which, as said before, must not be regarded as an anomalous
casualty, must rather be regarded as an indication that widely differing affections are designated by the common expression *pneumonia*.
And already anatomical investigations have begun to indicate a recognition of this. The names *croupous, hæmorrhagic, serous, embolic,
purulent,* and *putrid* or *septic* (jauchige) *pneumonia, lobular pneumonia,* &c., &c., represent varieties of such importance that they
must necessarily be regarded as different morbid processes. It must
also not be forgotten that forms of disease which may currently be
regarded as anatomically identical may yet diverge from one another

in very essential points; and that besides the different anatomical forms assumed by the results of the process, the varying ætiology may produce differences which essentially differentiate complaints which many persons comprehend under the same name.

The designation of any form of disease as pneumonia is about as superficial a classification as that which comprehends all diseases of the skin which run their course with inflammation under the name of dermatitis. But the term is useful and necessary, because it is very often impossible whilst the patient is living to make a more accurate diagnosis, and to differentiate from one another the different morbid processes; and partly so, indeed, because the essential distinctions themselves are, as yet, not clearly mapped out.

Symptomatology has indeed, already discovered a number of data which indicate different processes as taking place in the lungs in the diseases classed as pneumonias. But it must be conceded that the aids thus given to differential diagnosis are as yet exceedingly scanty. Thermometry is able to considerably increase these diagnostic means. Yet it must be acknowledged that many gaps yet remain to be filled up, and it cannot be denied that with all the aid rendered by the thermometer both our diagnosis and our prognosis of pneumonic patients is exceedingly fragmentary.

§ 2. In the first place, the thermometer by itself alone cannot decide as to the presence or absence of pneumonia. On the other hand, when pneumonic affections have already been diagnosed, thermometric observation is able to demonstrate differences which can be recognised by no other means, and to facilitate the diagnosis of these special forms;—

To determine the degree of the affections and its danger;—

To furnish a delicate standard (Maas-stab) of improvement or relapses, and thus to test the effect of therapeutic measures;—

To indicate the occurrence and persistence of complications;—

To determine the completion of the processes;—

To guarantee the certainty of convalescence and recovery;—

Or to give warning of the continuance of unresolved and lurking disorders, and of the supervention of sequelæ.

In other diseases also, where the access of pneumonia is especially to be dreaded, thermometry is able to indicate, with great probability, the earliest actual development of this complication (in measles, bronchial catarrh, hooping-cough, pulmonary consumption, and pleurisy).

24

It must therefore not be forgotten that thermometry in relation to pneumonic affections (in contradistinction to what occurs in abdominal typhus, &c.) has only the value of an accessory means of diagnosis. The more decisive, or, if one may call them so, ruder means of investigation, must give all the aid they can to diagnosis, and make it in the rough, and then first we learn what important practical questions, based on what has already been gained, can be quickly answered by thermometry.

§ 3. Besides the cases of pneumonia which run their course without any fever at all (always exceedingly rare cases), there are some almost equally rare cases of pneumonic affections, with almost momentary and very moderate elevation of temperature (i. e. lasting for only a few hours), cases in which even the lower limits of moderate fever ($38 \cdot 5°$ C. $= 101 \cdot 3°$ F.) are scarcely reached, and that generally on the first or second day of the illness, and the disease almost immediately becomes devoid of fever.

Somewhat akin to these are two different sorts of somewhat more pronounced pneumonic *febricula*. In one of them there occurs, generally with symptoms of a rigor, and in an abrupt manner, a more or less considerable elevation of temperature (even to above $41°$ C. $= 105 \cdot 8°$ F.), which is immediately succeeded by a rapid defervescence, so that by the second or third day the normal temperature has again been attained (ephemera with pointed peak—*akmeartige E.*). In a second series of cases the rise of temperature is more tedious, sometimes remittent. The highest point (lower than in the first form, scarcely $40°$ C. $= 104°$ F.) is not reached before the third day of the illness. The temperature then begins immediately to decline (ephemera protracta).

All these cases of febricula go along with slight local processes, and only occasionally become dangerous on account of their surroundings. They correspond to moderate, rather œdematous infiltrations, or such as continue very limited; the form of ephemera with pointed peak especially occurs in embolic pneumonia; the ephemera protracta occurs in attacks in which little pneumonic deposits (foci) occur in the course of catarrhal bronchitis. Pneumonic febricula also occurs not infrequently in secondary pneumonias, also in mild inflammations of the lung in young children, in very old or emaciated and phthisical patients, and those with declining powers, and in these cases the results may easily be very unfavorable. These two forms of febricula at once represent rudimentary types of the two chief forms of pneumonic fever. If we imagine the sharp peak of the first form of ephemera flattened out, the result is the continuous type, with its sudden commencement and rapid end; and if we imagine the ephemera protracta extended, we get the remittent type, with its gradual commencement and defervescence by lysis.

§ 4. The fever of pneumonia also shows another peculiarity whenever it is more fully developed, which is, indeed, met with in other diseases, but not so often nor so constantly in any other malady as in pneumonia—namely, the occurrence of isolated brusque elevations and of intercurrent falls of temperature.

This *brusque elevation* (like an acutely peaked ephemera, such as, for example, sometimes momentarily breaks the course of advancing convalescence in abdominal typhus) very often occurs in pneumonia, and not merely after decided advance has been made towards recovery, but very often immediately after defervescence, or even during the same, and, so to speak, interrupting it; and lastly, in the course of the fever itself, in which case we get a very considerable but transient rise of temperature to heights of 41·5° C. (106·7° F.) or more. The ephemeral elevations of temperature met with during defervescence, or subsequently, very usually amount to 39° C. (102·2° F.), and often even above 40° C. (104° F.), but very seldom approach 41° C. (105·8° F.) or exceed it.

§ 5. *The intercurrent falls of temperature* are in direct contrast to these brusque elevations. They may occur in the course of almost any form of pneumonia, so that the regular course of the temperature suffers a sudden interruption through a deep descent of the temperature, which sharply contrasts with both its preceding and subsequent course.

This intercurrent sinking occurs in the majority of pneumonic cases, whether slight, severe, or, indeed, fatal. The downfall generally occurs very rapidly, and may amount to from one and a half to four or even five degrees Centigrade (= 2·7° to 7·2° or 9° Fahr.), and the temperature more or less nearly reaches normal; indeed, it very often reaches it, and sometimes falls even below this. If the descent be comparatively trifling (1¼° to 2° C. = 2·7° to 3·6° F.), it only appears striking because it is thrust into an essentially continuous course, and, indeed, the most abrupt descents of temperature do occur intercurrently in this very kind of course.

The temperature, as a rule, remains only a very short time at this low level, for generally it rises again almost immediately to its old heights, or often falls a little short of these, but not very seldom rises even a little higher. The whole episode generally occupies only about half a day or, perhaps, even less. Yet sometimes this downfall of temperature extends itself to a somewhat more protracted apyrexia.

This intercurrent decline of temperature may occur at any time in the course of pneumonia, from the second day of the illness to the last day of the defervescence, or even to the death-agony. For the most part it is met with only once in the course, but sometimes twice or thrice.

The significance of this intercurrent downfall of temperature is affected by these varieties. Especially does it modify the course, and may even give rise to a false prognosis. It is easy to understand that such an event raises hopes that defervescence has already begun. If defervescence very quickly follows this, it looks as if the pneumonia had already completely developed itself. But the temperature again rises, and so its downfall proves to be only a deceptive *pseudo-crisis*, which momentarily interrupts the course, which afterwards goes on as before. Yet it may so happen, that when the temperature again rises it does not regain its pristine heights, but assumes a descending direction. Thus, the intercurrent downfall divides the fastigium into two portions of different character, and may even appear as the first beginning of a moderated course.

In more protracted pneumonias, such, namely, as last over a week, a pseudo-crisis very often occurs on the seventh day, and after this the course may go on with great severity and end fatally, or the intercurrent downfall may inaugurate a more favorable conjunction of circumstances. This intercurrent fall can be more safely regarded as the first beginning of moderation in the attack when it occurs, as it often does, although this cannot be prognosticated, on the day before the definite defervescence. Even then we may be in doubt whether to reckon it as the actual commencement of the process of shaking off the fever, in which case the fresh rise of temperature must be considered as a break in the defervescence; or whether we should reckon them both as a part of the fastigium. If the downfall of temperature is several times repeated, we get a transition to the *remitting* type.

If an abrupt sinking of temperature occurs regularly several times with great punctuality, the pneumonia becomes truly *intermittent*.

If the repeated succession of descending temperatures is less punctual and orderly, the course resembles the abrupt fluctuations of the *pyæmic type*.

If the low temperature persists for a longer time, and the fresh rise of temperature does not occur till after two or three days, we get the *relapsing form*, and if the temperature does not fall quite to normal the form with recrudescing fastigium.

The fall of temperature before the death-agony is equivalent to a pro-agonistic stage.

The true reasons for these intercurrent falls of temperature are by no means always easy to discover. In many cases the fall appears manifestly to result from energetic therapeutic measures, which have, however, proved insufficient to destroy the disease. In other cases, perhaps, very frequently it may depend on the local process having terminated in the part first attacked, and beginning afresh in some neighbouring place, or extending itself, in which it is very probable that the second development of pneumonia is less perfect than the first. But neither of these explanations will suit all cases, and the unusual frequency of this behaviour of the temperature in pneumonia gives rise to the opinion that this is an especial peculiarity of its course; and hence we can understand that therapeutic measures of no marvellous potency in themselves may easily produce this phenomena of intercurrent falls in pneumonia, which is a disease already so predisposed to such interruptions.

It is of the highest practical importance to distinguish the pseudo-critical downfall from definite defervescence, and from the moderation of temperature which precedes the latter. It is, however, not always practical. The earlier the downfall occurs, the more reason have we to expect a fresh rise of temperature, although there are plenty of cases in which the pneumonia actually and definitively terminates as early as the second or third day. Further, the more unexpectedly and, as it were, unpreparedly the downfall occurs, the less it harmonises with the progress of the case in other respects, the closer it follows some therapeutic proceeding, and the more rapidly the fall itself takes place so much the more must it be taken for a pseudo-crisis.

Besides, the preparatory rapid downfall which precedes defervescence by only a single day cannot be distinguished from true defervescence with anything like certainty in many cases, and we must therefore expect a fresh rise of temperature on the following day after every rapid fall.

§ 6. The *continuous* or *subcontinuous* type of pneumonia occurs chiefly in primary croupous[1] or lobar pneumonia, and very often also in secondary affections. The beginning of the disease is marked by an abrupt rise of temperature, generally accompanied with a rigor. The temperature in a few hours rises above 39° C. (102·2° F.) and still continues to rise, till it attains a height of about 40° C. (104° F.), or in severe cases even 41° C. (105·8° F.) or more.

During this first appearance of fever there is very often no other symptom which directs special attention to any disease of the lungs. Occasionally only do we find cough, pain in the chest, and dyspnœa. It is very seldom that any auscultatory symptoms can be found in the thorax. It is much more common to meet with head-ache, or even delirium, sometimes vomiting, generally loss of appetite, and the patient feels very unwell. Even on the second or third day the thoracic, and especially the auscultatory symptoms, are often wanting, and this may be the case even on the fourth day, whilst the fever continues with great fierceness.

The course of such cases resembles that of an exanthem, and if we are to make a distinction between attacks of " pneumonic fever " and cases with " febrile pneumonia," the cases with a continuous course of temperature belong, in overwhelming proportions, to the first category.

The temperature for the first few days remains at a considerable height, that is, generally from two to three and a half degrees above the normal (= 3·6° to 4·66° F.), or in mild cases at 39·2° to 39·6° C. (102·56° to 103·28° F.), in severe ones above 40° (104° F.), but shows slight fluctuations of ⅓° to 1° C. (= ·9° to 1·8° F.), sometimes by brief remissions occurring in the morning, with quickly returning exacerbations, sometimes by a second rise occurring about midnight, and sometimes by several exacerbations occurring in a single day, or quite anomalous fluctuations of plus and minus temperatures.

This course practically lasts as long as the process set up in the lungs progresses, which is seldom less than three days, seldom longer

---

[1] This awkward name is the designation given in Germany to what is generally called acute pneumonia in this country.—[TRANS.]

than seven. Intercurrent falls of temperature may break the regularity of the course on any day. Sometimes also, though very rarely, the daily maxima and the daily minima remain pretty stationary all through the stage.

More commonly one observes the daily average getting higher and higher, and the excursions or extent of the remissions becoming less and less (ascending exacerbations), and thus the maximum temperature of the attack is not reached till a late period. But in the great majority of cases the opposite happens. The maximum temperature is met with on the second or third day (generally some time in the afternoon), or on the day upon which observations are first taken, and from henceforth the height of the temperature declines from day to day, though, perhaps, only by a few tenths of a degree. Even in fatal cases this moderation of temperature often occurs. Moreover, it is conceivable that this customary and steady, although tedious, downfall of temperature from the very considerable heights observed at the beginning of the attack is the result of medical treatment, or of the careful nursing prescribed.

Even in cases which terminate fatally this descending direction is commonly enough seen in the fastigium. Yet more or less accidental irregularities are generally observed. Sometimes a morning remission is wanting, sometimes an unusually deep fall intervenes, or the regular remission occurs at unaccustomed hours; thus the exacerbations are unusually high, at least in the earlier days, and when they begin to moderate do so but partially. Sometimes before the disease unmistakably tends to death there occurs a very marked downfall. Death may occur with low temperature, but generally the temperature begins to rise again just before death, at first very slowly, and towards the end very suddenly. When death follows with symptoms of suffocation the height of temperature finally reached is by no means remarkable, generally less than 40° C. (104° F.). But if severe nervous symptoms precede death then a rapid final rise of temperature occurs to 41° C. (105·8° F.) or more, and even to 43° C. (109·4° F.).

In favorable cases there is often a visible preparation for improvement. The descending direction taken by the temperature becomes quite clear after the occurrence of the maximum, which is attained early, or after an intercurrent downfall of temperature, whilst the remissions become more striking and the exacerbations diminish in severity. On the day before the definitive defervescence a pseudo-crisis often takes place, in which the temperature falls to normal, which is followed by a transient but considerable final rise of temperature. On the last or last but one day of the fastigium a remarkable fall (amounting to $\frac{1}{2}°$ to $\frac{3}{4}° = 9°$ to $1·35°$ F., or if the temperatures have previously been very high as much as $1°$ C. $= 1·8°$ F.), or even more, is in contrast to the previous slow increase of evening temperatures, or in cases not marked by this in contrast to the continuous height of the fastigium. All these varieties in the course may be regarded as preparatory moderations of temperature preceding defervescence. On the other hand, it likewise happens, often enough, that immediately before the process of defervescence a considerable rise of temperature sets in (*perturbatio critica*), whether there has been any preliminary reduction of temperature or not. This generally lasts only one evening, or perhaps, though less frequently, a whole morning, or even twenty-four hours. But in this the temperature only exceeds the height of the previous maximum in exceptional cases.

The defervescence, in the majority of cases, begins late in the evening, though sometimes as early as the afternoon, or in others during the night, comparatively seldom in the morning or noon-time, and occurs most commonly between the fifth and seventh days, tolerably often on the third or fourth, or on the eighth, more rarely on the ninth or tenth, or at a later date; and the opinion advocated by *Traube*, and others who have followed him, that the crisis occurs in the majority of cases on the odd days, is quite erroneous. Compare *Thomas* on the doctrine of critical days in croupous pneumonia in 1865 ('Archiv der Heilkunde,' vi, 118).

Defervescence generally takes place rapidly, so that when the previous temperatures have not been excessive the normal point is very often reached in the course of one night, and, indeed, in most cases this occurs within twenty-four to thirty-six hours, and on the intervening evening the temperature usually continues to fall, but less rapidly, or is sometimes broken by a considerable rise (evening exacerbation).

It is not very rare, especially when there has been very high fever, for the defervescence to require forty-eight hours for its completion. It pretty frequently happens that the temperature in falling oversteps the normal, and collapse temperatures result. Other severe symptoms of collapse may also be met with in the stage of defervescence, which appear very dangerous to the uninitiated, but which may be considered as forming an essential portion of the transition to recovery.

In most cases of pneumonia the arrest of its extension and the remission of its symptoms first begin during the defervescence, or after its completion. On the other hand, the nervous symptoms, when such are present, generally last through the period of defervescence in great and undiminished severity, or even occur at this period for the first time, if they have previously been absent. The course of the defervescence may be varied by the simultaneous presence of very severe bronchitis or acute pleurisy along with the pneumonia, and also in cases where pneumonia attacks a patient who was suffering from some other disease beforehand. In general, when the normal temperature has once been fairly reached, the further progress of convalescence is not marked by any more deviations, but runs a regular course. Yet occasionally on the evening of the second or third day after, there are slight elevations of temperature, which, when repeated, justify us in assuming some complication to exist, or that the local process in the lung is imperfectly recovering. But during the early days of convalescence very considerable, although transient, elevations of temperature may occur without any unfavorable significance attaching to them.

Relapses also occur pretty often, but such cases cannot be distinguished from relapsing pneumonia.

When subnormal temperatures and other symptoms of collapse have set in, the low temperature and a very extreme degree of collapse may last for several days, marked by fluctuations, till at last the temperature settles at normal.

§ 7. Many cases of pneumonia show the continuous type *less perfectly*, since more or less deviations in the course of the temperature occur either in the beginning, middle, or end of the course, which do not materially affect the most important feature of the course. For example, its beginning may be less rapid and less abrupt, and it may last for two days or more, till the temperature has reached a high level.

Or the temperature in its course may remain at a lower level than in well-developed pneumonias, or may approximate to a remittent type by the fluctuations being very considerable, or to an intermittent or relapsing type by great falls of temperature.

Or on the other hand, the course of the fastigium may be both unusually severe and unusually prolonged, which happens in double pneumonias, or with acute pneumonia of the upper lobes, or when a whole lung is attacked with inflammation. In such cases the fastigium is generally prolonged into the second week, or even to its end. But then it is by no means stationary, but towards the end of the first week, or sometimes even earlier, there commences a stage of fluctuations, an amphibolic stage, with alternations of improvement and relapses. We must not expect a rapid defervescence in such cases.

In particular, the defervescence may be protracted and complicated, may occur less rapidly, and may exhibit slight subsequent elevations of temperature.

Such deviations from the normal fashion of the continuous course occur under very many different circumstances. On the one hand they occur in children, on the other in very old people, and especially in sick persons, whose idiosyncrasies predispose to irregularities of the fever course.

They occur in secondary croupous pneumonia, which, indeed, sometimes follows an identical course with that of primary, but in other cases exhibits more or less deviations from such a course.

And occasionally such variations occur in all kinds of pneumonic attacks, just as in other typical affections there are some epidemics in which irregular cases greatly preponderate.

Accidental complications of the case, sometimes with actual separate disease, sometimes only with isolated disturbances originating in other organs (severe delirium, obstinate constipation, or retention of urine, &c.), may, indeed, easily induce more or less considerable modifications in the course of the temperature, and this especially occurs with previously existing emphysema of the lungs or coincident acute pleurisy, the occurrence of bilious symptoms, of albuminuria during the course of the attack, and of severe diarrhœa or vomiting. In those cases, too, in which the fever supervenes on an already developed inflammation of the lung, which is most characteristically shown by traumatic pneumonia, deviations from the pure continuous type are almost constantly met with.

Deviations from the regular course of pneumonia are very often brought about by the operation of energetic therapeutic measures, or by some favorable event occurring, in which case they may be advantageous to the patient.

The most decided influence on the course of the fever is brought about by a sufficiently copious bloodletting or a free spontaneous hæmorrhage (bleeding from the nose, the menses, &c.). The immediate result of a considerable loss of blood is almost always a considerable reduction of temperature; but it depends on circumstances whether this may shape itself as a definite defervescence, or be followed by a fresh rise of temperature, and in the latter case a more or less complete approximation of the course to the relapsing type may occur. *Emetics* operate in a similar way to losses of blood; *digitalis* and *veratria* do so somewhat more slowly, whilst the influence of other medicaments (potassic nitrate, aconite, &c.) on the type of the temperature in pneumonia is either less striking or not so well established.

On the other hand, injudicious therapeutic measures and other accidental injurious influences may cause deviations from the type of an injurious nature.

Lastly, in many cases of pneumonia, in which the course of the fever exhibits certain irregularities, the true reason can sometimes be only surmised (as, for example, that the infiltration approximates to a hæmorrhagic form, or to œdema), and is generally not discoverable at all.

§ 8. A *remittent* course of fever occurs in those pneumonias which are developed after a longer or shorter course of bronchial catarrh, in catarrhal pneumonias and the pneumonia of influenza; but even in the latter case the pneumonia exhibits the remittent type most clearly when its course begins to be complicated by severe bronchitis. In the same way the pneumonia of measles and of hooping-cough is often distinguished by a remittent fever; but sometimes cases occur with a remitting type in which we are unable to demonstrate any particular bronchitis either before or during the whole course of the pneumonia.

Remittent forms of pneumonic fever are common enough in children and in very old people.

At many periods almost all cases of pneumonia exhibit a remittent course.

Even although the pneumonia may be developed in a person previously free from fever, the beginning of the rise of temperature is less rapid in the remittent type than in the continuous; sometimes it is even zigzag in character, like the beginning of abdominal typhus and influenza, yet it is generally rather more sudden and irregular than the first of them at all events.

If the lung-affection is developed in a patient who was previously feverish, although the course of the previous fever may have been very moderate, as, for example, during a mild feverish bronchial catarrh, the beginning of the proper pneumonic rise of temperature is generally not clearly defined.

During the fastigium the course of the temperature exhibits more or less considerable fluctuations, similar to the morning remissions and evening exacerbations of ileo-typhus (typhoid fever). In cases of moderate severity the exacerbations seldom reach the height of the daily maxima in abdominal typhus, and therefore fall short of the maxima which occur in the continuous course of pneumonia. In certain severe cases, however, they may equal or even exceed these, and more than one severe case has occurred in which the afternoon temperature amounted to 40° Cent. (104° Fahr.), or even a little more. However, the course of the disease is seldom so regular as in abdominal typhus—more often larger and smaller exacerbations, and more or less considerable daily remissions, alternate with one another.

On an average, the duration of remittent pneumonia exceeds that of the continuous, without, however, extending to the same length as abdominal typhus.

The termination of the fever only exceptionally happens by very rapid defervescence; it generally occurs in a protracted manner by the morning remissions gradually becoming greater and the evening exacerbations growing less, but always, however, more rapidly than in ileo-typhus.

It is pretty common, too, for the fever to terminate at the close, after the daily excursus has already become very considerable, by a sudden, final descent from a still very considerable evening exacerbation.

Imperfect convalescence is more commonly associated with the remitting than the continuous course.

Transitional forms between the continuous and remitting course are by no means rare, just as undoubtedly croupous and catarrhal pneumonia are closely allied to each other.

The truly characteristic remittent catarrhal pneumonia only exceptionally occurs sporadically, but, on the contrary, chiefly during the prevalence of a severe epidemic of influenza.

The diagnostic question, whether there is bronchitis or pneumonia during a remittent course, cannot be settled entirely by thermometry, but this must generally be done by taking into account the acoustic symptoms. But pneumonia is highly probable when the exacerbations exceed 40° Cent. (104° Fahr.) in height.

The differential diagnosis from abdominal typhus may present no little difficulty, more particularly as infiltrations of the lung may occur in this disease, and, on the other hand, the cerebral and abdominal symptoms are very similar to those of typhoid, and even the spleen may become enlarged. And it is not always possible to make a correct diagnosis when only a limited abstract of the course lies before us. But in favorably progressing pneumonias the diagnosis is generally possible after observation for some four days or so. If they are the first four days of the disease, the rise of temperature in pneumonia will be found less regular than in abdominal typhus. (See page 300.) If the days are at later periods, one generally observes in favorable cases of pneumonia a constant diminution of the high evening temperatures, and if the disease has already shown a decided decrease it may be taken as true that this makes more rapid progress than in ileo-typhus.

§ 9. A course with recrudescing fastigium not infrequently occurs as a modification both of the continuous and remittent types, and is remarked in those cases where, after the hepatization of one part of the lung, either a second lobe or the other lung is attacked (*saccadé* 'd progressing pneumonia).

After the previous temperature has been pretty moderate, or the course has already begun to moderate, there occurs all at once a rise of temperature, which is shortly succeeded by either a continuous or discontinuous course.

Unless death occurs, the convalescence generally resembles that of the other cases, though it sometimes displays irregularities, and is at least more protracted than in the simple continuous course.

§ 10. Sometimes the fever in pneumonia displays a relapsing course. This may occur after a general or large local abstraction of blood, and sometimes also without any external interference at all.

For the most part a rapid defervescence occurs unusually early, perhaps on the second or third day, although sometimes later, just as in recovery from croupous pneumonia.

The temperature continues fully normal, or it may be sub-febrile, for eighteen, twenty-four, and sometimes thirty-six hours or more, and it seems as if recovery would follow, yet there is no actual retro-cession, generally speaking, in the local symptoms.

All at once the temperature rises again rapidly, although it does not usually reach quite its former height, remains generally only a few days at the fastigium, and then tends towards a definitive defer-vescence, or the fever may thus renew itself a second or even a third time.

By imperceptible gradations these relapsing cases are allied to the one just described above (§ 9), in which there occur remissions or pseudo-crises, with an extended apyrexia.

During the febrile relapse the local changes either remain sta-tionary, or they become intensified in certain spots (the dulness becomes intensified, the bronchial breathing more perfect), or they extend further.

Sometimes, although not invariably, *erratic* pneumonias exhibit a relapsing form; by erratic, I mean those peculiar forms of the disease in which (like erratic erysipelas or many cases of polyarticular rheu-matism) the lung affection jumps from one spot to another, the places first attacked heal again, whilst new spots are invaded, and so infiltration and resolution succeed with extraordinary rapidity, as in-dicated by auscultation and percussion.

§ 11. The *intermittent* course is closely allied to the relapsing, and only differs by the fact that the apyrexiæ and the paroxysms alternate in tolerably regular rhythm, and are more sharply defined, one from the other, than is the case in the relapsing form. The fever paroxysms themselves resemble the pneumonic ephemera with acutely pointed peaks. The local anatomical symptoms may also diminish during the apyrexia or interval. This form is only ob-served in its most perfect development during epidemics of intermit-tent fever.[1] An intermittent type may also be observed in embolic pneumonias with a tendency to repetition (self-repeating).

Intermittent pneumonias may lead to erroneous opinions in a two-

---

[1] This intermittent form of pneumonia is occasionally found in malarious dis-tricts in England. I have myself observed it in patients from Barking Road, and I remember Dr. Nicholas Parker, late Physician to the London Hospital, pointing my attention to the same fact.—[TRANS.]

fold manner. The defervescence which occurs leads to the conclusion that the disease is at an end, and perhaps that some particular treatment has cut it short. And, on the other hand, after
repeated attacks and returns to apyrexia, we may easily fancy that
we have to do with an intermittent fever. However, in intermittent
pneumonia—at least so far as I have seen—the attacks become spontaneously weaker after two or three attacks, which seldom happens in
intermittent fever, unless specially treated.

Intermittent pneumonia may terminate either by no fresh rise of
temperature occurring after defervescence and the establishment of
convalescence, or by the intermittent character becoming obscured
after several repetitions, and later on the pneumonia terminates with
moderately high temperatures as a remittent form, which goes on to
convalescence by lysis. I have never seen it end fatally.

§ 12. The course with abrupt, and hence for the most part imperfect falls of temperature and fresh irregular elevations, exhibits the
greatest resemblance to *pyæmia*, and is doubtless pyæmia with a
preponderance of lung symptoms. Sometimes repeated embolic
processes in the lung with multiple centres (foci), sometimes septic
processes, display this course, which, as a rule, ends in death. If the
individuals are emaciated, the rising temperatures alternate with
more or less intense collapse.

§ 13. Pneumonias with *protracted* course generally display nothing
remarkable at the commencement of the attack. They are either
continuous or discontinuous in their course during the first few days.
Remissions occur later, if not beforehand. But instead of showing
a tendency to recovery, the fluctuations continue considerable. High
evening temperatures alternate with severe collapse. The daily
maximum generally occurs about noon. In the evening there is a
remission, which has a great tendency to collapse, and this is succeeded by a second, although slight, exacerbation about midnight.
Thus it may happen that, whilst the remissions continually increase in
depth, the exacerbations also increase, and thus the daily difference is
augmented.

But this tolerably regular course only lasts a few days; other modes
of temperature occur intercurrently, which again make way for the
great daily excursus. If the patient does not succumb, the case lasts
a long while, till the exacerbations diminish, and very often a course

which has almost advanced so far as to be free from fever, is again interrupted by fresh elevations of temperature for one or more days.

In those cases in which only moderate evening exacerbations continue for a long time, which may depend partly on imperfect recovery from the pneumonia itself, and partly upon the existence of marked complications (pleurisy, or purulent bronchiectasis), the transition towards a state free from fever, when it does occur, is always gradual and almost unnoticeable.

§ 14. Terminal pneumonias (pneumonie des agonisants) do not always necessitate an elevated temperature. And where this has previously existed it is by no means necessary that this should be altered by the occurrence of infiltration of the lungs.

Yet, on the other hand, in cases of patients previously very ill, whether the original disorder has been acute or chronic, the supervention of pneumonia very frequently leads to the fatal termination, and this is indicated by the temperature rising.

At first it only rises moderately, but may rise to very considerable heights in the last few days, or even at an earlier period. But it is quite exceptional, no doubt, to find a high febrile temperature produced by such a terminal pneumonia, and when this is met with it is pretty surely brought about by other circumstances, and not by the pneumonia itself.

§ 15. *Traube* has communicated some remarkable facts on the peculiar course of the temperature in pneumonia, in his paper on the effects of digitalis (1850, 'Charité Annalen,' i, 622), and on crises and critical days (1851 and 1852, 'Deutsche Klinik'). Consult, further, *my own* publications concerning pneumonia (in the 'Archiv f. phys. Heilkunde,' 1856, p. 17, and 1858, p. 27, and the 'Archiv der Heilkunde,' 1862, p. 13) ; *Ziemssen* ('Pleuritis und Pneumonie im Kindesalter,' 1862) ; *Thomas* (in the 'Archiv der Heilkunde,' 1864, p. 30, and 1865, p. 118) ; *Kocher* ('Behandlung d. croupösen Pneumonie mit Veratrum,' 1866) ; *Schrötter* ('Sitz-Ber d. Kais. Acad. d. Wissensch.,' Juli, 1868) ; *Kiemann* ('Prager Vjschr.,' 1868, iii, 72) ; *Grimshaw* ('Dublin Quarterly Journal,' May, 1869) ; *Maclagan* ('Edinburgh Medical Journal,' February, 1869, p. 684), &c.

For the curves of the fever-course in pneumonia see the diagrams at the end, Table VI.

XV.—AMYGDALITIS.

(Tonsillitis — Quinsy.)

§ 1. Tonsillar angina is analogous in many respects to pneumonia, and its various modifications ; though, if we exclude diphtheritic affections of the pharynx, the danger is never so great, and therefore its course in every respect exhibits less severe types.

As in pneumonia, so also in tonsillitis, there are two distinct species of fever, as regards their relation in point of time to the local symptoms. Whilst in a number of cases the fever, and the topical disorder are simultaneously developed, or the former only succeeds the latter ; there are also not a few cases in which (as frequently in croupous pneumonia also) an intense fever, resembling the prodromal fever of an exanthem, precedes the development of the tonsillar angina by some twenty-four to thirty-six hours, or even two or three days.

The latter course occurs in catarrhal as well as in parenchymatous tonsillitis : and is relatively more common in the first, although on the other hand absolutely less frequently met with, since febrile catarrhal anginas are not quite so numerous as those of the parenchymatous form.

No sharp boundary line can be drawn between the fever-type of these two forms of tonsillitis, but certain symptoms occur more frequently in one form than in the other.

§ 2. When fever sets in at the very *beginning* of the disease, whether any phenomena of the disease can be observed localised in the tonsils, or none can be seen so soon, there is almost always a rapid development of febrile symptoms ; very often accompanied with a rigor, and still more frequently with strong sensations of chilliness ; though it is not so very rare to find cases with an immediate feeling of heat. In this respect there is no essential distinction between the catarrhal and parenchymatous forms.

It is not possible to accurately state the form assumed by this initial rise of temperature, since the cases which come under observation during this period are not sufficiently numerous. The temperature generally reaches its maximum height during the first few days of the disease, most commonly on the third day of the illness, though often enough on the second or fourth. The *maximal heights* are on an average lower in the catarrhal, than in the parenchymatous form; in the former they seldom exceed 40° C. (104° F.), whilst in the parenchymatous form, though it may not be very common, still there are many cases which reach a height of from 40°—40·75° C. (104°—105·35° F.). In the great majority of cases the maximum temperature in the parenchymatous form remains between 39° and 40° C. (102·2° to 104° F.), whilst in the catarrhal it still remains under 39° C. (102·2° F.).

A descending direction can be generally noted in both forms, after the maximum is reached, although the crisis may not occur directly.

The course of the temperature in both forms is *discontinuous* during the *fastigium* : but in the catarrhal form when the temperatures are higher than those mentioned above, the fluctuations are greater, and the remissions sometimes almost descend to normal; whilst in cases of very high temperature, in the parenchymatous form, the course is actually wont to approximate more to a continuous type, at least in the first few days, or exhibits only an isolated peak of elevation. But very marked remissions, on the other hand, are more often seen in the parenchymatous form, when the temperature, after reaching its maximum, begins to moderate.

A critical perturbation precedes the crisis in some cases, although it is rare.

§ 3. A *rapid defervescence* is by far the commonest form in both kinds of amygdalitis, occurring in about two thirds of the cases of the catarrhal form, and in about five sixths of the parenchymatous cases.

In the great majority of cases the crisis begins between the third and fifth day, more rarely on the second, sixth, or seventh days, and still more rarely at a later period. In catarrhal tonsillitis a postponement of the crisis to the two last days of the week (of the illness) is relatively more common. On the other hand, the defervescence, if it takes place at all rapidly, is sooner over in this form (doubtless because the temperatures are less high than in the other form), and generally takes place in one night, whilst in the parenchymatous form, though often enough completed in a night, it just as often takes from twenty-four to thirty-six hours.

Sub-normal temperatures are sometimes met with after defer-

vescence in the parenchymatous form, but never occur at this stage
in catarrhal tonsillitis.   If, on the opposite, defervescence takes the
form of lysis, which especially happens in cases with moderate temperatures, slight elevations of temperature may be met with for
several days, and recovery is retarded.[1]

Consult *Thomas* (1864, in the 'Archiv der Heilkunde,' v, 170)
and *Treibmann* ('über Angina Tonsill.' Diss., 1865), who both
made their observations on cases in my wards.

XVI.—PAROTITIS.

(*Mumps, and Inflammations of the Parotid Gland.*)

Parotitis affords us an immense variety of varying curves of temperature, and indeed we cannot expect that it should be otherwise,
when we consider under what various circumstances the inflammatory
affections of the salivary glands and their surroundings occur; not
only as a primary epidemic affection (*Mumps*) in which the fever is
generally very slight;[2] as a catarrhal affection; as an inflammation
induced by contiguity; as a complication of the most varied infectious constitutional diseases; as a metastatic form in pyæmia; as a
terminal disorder in severe febrile and wasting diseases, &c., &c.

Many of these forms, and particularly such as are accompanied
by fever, do not occur sufficiently often to render it possible to lay
down rules for the course of the temperature in particular cases,
especially as such cases are almost always complicated, and therefore

---

[1] In addition to the croupous and diphtheritic affections of the tonsils, which
properly belong to diphtheria and croup, I think the following forms of tonsillar
affections are frequently met with:

1. Catarrhal (as described above), most common in xantho-tubercular, or
epithelio-rheumatic patients, generally young persons or children of either sex
commonly affects *both* tonsils.

2. Gouty, attacking *one* tonsil usually.

3. Erysipelatous, attacking one or both tonsils, and tending to spread (most
common in middle-aged or old people).

4. Consecutive, following the exanthemata (scarlatina being of course
excluded from this classification).

5. Syphilitic, attacking both tonsils.

6. Tubercular, analogous to tubercular pneumonia.

7. Catamenial (see note, page 102)—[TRANS.]

[2] I have often seen a *maximum* of 40° C. (104° F.), and sometimes a little
more, in the fastigium.—[TRANS.]

require a largely accumulated experience to enable us to eliminate the effects of the parotitis from those of the original disease.

It can, therefore, only be stated generally that in the various forms of parotitis the temperature behaves itself as follows :

There is either no alteration of the previously normal or febrile temperature (this happens pretty frequently) ; or there may be a moderate elevation of temperature ;

Ephemeral rises of temperature may occur, followed by either sudden or protracted downfall ;

There may be several days' continued fever ;

Or remittent fever ;

Or the course of the fever may assume a pyæmic form ;

Or final elevations of temperature to very high degrees ;—

Or collapse may occur.

XVII.—Meningitis.

§ 1. Many attacks of meningitis occur, which either run their course without any fever at all, or only display irregular elevations of temperature, which are by no means characteristic.   Such is the case in chronic and partial forms of inflammation of the meninges.

Even the acute and more extensive forms of meningitis do not correspond, one with the other, as regards the course of the temperature ; yet it is possible to lay down certain definite rules, which indeed are not very precise, nor are they invariable, but still serve for the great majority of cases.

In this way there are three special modifications of meningitis, which differ as regards the course of their temperature :—

(*a*) Acute sporadic inflammation of the pia mater of the convexity, or upper surface of the brain.

(*b*) The granular (tuberculous) form, which has its seat more especially at the base of the brain, in the fissure of Sylvius, and about the cerebellum.

(*c*) The epidemic form generally attacking the base and the convexity simultaneously, and extending itself even to the spinal cord (epidemic cerebro-spinal meningitis).

As these various forms differ in their ætiology and their special symptoms, so also they exhibit variety in the course of the temperature.

§ 2. The fever in acute meningitis of the convexity, according to the cause of the disease, sometimes begins very rapidly, sometimes more or less slowly.

So far as I can decide from not very numerous cases, the rise of temperature very soon becomes very considerable, and maintains itself at striking elevations (above 40° C. = 104° F.) in a continuous fashion; and rises still higher in the death agony, so that death usually occurs with hyperpyretic temperatures. The whole course lasts only a few days.

§ 3. In *granular basilar-meningitis* (tubercular meningitis), the commencement of the elevated temperature generally escapes observation, either because the insidious beginning of the disease has excited no attention, or because the previously existing disorders (tuberculosis of the glands, or of the lungs) have already caused the temperature to be high.

Sometimes the course of the temperature continues very slightly above normal, sometimes at moderate fever-heights with (usually) a remittent type; but it is not very unusual for it to reach the same height as the fever of abdominal typhus, and then to display isolated and striking falls of temperature, and sometimes pauses extending over several days.

When the fatal termination approaches, after a longer or shorter course, it is quite exceptional for the temperature to rise. In general it sinks rather, if it has been febrile, if not quite to normal, yet far below the previous degrees, *whilst the pulse is rising all the while.*

During the death agony this sinking may continue, or just before death there occurs a final more or less considerable rise of temperature; the pulse, on the other hand, rapidly increases in frequency, almost up to the very moment at which the heart ceases to beat.

§ 4. *Epidemic cerebro-spinal meningitis* is obviously a form of disease, which in spite of the actual identity [of the anatomical lesions] may present itself under apparently widely different symptoms.

Accordingly the temperature may pursue varied courses. As, however, observations on temperature have only lately been made at a few places in the last German epidemic, the materials are still too scanty to enable one to represent the manifold varieties of the fever course of this disease in an exhaustive manner.

From rather more than thirty cases observed by myself, it appears to me that three special varieties of the fever course can be particularly distinguished.

(*a*) In some *very severe* and rapidly fatal cases, the temperature displays a similar course to that of meningitis of the convexity. Though not invariably very high at the beginning of the disease, it reaches very striking heights in the briefest time, which persist continuously for some days, and rise just near death, and in the very moment of death to quite unusual degrees (42° C. (107·6° F.), and more; and in one case 43·75° C. (110·75° F.) in dying), and may even rise some tenths higher after death (three quarters of an hour after death in the case just mentioned, it was 44·16° C. = 111·48° F.). There were also some fatal cases, in which the temperature for some time was very moderate, and rose considerably all at once just near the end of the disease.

(*b*) On the other hand, relatively *mild* cases, exhibit only a fever of short duration, although there are sometimes considerable elevations of temperature (which contrast with the quiet pulse), and the course is generally discontinuous. Recovery does not take place by decided crisis, but generally happens rather with remittent defervescence [lysis]: and the pulse then begins to quicken just as the temperature has become normal, or nearly so. Here and there cases occur, which after defervescing, and apparently almost recovering, relapse all at once, with a rapid rise of temperature, and run a course like the cases marked (*a*).

(*c*) In contrast to these brief courses of fever with either very severe or slight character, we find cases which are more or less *protracted*, with a corresponding course as to the fever. The height of the temperature in these may be very varied, and indeed exhibit manifold changes in the very same case, though indeed this chiefly depends upon the varied complications which supervene, in the shape of bronchial, pulmonary and intestinal affections, and affections of serous membranes.

Sometimes the fever has the same duration, and the exacerbations of temperature the same height as those of typhoid fever, and its curves when projected may greatly resemble the latter; but there is not the regularity of abdominal typhus, and at the best the course is only that of the amphibolic period of that disease, or like that which occurs in very irregular forms of it. Fluctuations of considerable extent, apparent improvements, and fresh and sudden rises of temperature are met with. Sometimes the course resembles the fever of phthisical patients.

Defervescence may occur rapidly, but is, however, for the most part protracted [by lysis].

With a fatal termination, we may get either a rising or falling temperature, according to the kind of case, and the various immediate causes of death. I have related at some length a very remarkable case, in which both the course of the temperature and the other symptoms rendered the diagnosis doubtful for a long time, whether we had to do with abdominal typhus or cerebro-spinal meningitis, in the 'Archiv der Heilkunde,' vi, 271.

Compare also *my own* publications (1864, 'Archiv der Heilkunde,' v, 417, and 1865, ibid., vi, 268), also *Ziemssen* and *Hess* (1865, in the 'Deutschen Archiv für Klinisch Medicin,' i, 72 and 346), and *Mannkopf* ('über Meningitis cerebro-spin. epidem.,' 1866).

See lithographs, Table VI.

See also 'New Sydenham Society's Biennial Retrospect of Medicine for 1865-6' (pp. 55-62, &c.), and articles in Russell Reynolds' 'System of Medicine,' and Aitken's 'Theory and Practice of Medicine,' and the "Supplemental Bibliography" at the end.

XVIII.—Pleurisy, Endocarditis, Pericarditis, and Peritonitis.

Inflammations of the serous membranes of the chest and abdomen exhibit, in the great majority of cases, perfect absence of any typical character.

They may run their course without any elevation of temperature, for if they are occasionally found with high temperature, at another time we find them quite free from fever.

If they are associated with any other febrile diseases, they very often effect no change in the temperature course, or only cause it to be irregular, without any characteristic form. They generally retard the defervescence of the primary disease, making it protracted and imperfect, and they have a share in the fresh elevations of temperature which occur at a later date.

They may, however, themselves induce the temperature to rise, sometimes moderately, at other times to considerable heights.

Lastly, they may depress the temperature to sub-normal degrees, or even collapse-temperatures.

In spite of the great number of temperature curves of such cases which I possess, I have never been able to deduce more than a few general propositions as to the significance of temperature in these affections, which I may formulate as follows :

(1) There is no course of the temperature in these affections which can be regarded as denoting safety; whatever the course of the temperature, a fatal termination may ensue. No behaviour of the temperature guarantees that the disease shall end in perfect recovery.

(2) The most advantageous course, *i. e.*, that which renders a favorable termination most probable is—

When the temperature all through is either not affected at all, or when the temperature keeps within the bounds of sub-febrile temperatures, or of slight febrile movement, or only very slightly exceeds them, and especially when it does not fall to sub-normal degrees (Fundamental Propositions, § 15), or when a moderate fever with remittent character is present, and does not exceed a fortnight, and then gradually subsides, without any other suspicious symptoms supervening.

(3) Subnormal temperatures are especially common in peritonitis, and are always highly suspicious. Death very often occurs with temperatures below the normal, which may either result from a fall shortly before death, or they may have lasted some time already, or have alternated with normal and elevated temperatures.

(4) Temperatures of considerable fever height, and particularly rising temperatures, are *per se*, however, no argument for an unfavorable termination, although they certainly add another dangerous element to the case. If these high temperatures become moderated, the danger is not entirely removed, but this is better at all events than their persistence.

(5) It is not so much the actual height of the temperature, but especially its remaining stationary (the absence of remissions) which greatly increases the danger; and still more a long continuance of very high temperatures, and this is so even when the high evening exacerbations alternate with considerable morning remissions. In the first case the disease is very severe, in the second event a perfect recovery is at least doubtful. The return to normal temperatures after high ones, when it occurs in these affections (whether they are

independent, or only complications of other diseases), is often delayed, and greatly hinders complete restoration to health, and induces disturbances during convalescence, but does not prevent the temperature finally finding its level.

(6) Very considerable and irregular fluctuations between very high temperatures and very low ones, such as occur in pyæmia, are especially common in endocarditis; sometimes occur in inflammation of the pericardium, and of the pleuræ, and also in peritonitis : they are always most highly dangerous, and render a fatal termination very probable.

(7) Hyperpyretic temperatures are more especially met with in many cases of peritonitis; particularly in the puerperal form : and lead us to suspect that besides the inflammation of the serous membranes, another process (originating in infection) has been set up : whilst those forms of peritonitis in child-bed which run their course without much elevation of temperature are apparently to be grouped with simply local affections. The former (those with very high temperatures) are tolerably certain indications of a speedy termination in death, which occurs in such cases with more or less considerable degrees of temperature. A very interesting observation of *Kussmaul's* deserves to be mentioned here. It is contained in the ' Deutsch. Archiv für klinisch. Med.' for 1868, iv, 1. He noticed in cases of fœtid and purulent febrile pleurisies (empyæma), that after thoracentesis the temperature very quickly returned to normal. I have observed a similar case myself, whilst in a case of fibro-serous exudation (pleuritic effusion) the moderate fever which was present was not materially affected by the tapping.

[Dr. *Edwin Long Fox* (' Medical Times and Gazette,' and ' St. George's Hospital Reports') confirms the author as to the uncertainty of the temperature as a sign of pericardial or endocardial affections in acute rheumatism. Dr. *Herbert Davies'* cases show the same thing. Dr. *Habershon*, Dr. *Reginald Thompson*, and Mr. *J. F. Goodhart* (' Guy's Hosp. Reports,' N. S., vol. xv) all agree in the same statement : that uncomplicated pleurisy, peritonitis, and other serous inflammations seldom exhibit high temperatures (often not above 100° F. = 37·7 C.). My own observations entirely confirm these, so that we seem to be very nearly warranted in assuming as a law, that inflammations of serous membranes are generally attended by only slight fever. Mr. Stephen Mackenzie (Resident Medical Officer of the London Hospital) lately showed me a chart

of pleurisy, which exhibited no symptoms of pneumonia, but in
which the temperature throughout was high.   There appeared to be
no other complication.   No doubt, however, many cases of pleurisy,
pericarditis, and peritonitis, are complicated by renal or other
visceral disorders, if not originated by them.—*Trans.*]

XIX.—ACUTE RHEUMATISM.

§ 1. If one roughly compares a few accidentally varying isolated
cases of acute polyarticular rheumatism, its fever appears to show
remarkable and extreme differences in different cases.   Perfect
absence of fever, or intense fever; its duration very brief, or
protracted; a continuous, or remittent course; and the most sudden
elevations and intercurrent downfalls of temperature are all met
with under the same nominal diagnosis.   However, when a great
number of cases of this disease are compared, it becomes apparent that
certain forms of temperature-course are more commonly met with
than others, so that one may describe them as definite, or loose and
indefinite types of polyarticular rheumatism : although it is not
always easy to determine the reason why a given case should belong
to one or the other group; and although we may not be able to
determine the forces which cause the disease to pursue a definite
course, or why a certain number of cases deviate from it.

It may also be remarked, that whereas this multiplicity of courses
makes a very motley mixture amongst a few hundreds of cases only,
yet that they are not found to multiply themselves infinitely.   When
we greatly increase the number of cases observed, we rather find
these difficulties clearing up, and get an idea that there may be a possibility of reducing all of them to a few primitive forms.

§ 2. A very large number, indeed nearly half of the cases of
acute rheumatism, especially cases of slight or medium severity and
severe cases too for a time, display in the main a *moderate amount of
fever;* during which the temperature gradually rises at the commencement, and reaches its maximum height at the end of the first
week, or at the beginning of the second; lingers for a few days only
(or sometimes only for a single evening) at or near this height with
no fluctuations, or only slight ones; and from this time forth, under
good nursing, sinks by a protracted descent, generally with moderate

morning remissions: whilst, however, pretty sensitive to external influences, it appears strikingly little affected by the occurrence of inflammation of internal organs (unless they are of extreme severity). There is also very often a disproportion between the temperature and the frequency of the pulse, even when the heart itself is free from disease. Nothing like weekly cycles is to be observed. With good nursing (timely at hand) when the surroundings are also favorable, freedom from fever, or comparative freedom is already obtained in the course, or towards the end of the second week, or in severe cases during the third week.[1] These general characteristics of the course must, however, be considered with more detail.

The course naturally divides itself into three divisions; namely—

(1) The ascent of the temperature or pyrogenetic stage;

(2) The *height* of the fever, which sometimes rises to a solitary peak, or acme, and sometimes constitutes a fastigium of several days' duration;

(3) Lastly, the period of *descending* temperature, which gradually loses itself in defervescence.

(*a*) The *beginning* of the fever seldom comes under observation in polyarticular rheumatism, because the patients hardly ever come under our notice till the course has lasted for several days. But their statements allow us very fairly to conclude, that the fever does not commence in the sudden manner common in croupous pneumonia, and in most cases of acute exanthematous affections, but takes a more gradual development, which is sometimes more tedious than that of abdominal typhus.

Cases do occur, however, in which patients show a temperature of nearly 40° C. (104° F.) or even more, even as early as from the second to the fourth day; such cases are however exceptional. On the other hand, it is common enough to find that in the very middle, or

---

[1] That our *treatment*, if not our *medication* of acute rheumatism is improved, is, I think, evident from this fact, which is also true of more than half our English cases. It is not so long since that it used to be publicly taught that at least *six weeks* was required for rheumatic fever; and a little further back, *six months* was a rather common period. I myself believe that, with any treatment at all, and good nursing, no genuine case of this affection extends anything like so long as the latter date. Mistakes are of course easy between gouty, pyæmic, syphilitic, and albuminuric rheum*atoid* cases, and true rheumatism. As regards the absence of warning of serious complications, such as pericarditis, endocarditis, and pleurisy, see the note appended to the previous section.—[TRANS.]

even the end of the first week of the illness, the temperature is still very moderate, and begins to rise higher at a later period; or when the disease is well nursed, remains moderate.

(b) Even the *height of the fever* is very often not completely under our own observation. *For it is very remarkable, as regards the course of acute articular rheumatism, that in an overwhelming majority of hospital cases, the maximum temperature is reached either on the day of admission or almost directly after*, and that it generally falls on the first evening after their removal to the hospital, and that from this time either a gradual and steady decrease of temperature is observed, or at worst a descending direction becomes decidedly manifest, after a fastigium of from two to four days' stationary temperatures. This extremely common course appears to indicate, either that the removal of rheumatic patients is extremely injurious, and is able considerably to raise their temperature; or that good systematic nursing is able to very quickly alleviate the fever.[1] We cannot admit the hypothesis that, by a happy accident, the patients always come under treatment at the very moment the temperature has naturally and spontaneously attained its summit. For this maximum height at the beginning, and the speedy completion of the descent, occur just as commonly whether the patient is brought into the hospital at an earlier, or more advanced period of the disease; indeed it appears to me that the decrease of temperature takes place the more quickly the earlier the reception into hospital occurs, and accordingly the earlier good nursing enters into competition with the rising temperature.

If the maximum height does not occur only at the first taking of observations, but is observed after the occurrence of lower temperatures, still, in spite of this, the maximum often presents only a solitary peak, which often sharply contrasts with the lower temperatures before and behind it. In such a case we cannot talk of a proper fastigium stage, but only of a momentary elevation of temperature. This maximal point, which occurs in the evening hours, is generally by no means inconsiderable in height, usually indeed quite 40° C. (104° F.), and may often exceed the temperatures of the preceding and following evenings by at least 1° C. (1·8° F.), and those of the preceding and following mornings by even 2° C. (3·6° F.) or more. This acme-point generally occurs between the fifth and ninth day of the disease, but may occur even earlier (perhaps on the third day), or

[1] Will no one give us good cases from private practice?

at a later period in some cases. Very commonly, however, the summit extends itself into an actual fastigium. But this in the majority of cases is very brief in comparison to the whole duration of the disease, and is still shorter when very high temperatures are reached, though the case in itself may not be very severe. It lasts, as a rule, only from two to three days. It is only in very exceptional and in other respects severe cases, that temperatures of 40° C. (104° F.) or more, are reached or exceeded on three successive days. In a great number of cases of very perfectly developed articular rheumatism, the daily maxima, even at the height of the disease, remain between 38·6° and 39·5° C. (101·48° and 103·1° F.).

In such cases the fastigium lasts rather longer; but even when it lasts a week, it is almost always longer than the period which succeeds. The course of the temperature during the fastigium is sometimes continuous, sometimes exacerbating, sometimes subremittent, and sometimes shows remissions of no inconsiderable amount.

(c) The *descending* period shows a varied type according to the form assumed by the decrease, and the suddenness with which it occurs.

In favorable cases, and particularly such as come early under treatment, the downfall of temperature is proportionately quick and then occurs generally in a zig-zag manner like a rapidly recovering typhoid fever, and perhaps without any evening rise of temperature, just as many cases of scalatina behave. The downfall then takes the form of defervescence by *lysis*, which may perfect itself in from five to six days.

It is exceptional to meet with a more rapid downfall, almost like a *crisis*. More commonly the decrease is protracted, and sometimes halting (stockend). After the first decrease of temperature a moderate, and generally remitting fever, of tolerably stationary daily average persists for several days, and it is only by looking at the whole course that one can faintly recognise a descending direction. Or there may be a daily decrease, but so trifling in amount, that from ten to twenty days are required, before the temperature reaches normal, which happens, so to speak, almost imperceptibly.

After freedom from fever has been attained, and convalescence has set in, the temperature is accustomed to fluctuate for a while, on a plane which is a few tenths higher than that of a healthy person, or of one who is convalescent from any really typical acute disease. So that the evening temperatures may occasionally show an approach to even febrile degrees, and even higher transient elevations of temperature may occur here and there.

After all, the fever in these cases of acute rheumatism, is only of *moderate*, or at the most, *medium severity*. Apart from its brief acmé it remains at heights which only exceptionally *exceed* the bounds of moderate fever.

§ 3. There are, however, many, and varied *exceptions* to this medium, and throughout favorable sort of course; which, however, when all comprehended together, scarcely reach the number of the former kind.

Abnormally mild cases are particularly common, or rather cases in which the temperature is either very slightly or, perhaps, not at all affected; although the local condition is not always correspondingly insignificant. Indeed, we cannot always tell why the fever should remain so trifling, or perhaps be altogether absent, when the joint affection is very severe; and cardiac complications are by no means excluded by the absence of fever. Cases with slight fever (not above 38·5° C. (101·3° F.), or with only sub-febrile temperatures, constitute about one third of all the cases of acute rheumatism. All other deviations from the course described, comprehending more or less severe cases altogether, do not, at least in our country, amount to more than one sixth of the cases.

§ 4. One of the commonest forms assumed is the *protracted* (Lentescirende) type. The duration of the disease in this is essentially lengthened. The fever persists as late as the fourth or fifth week. The daily differences are usually far more considerable, and thus the temperature may fall to normal in the morning hours, whilst in the evening the fever is more or less considerable, and indeed, generally exceeds 40° C. (104° F.) Numerous abnormalities and changes of type are met with, and the temperature only very gradually returns to normal. Large daily fluctuations show themselves most strikingly when the affection of the joints and articulations becomes fixed; and thus fluctuations of three degrees or more (= 5·4° F.) may occur in one day.

Recrudescence of the fever, or apparently objectless intercurrent elevations of temperature are by no means rare. Right in the middle of a moderate course of fever, or even after return to a sub-febrile, or fever-free condition, there often occurs a more or less considerable rise of temperature (even a couple of degrees or so, = 3·6° F.), which is sometimes quite ephemeral, sometimes compensates itself after a day or two, or sometimes lasts rather longer. This fresh rise is not always dependent on fresh increase of the joint affection, nor yet on the occurrence of complications. It is especially difficult to find an explanation for the cases of very brief inter-current elevations of temperature, which only last one day or so : and this short fever paroxysm, of which the patient is often quite uncon-scious, has no influence at all upon the regular and proper termina-tion of the case. More slowly developing, and longer lasting elevations of temperature may be associated with a relapse in all the symptoms.

Those cases may be classed as *apparent* recrudescence, in which the temperature has been artificially depressed at the height of the disease, by medicine (such as Digitalis and Aconite), and has risen again when the influence of the medicine is exhausted, or when it is left off.

§ 5. Complications, especially pericarditis and endocarditis, in many cases have no effect at all on the *course* of the fever [see notes to pp. 393 and 395]. They sometimes occur without ele-vating the temperature even the tenth of a degree, or without at all affecting its downward progress. In other cases, however, the opposite is the case, and the course may be modified as follows :

(*a*) The course of the temperature during the fastigium and during recovery may, indeed, be unaffected, but during convalescence the temperature remains in a somewhat higher plane than is commonly the case with rheumatic convalescents, and sometimes in the further course of convalescence rises somewhat higher still; this occurs occasionally in pericarditis and in endocarditis, when this has pro-duced valvular mischief. It is sometimes a considerable time before the temperature descends from this elevated platform (Niveau).

(*b*) Associated with this, we find after actual recovery from the acute disease a protracted sub-febrile or actually febrile condition : sometimes in the temporary stage, paroxysms of fever, lasting several days, may set in. These sometimes consist of aberrant secondary fever, dependant pericarditis, made up of several isolated febrile *ex-peditions* of a week or more, which are only separated by a brief interval of sometimes only imperfect freedom from fever. With a fresh development of aortic valvular insufficiency through endocarditis, very considerable elevations of temperature sometimes occur late in the disease; whilst mitral insufficiency appears to have far less effect on the temperature.

(c) Sometimes, however, even during the fresh course, or relapse of acute rheumatism, more or less considerable rise of temperature is brought about by complications. The supervention of pneumonia most certainly, although not invariably, raises the temperature, yet without impressing on the course the characteristic type of pneumonia.[1] The remaining complications (pericarditis, endocarditis, bronchitis, urticaria, miliaria, &c.), only exceptionally produce this inflammatory rise of temperature, either when they are very severe, or perhaps on account of individual predisposition, or perhaps according to some special form of the complicating inflammation.

§ 6. When the disease becomes fixed in a joint or a bone, the articular rheumatism may hang about for a very long time, through recrudescence of the process or through successive complications.

Such *obstinate* attacks are not very frequent amongst my hospital patients. I think, however, that I am not wrong in saying that they occur much more frequently in private practice. Obstinate rheumatism with fixed or changing and successive localisations sometimes displays great intensity, but sometimes produces only very slight symptoms, differences which are very clearly indicated in the course of the temperature. On the other hand, severe incidents occur now and then without corresponding elevations of temperature.

§ 7. Amongst the *fatal* affections which accompany acute rheumatism, or have rheumatoid symptoms, we may notice two essentially different courses, in which there is a corresponding difference in the course of the temperature.

(a) In the one class of cases death occurs from a *fixed localisation*, particularly from heart affections or their results, sometimes in immediate sequence to the rheumatic affections of the joints, and sometimes not till after their recovery. The course of the tempera-

---

[1] This is one of those little touches so true to nature, as to show clearly that the author draws from life, and not merely from his own imagination.—[TRANS.]

ture during the rheumatism itself is not generally much altered, but it displays irregularities, and if death occurs at an early date, the characteristic descent is either wholly wanting or interrupted. Death, which results in these cases, not from the actual disease itself, but from the unfortunate course taken by some local manifestation of it, or some complication, may be preceded by a very marked fall of temperature.

(b) In other cases which are just as commonly included with acute rheumatism, a *malignant character* sometimes reveals itself from the very beginning, at other times during the further progress of the disease, at first in symptoms which may easily be misinterpreted, but further on shows itself more powerfully. The most commonly observed symptoms of a pernicious nature are rigors, very intense fever, various severe nervous symptoms, jaundice, hæmorrhages, diarrhœa, and enlargement of the spleen.

No one of these symptoms by itself is perfectly diagnostic, but the combination of several of them characterises the case as a malignant one. The pains in the joints are more or less severe, and generally extend to the muscles, over the head, chest, and abdomen. Death generally occurs with very considerable and sometimes enormous *elevation of temperature* (to 43° C. or even 44° C. and more = 109·4° Fahr. and 111·2° Fahr. Cases by *Quincke;* and *H. Weber* in London (' Transactions of the Clinical Society'), and by *myself* (Wunderlich).

These cases, which, perhaps, ought to be called rather *rheumatoid* affections, though regarded as genuine articular rheumatism, display as far as my observations have yet extended, peculiar differences, in three distinct directions = a *pyæmic*, an *icteric*, and a *nervous* form. They rank along with spontaneous pyæmia, with primary pernicious jaundice [acute yellow atrophy], and with those rapid and pernicious nervous catastrophes which are devoid of an anatomical basis; and they are only to be distinguished from these forms by the fact that the strongly pronounced articular pains, for some time at least, simulate acute rheumatism. These differences are, however, by no means strongly marked; and one might say that the nervous form was the least perfectly developed, the icteric form the most pronounced, and the pyæmic form the most complete. In the completest (pyæmic) form, indications of the malignant nature of the process may be very early recognised; the fever is very intense, whilst rigors, jaundice, and enlarged spleen are met with, and the only moderations of the course which occur are, transitive, deceptive, and imperfect.

Such deceptive remissions occur more especially in the proagnostic period, whilst on the very day of death the temperature regularly rises considerably.

The course of the temperature fashions itself thus when the centres of suppuration are not too numerous, but a complexity of grave disorders exists, corresponding to the jaundice.

In the cases which end fatally without multiple centres of suppuration, and without jaundice, the disease at first runs its course like a very severe articular rheumatism. A descending direction may even have set in as regards the temperature, but suspicious nervous symptoms show themselves simultaneously. These suddenly arise with very rapid fresh increase of temperature, and in the briefest time reach most extreme degrees, so that death occurs with hyperpyretic temperatures, whilst no anatomical lesion in the brain can be discovered in the corpse, or only very moderate degrees of meningitis. Post-mortem elevations of temperature may be met with.

[See papers by Drs. Herbert Davies, Fuller, Gull, Sutton, and E. Long Fox, in the 'London Hospital Reports,' 'Guy's Hospital Reports,' and 'Medical Journals' for 1870, *passim*. Dr. Wilson Fox ('Lancet,' July 2nd, 1870) gives two cases with præ-mortem temperatures of 110° and 110·8°, and Dr. E. B. Baxter has kindly given me notes of a case of acute rheumatism under Dr. Dufflin's care, whose temperature in dying was 111° Fahr. (43·9° C.). Dr. Edwin Long Fox (in one of a series of valuable papers in the 'Medical Times and Gazette' for 1870) also says that death often occurs when the temperature reaches 105°, but not invariably (the latter statement I can confirm from notes of several cases). He further observes that high temperatures usually correspond with a high pulse, but an *evening* temperature of 103° Fahr. may go with a pulse of 84° or 90°. The urine is generally acid with high temperature, but it may be alkaline. There may be profuse sweating with temperature of 103° and 104½° Fahr., and sudamina also." He thinks that blisters do not diminish the temperature; but many of Dr. Herbert Davies' cases lead to an opposite conclusion, especially those in which blisters were applied after recrudescence.—TRANS.]

[See the curves in Lithographs at the end, Table VII].

XX.—OSTEO-MYELITIS.

In acute osteo-myelitis, which resembles typhus [*typhoid* fever] in many respects, and has, therefore, been called "bone-typhus," the course of the temperature only very imperfectly and, it would appear, exceptionally, coincides with some typhoid attacks.

Of six cases which came under my own observation, five displayed a brief and somewhat continuous course till the fatal termination; in three it lasted eight days, in one fourteen days, in the fifth case the commencement was not accurately determined; the whole course even in this did not last over a fortnight. Four of these cases were observed in the last two to five days, and one was noted only on the day of death. This case died with a temperature of $40.7°$ C. ($105.26°$ F.), and after death the temperature rose to $41.1°$ C. ($= 105.98°$ F.). In the remainder the bounds of pretty high fever $40.5°$ C. ($= 104.9°$ F.) were never exceeded. The course of the temperature displayed irregular, but on the whole trifling fluctuations, and only isolated deeper falls of temperature (to $38.4°$ and $38.6°$ C. $= 101.2°$ to $101.48°$ F.). The contrast was always remarkable between the temperature, which was never immoderate, and the enormous frequency of the pulse (which in one case was 188 per minute, twelve hours before death), and this contrast was only absent in one case.

In contradistinction to these not very typhoid-like courses of temperature, there was one case which came under observation on the seventh day of the disease, in which the affection was pretty soon limited to the left femur, and gradually improved at a later date. During the whole of the second week this exhibited the remittent course of abdominal typhus (up to the twelfth day a daily maximum of $39.8°$ to $40° = 103.64°$ to $104°$ F., and a daily minimum of $38.6°$ to $39.2° = 101.48°$ to $102.56°$ F.; and from the twelfth day assumed a descending direction with considerable remissions), and, indeed, in such wise that even the brain-symptoms and those of the intestines and spleen corresponded to a severe attack of typhoid fever, and the diagnosis remained in suspense during the whole of that week. Further on, when the fever moderated, the course assumed a hectic type.

XXI.—Parenchymatous Inflammation of the Kidneys.

Acute inflammation of the kidneys (acute Bright's disease) exhibits very little regularity as regards the course of the temperature, which is apparently dependent on the varied rapidity and intensity of the attacks, and partly on the circumstances under which they are developed.

The temperature is often only febrile, and perhaps only moderately so; in other cases it attains a height of $39°5°$ to $40° = 103°1°$ to $104°$ F., or even more. In cases which recover there is a gradual defervescence by lysis; in fatal cases death may occur with either a rising or falling temperature.

Chronic inflammations of the kidneys (chronic Bright's disease) as a rule affects the temperature very little, and even in fatal cases terminal elevations of temperature are exceptional.

[I have notes of several cases (some of which are still attending at the London Hospital) in which, after acute desquamative nephritis for the most part of scarlatinal origin, the temperature has remained on an elevated plane, with occasional exacerbations, accompanied by other signs of renewed kidney mischief (such as alteration in the quantity of urine, or in the amount of albumen, or occasional hæmaturia, and the occurrence of casts and epithelium from time to time) for from two to three years; and in one case for four years. The noon temperature in these cases has remained sub-febrile ($99°5°$ to $100°4°$ F.), or slightly febrile ($100°4°$ to $101°3°$ F.), ever since, whenever noted (once or twice a week), although the other symptoms of kidney mischief have been comparatively slight.—TRANS.]

XXII.—Hepatitis.

Acute *parenchymatous* inflammation of the liver exhibits varieties which differ widely from one another as regards the course of the temperature; but these cases are too rare to allow one to deduce any definite common principles from them.

In the form with malignant (pernicious) jaundice, whether from phosphorus poisoning or not, the temperature is sometimes unaffected even till death, whilst sometimes it is moderately elevated, or begins to rise towards the end of the attack; and sometimes highly febrile, or even hyper-pyretic temperatures are met with. The course of the temperature in *yellow fever* has been made known to us through an interesting paper of *Schmidtlein's* in the 'Deutsches Archiv für klinische Medicin,' IV, 50. According to him the temperature is highest in the first few days of this disease, and very often reaches a height of from 40° to 41° C. = 104° to 105·8° F., very frequently with slight evening exacerbations. From the fourth to the fifth day the temperature steadily falls, and sinks down to normal, or even below this. In cases which end fatally it rises again towards the end some 2° C. = 3·6° F., or even more.

In suppurative inflammation of the liver, the temperature, with the abscess of the liver, may follow the same course as in pyæmia, or in chronic suppurations. *Fräntzel* (in the 'Berliner Wochenschrift,' 1869, p. 5) quotes *Traube* as saying, " Repeated attacks of severe rigors with great elevation of temperature are only observed in two diseases of the liver—in blennorrhœa of the gall-ducts, and in abscess of the liver." Further on (p. 13) he says: " With the exception of abscesses of the liver originating in pyæmia, endocarditis, and pyle-phlebitis;[1] all the other forms, directly they take on an intermitting fever, and pursue their course accompanied by attacks of rigors, constantly exhibit a perfectly regular course all through; that is, paroxysms of fever preceded by rigors, or febrile exacerbations occur; and it is a matter of indifference whether they maintain the type of a simple quotidian, or of a duplex quotidian, or that of a tertian; it is always just at or close to a definite period of time, as in malarial disease; whilst, on the other hand, those fever-paroxysms and exacerbations induced by pyæmia, endocarditis, and pyle-phlebitis,[1] which are preceded by a rigor, always exhibit an irregular rhythm throughout, with very much shorter intervals, occurring from three to four times in the twenty-four hours."

XXIII.—LUES (CONSTITUTIONAL SYPHILIS).

1. By the term Lues I mean those numerous and complicated affections which have hitherto been known by the name of secondary and tertiary syphilis. [See Note to page 247.]

[1] " Pyle-phebitis or pylo-phlebitis (πυλή, the vena porta—phlebitis, inflammation of a vein). Term for inflammation of the vena porta."—'Expository Lexicon,' Dr. R. G. Mayne.

By this I avoid, on the one hand, the ambiguous expression "syphilis," and, on the other hand, their doubtful relation to the local chancre is not either assumed or denied.

The luetic (syphilitic) symptoms may certainly occur without any fever, and there is, perhaps, no form of luetic manifestations which may not develop itself, and run its course perfectly free from fever.

On the other hand, with certain symptoms of lues, fever is far more common than is generally believed ; and this fever is somewhat peculiar ; and indeed so characteristic that it is by no means diffi-cult to at least suspect the nature of the disease by a glance at the course of the temperature. [See fig. 39 opposite.]

§ 2. In luetic (syphilitic) cases, elevated temperatures are most commonly met with at the time when the first extensive hyperæmic papular or pustular skin eruptions are developed.

The fever which accompanies the luetic (syphilitic) eruptions of the early periods may be very severe, and the maximal temperatures may reach nearly $41°$ C. ($= 105·8$ F.).

The course of the temperature is markedly remittent (pseudo-intermittent), with a daily downfall which descends quite to normal, or very nearly so. The alternation of these deep morning remissions with the high evening exacerbations is tolerably regular, but in spite of the rapid rise of the evening temperature rigors only accom-pany it in exceptional cases. It is also equally exceptional for a day quite free from fever to intervene between the days of fever, or for the fever subsequently to display a tertian type, or for greater and more moderate exacerbations to prevail alternately from day to day. The duration of the fastigium is indefinite, sometimes it is short, occupying a few days only, but it may last over a fortnight [and even longer than this.—TRANS.]. The fever subsides by the evening exacerbations gradually becoming less severe, in a manner which corresponds pretty closely with the behaviour of the tempera-ture in advanced periods of convalescence from abdominal typhus.

§ 3. In many of the acute internal luetic affections of the liver and brain, and also in those of the bones which occur from time to time, we sometimes meet with an analogous though less regular course of the temperature, which is marked by the alternation of considerable morning remissions, with more or less severe evening exacerbations. In that malignant form of lues which is marked by

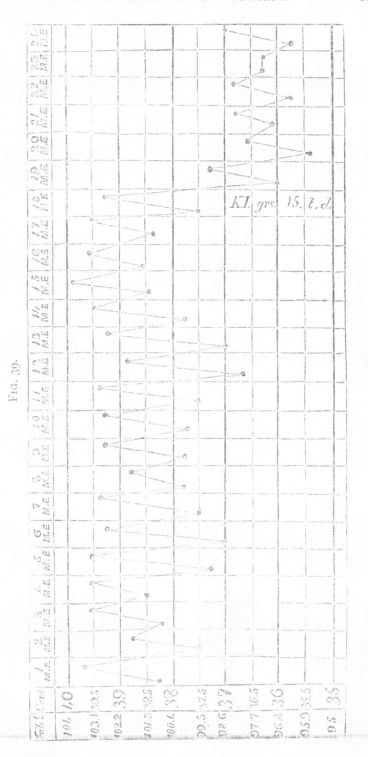

FIG. 39.

rapidly fatal attacks, similar considerable rises of temperature are met with (40° C. = 104° F., and even more) ; but the intervening remissions are less, or if they occur, less regular ; sometimes they are actually less in depth, and sometimes wholly absent. The fever observes no order in its course. The remissions of temperature are deceptive, and are by no means signs of a favorable termination.

On the course of the temperature in luetic (syphilitic) marasmus see Marasmus.[1]

XXIV.—GLANDERS AND FARCY.

I can only find one case of observations of temperature in glanders in the human subject (Goldschmidt's Giessen Thesis, 1866). This is somewhat interesting. He remarks (from observations commenced in the fourteenth day of the disease) that the fever displays a remittent course, which is of moderate severity at its commencement, from the nineteenth day of the disease it rose gradually, zig-zag fashion, and reached highly febrile degrees ; from the twenty-fifth day forward it never sank below 40° C. (104° F.), and in the last few

---

[1] The author's observations in the text, and those of *Dr. T. E. Cuntz*, in " Das syphilitische Fieber," Küchenmeister and Pross' Zeitschrift f. Médicin, Chirurgie and Geburtshilfe. N. Folge iv, 1865, p. 192) (for a reference to which I have to thank *Dr. Christian Bäumler*), as well as the cases of syphilitic rheumatism in Dr. Garrod's and his own practice reported by Dr. Duffin, at p. 81 of the 2nd vol. of the ' Clinical Society's Transactions ;' and the " Report of the Committee on Temperature in Syphilis," at page 170, in the 3rd vol. of the ' Transactions ' of the same society, may be referred to along with the *diagram* specially added to this English edition, as tending to prove that some forms at least of constitutional syphilis, particularly those resembling rheumatism, are at least as *typical* as most fevers. I have to return special thanks to Dr. E. B. Baxter for first directing my attention to this subject, and for kindly lending me his own notes and charts of several cases, which have enabled me to present an *ideal* chart (all the temperatures of which, however, are *real*) compiled from his careful observations, which in one case at least extended over more than two months. Besides showing the great fluctuations of temperature met with in these cases, the figure shows the striking effect of 10 gr. doses of Iodide of Potassium, in reducing the temperature—an improvement which coincided in some of the cases with a remarkable and striking gain in weight (20 lb. in fourteen days in one case). See also " *Lancereaux* on Syphilis," New Sydenham Society's Translations, by Dr. Whitley, vol. i, p. 125.—[TRANS.]

days (fifth week of the disease) it progressed in a pretty continuous course (41·3° to 41·6° C. = 106·34° to 106·88° F. being attained). No observations were taken during the last twenty-four hours.[1]

XXV.—ACUTE MILIARY TUBERCULOSIS, &c.

Acute miliary tuberculosis produces considerable alteration of temperature in the majority of cases, and this is in general so much the more, the more copiously and extensively the tubercle deposits are diffused, and the freer the person attacked was from other disorders, before the formation of the miliary granulations.

When the miliary tubercles are scanty and localised, or in patients who are already greatly under the influence of other serious affections (such as advanced pulmonary phthisis, pneumonia, or cerebral disease), miliary tuberculosis sometimes fails to affect the temperature at all, or at least its influence is very slight. The course of the temperature in miliary tuberculosis assumes the following leading types :—

(*a*) A type resembling that of catarrh at its commencement, with an intense hectic fever later on ;

(*b*) One resembling the course of the temperature in abdominal typhus ;

(*c*) A type resembling the course of intermittent fever.

These three different forms may succeed each other in one and the same case. The first form is met with in cases whose course is subacute.

The illness, at least as regards its temperature relations, perfectly resembles, at its commencement, the course of a severe attack of influenza, or one of catarrhal pneumonia. Only the obstinate persistence of the fever excites suspicion. Gradually deep remissions, which almost descend to normal, occur, and alternate with febrile evening exacerbations of considerable height. Yet even by this behaviour of the temperature it is not possible to distinguish acute tuberculosis from an acute non-tuberculous phthisis; and so it may remain even up to the time of death ; unless meningeal tubercles are developed, and the characteristic symptoms of basilar meningitis display themselves.

[1] A case, under the care of Mr. de Morgan, is reported in the 'British Medical Journal' for April, 1870. The temperatures in this were not very high, and death took place on the 20th day with a temperature of 104·4° F. (= 40·2° C.).

In the second form a diagnosis between that and typhoid fever is often for a long while, and perhaps even up to the time of death, impossible. However, the course of the temperature is more irregular in acute tuberculosis than is ordinarily the case in abdominal typhus; the remissions are generally somewhat greater than in the latter disease, and do not sink down to normal.

Those cases of acute tuberculosis which simulate typhoid fever are generally those which are most rapidly fatal. Should life, however, be prolonged, which[1] is exceptional, the fever later on assumes another character, it may be either the hectic or the intermittent type. Undoubtedly the intermittent fever type is the rarest form in acute tuberculosis. The course of the temperature of each fever-abscess (or local suppuration) may perfectly resemble that of an intermittent fever, and repeat itself with the same regularity, sometimes, indeed, with a tertian or duplicated quotidian rhythm. Yet the occurrence of the attacks, especially in the afternoon, and the fact that the heights reached by the temperature are somewhat less, or become so in time, than those met with in intermittent fever; whilst, on the other hand, the temperature of the intermission (or apyrexia) generally falls deeper below the normal than in that, may raise our suspicions of the presence of acute tuberculosis. In the further course of acute tuberculosis the intermittent type is generally lost, and the succession of an invariably less severe remittent fever renders the diagnosis certain, if that has not already been settled upon other data.

[See notes at end of the next section.]

XXVI.—ACUTE PHTHISIS.

§ 1. Acute phthisis may take its origin from a condition perfectly free from fever, upon which elevations of temperature supervene in a zig-zag fashion, with remissions and exacerbations of increasing severity; less regularly and more tediously, however, than is usual in abdominal typhus.

Or acute phthisis may closely follow the fever of an attack of bronchitis, pneumonia, or some other acute affection; in which case,

---

[1] So that, as has been well said, "The incautious practitioner pooh-poohs the attack at first as only a trifling cold, and in a week or two has to sign the death certificate."—[TRANS.]

when the phthisis sets in, somewhat lower daily remissions are met with, but the height of the daily exacerbations may either remain the same, or diminish somewhat, or even increase.

§ 2. In the further progress of the case, the course of the temperature generally shows pretty continuously, or at least for the most part, a non-continuous type.

The daily differences, as a rule, are very considerable, they amount to 3° or more (Centigrade = 5·4° Fahr.).

The daily maxima occur for the most part in the afternoon or evening, but not very infrequently in the morning also, and approximate to or even exceed 40° C. (104° F.)   Even heights of 41° C. (105·8° F.) or more are observed.   Sometimes they occur twice in one day, but only very exceptionally every two days.   Sometimes they are pretty nearly the same height for a series of days, sometimes from day to day they show a pretty regular slight increase or decrease, whilst sometimes there is a persistent alternation between higher and lower exacerbations, and this alike whether the type be simple or duplicated quotidian.   The daily falls of temperature are abrupt, and their minima may reach to normal or even sink beneath it.   Even profound collapse is not very rare.   An alteration from day to day is sometimes displayed in the amount of the remissions, though less commonly than is the case with the height of the exacerbations.

There is sometimes an intervening period, thrust in as it were upon the course, in which the remission becomes considerably less, and the course of the temperature becomes sub-continuous, or even somewhat ascending in its type, in which the exacerbation-peaks of the earlier stages are sometimes reached by the temperature.   Complications (such as intercurrent attacks of pneumonia) may bring about these modifications.   Yet they may occur independently.

The fever is often interrupted also by short (less often by longer) intervals of moderate fever, or of sub-febrile or even of normal temperatures.

On the other hand it is somewhat rare to meet with a persistent sub-continuous course with considerable or moderate fever from the very beginning to the fatal end.

§ 3. In the majority of cases the temperature falls from its previous height towards the approach of death, and the remissions become less distinct.   The daily differences become less, whilst the

daily average may either fall or rise.   Death indeed may occur with
a tolerably low temperature.   Or the temperature which had previously fallen may rise afresh during the death-agony, and sometimes
to hyper-pyretic heights.

On the other hand, it is seldom that death occurs with persistently rising temperature, in immediate sequence to the previous
fever.

NOTE.

[Dr. Sydney Ringer has rendered such good service to thermometry in England, especially by his book 'On the Temperatures of
the Body as a means of Diagnosis in Phthisis and Tuberculosis,'
1865, that I feel loth to differ from him; but if I understand him
aright, that there is an elevation of temperature in all cases of tubercular deposit, I am compelled to do so; if that statement be intended
to apply at all times, after the deposit of tubercle has once taken
place; and to express my conviction that Wunderlich is correct in
saying that there are intervals free from fever in some cases of
phthisis; and further, that in some cases miliary tuberculosis does
not affect the temperature at all.   I believe these *intervals* may
sometimes extend over three or four weeks, and I certainly agree
with M. Henri Roger when he says—"Si dans l'enfance, comme aux
periodes plus avancées de la vie, les tubercles donnent quelquefois
lieu à un accroisement de la chaleur animale, ce n'est point par eux-
mêmes, mais par leurs effects consecutifs, par l'irritation locale que
leur présence détermine dans les tissus.   Lorsque cette inflammation
n'existe point, ou qu'elle est devenue chronique, le thermomètre
monte à peine audessus du niveau ordinaire."   And again—
"M. Andral a constaté pareillement chez les adultes que la température reste normale, dans la phthisie pulmonaire, tant que la fièvre
ne s' allume point."[1]   *H. Roger*—"De la température chez les
enfants," &c., Paris, 1844-5.

MM. Hérard and V. Cornil assert confidently that, apart from

---

[1] "Although both in infancy and at more advanced periods of life tubercles
sometimes cause an increase of temperature, they do not do so on their own
account, but only by the effects which they produce, and by the local irritation
caused by their presence in the tissues.   When this inflammation is wanting,
or if it become chronic, the thermometer will scarcely rise above the average
degrees."   And again, "M. Andral has similarly established for adults that
the temperature remains normal, even in pulmonary consumption, so long as
there is no fever."

complications, there is no fever in the stage of deposit ('De la Phthisie Pulmonaire,' Paris, 1867, p. 200).

Dr. Finlayson also objects to Dr. Ringer's statement, that there is a continued elevation of temperature in all cases of tuberculosis and tuberculisation, and that the thermometer will always detect it. He thinks many of Dr. Ringer's temperatures are too low, which he ascribes to the thermometer being retained only five minutes. His own observations on children with tubercular disease (made in the Manchester Clinical Hospital for Children) lead him to believe that there are three principal types of tubercular disease, corresponding to Sir W. Jenner's clinical classification of "the insidious, the active febrile, and the adynamic." In this way he combines the views of Jochmann (Berlin) and of Wunderlich. These three types may be briefly expressed as follows:

First type.—The morning temperatures are normal, or rather less than normal, whilst the evening temperatures are more or less high. *E. g.*, a child has a temperature of 99·32° Fahr. (in the rectum) in the morning, whilst the evening temperature = 101·53 or 101·80° Fahr. This equals the insidious and often unexpectedly fatal type.

Second type.—The morning and evening temperatures are *both* high, whilst there are evening exacerbations. *E. g.*: a child has a morning temperature of 100·16° F. (rectum), whilst the evening temperatures are from 101·57° F. to 103·67° F. = the active febrile type.

Third type.—The morning and evening temperatures are both high, but there is a tendency to exacerbations at odd times. *E. g.*: on one day the child has a morning temperature in the rectum of 102° F., and in evening one of 102·33 F. On another day the morning and evening temperatures may be 102·6° and 104° F. respectively. This characterises the adynamic type.

Dr. Finlayson lays most stress on the continued absence of that evening fall in temperature which he considers as so characteristic of healthy children. He contends that the daily range of temperature in the healthy child is greater than in the adult, amounting to as much as two or three degrees Fahrenheit, and that there is invariably a fall of temperature in the evening, amounting to one, two, or three degrees Fahrenheit; the most striking fall usually occurring between 7 and 9 p.m., often before sleep comes on.

See 'On the Temperature of Children in Phthisis and Tuberculosis,' by James Finlayson, M.D., p. 32, Dunn and Wright, Glasgow, and the 'Glasgow Medical Journal,' November, 1869.   Dr. Hillier also admits that the morning and evening temperatures in phthisis may sometimes be normal, and even Dr. Ringer admits this.   It is therefore rather the *course* of the temperature than its height on a particular day which must be our guide.—TRANS.]

[Dr. Finlayson's table of the variations of temperature in twenty-four hours in healthy children is here combined with Dr. Ogle's tables of temperature in adults (male and female) referred to at p. 101, and for convenience represented by a diagram.—TRANS.]

FIG. 40.

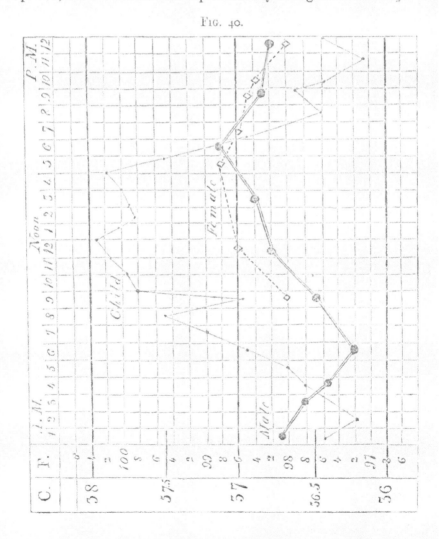

XXVII.—Trichinosis.

Trichinosis cannot have a typical form of fever; for the participation of the system in general is essentially determined by the numerical circumstance of the little foci of inflammation induced by the parasite being more or less numerous. Notwithstanding this, the course of the temperature in this disease is more than usually interesting, because it affords us almost the only certain proof that a considerable elevation of the general temperature of the body may be brought about by purely local, although enormously multiplied disturbances (inflammations), for a considerable time at least; for when the disease has lasted some time, and the deposits have reached a later stage, it is quite true that further mischief is developed; which is shown by the implication of the brain, lungs, and kidneys, and by the simultaneous disease of other organs in which there are no trichinæ. In such advanced cases it is clearly not possible to determine how much of the fever which is present should be ascribed to the topical inflammation of the muscles, and how much to the cerebral disease, the pneumonia or nephritis, and such like.

Observations on patients suffering from Trichinæ show—

(1) In spite of tolerably extensive muscular symptoms, and, doubtless, no inconsiderable localisation of Trichinæ, there may be perfect freedom from fever, or a sub-febrile condition, or at most a very slight febrile movement.[1]

(2) In the same manner the fever is either absent or only slight, when the muscles are first attacked.

(3) When the symptoms grow increasingly severe in the further course of the disease, the temperature may be very considerably varied, and even 40°—41° C. (= 104°—105·8° Fahr.) may be reached; only such high temperatures are interrupted by more or less considerable remissions, generally reaching the normal point, or

---

[1] In a man admitted into the London Hospital, under Mr. Curling's care, and who died almost immediately in consequence of having been run over in the street, almost all the voluntary muscles were thickly studded with trichinæ. Yet Dr. Bathurst Dove, who made the post-mortem which discovered this fact, found, on careful inquiries of his nearest relatives and friends, that he had never complained of any of the usual symptoms, and considered himself as almost a model of health.

even descending beneath it, so that there is then an almost daily compensation or re-establishment of an equilibrium of temperature.

(4) Such high degrees of temperature do not persist long. Even in fatal cases they are interrupted by the occurrence of either normal or only slightly elevated temperatures for several days together.

(5) These circumstances combined, render the course of the temperature in trichinosis somewhat characteristic, at least in those cases where the temperature reaches high degrees. In such cases there is little danger of confounding it with typhoid fever, and with the fever of articular rheumatism; it is more likely to be confused with acute tuberculosis, or with cases of internal suppuration running a rapid course.

On the other hand, when the fever continues to be very moderate and inconsiderable, all characteristic features are lost.

See the curves in lithograph at end, Plate VII.

XXVIII.—MALARIOUS DISEASES.

Only the intermittent form of malarious infection is accurately known as regards the course of the temperature. There is no opportunity in our country of making any observations on the remittent forms.

We must distinguish in this kind of disease between the course of the temperature in the several paroxysms and its course during the entire duration of the disease.

§ 1. The separate *paroxysms* are each characterised by a sudden rise of temperature (generally with rigors and " cold shivers"), to a height of extreme fever, and an equally rapid return to the normal or a little below it.

The temperature begins to rise before any other symptom of the incipient attack announces itself.

The rise of temperature is, however, comparatively slow just at first, that is, it may continue for a couple of hours without reaching more than $38 \cdot 5°$ or $39°$ C. ($= 101 \cdot 3°$ or $102 \cdot 2°$ Fahr.). As soon as the rigor occurs, which may begin at temperatures of varying height, the rise becomes more rapid, and in the course of about an hour has reached a height of $41°—41 \cdot 5°$ C. ($105 \cdot 8°$ to $106 \cdot 7°$ Fahr.), or only exceptionally a little higher. Meanwhile, the stage of dry heat (hot stage) may have set in, and during this, the rise of tempe.

rature may still go on. This ascent to the summit or *acmé* of the temperature of the paroxysm is generally quite steady and uninterrupted; at the furthest the temperature halts once or so, for a few minutes at some given point; or occasionally there occurs a slight fluctuation just close to the highest point [so that the summit is slightly bifid].

The *maximum* of the temperature is reached in the stage of dry heat, though sometimes perhaps, after the appearance of partial sweating. It only lasts for a few minutes.

When the sweating becomes general [moist stage], the temperature begins to fall again, only slowly for the first hour or half hour; and sometimes it fluctuates a little ; then it begins to fall somewhat more rapidly, without any fresh rise occurring : it does so, however, in such a way that the temperature halts for a quarter or even half an hour, and then falls about one or two tenths of a degree Cent. (= one fifth to one third of a degree Fahr. nearly), then rests again, then begins to fall again and so on (so as to resemble *terraces*) ; when this has continued some four hours or so, and the temperature has fallen to somewhere about 40° C. (104° Fahr.), it sinks somewhat more rapidly; requiring, however, some ten or twelve hours or more before it regains the normal point.

During the intermission or apyrexia which succeeds, the temperature is sometimes a little under the normal ; but if the apyrexia lasts more than one day, there is a very slight evening exacerbation, which scarcely exceeds the range of a normal daily fluctuation. Not infrequently, especially after the use of febrifuges (quinine, &c.), there occur paroxysms without any subjective symptoms, which only announce themselves by the elevated temperature, and run their course without a rigor and without any sweating or only very trifling perspiration. The maximal height in these attacks may equal, or very nearly so, that of the perfect fever paroxysm; the rise and fall of temperature are, however, compressed within a briefer period than is the case in paroxysms accompanied with a rigor.[1]

[1] As the two facts of the *rise* of temperature during the cold stage, and the existence of paroxysms of fever (as shown by the thermometer) after the apparent cure by antiperiodics—attacks which are scarcely known to the patient himself—are still unknown to a large number of medical men, and even denied by some, although recognised by de Haen (see Chapter II of this work), it is perhaps not superfluous to remark that I have often verified this observation, and have demonstrated the fact to others. Were it necessary I could easily furnish corroborative cases from my note-book.—[TRANS.]

This behaviour of the temperature in the paroxysm and the apyrexia which succeeds it, is itself so characteristic of intermittent fevers (agues, &c.), that it renders the diagnosis tolerably certain. There are extremely few forms of disease in which there is so rapid a rise of temperature from the normal level to a height of 41° or 41·5° C. (105·8° to 106·7° Fahr.), immediately followed by an equally rapid return to the normal temperature. Hardly any except ephemera, the solitary relapse into fever during convalescence from typhoid fever, the paroxysms of acute tuberculosis and those of pyæmia, display a similar course; and to distinguish between these diseases it is in general sufficient to wait for a second paroxysm, and at the same time to pay attention to the exact time of its occurrence.

However, even a single paroxysm is enough to enable us to distinguish intermittent fever from those affections for which it is most likely to be mistaken when its symptoms are severe, such as typhus, meningitis, and cholera. In these, which often resemble a very intense and pernicious intermittent in all the other symptoms, the course of the temperature is so perfectly different, that the use of the thermometer makes our diagnosis absolutely certain.

§ 2. In relation to the manner in which the paroxysms of intermittent fever succeed one another, it has long been known that this may happen in various kinds of rhythm. It appears to me, after making very numerous observations, that the most normal course, *i. e.* that which is undisturbed by individual peculiarities, complications, &c., is that in which the paroxysms are repeated after about forty-four to forty-six hours (tertiana anteponens).

Thermometry alone is often able to reveal the fact that the apparently pure quotidian, tertian, or quartan rhythm is duplicated; and that either stronger paroxysms alternate with weaker ones (in the apparently quotidian rhythm); or that between the separate paroxysms which are completely developed in all their symptoms, there are attacks interposed which only announce themselves by the elevated temperature.

In a similar manner complete recovery from intermittent fever can only be guaranteed by the thermometer. Thermometric observation teaches us that the disease does not generally terminate with a well-pronounced paroxysm, but that fresh attacks may succeed which consist only in a rise of temperature (which is sometimes very great), and announce themselves in no other way but

which may again give place to perfectly developed paroxysms if the treatment be too early discontinued. Besides *Zimmermann* and *Bärensprung*, special reference may be made to *Michael's* paper in the 'Archiv für physiol. Heilkunde' (for 1865), xv, 39, entitled, "Specialbeobachtungen der Körpertemperatur im intermittirenden Fieber."

See the curves in the lithographs at the end, Plate VII.

XXIX.—THE TEMPERATURE IN CHOLERA.

§ 1. Observations on temperature in cholera are attended with some special difficulties, and in particular the results derived from those taken in different regions of the body, require to be separately estimated, since they do not run parallel courses.

Temperatures taken in the axilla cannot be trusted unless taken with great precautions. The mercury rises very tardily, and sometimes takes half an hour before it becomes stationary, particularly in the cold stage. However carefully taken, these axillary temperatures in the cold stage afford no correct standard of the general temperature of the body (or temperature of the blood). However they are valuable, because they represent the conditions of the surface temperature (the heat of the skin). In the reaction stage, the axillary temperatures are once more trustworthy standards for the general temperature of the body.

The degree of surface warmth, or the extent rather to which the skin is cooled, is indicated far more perfectly on exposed parts of the body, and particularly in the hands and feet. But any accurate measurement of temperature in these spots is almost impossible, and the results obtained are, therefore, comparatively worthless.

During the algide stage temperatures taken in the mouth give hardly any idea of the general temperature. They may, indeed, be of some value, as giving indications as to the temperature of the expired air; though, indeed, these are complicated, and little trustworthy.

Only observations taken in the rectum or vagina can serve as a standard of the general temperature of the body. The former, however, are difficult to make at this period of the disease, and are easily disturbed by the action of the bowels. Vaginal measurements are by far the best, but cannot be had recourse to in some females; or, at least, cannot be repeated sufficiently often; and may be affected

by the croupous (diphtheritic) affections of the vagina which often
supervene in these cases.

There is very often a considerable contrast between the results
obtained by readings taken in various parts; and sometimes this very
contrast may afford us valuable hints (*lit.* winks) for prognosis.
Thus a great difference between the axillary and rectal or vaginal
temperatures is decidedly unfavorable, and in the progress of recovery we often observe the temperature in the mouth to rise, while
the vaginal temperature falls.[1] The behaviour of the temperature in
sporadic cases of cholera, when these are severe, does not essentially
differ from that of the epidemic form.   Only the average differences of
temperature are rather less, unless the choleriform attack accompanies
some special affection, which necessitates considerable alteration of
temperature.[2]

§ 2. Even *before the beginning* of any other symptoms, a fall of
temperature may be observed in patients previously suffering from
fever, when they become infected with cholera (as *Friedländer* has
shown from observations made in my wards); which although closely
connected with the still latent infection, yet demonstrates clearly,
that the decrease of temperature of the surface is in no way the
result of the evacuations alone; [perhaps, however, it does result
from the increased flow into the intestinal canal, just as a fall of
temperature succeeds internal hæmorrhages.—TRANS.]

In the *stage of evacuations* (cholera flux), in slight cases which
do not become asphyxiated, both the axillary, vaginal, and rectal
temperatures are, as a rule, normal, or (particularly the vaginal
temperature) a little raised.   As soon as there is any indication
of asphyxia, the temperatures are always more divergent; the
vaginal temperature appears somewhat higher, and the axillary
temperature somewhat lower than normal.   If the algide form is
developed, the temperature of *internal parts* in cases which recover,
is moderate, as a rule, although sometimes rather high (in a case of
Güterbock's it was 39·6° C. = 103·28° Fahr.), and it is exceptional
to find it normal or diminished.

[1] See note to page 153.

[2] Numerous cases in the medical journals, especially in 1866, when attention
was drawn to the subject by several physicians, show that all the appearances
of cholera may be perfectly simulated by many other affections—as perforating
ulcers, toxic influences, intestinal obstructions, hæmorrhages, &c. &c.—
TRANS.]

In cases in which death occurs in the asphyxiated stage, the temperatures in the vagina and rectum sometimes reach still higher degrees (40° C. = 104° Fahr.), or more, and in one case of Güterbock's, even 42·4° C. = 108·32° Fahr.). Any considerable rise of temperature, or any considerable fall, indicates great danger, and with either alteration quickened respiration.[1] Cyanosis, asphyxia, and suppression of urine, may be present.

Very profuse and violent alvine discharges are generally indicated by a fall of temperature, though sometimes only accompanied or preceded by a relative fall.

When the temperature rises, although the rise may be only relative, the alvine discharges cease, and if the temperature rise higher there is a tendency to coma (sopor).

Both a rapid fall of considerable amount, and a rapid and considerable rise of temperature are indications of approaching death.

On the contrary, the less the temperature fluctuates, the less it varies from the normal, the more probability there is of recovery. On the cutaneous surface, even in the axilla, the temperature during the algide stage is, as a rule, diminished, sometimes, indeed, very greatly so, yet not often below 35° C. (95° Fahr.). The axillary temperatures generally show less striking fluctuations than the heat of internal parts of the body. There is especial danger when the surface temperature of the body remains persistently low, or after being considerably lessened, rises rapidly, or sinks afresh after it had begun to rise. On the other hand, it is a good sign when the low temperature slowly and steadily begins to rise with only slight fluctuations, and thus the normal temperature is not exceeded or only slightly.

The temperature under the tongue may be still more diminished. In the stage of asphyxia, the temperature there seldom exceeds 31° C. (87·8° F.), and even in cases which recover may fall to about 26° C. (78·8° F.). If it falls below this, recovery would appear to be impossible.

§ 3. In the *post-choleraic* stage (period of reaction) the temperature in favorable cases is normal or approximately normal. In this stage, from its previously abnormal condition, it returns to the normal again.

---

[1] Quickened respiration is present in almost all cases of cholera, as it is in nearly all fevers, probably from failure of muscular power, or to compensate the pulse frequency.—[TRANS.]

Yet moderately febrile rises of temperature are by no means signs of great danger; they are, however, suspicious, and denote complications of some sort.

More considerable elevations of temperature are a sure sign of complications, and of the supervention of various local affections, and give little prospect of recovery. Very high temperatures are particularly induced by parotitis and erysipelas, and sometimes, though less invariably, by pneumonia, which only exceptionally pursues a typical course.

Patchy exanthems [roseola, &c.], do not invariably induce a rise of temperature.

A normal or approximately normal course of temperature in the post-choleraic stage is, however, by no means an absolute guarantee of recovery.

When the reaction assumes an actually typhoid form, the temperature in many cases is normal, or only slightly elevated. It is true these are in general favorable cases with but slight development and inconsiderable local affections, yet even in these all danger is by no means got rid of. However, the temperature may rise, and that pretty considerably, even in the typhoid form, and the type is for the most part remittent. These are cases which run a stormy course, with severe local disorders, and if they do not suddenly end fatally, they lead us to expect that the disease will be protracted. Parenchymatous nephritis occurs indifferently both in cases with moderate and those with elevated temperatures.

The most unfavorable thing in the post-choleraic stage, is for a previously normal or elevated temperature to suddenly sink below normal. Even a considerable diminution of the peripheral heat [surface-warmth] at this period, indicates considerable danger.

In many cases, the temperature of the body falls more or less suddenly *after death*. Yet in some cases when the temperature has previously been but slightly raised as well as more especially in those with already high temperatures, the temperature actually rises for some minutes, or about half an hour after death.

§ 4. The temperature in cholera has attracted attention for a long while, and from the time of the first appearance of the disease in Europe, thermometric observations have been published (*Czermak, Göppert, Lockstädt*). These earlier observations, however, were not worth much. The observations made in the years 1848-52 by *Ross*,

Mair, Reinhardt and *Leubuscher, Roger, Doyère, Briquet* and *Mignot, Hübbenet,* and *Bärensprung,* were more valuable. The most important facts in a diagnostic and prognostic point of view were discovered in the epidemic of 1866. Consult particularly *Charcot* (on the temperature of the rectum in cholera, 'Gazette Médicale,' 1866, 11). *Monti* ('Jahrb. d. Kinderheilk.,' 1866, p. 109) and *Güterbock* ("die Temperaturverhältnisse in der Cholera," 1867, in 'Virchow's Archiv,' xxxviii, 30).

[Particular reference may also be made to the authorities quoted in the notes to pp. 183 and 204. By an accidental omission in the latter place, Mr. E. Nettleship's name does not appear as it should amongst those who contributed largely to our knowledge of the temperature in the cholera epidemic of 1866. Dr. Thudichum's arrangement of some of the observations made in the London Hospital, appears in the 9th 'Report of the Medical Officers of the Privy Council.' For some reason Dr. Thudichum has, however, fixed the *line of normal temperature* at 36·8° C. (98·24° F.), which is a lower average temperature than that generally admitted as normal.—TRANS.]

XXX.—INJURIES OF THE CERVICAL PORTION OF THE SPINAL CORD.

B. Brodie (in 1837, in the 'Medico-Chirurgical Transactions,' xx, 146), first made the remark, as an addendum to Chossat's experiments, that he had observed a considerable rise of temperature in several cases of injury to the spinal marrow; and published his celebrated case of laceration of the lower portion of the cervical cord, in which death occurred after twenty-two hours, after the inspirations had fallen to five or six in the minute, and the thermometer applied between the thigh and the scrotum had marked 43·9° C. (111·02° Fahr.).

Since that time other observations have been made which confirm the influence of injuries of the cervical portion of the spinal cord in producing enormous elevations of temperature, by *Billroth* ('Langenbeck's Archiv,' 1862, rise of temperature to 42·2° C. (107·96° Fahr.); *Quincke* ('Berliner klinische Wochenschrift,' 1869, No. 29. Two cases with temperature of 43·4° and 43·6° C. = 110·12° and 110·48° Fahr.). *Weber* in London ('Transact. of the Clinical Society,' vol. i (1868), two cases, one with temperature

of 44° C. = 111·2° Fahr. ; the other with a post-mortem temperature of 43·3° C. = 109·94° Fahr.). *Fischer* ('Centralblatt,' 1869,
p. 259 ; a rise to 42·9° C. = 109·22° Fahr.).

On the other hand, the latter has observed two cases of injuries
of the cervical portion of the spinal cord with a diminution of temperature in one case to 34° C. (= 93·2° Fahr.), in the rectum, in the
other to 30·2° C. (= 86·36° Fahr.) in the axilla.

[See also *Binz* on alcohol in paralytic fever in the 'Practitioner,'
July, 1870, and a paper on the temperature of shock in surgical
cases by W. W. Wagstaffe, F.R.C.S., 'St. Thomas's Hospital
Reports,' vol. i, new series, p. 466, where (*inter alia*), a case is
given of fracture and dislocation of sixth cervical vertebra, which
died after forty-eight hours, when temperatures of 92·3° Fahr. on
admission, and 81·75° Fahr. (forty-five hours after injury) were
recorded. See also a paper by Dr. Frederic Churchill in the same
volume on shock and visceral lesions. Compare also remarks on
injuries of the nervous system at pages 145, &c.—TRANS.]

XXXI.—NEUROSES.

Uncomplicated neuroses, whether evincing their presence in
psychical, sensitive, or motorial functions, do not, as a rule, exhibit
any alteration of temperature at all, whether they are recently developed or long existing, or extremely chronic, or, at all events, the
alterations of temperature are very inconsiderable.

The following exceptions must be made :

(*a*) Sometimes intermittent neuroses are developed under malarious influences, and in their attacks there may be an elevation of
temperature.

(*b*) The hysterical neuroses, in which elevations of temperature
even to excessive heights may occur, like every other possible symptom, to all appearance without any motive at all.

(*c*) Those affections which we may designate as vaso-motor neuroses, which are by no means thoroughly understood as yet! In
these cases also there may be alterations of temperature.

In psychical neuroses, indeed, there is generally no particular
alteration of temperature to be observed, unless it is produced by
intercurrent corporeal affections. Yet a rather subnormal temperature may be constantly observed in many insane persons (Geistes-

kranken), and in others again moderate and apparently objectless elevations of temperature are sometimes seen which for the most part scarcely reach the limits of fever. In cases of extreme inanition, exposed to great external cold, the temperature of the insane may also sink in a most extraordinary manner. See the remarkable case by *Löwenhardt* already quoted on page 204. On the other hand, *Westphal* has published observations (in 'Griesinger's Archiv für Psychiatrie,' i, 337), according to which very considerable elevations of temperature occurred in an intercurrent manner in paralytic lunatics. However, they occurred along with epileptic and apoplectic attacks; but Westphal implies that they had no relation to the muscular spasms or their intensity, and even when the muscular movements were very slight they occurred, and sometimes when these were altogether absent, and also that the epileptic attacks in themselves caused no very special elevation of temperature. He believes just as little in the dependence of the elevated temperature on the generally co-existent acute affections of the respiratory organs, since the latter are by no means always present in the attacks with elevated temperature. [The observations of *Dr. T. S. Clouston* in the 'Journal of Mental Science,' 'Edinburgh Medical Journal,' and elsewhere, of which there is a very good abstract in the New Sydenham Society's 'Year Book' for 1863, p. 110, would seem to show that tuberculosis is present in a large number of cases of insanity.]

It is also quite proper to note, as only apparent exceptions—where there are latent processes going on in a case in which, at the same time, only the neurosis is to be recognised, and deviations of temperature result; or where complications interrupt the quiet course of a neurotic affection, and although by no means visible, constantly affect the temperature. On the other hand, there is a very peculiar symptom to which I first drew attention, although it has since been confirmed by several observers (*Billroth, Leyden, Elmier, Ferber, Erb, Quincke*, and *Monti*); namely, that in the last stage of fatal neuroses, and more particularly in *Tetanus*, although met with in very many other disorders of the nerve-centres (of the brain), the temperature begins to rise, and rises in the briefest space of time to extraordinary heights; to heights, indeed, which are only exceptionally reached in diseases which are of distinctly febrile origin (sometimes to 43° C. (109·4° Fahr.), or even to above 44° C. (111·2° Fahr.) and in one case of tetanus to 44·75° C. (112·55° Fahr.), which is usually succeeded by a still further post-mortem rise of temperature amounting to a few tenths of a degree. Herr Hofrath *Unterberger*, Professor of Veterinary Surgery in Dorpat, has informed me in a letter, that he has observed temperatures of above 42° C. (107·6° Fahr.), in fatal cases of tetanus in horses.

These facts, taken in conjunction with the equally extraordinary high temperatures which are observed in tissue changes of the brain and upper part of the spinal cord, appear to show as has been adduced already (pp. 150 and 195) that there are, apparently, moderating centres or apparatus in the brain, the paralysis of which is succeeded by a morbidly increased action of the processes which produce warmth.

This observation is of practical importance, because it indicates that any considerable elevation of temperature in patients suffering from neuroses, when no particular reason can be assigned for the fever which is developed, affords the worst possible prognosis.

My own publications on this behaviour of the temperature may be found in the 'Archiv der Heilkunde' for 1861, ii, 547; 1862, iii, 175; and 1864, v, 205; and those of *Erb* in the 'Deutsch. Archiv für klinische Medicin,' 1866, i, 175.

[In addition to the author's remarks on neuroses, I may just remind the reader of the remarks made at pp. 106—145, &c., 195 and the note to p. 225. In studying the temperature in neuroses, we have, of course, to eliminate the influence upon temperature of the primary cause of the neurosis; thus, for instance, in most of the *fatal* cases of *chorea*, this symptom supervenes upon acute rheumatism or scarlet fever, whilst in most of the cases which *recover* the ætiology is obscure or utterly unknown. Of the latter class of cases, *Dr. Finlayson* states that in a girl aged 9¼ suffering from chorea, the average of six observations of morning temperature was 99·01° Fahr. (37·22° C.) in the rectum, whilst the average evening temperature of eleven observations was 103·21° Fahr. (39·56° C.). In a boy aged 10½ the average of eleven *morning* observations was 99·44° Fahr. (37·46° C.) ; and that of thirteen evening temperatures was 98·93° Fahr. (37·18° C.). *H. Roger* also states that in chorea there is little or no alteration of temperature. *Dr. Long Fox* ('Med. Times and Gazette,' 1870), says the temperatures in chorea are seldom over 99° Fahr., often less, or below normal. I myself have often observed sub-normal temperatures (97° and 96° Fahr. = 36·1° and 35·6° C.), in feeble children suffering from the common forms of chorea ; whilst in two cases supervening on acute rheumatism, I observed temperatures of 105° and 106° Fahr. for two or three days preceding death (= 40·5° and 41·2° C.).

In epileptic attacks also, the co-existence of tubercular or syphilitic disease must greatly affect the temperature. Refer also to *Binz* on "Alcohol in Paralytic Fever," in the 'Practitioner' for July. I am indebted to Mr. Semple for an account of a case of general paralysis, in which the temperature was perfectly normal.—TRANS.]

XXXII.—CHRONIC DISORDERS OF THE BLOOD, OF THE TISSUES, AND OF SECRETIONS.

Very many changes of essentially chronic course, affecting the composition of the blood, and the formation of tissues and secretions, may influence the course of the temperature. But the true relations of the former to the latter are by no means exactly or entirely determined. Sometimes the temperature is found normal all through the course of the disease; whilst at other times there are more or less considerable elevations of temperature, which very commonly belong to intercurrent acute processes ; sometimes chronic fever of various kinds is met with, or on the contrary, the temperature may be persistently subnormal. Even when these chronic diseases end fatally, their closing course may exhibit numerous differences.

Jochmann (in his 'Observations on the Temperature of the Body in Chronic Febrile Diseases,' published in 1853) has published a number of facts, especially taken from thermometric observations in phthisical patients, and has determined several types of chronic fever.

It may be sufficient for our purpose to lay special stress upon the following empirical discoveries relating to the course of the temperature in chronic diseases affecting the blood, nutrition, and secretion.

§ 1. An abnormally low temperature is very commonly met with in conditions of inanition, and such temperatures are more particularly met with during the last days of life in a great many chronic conditions which are associated with marasmus, although marasmus in itself by no means excludes the possibility of an elevated temperature.

Inasmuch as inanition is so commonly both a sequel and a concomitant of very many chronic diseases, the course of the temperature may be modified by it in very many ways. Not only does it very frequently depress the temperature persistently, and sometimes also without any recognisable reason, depress it even to the extent of collapse; but in conditions of inanition, any considerable or extreme cooling of the body, deprivations of nourishment, muscular exertions, perspirations, vomiting, or diarrhœa, and losses of blood, have generally a very unusual (ungleich) effect in considerably lowering the temperature, because the diminished production of heat in these cases is no longer able to compensate and conceal the effect of the loss of warmth. This is especially noticeable when the fatal end is approaching. The decrease of temperature in emaciated children just before death is very great, and is especially to be noted in children who are subjects of luetic (syphilitic) marasmus whilst at the breast.

In one such case, which was recently under my care, the temperature began to be subnormal six days before death, and by a gradual process of sinking it fell at last to 25° C. ($=77^\circ$ F.) as measured in the rectum. In another case of common atrophia infantum (marasmus) it was only $28\cdot6^\circ$ C. ($83\cdot48^\circ$ F.).

§ 2. According to the observations of *H. Roger*, the temperature (at least in the axilla) is extraordinarily diminished in congenital induration of the areolar tissue (sclerema of new-born children). He says that the average of twenty-nine cases was only 31° C. ($87\cdot8^\circ$ F.), and in seven cases was less than 26° C. ($78\cdot8^\circ$ F.).[1] As regards this behaviour, *Bärensprung* reminds us of the effects of experiments artificially preventing the action of the skin [see page 143].

§ 3. It has been thought that thermometry might afford an aid to diagnosis in distinguishing tubercular and non-tubercular phthisis [see notes to p. 412], or, perhaps it is better to say, to enable us to determine the presence or absence of tubercles in a phthisical patient, even in life.

This hope is, for the most part at least, illusory. As the same meaning is not always now-a-days attached to the word tubercles, it may not be superfluous to express my meaning in the following propositions :

(*a*) The existence of cheesy (caseous) deposits cannot in any way, and still less in phthisical patients, be recognised by any thermometric peculiarity.

[1] I have slightly altered the text in accordance with Roger's own statement. —[TRANS.]

(*b*) Thermometry only affords us data for detecting the development of phthisis from caseous pneumonia, when the observations were commenced whilst the pneumonia was still recent, and when they are continued throughout the period of transition. The suspicions that the relics (Reste) of the pneumonia are undergoing casefaction may be justified by the persistence of high temperatures at the end of the fastigium of a remittent type, and by considerable elevations alternating with low temperatures.

(*c*) All the symptoms of hectic fever, whether they present themselves in the form of moderate febrile movements, or of a remittent, subcontinuous, or fragmentary continuous fever, may, however, be induced simply by chronic suppurative bronchitis, with progressive dilatation of the bronchi, peribronchitis, chronic pneumonias, repeated lobular and vesicular pneumonias without any casefaction, and also without any development of granular tubercles. And just in the same manner the fatal termination of non-tubercular phthisis may be heralded either by a fall or a rise of temperature; and the latter may succeed in a zig-zag, continuous, or sharply-peaked pattern.

(*d*) The mere presence of sparse, or even tolerably numerous tubercle-granules in the lungs, pleura, spleen, or liver, is absolutely devoid of effect on the course of the temperature.

(*e*) It is only when extraordinarily numerous and closely studded miliary tubercles are rapidly deposited, that we sometimes meet with a modification of the course of the temperature in phthisical persons; which then approximates closely to the course it is accustomed to take in what is (relatively) called primary miliary tuberculosis. The same modification may, however, be brought about by complications of other kinds (for example, protracted pneumonia).

(*f*) However, very copious deposits of miliary tubercles in the peritoneum, and especially the development of granular meningitis, may affect the course of the fever in phthisical patients.

§ 4. It is a peculiarity of cancer cases that elevated temperatures are comparatively rare, and that the temperature generally maintains itself on a normal, or even subnormal plane, which, however, by no means precludes the occurrence of high temperatures through intercurrent complications, or at the close of the disease. But fever temperatures of long duration are at least rare in cancer patients.

[*Dr. Finlayson* (loc. cit.) states that he made observations of temperature in cancer of the uterus and ovary in a woman, aged forty seven, and found in eight observations of morning temperature an average of 98·47° F. (36·92° C.) in the vagina, and in seven observations of evening temperature (also in vagina) an average of 98·51° F. (36·95° C.), which is decidedly sub-normal.

He also refers to observations by *Da Costa* on the same subject in the 'American Journal of Medical Sciences,' vol. liii, p. 156, Philadelphia, 1867.

I am indebted to Dr. E. B. Baxter for notes of the temperature of a case of medullary cancer of the liver in a patient of Dr. Garrod's in King's College Hospital, in which the temperatures on the six last days of life were as follows:

> 1st day, *M.*, 99·5° F.; *E.*, 100·0 F.
> 2nd „ *M.*, 99·5° F.; *E.*, 98·4 F.
> 3rd „ *M.*, 99·5° F.; *E.*, 99·5° F.
> 4th „ *M.*, 98·2° F.; *E.*, 99·0 F.
> 5th „ *M.*, 97·6° F.; *E.*, 99·4° F.
> 6th „ *M.*, 98·9° F.; *E.*, Died.

The few observations I have myself made of carcinoma of the liver, uterus, and breast, before marasmus had set in, only show very slight elevations of temperature, or none at all; never above 101° F. (38·4°), unless from some complication; whilst I have found sub-normal temperatures with rapid pulse in several cases of advanced cancer, with emaciation. See paragraph 1 of this section.— TRANS.]

§ 5. Chronic cases of heart disease generally exhibit considerable elevations of temperature only when acute attacks supervene. In congenital malformations of the heart connected with cyanosis, such as stenosis of the pulmonary artery [which Dr. Peacock has shown to be the most common cause of cyanosis], sub-normal temperatures are by no means uncommon.

§ 6. In diabetes mellitus (glycosuria) it is quite exceptional to find an abnormally high temperature, whilst it is by no means rare to find it persistently sub-normal; and even the formation of abscesses, pneumonia or pulmonary consumption, very often fail to elevate the temperature of diabetics. [See Dr. B. W. Forster's Remarks in the 'Journal of Anatomy and Physiology;' London, 1869, p. 377.]

§ 7. Jaundice runs its course without elevation of temperature, unless it is of a pernicious kind, and on this account any elevation of temperature in the subjects of jaundice is always ominous.   [The author probably refers to the jaundice of intermittents, and that met with in hepatic abscesses ; or perhaps the word pernicious takes in a wider range, and refers also to the latter stages or complications of cancerous tumours.]

§ 8. Dropsical patients very often have a low axillary temperature; yet rises of temperature frequently occur in such cases.   [Especially if the dropsy be associated with nephritis.]

§ 9. When alterations of temperature occur in chronic diseases, they generally show great variety in their course, even in one and the same case, in the course of time.   Yet sometimes a pretty stationary and even course of temperature may be met with, lasting for not weeks only, but whole months; indeed, I have observed a chronic fever with a perfectly steady and even, though very peculiar, course, extending over a whole year.

§ 10. The commonest behaviour of the temperature in chronic diseases is for it to show great mobility and susceptibility to external influence; and for its daily fluctuations to be rather more considerable, although somewhat disorderly, so that the exacerbations very often begin at an earlier time in the day, and thus frequently approximate to the ranges of slight febrile movements, or actually reach them; and very often, too, whilst the daily remission is not quite normal (it is seldom too low, generally too high, frequently alternating) ; the general temperature moves, so to speak, upon a somewhat higher plane as regards the daily average, than it does in the healthy condition; and besides this, there are occasional rises of considerable amount (not infrequently to over 40° C. = 104° Fahr.), lasting only for a few hours or a few days, and thrusting themselves in after the manner of an ephemera.   This course of temperature may occur under the most varied conditions, and contributes next to nothing to our accurate knowledge of the given cases, only tending to show that the condition is not a normal one.

§ 11. Whilst the morning temperatures are normal or very nearly so, or, perhaps, even subnormal; the temperature in the evening hours may rise more or less considerably, even as much as some 4° to 6° C. = 7·2° to 10·8° Fahr., in which case it is common enough to find collapse temperatures alternating with highly febrile elevations (a course resembling that of an intermittent.) This kind of course may last for a long time with tolerable regularity, unless, indeed, the extent of the daily excursion is too great, and the breadth of the exacerbation too striking. Sometimes two exacerbations may occur in one day, separated by a perfectly normal temperature, or one nearly normal, and one of these exacerbations may be much more severe than the other (like a duplex quotidian.) Sometimes when there is only a single daily exacerbation, a stronger and a weaker one alternate very regularly with each other from day to day; less commonly, the exacerbation is altogether absent on the alternate days (tertian rhythm); or still wider intervals may occur (quartan and sextan rhythms.)

In the latter sprawling kind of return, the exacerbation in many cases no longer keeps its appointed day with punctuality, but the course imperceptibly merges into one with irregularly repeating elevations of temperature of an ephemeral type.

Such a course of chronic fever, resembling that of an intermittent, is tolerably common, but its determining causes and conditions cannot be formulated. It occurs in chronic suppurations and phthisical conditions, although not as the usual type of fever in these. It occurs also in diseases of an obscure sort, in which we sometimes find this course of fever lasting for months, associated with some enlargement (intumescence) of internal organs, and no other demonstrable morbid symptoms; in such cases recovery may occur, or before their fatal end such farther developments of disease occur, with alterations of the fever type, that the relations of the intermitting course of temperature to the original disease still remain unexplained. It is, however, worthy of note, that *quinine* and in a higher degree *arsenic*, have an indubitable influence upon the course of the chronic fever. The attacks become less severe and sometimes are even completely suppressed.

[Reference may also be made to the report of Drs. Murchison, Symes Thomson, and H. Weber, to the Clinical Society, on the "Value of Quinine in Pyrexia," vol. iii of the Clinical Society's 'Transactions,' pp. 201—238, which besides including acute diseases such as typhus, typhoid and scarlet fever, pneumonia, measles, erysipelas, and rheumatic fever, includes a number of cases of phthisis. The reporters state that the effect of the quinine in these was generally " to lower the temperature, pulse, and respiration, to mitigate the severity of the paroxysms, and often to postpone the attack of the following day, and lessen its severity. The effect of the quinine rarely lasted more than thirty-six hours; it was sometimes apparent in half an hour after the dose, but in other instances was not observed for three or four hours, and was most marked when given at the end of the attack." Other notices of quinine will be found at pp. 139 and 325.—TRANS.].

§ 12. Chronic fever very often assumes a *remittent* type, in which the temperature during the remissions is usually only a little above the limits of slight febrile movement, whilst during the exacerbations it amounts to as much as 39·5° to 40° C. (103·1° to 104° F.), or even more. The remissions usually occur early in the morning, and the exacerbations in the afternoon and evening hours. Yet it is not uncommon to find the highest temperatures at noon, or for two exacerbations to occur, one at mid-day and the other usually less severe at midnight. This course of temperature, however, seldom lasts long, or persists with even tolerable steadiness. It soon slides into some other type, either more dangerous or less severe. Even in itself it appears to work very prejudicially and exhaustively. It is found in chronic suppurations, phthisical affections, and large fluid exudations, and is more particularly related to the rapid progress, relapses, and complications of the essential process.

§ 13. Chronic fever may sometimes very closely resemble the *continuous* type. The temperature in such a case is generally rather high, or, indeed, very high. Such a fever, particularly when there are very high temperatures, produces rapid consumption, and, therefore, burns too fiercely to last long. It therefore either speedily moderates and merges into other types, or it quickly pulls the patient down. It is met with in intercurrent relapses and complications, and at the conclusion of fatally ending chronic diseases.

§ 14. Intercurrent relapse may occur in any form of chronic fever, and a repetition of such an evil is far from rare. It is most commonly seen when the state of the temperature has previously been very high. After the collapse the temperature sometimes quickly rises again to the former level, or sometimes this occurs very slowly; sometimes also collapse may set in without the preceding temperature having been very high, and towards the fatal close of a chronic disease it is very common to meet with repeated falls of temperature below the normal.

§ 15. Those almost critical downfalls of temperature which sometimes occur after a remittent or continuous course of chronic fever have many points of resemblance to collapse, especially when the crisis is immediately preceded by a considerable rise of temperature (Perturbatio critica). But the downfall does not happen so rapidly as in collapse, and does not go down so low as in that, only reaching the normal or a little below it. These defervescences are sometimes really favorable, and in such cases sometimes show that the effect of a complication has ceased. In the majority of cases they are, however, deceptive pseudo-crises, and after remaining normal for a few days the temperature again rises rather slowly or suddenly.

§ 16. Very great irregularities are displayed by the course of the temperature during the course of many chronic diseases; rude and apparently objectless (unmotivirte) fluctuations occur; and although very considerable rise of temperature is always a symptom worthy of attention, no hopes must be based upon the occurrence of lower temperatures, partly because they are often transient, and partly because the disease may go on to a fatal termination with the diminished temperature. The more abrupt the changes of temperature the less are they to be trusted.

§ 17. Towards the fatal close of chronic diseases, and in the death agony, the course of the temperature may be widely different in different cases, which need not surprise us, since death may be brought about in so many different ways in chronic diseases, and very often with only slight connection with the essential process.[1]

---

[1] As, for instance, death in cancer may happen (1) from hæmorrhage; (2) nervous exhaustion (as when pain has become unbearable); (3) starvation, either immediate, from direct pressure on thoracic duct, or direct interference with organs essential to digestion; or mediate by the enormous growth of the tumour diverting other supplies; (4) by asphyxia, when it presses upon or invades the air-passages; (5) by septic and pyæmic processes being induced; (6) by invading organs whose integrity is essential to life, as the lungs, for example, or the nervous centres, and perhaps in other ways.—[TRANS.]

As a general rule, the temperature in chronic diseases more often falls than rises before death; sometimes it falls only a little, and rather in comparison with previous heights; and in other cases very considerably, indeed, very often to extraordinarily low degrees, as in marasmus, particularly the marasmus of children, that of the insane, and luetic marasmus (syphilitic atrophy) as has been already mentioned (p. 428).

§ 18. The opposite conditions or final elevations of temperature do, however, occur. The temperature which had before been normal or but slightly raised, begins to rise a short time before death, and this increase of heat which begins slowly and moderately may at a later period become more rapid and more considerable; in from twelve to thirty hours a height of from $40°$—$41°$ ($104°$ to $105.8°$ Fahr.) or more may be reached; *terminal fever.*

Sometimes a cause for this rise of temperature can be found in some special circumstances affecting the dying patient—a terminal erysipelas, parotitis, meningitis, or pneumonia, but in very many cases the real cause of these final elevations of temperature remains undiscovered.

CHAPTER XIII.

ON THE INFLUENCE OF ALTERATIONS OF TEMPERATURE UPON THE SYSTEM.

§ 1. Every one must agree that any considerable change in temperature must produce more or less effect upon the general system and its separate component parts and their functions, upon the secretions and upon the nutrition of parenchymatous tissues. It has long been acknowledged that both the presence and degree of fever in a given case affect the subjective sensations of the patient and the frequency of both the pulse and the respiration, as well as causing changes in the patient's urine and perspiration; and, still further, that consumption may be produced by fever.

As regards the physiological aspects of the question, it has been demonstrated experimentally that alterations of temperature produce remarkable effects upon the irritability of muscles and nerves. Consult *Eckhard* ('Zeitschrift für rat. Medicin,' 1850, x, 165); *Calliburcès* ('Comptes rend.,' xlv, 1095, and xlvii, 638); *J. Rosenthal* ('Allg. med. Centralz.,' 1859, 761); *Harless* ('Zeitschrift für rat. Med.,' 1860, cviii, 122); *Schelske* ('Ueber die Veränderungen der Erregbarkeit durch die Wärme,' 1860); *Afanasieff* ('Reichert's Archiv,' 1865, 691).

[See also, on kindred subjects, the following memoirs, &c. :— *Chmoutevitch, J.* ("Sur l'influence de la chaleur sur le travail mécanique du muscle de la granouillo," 'Révue Médicale,' 1867 (2), p. 491); *M. Andral* (ibid.), 1869 (2), p. 716); *J. Moutier* (" Mém. sur la théorie mécanique de la chaleur," ('Ann. de Chimie, &c.,' tom. xiv (4me série), p. 247); *Hirn* (" Mémoires sur la Thermodynamique" (ibid., tom. x (4me sér.), p. 32, tom. xi, p. 5); *Berthelot* (several papers in ibid., tom. xviii, 5—196, entitled "Nouvelles recherches du themochemie"); MM. *A.* and *P. Dupré* (five memoirs, " Sur la Théorie mécanique de la chaleur," ibid., tom. ii (4me série),

p. 185, tom. iii, p. 76, tom. iv, p. 426, tom. vi, p. 274, tom. vii, pp. 236, 406, tom. xi, p. 194, tom. xiv, p. 64) ; *Tscheschichin* ("Zur Lehre von der thierische Wärme," 'Reichert's Archiv," 1866, p. 151); *Schiffer, Dr. Julius* (Berlin), ('Ueber die Wärmbildung erstarrender Muskeln," ibid., 1868, p. 442) ; *E. Cyon* ('Der Einfluss der Temperatur veränderungen auf Zahl u. s. w. der Herzschläge," 'Arbeiten aus d. phys. Anstalt zu Leipzig, von J. 1866, Leipzig, 1867, pp. 77—127) ; *Cavagnés* ("Versuch über die Tastempfindlichkeit," 'Ann. Univers.,' cci, p. 268, Agosto, 1867, quoted in 'Schmidt's Jahrbücher,' 1868, Bd. 137, p. 157) ; and Supplemental Bibliography at end.—TRANS.]

E. Cyon's work is still more closely connected with clinical experiences, since it treats " on the influence of changes of temperature on the number, duration, and strength of the beats of the heart" ('Berichte über die Verhandlungen der k. sächs Gesellschaft der Wissenschaften,' 1866, xviii, 258 ff.), for by means of an ingenious apparatus he studied the effects of serum, at various temperatures, circulating by means of glass tubes through the heart of a frog separated from the body of the animal. The results of gradually rising temperatures are of special interest, for they first produced a slow increase in the number of the cardiac contractions, but when the rise of temperature was carried further there was observed a sudden decrease in the number of contractions, and they began to be irregular, till finally they ceased altogether; and, besides, the extent (Umfang) of the contractions of the heart was equally increased at the beginning of the experiment, but always diminished again, whilst the number of the beats increased for a greater length of time, which seems to indicate that the heart is best able to deal with the blood-stream at certain temperatures only. Cyon's experiments on sudden changes of temperature are, on the other hand, not applicable to pathology, since the temperature never takes such sudden plunges in actual disease.

Even in these experiments, however, it was noticed that all hearts did not behave exactly alike under similar circumstances, for the definite effects named occurred in some hearts with a rather low temperature, and in others with a much higher one.[1] How much more must these individual differences make themselves felt in pathological cases! Indeed, it is easily conceivable that the conditions in diseased human beings are essentially far more involved and com-

[1] See also 'Biennial Retrospect' (New Sydenham Society) for 1867-8, p. 11.

plicated than in an experiment which strives to represent the phenomenon in its full and uncomplicated simplicity.

Thus, in morbid conditions, the varied operations and effects
must be studied within somewhat narrow ranges of temperature degrees, both as regards the varied influence of suddenly or slowly
occurring alterations of these, as well as of their longer or shorter
duration.

It must further be very important whether the altered temperature in a given case depends on a disorder of heat-production or from
altered giving off of heat, or how far it may depend on both these
combined. The idiosyncrasies of the patient must also concur in the
production of these effects, and peculiarities in his structure, which,
in any case, will probably differ quite as much as the individual dis-
positions of extirpated frogs' hearts do from one another. More especially must the co-operation of pathological changes in the organs of
the body and in the secretions—and particularly in many forms of disease, the co-operation of the original cause of the disease itself, and
in all, the combined influence of factors which cannot be estimated,
and of the most widely differing influences during the course of the
disease—be reckoned up and eliminated, if we want to estimate the
influence of altered temperatures on the behaviour of the organism
and its several members, in all its simplicity and completeness
(Reinheit). Such results are out of our power.

If we only represent to ourselves in this manner the uncertainty
attending such a determination in special cases, we are led to doubt
even the possibility of an approximative determination of the influence of an abnormal temperature on the system or its members in
any particular case.

§ 2. Nevertheless, the attempts made by Liebermeister, are none
the less valuable on this account, to determine at any rate the effects
of febrile rise of temperature ('Deutsches Archiv für klin. Medicin,' i,
298, ff.). He has, very properly, greatly simplified the question by following out more particularly the effects of only highly febrile degrees
of temperature, and he appears to imagine that there is a sort of individual sliding (wechselnde) scale of elevated temperature at which the
unfavorable influence begins in different diseases. He particularly believes in the malignity of many attacks of disease, certain wide-spread
processes destructive to tissues, many disorders in the functions of the
central organs of the nervous system, the occurrence of multiple

hæmorrhages in severe febrile diseases, and many of the shapes assumed by local processes, to be properly assumed as the results of high febrile temperatures; and he has adduced a great many observations of his own, and quoted copiously from others, in support of his views.

Unless I deceive myself, his views have met with nothing but applause, and the recent and extending preference for the cold-water treatment of febrile disease (which is certainly reasonable) is based in great part on this exposition of the dangers of high degrees of temperature, as, on the other hand, the favorable results of this therapeutic method have afforded strong support to the opinion as to the injurious effects of fever.

§ 3. But however we may be inclined to admit that alterations of temperature *may* exert a considerable influence on the system and its several parts, we cannot on this account exclude from view the facts, which are not isolated, but accumulated, which teach us that in general this effect is far from being clearly manifested. The conviction is forced on us that there must be regulators (Einrichtungen) in the system which are able to paralyse and compensate more or less completely the influence of an abnormal temperature, as well as the influence of many other disturbing forces, up to a certain point at least. In this point of view (as also in many others) no disease is more instructive than relapsing fever, in which not only enormous, but in nowise transient, extremes of temperature, which in any other case would be infallibly fatal, are borne without much injury or distress; in which also not only the extremest and most sudden changes of temperature leave scarcely a trace behind, but in which, moreover, the very same individual during the insignificant and brief intermediate rise of temperature in the apyretic stage exhibits severe brain symptoms, and disordered sensations, &c., whilst, on the other hand, in the severe paroxysm with abrupt rise of temperature amounting to from $4°$ to $6°$ C. ($7 \cdot 2°$ to $10 \cdot 8°$ F.), and sudden falls of temperature of some $5°$ to $7°$ C. ($9°$ to $12 \cdot 6°$ F.), the patient is actually far less affected.

§ 4. The organs and parts of the body which *may* be influenced in their functions, and in the degree of their nutrition, by alterations of temperature, are, without doubt, very numerous; or rather, there seems to be no part of the body which is not sometimes affected in this way.

The following are some of the commonest and most striking results of this effect in different parts, under different circumstances :

(a) On the *general nervous system* : although it must not be forgotten how susceptible the nervous system is to manifold processes and influences, and what the degree of its impressibility is in different individuals. On this account the influence of the temperature in special cases can least of all be conclusively demonstrated by mere functional disorders of the brain or the nerves. This much is certain, that the brain functions may continue in all their integrity at any degree of temperature which is compatible with life, at least so long as increased exertions are not demanded from them. In hyperpyretic temperatures, such as occur shortly before and in the death agony, there is seldom wanting a certain strangeness (Benommenheit) and confusion of manner (Verwirrung); only in such cases the original cause of the brain disorder must not be sought for only in the temperature, but generally also in numerous and extensive lesions of those organs. But once now and then restlessness, headache, sleeplessness, startling dreams, and sometimes even delirium, may result from the height of the fever, but the cases are rare in which these symptoms can be attributed solely to this circumstance.

(b) *On the movements of the heart.*—Although quite independent of any local cardiac disease, there are many other subordinate influences, and the contrast of the frequency, as well as their potency, with the degree of temperature, is so common that it is met with at some time or another in almost every case.

None the less must we admit that there are certain relations between the behaviour of the pulse and the temperature. It is particularly certain that with high febrile temperatures we no longer meet with quiet and satisfactory contractions of the heart, but, quite otherwise, that they generally not only become more frequent, but insufficient, and generally irregular. However, it is by no means certainly determined that the cardiac contractions are determined by the temperature; it is rather more common to find that the changes in the pulse have slightly preceded the alterations of temperature, and, as it were, announced the occurrence of the latter.

(c) *In the fulness of the capillaries,* for since their behaviour reacts upon the giving off of warmth, and, therefore, has great influence on the degree of temperature, their relations are at least somewhat complicated.

(*d*) *On the frequency of the respirations,* of which, however, the same may be said as about the heart's contraction, with this super-added, that in almost all severe diseases it is tolerably common for local disorders to develop themselves in the organs of respiration, which produces an effect upon the frequency of respiration.

(*e*) *On the tongue.*—Although the extremest degrees of dryness are very often observed with normal temperatures, and without any local affection of the cavity of the mouth.[1]

(*f*) *On the digestive faculty.*—Although through the frequency with which gastric catarrh sets in in almost all diseases, the direct influence of the temperature on digestion is by no means a simple question.

(*g*) *On the integrity of the functions of the muscles* (functions beeinträchtigung), which may, however, have many other causes affecting it.

(*h*) *On the secretions,* especially that of urine; although the relations of this to the changes of temperature are far from being accurately determined as yet.[2]

(*i*) *On the composition of the blood,* and especially in the diminu-tion of its red corpuscles, which, however, may take place through exudations and deprivation of nourishment.

(*k*) *In the tendency to extravasations and transudations,* and to the *aggregation of deposits,* which are, indeed, every one of them possible effects of the most widely differing factors.

(*l*) On extensive *parenchymatous* processes of a destructive nature (acute fatty degeneration), although, indeed, this too may occur without any considerable alterations of temperature (as in poisoning by phosphorus).

(*m*) *On the general nutrition of the body;* on its arrest, on its

---

[1] It is almost superfluous to remind the reader that dryness of the tongue may be produced (*a*) by breathing through the mouth instead of the nose, as in sleep, especially when the surrounding air is deficient in humidity; (*b*) from defective water supply, which often happens in bad nursing; indeed, I believe, that if the patient be liberally supplied with drinks, extreme degrees (such as sordes) of dryness of the tongue are seldom met with.   (*c*) From the effect of certain medicines, or tonic agents.   (Opiates are often credited with this, yet, in common with Graves and Trousseau, I have often seen the tongue grow moister and cooler under their use.)   (*d*) From local affections of the mucous membrane, and perhaps other causes.—[TRANS.].

[2] Although Professor *Parkes* has ably led the way in researches of this nature.

diminution; although, indeed, consumption or wasting never appears to be produced purely by fever, or by collapse; and the share of the other morbid processes of the disease in the diminished nutrition can as little be calculated as the influence of the temperature upon it.

§ 5. If one tests a very large number of separate observations it becomes impossible to escape the following conclusions:

(*a*) When the *changes of temperature are moderate,* either in a rising or falling direction, nothing can be detected in the system which need necessarily be attributed to the abnormal temperature or which may not often enough occur without any such alteration of temperature.

Yet even in such cases it rather seems that the subjective feelings, the general turgescence, and the aspect of the patient dependent upon it, the faculty of digestion, the free and perfect co-ordination of the functions of the brain and of the muscles, the quantity and quality of the urine, and, perhaps, of other secretions also, are simultaneously affected by the change of temperature. These effects generally appear much more evident when the system at the same time is called upon to make any considerable effort.

(*b*) *When the temperature rises abruptly* from normal or almost normal degrees to considerable heights, it is very common to meet with striking nervous and other functional disorders; yet in not a few cases not the slightest symptom of these is observed, and the patient and those around him have not the slightest suspicion of the processes going on, which can only be recognised at such a time by thermometric observation.

It is also remarkable that even in the cases when the abrupt rise of temperature is accompanied with many and severe symptoms, it is uncommonly rare to find delirium associated with them, whilst headache, absence of mind, fainting, or even sopor, are by no means rare.

(*c*) *Even rather considerable elevations of temperature, when they alternate with daily remissions of tolerable extent,* may last for a considerable time without being accompanied at the moment by any particular phenomena, dependent (with any probability) simply upon the anomaly of the temperature.

The functional disorders which display themselves at such a time are, at least extremely often, by no means parallel with the height of the exacerbations, and in such cases at least the perhaps immediate effects of the change of temperature are dominated by the influence of the primary cause of the illness and the manifold changes in various organs which are set up by the disease itself. This, however, does not preclude even remitting febrile temperatures having their share in impoverishing the blood, in the alteration of secretions, and in diminished nutrition. These results appear, however, to be far more dependent upon the duration than upon the intensity of the remittent febrile course.

(*d*) *In sub-continuous and continuous elevations of temperature of considerable amount* there are either so many other serious conditions present that it would be inappropriate to attribute special functional phenomena and consecutive disorders of tissues to the increased temperature, or they are special obscure cases, which cannot well be made use of as bases for general conclusions, or as illustrative arguments.

In any case there is no particular morbid symptom which can be shown to display anything approaching to a regular parallelism with the degrees of temperature, or of which it can justly be said that it must infallibly occur with certain degrees of temperature. But, again, this by no means precludes the anomalies of temperature from being followed either directly or mediately by certain subsequent results.

(*e*) *But it is undeniable that there is a definite relation between the temperature and the event of death,* inasmuch as the continuance of life is clearly incompatible with certain heights of temperature, although the reason is certainly unknown, and can scarcely be that propounded by *Weikart* ('Archiv der Heilk.,' iv, 193), who mentions that fibrine begins to be separated from the blood at certain high degrees of temperatures. Even in this respect relapsing fever has taught us that the limits of bearable temperature must be extended further than was at one time believed to be possible.

(*f*) *With a fall of temperature from high degrees to normal or below it,* we generally find remarkable anomalies of function, under circumstances which prove by no rise unfavorable to the patient, and it may be in the direct road to recovery. In exanthematous typhus the delirium often lasts some days after the fever, and even in abdominal typhus the greatest disturbance of the brain sometimes coincides with the period when the temperature has decidedly taken a descending direction. In pneumonias the severe functional disorders of the brain, as well as delirium, occur far more frequently *after* the maximum of the temperature has been attained, when the temperature is quickly falling, or has again become normal, rather than at the height of the fever.   And the same is true of any other kind of disease.

But just as frequently very abrupt downfalls of temperature occur in which neither the functions of the brain nor those of any other organ appear to be disturbed in any way.

(*g*) *In subnormal temperatures* there is, indeed, generally, an influence on the turgescence of the surface of the body [washerwoman's hand of cholera], and, therefore, not to be overlooked in the aspect of the face.   Other parts of the body also may be disturbed in their functions.   But in any considerable downfall of temperature the circumstances of the case are always so complicated and intricate, that it appears impossible to attribute the symptoms simply to the decrease of temperature.

APPENDIX No. I.

Note to pages 105 *and* 115, *on the Influence of Rest and Work, and the Influence of Atmospheric Pressure, on Temperature.*

Lortet has made very interesting observations on variations of the temperature in conditions of rest, and of muscular movement, on level ground and on high mountains, and has lately published them in the 'Comptes Rendus' (1869, p. 709, séance pour 20 Sept.). The temperatures were taken under the tongue.

In Lyons (200 mètres = 218¾ feet elevation), with an atmospheric temperature of 22·7° C. (72·86° Fahr.), the temperature during rest was 36·4° C. (97·52° Fahr.), whilst with bodily exercise it was only 36·2° C. (97·16° Fahr.). On the other hand, *Lortet* found in two ascents of Mount Blanc on the 17th and 26th of August, 1869, the temperature affected as shown in the table on page 446.

No doubt the diminished chemical processes resulting from the rarefaction of the atmosphere were quite sufficient during bodily rest to maintain a normal temperature. But as soon as exertions were made, and the chemical forces had to resolve themselves into motion, they no longer sufficed to produce the warmth which is necessary for the maintenance of the normal temperature. The temperature suddenly sank several degrees, even as much as nearly 5° C. (9° Fahr.). But directly a few minutes' rest intervened the chemical forces again produced warmth, and the temperature quickly began to rise to normal again. On the summit of Mont Blanc, however, it required half an hour's rest before the temperature regained its normal height.

During digestion, on the other hand, this discrepancy between rest and movement was no longer remarkable. In spite of continued exertion, the temperature remained between 36° and 37° C. (96·8° and 98·6° Fahr.), and, indeed, reached as much as 37·3° C. (99·14° Fahr.) However, the compensatory influence of nourish-

Place	Height in Metres.	Height in English yds.	Temperature of the air.		Temperature of body whilst resting.		Temperature of body whilst walking.		Temperature of the air.		Temperature of body whilst resting.		Temperature of body whilst walking.	
			Cent.	Fahr.	Cent.	Fahr.	Cent.	Fahr.	Cent.	Fahr.	Cent.	Fahr.	Cent.	Fahr.
Chamounix .	1050	= 1148	+ 10·1°	= 50·18°	36·5°	= 97·7°	36·3°	= 97·34°	+ 12·4°	= 54·32°	37·°	= 98·6	35·3°	= 95·54°
Cascade du Dard .	1500	= 1640	+ 11·2°	= 52·16°	36·4°	= 97·52°	35·7°	= 96·26°	+ 13·4°	= 56·12°	36·3°	= 97·34	34·3°	= 93·74°
Chalet-de-la-Para	1605	= 1755	+ 11·8°	= 53·24°	36·6	= 97·88°	34·8°	= 94·64°	+ 13·6°	= 56·48°	36·3°	= 97·34	34·2°	= 93·56°
Pierre per-duc . .	2049	= 2240	+ 13·2°	= 55·76°	36·5°	= 97·7°	33·3°	= 91·94°	+ 14·1°	= 57·38°	36·4°	= 97·52	33·4	= 92·12°
Grands Mulets . .	3050	= 3336	— 0·3°	= 31·46°	36·5°	= 97·7°	33·1°	= 91·58°	— 1·5	= 29·30°	36·2°	= 97·16°	33·3°	= 91·94°
Grand Plateau . .	3932	= 4300	— 8·2°	= 17·24°	36·3°	= 97·34°	32·8°	= 91·04°	— 6·4	= 20·48°	36·7°	= 98·06°	32·5°	= 90·5°
Bosses du Dromadaire	4556	= 4973	— 10·3°	= 13·46°	36·4°	= 97·52°	32·2°	= 89·96°	— 4·2	= 24·44°	35·7°	= 96·26°	32·3°	= 90·14°
Sommet du Mont Blanc	4810	= 5260	— 9·1°	= 15·62°	36·3°	= 97·34°	32·°	= 89·6°	— 3·4°	= 25·88°	36·6°	= 97·88°	31·8°	= 89·24°

ment was not lasting. An hour after the meal the cooling of the body by exercise recommenced.[1]

APPENDIX No. II.

Table of Thermometric Equivalents, according to the Celsian (or Centigrade), Réaumur's, and Fahrenheit's Scales.

[N.B.—Any numbers not included in the table can be easily converted if once the principle of division of the scales be mastered. The principle of the Centigrade or Celsian thermometer is to divide the space between $32°$ of Fahr., or freezing-point, from which the Centigrade starts, and $212°$ of Fahr., or boiling point, into $100°$. Therefore, every $180°$ Fahr. $= 100°$ C., or every $1°$ C. $= 1·8°$ Fahr.

In Réaumur's thermometer the same space is divided into $80°$ only. Therefore, $1°$ C. $= 1·8°$ Fahr., or $1·25°$ R.; or $1°$ Fahr., $= \frac{5}{9}°$ C. or $\frac{4}{9}°$ R. Therefore, the relation between the degrees of Fahrenheit, Centigrade, and Réaumur, is explained by the numbers 9, 5, 4.

In converting from Fahrenheit into Centigrade or Réaumur we must *first subtract* 32, and then reduce ; whilst in converting *into* Fahrenheit from either Centigrade or Réaumur we must *add* 32 *after* the multiplication and division are completed. The following arbitrary rules may be found convenient :

(1) To convert Centigrade into Fahrenheit, multiply by 9, divide

---

[1] In the 'Lancet' of Jan. 1st, 1870, I find the following observations of Dr. *Marcet* (see also ' Archives des Sciences physiques,' xxxvi, 247, and the ' Bibliothèque Universelle et Revue Suisse,' Nov. 15th, 1869), who gives an account of some observations, made in an expedition to the Mont Blanc chain of mountains, on the influence of altitude on temperature. His observations were made with a thermometer in the mouth, by means of a mirror attached to the instrument. It will be seen that they substantially confirm Lortet's researches.

1. The temperature of the human body in a state of repose is not less elevated at the summits of high mountains than at the level of the sea.

2. During the act of ascent the temperature appears to diminish progressively—the time from the last meal is one of the chief factors. As a general rule, rapid mounting, with free cutaneous transpiration, produces the greatest depression of temperature.

3. The temperature soon rises again when at rest, or by moderating the speed.

4. The cardiac oppression and general feeling of indisposition, &c., is accompanied at great altitudes by remarkable depressions of bodily temperature."—[TRANS.]

by 5, add 32, or multiply by 1·8 and add 32. Example: 20° C. = 20 × 1·8 + 32 = 68° Fahr.

(2) To convert Centigrade into Réaumur, multiply by 4, divide by 5, or multiply by 0·8. Example: 20° C. × 0·8 = 16° R.

(3) To turn Fahrenheit into Centigrade, deduct 32, multiply by 5, and divide by 9. Example: 104° Fahr. − 32 × 5 ÷ 9 = 40° C.

(4) To turn Fahrenheit into Réaumur, deduct 32, divide by 9, multiply by 4. Example: 104° Fahr. − 32 ÷ 9 × 4 = 32° R.

(5) To turn Réaumur into Fahrenheit, multiply by 9, divide by 4, and add 32.

(6) To turn Réaumur into Centigrade, multiply by 5, divide by 4. The following figures will still further explain.

		Freezing.			Boiling.
Fahrenheit . .	0	32	77	122	212
Réaumur . .		0	20	40	80
Centigrade . .		0	25	50	100

C.	R.	F.	C.	R.	F.
0	0	32	33	26,4	91,4
5	4	41	33,1	26,48	91,58
10	8	50	33,2	26,56	91,76
15	12	59	33,3	26,64	91,94
17,5	14	63,5	33,4	26,72	92,12
20	16	68	33,5	26,8	92,3
22,5	18	72,5	33,6	26,88	92,48
25	20	77	33,7	26,96	92,66
27,5	22	81,5	33,8	27,04	92,84
30	24	86	33,9	27,12	93,02
30,5	24,4	86,9	34	27,2	93,2
31	24,8	87,8	34,1	27,28	93,38
31,5	25,2	88,7	34,2	27,36	93,56
32	25,6	89,6	34,3	27,44	93,74
32,5	26	90,5	34,4	27,52	93,92
32,6	26,08	90,68	34,5	27,6	94,1
32,7	26,16	90,86	34,6	27,68	94,28
32,8	26,24	91,04	34,7	27,76	94,46
32,9	26,32	91,22	34,8	27,84	94,64

C.	R.	F.	C.	R.	F.
34,9	27,92	94,82	38,75	31	101,75
35	28	95	38,8	31,04	102,84
35,1	28,08	95,18	38,9	31,12	102,02
35,2	28,16	95,36	39	31,2	102,2
35,2	28,24	95,54	39,1	31,28	102,38
35,1	28,32	95,72	39,2	31,36	102,56
35,5	28,4	95,9	39,25	31,4	102,65
35,6	28,48	96,08	39,3	31,44	102,74
35,7	28,56	96,26	39,75	31,5	102,875
35,8	28,64	96,44	39,4	31,52	102,92
35,9	28,72	96,62	39,5	31,6	103,1
36	28,8	96,8	39,6	31,68	103,28
36,1	28,88	96,98	39,7	31,76	103,46
36,2	28,96	97,16	39,75	31,8	103,55
36,25	29	97,25	39,8	31,84	103,64
36,3	29,04	97,34	39,9	31,92	103,32
36,4	29,12	97,52	40	32	104
36,5	29,2	97,7	40,1	32,08	104,18
36,6	29,28	97,88	40,2	32,16	104,36
36,7	29,36	98,06	40,25	32,2	104,45
36,75	29,4	98,15	40,3	32,24	104,54
36,8	29,44	98,24	40,4	32,32	104,72
36,9	29,52	98,42	40,5	32,4	104,9
37	29,6	98,6	40,6	32,48	105,08
37,1	29,68	98,78	40,625	32,5	105,125
37,2	29,76	98,96	40,7	32,56	105,26
37,25	29,8	99,05	40,75	32,6	105,37
37,3	29,84	99,14	40,8	32,64	105,44
37,4	29,92	99,32	40,9	32,72	105,62
37,5	30	99,5	41	32,8	105,8
37,6	30,08	99,68	41,1	32,88	105,98
37,7	30,16	99,86	41,125	32,9	106,025
37,75	30,2	99,95	41,2	32,96	106,16
37,8	30,24	100,04	41,25	33	106,25
37,9	30,32	100,22	41,3	33,04	106,34
38	30,4	100,4	41,4	33,12	106,52
38,1	30,48	100,58	41,5	33,2	106,7
38,15	30,5	100,67	41,6	33,28	106,88
38,2	30,56	100,76	41,625	33,3	106,925
38,25	30,6	100,85	41,7	33,36	107,06
38,3	30,64	100,94	41,75	33,4	107,15
38,4	30,72	101,12	41,8	33,44	107,24
38,5	30,8	101,3	41,875	33,5	107,375
38,6	30,88	101,48	41,9	33,52	107,42
38,7	30,96	101,66	42	33,6	107,6

C.	R.	F.	C.	R.	F.
42,11	33,68	107,78	43,375	34,7	110,075
42,125	33,7	107,825	43,4	34,72	110,12
42,2	33,76	107,96	43,5	34,8	110,3
42,25	33,8	108,05	43,6	34,88	110,48
42,3	33,84	108,14	43,625	34,9	110,525
42,375	33,9	108,185	43,7	34,96	110,66
42,4	33,92	108,32	43,75	**35**	110,75
42,5	**34**	108,5	43,8	35,04	110,84
42,6	34,08	108,68	43,9	35,12	111,02
42,625	34,11	108,725	**44**	35,2	111,2
42,7	34,16	108,86	44,1	35,28	111,38
42,75	34,2	108,95	44,2	35,36	111,56
42,8	34,24	109,04	44,3	35,44	111,74
42,875	34,3	109,175	44,375	35,5	111,875
42,9	34,32	109,22	44,4	35,52	111,92
43	34,4	109,4	44,5	35,6	112,1
43,1	34,48	109,58	44,6	35,68	112,28
43,125	34,5	109,625	44,7	35,76	112,46
43,2	34,56	109,76	44,8	35,84	112,64
43,25	34,6	109,85	44,9	35,92	112,82
43,3	34,64	109,94	**45**	**36**	**113**

APPENDIX No. III.

The following notes came under my notice too late for insertion in their proper places:

1. K. Th. Schmalz (in Schmidt's 'Jahrbücher,' B. 137, p. 212 (1868) gives the following as the average temperature of several domestic animals taken in the rectum, the vaginal temperatures being about 0·2° to 0·5° Reaumur, $= \frac{9}{20}$th° to 1·125° Fahrenheit *lower* than these :

Bulls	= 31·3° R.	= 102·41° F.
Cows	= 31·2° R.	= 102·20° F.
Calves	= 31·4° R.	= 102·65° F.
Sheep	= 32·2° R.	= 104·45° F.
Lambs	= 32·5° R.	= 105·12° F.
Horse and ass	= 30·7° R.	= 101·07° F.

Some of these differ rather considerably from those given at page 85.

2. *Lombard* has found, by means of a very delicate thermo-electric

apparatus registering $\frac{1}{1000}$° C., that the temperature of the skin over the radial artery at the wrist falls for a few seconds after suspending respiration. [See p. 108.] Quoted in 'Medico-Chirurgical Review' for January, 1871, to which also I am indebted for the following reference.

3. Drs. Brown-Séquard and Tholozan find that pinching a limb raises the temperature of that limb, but lowers the temperature of its fellow on the opposite side ; also, that pinching one leg often raises the temperature of the arm of the same side, and lowers the temperature of the other (opposite) arm, as well as of the opposite leg.

They consider all these to be phenomena of a reflex kind, and due to vascular contraction or dilatation. ('Gazette Médicale de Paris,' 1870, p. 142.)—[TRANS.]

APPENDIX No. IV.

Supplemental Bibliography.

Allbutt, T. Clifford, two articles "On Medical Thermometry," including review of Wunderlich, 'Brit. and For. Med-Chir. Rev.,' 1870, April, p. 429 ; July, p. 144.

Alcock, Assist.-Surgeon, "On Nervous Power in relation to Temperature, and Rise after Death," 'Med. Times and Gaz.,' 1869, vol. i, p. 206, vol. ii, 621.

'American Journal of Medical Sciences,' 1866, p. 241 ; 1867, p. 506, 525, 245 ; vol. ii, 539 ; 1868, 1, 495, 557 ; 1869, 243, 425, 521.

Andral, M., "On Temperature of Infants," 'Med. Times and Gaz.,' 1870, vol. i, 526. 'Comptes Rendus,' t. 70, p. 825. 'Archiv. Générales,' 1869, 2, 716.

Aufrun, M., "Thermométrie Médicale," 'Bulletin Gén. de Thérap.,' 1869, iii, 50.

Barclay, A. W., " On High Temperatures in Acute Rheumatism," 'Lancet,' July 30th, 1870.

Baümler, C., "On Treatment of High Temperatures by external Application of Cold," 'Lancet,' August 6th, 1870 (ii, 181).

Becquerel, E., " On Thermo-electric Piles and Thermo-electrics," 'Annales de Chimie et de la Physiologie,' 1866, tom. viii, sér. 4, 389.

Beddo, John, "A peculiar case of Fever [high temperature ($103 \cdot 8°$ F.) with slow pulse (60)]," 'Edinburgh Med. Journal,' 1870.

Bergeron, M., "Recherches sur la Pneumonie des Viellards," Paris, 1866.

Berns, F. W. C., "On Temperature," 'Nederlands Archiv.,' Bd. v, p. 179. 'Brit. and For. Med.-Chir. Rev.,' January, 1871, p. 233.

Berthelot, M., "Des Carbures pyrogénés," 'Annales de Chimie, &c.,' tom. xii, sér. 4, p. 94, &c. (1867).

Binz, C., "Pharmak. Studien über Chinin," 'Virchow's Archiv,' 1869, Bd. 46, Heft. 1, p. 67, Heft. 2, p. 129.

Binz, "On Quinine and Alcohol in Paralytic Fever," 'Practitioner,' vol. iv, July, 1870, p. 1.

Binz, C., "On Effects of Quinine and Alcohol," 'Virchow's Archiv,' Bd. 51, Heft. 1, p. 6, and Heft. 2, p. 153.

Bird, R., "Effects of Sulphurous Acid on Temperature," 'Practitioner,' vol. ii, p. 247.

Blake "On Inequality of Temperature on two sides, &c.," 'Med. Times and Gaz.,' 1870, vol. i, p. 676.

Blum, A., "Étude sur la Fièvre traumatique primitive," 'Archiv. Générales,' 1869, tom. i, sér. 6, p. 414.

Bosscha, M., "On Air and Mercurial Thermometers," 'Comptes Rendus,' 1869, tom. lxix, pp. 875, 879, and 1185.

Braune, Wilhelm, "On Intermittents with several months' intervals," 'Archiv. der Heilkunde,' 1870, Heft. 1, p. 68.

Breuer, "On Senator's Paper," 'Virchow's Archiv.,' 1869, Bd. 46, 3rd Heft., p. 391.

'British and Foreign Med.-Chir. Review;' various papers in vol. xxxviii, p. 93 (July, 1866), vol. xlv, pp. 260, 279, 168, July, 1870, pp. 241-2-3, January, 1871, p. 233.

Brown-Séquard, and *J. E. Lombard,* "On effects of Irritation of Sensory Nerves on Temperature," 'Archives de Physiologie,' 1868, p. 688.

Buzzard, Thomas, "Effects of Aconite on Temperature and Pulse," 'Practitioner,' vol. ii, p. 127.

Carter, Thomas, "On Thermometer as a Test of Death," 'Lancet,' 1867, vol. ii, p. 544.

Charcot and Vulpian "On Temperature," 'B. Séquard's Archives de Physiologie' (1870), iii, 451.

Clark, Le Gros, "The Temperature in Diseases," 'British Med. Journal,' 1868, i, 451.

Clouston, *T. S.*, "On Bromide of Potassium in Epilepsy," 'Journal of Mental Science,' October, 1868, p. 305.

Colin, *M.*, "On Temperature of Venous and Arterial Blood," 'Archives Générales de Médecine,' tom. ii, Sér. 6, p. 45 (1865).

Compton, *T. A.* (*and S. Warter*) "On Temperature in Acute Diseases," 'Dublin Quarterly Journal,' August, 1866, p. 60.

Da Costa, "Temperature of Body in Cancer and Tuberculosis" (review), 'Brit. and For. Med.-Chir. Rev.,' vol. xxxix, April, 1867, p. 535.

Davies, *Dr. Herbert*, "On Temperature in Acute Rheumatism, and Effect of Blisters," 'Med. Times and Gazette,' 1870, vol. i, p. 47.

Deville, *H. Sainte Claire*, "On variations of Temperature by Mixture of Two Liquids," 'Comptes Rendus,' 1870, tom. 70, p. 1377.

Ehrle, *Carl*, "On Registering Thermometers," 'Deutsch. Archiv.,' Bd. vii, June, 1870, p. 345.

Falck, *C. Ph.*, "Experiment. Studien, &c., der Temperatur curven der Acuten Intoxicationen," 'Virchow's Archiv.,' 1870, Bd. 49, Heft. iv, p. 458.

Fastre's "Spirit Thermometers," 'Schmidt's Jahrbücher,' Bd. 139, p. 144 (1868).

Faye, *M.*, "On Zeuner's Traité de Thermo-dynamique," and other papers, 'Comptes Rendus,' 1869, tom. lxix, pp. 101, 858, 1057.

Fergus, *Walter*, "On Inequality of Thermometers," 'Med. Times and Gazette,' 1870, vol. i, p. 696.

Fox, *Cornelius B.*, "Remarks on Clinical Thermometers," 'Med. Times and Gazette,' vol. ii, 1869, p. 459; 'Lancet,' 1870, vol. ii, 180; 'Brit. Med. Journal,' 1869, ii, 247.

Fox, *E. Long* [a series of valuable papers on Temperature, with charts], 'Med. Times and Gazette,' 1870. "On relations of Phosphoric Acid to Temperature," 'British Med. Journal,' 1867, vol. i, p. 544. "Clinical Observations on Acute Tuberculosis," 'St. George's Hosp. Reports,' vol. iv.

Frese, *J. B.*, "On the Temperature after transfusion of Healthy Blood," 'Virchow's Archiv.,' 1867, Bd. 40, Heft. ii, p. 302.

Gibson, *F. W.*, paper in 'Journal of Mental Science,' Jan., 1868, p. 497.

Gibson, F. W., "On Temperature," 'Brit. Med. Journal,' 1866, i, 249, 278.

Goodhart, J. F., "Thermometric Observations in Clinical Medicine," 'Guy's Hosp. Reports,' 1869 (3rd ser., xv, p. 365).

Greenhow, Dr., "On progressive fall of Temperature [to 84° in axilla]," 'Brit. Med. Journal,' 1870, i, 652.

Grimshaw, T. W., "Observations of Temperature in Pneumonia," 'Dub. Quarterly Journal,' May, 1869, p. 335. "On Temperature in Typhus," 'Dub. Quarterly Journal,' May, 1867, p. 313. "Thermometric Observations in Fever," Dublin, 1866 (reprint from 'Med. Press and Circular).

Gruber "On Temperature in Pregnancy," 'Schmidt's Jahrbücher,' 1868, Bd. 139, pp. 197-8, 246.

Hamilton (Royal Artillery) "On Effects of Quinine" (from 'Indian Medical Gazette'), 'Lancet,' January 14th, 1871.

Hankel, Ernst, "On a Thermo-electric Apparatus of spirals of iron and virgin silver wire," 'Archiv. der Heilkunde,' 1868, ix, 4, 321.

"*Hawksley's* Thermometers," 'Lancet,' 1870, vol. ii, 12.

Hayden and Cruise, Drs., "On Temperature in Cholera," 'Dub. Quarterly Journal,' May, 1867, 396.

Hirsch, Dr., "On development of Doctrine of Fever," 'Archiv. der Heilkunde,' Heft iv, 1870, p. 400.

Hirz, M., "Chaleur dans les Maladies," 'Nouveau Dictionnaire de Med. et Chirurg. Pratiques,' 1867.

Hollis, W. Ainslie, "On value of Thermometer to Physicians," a very valuable paper, in 'St. Bartholomew's Hosp. Reports,' vol. ii (1867), p. 285.

Horwath (of Kiew) "On Temperature," in 'Wiener Acad. Anz.,' 1870, No. 11; 'Centralblatt f. d. Med. Wissenschaften,' No. 35, 1870; 'Brit. and For. Med.-Chir. Rev.,' Jan., 1871, 233.

Huppert, H., "Ueber die Ursache der postmortale Temperatur steigerungen," 'Archiv. der Heilkunde,' viii, 6, p. 321, 1867; also in 'Schmidt's Jahrbücher,' 1868, Bd. 138, p. 79.

Jacobi, Professor, "On Antiphlogistics in Diseases of Children" (lectures to New York Med. Journal Association), 'New York Medical Record.'

Jacobson, Heinrich, "On normal and pathological Local Temperatures," 'Virchow's Archiv.,' Bd. 51, Heft. ii, p. 275.

Janim, M., " On Temperature in mixtures of Alcohol and Water," &c., ' Comptes Rendus,' 1870, tom. lxx, pp. 1237, 1309.

Jordan, Furneaux, "Temperatures in Shock," 'Brit. Med. Journal,' 1867, vol. i, p. 164.

Kettler, C., " On Fresé's Paper on Transfusion," ' Virchow's Archiv.,' 1867, Bd. 41, Heft. iv, p. 542.

Labbée, Leon, " On Effects of Veratrum Viride," ' Gaz. de Paris,' 44, 45; 'Schmidt's Jahrbücher,' 1870, Bd. 145, 273.

' Lancet,' Oct. 23rd, 1870, p. 584; Oct. 29th, p. 624, " Effects of Medicines on Temperature," by F. J. Mavor.

Laschkewitsch " On causes of Depression of Temperature in Suppression of Perspiration," ' Reichert und Du Bois Raymond's Archiv., 1868, p. 61.

Leriche, M., " Effets variés des traumatismes du rachis," ' Lyon Médicale,' tom. v, No. 18, p. 598.

Le Roux, F. P., " On Thermo-electric Currents," ' Annales de Chimie,' &c., tom. x, sér. iv, p. 201 (1867).

Lewizky, P. (Kosan), " On Sulphate of Quinine," ' Virchow's Archiv.,' 1869, Bd. 47, Heft. iii, p. 352.

Liebermeister, " On Antipyretic Effect of Quinine," ' Deutsch. Archiv. f. Klin. Med.,' 1867, iii, 23-66.

Lombard, J. S. (Harvard, U. S.), " Influence of Respiration on Temperature," ' Brown-Séquard's Archives de Physiologie " (1869), tom. ii, p. 1.

Lombard, J. E., " New Thermo-electric Apparatus," ' Archives de Physiologie,' 1868, p. 498.

Maclagan, T. J. (Dundee), " Notes on Fall of Temperature in Infants for a few days after birth," ' Proceedings of Royal Society of Edinburgh.'

McDonnell " On Temperature in Injuries of Spine," ' Dublin Quarterly Journal,' August, 1866, p. 28.

Mantegazza Paolo " On Pain in relation to Generation of Heat," ' Gaz. Lombard,' Nos. 26-29, 1866.

Mendel, E., " D. Temperatur der Schädelhöhle in normalen und pathol. Zustände," ' Virchow's Archiv.,' Bd. 50, Heft. i, p. 12.

' Medical Times and Gazette,' 1866, i, pp. 177, 201, 311, 394, 418, 228, 311, 666, 659, 251, see E. Long Fox, &c.

Meding, Dr., " A case of very High Temperature (108·5° F.) with Preservation of Life," ' Archiv. der Heilkunde,' 1870, Heft. v, p. 467.

Moore, J. W., "Mean Temperature in relation to Disease, &c.," 'Dublin Quarterly Journal,' Nov., 1869, p. 107.

Muirhead, Claud, "On Relapsing Fever in Edinburgh in 1870," 'Edinburgh Med. Journal,' 1870, July, p. 1.

Murchison, Charles, "High Temperature in Acute Rheumatism," 'Clinical Society's Trans.,' vol. i, p. 32.

Naumann, Osw., Dr., "Influence of Epispastics on Pulse and Temperature," 'Schmidt's Jahrbücher,' 1867, Bd. 133, p. 158.

Naunyn, B. & H. Quincke, "Ueber den Einflusz des Central Nerven-systems auf die Wärmebildung im Organismus," ' Reichert und Du Bois Reymond's Archiv.,' pp. 174, 521, 1869.

Naunyn, B. (Dorpat), "Beiträge zur Fieber-lehre," ' Reichert und Du Bois Reymond's Archives,' 1870, Heft. ii, p. 159.

Obermeier, "Ueber das wiederkehren des Fiebers," 'Virchow's Archiv.,' Bd. 47, 4tes Heft., 428.

Oehl, E. de Rienzi, and Traube, "On Temperature in Cancer and Tuberculosis" (Review), ' Brit. and For. Med.-Chir. Review,' July, 1867, vol. xl, p. 249.

Oehl, "Die Beziehungen des Vagus zur T. der Bauchhöhle," 'Schmidt's Jahrbücher,' Bd. 143, 1869, p. 280 [section of vagus; temperature of abdomen].

Onimus and Viry, "Relations de l'activité musculaire avec la Température," &c., (review of), ' La Revue Médicale' (Paris), 1868, tom. i, 607.

Parkes, E. A., and *Count Wollowicz,* "On Effects of Alcohol," ' Proc. Royal Society,' vol. xviii, No. 120, p. 362, ' Lancet,' August 20th, 1870.

Peter, Dr., "Modifications de la Température," ' Archives Générales,' 1867, tom. i, sér. 6, p. 616.

Pick, Thomas P., "On Traumatic Fever," ' St. George's Hosp. Reports,' vol. iii, p. 73.

Pochoy, M., "Recherches expérimentales sur les centres de Température," Paris, 1870, v. ' Lyon Médicale,' Oct. 23, 1870, No. 22, tom. vi, p. 197.

Potain's Alcoholic Clinical Thermometer, notices of, ' La Revue Médicale,' 1868, tom. i, p. 631 ; ' Med. Times and Gazette,' 1868, vol. i, 238.

Prior, C. E. (Bedford), "On Temperature, &c.," ' British Med. Journal,' 1868, vol. i, p. 451.

Rattray, Alexander, "On Effects of Tropical Climates on Temperature, &c., of Body," 'Proc. Royal Society,' vol. xviii, No. 122, p. 513.

Redwood, T. H., " Temperature in Typhoid," 'Lancet,' 1868, vol. i, pp. 497-528.

Ringer, Sydney, and *W. Rickards* " On Effects of Alcohol on Temperature," 'Lancet,' vol. ii, 1866, p. 208.

Richardson, B. W., "Effects of High Temperature on Animal Substances," 'Medical Times and Gazette,' 1869, vol. i, pp. 29, 53, 84.

Robin, Edouard, "Effects of Temperature on Growth of Horns, Feathers, &c.," 'Révue Médicale,' 1869, i, 139, 272.

Roch, Staff-Surg., "On Heat Apoplexy," 'Medical Press and Circular,' 1868, vol. i, 519 [records a temperature of 113° F.].

Rosetti, F., " Sur l'usage des couples thermo-electriques dans la mesure des températures," 'Annales de Chimie, &c.,' tom. xiii, p. 68 (4 série).

Ruge, Paul, " Wirkung des Alkohols auf dem thierische Organismus," ' Virchow's Archiv.,' 1870, Bd. 49, Heft. ii, pp. 252, 265.

Sanderson, J. Burdon, "High Temperatures in Acute Rheumatism," 'Clinical Society's Trans.,' vol. i, p. 34.

Schiff, Moritz, and Levier, "Recherches sur l'echauffement des nerfs, &c., à la suite des irritations sensorielles and sensitives," ' Archiv. de Physiologie ' (B. Séquard), 1869, ii, 157.

' Schmidt's Jahrbücher ' (besides papers quoted elsewhere), Band 133, p. 241, Bd. 135, pp. 6, 237, 248, Bd. 136, pp. 92, 112, 116, 119, 217, 263, Band 137, pp. 213, 232, 248, 249, 250, Band 138, pp. 77, 78, 95, 104, 129, 303, 334, Band 139, p. 94, Band 140, pp. 139, 155, 167, 171, 210, Band 141, pp. 98, 100, 214, 250, Band 143, pp. 134, 221, 225, 293, Band 146, pp. 13, 14, 16, 19, 23, 93, 204, 205, 304.

Schröder (of Bonn), "Temperatur-beobachtungen im Wochenbette," ' Monatsschrift f. Geburtskunde,' xxvii, p. 108, February, 1866.

Senator, H., " Beiträge zur Lehre v. d. Eigenwärme u. d. Fieber," ' Virchow's Archiv.,' 1869, Bd. 45, Heft. iii, p. 351. " Ueber das Verhalten der Körperwärme bei Abkühlung der Haut," ' Virchow's Archiv.,' Bd. 50, Heft. iii, p. 354.

Simons, R., Inaugural Dissert., Bonn, 1870, " On Gases (CO_2, &c.) depressing Temperature," 'Brit. and For. Med.-Chir. Rev.,' January, 1871, p. 233.

Smyth, W., " On Effects of Alcohol on Temperature," ' Med. Times and Gazette,' 1869, vol. ii, 744.

Spring, A. F. (Luttich), " On the Relation of Sense of Touch, Temperature, and Pain," ' Med. Press and Circular,' 1866, vol. i, 400.

Squire, W. (papers " On Puerperal and Infantile Temperatures " already quoted), " On Temperature Variations from Vaccination," ' Lancet,' 1869, ibid., 1870, vol. i, 806.

Squarey, Charles, " Observations on the Temperature, Urea and Chlorides in Typhus Fever," ' Trans. Med.-Chir. Society,' 1867, and ' Lancet ' in 1866.

Stieler, Guido, " On Ten Fatal Cases of Cold Water Treatment of Typhus Fever," ' Zeitschrift f. Rat. Medicin ' (Henle and Pfeuffer's), xxvi Bd., 3 Reihe., p. 254.

Sutton, H. Gawen, " Cases of Acute Rheumatism," ' Guy's Hosp. Reports,' 1866 (3rd series, xii), 509.

Theurkauf, J., " Ueber Typhus," ' Virchow's Archiv.,' Bd. 41, Heft. iv, 443 ; Bd. 43, Heft. i, p. 35.

Thompson, R. E., " On Temperatures in Typhus Epidemic, 1864-5," ' St. George's Hosp. Reports,' vol. i, p. 47. " Temperature Observations in Typhoid Fever," ' St. George's Hosp. Reports,' vol. ii, p. 75. " On Rheumatic Pericarditis," ' St. George's Hosp. Reports,' vol. iv.

Traube and E. Leyden " On the Temperature in Puerperal Fever," ' Annalen der Charité,' Berlin, 1863.

Troost and Hautefeuille, " Chaleur due à des actions chimiques," ' Comptes Rendus,' 1869.

Tscheschichin, M., " Zur Lehre von d. thierische Wärme," ' Reichert und Du Bois Reymond's Archiv.,' 1868, iv, 151.

Vallin, M., " On Insolation," ' Archives Générales,' tom. i, sér. 6, p. 113. Also a paper ' On Convulsions,' ibid., p. 129, 1868.

Veratrum viride, effects of, on Temperature. See ' Schmidt's Jahrbücher,' Bd. 139, p. 282 ; Bd. 140, p. 156 ; Bd. 143, pp. 11, 136, 139, v. Labbée.

Wagner " On Temperature in Phthisis, &c.," ' Schmidt's Jahrbücher," 1854, Bd. 81, pp. 117-120.

Warter, S., papers in ' Med. Times and Gazette,' 1866, vol. ii, pp. 416, 483. Also vol. ii (1866) ' St. Bartholomew's Hosp. Reports,' p. 65.

Weber, Hermann, " Remarks on Hæmoptysis," 'Clinical Society's Trans.,' vol. ii, p. 143.

Williams, Dr., " On Temperatures in Insanity," 'Med. Times and Gazette,' 1867, ii, 224.

Wiltshire and *Squire* "On Puerperal Temperatures," 'British Medical Journal,' 1867, vol. ii, p. 410.

Wolf and *Schroder* "On Temperature of Childbed" (Review), 'Brit. and For. Med.-Chir. Review,' vol. xxxviii, p. 280.

Wunderlich and *Hirz*, review of, 'Med. Times and Gazette,' 1869, vol. ii, p. 19.

APPENDIX No. V.

Explanation of the Lithographic Plates.

The first plate affords a model for the registration of the frequency of the pulse and respirations, and for the temperature.

The publishers keep such ready for use, at a cost of two silbergroschen each = 2½d., or thirty for one thaler, ten silbergroschen = 3s. 10d., or 100 for 3½ thalers = 8s. 8d. nearly.[1]

On this, as in the remaining tables, the strong perpendicular line indicates midnight, the finer perpendicular line mid-day. The space between these vertical lines may be employed to note measurements taken at different hours of day or night. For convenience, the Celsian (Centigrade) and Réaumur's scale are placed side by side. [Centigrade and Fahrenheit's are substituted in our copy.]

In order to facilitate the use of this chart, I have noted the particulars of a case, which is interesting even in itself, on account of its changing fortunes. It will be easily seen how such curves assist

---

[1] Mr. Hawksley, surgical instrument maker, of 80, Blenheim Street, Bond Street, W., keeps charts of large and small size (the latter bound for the pocket). He has also made considerable improvements in clinical thermometers, particularly in the graduation.

Messrs. Harvey and Reynolds also supply charts at a moderate cost; and have lately made an improvement by introducing a chamber at the upper end of the thermometer, by which the index can be recovered, if it has been shaken down into the bulb, in accordance with a suggestion of the late Professor Phillips.—[TRANS.]

in rapidly gaining a correct idea of the whole disease. A few remarks on the special occurrences of the case, and on the therapeutic measures employed, suffice to show *at one glance* all that is worthy of note in the case. After some details of a personal nature, the beginning and common diagnosis of the disease, and the number of the thermometer, the days of the month are appended in Arabic numerals, the days of the disease in Roman figures. Besides this, the principal therapeutic measures employed are recorded; then follows the temperature curve, with, on an average, six daily observations, which is succeeded by curves of the pulse (taken morning and evening), and then the curve of the frequency of respirations.

At the lower part of the chart there are the weights of the patient at different periods [in kilogrammes—a kilogramme = 2·2046213 English pounds avoirdupoise, and the reduction has been made in our copy], and some further remarks are also appended. It is very easy to supplement and complete a table of this kind by adding, for example, a diagram or curve of the size of the spleen, or of a pleuritic exudation, and by noting down the chief and special symptoms as they occur.

For a beginner it may, perhaps, be useful to mark the space between 37·5 and 36·5 C. (99·5° and 97·7° F.) in some way; with a red pencil, for instance, in order to denote the range of normal temperatures.

The case which I have used to exemplify the mode of using the table was one of extraordinarily severe and much complicated abdominal typhus, with recrudescence in the middle of the fourth week, in which the treatment was somewhat varied. The action of the calomel given is recognised by a sudden fall of temperature, but any lasting effect from the remedy could not be expected, because the disease had already made considerable progress when it was prescribed. When the temperature again rose, in spite of a good deal of bronchitis a cold bath of 18° C. (64·4° F.) was given for twenty minutes on the twelfth day, and douches of iced water were applied at the same time, and repeated three times in the course of twenty-four hours. The immediate effect of the baths on the temperature may be seen in the dotted lines (temperature taken in the rectum); after the first bath the temperature fell from 40° C. (104° F.) to 39·5° C. (103·1° F.); after the second bath from 40.3° C. (104·5° F.) to 39·5° C. (103·1° F.), and then sank spontaneously (see the continuous line) to 39·1°C. (102·38 F.). After the third bath from 39·9° C. (103·9° F.) to 38·3° C. (101·12°); after the fourth bath the immediate effect was barely ⅓th of a degree (Fahr.). Between the baths the trunk was covered with ice-bags. But although all the symptoms improved under this treatment, and the dry smoky tongue perfectly cleaned, the appetite returned, the meteorism diminished, the spleen decreased in size, and the brain symptoms in particular were essentially improved; although the bronchitis also became better, the patient complained so bitterly of the torment of the cold baths that the next baths employed were only lukewarm (25°—32° C. = 77°—89·6° F.). The results, as the dotted lines show, were proportionately small. From the fifteenth day the patient positively refused to take the baths. Soon after they were discontinued the temperature rose in spite of persistence in the application of cold compresses; however, after the seventeenth day the disease appeared to take a favorable turn. An increase of fever on the seventeenth day, which the patient herself found very uncomfortable, determined her, partly also because she observed the favorable effects of the baths in a fellow patient, to take another bath, and the same on the next day. The result was favorable; the remissions became more marked. However, an exacerbation on the twenty-first day again made the patient refuse the baths, and they were not persisted in, because the symptoms on the whole appeared to take a favorable aspect. But from the twenty-fifth day the exacerbations again became more severe, and at the same time the remissions grew less from day to day. The spleen now began to enlarge again; at first, however, there were no particular subjective feelings of discomfort, and the patient continued most decidedly to refuse to resume the baths, and still did so, whilst all the symptoms of a fresh fastigium gradually developed themselves: the head symptoms grew worse and worse, till persistent delirium, a dry, fuliginous, and tremulous tongue, increasing meteorism, the spleen growing bigger, fresh rose-spots, and extreme prostration, set in. To these were added severe bronchitis, with infiltration of the lower lobes of both lungs, great debility, and frequency of cardiac contractions; the urine became albuminous, and there was painful thrombosis of both lower extremities, with severe œdematous swelling. It is true that the high fever temperature was lowered on the thirty-fifth day by the use of digitalis, but the patient became collapsed, and whilst the cheeks had a circumscribed flush of redness, the rest of the surface was pale, the nose, ears, hands, and

feet cold, the breathing irregular and shallow.   She quite lost consciousness, and only murmured incoherently, and exhibited automatic
movements of the facial muscles and of the hands.   The second
sound of the heart grew indistinct, and was almost lost, and the
patient appeared to be in the death-agony.   She was, however, then
plunged into the baths (at a warmth of 22.5° C. $= 72.5^\circ$ F.).   The
effect, which could scarcely have been hoped for, was overwhelming.
All the threatening symptoms vanished after only a few baths.

Not only was their influence on the temperature very considerable,
but the tongue very quickly cleaned, the spleen began to diminish,
consciousness was restored, sleep returned to her, she passed a large
quantity of urine free from albumen, the breathing became regular,
both the infiltration of the lungs and the bronchitis were amelio-
rated, the swelling of the legs subsided, and after only six days
convalescence set in, and no further baths were required.

The remaining tables give examples of the more important forms
of the course taken by the temperature in various diseases.   They
are, however, all taken from actual (concrete) cases.   The apices
of the curves between midnight and noon generally correspond to
the daily *minimum*, although generally but little regard has been had
to the exact hour of the forenoon on which this occurred.   The
apices of the curves between noon and midnight correspond in the
same manner to the daily *maximum*.

It often seemed necessary to draw more perpendicular lines, to
accurately represent the intercurrent elevations of temperature
which sometimes occurred.   However, they cannot well be misunderstood.

As regards other matters, the letter-press will, doubtless, afford
sufficient explanation of the several curves represented.

INDEX.

Abnormal temperatures always suspicious, 2

Acme or fastigium (see also special diseases), 9, 10

Acute rheumatism, 394

Age, effects of on temperature, 97, 158, 209, 320, 414

Ague, see "Fever," intermittent, 16, 416

Air, effects of cold, 96, 109

Aitken, Dr., on temperature, 42, 62

Alcoholic liquors, effects of, 117, 137, 424

Amphibolic period (see also "Fever"), 9, 11, 263, 315

Amygdalitis, 385

Andral's theories, &c., 30, 142

Anæmia, in typhoid, 321

Animals, immunity of some to poisons, 126

—, temperature of lower, 84; see "Appendix"

Animal poisons, see "Putrid"

Approximatively typical diseases, 5

Arteries, ligatures of, 133

Atmospheric pressure, effects of varied, 115; see "Appendix"

Atropine, effects of, 138

Atypical diseases, 5

Auerbach's fever theory, 188

Average temperatures, see "Normal temperature," &c., 1, 83, 230

Average height of temperature in special diseases, 248

Axilla, best place for thermometer, 68

— normal temperature of, 1

— should be closed, 70

Axilla, temperature of right and left not always same, 166

Bailly's memoir, 27

Bärensprung and Traube, 37, 97

Barnes, Robert, 139, 155

Barral's calculations, 88

Baths, cold, effects of, 109, 112, 322

Bäumler, C., 42, 71, 135

Beclard, J., on muscular contraction, 44, 87

Becquerel and Breschet, 27, 93, 107, 113, 161

Beer and brandy lower temp., 117

Bérard, P. H., 28

Berger's treatise, 28

Bergmann's researches, 34, 141

Berlinghieri Vacca, 25

Bernard, Claude, on nerves in relation to heat, 43, 93, 131, 147, 185

Berthelot, 43

Bilious typhoid, 333

Billroth and Weber on traumatic fever, &c., 41, 140, 162, 188

Biot, quotation from, 28

Blagden's experiments, 23

Bleeding, effects of, 118, 134, 378-9

Blisters, effects of (see also "Mustard") 402

Blood, loss of, see "Hæmorrhage"

— temperature of venous and arterial, 92

— composition of, 142, 441

Boerhaave on thermometer, 20

Bouillaud's observations, 28

Bright's disease, temperature in, 404

Brodie's, Sir B., views and cases, 25, 29, 145

Bronchitis, 365

Brown-Séquard and Tholozan, experiments of, 44, 112, 114, 133, 145, and Appendix

Budge and Waller's experiments, 147

Buntzen, 25

Calomel, effects of, 324

Calorimetry, 26, 67, 87, 190

Calorien (heat units), 87

Camphor, curare, coffee, and musk, raise temperature, 139

Cancer, temperature in, 429, 431

Casella first maker of registering clinical thermometers, 62

Catamenia affect temperature, 102, 135

Catarrhal affections of mucous membrane, 365

Causes of specific heat, 85

— of alterations of temperature, 120, 192

Cerebro-spinal meningitis, 222

Charts, thermometric, 78, see "Appendix"

Cheesy deposits not recognised by thermometer, 428

Childbed and labour, 102, 359

Children, typhoid diagnosed with difficulty in, 320

Children, temperature of, 96, 98, 413

Chloroform, 32, 137

Chloral-hydrate, 137

Cholera, temperature of, 94, 183, 313, 419

Chomel on temperature, 28

Chorea, 225, 426

Chossat's experiments and theories, 26, 31, 135

Chronic diseases, temperature in, 16

Chronic fever, 16, 431

Clark, Andrew, and *Crisp, Edwards,* on tuberculosis, 113-4

Climate, effects of tropical, &c., 114; 116, 131

Clothes must be free of thermometer, 71

Cold, effects of, 128, see "Baths, thermal, &c.," 322

Coleman's dissertation, 25

Colin's experiments, 93

Collapse, temperature in, &c., 4, 7, 179, 200, 207, 421

Collard de Martigny, 28

Compensation of temperature, 89

Constipation, effects of, 136

Convalescence, 221, 265, &c.

Constancy of temperature in health, 1

Course of temperature in febrile diseases, 241, 249

Course, varied, in different fevers, 13

Crawford's experiments, 24

Crisis, 9, 268

Cord, injuries to spinal, 29, 145, &c., 205, 423

Croupous and diphtheritic affections, 367

Croupous pneumonia, 368, 374

Currie, James, in advance of his times, 24, 25

Curves of temperature, 8, 78, 244, &c., see also Lithographs at end

Daily fluctuations of temperature, 8, 101, 226 (Chart of, 414)

— in disease, 255

Dalton opposes Brodie, 26

Damrosch on temperatures, 101

Davies's, Dr. Herbert, observations, 393, 402

Davy, John, experiments of, 26, 30, 33, 99, 107, 108, 114, 116

Death, temperature at time of, 13, 283

Defervescence, 12, 223, 265, 308, 317, 330, 345

De Haen on thermometer, 22, 30

Delirium, 410, 413

Demarquay and *Dumérril* on ether and chloroform, 32, 137

Depression of temperatures (see "Collapse," &c.), 127

De Rayter and *Donders* on temperatures, 148

Deyeux, 27

Diabetes, 430

Diarrhœa, 365

Digitalis, effects of, 137, 325

Directions taken by the temperature, 259

Diseases obey fixed laws, 39

Dobson's experiments, 23

Donné on temperature, 28

Drinks, effects of various, 114, 117

Dropsy, 431

Drugs, effects of various, 137, &c., 264, 324, 379, 432, 407, 408

Dulong and *Despretz,* 26

Earle, experiments of, 26, 152

Edwards' résumé, 27, 28

Effects of altered temperatures, 436

Elevated temperatures, causes of, 127

Endocarditis, 351, 399

Ephemera, 14

Ephemeral fever, 209

Epicritical period (see "Fever," &c.) 10, 12

Epilepsy (see "Neuroses") 225, 352, 425

Erysipelas, 222, 351

Exercise (muscular), effects on temperature, 105, 154

Fahrenheit invents thermometer, 21

Fastigium (see "Acme"), 9, 10, 247

Febricula (see "Ephemera") 355

Febrile temperature (see "Fever," "Smallpox," &c.), 7

Fæcal accumulations, 198

Fever, continued, 15 (see "Typhus," "Typhoid," &c.)

'ever, intermittent, 16, 223, 416
— or pyrexia, 4 ; theory of, 184
— peculiar remittent, 354
— relapsing, 16, 333
— remittent, 15
— terminal, 14, 435
— yellow, 405
Fingers, temperature in, 70
Finlayson and Förster on temperature of children, 98, 413, (chart) 414
Fluctuations of temperature, 8, 80, &c. (see "Daily" also)
— in disease, 92
Food, effects of, 115
— see Appendix I
Fourcault and Flourens, 34
Frese's experiments, 140
Fricke's experiments, 29
Friedländer's observations on cholera, 313
Fröhlich, Anton, 27

Garrod, A. H., on minor fluctuations of temperature, 40, 95
Gavarret on de Haen, 30
— thermo-electric pile, 66
Gentil on variations of temperature, 27
Gierse's dissertation, 30, 31, 162
Glanders and farcy, 408
Grainville and Horae, Sir E., 27
Grimshaw, T. W., 42
Groin, Levier takes thermometric observations in, 69
Grünewaldt and Winckel on temperature in labour, 103

Hæmorrhages lower temperature and then raise it, 118, 134, 313
Hale's communication, 26
Haller-Marcard, 23
Hallmann on typhus, 31
Hand, not reliable as a standard of temperature, 60
Harvey and Reynold's portable thermometers, 63
Health, temperature in (see "Normal temperature," &c.), 80, 82, &c.
Heat, effects of great, 130, 132, 208
Heart, disease of, 430 (see "Endocarditis," &c.)
Heart (of frog), effects of temperature on, 437
Heat equivalent to mechanical force, 35, 36, &c.
Heat, specific, 83 (see also "Animals," "Temperature," &c.)
Heat-units, 36, 87
Hegewitsch on Currie, 25
Helmholtz demonstrates heat from motion, 34, 35, 87, 105

Hemiplegia, temperature of, 165
Hepatitis, 404
Herpes labialis often preceded by severe fever, 360
High temperatures observed in life, 2, 131, 132, 204, 208, 350, 401, 425
Hippocrates, opinion of, 19, 308
Hirn (Colmar) on consumption of oxygen, &c., 37, 43, 106
Hooping-cough, 222
Hospital wards, use of thermometer in, 77
Hufeland on Currie, 25, 27
Hunter, John, experiments of, 23, 161
Hutchinson, J., on injuries to nerves, 153
Hydrocele, temperature after operation for, 161
Hydrogen, more consumption of in fever, 188
Hyperæmia, effects of, 133
Hyper-pyretic temperatures, 7
Hysterical neuroses, 166, 424

Iatro-mechanical theories, 19
Ice-bags, Hagspiel on effects of, 113
Idiosyncrasies affect temperature, 100 and passim
Inanition, 135
Index, how to set the, of registering thermometers, 63
Initial or pyrogenetic stage (see "Fever," &c.), 9, 10
Inflammation raises temperature, 161
Influenza, 222, 336
Insanity, temperatures in, 171, 204, 426
Interior of body, temperature of, 93
Iodide of potassium, effects of, on temperature, 407-8
Irregularities of temperature, 255
Irritants, effect of, 133

Jaundice, 225, 431
Jochmann on types of chronic fever, 427
Joule (Manchester) on heat-equivalents, 36

Kidneys, diseases of, 404, 431 (see "Cancer," "Tubercle," &c.)
Kilogrammeter, 36
Kussmaul and Tenner, 44, 133, 150, 393

Labour (see "Childbed," "Exercise," &c.), 102
Lavoisier's theories, 24, 25, 34, 83
Law, domain of, in disease, 39, 51
Legallois, 26

Lepine on hemiplegic temperatures, 165

Leyden's experiments, 190

Lichtenfels and *Fröhlich*, 40, 45

Liebermeister's researches, 44, 47, 71, 108, 112

Liebig's chemical theories of heat, 31, 93

Limits of human temperature in disease, 2

Liver, diseases of, 404, 431

Livingstone and *Thomsen* on effects of race, &c., 99

Local variations of temperature, 3

Lombard's thermo-electric apparatus, 66, 95

Low temperatures (*see* "Sub-normal," "Collapse," &c.), 204

Löwenhardt's cases, 204

Lucas's dissertation, 27

Ludwig's speculations, 90

Lues, or syphilis, 405

Lysis, 271

Mackenzie, F. M., 183, 204, 287

Magendie, F., 34

Malarial diseases, 16, 22, 382, 416

Malignant rheumatism, 401

Malingering, thermometer aids detection of, 53, 212

Marasmus, 428

Martin, Charles, 23

Marey's thermograph, 66

Maximum temperatures, 204 (*see* "Height in life")

Mayer, J. R., on correlation of forces, 35, 106

Mean temperature (*see* "Normal," "Health," "Average," &c.)

Measles, temperature, 221, 342

Meningitis, 222, 388

— cerebro-spinal, 389

Menstruation (*see* "Catamenia")

Mental exertions raise temperature, 95, 108

Michaelis translates Currie, 25

Miliary tuberculosis, acute, 143, 409, 427

Milk fever, 105

Mobility of temperature a bad sign, 3

Montgomery, E., observations by, 66, 162

Morphia, effects of, 138

Mouth, inside of, temperature, 68, 72

Mumps, 387

Muscles (*see* "Exercise")

Mustard epithems, 133, 164

Nasse supports Brodie, 26

— *F.* and *H.*, 29, 30

Nasse, F., 34

— 33

— *H.*, 43

Naunyn and *Quincke's* experiments, 151

Nerves, effect of injuries to, 152

Nervous system, effects of, on temperature, 25, 27, 43, 145, &c., 225

Neuroses, 424 (*see* "Chorea," "Cord," "Nervous," &c.)

New-born, temperature of, 97

Normal types of disease, 291

— temperatures (*see* "Average," "Axilla," &c.), 1, 7, 82

— temperature need not mean health, 2, 53

Nurse or friends may take temperatures, 74

Obernier on heat apoplexy, 131

Observations, mode, and precautions for thermometric, 70

Ogle, W., on diurnal variations, 45, 95, 99, 101, 116, 414

Operations, fever after (*see* "Traumatic," and "Wounds"), 356

Osteo-myelitis, 403

Parotitis, a complex designation, 387

Paralysed parts, temperature of, 152, 164, &c.

Paroxysms of ague only recognisable by thermometer, 417

Pericarditis, 391, 399

Peritonitis, 391

Perturbatio critica, 10, 11

Phlyctenular eruptive fever, 355

Phthisis, acute (*see* also "Tubercle," "Miliary," &c.), 410

Pickels' dissertation, 23

Piory, remarks on, 29

Pitschaft's essay, 27

Pleurisy, 222, 391

Pleural cavity, temperature of, 94, 393

Pneumonia, 197, 222, 368

Post-mortem temperatures, 205, 286

Pregnancy, effects of, 102 (*see* "Childbed")

Priestly and *Scheele* discover oxygen, 24

Private practice, thermometer in, 77

Pro-agonistic or pro-lethal temperatures, 10, 13, 207, 277

Pseudo-crises, 253

Pulse, ratio to temperature of the, 213, 281, 317, 389

Pus (*see* "Putrid," &c.)

Putrid products, effects of, 140

Pyæmia (*see* "Billroth," "Weber," "Putrid," "Pus," &c.), 361

Pyrexia, 4, 177, 200
Pyrogenetic stage (see "Fever," &c.), 9, 10, 213

Quinsy, 385

Race, station, and occupation, 99
Range of temperature in disease, 2
Rectum, temperature of, 1, 69, 72, 163, 183
Relapsing fever, 333
Relation between certain temperature and death, 443
Removal of patients, effects of, 155
Respirations and temperature, 214, and Appendix
Retention of urine, &c., 136
Reuss's essay, 27
Rigors, temperature is increased in, 4, 17, 172, 199
Rilliet and Barthez on normal cases, 291
Ringer, Sydney (and Stewart, A. P.), on temperature in health, 41, 97
Ringer, S., 42, 118, 412
Rise of temperature in typhoid fever, 300
Röderer on animal heat, 23
Roger, Henri, important services of, 31, 98, 412, 426, 428
Rubeolæ or Rötheln, 351

Saissy on hybernants, 25
Sanctorius the father of thermometry, 20
Scarlatina, 204, 221, 347
— resembles typhoid, 305
Schäfer on temperature of infants, 97
Schiff, M., on temperature, &c., 44, 149, 185
Schmitz, J. P., makes 300 observations, 33
Schröder on temperature in labour, 103
Secondary fever, 358
Senator, H., 190, 285
Sequelæ, 276
Sex, effect of, on temperature, 99 (see "Childbed," &c.), 158, 210
Serous cavities, temperature of, 164
Simon, John, 42, 162
Single observations, value of, 6, 7, 202
Skin, checking action of, 143
Smallpox, 222, 335
Squire, Wm., observations by, 98, 105
Stages in febrile diseases, 9
Starvation, 135
Sub-febrile temperatures, 7
Sub-normal temperatures, 7, 18, 171, 199, 428, 421, 444
Sunstroke, 132, 208

Syphilis, constitutional, 405

Tea, effects of, 118
Temperature the expression of many processes, 3
Temperatures, general significance of certain, 7, 205
— effects of very high, 17
Tension, effects of, 95
Terms used in medical thermometry, 227
Tetanus, temperatures in, 204, 425
Therapeutics, thermometer as a controller of, 59, 133, 135
Thermometers, mercurial, 61, &c.
— registering, 62
— thermo-electric, 66
— require testing, 63
— how to use, 72
— metastatic, 64
— where procured, 62 (see Appendix also)
— characteristics of clinical, 61
Thermal influences, &c., 109, 131
Thermograph, Marey's, 66
Thierfelder on abdominal typhus, 39
Time of observation should be noted, 73
Thoracentesis, effects of, 393
Todd's 'Cyclopædia,' 28
Tonsillitis, 385
Traube (see "Bärensprung"), 186
Traumatic fever, 356
Trichinæ, effects of, on temperature, 415
Tropical climates, Dr. Day's observations on, &c., 114, 116
Tscheschichin's observations, 47, 150, 190
Tubercular disease (see "Miliary," "Meningitis," &c.)
Tubercle does not raise temperature, 412, 427
Typhus fever, 327
Typhoid fever, diagnosis of, 306
— 221, 292
Typical diseases, 5

Units of heat, 36, 67
Urinary constituents, 102, 142, 155
Uterus, temperature of the, 102

Vagina, normal temperature of, 1
Vaginal temperatures, 69, 163, 183
Value of thermometer, 47, &c., 53
Van Swieten on thermometer, 21
Variation of temperature in disease, 1, 7
Variations of temperature in health, 1
Varnishing skin, effects of, 143
Variola (see "Smallpox"), 337

Varicella, 344
Villemin on tuberculosis, 143
Virchow's theory of fevers, 184
Vireaot's experiments, 115

Wachsmuth's theory of fever, 188
Walferdin's metastatic thermometers, 64
Walther's experiments, 45, 128, 131
Warmth, production of, 23, 34, 85
— giving off of, 87
Warter, J. S., 42
Water-treatment (see "Cold"), 97, 322

Weber, H., hyperpyretic temperatures, 42, 401
Weber, O., 140, 163, 190
Wistinghausen, dissertations of, 29
Wounds, temperature of, 161, &c.
Wunderlich collects several million observations, 38, 46
Wunderlich's assistants, 40

Yellow fever, 405

Zimmermann, George, industry of, 32, 33, 185

TABLE OF ERRATA.

PAGE.	LINE.	
30,	9 from bottom, for "*Auschaung zu bingen*" read "*zur Auschauung zu bringen.*"
31,	12, for "*starch*" read "*starvation.*"
42,	8 from top, for "*Lewick*" read "*Levick.*"
42,	18, for "*Sidney*" read "*Sydney.*"
42,	20, for "*Aitkin*" read "*Aitken;*" the same mistake also occurs at pp. 213 (note, line 1) and 351, line 15 from bottom.
94,	3 and 4 of note, transpose the symbols "*Fahr.*" and "*C.*"
126,	15 from top, for "*trying*" read "*tying.*"
118,	1, for "*Bonvier*" read "*Bouvier.*"
153,	13 from bottom for "*ulna*" read "*ulnar.*"
161,	(Chapter VII), the heading should be "*Local Alterations of Temperature in Disease.*"
213,	7 from bottom, for "*Liebermerster*" read "*Liebermeister.*"

PRINTED BY J. E. ADLARD, BARTHOLOMEW CLOSE.